ALSO BY NICHOLAS MOSLEY

HOPEFUL MONSTERS

Nicholas Mosley

Introduction by Sven Birkerts

Dalkey Archive Press

Originally published by Martin Secker & Warburg Ltd., England, 1990
Copyright © 1990 Nicholas Mosley
First Dalkey Archive hardback edition, 1991
First Dalkey Archive paperback edition, 2000
Introduction copyright © 2000 Sven Birkerts

Library of Congress Cataloging-in-Publication Data:

Mosley, Nicholas, 1923-
        Hopeful monsters / Nicholas Mosley. — 1st Dalkey Archive pbk. ed.
            p.   cm.
        ISBN 1-56478-242-5 (alk. paper)
        1. Physicists—Fiction. I. Title.

        PR6063.O82 H67 2000
        823'.914—dc21   00-020968

Partially funded by grants from the National Endowment for the Arts, a federal agency, and the Illinois Arts Council, a state agency.

Dalkey Archive Press
www.dalkeyarchive.com

Introduction

Novels, like Prufrock's women, come and go, and only a very few manage not only to outline their moment but protrude into the future. Nicholas Mosley's grandly panoramic intellectual and moral odyssey, *Hopeful Monsters,* is such a work, and as the 20th century slowly recedes, it will come ever more clearly into focus not only as a trenchant diagnosis of ideological struggles of the modern epoch, but also as a kind of prophecy of what being human may hold in store for all of us living in the post-atomic information age. On top of this—rather, inextricable from it—the novel tells one of the great modern stories about love, love in the ruins, if you will.

Mosley, who was born in London in 1923, is far better known in Europe than on these shores. A commanding literary figure, son of the late Sir Oswald Mosley, who was leader of the Fascist Party in England in the 1930s—a period studied from a very different political vantage in sections of this novel—he is prolific as a writer of nonfiction as well as novels.

Hopeful Monsters is, in fact, the fifth book in a series of linked but individual works, beginning with *Catastrophe Practice* (1979), which introduced the six characters who appear in various combinations in the novels *Imago Bird* (1980), *Serpent* (1981), *Judith* (1986), and then *Hopeful Monsters* (1990). Mosley's explanatory synopsis of the project (appended to the text) gives some warrant for seeing the saga of Max and Eleanor, the protagonist-narrators of *Hopeful Monsters,* as the main narrative axis of the series. In any case, the work is massive and complex enough in its own right to be considered in isolation, and readers who would situate it in its larger context will have to proceed on their own.

Hopeful Monsters braids, overtly and through a hundred twists of suggestion, the lives and careers of Max and Eleanor. Both are highly articulate thinkers from families of thinkers. Eleanor, a German Jew, is the daughter of a prominent physicist-philosopher and a left-wing radical. Max grows up in the hothouse atmosphere of prewar Cambridge—his father is a biologist, his mother a student of psychoanalysis.

Max and Eleanor first meet in Germany's Black Forest during a youth festival in the late 1920s, after which the tides of their lives pull them apart. The mainspring of the plot is their eventual reunion and marriage, for the reader is convinced, as indeed are Max and Eleanor themselves, that they are meant to be together. They write, address the accounts of their lives to one another, cherish the flame of their first contact. They have agreed to leave their next meeting entirely to chance: History will make the arrangements. "My beautiful German girl," exclaims Max at one point, "will one day rise again sword-in-hand from a lake; she will help me to slay the dragons that entrap me in dreams. . . ." The two are like Stanley and Livingstone heading for rendezvous in Darkest Africa and our expectation of their fated encounter sets the pages aglow.

Max and Eleanor are romantic searchers, though they are both intellectuals immersed in the thought and politics of their time, they are also dreamers of some elusive synthesis of the personal and the collective, the subjective and the historical. The tantalizing premise that they will each have to fulfill a near-epic course of wanderings (and challenging self-interrogations) before finding on another, gives the novel the tension needed to support Mosley's many episodic excursions into the unfolding drama of our century's history. By the time Eleanor finds Max in a Spanish monastery in the late 1930s, we have been present at, or very near, a number of crucial historical scenes, among them the murder of Rosa Luxemburg, the Reichstag Fire, the first attempts by theoretical physics to dismantle the atom, and the eruption of the Spanish Civil War. We have also encountered, if only in cameo roles, Albert Einstein, Ludwig Wittgenstein, Martin Heidegger, and Generalissimo Franco, to name a few.

Such a characterization allows us to isolate right away what is remarkable about Mosley's conception, which is that he has engineered his narrative in such a way as to allow many of the headline developments of the 20th century European history—indeed History itself—to assume a heightened, very nearly protagonistic role in the novel. But careful—this is no glibly postmodern playing with the facts, as in, say, E. L. Doctorow's *Ragtime*. Nor is it, as the reader quickly discerns, a framing of iconically significant tableaux. For while we do feel present at a number of signal events, we are so only at an angle, obliquely. We do see Wittgenstein, but he is not writing the *Tractatus,* he is sitting in a chair at a party, trying to balance his plate on his lap. Franco? We glimpse him as "a small dapper man who flung his arm up in a Fascist salute and jerked his hips forward as if he were being propelled to the edge of the balcony from behind."

As Max observes, surely voicing Mosley's own view in the matter: "History is put together from what people want to say or to remember: but how little of what is written seems to do with what an individual on the spot has experienced!"

This collision of perspectives drives the novel from the first page on. The reader's work is to keep reconciling the struggles of Max and Eleanor—struggles shaped at every turn by the pressure of circumstances upon their ideas and beliefs—with the public unfolding of events. The to-and-fro movement between perspectives affords the reader a sense of historical engagement unusual for the genre.

Neither a work bound to the conventions of realism, nor simply a novel of ideas, *Hopeful Monsters* navigates its own border zone. Mosley's knack, his art, is not so much to give Max and Eleanor ideas—fascinating, compelling ideas—but to bring these characters to life by way of a sustained exposition of their authentic thinking selves. As the novel proceeds, Max and Eleanor, in ways that even they cannot always recognize, live out the growth and change—the evolution—of those ideas.

When we first meet Max, for instance, he is a precocious boy growing up in the intellectually contentious atmosphere of Cambridge. Through his parents, his mother in particular, he becomes interested in the experiments of their visitor, the Viennese biologist Kammerer, who is trying to demonstrate the possibility of the genetic transmission of acquired characteristics. This interest leads Max, eventually, to set up his own experiment with two salamanders, Adam and Eve, which he calls his "hopeful monsters." When his mother asks him what that means, he answers—this young teen—" 'They are things born perhaps slightly before their time; when it's not known if the environment is quite ready for them'."

The notion, of new life given unforeseeable shape by pressures and circumstances that are new in the world, becomes one of the formative tropes of the novel. What are Max and Eleanor if not themselves just such "hopeful monsters"? But the concept, living in the "not yet," the subjunctive, resonates through Max's whole intellectual career, affects everything from his involvement in the Left politics of the 1930s to his work as a physicist before and after the discovery of nuclear fission. Mosley is theorizing—as only a novelist can theorize—about the conditions under which new modes of being may emerge in the era to come.

Central as it is, the "hopeful monsters" thread is only one of a great many. The novel is tightly patterned with echoing themes—leitmotivs—which take on a growing profundity through recurrence. We begin to believe, as surely the author wants us to, that ideas are not so much bounded cognitive constructions as they are organisms that propagate, flourish, and die in the context created for them by historical events.

Though the comparison will maybe seem farfetched to some, I would put *Hopeful Monsters* in direct lineage of Thomas Mann's *The Magic Mountain*. Like Max and Eleanor, Mann's Hans Castorp also lived out the intellectual and moral dilemmas of Europe. But where Mann had to put his hero through the crisis of isolation—Hans spends seven years in the seclusion of a mountain sanitorium—in order to make the slow movement of his ideas plausible, Mosley opted for the contrary expedient. His characters would live their thoughts right in the teeth of catastrophic events. And what a difference! Against the great German's stately examination of values and philosophies, the dialogues that are almost Platonic in their purposeful progress, we have Mosley's urgent, at times almost improvisational reckonings. His ideas at every point take the touch of events, and—no less important—they impart to specific actions their defining character. Still, in terms of scale and seriousness, we have to look back to Mann to find a work of comparable ambition.

There is so much to say about *Hopeful Monsters* and Mosley's angle on the life of our recent era that I feel a wonderful arbitrariness about finding a thought with which to conclude. Probably I should convey some further sense of how the novel keeps mattering; how it impinges upon the future.

For me, one exemplary instance—an instance that allows us to savor both style and intellectual thrust—comes in an exchange between Max and Eleanor after they have reunited and gotten married, and after Max has taken up his work in physics again. The narrating voice in this passage is Max's:

> We settled, you and I, in two rooms in a boarding-house on the outskirts of the town. We were very happy. I thought – But could not we, with our particular story, be involved in some experiment to find out what goes on in the heart of being human?
> I said 'The real race, do you think, is between people or forces intent on self-destruction, and the chance of being able to begin to stop it because one can see what is happening?'
> You said 'You mean for thousands of years people have just liked war?'
> I said 'But now, with the chance of this Bomb, people surely won't like what they may be able to imagine.'
> You said, 'You mean, it is necessary that at this time there should be discovered this explosive force in the nucleus of the atom, to give a chance to a change in people's minds.'
> I said, 'Necessary, I suppose, for continued existence.'
> I thought – Minds, matter, flying apart, coming together again –
> For some renewal, yes, of what might be called 'spirit.'
> You said, 'But how odd, that by seeing something one might stop it!'
> I said, 'But there's been for some time the idea that by seeing things we affect them. And then there's that other crazy vision I had in Spain – that we are in some sense part of a self-creating universe.'
> You said, 'Well you and I, before we could begin again, had very nearly to hit rock bottom.'

Such an elegant, compressed exchange—such a distillation for the reader of motifs present in one form or another from the very outset. But coming as it does after Max and Eleanor have fought their way through some of the darkest contortions of history, the words—the paradox of salvation they outline—also have a luminous clarity. We grasp the serious yet parrying responses, as we eventually grasp everything in the novel, as the peculiar self-reflexive interrogation that is the calling card of wisdom in our age. Mosley leaves us where he wants us—excited, full of querying spirit, feeling as if we ourselves were part of an equation being worked by a visionary intelligence. I don't know that a late-modern novel can achieve much more than this.

SVEN BIRKERTS
2000

ONE
We know the predicament

I: Eleanor

If we are to survive in the environment we have made for ourselves,
may we have to be monstrous enough to greet our predicament?

In the winter of 1918–19 when I, Eleanor Anders, was nine years
old, I was living with my parents in an apartment in the Cranachstrasse in a respectable area of Berlin. My father was a lecturer in
philosophy at Berlin University: my mother was a left-wing socialist
politician. My earliest memories of Berlin are to do with the ending
of the 1914–18 war – soldiers keeping to the shadows with their eyes
cast down, the impression that they were looking for even more
terrible events round some corner. At the very end of the war there
was the socialist revolution that my mother's friends had for so long
foretold; civilians with rifles suddenly appeared in the streets – men in
thick dark suits with caps and bowler hats who stood and stared at
you as you went past, who clattered to and fro hanging on to the sides
of cars and lorries. It was as if, after all, they might find a new enemy
to provide from defeat some futile victory. It was at this time, I think,
that I began to have the impression of myself as needing to be
somehow invisible to people in the streets, if I were not to be caught
by whatever it was round some corner.

The apartment in which my parents and I lived in the Cranachstrasse was at the top of a building at the centre of which there was

a wide spiral staircase that seemed like something placed in water for the construction of a bridge: there was a skylight at the top through which thin sunshine filtered; the bottom was murky as if at the depths of the sea. In the streets an impression of being at a depth continued: the walls of high apartment buildings rose like rock-faces on either side; the lorries and cars that went past festooned with men with rifles were like lobsters or crabs with heavy claws. It was necessary to get past these to climb up the spiral staircase to our apartment where there was airiness and light. High narrow windows jutted up into a slightly sloping roof; walls were panelled in a soft wood which was like the lining of my father's boxes of cigars. My earliest memories of our apartment are of the evenings when I would sit with my father in his study and he would read me stories from mythology or from children's magazines. There was a vogue at the time for an early type of science-fiction magazine, and I suppose it was from these that my mind picked up some of its lasting images. When I was in my father's study it would seem that we were in the cabin or gondola of an airship; we were gliding above the rooftops of the grey and watery city; my father was the captain and I was his mate; we were looking for somewhere to land where we would make a new home, or perhaps we would carry on forever like that bird I suppose that first flew out of the ark.

My father was a tall man with a pale drooping moustache and short fair hair that was brushed up so that he often seemed amazed or even about to shoot upwards like a rocket. The other occupants of our apartment – or airship, or ark, or whatever – were Magda the cook, Helga the parlourmaid and my governess Miss Henne who came in to teach me each day. There was also, of course, my mother.

My mother was a small dark woman with flashing eyes: she was Jewish (my father was not): she came from a family who lived near the frontier with Poland. My mother was the driving force or power-house in whatever my father and I dreamed of as our lofty world; it was around her that there was the clatter and hum of the machinery to do with the running of the airship – the obtaining of fuel and food, which was difficult in the last years of the war. There were also the occasional meetings of my mother's political associates. My father and I would sit behind closed doors and listen to the business of practical life going on. I sometimes wondered – or it seems to me now that my father and I must have wondered – where in fact does power reside within something like an airship? Is it in the engine-room, or with the people who sit with their knobs and levers and dream that they are in control?

I suppose not much is remembered now about German politics during those years. The war was brought to an end in November 1918 by an almost bloodless revolution in Germany; an alliance was made between the moderate socialists and the conservative militarists who had been running the war; one of the aims of the alliance was to keep out of power the extreme left-wing socialists, who were the people around my mother. There was skirmishing in the streets between government forces and the extremists who felt they had been cheated of their true revolution; but there was a general exhaustion in the aftermath of war, and there was dissent even among the extremists. The questions at issue among the extremists were: should a revolution be organised with central control – should there be tactical planning and the making of alliances and concessions – or should the proper business of revolution be left to the spontaneous uprising of the masses (it is impossible to write of left-wing politics without the jargon!)? Karl Marx had foretold (or it was believed he had foretold) that history would in time inevitably lead to the take-over of power by the masses, so might not attempts at human planning only divert the course of history from going on the way that was just what was desired? Was it not the moderate socialists who had planned and schemed – and see how they had betrayed the revolution! This was the argument of the extremists. Should it not be the business of leadership just to keep the doctrine pure and to analyse accurately what in the jargon was referred to as the 'concrete situation' – and then, would not history be free to go its own spontaneous way?

These were the arguments of Rosa Luxemburg – the most popular and most bewitching of the leaders of the extremists. My mother was a disciple or devotee of Rosa Luxemburg. Rosa Luxemburg came from the same Jewish background as my mother. She was a small bright-eyed woman who seemed sometimes to purr, and sometimes to spit, but always to have claws like a cat.

Some of the most striking of my earliest memories are to do with the meetings that my mother's friends used to hold in our apartment. Into the quiet world that my father and I dreamed of as our airship there came, climbing from the depths of the streets, men in thick dark suits and stiff white collars, women in long skirts and blouses buttoned up to their chins. The men would stand in the hallway looking for somewhere to hang their hats; the women would embrace my mother underneath their hats which were like nests or umbrellas. They would flow from the hallway into the dining-room where they would stand or sit round the table; they would talk or shout and make speeches, sometimes singly and sometimes all at once; they would pass bits of paper like food to and fro across the table. Perhaps this image came mostly from the sounds they made: on the few occasions on which my father opened the dining-room door and I caught a glimpse of them, they would seem to freeze, turning to the door as if alarmed or posing for a photograph. Then after the meeting they would flow out into the hall again and the men would look for their hats and the women would be putting their arms again round my mother. I suppose I came to see the grown-up world as containing creatures who just behaved in this way – who clattered through streets hanging on to cars and then came together and stood and shouted round dining-room tables; and then were suddenly silent, as if they needed to be caught within a photograph.

My father did not play much part in these activities. He and I would sit in his study and listen, or occasionally get glimpses. I would think – So if this is the grown-up world, what is my father then? I understood that he was sympathetic to what my mother and her friends were trying to achieve, but that he did not think they were going about it the right way. I wondered – But are he and I going the right way with our stories about our airship?

I would try to talk to my father about this: I would say 'But what do you think my mother's political friends should do: should they do nothing? Should they fight? What is this word that you say they use – "spontaneous"?'

My father would say 'I think the trouble is that they don't have the ability to see just what it is they are doing.'

I would say 'Is that difficult?'

My father would laugh and say 'Yes, it's difficult.'

Once or twice Rosa Luxemburg herself came to the apartment. These meetings seemed more orderly because she did most of the talking. Her voice was sometimes a purr and sometimes a spitting. I would wonder – She is trying to make them see just what it is she is doing? My father once said 'She could make a snake rise up from a basket.'

I thought – What it is difficult for them to see is that they are snakes rising up from baskets?

After these meetings at which Rosa Luxemburg had been present, my mother would come into the study where my father and I were sitting and her eyes would be shining and she would say 'We will win!'

My father would say 'Yes, my dear, but what is it you think you will win?'

At the end of December 1918 I was sent away with my governess, Miss Henne, to stay with my mother's relations in the provinces. I understood that some uprising of the extremists had been planned in Berlin. I gathered this much at the time, though I learned much of the details of course only later. The planned uprising had been agreed to reluctantly by Rosa Luxemburg: she did not believe in planning but she believed in activity: but what does a revolutionary do when there is no spontaneous activity? Rosa Luxemburg had hoped that the masses would come out in a general strike; but when there was no general strike what had to be encouraged, it seemed, were bits and pieces of violence.

I said to my father 'You mean, I am being sent to the country because it is dangerous?'

My father said 'Your mother wants you to go to the country. Who knows what will be dangerous!'

I thought – But as the captain of our airship, are you not in charge?

– Or you mean, your business is to see just what we are doing.

In the town in the provinces where my mother's relations lived there were tall bearded men with long black coats and wide-brimmed hats; they spoke a strange language; they seemed to spend much of their time reading. The women were rounded and tightly strapped into their clothes as if they were things about to be cooked; they would dab at their faces with bits of lace or cloth, although it was very cold. These people seemed to be of quite a different kind from those I was used to at home: it was as though I had landed from my father's airship on a strange planet. This was another impression that I suppose formed in my mind at this time – of people naturally forming self-contained and easily distinguishable groups: perhaps because like this they need not see what was happening when there were things like dangerous uprisings –

– But my father and I, we were above all this in our lonely airship?

My father used to laugh when I said such things: he would say 'But you cannot talk like that!'

I would say 'Why not?'

7

He would say 'Perhaps people have guns that can shoot down our airship!'

Soon after we had arrived to stay with my mother's relations in the provinces my governess, Miss Henne, seemed to have a fit. She had had a headache; she stayed in bed; then one morning she was shrieking and rolling her eyes and going rigid. My great aunts and cousins came in and stood by her bed; they too raised their eyes and waggled their heads; one of the men in a long black coat read a bit from one of their books above Miss Henne, but it seemed to be this sort of thing that was making Miss Henne have her fit. After a day or two it was decided that Miss Henne and I should return to Berlin. Telegrams were sent to my father and my mother. I wondered – But is there any connection between Miss Henne's fit, the uprising of the extremists, and a snake being drawn up out of a basket?

When Miss Henne and I arrived back at the railway station at Berlin neither my father nor my mother were there to meet us. I thought this strange. There were not so many lorries and cars in the streets; there were occasional groups of men on street corners. Miss Henne and I had to walk because the trams were not working; men watched us as we went past; I wondered how it might be possible to make myself invisible. There was an extraordinary amount of litter in the streets – paper and bits of metal and stone like things that have ended up at the bottom of the sea. Miss Henne rolled her head and muttered. I wondered if it would be proper to leave her and make a dash for the safety of our airship, if she began again to have a fit.

When we reached the door of our apartment at the top of the wide spiral staircase there were voices coming from inside; when Miss Henne knocked the voices stopped. After a time we could hear the door being unbolted; it was opened by my mother. Behind her in the hallway were a group of her friends: they were facing the door as if they were alarmed, or expecting to be photographed.

My mother held out her arms to me; she did not usually do this; it seemed that I had to be seen being embraced by my mother. My mother had a belt with a cold silver buckle on it. One of the people in the group behind my mother was Rosa Luxemburg. I thought – Oh I suppose it is because of her that I am having to be embraced by my mother.

The people in the hallway began talking again; they moved off down the passage, led by Rosa Luxemburg. They seemed to be looking for something: there is that children's game in which an object is hidden and then you have to come in from another room and find it. In our apartment there was the hallway off which, on one side, was my father's study and the dining-room and the drawing-room; then the passage down which there was my mother and father's bedroom and then Helga and Magda's bedroom and the kitchen; my own bedroom and the bathroom and the airing cupboard were on the other side of the passage. Rosa Luxemburg led the way down the passage; she was like a goose or a duck with the rest of us following her. Miss Henne had disappeared as soon as she had delivered me at the door of the apartment. My father did not seem to be at home. I thought – But we are being invaded: these people are taking over our airship.

We went first into my mother and father's bedroom; someone looked under the bed; someone looked in a cupboard. I thought – What are we searching for: something that has been lost in the uprising of the extremists? My mother went to the end of the passage and knocked on the door of Helga and Magda's room; after a time Magda came out and stood with her back against the door; she put her arms out like a crucifix. Rosa Luxemburg spoke to Magda in her soft purring voice and after a time Magda lowered her arms and put her head on Rosa Luxemburg's shoulder; she seemed to weep. I thought – There are illustrations like this in stories about myths. Someone opened the door into my bedroom; my mother seemed to protest; the door into my room was closed. Then Rosa Luxemburg left Magda and held her arms out to me. I thought – I am to become part of this odd story? When I was in Rosa Luxemburg's arms she had a strange musty smell like something kept in a sack in an attic.

Amongst the group with my mother there were a young man and a girl whom I had not seen before; they were holding hands; they were not playing much part in the discussions. After a time I realised from the talk that the point of all this activity was not to find some hidden object, but to find some place where this young man and the girl might hide; they were being hunted, it seemed, perhaps by one of the groups of men in the streets; they had been brought by my mother's friends to our apartment for refuge.

My mother had opened the door into the airing cupboard; we all looked up at the shelves containing sheets and towels and blankets: I thought – Oh yes, this is another picture from one of the stories my father used to read to me: of an empty tomb? It seemed to be being agreed that the best place for the young man and the girl to hide would be the top shelf of the airing cupboard. Rosa Luxemburg went to them and put her hands on their shoulders; there was always some sort of aura of light, of smell, around Rosa Luxemburg. The young man began climbing to the top shelf of the airing cupboard. Then Helga came running out of her room and pushed her way through the crowd and stood with her back to the shelves of towels and blankets and sheets and held her arms out like a crucifix. The young man had reached the top shelf by this time and was sitting there with his arms around his knees and his head against the ceiling. Rosa Luxemburg went and put her hand, and then her head, against Helga's shoulder. Helga began to weep. I thought – What does it mean, that we are all behaving as if we were pictures in some religious fairy story?

Then there was the voice of my father in the passage. He was saying 'You gave me the wrong time of the train at the station.'

My mother said 'I'm sorry, but I have other preoccupations than the wrong times of the trains.'

My father said 'But she might have been in danger.'

My mother said 'Well it's not she who is in danger now.'

My father came to the door of the airing cupboard. When he saw me he said 'Are you all right?' I said 'Yes.' He did not come and put his arms around me. He looked up at the young man who was on the top shelf of the airing cupboard. I thought – Well, he will understand all this business of behaving as if in a story. My father said 'Why don't they just stay for supper? Then I can say they are two of my students.'

My mother said 'And what good will that do?'

My father said 'Don't you want to protect them?'

Rosa Luxemburg came out of the airing cupboard and she stretched a hand out towards my father; then she swayed, put a hand to her eyes, and seemed about to fall over. People caught her, gathered round, helped her to a seat in the hallway. They were saying that she must rest, my mother was saying that a bed could be made up for her in the airing cupboard. The young man and the girl were now standing hand in hand in the passage. Rosa Luxemburg was shaking her head and smiling; she was holding her hands against her breasts. I wanted to say to my father – But they are really illustrating something else, aren't they, these religious pictures? My father was watching Rosa Luxemburg. Then suddenly she stood up and swept out of the apartment; she took most of the crowd with her, as if they were the tail of a kite or a comet. The young man and the girl were left behind. My mother was standing in the hallway chewing the insides of her lips, which she did when she was angry with my father.

Helga had gone back into her bedroom and slammed the door. Magda was banging pots and pans about in the kitchen.

My father said to the girl who was with the young man in the passage 'You are at the university?'

The girl said 'Yes.'

My father said 'What is your subject?'

The girl said 'Physics.'

My father said 'Ah then we will have a lot to talk about!'

He held an arm out to the girl. The girl was blonde with a squashed face as if there were a wind blowing against it. I could not understand why my father was not paying more attention to me. I went and stood by my mother.

It is relevant to put in here (relevant I mean in the way that this comes up in memory, relevant in the way that these occurrences were roughly coincidental in fact) what I remember of the conversations I used to have with my father when we were not reading stories: these conversations having begun around the time when the group with Rosa Luxemburg came looking for a hiding-place in our apartment; their subject also being to do with what my father talked to the young man and girl about at supper.

Sometimes when I sat with my father on the sofa in his study and he had been reading to me stories or articles about science from children's magazines, I would, at the end of whatever voyage of discovery or imagination we had been on (I was, I suppose, quite a precocious little girl), ask my father about the work he was doing at the university. He told me something of his regular work of lecturing and teaching, but I do not remember much about this. Then he told me of the work that really interested him at this time, which was outside his regular curriculum, and was to do with his efforts to understand, and to put into some intelligible language, the theories that were being propounded about physics at this time by one of his colleagues at the university – a Professor Einstein. I do not think that my father knew Einstein very well, but he venerated him, and he was enough of a mathematician to be able to try to grapple with some of his theories. I, of course, could have comprehended little of the substance of what my father said: but because of his enthusiasm it was if, on some level, I was caught up in his efforts. I had a picture of Professor Einstein as some sort of magician: there was a photograph of him on the chimney-piece of my father's study which was a counter-balance to my mother's photograph of Karl Marx on the chimney-piece of the dining-room. Professor Einstein's head, set rather loosely on his shoulders, seemed to have a life of its own; Karl Marx's head seemed to have been jammed down on to his shoulders with a hammer. I would say to my father as we sat above the wonders of the world in our airship 'What is it that is so special about the theories of Professor Einstein?'

My father said 'Shall I try to explain?'

I said 'I like hearing you talk. It doesn't matter if I don't understand.'

This was the time – the winter of 1918–19 – when Einstein had recently published his paper concerning the General Theory of Relativity (the papers concerning the Special Theory had been published some years previously), but the conjectures put forward in the General Theory had not yet been verified. Nothing in these theories had yet much caught the public imagination: people seemed not to be ready for such images as they might evoke. But my father had become obsessed with trying to make intelligible an interpretation of the General Theory: it was this, he said, that should alter people's ideas about the universe and about themselves.

My father said 'All right, I'll try to tell you. I'm not sure, anyway, just what it means to understand.'

I think my father had already tried to explain – usually more to himself in fact than to me – the Special Theory of Relativity. I remember the phrases about there being no absolute space nor absolute time: my space is my space; your time is yours; if I am travelling at a certain speed in relation to you it might as well be you who are travelling at a certain speed in relation to me; the only thing that is absolute is the speed of light. The speed of light is constant no matter if it arises from this or that travelling hither or thither: if there seem to be contradictions, these are because the measuring devices themselves get bigger or smaller and not the speed of light. I do not suppose I grasped the latter idea: but I do not think I found it difficult to see the idea of each person, each observer or group, having his or her or its own world: was not this, after all, what I had come to feel about the people in the streets, my mother's friends, her cousins in the country? I felt sometimes that I understood even about the absoluteness of the speed of light – was not this something that my father and I felt ourselves in touch with as we looked down on all these separate worlds from the super-world of our airship?

I said 'You are going to tell me about the new thing, the General Theory.'

My father said 'Ah!'

There are two or three particular and personalised images that stick in my mind from my father's efforts to explain to me, aged nine, Einstein's General Theory of Relativity. These images arose from the conjecture that light itself had weight, so that it could be bent or pulled in the proximity of matter by what used to be called 'gravity': that if there is enough matter in the universe (which Einstein thought there was) then space itself would be bent or curved – and it would be just such curvature that could properly be called gravity. The particular images suggested by my father that have stuck in my mind are, firstly, of a small group of people standing back to back on a vast and lonely plain; they are looking outwards; they are trying to see something other than just their surroundings and themselves. But they can never by the nature of things see anything outside the curve of their own universe, since gravity pulls their vision back (my father drew a diagram of this) so that it comes on top of them again like falling arrows. The second image is that of a single person on this vast and lonely plain who has constructed an enormously powerful telescope; by this he hopes to be able to break at last out of the bonds of his own vision; he looks through it; he sees – what appears to be a new star! Then he realises that what he is looking at is the back of his own head – or the place where his head now is billions of years ago, or in the future, or whatever. Anyway, here he is now with the light from him or to him having gone right round the universe and himself never being able to see any further than the back of his own head. But then there was a third image that my father gave me, different in kind from the others: which is of gravity being like the effect of two people sitting side by side on an old sofa so that the springs sag and they are drawn together in the middle: and there were my father and I sitting side by side on the sofa in his study.

I would say to my father 'But is this true?'

My father said 'Mathematically, it seems to be true.'

'But is it really?'

'Ah, what is really!'

I would think – But together, might not my father and I get beyond the backs of our heads in our airship?

Sometimes when my father and I had our arms around one another sitting like this my mother would put her head round the door of his study and say 'Are you coming?'

My father would say 'Coming where?'

'To supper.'

'Ah yes, supper.'

Then my mother would perhaps advance into the room and say 'What have you two been doing?'

'Talking.'

'It didn't sound like talking to me!'

'Thinking then.'

'Do you have to sit like that when you think?'

And I would think – Oh do let us get through, yes, into some other dimension!

It was such conversations I had with my father that seemed relevant to the evening when the group of people round Rosa Luxemburg had been in our apartment (they being like the people on the vast and lonely plain) and when the young man and the girl stayed for supper.

My mother had gone to argue with Magda in the kitchen. Helga was banging plates down on the sideboard in the dining-room. My father had said to the girl, who was quite pretty, 'What is your subject?' The girl had said 'Physics.' My father had said 'Then we will have a lot to talk about!' And I had wondered why my father was not talking more to me.

My father said to the young man 'What do you do?'

The young man said 'My subject is philosophy but at the moment I am occupied in politics.'

My father said, as he so often said, 'Ah.'

During supper my father sat at the head of the table: I sat on one side of him and the young man sat on the other: the girl sat next to the young man. I remember the atmosphere, the style, of this supper quite well – perhaps because it was almost the first time I had been allowed up so late; out of deference, I suppose, to the tensions of the evening. Whoever remembers the exact words of conversations? but I imagine I can recreate the style, the attitudes, of my father.

He said to the girl 'What do you know of the theories of Professor Einstein?'

The girl, who had a scraping voice that did not go with her soft squashed face, said 'I understand they have not been verified.'

14

My father said 'What do you think might count as verification?'

The girl said 'I understand verification is unlikely.'

My father turned to the young man who had small steel pince-nez from which a black ribbon hung down. My father said 'And what is the opinion of a philosopher or a politician on these matters?'

The young man said 'I think these are matters for scientists and mathematicians.'

My father said 'Should not a philosopher have ideas or opinions about what might be called reality?'

The young man said 'It is the job of philosophers to clarify concepts. It is the job of scientists to uncover facts.'

My father said 'But are not concepts seen to be of the same nature as facts?'

The young man said 'And it is the job of politicians to separate practical sense from nonsense, which is the tool of exploitation.'

My father said 'I see.' He used to say 'I see' when he was disappointed; this was slightly different from when he said 'Ah!'

At some such moment in this conversation my mother came in; she banged plates about with Helga or Magda at the sideboard. She said 'It might make more sense to talk about the practical difficulties of getting the materials for this soup.'

The young man said 'Indeed.'

The girl said 'I'm sorry.'

My mother said 'It is not your fault.'

My father raised his eyebrows; he seemed to be hoping he might take off, as if he were a rocket.

My mother sat down at the other end of the table. Helga handed round the soup. After a time my mother said 'Some people do not seem to realise that even at this moment there are people being killed in the streets.'

My father picked up his napkin, put it down, looked at the girl, looked at the young man, looked at me. I thought – Well, you did not put your arms around me: what am I supposed to do alone in our airship?

Then my father said to my mother 'But haven't you been looking forward to the time when people would be killed in the streets? Haven't you said that the revolution could not come until there were people being killed in the streets?'

My mother said 'That is an insult!' She banged her knife and fork down on the table.

I thought I might now join in by saying – But didn't you want my father to protect this young man and the girl by saying that they were two of his students at the university?

My mother went out of the room. We could hear her talking, or crying, with Magda in the kitchen.

The girl said to my father 'Don't you care?'

My father raised his eyebrows; gazed at a corner of the ceiling.

The young man said 'In my opinion, the scientific reality is that there is this repression of the masses.'

My father said 'I see.'

After a time the girl said 'Excuse me, I will go and see if your wife is all right.' She left the room.

We sat at the table and drank our soup – my father, the young man with pince-nez and myself. I thought – Oh yes, our various visions, like arrows, are going out and coming crashing round on to the backs of our own heads.

Then – But it is true that my mother must have had difficulty in getting the materials for the soup?

After a time the young man said 'But the masses have the real power according to the iron laws of history.'

My father said 'Then for God's sake join them.'

The young man stood up and bowed, and went out – presumably to join my mother and the girl and Helga and Magda in the kitchen.

I thought – So now, yes, my father and I are alone in our airship.

My father sat staring at a corner of the ceiling. I thought – But it is all right, it is all right, even if there are things one does not understand and cannot say: is not this what you have taught me?

Eventually a bed was made for the young man in the drawing-room; the girl was to sleep on the floor of my room.

Sometime during the night people did in fact come knocking at the door of our apartment; I heard my father going to answer the door; he was calm, authoritative; after a time the people who had knocked went away. What my father had said was that there was no one in the apartment except his family and servants; he could give his assurance on this point on the authority of his position at the university. I was in my bed with the girl beside me on a mattress on the floor. I was thinking – Well what does one understand? What is truth? What is authority? What is caring for others, in this lonely business of our airship?

It was a day or two after this, I think, that the revolution of the left-wing extremists that had been simmering came to the boil in Berlin:

this was the second week in January 1919. The eruption of the left wing brought out the right-wing extremists; there were gangs in caps and thick dark suits running through the streets; gangs in makeshift uniforms clanking about in lorries. I saw comparatively little of this; for a week I was not allowed out of the apartment. I would stand at the window and look down. What I understood vaguely at the time and in more detail later was that the left-wing extremists, or Spartacists as they were called, had emerged with rifles and machine-guns; had attacked, and taken over, three or four newspaper offices (this might have seemed apt to my childish vision, since I saw their business as being to do with the banging about of bits of paper). There was sporadic shooting, a few hundred deaths, a failure in storming government buildings. Railway stations and the Telegraph Office were occupied: but all this was being done not so much by the workers as by people who had said that it should be being done by the workers – in accordance with the iron laws of history. Workers for the most part stayed at home. And the right-wing gangs took time off from their clattering in lorries to retire to cellars and drink beer – and to wait for the time perhaps when they could re-emerge and deal with the left-wing extremists who in the end would have to emerge from the newspaper offices without even having had any beer.

I would sometimes hear the sound of firing in the streets; sometimes see the lorries going past with the men hanging on like the claws of crabs. Once there was a column of people with banners going past and they were shouting 'Out! Out!': later there was a column with banners containing slogans of the other side going past and they were shouting 'Out!' I would think – But where are the people dying in the streets? Or are they being kept like a score, as in a game of cards.

My father stayed in the apartment for a few days; then he was needed at the university. The young man and the girl had moved on to another hiding-place. Some of my mother's friends would come to the door now and then and there would be whispered consultations in the hallway; they would sit for a short while on the chair on which Rosa Luxemburg had sat. I thought – They are like tops that have been whipped up by Rosa Luxemburg, and are now running down.

Once a day Magda or Helga or my mother would go out to try to get food; they would have to queue in streets where there was the sound of firing. When they came back they would rest in the

chair in the hallway, and we would gather round: I thought –
Perhaps tops are kept spinning by the sound of firing.

I tried to talk with my mother. She would sit with her back to
me at her desk in the drawing-room or at the table in the kitchen. I
would say 'But what is happening?'

She said 'It will not be a defeat. It will be a victory.'

'But where is Rosa Luxemburg?'

'In hiding.'

'How will it be a victory?'

'In the end, it will be a victory.'

I imagined Rosa Luxemburg crouched like a small hawk at the
top of someone's airing cupboard.

Then there was an evening when there were more than the usual
comings and goings at the door of our apartment. My father had
come home; he went to join in whatever was happening. I sat on
my own in my room. I was often on my own in my room at this
time; I used to plan how, if the gangs from the street came to get
me, I would climb out of the window and up the ventilation area in
the centre of the building. But then what should I do – fly above
rooftops? This particular evening, after the more than usual comings
and goings in the hallway, there were just the sounds of my father
talking quietly to my mother and my mother crying; then my
mother began to make a noise like howling. I went out of my room
and along the passage. My mother was sitting on the chair in the
hallway and my father was standing over her. My mother was
hitting him with her fists. I said, as I so often said, 'What's
happened?'

My father said 'They've found Rosa Luxemburg.'

My mother said 'They've killed her.'

My father said 'Come to bed.'

My mother said to my father 'You killed her!'

I thought – Do you mean my father's thoughts, like arrows, went
right round the universe –

My father said 'You go to bed.'

I said 'Me?'

My father said 'Yes.'

I thought – But I don't think you've killed her!

My father sat up with my mother most of that night. Sometimes
she became calm; sometimes she cried and shouted. It did not seem
that anything my father said made any difference to my mother. I

sat in my room and listened. I thought – You mean, my mother doesn't want to see what it is she herself has been doing?

The next morning details came through about what had happened – or what people thought must have happened – to Rosa Luxemburg. She had been found hiding in someone's house by one of the right-wing gangs roaming the streets; she had been taken to the Eden Hotel to be interrogated; then the gang had said they were going to hand her over to the police. On the way out of the hotel she had been hit on the head by a rifle butt; she had been pushed into a car half dead. In the car she had probably been shot, and her body had been dumped in a canal. The official story put out was that on the way to the police station the car had been stopped by a mob and Rosa Luxemburg had been dragged from it and lynched. No one bothered to try to believe this. But with her death the revolution was effectively over. Her body was recovered some months later from the canal. A few of her followers continued to imagine that she must still be alive, and that the whole story was a ruse so that she could remain in hiding and eventually emerge.

My father said to my mother 'There is a sense, you see, in which something like that might be true.'

My mother said 'What sense?'

My father said 'She always knew that that sort of revolution wouldn't work. Now she can become a symbol.'

My mother said 'You and your symbols!'

My father said 'Unconsciously, she might have known this.'

My mother said 'I don't want to hear about your unconscious!'

My mother used to sit in the chair in the hallway in which Rosa Luxemburg had sat. I thought – She is waiting for Rosa Luxemburg to have gone right round the universe and to come back in through that doorway.

Later that winter my father took to going for long walks on his own; there were no more civilians with rifles in the streets; occasionally there were soldiers. I thought – My father is looking for his own way out of whatever predicament we might be trapped in.

My mother for a while spent much of the time in bed. She would lie on her back with her hands above the bedclothes and her fingers intertwining as if they groped through a grating. I sometimes sat with her. I wanted to say – It is all right! Then – But are you not where and as you want to be?

She once said 'Your father is a good man! I am so sorry!'

I wanted to say – What are you sorry about?

She said 'You know, Rosa Luxemburg was very grateful to your father. I mean, that night, when the two students stayed in the apartment.'

I said 'Then why don't you say so?'

She said 'Your father has never loved me. He loves you.'

I thought – You are trapped, all laced up, like your relations in the country: you don't want to make yourself lovable!

In the spring – I was doing lessons with Miss Henne again; my mother had begun to go out to work in a soup-kitchen in one of the poorest districts of Berlin – in the spring my father sometimes took me with him on his walks. We would go to the Tiergarten; we would look in at the zoo where there were a few sad animals in cages; suddenly there was blossom on the trees. I thought – But of course we will get out of our predicament! The high point for my father and me in our walks was to go and have tea in the Adlon Hotel – this being the meeting-place for rich and cosmopolitan Berlin, also for the French, English and American officers of the Allied Commission who were overseeing the peace terms being imposed on Germany. These Allied officers were elegant and languid; they had bright belts and boots and even hair that seemed polished; they stood in groups with the sort of vision, I hoped, that would tumble back like cannon balls on their own heads. Occasionally they were joined by one or two of their Prussian counterparts who were elegant in something of the same way except that their hair, like that of my father, was brushed upwards at the back, so that it was as if they might take off like fireworks. But there were also in the hotel groups of a kind that I had not seen before: these were short, rather orange-faced men who seemed to be slightly too big for their clothes; who were like drops of oil or ointment on the point of touching a surface and spreading. They sat round tables with their heads facing inwards: with them sometimes were women of a kind I also had not seen before – younger or at least made up to seem younger than the men; they perched on the arms of chairs and smoked cigarettes and kicked up their feet with pointed shoes. It was as if they might puncture the surface of the men so that there would be oil or ointment, spreading.

My father and I would arrive on the threshold and survey the scene. Between and around the various groups there whizzed waiters who were neat and dapper young men who balanced trays on the tips of their fingers: they wore short jackets and tight trousers: they were like acrobats, or balls in a game of bagatelle. And there were my father and I, having landed on this strange world from our airship.

We would settle at a table and order tea. The women on the arms of chairs tried to blow smoke rings; the men with their heads together were like bubbles on the surface of a cauldron. Occasionally one of the French or English or American or Prussian officers would look without expression at the men and women gathered round a table; then he would call to one of the waiters going past with a tray, and he and the waiter would laugh and chatter.

One day I said to my father 'But how can you fight a war and then be friendly with the people you have been fighting?'

My father said 'People quite like fighting wars; then after a time they've had enough.'

I said 'And they aren't able to look at what they've been doing?'

My father said 'You're right!'

There was one particular waiter with smooth blond hair who whirled to and fro and who seemed to have special attention paid to him by the officers. I wondered – There is a glitter about him, as if of the same sort as there was around Rosa Luxemburg.

I said to my father 'What happened about that theory of Professor Einstein's – the one that said however far you tried to look outwards, you would come up against the back of your own head?'

My father said 'How interesting you should say that! They think they have found a way, as a matter of fact, of either proving or disproving the theory. The English are sending expeditions to South America and to Africa – '

One of the women who was perched on the arm of a chair at a table near us had fallen backwards on to the lap of one of the men who was like a drop of oil. She kicked her legs up into the air. Ash from the man's cigar fell on to her dress; she brushed at it, and seemed to be making out that it had burned her.

My father was saying 'At these particular places there is going to be a total eclipse of the sun. The expeditions are taking with them telescopes and instruments which will discover what happens when light from a distant star passes close to the sun. Normally light from such a star would not be visible because of the brightness of the sun, but if there is a total eclipse – '

The woman who was on the lap of the man with the cigar was holding a piece of her dress and was looking at him reproachfully.

Then she put her hand into his jacket and took out his wallet and looked inside. The man seemed to pay no attention to her; he was puffing at his cigar.

My father was saying 'By an extraordinary coincidence, just at the time when there is a total eclipse at these places there is also just such a bright star almost directly behind the sun – '

Some of the Allied and Prussian officers were looking down at the man and the woman in the chair. The woman was taking money from the wallet of the man; she leaned and kissed him on the forehead. Then she looked up at the Allied and Prussian officers. One of them looked away and seemed slightly to spit, as if he were taking tobacco off his tongue. The woman who had taken the money put her tongue out at him. I wondered – But why is the man who is like a drop of oil or ointment paying no attention?

My father was saying ' – So they will be able to tell, from the observations recorded by their instruments, whether or not, when the light from the star passes close to the sun, it is bent or curved or whatever; and so whether or not the nature of space is bent or curved. I mean they will know from calculations where the star behind the sun will actually be and they will see from their observations where it will appear to be – ' My father broke off. He too was now watching what was happening between the woman and man in the chair and the Allied and Prussian officers.

I said 'I'm listening.'

My father said 'But how will they have made their calculations except through observations?'

I said 'What?'

My father said 'Where was I?'

The woman was climbing off the lap of the man in the chair. The Allied and Prussian officers were moving away. I wondered if I should talk about the scene with my father: then I found that I did not want to.

I said 'So you mean, they won't be able to prove it.'

My father said 'Oh well, they may think they've proved it.'

I thought – But is it about this, or the scene in the hotel, that I want to talk with my father?

Sometimes during these days I went with my mother to her soup-kitchen in one of the poorest parts of Berlin. There was the impression of going down into ever greater depths under water; it was as if I now had to imagine myself in some diving-bell or bubble. The soup-kitchen was in a cellar; there were grey women and children like shadows against walls. I thought – If they or I touched, there would be no oil or ointment to spread! I helped with the handing-out and washing-up of plates. My mother seemed at home among these shadows. She told them what to do; she arranged them in formations against the walls. I thought – Perhaps it is easier to feel what should be done with shadows.

My mother said 'This is not like the grand tea-parties you go to with your father!'

I thought – But why do you say that my father does not love you? Is it because you see him as a shadow?

Sometime during that summer I became ill; I had a fever; I lay in bed and stared at the wall. I thought – There, and there, are shadows! But the sun is too dangerous; you are bent, this way and that, by gravity.

There was one other particular occasion that I remember from the times when my father and I used to have tea in the Adlon Hotel. This must have been later in the summer when the terms of the Treaty of Versailles had become known, because the Prussian and Allied officers were no longer easily speaking to one another. A scene occurred between one of the French officers and one of the Prussians (must not memory depend on events having some connection with symbols?). A group of French officers had been drinking. One of the Prussian officers stopped and spoke to one of the waiters – this was the one with blond and glittering hair – and the waiter smiled and put an arm round the Prussian officer's waist. One of the French officers made a remark that seemed to be about the Prussian officer; the waiter looked at the French officer and rolled his eyes and bit his lip. Then the Prussian officer went up to the French officer and clicked his heels and bowed (how can there be this sort of behaviour unless there are archetypal images?); he said something to the French officer while the French officer languidly fitted a cigarette into a holder. Then the French officer was turning and bowing and clicking his heels; I suppose in a moment there would have been the business with leather gloves and face-slapping; but then an older Prussian officer – one with a monocle, yes, and a shaved head and wrinkles at the back of his neck – was going up to the French officer and laying his hand on the arm of the young Prussian officer and was speaking to the Frenchman in loud and bad French. I understood what he was saying just because he articulated so carefully. He said 'Gentlemen, we do not have to quarrel amongst ourselves, surely, when we have amongst us a more natural enemy.' And then he turned to a table at which there was one of the groups of men who were now like drops of oil or ointment perhaps having touched a surface and spread. This group did not have any women with them: they were just, with their heads bent over a table, like one of the diagrams that my father used to draw to illustrate how people's visions might rebound on themselves.

Then the French and Prussian officers laughed; they put their hands on each others' arms; they were no longer clicking and bowing: the incident was over. And so for a moment there was not the renewed enmity between the Prussians and the French. But it was as if the men who had their heads together had still noticed nothing; they were content to show to the outside world just the backs of their large, vulnerable necks.

When my father and I were walking back through the Tiergarten – it must have been late summer because there were a few falling leaves – my father hit at the leaves with his stick and said 'Oh dear, oh dear!' I knew that this time he had been watching the whole of the incident in the hotel: it did not seem sensible now not to talk about it. I said 'What was all that?' He said 'What was all that?' He sat down on a seat by the path and stretched out his legs. He said 'How much do you know about that sort of thing?'

I thought – You mean, about the Prussian officer and the waiter with blond hair: that sort of thing?

He said 'You know your mother is Jewish?'

I said 'Yes.'

He said 'And you are half Jewish.'

My father had his hands in his pockets. He had stretched his feet so far out that he was almost horizontal.

I thought – Oh you mean, that sort of thing.

He said 'Perhaps it is one of the things impossible to talk about.'

I said 'You once promised to tell me anything I wanted to know.'

He said 'What do you want to know?'

I thought – How can I tell you if I don't know?

Then – You mean, those men in the Adlon Hotel were Jewish?

Then – They are not what I call Jewish!

My father said 'The Jews are the most remarkable people in the world. It is difficult even to say this, because for some reason it is taken to be condescending. But they have some sort of knowingness that other people have not got. They know this themselves; other people know it. But no one quite knows what it is. Something has gone wrong. Jews should be running the world, but they are not. I think they know this, but don't want to talk about it.'

I said 'Why not?'

My father said 'I don't know; and I mean, even if I thought I did – '

Then he sat upright and hit at the leaves with his stick. He said 'Damn!'

I said 'Professor Einstein is a Jew.'

He said 'Yes.'

I said 'And my mother's friends – '

He said 'Some of them.' Then he murmured as if to himself 'They won't take the responsibility.'

I said 'For what?'

He swung his stick to and fro on the ground as if it were a mallet. He said 'For being the children of God, for taking a chance to be the grown-ups of God: but then, how can you grow up if you are the children of God?

I said 'And can't you help them?'

He said 'Help them?' He seemed puzzled.

Then he turned to me and said 'Your mother is a fighter.'

I thought – But I know my mother is a fighter!

He said 'One day you will see the point of your mother.'

I thought – But of course I see the point of my mother!

I suddenly felt very tired. I wanted to go home.

I thought – When things get too difficult, it is as if there is a bright light coming down.

I said 'Is that why people don't like them?'

He said quickly 'Oh of course, people are envious of them.'

I thought – Anyway, people do like them!

I said 'Let's go home.'

It was during that autumn of 1919 that there occurred the event that my father had so long awaited – the publication of the results of the observations that the British expeditions to Africa and South America had made to test Einstein's theory: to see whether light was bent by gravity, whether space was curved, and whether it was this that we understood as gravity. My father came back from the university one evening carrying a file of papers under his arm and went straight to his study, and although I hung about outside to see if he would talk to me he did not come out or call me in. My mother, as usual, had to summon him to supper. I remember him in the dining-room at first not speaking; then turning to me and saying 'It's true, I've got the results. Light is affected by gravity.'

My mother said 'I thought you might have some interesting news to tell us.'

My father said 'Such as what?'

My mother said 'Such as whether President Ebert has made a deal with General von Lüttwitz.'

My father said to me 'But there's still something not quite right. It's not in the measurements. It's in the language.'

I said 'What is in the language?'

My father said 'What is true, is usually in the form of a myth.'

It is difficult now to imagine the interest that was in fact aroused by the publication of the results that seemed to confirm Einstein's General Theory of Relativity. The earlier Special Theory had, as I have said, made little public impact; then for a time the General Theory had been no more than a conjecture. But there was something in the mood of the times, I suppose, that required a liberating vision – a longing in the aftermath of war for old patterns to be broken up – and it was felt that this had in some way been achieved by the confirmation of the General Theory. Also there was something romantic, I suppose, in the story of the conjectures of a comparatively obscure German physicist being confirmed at great trouble and expense by British expeditions to the tropics. Whatever the background, there were headlines in the papers the next day: 'Revolution in Science'; 'Ideas of Newton Overthrown'; 'New Theory of the Universe'. The evidence was, yes, that light from a distant star had been bent as it passed close to the sun; it was thus as if light had weight and mass; 'gravity' was a word for the curvature of the universe. The language used to describe all this might not exactly seem to make sense; the sense was in the mathematics. Language, it was suggested, was after all a second-rate way of trying to explain what in mathematics could be trusted.

All the reports seemed to agree that something liberating had occurred; old systems in which minds had been trapped had been broken; thoughts were freed to wing this way or that round the universe. I remember kneeling on the floor of my father's study and trying to understand the newspaper reports spread out on the floor. I said to my father 'But I thought you said that, if the theory were proved, it would mean something quite different.'

He said 'Yes.'

I said ' – That everyone would see that they could never see anything much beyond the backs of their own heads.'

My father said 'Something like that.'

I said 'Then what has happened?'

My father said 'I suppose it might be by seeing that they can't get out of their own vision, that people might get out.'

I said 'And that was what you were saying?'

He said 'Yes.' Then – 'You're brilliant!'

I thought – What's brilliant? I said 'So they haven't got out.'

He said 'Not if they don't see, they haven't.'

I said 'That's difficult.'

He said 'Yes.'

I remember my mother being somewhat grimly humorous during these days. She would move in and out of the apartment with baskets of groceries both for her own family and for others; she would walk with her shoulders slightly hunched like Rosa Luxemburg. It was as if she were battling against a world gone slightly mad: she even made jokes, which she did not often do. She said 'So it is light that has weight: perhaps it is that which explains the heaviness of these groceries!' My father would say 'Yes, my dear, you are quite right to make jokes.'

She said 'Perhaps we can scoop up some of this light and with it make bullets to use against General von Lüttwitz!'

My father would say 'Yes, my dear, one day we might even be able to do something like that.'

This was the time – the winter of 1919–20 – when there were barricades again going up in the streets: when there was apparently the threat of a revolt by right-wing extremists against the moderate socialist government.

I would say, as I so often said – 'But what is it really that is happening?'

My father said 'What was that thing you said the other day?'

I said 'That *I* said?'

He said 'That just by seeing that we can't get out from our own vision, we might be out.'

I said 'I said that?'

My father used to walk up and down in his study at this time as if he were very excited. I remember an evening when we, he and I, could hear my mother, as usual, banging plates and cutlery about in the dining-room: my father turned to me and said 'We might even go out to your mother and say that we are ready for supper!' He did this, and my mother looked amazed. I thought – Well, that was brilliant!

During that winter my father struggled to put into words what might make sense at least to himself about what was happening in physics. I think he planned to write some short book or pamphlet on the General Theory, though there were no traces of such a manuscript in what later was found of his papers. There were however some notes in a notebook. What he was trying to do, it seemed, was to say that there were two problems – one was to try to understand Einstein's mathematics, and the other was to try to understand what mathematics in general was doing. These, he said, were problems on different levels. The second problem had, as it were, to look down on the first: what was required was a type of language that could talk both about mathematics, and about what mathematics is.

There was a sentence in his notebooks – 'Reality is not a metaphor we construct from mathematics: mathematics is one of our metaphors for reality.' Also – 'If we try to put knowledge on this level into words, are we not back in the trap of language?'

During this winter (I was now perhaps ten) my father and I continued with our reading from story books and science magazines; these often seemed curiously relevant to what we tried to talk about. There was one story that I remember in particular which was to do with some people who were on a trip to outer space; they were, yes, in an airship. They were led by a man called Captain Steadfast; their second-in-command was a boy called Max. There was even a supposedly mad scientist whose head seemed to be set loosely on his shoulders. Captain Steadfast was on a mission to an outer galaxy where there was an evil demon about to dominate the universe; this was to be done by means of noise; the earth was being bombarded with inaudible but unbearable frequencies of noise; this was sending people mad; they were jumping about, bashing one another, starting wars; they could not tell what was plaguing them. Captain Steadfast and his crew had to find and destroy the evil demon before people on earth destroyed themselves. Also on the demon's star there was a beautiful girl imprisoned who might, if freed, lead Captain Steadfast to the source of the terrible noise. My father would look up every now and then and say 'This really is a very good story!' I identified, of course, with the boy called Max. The climax came (I remember it well!) when Captain Steadfast's airship was approaching the demon's star; the airship came up against a solid barrier of noise; the evil demon had put out sound waves so that they were like a wall; the airship banged against this wall but could not get through; the airship was breaking up! Captain Steadfast was being defeated. Then someone aboard had the idea (was it the mad Professor? was it Max?) that what had to be done was to create a vacuum in front of the airship – sound cannot travel through a vacuum – so that if the vacuum could be made the airship could get through. So the propellers at the front of the airship were put into reverse; they went faster and faster; the propellers at the back drove the airship forwards; somehow or other the propellers at the front created a vacuum! And so Captain Steadfast and his crew got through. And they destroyed the evil demon and rescued the girl; and people on earth stopped hopping up and down as if they were demented.

My father and I were quite carried away by this. We sat side by side staring at the ceiling.

I said 'But could that sort of thing be true?'

He said 'Well, it is true that sound cannot exist in a vacuum.'

I said 'What about light?'

He said 'Ah yes, light.' Then – 'What we want to do, perhaps, is to make a vacuum in our heads, and then light might break in; and then it might not even have to be us who break through!'

We sat with our arms round each other staring at the universe. Sometimes there did seem to be outlines of dark light around the objects in the room in front; as if we were through to a strange planet.

At night I would lay in bed and would try both to think and to stop thinking of all this: there were all these lumps of light coming down – had it not been proved that light had weight? a hundred and sixty tons of it fell on the earth each day! – so what would become of us? Would we be crushed? Would we be made full of holes like a sieve? Was it true that if one made one's mind a blank then such images might fall through? There would be bits of gold and diamonds at the bottom of the sieve.

Sometimes at night there would be the sounds of my mother's and father's voices across the passage: my mother was nagging at my father; my father was being so reasonable; but it seemed to be his very reasonableness, like the demon's unheard voice, that was sending my mother mad. My mother would shout 'You think I don't know about the beautiful things you talk about with Eleanor!' My father would say 'Indeed I would like you to be interested in the beautiful things I talk about with Eleanor.' Then occasionally (as almost happened with Captain Steadfast's airship) my father's patience would break; he would roar and rage at my mother. I would want to shout – But the vacuum! The vacuum! Then I would think – Do we each of us have our evil demons and our Captain Steadfasts in our universes? I would try to go to sleep. But how do you make your mind a vacuum in order to go to sleep? I thought – There must be some trick: how does it happen, just when you are not looking, that you get tipped over on to another universe.

Of course, there were a myriad other things going on in my life at this time: there was my work with Miss Henne; the tea-parties at the houses of friends. But it was my relationship with my father that was like a thread through the maze; it was because of this, of course, that I remember it; one does not remember what is random in a maze.

There are two more instances that pick themselves out from the oddities of this time – the thread of memory bumping me into this or that corner of the maze.

The first was to do with the occasion that became known in history as the Kapp Putsch: this occurred in Berlin in March 1920. There had for some time been rumours – coincidental with the excitement over the confirmation of Einstein's General Theory – of a possible *coup* by right-wing militarists: these were objecting to what they saw as a too easy acceptance of the terms of the Treaty of Versailles. In particular there was said to be danger from General von Lüttwitz whose trooops did in fact move in from where they had been encamped in the suburbs; members of the socialist government under President Ebert fled to Stuttgart; a new government was proclaimed with at its head a conservative politician called Kapp. But then there was the question – as indeed had occurred before to other revolutionaries – what are troops to do after they have marched into the centre of their own city? There they are with their baggage-wagons and bedrolls and field kitchens; where have they to go, what have they to do, except in the end to march out again?

I remember that for two or three days I was again not allowed out of the apartment; I stood at the window and looked down; there did not seemed to be anything much happening in the streets. I understood from my father and mother that the moderate socialists had successfully called for a General Strike; this of course was just what had been advocated by Rosa Luxemburg, but the workers had never heeded Rosa Luxemburg, so why were they now obeying the moderate socialists? They seemed now at last to be acting spontaneously according to whatever were the mysterious laws of history. Water and gas and electricity were cut off; shops and factories were closed; public transport was not working. But still none of this was happening in the style that had been envisaged by Rosa Luxemburg. She had envisaged the iron necessity of history as something forceful and passionate and heroic; that in a General Strike (I remember the speeches of my mother's friends) there should be crowds charging with banners; men with pince-nez urging them on from makeshift platforms on street corners. But now, in this actual General Strike, it was just nothing that seemed to be happening. Soldiers lounged here and there with their bedrolls and mobile kitchens. There was not even the impression of an enormous event round some corner.

I listened to my father and my mother trying to analyse (as my mother's friends would have said) the concrete situation.

– But what on earth can troops do in the centre of a city? –

– They can kill –

– Who can they kill? –

– Are you saying that there is no violence nor oppression in a counter-revolutionary situation? –

– I am saying that in this particular situation, if there is no particular enemy, and if the situation is left alone, then in the end there is nothing for the counter-revolution to do but to withdraw –

– That is ridiculous –

– Yes, it is ridiculous –

– You think it is so easy! –

– No, I think it is very difficult –

– And in the meantime there are people being killed –

– Who in fact is being killed? –

And so on. I thought – I suppose my father, at least, is trying to create a vacuum.

Then on the third day there were indeed crowds coming out on to the streets; but they were still not the sort of crowds that had been imagined in a revolutionary situation; they were holiday crowds – girls on the arms of young men, families with children, individuals wandering and looking for people to make friends with. It was as if, after all, the event round some corner might be a carnival: what indeed should a General Strike be except an occasion for a holiday?

We could see something of this from our windows. My father announced that he was going to take me on one of our walks. My mother said 'You are not taking that child out of this apartment!' My father said 'But there is nothing happening in the streets.' My mother said 'You cannot tell what will happen in such a situation!' She stood with her arms out and her back against the door of the apartment. I thought – Why are there these sorts of religious images in a revolutionary situation?

My father watched my mother with his air of amazement. He said 'But you always wanted a General Strike!'

She said 'Not this General Strike!'

He said 'But it seems to be working.'

She said 'Some sort of joke, you call this working!'

I do not remember how we got past the outstretched arms of my mother. Perhaps in the end she let us go: she wanted herself to see what was happening. I remember my father and I going out into the street, my mother emerging and following some distance behind us.

There were, yes, all these people in the streets; they were moving towards the centre of the town as if on their way to a fairground. When water and electricity have been cut off, and public transport is not working, what better can people do than wander out into the streets? And had not the presence of soldiers always been characteristic of a carnival?

My father and I moved along with my mother not quite catching up with us. I suppose my mother was beginning to be slightly mad at this time; I do not know what my father could have done about her. He was now pretending to ignore her. I wonder now sometimes if it suited him for her to be going slightly mad; then he could wander in his own way dreamily forwards. I imagine I wanted to say to him – Stop! (You think I really wanted to say to him – Stop?) I might have felt suddenly – What is the worth of our breaking through barriers if we drag along in our wake this piece broken off from us, my mother?

At the bottom of Wilhelmstrasse there were, yes, soldiers, sitting on the edges of pavements with their arms round their knees; reclining on their bedrolls against the walls of buildings. Their rifles were stacked in tripods; their kitchens were like small steam-engines on wheels. It was as if everyone was at the end of a picnic. The soldiers watched the crowds go past; the crowds both were and were not quite watching the soldiers; it was as if it were not exactly clear who were the carnival performers and who were the audience. An aeroplane went overhead dropping leaflets like confetti. Within the covered wagons of the soldiers there were glimpses of machine-guns. From the lines of girls that paraded arm-in-arm one girl broke off to offer to the soldiers a bunch of snowdrops: the soldiers looked away. They were unhealthy-looking, rather dried-up men: their uniforms were like bits of old skin peeling off them.

There was a group of civilians round a movie camera set up on a tripod. They were trying to get the girl with snowdrops to go through the motions of offering them to the soldiers again. This time one of the soldiers accepted the snowdrops.

My father and I pushed our way up Wilhelmstrasse towards the Adlon Hotel: my mother followed twenty or so paces behind. When we stopped she stopped; when we went on she came after us. I could not make out if I was angry with or sorry for my mother: I thought – What is the difference. Or – Perhaps my mother will always haunt me thus like a ghost. The crowds were thicker at the end of the street by the Adlon Hotel: there was a semi-circle of bystanders round the hotel's side entrance; it did seem, yes, as if there was taking place some performance. Some waiters were in a cleared space by this side door: one of them had got hold of two rifles and a soldier's helmet; he was holding the rifles so that they stuck up past the sides of his helmet like the horns of a bull. He lowered his head and charged at another waiter – this was the one with fair, glittering hair – who stood and languidly twirled a tablecloth round his hips. I did not know the connotations of these bullfighting images at the time; what was evident was that the soldiers were being mocked. The waiter with the helmet and horns went lumbering past the other who twirled his tablecloth prettily: the crowd jeered and laughed. After a time the good-looking waiter snatched one of the rifles from the other and, with the latter still bent over, pretended to stick the rifle up his behind. Then he turned to the crowd and made his mouth into an 'O' and waggled his tongue up and down. The crowd cheered and whistled. My father and I had made our way to the front of the crowd. Somewhere at the back was my mother; and, of course, the soldiers.

This must have been the day when the so-called Kapp government resigned (or have I run two days together? in my memory my mother has by now come up with us and we are all three standing hand in hand). Anyway, on the third or fourth day of the occupation of the city the rebel politicians and soldiers gave in; they had run out of water and food; the banks would not give Kapp any money. (Oh the effectiveness indeed of a truly general strike!) So on this afternoon the soldiers lined up ready to move out of the city; they would go back to their camps on the outskirts where they would be able to feel at home. While they were preparing, my mother had joined us; we were standing with our backs against a wall at the top of Wilhelmstrasse; we were waiting to watch the troops move out. I remember my mother's bright-eyed face beside me like that of a bird; or like something on the prow of a ship – there was often an impression about my mother of someone moving through spray.

Perhaps I have not always been fair about my mother: I have so many fewer memories of her than of my father. Or I feel guilty about my mother. There were many times when she was good to me, after all: she had sat up with me when I was ill; she had taught me to play the piano; she made for me the dresses in which I went out to the tea-parties of friends. And now here we were hand in hand as a family at the top of Wilhelmstrasse. Most of the crowd had stayed to jeer at the soldiers as they marched out. But I suppose the revolution or counter-revolution could never be a laughing matter for my mother.

The soldiers were like strange animals caught in a desert without water. They moved off round the corner of Wilhelmstrasse and into Under den Linden. There were glimpses of machine-guns in the wagons. From the crowd there were whistles and catcalls and booing. The columns turned left towards Pariser Platz and the Brandenburg Gate. When the last of the columns had gone round the corner the crowds broke and drifted after them. My mother and father and I at first stayed with our backs against our wall; then my father moved off in the wake of the crowd. He held me by the hand; my mother pulled me back by my other hand; she would not let me go. I was thinking – She wants to protect me; but I have been on so many journeys with my father! Then my father let me go; he went off in the wake of the crowd. I was angry both with my father and my mother – how could I be left behind! I broke away and went after my father. I thought I would just go round the corner into Pariser Platz and then I could say that I had been with my father and then perhaps I could go back to the safety of my mother: or I could be on my own. Then suddenly there were shots. I had got round the corner, I could see the Brandenburg Gate, I did not at first recognise the sound of shots; it was like fireworks going off. These were the only shots fired during those three or four days. But then there were people running back from the direction of the Brandenburg Gate. Some were screaming. I stayed where I was because I wanted to find my father. There was a girl just next to me who was not much older than myself; she had been knocked backwards as if something like a tram had hit her; she had sat on the ground. Then she rolled over, holding her middle. The crowd trampled over her. Then my father came up and grabbed me. What had happened I learned later (there were photographs of this in the illustrated magazines) was that as the end of the last column of soldiers was going through the Brandenburg Gate the crowd, coming up behind, had given it a valedictory jeer; and the soldiers sitting on the backs of baggage-wagons had opened fire for a moment with machine-guns. And now there was the crowd running back to the safety of Wilhelmstrasse. I think both my father and my mother grabbed me at the same time – the one running back and the other running forwards – and then we were all going back round the corner to our wall. But my mother was once more shouting and yelling at my father. Then my father and I stood in an alcove while my mother went back into Pariser Platz; this was now almost emptied of the crowd; there were just bodies here and there and my mother picking her way amongst them like a bird. She knelt down by the young girl who was lying on her side holding her middle. My father and I watched her. I thought – She is like an angel, or a vulture. Then – But what my mother shouted at my father was: 'You murderer!'

The other incident that has stayed in my memory of this time (a bump from a corner of the maze; a nugget left behind in the sieve) was to do with the rocketing to fame of Professor Einstein.

The publicity given to the corroboration of the General Theory of Relativity, combined with the apparent need of the public for at least the illusion of a liberating vision, had resulted in adulation for Einstein but also a growing hostility. In particular there was animosity towards him on the part of some scientists in the Berlin Academy, who either did not understand what he was proposing, or did not like it if they did. They complained not only that his physics was incorrect, but that his theories were undermining objective principles about right and wrong. In particular there was a physicist called Lenard, a Nobel prizewinner, who led the attack

35

against Einstein. After a time this took the form of a crusade against what came to be called 'Jewish' physics. It had been a characteristic of German anti-Semitism, I suppose, that Jews were held to be subversive to objective standards of right and wrong.

These so-called 'true German' scientists embarked on a series of public lectures to try to warn what they saw as the gullible public about the machinations of the wicked Professor Einstein. My father got tickets for one of these lectures; he wanted to attend it so that, of course, he might be better armed to defend Professor Einstein. He got two tickets, intending to go with my mother, but my mother was becoming more and more distant from both my father and me at this time; she would spend two or three nights at a time away at her soup-kitchen; she was becoming increasingly involved again in Communist politics. When she came back to the apartment now she would sleep in the dining-room which had been rearranged to take a bed; my father and I ate and sat in the drawing-room. At the time of the shooting in Pariser Platz I had felt some kinship with my mother; it was as if some light had entered my mind about the prevalence of death. But my mother did not seem to want to take any notice of this; it was as if she wanted quite openly now to hand me over to my father.

So when my father asked her to go with him to the anti-Einstein lecture, saying that there might be a chance here of their joining hands in their work, she just said 'Take Eleanor.'

My father said 'Eleanor's too young.'

'She's not too young for most of the things you get up to.'

So my father said to me 'Would you like to come to this lecture?'

I said 'Can I?'

He said 'There's no reason why not.'

I thought – I still do not know if she wants to damage me, or encourage me, my mother.

I remember that I tried to dress up to appear as old as I could for this lecture: I put on one of my mother's hats; it looked ridiculous; I took it off. In the end I wore just one of my mother's shawls. The lecture was in the old Philharmonic Hall; there were boxes in tiers; there did not seem to be any empty seats in the hall. I suppose it was brave of my father to take me; many of his colleagues were there; they looked at me curiously. I think my father had told them that I was some sort of mathematical prodigy – which I was not. We sat in the stalls. The audience did not seem to be so different from that at a concert of Wagner's music that my father had taken me to not long before in the same hall; the music had made my mind go blank; I had thought – If I were a snake, yes, I would be being drawn up out of a basket. Now I thought – Will this lecture be about Jewishness and non-Jewishness? I must pay attention: I have to study, after all, what is it to be half Jewish and half not.

The first speaker was a large man in evening dress who had a purple sash across his chest. He spoke about the Theory of Relativity being contrary to the German Spirit; this Spirit was to do with the Fatherland and blood and God, while Relativity was to do with atheism and decadence and chaos. According to him Relativity was also, in some contradictory way, to do with a highly organised conspiracy for world domination. The Absolute German Spirit, he said, if it did not take heed, would be overwhelmed by an alliance of rampant subjectivity and alien invasion. The man made strange gestures with his arms as if he were throwing stones. I thought – How long will it take the stones to go right round the universe and hit him on the back of the head?

The next speaker was a small neat man with a beard. He explained how the so-called 'corroboration' of the General Theory was anyway not scientific because it was probable that any peculiarities in the experimenters' measurements were caused by the deflection of light by the murky atmosphere round the sun. And anyway, he added – was it not significant that the theory of Professor Einstein had been confirmed, if that could be the word, by the British! This last remark brought forth a growl of approval from the hall. My father was sitting with his hair seeming to stand on end. I thought – But he will not shoot up and make some public protest, will he? Is it not best, in this strange territory, if we remain somewhat secret; then according to the theory will not these people find their criticisms coming down upon themselves?

Then at a certain stage of the evening there was a slight disturbance in the hall; heads were turning as if a wind were blowing them; there were people entering late and settling down in one of the boxes in the first tier. One of them, sitting at the front, even looked like Professor Einstein. People around us began to whisper; my father was looking up at the box as if he were indeed now transfixed by light; then he murmured to me that the man in the box was, to be sure, Professor Einstein. There·was the dark halo of hair; the humorous look that seemed to be going far outwards and inwards all at once. This was the only time that I saw Einstein in the flesh. From the front of the box he bowed slightly to the audience; he seemed to be acknowledging their whisperings. The speaker on the platform had paused; Einstein waved at him as if he were encouraging him to continue. The whispering in the hall subsided. (This was on 27 August 1920; I have checked the date; do you think it makes it more telling if I can say 'I have checked the date'?) Einstein sat back in his box. The speaker went on. He was suggesting what a dangerous and terrible thing it was to have no objectivity. Einstein was nodding and smiling; he leaned back and spoke to one of the people behind him; this person laughed. The man on the stage paused again; he seemed both at a loss and furious. I thought suddenly – But what of that crowd, those waiters, the people who jeered at the soldiers! Einstein leaned forward and clapped, sardonically, at the speaker; it was as if the performance might be over. Then my father whispered 'Oh don't overdo it!' I remember this whisper quite clearly: I thought I understood it. I put my head in my hands. Several images had come into my mind all at once: there was my mother walking like a bird amongst the dead or dying bodies as if on a battlefield; there was the girl curled up with her hands to her middle (I read later that she had died); then there was a photograph I had come across recently when I had been looking through some of my mother's papers, which was of the body of Rosa Luxemburg when she had been dragged from the canal some months after she had been killed. Her face was like that of a wooden doll, half eaten by worms. So I felt I understood when my father whispered 'Oh don't overdo it!' When the small furious man on the platform began speaking again his beard pointed and waggled up and down like a machine-gun. Professor Einstein seemed only to have his halo of hair to protect him.

II: Max

If we are talking about an environment in which the acceptance of paradoxes might breed, then this can happen in an English hothouse, I suppose, as well as in a melting-pot of Berlin streets.

Then the products might come together, as a result of what it seems you called 'gravity'?

After the First World War the centre of the intellectual and cultural life of England was at Cambridge. When I, Max Ackerman, was ten or eleven years old – I was born two years after you (I need to tell you!), Eleanor – I was living with my parents in a village just outside Cambridge. Pretty redbrick cottages were on either side of a winding street; larger houses were set back within lawns behind walls. Our house was one of the largest in the village. White-framed windows were like the backdrop to a stage-set: there was room for both tennis and croquet on the lawn.

My mother came from a family that had for long had connections with Cambridge. She had been brought up on the fringes of what was even then known as the Bloomsbury Group; this had at one time been seen as a London outpost of Cambridge. The intellectual atmosphere of both Cambridge and Bloomsbury had been set by the philosopher G. E. Moore who taught that the aim of humans should be to cultivate beautiful states of mind – the pleasures of human intercourse and the enjoyment of exquisite objects. He had begun one lecture with the words 'We should spread scepticism until at last everybody knows that we can know absolutely nothing'; and then apparently had been overcome with laughter.

My father also came from a Cambridge family but one of a more austere intellectual tradition. He was a scientist: his father and grandfather had been scientists – one a biologist and the other a physicist. My father was a biologist specialising in the field of genetic inheritance. There was a good deal of controversy in this area as he grew up; orthodox Darwinists were under attack; it was difficult for them to explain how evolution could have occurred simply through chance mutations and natural selection. There seemed to be too many coincidences required for the emergence, by these means, of complex organic forms.

I was an only child. I do not know why my father and my mother did not have more children. Perhaps too many coincidences have to be taken into account for the answering of such questions.

I had a bedroom on the top floor of our house, from which I could look down on what went on in the world below. There were the red-tiled roofs of the village; the tops of creeper-covered walls along which squirrels ran. My mother might be talking to Mr Simmons the gardener by one of the herbaceous borders; my father might emerge on to the lawn from the greenhouse where he had once kept the famous collection of sweet peas with which he had been able to confirm some of the ideas about genetic inheritance put forward by Mendel. These had made it easier to understand the evolution of complex organic forms.

I had been allowed the use of an attic room of our house in which I could set up my toys. At an earlier time in my childhood I had created a model village complete with houses and shops and a church; there were roads and a railway system that ran right round the room; at the door there was a drawbridge to allow giant humans to go in and out. It had seemed important to me to try to make a model of the real world in my attic; not exactly so that I could control it, but rather perhaps so that there should be somewhere orderly and exact in which I might feel at home. At the time about which I am writing my model village was still intact: but now I spent more time with my electricity and chemistry sets, which I suppose were like factories springing up and polluting the once pristine countryside.

Beyond a green baize door on the top floor of the house there were the rooms of Mrs Elgin the cook and Watson the parlourmaid (what complex evolution of forms must have been required for a cook but not a parlourmaid to have acquired the prefix 'Mrs'!). On the floor below there were my mother's bedroom and my father's separate bedroom and their bathrooms and two spare rooms. There was a primitive bathroom next to my bedroom, which had pipes that shuddered and bubbled like pieces of my chemistry set.

The times when I felt most at home outside the fastness of my attic were when my father was away; he used to go on lecture tours to the Continent and to America. Then I could ride my bicycle in and out of the croquet hoops of the lawn; in the evenings I could stay in the drawing-room and be read to by my mother. My mother and I would sit side by side on the curved seat on the inside of a bow window; our backs would be to the setting sun; there would be the cool touch of flames at our necks. When I was younger my mother had read to me fairy stories; I think we went on being interested in fantasies and myths somewhat after a time when they might have been thought suitable for a boy. My mother had a professional interest in fairy stories since she was studying psycho-analysis and saw that useful insights might be gained by an analysis of such matters: I suppose I liked whatever was of interest to my mother. In particular I enjoyed stories in which a person went on a journey for the sake of some precious object that had to be found or some person to be rescued; on the way there were meetings with birds, magicians, rings, wells, animals; there had to be an understanding of portents and tricks, an answering of riddles.

I would wonder – Is this or is this not to do with the real world?

Or – This is one of the riddles?

Most of all during these evenings I would like the proximity of my mother; I would put my head against her shoulder so that I could better follow the words that she was reading; with the sun behind us, it was as if we were in long grass on a summer's day. My mother was a large golden-haired woman who sat straight-backed; there was a way in which the top half of her body seemed to be like milk contained miraculously by the air. I would put my arm around her; when she had finished reading she would hug me.

She would say 'You shouldn't be stuck with your old mother! You should be out playing with friends.'

I would say 'I haven't got any friends.'

She would say 'Do you want any?'

I would say 'No.'

She would say 'Why not?' Then – 'Don't tell your old mother!'

Often when my father was working in Cambridge he would bring a gang of his friends home at weekends. They would arrive in cars or on bicycles; they would come on to the lawn pulling off scarves and caps or goggles; they would be laughing and nudging one another and chattering. They broke into my mother's and my quiet world like Vikings in longboats from the sea. My father kept in the hall an enormous bag of shoes suitable for croquet or tennis; he would bring this bag out and toss shoes to people even as they came on to the lawn; they were supposed to catch them; this was a game even before the start of a proper game; it was as if there had to be established from the very beginning of a visit the style that the guest was expected to conform to.

My mother would move graciously from one to another of my father's guests. She often wore a long white skirt nipped in at the waist. The people she spoke to would stand awkwardly and hit at their legs with a mallet or a racket. My mother would stay with them for a time; then move back through the windows into the drawing-room.

Once, after my mother had gone, my father's friends played leap-frog on the lawn.

My father would call to me 'Where are you off to?'

I would say 'I thought I'd just go upstairs.'

'Don't you want a game of croquet?'

'I've just had one, thanks.'

'Who with?'

'Myself.'

'Don't strain yourself, will you.'

My father was a large, thick-set man with a moustache that came down over the lower part of his face like a portcullis. He would wear a panama hat when he played croquet. He would crouch over his ball, then go bounding after it. I would wonder – Why can he not let it go its own way; would he then have to trust to birds, rings, portents, riddles?

I understood that my father was quite famous for the work he had done in biology. From books I had in my room I did not find it difficult to understand the business of natural selection: all life evolved by means of chance mutations in genes, the products of which are put to the test by the environment; most mutations die, because of course what is established is what is suited to the environment. But occasionally there is a change in the environment coincident with a genetic mutation, the result of which is suited to the change – suited in the sense that it is more likely to survive in the new conditions than the established stock from which it comes. So then it is the mutation or mutant that survives and eventually the old stock dies. But what seemed mysterious to me – what had once apparently seemed mysterious to my father – were the questions of what occasioned these mutations; what is called 'chance'; how many and how frequent coincidences had to occur for it to be possible for a new form of life to emerge? Was it not what might be called 'miraculous', that so many coincidences seemed to have to happen all at once for a new strain to occur?

At Sunday lunches my mother would say to my father 'Can you explain to Max?'

My father would say 'It's really a matter of statistical analysis.'

My mother would say 'I understand that it is a matter of all sorts of mutations being latent and potentially available in the gene pool.'

My father would say 'Lovely bits of mummy and daddy swimming in the gene pool.'

My mother would say 'I do think it a pity that you cannot be serious with Max.'

My father would say 'You can use such images if you like. But such language does not help explanation.'

My mother would look away as if she were someone in a fairy story imprisoned in a castle.

There were times, nearly always when my father was away, when a group of my mother's friends came down from London. They would emerge on to the lawn having walked perhaps from the station; they were unlike my father's friends in that they did not make much noise. There was a rather ancient young man with steel spectacles and beard; a much younger-looking young man in white flannels who danced up and down in front of him. There were two tall ladies in floppy hats and with beads who went and gazed at the herbaceous border. Then they would all sit in deckchairs and seem to be waiting to be photographed. When they talked it was as if they were trying out lines for a play.

After they had gone, and my father had come home, he would say 'And how are the Wombsburys?'

My mother would say 'Very well, thank you.'

My father would say 'Bedded any good boys lately?'

My mother would say 'Please don't talk like that in front of Max.'

I would want to say – But of course he can talk like that in front of me!

My father once said to my mother 'If I were you, I'd watch out for them having a go at Max.' My mother got up and left the table.

I suppose I wondered why my father and my mother went on at each other like this; but their style seemed to be just part of the grown-up world. There was all the battling and jockeying for position. I would wonder – This is something to do with the needs of natural selection?

Quite often I went through to talk to Mrs Elgin and Watson in the kitchen. In their separate world they would be banging pots and pans about and getting on with polishing the silver.

I would say 'Who do you like best, my father's or my mother's friends?'

Mrs Elgin would say 'I've got something better to do all day than think about things like that!'

I once said 'I think that man with the beard is going to ask the man in white flannels to marry him.'

Watson said 'One day the wind will change and you won't be able to get rid of those ideas!'

I would think – Oh one day will I find someone with whom talk is not a testing or a battle?

Then sometime in 1923 (this was the summer of my eleventh birthday) there appeared on the Cambridge scene – I mean by 'Cambridge scene' not only the academics in their lecture-rooms and laboratories but also, on this occasion at least, the concourse on my father's lawn – a biologist from Vienna called Kammerer. The story of Kammerer is quite well known; but I have this particular memory of him among the men in white flannels and knickerbockers and the croquet hoops on our lawn. Kammerer was a thin, youngish middle-aged man with a high forehead and brushed-back hair; he wore a dark suit of a strangely hairy material. His eyes were alert and watchful; he seemed puzzled, yet not put out by the things going on around him. When my father introduced him to my mother, he kissed her hand. Then he held on to her hand for a moment, as if his attention had been caught by something just behind her eyes. My mother put one foot behind the other and rubbed her ankle with it; it was almost as if she were doing a curtsey.

I thought – But he is like someone come down from a strange planet: a mutation?

My father stood hitting a tennis racket against his leg.

Now what I had heard of this Dr Kammerer was that my father looked on him as a great enemy: they had been having some dispute about the nature of genetic inheritance. Dr Kammerer (so I had understood from my father) was a heretic – something called a 'Lamarckian'. What he was supposed to believe in (it is impossible in such areas, as you say, to avoid the jargon) was the inheritance of acquired characteristics.

What Darwinists such as my father believed in (arguments about dogma go round and round; it is impossible also not to repeat oneself) was that parents can transmit through heredity only what they have inherited themselves – they cannot pass on the skills or faults or features that they have acquired during their lifetimes; though they can, of course, pass on something of these by teaching. Evolutionary jumps take place when mutations in genetic material occur by chance; 'chance' means here just what cannot be explained scientifically in terms of what is predictable. There was even a theory that genetic mutations might be caused by cosmic radiation, but this conjecture could not be tested.

Lamarckians (taking their name from a French biologist who lived in the early nineteenth century) claimed that it is impossible to explain evolution by chance occurrences: for such huge steps to have occurred as, for instance, the emergence of the human eye, there would have to have been such myriad interlocking coincidences as to be inconceivable: what possible evolutionary advantage could there have been in the emergence on their own of one or two still useless facets of the complex totality of the human eye which only functions when it is complete? For explanations to make sense there had to be taken into account the likelihood of some directing or at least coordinating force among the plethora of required mutations: and it did seem, yes, that this might be provided by the possibility of what had been of advantage to parents being in some way genetically passed on. This would not mean, for instance, that a parent who had lost a limb would pass on to an offspring this lack of a limb: Lamarckians suggested that only such characteritics might be passed on as would be of advantage in coming to terms with the environment.

But this sort of talk was anathema to Darwinists, ostensibly because there was no means of explaining scientifically how this learning on the part of parents could be transmitted to the genetic material, the cells of which could be shown (or so it was believed) to be quite separate from the cells of the other parts of the body. But it seems to me now (of course, no scientist talked like this at the time) that there was some rage or even terror amongst biologists at the suggestion that what a person had acquired (or not acquired!) during a lifetime might be passed on to offspring: what a burden of responsibility this would place upon a parent! Every failure would be perpetuated; every fault would make a person accountable for ever.

During the early years of the twentieth century the situation remained confused: neither Darwinists nor Lamarckians seemed able to answer the objections that each put up against the other. Then there was the rediscovery by people like my father of Mendelian genetics – theories about inheritance suggested by Mendel fifty years earlier but not at the time taken up. These described how innumerable small differences occurring naturally in genetic material could be seen, by an understanding and application of mathematics, to account for the larger changes in living forms seeming to occur just when a change in the environment, as it were, provoked or required them: it was as if (my mother had used an image that was coming into vogue at the time) there were indeed all sorts of latent mutations hanging about waiting to be encouraged to emerge from what might be called a 'gene pool'. This image, it was true, did not seem very explicit about what it actually referred to; but then experts such as my father could retreat behind their jargon – or behind their claim that such a matter could properly only be understood by mathematicians.

But then, just when geneticists like my father seemed to be getting the business sorted out, or at least protected, there turned up on the scene this Viennese biologist called Kammerer who appeared to claim once more that Lamarck was probably right – in certain circumstances parents could, yes, be shown to transmit by heredity to their offspring characterics which they had acquired during their lifetimes.

Kammerer was this thin man with a high forehead and brushed-back hair; he had come on to our lawn and had kissed my mother's hand: my father was banging his tennis racket against his leg.

This was on a Sunday afternoon; there were the men in blazers and white flannels on the lawn. They were playing croquet; at any moment they might be playing leap-frog. Dr Kammerer was looking round the garden as if he were sizing up possible escape routes; or perhaps manoeuvres for survival on this strange planet.

My father said 'Do you play tennis?'

Dr Kammerer said 'I sometimes play.'

My father said 'I can lend you a pair of shoes.'

Now I knew about my father's ways of playing tennis: he used a tennis court as some sort of battle-ground on which to engage with the people (and these seemed to be most people) against whom he felt aggression. He was, I suppose, quite a good player for his age; he put great energy into his game; he would serve and rush to the net; he would leap to and fro volleying; he would prance backwards towards the baseline slashing at high balls as if they were seagulls or vultures attacking him. Sometimes I would be his partner in a foursome and it seemed to be his aim, at the net, never to let a ball reach me. Once there was a very high lob and my father came staggering back; it was obviously my ball; I tried to get to it; my father and I collided and he fell on top of me. I remember the bright amused look in his eye as people ran up to us as if he might have done me some injury.

Now Dr Kammerer was saying 'Oh I don't need any shoes!'

My father said 'You can't play in those.'

Dr Kammerer said 'I will play in bare feet.'

He sat on the grass and took off his shoes. My mother watched him. When he looked up he seemed to wink at my mother.

Then he took off his jacket and jumped up and down on his toes. He had trousers that were much narrower than the trousers of my father's friends. He looked elegant. Trousers at that time were apt to be like the screens behind which one undressed in a doctor's consulting-room.

My father said 'Well I suppose you'll need a racket!'

Dr Kammerer said 'Or shall I use my bare hands!' He smiled, not quite catching my mother's eye.

She said 'You don't have to play, you know!'

He said 'Oh I think I do!'

In fact Kammerer played tennis well. But he seemed to treat it not so much as a game – an activity in which someone had to win and someone to lose – as an exercise in practising some quite solitary proficiency. He stood halfway up the court near the service line and played most of his shots from there; he did not rush to the net nor come prancing back; he stayed roughly where he was and when balls came near him he volleyed or half-volleyed them for the most part expertly, and when balls did not come near him he turned and watched his partner solicitously. When it came to his turn to serve he seemed reluctant and even slightly bewildered about this; but then he pulled off some quick cutting serves that went into the corners of his opponents' court and were quite often aces. He appeared to be somewhat apologetic about these: but not too much, as if he were anxious lest this might seem condescending.

My father on the other side of the net heaved and leaped and dashed about like a seal: I thought – Kammerer is a keeper at a zoo and he is throwing my father fish. When the score had reached something like six all my father said 'You've played quite a bit!'

Dr Kammerer said 'In my time.'

My father said 'Shall we play sudden death?'

Dr Kammerer looked to where my mother and I were sitting, and where Watson was coming out with tea-things on to the lawn. He put his hand on his heart. He said 'As a matter of fact, I think what I would love is some tea!'

My father said 'Ah, it's a business keeping fit!'

We sat on deckchairs on the lawn. Dr Kammerer sat next to my mother. He glanced at her sideways quickly from time to time; my mother seemed to know that he was doing this but to be pretending not to know; but in such a way that Dr Kammerer would know that she knew. I was thinking – If Dr Kammerer is some mutation, is it that he knows, without talking, what people are up to?

Sometime in the course of tea Dr Kammerer turned to me and said 'You do not like tennis?'

I said 'Not really.'

He said 'Why not?'

I said 'I don't think I like winning.'

He seemed to think about this. Then he said 'You are very lucky.'

My father, who had overheard this conversation, said 'Not winning would seem to be an accomplishment extraordinarily easy to achieve.'

Dr Kammerer said 'Oh no, it is very difficult! Very paradoxical!'

I was pleased about this. I thought – Dr Kammerer, my mother and I, we are each a mutation that knows what the others are up to?

After tea my father took Dr Kammerer off to his study. Before he went Dr Kammerer said to my mother 'I will see you before I go?'

She said 'Yes.'

I thought – But will he be able to survive, in this environment!

While he was gone I talked with my mother about what she knew about Dr Kammerer. He came from a prosperous Viennese family;

he had originally trained to be a musician but had turned to biology because of a passionate love for animals. He was often able to keep delicate animals alive for his experiments in circumstances in which others could not.

One of the experiments for which he had become famous just before the First World War (I learned about these in the weeks or months following the visit of Dr Kammerer) was to do with two species of salamander (small newt-like amphibians) known as *Salamandra atra* and *Salamandra maculosa*. The former are found in the European Alps, and the latter in the Lowlands. The two species have different breeding characteristics: the alpine female gives birth on dry land to two fully formed young salamanders; the lowland species gives birth in water to up to fifty tadpole-like larvae which only months later turn into salamanders. Kammerer's experiment had been to take alpine salamanders and to put them in lowland conditions and see whether, as a first step, they would acquire the breeding characteristics of lowland salamanders; and then, if they did, to see what would be the breeding characteristics of the offspring of these salamanders in so-called 'neutral' conditions – would they have inherited the acquired characteristics of their parents, or would they have reverted to the original breeding habits of their ancestors? Kammerer claimed that he had, first, succeeded in getting alpine salamanders to breed in lowland conditions in a lowland manner – they had produced, that is, tadpole-like larvae – and then the offspring of these salamanders in so-called 'neutral' conditions had continued to produce larvae: and so from this Kammerer suggested that they had inherited the acquired characteristics of their parents.

It seems to me now (you think it could not have struck me like this at the time?) that there was a dubiousness about these experiments and the claims that Kammerer seemed to make from them: for instance, what could have been the 'neutral' conditions in which offspring were placed that would have been suitable for demonstrating their inheriting (or not) the acquired characteristics? Might not the conditions provided be simply those that encourage the emergence of either one set of characteristics or the other? But what was striking about the objections to Kammerer on the part of mainstream biologists (this was what much later came particularly to interest me) was that they did not point out rationally, as they might so easily have done, the flaws in his arguments and procedures; they seemed intent on impugning emotionally his honesty and even his sanity; they claimed that he was 'cooking' his results – even those that were so obviously tentative.

One of the difficulties about all this in 1923 was that Kammerer's experiments with salamanders had been done before the First World War; during the war his laboratory had been dismantled and most of his specimens destroyed; in the post-war inflation in Vienna he had found it impossible to get money to set up his experiments again. And then there was the fact that when other biologists tried to repeat his experiments, they could not keep alive long enough to get any results the animals that Kammerer had managed to keep alive through several generations. It was perhaps annoyance at this that drove mainstream biologists to hint that Kammerer must be a charlatan.

Nevertheless his reputation was still such that he was invited to Cambridge in 1923: he was only the second ex-enemy-alien to be invited to Cambridge since the war. (The first – you will be pleased at the coincidence! – had been Einstein.)

I picked up bits and pieces about all this at the time: I learned details later. But the picture I had in my mind about Kammerer did not have to be much amended later.

At the end of that day when he had played tennis on the lawn and after he had gone along with the rest of my father's guests – I had not properly said goodbye to him: I minded about this: I had run out on to the drive just in time to wave as he drove away; I think he waved to me; but of course it was more probable that he was waving to my mother –

– At the end of this day, when my mother and father and I were settling down to some plates of cold meat for supper, my father said –

'Well, what's the verdict?'

My mother said 'The verdict about what?'

'Dr Kammerer, of course.'

'He is certainly very charming.'

'Yes, "charming" is the word I would use myself.'

'You use it with a certain distaste.'

'It is not a word held in high regard in scientific circles.'

'But this afternoon we were not in scientific circles.'

'No indeed we were not.'

And so on.

This was the sort of conversation that had to be suspended while Watson the parlourmaid came in with dishes. Watson was a tall craggy woman like a member of a military band. She would bang her plates and cutlery about at the sideboard like percussion.

The word 'charming' was one I had not heard my mother use before. I thought – Well, no, you could not call my father's friends charming: and my mother's friends, well, but their charm is like that of witches around a lukewarm cauldron. But Dr Kammerer was like a wizard with his hands round a crystal ball –

My mother said 'He played tennis very well.'

My father said 'He never moved.'

'How lovely to find someone who hardly needs to move!'

'Well in his line of business he certainly moves one or two pieces around on the board, when no one is looking, I can tell you!'

When my father and my mother went on like this I usually switched my attention off: but every now and then I cared about something enough to want to try to divert them.

I said 'But why do you think Dr Kammerer was able to keep his salamanders alive in captivity, while others could not?'

My father said 'That is indeed a subject on which we have little information.'

My mother said 'Perhaps he loved them.'

My father said 'Loved them!'

My mother said 'Haven't you heard that things are sometimes helped to stay alive if they are loved?'

Perhaps Watson clattered in or out again at this point with some dishes. I sometimes wondered – Might one of the reasons why people employ servants be so that they can be rescued at regular intervals from their dreadful conversations?

But now my father ploughed on. 'Yes indeed Dr Kammerer is said to have an amazing way with animals. Once, when he was out on one of his walks looking for specimens, he is said to have picked up a toad and to have kissed it.'

My mother said 'I'm sure it turned into a princess.'

Watson had become curiously quiet at the sideboard.

I said 'But you haven't answered my question.'

My father said 'What was your question?'

'Why do you think Dr Kammerer could keep his salamanders alive while you could not.'

I thought this quite brave. I knew that my father had tried, and failed, to reproduce some of Kammerer's experiments. To be able to ask a question like this, I was probably on the edge of tears.

My father said 'Are you suggesting that there was some flaw in my handling of the breeding experiment? Do tell us. Do give us the benefit of your experience.'

My mother said 'It is interesting you should put it like that.'

My father said 'Like what.'

My mother said ' "Are you suggesting some flaw in my handling of the breeding – " ' Then she broke off and said 'Oh never mind!'

My father said 'Oh we're now going to have your expertise about the hidden meaning behind the meaning of words, are we?'

My mother said 'Max asked you a question which you would not answer.' I did not think my mother was on the point of tears.

Watson had completed her performance at the sideboard. But we anyway ate the rest of the meal in silence.

I would think – Well, God protect me from inheriting any of the acquired characteristics of my father!

And – There is no reason, is there, why I should not be a mutation?

After such an evening my mother would come up to say goodnight to me in my room and she would lie back on the bed as if she were exhausted. She would say 'What a comfort you are to your old mother!'

On this occasion I wanted to say – But what do you really feel about Dr Kammerer? It is different from what you feel about my father?

But sometimes with my mother sprawled on my bed like this my mind went blank; it was as if we were somehow on hot sand; as if I were an insect that could be crawling on her.

I do not know if I make sense in my descriptions of my mother: she was this large blonde woman who was sometimes girlish and sometimes queenly; sometimes apparently a victim and often victorious. In relation to my father she often seemed to be all these things at once: she would sit with her legs curled underneath her and her eyes cast sadly down like a mermaid on a rock; then, as if glistening with spray, she would be a siren luring helpless sailors to their doom. In arguments with my father she would sometimes seem to yield to his heavier weight; then suddenly, with a ju-jitsu-like flick of her wrist, as it were, it was as if she had him flying over her head and into the shrubbery. Or more prosaically, he would be rushing out to his car to go to Cambridge. There are tricks like this that people can do who practise psychoanalysis: opponents can attack you; you can say 'Now it is interesting why you say that!' and there they are, in the air on their way into the shrubbery.

This evening when my mother was lying on her back in my room she looked at me with her eyes that even I could tell were somewhat wicked; and she said 'Shall we ask him again?'

I said 'Who?'

She said 'Dr Kammerer, of course.' Then – 'I know he liked you. Did you like him?'

I said 'Yes.'

I wanted to explain – It was somehow as if we all three, she and I and he, were agents in an occupied territory.

Sometimes when my mother came up to talk to me in my bedroom like this she would after a time start pulling her skirt up and say 'I must pee.'

This sort of thing between mother and son was, I suppose, unusual for the time: perhaps it came from ideas that arose out of psychoanalysis about the need for relationships between parents and children to be open. My mother would go next door to the bathroom and would expect me to go on chatting through the half-open door while she sat on the lavatory.

I said 'What did you think was so special about Dr Kammerer?'

She said 'He didn't show off. At least not to others.'

She sat with her legs apart: her arms hung down between her knees.

I said 'And that's a good thing?'

She said 'Yes.'

I said 'Why?'

She said 'I think he was interested in getting on with what he wanted.'

She gave herself a wipe with some paper between her legs.

My mother's interest in psychoanalysis had begun, I suppose, when she had found herself on the edge of the Bloomsbury Group and, possessing like other women in the group considerable energy which she did not want to expend in social or domestic chores or on the taking of buns and tea to the poor of the village – but, unlike some women in the group, finding that she had no literary or artistic talent – she had turned to what seemed to be the latest intellectual challenge, which was psychoanalysis. And what more effective business indeed can be turned to by people who have creative energy but no artistic talent (you think I am having a dig at you? but I am having a dig at myself! you know how I admire psychoanalysis!) than this discipline which can make people feel, if they wish, that they are creative in a way even superior to those

53

who create artistically. For do not analysts feel that they can explain away the mechanisms of artistic creation? And how well, ju-jitsu-like, can they defend themselves against those who try to explain away the mechanisms of psychoanalysis! (And you know how I admire people who defend themselves without appearing to defend themselves.)

Anyway, psychoanalysis had begun to make an impact on Bloomsbury at this time: James Strachey, brother of Lytton, had gone to Vienna in 1919 to be analysed by Freud; Adrian Stephen, Virginia Woolf's brother, had become a practising analyst in London. My mother, when I had begun to go to school, had become a founder member of a group studying psychoanalysis in Cambridge. Now in 1923 and 1924 she was going up once a week to whatever lectures were being given in London.

I once said to her 'Tell me about these lectures.'

She said 'You want me to explain about psychoanalysis?'

I said 'Yes.'

(I do not think even my mother could have had this conversation while she was sitting on the lavatory: she was probably sitting in the bow window of the drawing-room, with her legs pulled up underneath her like a mermaid.)

She said 'Psychoanalysis is to do with the idea that certain patterns are set in the mind, probably as a result of a person's experiences in early childhood. These experiences have been frightening; so a child protects himself by pushing his feelings into that part of the mind that is called the unconscious. There he need not think of them, but they go bad, like things rotting in a cellar. Psychoanalysis is the process of trying to bring them into the sun.'

I said 'I see.'

She said 'How funny to be talking to you like this!'

I wanted to say – What frightening experiences did I have in childhood?

I said 'And do they get better in the sun?'

She said 'Yes.' Then – 'Not always.' Then – 'I think so, if you are brave enough to let them.'

I said 'What sort of experiences did I have in early childhood?' I laughed.

I thought – Why am I laughing? Then – You mean, I am protecting myself?

– From whatever things are rotting away in my cellar? From my mother?

My mother seemed to think for a time. Then she said 'They are usually, yes, to do with your parents.'

You know those experiences we have always been interested in, you and I – those moments when what one is talking about seems to coincide with what is happening: it is then that it is as if there is a white light coming down; some performance on a stage is over, and an audience is getting up to leave the theatre. Well, this was the first time I remember being conscious of such an experience: there I was with my mother in the bow window of the drawing-room; the sun was at our backs; she had her legs underneath her like a siren; I was a sailor who had swum to the edge of her rock and was about to pull myself up out of the sea.

I said 'Well, tell me.'

She said 'What do you want to know?'

I thought – How do I know if it is unconscious?

Then she said 'In fact, of course, it is only you who know. The analyst can only help you to remember.'

I said 'I see.' Then – 'How?'

She said 'He or she listens for what is behind your words; for what is still in the dark, and not in the sun.'

I said 'And can that be heard?'

After a time she said 'I think so. Can't it?'

I was thinking – There is, yes, this feeling of ants crawling over the earth, my mother.

I said 'But how much does all this tie up with what my father is doing in biology?'

She said 'Good heavens, in no way at all, as far as I know.' She looked disappointed.

I said 'But shouldn't it?'

She said 'Why?'

I said 'Aren't they both to do with the things that go on between parents and children?'

She said 'I hadn't thought of that.'

I thought – But why haven't you thought of that?

– You mean, it might be because of something that happened in your early childhood?

I was quite pleased with this. I thought that I would like to tell it to my father.

Then – But why is it, yes, that I seem to want to score off my mother?

Dr Kammerer's visit to us was in 1923, the summer of my

eleventh birthday. These conversations with my mother, and then with my father, might have taken place a year or two later. But I was quite a clever little boy; I was at a good school to which I went each day; I liked listening to and joining in the conversations of grown-ups. I had few friends of my own age at this time.

I sometimes hung about outside the conservatory when my father was tending to what was left of his collection of sweet peas. His serious work was now done in his laboratory in Cambridge.

He would say 'Come in! Don't moon about!'

(He once said to me 'I used to have a goose like you who mooned about outside windows looking at itself in the glass: it thought its reflection was its lost lady-love, which I had eaten.')

I said 'Can I ask you something?'

'Fire away.'

'How much is the work that you are doing in genetics to do with what Mother is interested in in psychoanalysis?'

'Nothing.'

'Nothing?'

'Absolutely nothing.'

'But why not?'

My father was snipping bits off sweet peas. At some times of the year he would stroke them tenderly with a small artist's brush.

He said 'Scientists are interested only in what you can test and measure and tabulate. Psychoanalysis is a set of ideas and practices wholly outside this discipline. People are foolish only if they claim that it is not.'

I said 'Was that the trouble with Dr Kammerer?'

My father laughed. He seemed to spray bits of moisture from his moustache on to his sweet peas.

He said 'Yes, I think you might say that that is a trouble with Dr Kammerer.'

I said 'But suppose there are things that affect things, you know, but they can't be tested and measured – '

He said 'They wouldn't be science.'

I said 'But they might exist.'

He said 'Such as – '

I said 'I don't know.' I wanted to say – I mean the sort of things that might go away if you look at them; that work through the unconscious.

He said 'Have you been talking to your mother?'

I thought – But you must know there are things going on behind the arguments you have with my mother; or if you don't, isn't this why you have such stupid arguments with my mother?

So – What was it that could have happened to my father in early childhood?

It was in the summer holidays of 1924 or even 1925 perhaps that my father went away on a long lecture tour of America. While he was away there came to stay with us a young student from Berlin University called Hans. Hans was the son of a professor who was in correspondence with my father.

(You say you did not know Hans in Berlin? And what had been imagined then of coincidences in a universal unconscious!)

I remember a conversation at the breakfast table just before my father left for America. He was reading a letter he had received from Berlin. He said 'This boy wants to come here and learn English.' My mother said 'How old is he?' My father said 'Eighteen.' My mother said 'He will make an interesting companion for Max.' My father said 'But it will be just at the time when I am away.' My mother said 'Well I suppose Max and I can speak English even when you are away.' My father said 'You know what I mean, you are not stupid.' I thought – Well I haven't any idea what he means: then – You mean, my mother might get up to no good with this boy? Then – But that is stupid!

My mother said 'And he can teach Max German.'

My father said 'That's a point.'

My mother said 'And Max can look after me, can't you, Max.'

So my father went away, and it was arranged that Hans would come to stay with us.

When Hans arrived he was a fair-haired, blue-eyed young man with a soft round face and a large mouth. He might have been my mother's younger brother. From the window of my attic I could watch him and my mother on the lawn. They stood facing one another, laughing and talking. I thought – They are like the Queen and Jack of Hearts in a fairy story: perhaps my father knew what he was talking about after all; he knew what might be going on in my mother's unconscious or, indeed, her conscious?

During the first few days of Hans's stay I kept out of the way of him and my mother; they spent much time together. I both did and did not see why I was doing this. I thought – Of course, it is in my unconscious; but of this fact I am conscious? Then – But participants in a fairy story have to be cunning to survive. I would watch my mother teaching Hans to play croquet on the lawn; she would stand behind him and hold his hands and show him how to swing the mallet between his legs. My mother never played croquet with my father's friends. I thought – This is ridiculous.

I found myself bored with my chemistry set and my electricity set in my upstairs room. I would go down to my father's study and sit in his chair and put my feet up on his desk. It was unlikely that my mother would catch me, because she would be out playing croquet or picking fruit in the kitchen garden with Hans.

On my father's shelves there were some papers to do with Kammerer. There were cuttings from newspapers in England and America – the headlines were: 'Vienna Biologist Hailed As The Greatest Of The Century'; 'Scientist Claims To Have Found How To Transmit Good Qualities'; 'Transformation Of The Human Race'. There were pencilled exclamation marks by my father at the sides of these cuttings: there was a letter to my father from someone in America expressing disquiet and even disgust at the fame that Kammerer had gained in America, where he had been on a lecture tour just before my father.

I thought – My father has gone to America to fight some sort of duel with Kammerer? They will meet like knights on a hot and dusty Midwestern plain –

Then – But who do I want to win in a battle between my father and Dr Kammerer?

There were other papers on my father's shelves. Most of them I did not understand. There were mathematical symbols like small fishes trying to crawl up out of the sea on to dry land.

I thought – But then what is the battle between me, and my mother, and this young man called Hans?

– It is a help, if you imagine your unconscious as a participant in a fairy story?

– I mean in the end, some of us may be fitted to the environment and some may not?

Then – Who am I talking about? Who am I talking to? Myself? My father? Dr Kammerer?

– Or that person, whoever it is, with whom one day I will have no battle with words.

Once I went up to my mother's bedroom to look through the books that she kept by her bed. It had begun to strike me – Why does she sleep in a room separate from my father? Beside my mother's bed there was a book called *The Interpretation of Dreams*. She had marked some passages in the margins with a pencil. I sat down on my mother's bed to read some of these. I could not be caught, because my mother had gone out bicycling with Hans.

I read –

It may be that we were all destined to direct our first sexual impulses towards our mothers, and our first impulse of hatred and violence towards our fathers; our dreams convince us that we were. King Oedipus, who slew his father Laius and wedded his mother Jocasta, is nothing more or less than a wish fulfilment – the fulfilment of the wish of our childhood. But we, more fortunate than he, in so far as we have not become psychoneurotics, have since our childhood succeeded in withdrawing our sexual impulses from our mothers and in forgetting our jealousy of our fathers.

I thought – Good heavens! Then – Well yes, indeed, but I have felt there is some style of truth in fairy stories.

I went and played tennis by myself against a wall. The ball flew off old bricks at odd angles. I thought – This is practising, I suppose, to be ready for some random occurrence.

That evening when my mother came up to my room to say goodnight – I had had supper early in the kitchen with Mrs Elgin and Watson; I had said that I was tired and hungry – that evening when my mother came up she appeared somewhat sombre, watchful. I thought – Well where are we: on a hot and dusty plain?

She said 'What's the matter?'

I said 'Nothing.'

'You've been avoiding me.'

'Have I?'

'Is it Hans?'

'Is what Hans?'

She said 'He is our guest! I have to be nice to him.'

She sat on my bed. She leaned back on her elbows with her head against the wall.

I said 'I've been reading that book by Dr Freud called *The Interpretation of Dreams*. I mean – do you believe all that sort of stuff?'

She said 'It's not Frood, it's Froid.' Then – 'Good heavens, where did you find it?'

I said 'I found it by your bed.'

'What were you doing by my bed?'

If I had been older, and wittier, I suppose I might have said –

You've been reading *The Interpretation of Dreams*, and you're asking me what I was doing by your bed?

I said 'I wanted to see what you were reading.'

She said 'And what did you find?'

'There were those bits you had underlined.'

'What bits had I underlined?'

She had her legs hanging over the edge of the bed. I was both looking at her and pretending not to be looking at her. I thought – I am being like Dr Kammerer.

I said 'About it's not just parents doing terrible things to children, but children wanting to do terrible things to parents.'

She said 'Oh I don't call them terrible!' She looked away. I thought – There is that impression again of being on hot sand, or in long grass.

I said 'Neither do I.'

She said 'Oedipus Schmoedipus.'

I said 'What?'

She said 'It's a Jewish joke.' Then – 'It is Hans!'

I said 'What is Hans?'

She said 'Oedipus Schmoedipus, so long as he loves his mum!' Then she laughed.

She was like one of those people in fairy stories with snakes in their hair. I thought – Was it a snake that was crawling over me in the hot sand?

Then she said 'Hans likes you. Hans wants to get to know you.'

I said 'Good.'

I thought – But if all this is what happens in fairy stories –

– What happened in early childhood?

My mother got up suddenly and kissed me and left the room.

For a day or two I continued to keep clear of my mother and Hans; I went off on my own on my bicycle; I kept banging away at balls that came at odd angles off walls. Then Hans began to go during the day into Cambridge; my mother would drive him in and then return and look for me. But I would be climbing up trees or over walls. I would try to eat with Mrs Elgin and Watson in the kitchen. I would explain that I had to do holiday work in the evenings. Sometimes I found Hans watching me.

You think children do not know why they are doing these things? Surely it is often a question more of power than of sexuality. Certainly by acting like this I was managing to get my mother's and even Hans's attention directed more and more towards me. So one night there were Hans's footsteps tramping up the stairs to my room. I assumed, yes, that my mother had told him to come and try to make friends with me.

He knocked and said 'May I come in?'

I was sitting up in bed. Perhaps I had my legs underneath me and my eyes cast down like a mermaid.

Hans said 'I felt I should like very much to have a talk about your work. Your mother tells me that you are interested in biology.'

I said 'What I am interested in is physics.'

Hans said 'Ah that is my subject!'

I thought – Oh I thought it was biology.

He said 'There are some extraordinary affairs occurring at your University of Cambridge! Your Professor Rutherford, some years ago, has bombardiered the nucleus of a nitrogen atom with particles alpha; a proton emerged, and the nucleus of the nitrogen atom was changed into oxygen, wonder of wonders!'

I said 'It sounds like a fairy story.'

He said 'Indeed, it is the transformation that alchemists dreamed about!'

I said 'But couldn't you do that in biology?'

He said 'Do what?'

I said 'Bombard – it is "bombard", by the way, not "bombardier" – bombard, yes, wherever it is, so that there are, when you might want them, these mutations.'

He said 'That is an extraordinary interesting idea!' He sat down on the bed beside me.

I thought – Oh well, here we are: and what do those mermaids and sirens do? Smooth down with a hand the soft sea of the bedclothes beside them –

(Of course, children learn these things! From relationships at school, if not from their mothers.)

Hans said 'Perhaps you will be a great scientist one day.' He leaned on an elbow so that he was reclining almost behind me.

I said 'But do they exist, these atoms, particles; can you touch them, measure them?'

Hans said 'No, but you can measure their effects.'

I said 'My father says it is not scientific what you can't test, measure.'

Hans said 'You can measure the collective effect. You cannot measure the individual within that effect.'

I said 'You cannot measure the individual?'

Hans said 'No.' Then 'The individual is sacred. The individual goes his own way.'

I looked up from under my eyelashes. Hans had put his hand round behind me. I thought – But this is ridiculous.

Then – But what are we after in this story we are engaged in? What is being told us by a stone, a ring, a bird, a pool of water, a tree?

After a while my mother was calling to Hans from the first-floor landing.

Sometime during these days I went to visit my father's laboratory in Cambridge. My father's chief assistant was Miss Box, a pretty brown-haired lady. I suppose this was a time, yes, when I was beginning to be haunted by sex. Miss Box spent much of her time in a specially heated room where there were the glass cases which were the settings for my father's experiments with newts and toads and salamanders. Miss Box took me round; I was particularly interested in the salamanders which were small bright lizards that lay or stood so still that it was as if they were made of enamel. When Miss Box lifted the lid off one of the cases there was the smell of sand and piss. Miss Box had soft gold hair under her armpits. I wondered if my father ever went and sat on Miss Box's bed at night.

I said 'I'd like to do an experiment with salamanders.'

She said 'You wouldn't have time.'

I said 'I wouldn't want to see what they passed on to their offspring. I'd just like to see if I could make them stay alive long enough to breed.'

Miss Box said 'It's difficult.'

I thought – But who would want to live and have offspring in a place like this, which is like the waiting-room of a railway station?

I said 'Do you go home at night?'

Miss Box said 'Of course I go home at night!' She looked at me as if I had made an improper suggestion.

I said 'I mean, I just thought that the salamanders might need to have someone with them at night.'

When I got home there were my mother and Hans on the lawn; he had apparently hit a croquet ball so that it had caught her on the ankle; she was leaning back on her elbows with her foot out on the grass. Hans was kneeling in front of her putting a hand forward, taking it back; putting a hand forward, taking it back. I thought – Oh carry on, do, in your glass case; and she'll have you head over heels, or whatever you want, in the shrubbery.

I suppose I was quite angry with my mother at the time. I had begun to feel sympathy with my father. For all his faults, one could have a straight conversation with him: with my mother journeys through the maze were tortuous.

My mother still came up to my room, of course, to say goodnight. One evening there was some sort of glow about her. I thought – Perhaps she and Hans have got wherever they want to get to.

She said 'I've got a new book for you.'

I said 'What?'

She said 'It's called *Beyond the Pleasure Principle*. It's by Dr Freud.'

I said 'Oh yes.'

She said 'He seems to have changed his ideas slightly. He says that basically there are two instincts, the life instinct and the death instinct.'

I thought I might say – Oh how brilliant!

She said 'And they're not particularly to do with sex. But a battle goes on between the two.'

I said 'And which was the instinct that made King Oedipus want whatever he wanted.'

She said "Don't be difficult.'

I said 'I'm not being difficult!'

She said 'On the deepest level, everything is paradoxical.'

I had become interested in this word 'paradoxical': I had looked it up in my father's dictionary. This had said that a paradox was something seemingly self-contradictory or absurd, but possibly well-founded and essentially true. I had thought – Yes! And there had been something like that white light coming down.

I said to my mother 'Is that why we find it difficult, you and I, to talk about things?'

She said 'I didn't know we did find it difficult to talk about things.' She was looking through some of the work I had been doing recently in German with Hans.

I said 'Are you in love with Hans?'

She said 'No, I'm not in love with Hans.' Then – 'Hans is a boy.' Then – 'I'm very fond of Hans.' Then – 'Aren't you?'

I thought – I've got her blushing!

Then there were evenings, yes, when Hans and I would work late in my room: he would read to me bits from Goethe or Schiller; he would not do much more than lean against me, rest his hand on my knee, half tumble sometimes on top of me. He would tell me

63

stories of walking-tours he went on with his friends in the Black Forest; how they would go singing over the hills during the day and there would be music and discussions round the camp fire at night; and sometimes at midnight they would bathe in moonlit lakes – of course, with no clothes on. This, Hans explained, was to do with the spirit of the Greeks (ah, what signals are given by a mention of the spirit of the Greeks!) – a perfect blending of passion and form, didn't I think? Hans's soft face as he leaned close to me was like an apple which wasps have been at. He said 'One day, when you are old enough, you must come with me on one of these walks in the Black Forest!'

I said 'How old would I have to be?'

He said 'I will ask your mother.'

I thought – For goodness' sake don't ask my mother!

But I had been given an image of this place called the Black Forest – which was where fauns and satyrs played, and witches.

Then there was one particular night just before the end of Hans's visit to us –

– Oh sometime before this, yes, I had been behaving as if I were more at ease with Hans and my mother; I no longer had meals with Mrs Elgin and Watson in the kitchen; Hans would practise on his own his croquet shots on the lawn; my mother would read out to me bits of letters that she had had from my father in America. She would say 'He seems to be having a good time!' and would look through the window at Hans on the lawn. I would think – Well aren't we all having a good time –

Then there was this particular night when Hans had come up to my room and he was reclining on my bed and was reminiscing, I suppose, about white and gold bodies flitting in the moonlight of the Black Forest; and I was at the washbasin, perhaps with one arm raised like some Greek statue by a fountain; and perhaps it was true that just before this I had had to hop out from underneath one of Hans's vague lunges at me on the bed; and then the door banged open and there was my mother on the threshold, all flashing eyes and hair like snakes and marble forehead; and she was glaring at Hans and pointing to the door; and he was getting up and going meekly past her even if with his tail, as it were, I suppose not exactly between his legs. And I with such sad, affected innocence was turning to my mother – a toothbrush halfway to my mouth (what else?) – and wide-eyed was suggesting – Have you gone mad? What on earth do you think you are up to? And my mother had to sit on the edge of my bed and explain how she had been concerned about my not getting enough sleep; she had been angry with Hans because she thought he was preventing me from getting enough sleep; she was sorry she had over-reacted; and so on. And I was thinking – Oh yes; but aren't you listening to what is going on behind your words? (Oh so-called 'innocence', to be sure, can be cunning!) And then my mother was kissing me goodnight. And there were sounds of her going on and on talking with Hans through the night. And I was thinking – But the point of a fairy story is that someone has to win and there is something to be won, isn't it?

Then – Who was my mother jealous of: me or Hans?

Or – But is this an area where things are paradoxical?

This incident occurred only a day or two before Hans was due to leave us anyway. Before he went he managed to make with me a few half-whispered plans about possible future walks in the Black Forest.

Then when he had gone it seemed that I had nothing much to do. My mother went to London for a few days: I did not question why she had gone. But I did sometimes wonder, because I was lonely – Who is it after all who might have landed up in the shrubbery?

Then – But of course there is more going on than anyone quite knows about in a fairy story.

Now let me look at this timing again. I think the summer when Hans came to stay must have been in 1925, when I was nearly thirteen, because it was after Hans's visit, and after my father had got back from his tour of America, that my mother and father started talking about sending me away to a boarding-school. Up to this time I had been going to the day-school in Cambridge. I could hear my father's and mother's voices from behind closed doors – 'Max is too old to be hanging all day around his mother'; 'Yes, I agree, I have tried to encourage him to spend more time with people of his own age.' I thought – Well at least Hans's visit has given them something to agree about. It was decided that next year I should go to a boarding-school.

(It matters that I try to get the timing right? One's mind makes patterns: but what coincidences there are between these and the outside world!)

After he had been away my father would make a point of coming up and talking to me in my room. He would stand with his hands in his pockets and his head seeming to be pressed against the sloping ceiling. He was like an elephant that has wandered into a cave in the jungle.

He would look at the books I was reading. There were the fantasy adventure stories; the encyclopaedias which tried to explain the way the world worked. I would go on asking my father questions about this: I would say 'But what are these things that you can't taste, touch, smell: what are atoms: what are those things you work with – can you see, touch, genes?'

My father would say 'No.'

I would say 'Then what is it that scientists think they are testing, measuring?'

When my father sat on the end of my bed it was as if it might collapse, like some beanstalk.

He said, as Hans had done, 'You set up experiments. You observe results. You measure the results. Of course, you may not be able to talk about what it is that is causing them.'

'Why not?'

'Why should you?'

'You mean, you make up words for this.'

'Whenever you speak you make up words anyway.'

'The things might not exist.'

'Something must exist. Or how would there be the results?'

I thought – But then why not talk about how we don't know what exists; wouldn't things then seem more like being on a journey in a fairy story?

When my father bent down to kiss me goodnight, there was the impression of the roof of the cave in the jungle being in danger of caving in.

I was still on my own much of this time: my mother often went up to London. (It still did not occur to me to ask her what she did.) There was a week or so left of the summer holidays. I was considering the question: But if you are a scientist doing an experiment, then would not part of it be to see in what way you yourself are part of the experiment? I mean if you make up words for what you taste, touch, see –

– But if you see this, is not the experiment different?

Then – Do other people think like this?

One day I knocked on the door of my father's study.

'Yes?'

'You know those experiments you have been doing with salamanders – '

'Presumably.'

'I'd like to try one.'

'We're packing them up.'

'I know. I'd like to take one over.'

In his own room my father seemed smaller, more compact. He was in one of those chairs that tipped back so that he could put his feet up on his desk. I thought – With one flick, could I get him flying into the shrubbery?

He said 'You wouldn't have time.'

'I've talked to Miss Box.'

'You've talked to Miss Box?'

'Yes. I know I wouldn't have time to do the whole experiment – '

'What did you make of Miss Box?'

'I like her. I thought I could just see if I could get one or two salamanders to stay alive – '

He said 'What did you talk about with Miss Box?'

I thought – This is ridiculous.

Then – You mean, my father does carry on with Miss Box? They lie about on damp sand as if in one of their experiments –

My father said 'Sorry. You want to do some experiment – '

I said 'Yes. I just want to see if I can look after two salamanders and perhaps get them to breed. I mean, those highland salamanders in lowland conditions, or whatever it is, or vice versa.'

My father said 'Nothing to do with the inheritance of acquired characteristics.'

I said 'No, nothing to do with the inheritance of acquired characteristics.'

He said 'Then try it vice versa.'

I thought – But why don't you want me to have inherited any of your characteristics?

He said 'We have got some set-up like that, as a matter of fact.'

I was going out of the door when I thought it was worthwhile stopping and saying 'But I don't see in fact how you could ever tell.'

He said 'Ever tell what?'

'What it was that was influencing things: I mean about heredity, and characteristics.'

'Why not?'

'Well, you can measure results, but you can't measure what is causing them. You can do statistics, but how can you measure what is individual?'

He said 'Who have you been talking to?'

I said 'Hans.'

He said 'Oh yes, I've been wanting to ask you about Hans.'

But my father did not, really, want to ask me about Hans. He turned away and looked out of the window. I thought – He wants me to think he wants to talk about Hans. Then – But how would anyone know what was going on in that experiment?

Anyway, it was arranged that as soon as I had got the equipment for my experiment ready, I could pick up two salamanders from Miss Box.

I had tried to keep up with what had been happening to Dr Kammerer during these two years: I knew from the papers in my father's study that he had achieved extraordinary notoriety: for a time (do you not think?) he was quite like Einstein. But there were, in spite of the difficulties, actual stars in the sky for Einstein's theories to be tested against; whereas Kammerer's specimens had died, and other experimenters had found it impossible to keep their specimens alive, so that the hostility to Kammerer that came naturally with the notoriety had nothing to stop it; it spread like fire. I gathered from my father's papers that Kammerer was in danger of falling into terrible disrepute. Perhaps it was because of this that I wanted to see if I, like he, could at least keep some salamanders alive.

I discovered that my mother had kept her own small heap of newspaper cuttings about Kammerer: they were in a drawer of her desk: she seemed to have got some psychoanalyst friend to send her them from Vienna. Some of them gave details of Kammerer's private life (I could put to good use here the German I had learned from Hans). The cuttings referred to Kammerer as a Don Juan, a Byron, a Lothario: he had left his wife, married a painter, then later his wife had taken him back. There were innumerable women, the writer suggested, who were dying for the love of Kammerer: how terrible it was to let oneself be loved thus by women!

I thought – Well, what is all this about death instinct; life instinct: was it not Kammerer's salamanders that had been able to stay alive, and other people's that were dying?

I tried to talk to my mother about this. I could not let her know that I had been going through the drawers of her desk.

'Did you ever see Dr Kammerer again?'

'No, why do you ask that?'

'I expect a lot of people fall in love with him, don't they – '

'Why do you say that too – '

'I remember your saying that you thought his salamanders must love him.'

'What I think I said, surely, was that he must love them.'

'What do you think he does to make things love him?'

'Perhaps he just makes people think he loves them!'

'But then why do people talk about dying for love – '

'Hey, hold on, what have you been reading – '

My mother had become dreamy again; glowing; as if she was listening to music round some corner.

I thought – Dr Kammerer himself couldn't have sent her those cuttings from Vienna?

Then suddenly – She couldn't have been meeting Dr Kammerer in London?

She said 'Perhaps what you think is love isn't true. Or perhaps sometimes you love, or want to love, and then there is no set-up, or framework, in which you can.'

I said 'I see.' Then – 'Can't you make a framework?'

She said 'How?'

I said 'I don't know.' Then – 'Do you think Dr Kammerer made one?'

She said 'For whom?'

I said 'For his salamanders.'

That autumn, in my evenings and weekends away from school, I set about preparing my experiment with my salamanders. My idea was: how can animals be expected to live – let alone reproduce; let alone be recipient to a chance mutation – if they are kept in glass boxes like those which contain sandwiches in a railway station. Kammerer had perhaps loved his salamanders: but what was love? I wanted to provide for my salamanders a suitable setting. Was it not something like this that my mother's psychoanalysis books were suggesting too – that settings are important, but human beings for the most part are no good at providing settings for love: they liked running things down, displaying jealousy and envy. Well perhaps I did too: but if I saw this, could I not provide at least my salamanders with some setting in which love could operate?

I obtained materials from Miss Box and constructed a glass case that was larger than the ones in which she and my father had kept their salamanders. I went out each evening to gather objects which would be fitting for my salamanders' setting. I found clean white sand and stones shining with crystals: I picked out sticks that were shaped and polished like ivory. I put on the sand some shells and even a starfish. I thought – Why should not landlocked salamanders have a glimpse of something outlandish from the sea? I collected red earth, and alpine plants, and one or two very tiny and expensive trees: I made a shelter of wire and bark and moss and leaves and coral. I constructed a mountain stream out of Plasticine and silver paper and a hidden electric motor and a pump: I bought (with money borrowed from my mother) a lamp that shone like the sun. I was aiming to produce for my salamanders a setting that would be surpassingly ethereal and strange. I looked down on my creation from above. I thought – I think I am God, and this is my Garden of Eden.

The two salamanders that I was going to pick up when my garden was ready were another breed of lowland salamanders, known as *Salamandra salamandra*, or Fire Salamanders: their usual habitat was dark and damp woods. They stayed for the most part during the day under rotting bark or leaves; they came out in the evenings to get food. I learned what I could about them from books lent to me by Miss Box: my father, when he overheard me talking to Miss Box, would smile and look away (I thought – His feelings about Miss Box are what are called 'paradoxical'?). My plan had been originally to make for these lowland salamanders something that could be called an alpine setting. But my enthusiasm had now gone beyond this: I wanted to make for them something beautiful like a setting for jewels, or the inside of a painting. Then I would see how my salamanders might stay alive! The inside of a painting, it seemed to me, was to do with what is immortal.

The breeding habits of these lowland salamanders was that they mated in the spring and then fifty or more tadpole-like larvae were born in water the following year. I had been told by Miss Box that the two salamanders designated for me had been together for some time. I did not know if they had mated: I assumed they were male and female. The point of my experiment had at one time been to see whether these lowland salamanders, in their new setting, might produce offspring in the manner of alpine salamanders – which was to give birth not to larvae but to two fully formed offspring. But this was what I had put out of my mind: my plan now was not to expect, but just to let things occur on their own. I thought – Things grow, develop on their own, don't they; once you have provided a setting.

The day came when my garden (in the books it was called an 'aquaterrareum') was ready: I bicycled in to Miss Box to pick up my salamanders. They were two small bright lizards about six inches long: their skin was mainly black but had golden patches and hoops. They seemed to sit, or lie, or stand, completely still, even when I was transporting them in a cardboard box on my bicycle from the laboratory. And then, when they were in the bright fair world that I had constructed for them, they were, yes, like jewels! they were so beautiful.

I had set up my aquaterrareum in my bedroom: I wanted it here rather than in the room with my chemistry set next door because I wanted to be with my salamanders at night. I do not know why I felt particular about this. Perhaps I felt – What strange influences, chances, flit about beneath the moon at night.

My salamanders sat or stood or lay sometimes parallel, sometimes apart, sometimes with their noses close together like an arrow. I hardly ever saw them move. They would be, yes, on the silver sand, by the stones like gold or diamonds, like things made immortal by a painting.

My mother came up to look at my aquaterrareum. She had that expression on her face that my father sometimes had when it was as if he could not make up his mind whether to be deprecating or impressed. She said 'That's beautiful!'

I said 'Yes.'

'What are they called?'

'Adam and Eve.'

'What good names!'

I said 'I think they might also be what are called "hopeful monsters".'

She said 'What are hopeful monsters?'

I said 'They are things born perhaps slightly before their time; when it's not known if the environment is quite ready for them.'

She said 'So you have made an environment that might be ready for them!'

I said 'Yes.'

She put her arms round me and hugged me. She said 'You are my hopeful monster!'

I thought I might say – But hopeful monsters, don't you know, nearly always die young.

– Because the Gods love them?

Then – But was God ever with his mother, by that garden, looking down?

Much of my spare time that winter was spent in collecting food for my salamanders: I got worms from the herbaceous borders, slugs from underneath stones, insects from behind the bark of trees. I dropped these like manna into my salamanders' garden. I once put a long black centipede in and it crawled over their still tails: I wondered – But have I introduced a snake into their garden! Then – Poor snake! But my salamanders paid no attention to it, and after a time it died.

I seldom saw my salamanders eat. Sometimes at night I imagined I had glimpsed a tongue flashing out; but it seemed to have travelled faster then light. I thought – Perhaps their tongues move in the jumps that Hans used to talk about; the jumps of those particles that are on one level and then instantaneously they are on another.

I had one or two letters from Hans: my mother also had one or two letters from him. We would eye each other's letters over the breakfast table.

Throughout that winter I cared for my salamanders; then in the spring they seemed to be spending more and more time within their shelter; there would be just their tails sticking out, like fishes that have managed to crawl up on to dry land. I thought – They can do whatever they want! I am not that fussy old God of the Garden of Eden.

Except when I was at school I was on my own a lot of that summer. My mother was going up to a new series of lectures in London; my father was working in Cambridge. Then halfway through the summer term there was a fire in my day-school and the school was closed. It was thought to be not worth while to send me anywhere else, because I was due to go to boarding-school anyway in the autumn.

So I went out on my bicycle and explored the countryside. I still collected food for my salamanders, though I was now not caring about them quite as much, since I knew I would have to leave them when I went away to school. However I felt that in some way just by riding about the countryside I was keeping in touch with my salamanders: I too was finding myself in a strange world; I thought it beautiful, but there now seemed to be something frightening growing in myself. I wondered – In learning about myself, might I not be discovering something for my salamanders –

– What is going on here might be connected to what is going on there –

– For something interesting to happen, should not that old God in Eden have been trying to find out more about himself, rather than hanging about and nagging his salamanders?

On my journeys on my bicycle I came across a country house that was empty and had fallen into disrepair: there was a lake and a boathouse and a punt: I could push myself across to an island where there was another rotting boathouse with a loft which had a table and a few broken chairs. Here it seemed that a hermit might once have lived: there was a crucifix with one arm dangling away from the wall. I felt as if I might have come to some aquaterrareum prepared for myself; the inside of a picture, yes; but of something rotting like that which was going on in my own head. I would sit cross-legged on the floor and close my eyes and try to breathe slower and slower; I had read about this in a book I had borrowed from my mother; I felt I needed to find some stillness, or suffer some explosion.

That summer it was as if there were some blockage inside me: there was an ache in my groin, stomach, heart; it shot up into my head. Well, what do adolescent boys do about sex? Oh we have been liberated from ghostly fears about masturbation, have we not! But how dispiriting can be this lack of haunting. Which is worse, to suffer from a lack of spirit or of sex?

It was as if I were one of those primitive organisms in which food and waste-matter go in and out of the same hole: nourishment and shit become confused; this seemed to be happening in my head. What I required, I felt, was one of those rods that plumbers use to unblock drains; you push it up, give it a few twists and tugs, then out comes all the slime and shit.

I thought – So indeed what is wrong! This is pleasure. Get it out, get it out.

There was a beam, and the half-broken chairs, and bits of old rope in the boathouse. I thought I might stand on a chair and put a bit of rope round my neck. Then, if I gave it a jerk, some blood and energy might be freed: machinery might start up again, like that of an outboard motor.

Once the chair broke – then the rope. I thought – I am ill: I am mad! Call this a quantum jump: for life, for death. Then – This is ridiculous.

I sat cross-legged on the floor and hoped – Cannot a bird like a woodpecker come down and make holes in my skull, my brain, through which messages might flow or, in a wind, make music.

Once when I got back from one of these trips to the boathouse I found my mother sitting on a chair in the hall staring straight in front of her. She had just come back from London. I thought – She has been, do you think, in whatever might be her form of boathouse –

She said 'Good heavens, what's happened to you!'

I said 'I fell through the floor of a boathouse.'

She said 'The things you do!'

I said 'I was collecting food for my salamanders.'

I did notice now that my mother was sad. But children have little capacity for bearing in mind that their parents are sad.

Then there was an evening when my father came back from Cambridge and he had been opening his letters in the hall and he was a long time reading one letter and he was looking up to the door of the drawing-room as if he were waiting for my mother to emerge. (I wondered – Had he noticed that she was sad?) But then when she did appear, he just said 'Your friend Kammerer has been caught cheating.'

She said 'My friend Kammerer?'

He said 'He's been caught faking the evidence.'

My mother said 'You do really hate people, don't you.' Then she began to go up towards her room.

My father called after her 'Yes, I do dislike people who don't tell the truth!'

My mother stopped on the top step of the stairs and said 'What do you know about truth!' Then she shut herself in her room.

I thought – But could it in fact be Dr Kammerer that my mother has been seeing in London?

What had been happening about Kammerer was, I found out later, both from my father and from press-cuttings in his study –

In the course of experiments with another species of animal called the Midwife Toad, Kammerer had claimed that he had created circumstances in which toads had demonstrably inherited acquired characteristics. First he had induced these toads which normally mate on dry land to mate in water, which other toads do; and in the course of time they had acquired 'nuptial pads' similar to those of other toads – pads on the palms and fingers of the male by which he clings to the body of the female under the water. Then after several generations Kammerer found, or so he claimed, that these pads acquired by his male toads had become a feature transmitted by heredity.

Now some time later, as a result of examination by so-called 'disinterested' scientists, it had been found that one of Kammerer's mummified specimens that he had used as evidence for the inheritance of these characteristics had been injected on the palms and fingers with Indian ink, so that this had simulated the colouring of nuptial pads, and now anyone might be able to call Kammerer a cheat and a forger with some justification. But in fact there was no evidence that Kammerer had known about the injections of ink: he himself had encouraged the examination of the specimens by neutral scientists and the injections might have been done by a laboratory assistant out of hate or even love of Dr Kammerer – the particular specimen was tattered, and the marks of the pad were fading. But no considerations such as these weighed in the balance against the opportunity that Kammerer's opponents now had publicly to discredit him.

That evening when the news about Kammerer's co-called 'exposure' reached my father and my mother went up to her room – she stayed in her room saying she had a headache and asked for supper to be sent up to her – that evening I talked with my father in a way in which, I think, I had not quite talked before.

'But why is it so important to you that there should not be the inheritance of acquired characteristics?'

'Because it's not true.'

'But you seem to care more than about its not being true.'

'Do I? Well, perhaps it's because if it was, there would be less chance of adaptation.'

'Why would there be chaos?'

'Folly, depravity, lying – they'd be dug in for ever.'

'But might not good things be dug in for ever?'

'No. When it comes to power, bad things win.'

'But couldn't human beings choose for the good things to win?'

'Who would do the choosing? It would be done by the people in power. God help everyone if people in power have more power!'

'But don't you think humans will ever be fitted for that sort of power?'

'No.' Then – 'Leave it to nature. Leave it to chance.' Then – 'Though I wouldn't be surprised if, sooner or later, humans wipe themselves out.'

I thought – My father must be going through an especially bad time with my mother?

The day was coming closer when I was due to go to boarding-school. My mother was still spending much of her time in her room; my father went off each day to Cambridge. I was sad about going to school, mainly because I would have to give up my salamanders. It had been arranged that when I went I would hand them back to Miss Box. I did not like to imagine what would become of them. I had recently taken less and less notice of the garden I had created. I said to them 'I'm sorry, I'm having a hard time myself, my salamanders.'

They still seemed to be spending most of their time in their shelter. I thought – They are like my mother: or is it that they know I am going away to school?

Then there was a day when my mother had been up to London and my father was in Cambridge and I had been walking round the village saying goodbye to it, and when I got back I saw that my mother had returned from London early; there was her handbag and umbrella in the hall. I went up to her room because I was sad and wanted to talk; but her door was locked. I knocked and called, and there was no answer. Then when I came downstairs Watson was in the hall and she was chewing the inside of her lips which she did when she was anxious. It appeared that my mother had come back some time ago and had gone straight up to her room; she had not answered when Watson had knocked. Mrs Elgin came out from the kitchen and she and Watson both went up to my mother's room and called; the door remained locked. They came back down the stairs and Watson went out into the garden and looked up at the windows of my mother's room; Mrs Elgin said 'Your mother was in a state when she came home.' I said 'What sort of state?' Mrs Elgin said 'Oh you boys, you would never notice anything!' I thought – But I did notice, yes, that my mother was sad. Watson was out on the lawn talking to Mr Simmons the gardener: they were both looking up at the windows of my mother's room. They seemed to be discussing whether or not to get a ladder. I thought – But this is terrible! I said to Mrs Elgin 'You mean, something might have happened to my mother?' Mrs Elgin said 'Oh yes, something has been happening to your mother in London!' Mr Simmons seemed to be going off to get a ladder. Mrs Elgin went back into the kitchen. I thought that what I would do was to go up to my room which was above my mother's and I would try and climb out on to the wisteria or magnolia or whatever it was and then down to the windows of my mother's room. I did not dwell too much on what Mrs Elgin or Watson and Mr Simmons seemed to think might have been happening to my mother: it seemed that there were just things to be done, one after another. Then when I got to my room and opened the door, there was my mother sitting on my bed. She was facing me, with her arms hanging down between her knees, as she sometimes sat when she was on the lavatory. I could see she had been crying. I said 'What's the matter?' She said 'I'm so sorry!' She went on crying. I went and knelt in front of her; I tried to put my arms around her; she was hot, as if she had been running or lying a long time on burning sand or in long grass. There was the smell of something growing, glowing, rotting, about her; it was like the smell in my boathouse; like the smell from my salamanders when they had been lying in their sun. The salamanders were in their glass case just behind her. She said 'I'm so sorry I came up here, I was so sad, I didn't want the others to find me.' I said 'Well that's all right then.' I thought – You wanted me to find you! She was on the very edge of the bed; I was kneeling close to her; she had put her arms around me. Oh what is it about grief that is so sensual, do you know? I was saying 'But what is it?' She was pulling me towards her; one of her knees was digging into me; I lifted myself so that my knees were on either side of her knee; she toppled slowly back, with me on top of her. I said 'Is it about Dr Kammerer?' She said 'Dr Kammerer!' She pushed her hair away from her face. Her mouth seemed swollen, crushed, like Hans's had sometimes been. I thought – Oh I see. I said 'It is about Hans?' I had not really thought much recently about my mother and Hans: perhaps at the back of my mind I had somehow known she had probably gone on seeing him. She took one hand from my back and stroked my face; she said 'Hans, why do you talk about Hans?' Her voice seemed to come from a long way away; or as if there were a rope tightening around it. She said 'Hans is very beautiful!' Then – 'And so are you.' Her body began tightening under mine. She rolled her eyes back: she seemed to be looking up at the glass case in which there were my salamanders. Then she said 'Did you and Hans ever do anything?' I said 'No.' She said 'How did you know what I meant – did you and Hans ever do anything?' There were only the whites of her eyes; she was arching her back; all this was happening very quickly. I thought – Well, my mother and I, we are in some Garden of Eden. I said 'Of course I know.' She said 'Don't go!' I thought –

77

Of course I'm not going to go! I had got used to something like this, after all, by myself; on my bed, in my ruined boathouse. Then my mother opened her mouth and made some sort of noise like air coming in from beyond her. And then it was as if it were my turn to be saying 'Don't go!' There was the tightness at my throat; the sweetness at the centre; at the top of my head and beyond me. Then there was nothingness, everythingness: the unblocked flow of blood, guts, air, liquid. After a time my mother said 'There.' Then – 'Are you all right?' I said 'Yes.' She said 'Your silly old mother!' She said this quite dispassionately. I was lying on top of her with one of her thighs between mine. After a time she began to push me gently off her.

She said 'You don't feel bad?'

I said 'No.'

She said 'Good.' Then – 'Well I don't feel bad.'

I said 'Good.'

She sat up and pushed the hair back from her face. Then she looked at my salamanders. She said 'Those poor things, will they be all right?'

I said 'I hope so.'

She turned and put her head down against mine. Then she said 'You won't tell anyone about Hans, will you.'

In the day or two that was left before I went to school my mother was at her most composed, regal: she floated round the house chatting with, giving orders to, Mrs Elgin, Watson, Mr Simmons. It was as if she were taking pains to put out the message – Ah yes, there are strange times of distress, of darkness, are there not: but then, look! we can come out on to another level!

I had a letter from Hans saying that he was sorry he had missed me in London, but he very much hoped that one day our plans would come to fruition about going on a walking tour in the Black Forest.

My mother saw that I had received the letter, but made no mention of it.

I thought – I see. Then – But what do I see? What means have I to know, let alone talk about, what is really happening?

I did not do anything about my aquaterrareum until the very day that I was going to my new school. So at the last moment there was a fuss about why I had not dismantled it before; how was I now going to get it to Miss Box? My mother was going to drive me to school. But I had this enormous glass case. In the end it was arranged that my mother would drive me and my aquaterrareum into Cambridge on our way to school so that I could drop it off at the laboratory with Miss Box. Then just before we left my mother was caught up in a long conversation on the telephone, so we were going to be late; but what did I care, I was having to leave this fine new world I had created; I was going to dump it, carrying it in my arms. I was still saying to my salamanders 'I'm so sorry; so sorry!' This was what my mother sometimes said. For some days I had not seen my salamanders; they had been in their shelter; I had not wanted to disturb them. I thought that when I got to the laboratory I would take the top off the shelter so that I could say goodbye to them there; but what sort of goodbye would this be! We make our beautiful worlds: we abandon them.

My mother was silent in the car. When we got to the laboratory building I staggered up the stone staircase carrying my made-up world like Atlas: my mother stayed in the car. My father was somewhere in the building: I would have to say goodbye to him too. Miss Box was in the room with the dim glass cases like those in which are kept sandwiches. I put my aquaterrareum down: I did not take the top off the shelter yet: I thought I would say goodbye to my father before I said goodbye to my salamanders. I found my father coming out of his room.

He too looked sad; I did not know why. He was coming towards me along the passage. I thought – Well it can't be just that I'm going away to school. I said 'I'm off. I've come to say goodbye.' He put his arm round my shoulder. He said 'Something rather terrible has happened.' I said 'What?' We were going back along the corridor to the room in which I had left my salamanders. He said 'Your mother's taking you?' I said 'Yes.' He said 'Kammerer's shot himself.' I said 'Dr Kammerer's shot himself?' Miss Box had taken the lid off my aquaterrareum; she was staring down at it. I said 'Why?' My father said 'I don't know.' Then – 'I believe he had some trouble with women.' My father and I had come up beside my aquaterrareum and we were staring down at it with Miss Box; she had taken the top off the shelter. On the sand, which had turned rather yellow and green in the course of time, there were my two salamanders parallel and facing the same way; and in between them, as if it were completing some hierogram, some coded message, there was a smaller but perfectly formed third salamander, with the same colouring, black and gold. Now you remember (oh do you!) what might originally have been the point of my experiment until it became simply about what might happily live or happily die – the point had been to take two lowland salamanders which normally produce tadpole-like larvae and to put them in alpine conditions (or in conditions of such beauty that who would care whatever occurred) and to see whether – as Dr Kammerer had claimed, and for which he had been ridiculed – two fully formed offspring would be produced. Well here there seemed to be just one perfectly formed offspring: but was not that enough! It was lying between its parents as if they might be three sticks cast by some augur on the ground; to give, indeed, some message, but what? Or of course one could say – Nothing. Myself and my father and Miss Box were looking down. My father said 'When did this happen?' Miss Box said 'I don't know.' My father said 'But these are *Salamandra salamandra*.' I said 'Yes.' I was thinking – Well, indeed when might this have happened? When was the last time I saw my salamanders? Miss Box said 'It's not some trick?' I thought – Of course it's not some trick! What do you mean, I ran round a corner and bought a third salamander? then – Oh but what if it happened when my mother and I were doing whatever it was we did that evening together: would that be a trick? I said 'No.' I thought I heard my mother hooting the horn of the car in the street below. My father said 'You didn't keep a record of your experiment?' I said 'No.' Miss Box said 'Then we can't of course tell.' I was thinking – But there would be no need now for Dr Kammerer to shoot himself! My father said 'No, we can't of course tell.' There was another hooting from the street below. My father said 'You'd better go.' I said 'Yes.' My father said 'We'll look into your experiment!' I said 'Thank you.' Miss Box was putting the lid on my aquaterrareum. I was thinking – But what will they do, nothing? But what will that matter: what has happened has happened: and is not everything that matters a unique experiment? I said 'Goodbye then.' My father said 'Goodbye.' Then he said 'You'd better say nothing to your mother.' I thought – About my experiment? About Dr Kammerer? Then – But of course I will say something to my mother! My father was still looking down into my aquaterrareum. I ran down the staircase and out into the street. My mother was sitting in the car still staring in front of her. I said 'Something rather terrifying has happened.' She said 'Yes, I know.' I thought – How do you know? Then – That was a telephone call from Hans? From London? I said 'Dr Kammerer's shot himself.' My mother said 'Is your father pleased?' I said 'No.' I was sitting beside her in the car. She drove off. I thought – But what if my mother and I have changed; and on to some different level. I found that I did not want to tell her about how my two lowland salamanders seemed suddenly to have produced one highland salamander; perhaps this was after all a thing that one should not talk about too much.

III: Eleanor

If, for the sake of change, old ground has to be broken up, one or two seeds lie secret – what terrible opportunities there were during those years!

You did not notice politics in England? Well what did happen to your salamanders?

In Berlin in 1923 there was the inflation: you have imagined the scene. People carried suitcases of million-mark notes to pay for a train ticket: a promise-to-pay in the morning might be settled for a third of the cost in the afternoon. Those who lived on fixed incomes were ruined – the unproductive, the bourgeoisie, stern keepers of the spirit. Those who flourished (and might not those who were ruined be being given a chance to flourish?) were the manipulators, the tricksters, the liberators of the spirit. They had been ruined a long time ago, perhaps, but had learned that the survival of a tribe is by no means impaired by groups being broken up. There appeared on the streets of Berlin – or perhaps it was at this time that I became aware of them on the streets of Berlin – people known as *Schieber*: at a later date they would be called 'spivs' or 'black marketeers': it was from them that one could obtain food, fuel, clothing, medicine. One obtained these by barter; it was important never to have thrown away from a bottom drawer or attic any trinket, bedspread, pair of boots, ancestral ornament – anything saved and hidden might suddenly become life-giving (was this like your so-called 'gene-pool'?). Of course, many *Schieber* were Jews – how practised at this sort of thing had Jews become over the years! – their tribal identity having been maintained indeed by their response to a hostile environment. Or was it that other people for their own protection (not survival!) were apt to notice only the *Schieber* that happened to be Jews? Certainly Jews, as usual, took no trouble to disguise themselves. There was still the question, yes – was all this exposure, immolation, necessary for survival?

There would come to our apartment in Berlin two of my mother's relations from the provinces – Cousin Walther and Cousin Jakob. They would arrive with their suitcases and long black coats and trilby hats and beards. I would hope – Might they not after all be taken to be people just out to buy a train ticket? They would open their suitcases in the hall: there would be vegetables and butter and eggs and perhaps a chicken or two: my mother would greet them but then retire to her room: well how does a good Communist maintain her dignity under the necessity of capitalist manipulation? My father and Magda usually did the bargaining. They would hand over a sheet or a blanket, perhaps, from the store in the linen cupboard; a few books; an heirloom that had come from my mother's family anyway. And so we stayed alive. Cousin Walther and Cousin Jakob would sit side by side on the sofa in the sitting-room like primeval images that had come floating across the sea in canoes. I would think – But, still, should not survivors, saviours, be more secret? Otherwise how easy it is for people to want to kill them! There are such opportunities for envy in the business of salvation: is this why it seems to go hand in hand with ruination?

There were in fact outbreaks of anti-Semitism in the streets of Berlin at this time. I had not noticed overt manifestations of it before – it had seemed no more than an oddity among the sophisticates of the university or of the Adlon Hotel. But it was now being said that Jews were taking over property cheaply from non-Jewish families who were hungry: Jewish shops were broken into and goods were looted. Of course there is envy of those who can adapt and look after their own kind on the part of those who cannot. (How would you put it? That there is hostility to mutants not only from the environment but, if the environment changes, from those who do not change?) Defence forces were organised by

Jews; a looter was shot and killed. I thought – Good. Then – But is it not the sign of a survivor to be different from those who are not?

I said to my father 'Would it not have been better if, from the beginning, Jews had remained secret?'

He said 'Then how could they have been agents of salvation?'

I said 'But people do not imitate them.'

He said 'I mean, perhaps they had to be scattered; to spread.'

I thought – You mean, what it is they spread still remains secret?

My father tried to explain about the inflation – about the post-war reparation payments that Germany was supposed to be making to France and England and America. The payments themselves were not affected by the inflation because they were in terms of gold; but it was the cost of them that was said to be causing the inflation in Germany. My father said 'But also the inflation might be a way of Germans saying to the French and English and Americans "Look, it makes no sense if this is what happens when you press us for payments: you will get nothing more from us if we are ruined."'

I said to my father 'But can't they just announce this?'

My father said 'But then they would seem to be plotting; they wouldn't seem to be helpless.'

I said 'So it's a game.'

My father said 'But one of the rules is you can't call it a game.'

I thought – So some things, yes, do have to remain secret.

The inflation, in fact, ended more suddenly than it had begun. For a week or so there was no paper money of any value at all (there was a joke – a billion-mark note was the cheapest form of lavatory paper) then one day there were new clean banknotes with eight or nine noughts knocked off. And these were accepted. I said to my father 'But how can money be stabilised, or whatever it is called, just by knocking eight or nine noughts off?'

He said 'Well, just as it might suit people to have chaos for a time, so it usually suits them suddenly to stop.'

I said 'Why?'

He said 'They get bored.'

I said 'No one controls it.'

He said 'No, no one controls it.' Then – 'I think one can have a feel of it.'

I said 'But not talk about it.'

He said 'No.'

84

I thought – You mean, one might influence it if one has a feel of it?

Then – We are like agents in occupied territory.

I was not having much contact with my mother at this time: she had moved out of our apartment except at weekends and was staying in a room in the east side of Berlin where she worked at one of the Communist Party offices. I thought – She is a fighter: fighters do not want to remain secret; fighters often die. Then – It is more straightforward, of course, to have an instinct to die?

Every now and then I would become slightly ill again at this time; I would spend a few days in bed. I would think – When I do imagine I understand things, it is as if a white light is coming down: indeed it seems difficult sometimes to stay alive.

My father would come and sit on the edge of my bed and talk to me. He once said 'As a matter of fact there is an old Jewish tradition that the real saviours of the world – those who stop the human race from destroying itself – are very few; perhaps no more than seven, seven just men, and they do remain secret! They are not known even to each other; perhaps in this guise they are hardly known to themselves.'

I thought, of course – Perhaps I am one of them!

Then – But if I were, I suppose I would not know this myself.

In the summer of 1925 I was fifteen and I was for the first time allowed out in the streets on my own: I was aware of the enormous changes that had taken place in Berlin since the days of my earliest memories. I had not noticed much of this going on at the time (change does indeed often seem to take place secretly) but now there were no more left-wing or right-wing militants in the streets; no more men with rifles hanging on to lorries like claws; no more soldiers with their helmets and bedrolls like chickens just out of eggs. There was suddenly an energy, a polish, a surface glitter in the streets: it was as if something garish had broken through a skin: something to do with the sun, perhaps; or with disease, or with cosmetics.

At the school I was going to at the time I had a girlfriend called Trixie and a boyfriend called Bruno: we went around together as a gang. Trixie was blonde with blue eyes and curly hair; Bruno was olive-skinned and Jewish. Bruno was our manager and clown; Trixie was our figurehead. I imagined myself as some sort of charioteer with reins in my fingers in the background.

I said 'My father has the idea that there may be seven or so just men, people, who hold the world together; and they may not even know each other.'

Bruno said 'Then thank God they are not us!'

I said 'Why not?'

He said 'Do we not know each other?'

Trixie was anxious because she feared that she would still be a virgin at the age of sixteen: she felt this would be a hindrance to her becoming grand and powerful and rich. She said 'It's not that I care about the business of becoming not a virgin, it's just that I think one should start practising how to get what one wants now.'

Bruno said 'Practising what?'

Trixie said 'How should I know? You tell us, Bruno.'

Bruno put a hand to his throat and made out that he was being strangled; he fell against a wall; he sank down on his haunches.

Bruno came from a family who were some sort of high-class *Schieber*: he seemed always to have cigarettes, new clothes, watches, money. He told us about the night-life of Berlin where there was a whole new world behind the façades of rock-like buildings – of Aladdin's caves that opened up with a dazzle of lights and jewels.

I said 'Well why don't you take us?'

He said 'Because I'd be responsible.'

I said 'Responsible for what?'

He said 'For the poor men, God help them, who might want to make you not virgins.'

At weekends Bruno and Trixie and I would go out to the woods and lakes on the outskirts of Berlin; we would hire a boat and row out on the lakes; we would watch the courting couples who lay under the trees. One of the conventions of our relationship seemed to be that neither Trixie nor I became sexually involved with Bruno: we did not question this: I thought – It just seems to be necessary if our three-sided relationship is to continue.

Trixie said 'I don't believe you know where to take us.'

Bruno said 'It costs money.'

Trixie said 'Then how do we make money?'

Bruno said 'Trixie, Trixie, you want me to tell you how to make money!'

I thought – But none of us are really meaning what we are saying.

Near one of the lakes we visited on the western outskirts of Berlin, the Wannsee, was the grave of the writer Heinrich von Kleist who had shot himself at this spot together with his girlfriend in 1811. A fence had been put up round a tombstone which was inscribed with Kleist's name and the dates of his birth and death and then the words 'He lived, sang and suffered in hard and sorrowful times: he sought death on this spot and found immortality.'

We were all three passionate admirers of Kleist. We would stand and stare at his grave; we did not know what more to do about it.

I said 'Why did he shoot himself!'

Bruno said 'Because he thought he could see only what was in his own head, and no one understood what he was saying.'

Trixie said 'Why did he shoot his girlfriend?'

Bruno said 'Because she had cancer.'

I thought – You mean, what are the connections between one thing and another?

Trixie and I went on pressing Bruno to take us to see the night-life of Berlin. He was a year older than us; he was used to going to bars and cafés on his own. Trixie said 'But what exactly do you have to do there?'

Bruno said 'Not much.'

I said 'I mean, what do you let men do to you?'

He said 'Nellie, you are not supposed to know about such things!'

This was a time when people called me Nellie. I have been known at different times as Eleanor, Helena, Elena, Nell, Nellie.

Then Bruno said 'But it is probably true, yes, that you could make money and still be virgins.'

Trixie said 'How?'

Bruno said 'Oh for God's sake, all right, do I have to show you?'

It was arranged that Trixie would tell her parents that she was staying with me for a night and I would tell my father that I was staying with Trixie for a night; Bruno apparently did not have to say anything to his parents. I tried to say what I had to say to my father in such a way that he would both believe and not believe me. He said 'But you will be all right?'

I said 'Yes, I'll be all right.'

I thought – This saying of things without saying them – this is the sort of thing we have often talked about, isn't it?

Trixie and Bruno and I met in a café. Trixie was wearing high-heeled shoes and stockings and a short skirt. I was wearing flat shoes and socks and a skirt like a kilt. Bruno was wearing a pale grey suit with a waistcoat. He said 'Oh my God, you two, may you suffer for the guilt of your innocent friend!'

Trixie said 'But you keep on telling us nothing will happen.'

Bruno said 'Promise me, nothing will happen!'

I said 'Bruno, stop acting.'

Bruno 'You want me to stop acting? You want nothing to happen even before it has begun?'

Bruno began to explain what it was we had to do. Every now and then he broke off and rolled his eyes and put his head in his hands. I thought – You mean you have to act in order to make things both happen and not happen?

He said 'It's not really very difficult. People are lonely. One of the ways they think they can stop being lonely is by talking to people and giving them money.'

Trixie said 'They just give us money?'

Bruno said 'You won't believe this.'

I said 'But what do we have to do?'

Bruno said 'I keep telling you, there's nothing you have to do. You just sit and be nice for a time and talk, and then people give you their money.'

Trixie said 'Who?'

Bruno said 'You want me to stop acting? You want nothing to happen even before it has begun?'

Trixie said 'And what do they do when you've got the money?'

Bruno said 'I've told you you won't believe this. You tell them you have to go home. They're quite relieved at this.'

I said 'Is this true?'

Bruno said 'Nellie, you're not allowed a direct question!'

Bruno and Trixie and I got a bus to a part of the town where I had not been before; it was somewhere off the road on the way to my mother's soup-kitchen. There was a traffic jam with bright lights beyond it. I thought – People are queuing up here for some sort of food from a kitchen.

Trixie went on 'We say we want money for – what? – a hotel room or something?'

Bruno said 'Look, let's call this off, shall we?'

I said 'We say we have to go and book a hotel room and then we bugger off somewhere quite different with the money.'

Bruno shouted 'Let me out of here!' He began to stagger along the central aisle of the bus.

I thought – But, of course, this is just the place where we should be getting off the bus anyway.

In the streets there were women of the kind I had seen here and there in other parts of the town – tall, top-heavy women like square-rigged sailing-ships in a high wind. Some were being pulled along by small dogs; some carried canes or even whips. One called out to Bruno as we went past 'Don't sit down, ducky, or you'll cut your arse on eggshells!' Bruno called back 'It would take more than eggshells to make a dent on yours!'

Trixie said 'How did you learn that?'

Bruno said 'Now just one look and then we'll go home.'

I said 'But we can't go home.'

Bruno said 'Why not?'

I said 'Because we have told our parents we are staying out for the night.'

Bruno said 'All right, we'll get a hotel room. If I tell you the name of a hotel, will you remember it if we get separated?'

Trixie said 'We're getting the money for a hotel room anyway.'

I said 'But it'll be a different hotel.'

Trixie said 'I don't see why if we're going to be on our own anyway.'

Bruno said 'Will you two be quiet?'

The place we were heading for was a café-theatre called the Resi. Here the audience or clientele sat in a semi-circle in tiers in small wooden compartments like stalls: in each compartment there was a bench and a table and a telephone, and the receiving and delivering end of a network of pipes through which, by means of a vacuum pump, messages could be passed in small cylinders from one compartment to another. On the stage there were displays of spurting and cascading water; on these were shone coloured lights to an accompaniment of music. The whole set-up I suppose was controlled by one of those mechanisms like that of a steam organ – the unwinding of a giant roll like lavatory paper. The effect was indeed like being in the presence of some giant's insides: on the stage water sprayed and splashed and squirted; at one's table one waited for little cylinders to pop in and out of holes; all this was supposed to be to do with the satisfying of desire; even love.

Trixie and Bruno and I sat at our table and hoped for a message to pop out from our particular hole. I said 'Or shall we shove a message in?' Trixie said 'Which hole is which?' Bruno said 'At your age, darling, and you still don't know.' After a time Trixie said 'All this splashing, it makes me want to pee.' Bruno said 'Trixie, you'll make a fortune at this game.'

I said 'I think it's like some sort of practice about how to stay alive.'

Bruno said 'Nellie, if you were Jael, wife of Heber the Kenite, and you were about to bang a tent-peg through the temples of Sisera the Captain of the Canaanites, you would say that it was all some practice about how to stay alive.'

I said 'Well it was, wasn't it?'

Bruno was in fact the first one of us to be picked up. One of the tubes by our table began to wheeze and fart: then out popped a little cylinder with a rolled-up message inside. The message said 'Zeus awaits his Ganymede at Table 27.' Trixie said 'How do you know I'm not Ganymede?' Bruno said 'Tell her, Nellie, will you.' I said 'Ganymede was a boy.' Trixie said 'As a matter of fact, I think Nellie's much the most beautiful boy here.'

Then I felt suddenly as if my insides were turning to water; splashing and churning with coloured lights and music.

Bruno said 'Now remember what I've told you: only go to the tables of English or Americans; don't leave this place without me; sit or dance with them here. I'll come back, and then we'll go to the hotel.'

Trixie said 'We'll have to get money before we go to a hotel.'

I said 'We'll tell them we've got an old grandmother who is starving.'

Bruno said 'Tell them you've got a boyfriend for whom you've got to put up bail for pimping.'

Trixie said 'Bruno, we love you, we're grateful, really.'

When Bruno had left us Trixie and I sat in our compartment and held hands. Trixie was a blonde girl with a mouth like a hot dusty cornfield. Bruno had got us a drink which was some sort of false champagne. I thought – But I did know, did I, that with Trixie there would be these coloured lights, shapes, music; this message at my throat like flashing tongues –

Trixie said 'What do you think Bruno does with his men?'

I said 'I suppose they kiss, don't they?'

Trixie said 'Can I kiss you?'

I said 'We can go to the hotel?'

Trixie and I kissed, holding hands. I suppose we had drunk quite a bit of champagne. I put my head down on her shoulder: she put her hand at the back of my neck. Sometimes our telephone rang; sometimes a little cylinder popped out of one of the holes. But the messages were mostly from German boys who just wanted to be witty – to show off their prowess at sending bits of paper in and out of holes. One of the messages said 'Greetings to the two most perfect daisies in the chain.' Trixie wrote 'Greetings to those who sit underneath the chain.' She said 'Do you think that's witty?' I said 'Trixie, I love you.' Trixie lifted the flap at the end of one of the pipes and put the cylinder in and it was sucked into the hole. She said 'I love you too.'

There were two American couples at a table just above us: at least they looked like Americans – the women had scraped-back hair and the men were like the casings of Egyptian mummies. They had been leaning over the front of their compartment watching Trixie and me; then after a time the two women got up and left. I thought – Well this might be all right. Our telephone rang and it was the two American men asking us to join them. Trixie had handed the telephone to me because she did not speak English. I said 'I'm afraid we are waiting for our friend.' Trixie said 'Are you mad?' I said into the telephone 'But we'll join you for a minute.' Trixie said 'Oh I see.' On our way to the Americans' table I said 'But we can really go to a hotel?'

The Americans were in their late twenties or early thirties; they ordered some more so-called 'champagne'. They were already quite drunk. When I looked round the auditorium I could see no sign of Bruno. The display of water and coloured lights had stopped; a dance-band had appeared at the back of the stage: people were dancing with the strange shaking movements that were fashionable at the time – as if they were being attacked by bees; as if they had not even been looking for honey. One of the Americans asked Trixie to dance. I thought – Of course I have always loved Trixie: I did not know until now about feelings like messages being sucked into holes; about putting my tongue inside her.

The American I was with said 'How old are you?'

'Seventeen.'

'You don't look seventeen.'

'No, we are not seventeen.'

The American kissed me; he was like crumbling plaster; I thought – He is a fungus growing out of a crack in a wall.

Then – Will there be a basin in which I can wash his taste from me in the hotel room where I will be with Trixie?

When Trixie came back from the dance-floor she said 'Has yours said anything about money?'

I said 'No.'

Trixie said 'I don't think these two nose-pickers know they're supposed to give us money.'

Trixie's American said 'What does your friend say?'

I said 'She says she has a grandmother or something who is starving.'

Trixie and I began to fall about, laughing.

My American said 'Do you two girls want to go to a hotel?'

I suppose Trixie and I were quite drunk by this time. What is the feeling – that things are worth a risk? That of course nothing that one doesn't know about happens without a risk? Well it is true, isn't it. I said to my American 'Those were your wives you were with just now?' My American said 'Yes.' I said 'You want us to book into a hotel?'

Trixie's American said 'You'll say you are our wives?'

I said to Trixie 'This will be all right.'

Trixie and I and the two Americans went into the street to find a taxi. Trixie gave the driver the name of the hotel that Bruno had told us about. I said 'Is that wise?' The driver said 'You two girls shouldn't be going to that hotel.' Trixie said 'Oh we're not really going to that hotel.' The driver said 'Oh I see.' My American said 'Did I hear you say we wouldn't be going to that hotel?' I said in English 'I said that for the driver.' Trixie's American said 'Oh I see.' When we got to the hotel Trixie said 'Tell them we'll have to have quite a lot of money in order to fix the man behind the desk.' I said in English 'We'll have to have quite a lot of money to fix the man behind the desk.' My American said 'Why, if you're going to say you are our wives?' I said 'Because we're only fifteen.' Trixie and I were falling about, laughing. Trixie's American was going to sleep, he kept toppling sideways, he had to be propped up by my American. The driver said 'Well do you or don't you want to go into the hotel?' I said in English to my American 'We will have to get two double rooms for you and your wives.' Trixie said 'Are you saying that for the driver?' Trixie and I hung on to each other, laughing. My American said 'You two girls seem very fond of each other.' Trixie's American said 'Give them the money.' My American said 'Why?' The other said 'They're only fifteen.' After a time my American pulled out a roll of notes and gave to me what seemed an enormous amount of money. I said 'Thank you very much.' I kissed him. Trixie and I got out of the taxi and ran into the hotel.

The man behind the desk started saying 'You two girls can't come in here on your own.' Trixie said 'We're not, we're with those two Americans.' The man behind the desk said 'Oh I see.' While he was turning to get the key we heard the taxi drive away, with the Americans still in it; the man behind the desk paused; I said to him 'It's all right, they've gone to get their wives.' Trixie said 'Oh I see.' We went on laughing.

I remember that hotel room: it was orange and brown; there was a pink advertisement-light outside the window. Trixie and I stood facing each other; we put our hands on each other's shoulders; it was not really like those flashing lights and music and spurting and cascading water: that was outside: this was within: this was something like a religious ceremony. Well it was the first time, wasn't it: what else is love? There are hands that shape the transformations of the body: spittle on the tongue like blood. Trixie said 'I didn't know it would be like this.' I said 'No, I didn't know it would be like this.' Trixie said 'How have we managed it?' I said 'I don't know.' I thought – So this is where you get to, where there are no words left; where there is no light but pressure as if at the bottom of the ocean.

Sometime in the middle of the night there was a quiet knocking on our door and I thought – The police? The man behind the desk? Dear God, those two Americans and their wives? Then Bruno's voice said 'It's me, Bruno.' I said 'Bruno!' I jumped out of bed. I thought – But we have forgotten Bruno! When he came in he looked white and sad in the pale pink light. He said 'What have you two been doing?' I said 'Bruno, Bruno, we're all right!' I jumped back into bed: Trixie was on her front sleeping. Bruno said 'The man downstairs said you were here with two Americans and their wives.' I thought – Oh I could manage, now, even the two Americans and their wives! I said 'And what have you been up to Bruno?' Bruno sat down on the edge of our bed: it seemed as if he were about to cry. I said 'Bruno. Bruno!' I put my arms around him. He said 'It's so awful.' Trixie half woke up and said 'What is it?' I said 'It's Bruno.' Trixie said 'Tell him to get into bed.' I pulled back the bedclothes and said 'Get in.' Bruno said 'Is that all right?' I thought – He has been so good to us, we are so lucky, he can be our child. Trixie said 'Put him in the middle.' I said 'Come in the middle.' He said 'Aren't I lucky!'

Sometime in the middle of the night I woke and it seemed that Bruno and Trixie were making love. I lay with my back to them. I thought – Well, I am not jealous: am I supposed to be jealous?

In the morning Bruno said 'Now it's your turn, Nellie.'

I said 'You never, Bruno!'

Trixie watched us. She said 'Am I supposed to be jealous?'

I thought – I suppose things may never be so good between the three of us again.

When later that morning I got home to our apartment my father heard me and came out into the hall. He looked as if he might be somehow frightened of me. He said 'Are you all right?' I said 'Yes, I'm all right.' He said 'Trixie's mother telephoned last night and asked if she could speak to her.' After a time I said 'So what did you say?' He said 'I said that you and she were taking the cat for a walk.' I thought – But one doesn't take cats for walks. Then – Oh I see. I said 'Thank you. Thank you very much.' He said 'But you are all right?' I said 'Yes, I'm all right.' My father said 'You look all right.' He came and put his arms around me. He said 'You will always tell me, won't you, if you are not?' I said 'Yes, I will.' I thought suddenly – But perhaps now I will not be so close to my father. He let go of me, and stepped back. I said 'You do know, don't you, that I've learned everything from you.'

He said 'Oh you needn't say that.'

I said 'Oh but that's something I can say!'

In 1926 my father moved to Heidelberg. I think he left Berlin because he felt he could do nothing more for my mother.

I went with him, and to a new school in Heidelberg. By this time I hardly missed my mother. I wondered – There must have been a time when I was close to her; she may indeed one day come back to haunt me. Occasionally in the holiday I visited her in Berlin: she worked in a room with an old printing press like a steam-organ. I thought – Here are the rolls of paper that provide the coloured lights, shapes, music, that my mother thinks are suitable for the masses.

Sometimes I still went with her to her soup-kitchen. Wooden compartments had been set up in which people reclined and tried to sleep with their heads on each other's shoulders. I thought – But there are no messages getting through: there is a blockage in intestines.

Nothing much remains in my memory of my time at Heidelberg: I suppose I was in some sort of limbo. I missed Bruno and Trixie: I made no real new friends. Bruno and Trixie and I wrote to each other – messages that tried to be sophisticated, witty. We did not talk about feelings. I thought – But I am happy when I write to Bruno and Trixie: you do not talk about happiness.

Bruno and Trixie visited me one weekend; we went on a walk through forests, over hills. This was the time of the *Wandervögel* in Germany – when troupes of people, mostly young, went striding across landscapes, singing, talking, sleeping out, living rough; sharing what they had in the way of food and money. But Trixie now was rather grand: she had a girlfriend in Berlin who was older than she and who gave her money. Bruno seemed sad: he looked for boys he might pick up in the forest. On our walk it rained most of the day, and at night we had to take shelter in a youth hostel. Bruno was put in a separate dormitory: Trixie and I remained in separate beds.

I said 'Perhaps one can never repeat things.'

Bruno said 'But in a way one does nothing else.'

Trixie said to me 'You must come to Berlin, darling.'

I thought – Perhaps it was because it was unrepeatable, that that time in Berlin was so good.

When the time came for me to leave school and go to a university, I said to my father 'Do you think I should stay here in Heidelberg, or do you think I should go somewhere else?

He said 'What do you think?'

I said 'I suppose I should go on.'

He said 'You sound as if you don't want to.' Then – 'That's probably right.'

I said 'I can always come back.'

He said 'Yes, you can always come back.'

I thought – But I will be carrying it with me, what I have got from my father.

I went to the University of Freiburg in 1928. I was to study medicine, but I also wanted to take a course in philosophy. Freiburg is a hundred miles from Heidelberg: four hundred miles from Berlin. I thought – I could walk to Heidelberg in about three days: I will not want to get to Berlin.

Conditions in German universities had always been different, I suppose, from conditions in British universities in that one arranged one's own accommodation and could go to what lectures one liked; one could move from discipline to discipline and could work (or not) in one's own time. I got a room with a family who were acquaintances of my father, but I spent as little time with them as I could. I wanted to be on my own. I thought – But what is this extraordinary condition in which one wants to be alone, and yet is always making arrangements so that one is not.

This was a time when student life in German universities was still dominated by what were called 'corporations' or 'fraternities'. There were nationalist fraternities, socialist fraternities, liberal fraternities, Catholic fraternities: inside each a boy might feel he was at home. Members of one fraternity were distinguished from those of another by the coloured ribbons they wore round their caps; otherwise the style of each was much the same. Members put up barriers against others to feel protected; but they did not feel seriously threatened because they knew that others were doing the same. The conventions were that members of fraternities should strut about carrying sticks and flaunt themselves during the day; then at night they should meet in beer-halls and drink and sing till they passed out. In this way they could imagine that they had asserted themselves without having incurred the dangers or indeed the responsibilities of self-assertion.

There were no such organisations for women. Girls to some extent felt themselves above such things; yet they were apt to hang about the boys' fraternities as if they were casual labourers waiting to be picked by gang bosses.

I thought – Of course I feel myself superior: but am I then hanging about on street corners in order to start a revolution?

There was a boy at Freiburg called Franz who was a member of the most élite of all fraternities, which was called The Corps (fraternities were graded strictly in terms of caste: members of one fraternity could properly have social contact only with their fellow members or with those of a fraternity immediately above or below it). Franz seemed to be aloof from even his élite fraternity. I understood that he was some sort of aristocrat; that he would have had to make no special effort to have become a member even of this élite fraternity; that he would have been included perhaps without even his wishing to be included. (I wondered – Does this make him more arrogant or less than other members of fraternities?) Franz would sit with other members of The Corps in the cellars of beer-halls in the evenings and he would drink and sometimes join in the songs, but for the most part would recline with his chair tilted back and his cap on the back of his head and smoking a pipe as if he were on a tightrope. I thought – He is like one of those people who show off by pretending to carry on normal life when on a tightrope. He was a tall thin boy with fair hair. His pipe was one of those long curly things that went down to a bowl like a stove with a lid on. The other boys at their long narrow table would all be yelling and banging their beer mugs up and down and becoming red in the face and sweating: Franz, balanced, seemed to be keeping his head just above water – or perhaps above fire, his pipe going down like some sort of lifeline. The other boys seemed to be in awe of Franz and yet to pay little attention to him. I thought – It is as if he were some sort of god, yes: and they are so hot and sweating because it is as if they are some sort of offering in cooking pots to him.

I wanted to get to know Franz. I did not feel about him in the way I had felt about Trixie or even Bruno, but I thought – He is on his own: there is that sort of glow about him as there was about – who? Rosa Luxemburg? That fair-haired waiter?

Then – Or perhaps he is like my father?

There was a girl student I was quite fond of at the time called Minna. Minna was a nature-worshipper: she would sit in the sun whenever she could and take off her clothes. Minna was a bit in love with Franz. She and I and a few other girls would go into beer-cellars in the evenings and sit and watch the boys sizzling and bubbling as if in their cauldrons. Franz remained impervious, like a salamander. Towards the end of the evening many boys had to be carried out vomiting or unconscious.

I thought – Well of course women don't want to be like this: we do not want now even to carry off their bodies to Valhalla.

I said to Minna 'Perhaps they need help.'

Minna said 'They don't need help, they need to be sacrificed.'

I said 'Sacrificed to what?'

Minna said 'To Akhenaton the son of the great sun.'

Minna had huge blue eyes that were like the empty spaces between stars.

I thought – Oh but in the end I want someone with whom I do not have to struggle to feel at home with!

I took to following Franz when I came across him in the street. I found out where his lodgings were, and to what lectures he was going. He seemed to be studying both philosophy and physics. I thought – I can bump into him and say 'I am interested in your opinion on the connections between philosophy and physics' –

Then – In this I would be treating him like my father!

The philosophy in fashion at that time was that of Husserl, who was Professor of Philosophy at Freiburg. Husserl taught that there could be no certain knowledge of a so-called 'objective' world: what were called 'objects' were always structured by the operation of ideas. What there could be certain knowledge about was the mechanisms of these ideas; the mind could be turned scientifically to investigate itself; there were operations of ideas that were common to all humanity.

I did not find it difficult to feel that I understood this: was it not to do with that vision of which my father and I had seen the possibilities as well as the limitations – the image of people looking at just the backs of their own heads? As my father used to say 'But once you see this, what worlds open up together with people who see the same!'

But could I come across Franz as if unexpectedly on some corner and say 'We might have a lot in common, you and I, looking down from such a lofty height on what we know are the ideas in our own heads!'

I had once said to my father 'But there would still be no certainty.' He had said 'Oh no, but what a thing to want, certainty!'

After lectures Franz would sometimes walk up into the hills at the back of the town. He would carry a satchel which I imagined contained books. I did not think it would be difficult to follow him: there were just one or two paths that went zig-zagging up the hill. If he stopped, I could myself stop and smile; or I could carry on past him.

I thought – There is some image in my mind here of a rock, a fork in the pathway, a gate: a road along which a traveller might go for ever.

There was a day when I followed Franz into the hills. He went on a path which, in fact, I had been on before: it did come, yes, to an outcrop of rock where the path doubled back on one of its zig-zags. But there had also been, when I had been here before, a faint track through the trees across pine-needles. I had followed this track and had come to a cave: I had thought – It might be Aladdin's cave: there were the signs of a fire in front of it, as if someone had recently camped there. But further inside the cave there had seemed to be bats, so I had not gone in.

Franz was on a level of the zig-zag path above me; I caught glimpses of him as he moved between trees. I thought – If he stops, why in fact should I not come up to him and say 'I am interested in the connections between philosophy and physics?' I had an image of Franz as Moses going up into the mountain to talk to God: in his satchel he might carry his tablets or whatever. Or was he, as Minna had suggested, a devotee of some nature god; would he lay himself on an altar and offer himself to the sun? I was daydreaming like this – following haphazardly a path in my mind – when I saw that I had come to the outcrop of rock at which I had left the path before. Franz was going straight on across the pine-needles; he had his satchel over his shoulder; he was going towards the cave. Then I saw that in his hand he carried a pistol. At least it looked like a pistol: I thought – He is going to shoot deer? Hares? Rabbits? But you do not shoot such game with a pistol! Then – He is going to shoot himself? This was an idea quite likely to occur to someone at this time: there had been an alarming increase in suicides amongst students recently. There was the fashionable prototype of Werther who had killed himself because what else was there to do about love; there was the story of Kleist – often in my mind since the days when Trixie and Bruno and I used to visit his grave – who had shot himself because what else was there to do if one saw that one was trapped within one's own mind; and there were the suicidal characters in Dostoevsky, whom I also much loved and who was in vogue amongst students at this time. I thought – Well, yes, indeed, there are these patterns in people's minds.

I had stopped by the outcrop of rock where the path doubled back on one of its zig-zags. I thought – I can go on; I can turn back; what does it mean that the way in front might go on for ever?

I left the path and went off across the pine-needles following Franz who was now out of sight. I wondered – One has an impression of choice? Or one chooses to imagine one has a choice? I was trying not to make any sound as I moved over the pine-needles: it was as if I were slightly above myself, watching myself. I wondered if Franz was going to the cave that was full of bats: would he shoot at the bats; would he perform some ceremony there, to get rid of devils? When next I saw him he had stopped and was undoing the flap of his satchel and was pulling out a length of rope. I thought – So what is he going to do, hang himself as well as shoot himself? Go rock-climbing in the cave like a bat? Then – This is ridiculous. Franz went on towards the entrance of the cave. I had stopped at some distance away. I thought – To go any further might be like breaking into the back of someone else's head. I seemed to be listening – for the sound of the pistol? For noises unheard like those of bats? After a time I went on. I still trod carefully. I got to where I could see into the cave. Franz was sitting on the ground just inside: he had taken his clothes off; he seemed to be tying the rope round his feet. I thought – Oh but I have no patterns in my mind that I can connect to something like this! He will hang himself upside down? He will be a sacrifice to something – what? – that which demands sacrifices of gods? Then again – This is ridiculous. I could not see the pistol. It might be under his bundle of clothes. Franz stood up and put one end of the rope through or over some aperture or projection in the roof of the cave; he pulled the end down; then he lay on his back and went on pulling so that his feet at the other end of the rope were heaved up towards the ceiling. He was then in the position of a piece of meat in a butcher's shop; or, yes, like a bat. I thought – But was not St Peter crucified like this? And there are all his poor insides, his cock and balls, hanging out! You mean, men might need to do something like this to give themselves a proper airing? When Franz was almost suspended, with his head just touching the ground, he slowly, through some inner momentum, swung so that his face was towards me: he seemed to see me: though it was difficult to imagine just what he saw, being upside down. I wondered – But doesn't the brain normally see things upside down? Might he not be doing some experiment to see things the right way up? There were, in fact, I knew, strange rituals being performed by nature-worshippers at this time. I thought that if I just stayed still, he might see me as some nymph of the forest. Then Franz let go of the end of the rope so that he collapsed, slowly, in a somersault. I thought I should bend down and pretend to have been doing something to my shoe. I picked up one or two pine-needles on the floor of the forest: the pine-needles seemed to be a representation of the fork in the road. I thought – Oh yes, there are connections between inside and outside worlds: you could say this is some turning I have taken. When I looked up again Franz was sitting with his feet underneath him and his bundle of clothes in his lap and he was holding the pistol which he was pointing sideways. There was no sign of the rope. I thought – He has not had time to untie the rope so that is why he is sitting with his feet underneath him. It did not seem that I could go either away or towards him. I thought – So I will stay here, on this my tightrope, just beyond the fork in the roadway.

After a time Franz, still watching me, raised the barrel of the gun so that it was in his mouth and pulled the trigger. I leaped into the air with my arms and legs flying out like those of a puppet. I thought – Oh it is I who have been shot, and am flying off round the universe!

Then – But this has got me moving.

I began walking towards Franz. The pistol had not gone off. I thought – He put only one bullet in it?

Franz watched me as I walked towards him. He held the pistol in his lap. The pistol was of the revolver type with which you can put as many bullets as you like into the cylinder and spin it.

I said 'I've come here before. I often come here.' I do not know why I said this. I suppose I was offering some sort of explanation.

He said 'You often come here.'

I said 'Yes.'

He said as if quoting ' – and must we not return and run down the lane in front of us, that long and terrible lane, must we not return, you and I, eternally – '

I said 'Oh yes, who said that?'

He said 'Nietzsche.'

I said 'Oh yes, Nietzsche.'

I had moved to the wall at the side of the cave which was opposite him. I leaned with my back to the wall. He still had his feet underneath him as if he were a mermaid.

I said 'And what happens then?'

He said 'What happens when?'

'At the turning. Doesn't he, Zarathustra, bite off the head of a snake, or something?'

'He comes across someone else who has a snake halfway down his throat, so he tells him to bite the head off.'

'And does he?'

'Yes.'

I said 'And then what?'

He said 'He is free. He is laughing.'

I said 'Can't you do that?'

After a time Franz raised the revolver and pointed it into the cave. Then he pulled the trigger. There was an explosion in which it seemed that my eardrums were going in and out together with the roof and walls of the cave; then hundreds of bats were flying around me like bits of black glass, like broken shadows, they bumped into walls, they almost bumped into me, I put my arms over my head. I thought – God damn you! Then – Oh well, have the shadows gone from the walls of the cave?

After a time I could see between my fingers that Franz was untying the rope from around his feet. When the bats had all gone I looked up. I said 'Had you got just one bullet in it? You could have known where the bullet was!'

He said 'Oh yes, I might have known where the bullet was.'

I said 'I mean, that would have been sensible.'

He said 'You think it right to be sensible?'

I said 'Yes.'

He said 'In this game?'

I said 'What game?'

He was still untying the rope from his feet. Then he said 'Why did you come here?'

I said 'I was following you.'

'Why?'

'I wanted to ask you about the connections between philosophy and physics.'

'You wanted to ask me about the connections between philosophy and physics.'

'Yes.'

He stretched his feet out in front of him. He leaned fowards and rubbed his ankle, which seemed to be hurting him.

He said 'In philosophy you are stuck within your own brains. In physics you are stuck within your own brains. So why not give your brains an airing.'

I said 'That's what Kleist thought.'

He said 'Yes, that's what Kleist thought.'

I said 'Why is it like that in physics?'

He leaned back and rested his head against the wall of the cave.

He said 'In physics what you observe is dependent on the fact that you observe: there is no way of observing anything apart from you as observer. You shine a light on an object and you alter it by the fact that you shine a light: you do not shine a light and then you cannot observe it. In some experiments light appears to be waves: in other experiments it appears to be particles. You can tell a particle's exact velocity, or location, but you can't tell both at the same time. There is no way of saying what anything is, apart from the way in which you are observing it.'

I said 'And you don't like that.'

'No.'

'Why not?'

He said 'There are such terrible things that go on in these heads in which we are trapped. They will destroy us. Why should we not destroy them.'

I said 'Yes, but once you know that – '

He said 'What?'

I said 'Let me see your ankle.'

I went across the floor of the cave to him: I looked down at his ankle, where the rope had chafed him. I said 'You let them out, you let them out, all those bats.'

He said 'Where?'

I said 'From the cave. From the mind.'

He said 'Yes, but where do they go to?' He banged his head gently against the wall of the cave.

I said 'That is not your business.'

He said 'What is my business?'

I said 'Where does it hurt you?'

He said 'You want to save me, do you?'

I said 'Yes.'

He said 'Why?'

I said 'That would be one of the things I'd like if I have to be going on doing it for ever.'

One of the ways in which members of fraternities maintained their senses of belonging and identity was in the matter of duelling. Boys seemed always to be on the look-out for an insult and for the opportunity to avenge it: in what simpler way could solidarity be demonstrated? Serious duelling occurred when a challenge was made and accepted between individuals. But when there was not much of this sort of duelling, a number of members of two fraternities came together for a ritual fight called a *Mensur*. In both events there were safeguards by which a fighter could achieve his sense of belonging with only a ritual wounding.

In a *Mensur* the boys from the two fraternities met in a gymnasium; they lined up opposite each other in pairs. (This was still happening, yes, in the late 1920s.) They carried swords with long thin blades. Their hands and arms and bodies were bandaged; only their heads were unprotected. (I would think – Dear God it is, indeed, as if they want to be hit just on their own heads!) At a signal, each boy put a hand behind his back and in the other raised his sword to a level slightly above his head. The fight consisted of queer flicking movements of the wrist with the forearm held straight: these were the rules: the idea was, in fact, that the boys should become cut about the face and head. And the aim was less that one should cut one's opponent's face than that oneself should be cut: once one's cuts were deep enough, clear enough, then the fight was over. One had received one's accolade – one's mark of loyalty to the tribe.

I had once said to my father 'But if this sort of thing is a ritual, is it more sophisticated or more silly than just to be decorated by tribal witch-doctors with knives?'

He had said 'What would be sophisticated, I suppose, would be to be able to look at why one wanted to be cut by knives.'

Shortly after the time when I had come across Franz in the cave in the mountain, there was one of these fights in Freiburg in which Franz's fraternity, The Corps, was involved. Franz was one of those chosen to represent The Corps. I wondered if they had chosen him because he was good at duelling; or because, since he was so aloof, they wanted to involve him as an active member of The Corps.

Franz had half tried to avoid me since our time on the mountain. I imagined – But perhaps he likes to know that I am here.

Minna and I and some other girls watched this ritual *Mensur* through the windows of the gymnasium. Franz in fact fought quite well: he seemed both bored and yet purposeful; even sometimes alarmed. He flicked at the other boy's face; then when he had cut it – once, lightly – he lowered his sword and stood still. The other boy pointed his sword at him but Franz did not move. Then after a time he turned his back and went to the chairs at the side of the gymnasium and put down his sword and picked up his clothes and went out. This was against the conventions, because he himself had not yet been cut on the face.

I ran after Franz when he appeared in the road. He seemed to be heading for the path into the mountains.

I said 'Hey, can I borrow your pistol?'

He said 'Why?'

I said 'I want to shoot some bats.'

He said 'Do you want to save just me, or half the human race?'

I said 'I think about a third would be enough, don't you?'

He said 'Yes, I think a third would be about the right number.'

We walked up the path into the mountains. He walked slightly ahead of me. I thought – I am acting the part of someone trotting along behind him.

He said 'But have you heard the news, the human race doesn't want to be saved.'

I said 'How can they know they don't want to be, until they have been?'

He stopped somewhere short of the turning to the cave. He sat on an outcrop of rock. He held his hands underneath him.

He said 'Human beings are not viable. They make sense on their own, yet they can't be on their own, they have to be in relationship to others. I am grateful to you for having been good to me. Yet it's this need to be in relationship that is destroying them.'

I said 'How have I been good to you?'

He said 'By not talking about what you have seen.'

I said 'But if you know all this – '

He said 'There you go again!'

I thought – I suppose I feel stupid with Franz because I am a bit in love with him.

I said 'If I'm good to you it's because I want to be. But there's no special virtue in loyalty. Most of the crimes of the world seem to be committed in the name of loyalty – '

He said 'Oh very true.'

I said 'So why do you do it?'

'Do what?'

'Go along with these ridiculous fraternities.'

'Where else would I go?'

I wanted to say – Here.

He said 'Unfortunately one carries whatever one is in one's head.'

I was going to say yet again – But once you know this –

He laughed and said 'Get it out, get it out.' Then – 'I know what you were going to say!'

I said 'What?'

He said 'Nellie, it will do for your epitaph.'

I thought – Well that's all right, isn't it?

That evening in the beer-cellar there was talk about how Franz had walked out of the *Mensur* before he had received his own wound: this was of course strongly criticised. But there were one or two of The Corps who argued that Franz might have been justified in that he had been wrongly paired in the first place; and this was why he had walked out.

I have mentioned the caste system that affected the relationship between members of fraternities: this was especially relevant to the matter of fighting duels. Challenges could only be made or received by members of fraternities one above or one below each other in caste. And at the lower end of this caste system were the Jewish fraternities. There were two main sorts of Jewish fraternities -- the pro-Zionist and the pan-German. Both of these sang and strutted about and drank themselves unconscious at night in the style of the others; but it was the custom amongst members of most non-Jewish fraternities that they should not fight duels with members of Jewish fraternities. If a challenge by one of the latter was made, it was turned down. It seemed to me that this was due not only to ingrained anti-Semitism but to the fact that Jews, by their nature and their situation, would be likely to have trained so well that they would be better as fighters than most non-Jews – Jews being apt to introduce a touch of reality into such ridiculous games.

Now, however, it was being suggested that the reason why Franz had not waited to let himself be cut about the face by the boy he had been paired with was because he had suspected that this boy might be a Jew. He wasn't. But it was being suggested that Franz might have suspected that he was, and so might have been justified in walking out.

I said to Minna 'But all this is typical of the pathetic games of Christians. It is the explanation that Franz would hate more than any other!'

Minna said 'I would like to fight a duel with the people who say this, on behalf of Franz.'

I said 'Ah Minna, you would be good at fighting duels!'

Minna said 'I could take on most of those boys with one hand behind my back!'

I thought I might say – But Minna, you would anyway have one hand behind your back!

Minna said 'Hoop! Hoopla!' She made slashing movements as if at a boy's loins.

In the matter of duelling there was one caste of persons of course far lower in the pecking order than Jews, and this was women. It was inconceivable that a boy could think of fighting a duel with a woman. I thought – Indeed, they might be frightened of confronting some reality.

I said 'But Minna, you would want to win!'

She said 'Of course I would want to win!'

I said 'But the point of duelling, amongst boys, seems to be to get exquisitely beaten.'

Minna said 'Then I would exquisitely beat them!'

That evening in the beer-cellar when members of The Corps came in they did not, as usual, pay much attention to Franz; but it was now as if they were almost consciously leaving a small space around him. I thought – He has broken, yes, a taboo, by refusing to become a ludicrous sacrificial victim. It had been rumoured that members of a Jewish fraternity were going to come to the beer-cellar that night: that they had been told that Franz, by walking out of the *Mensur*, might have insulted someone he had supposed to be a Jew; so they felt themselves insulted even though this person was not a Jew. So it seemed that there might even be a serious fight that night: for if it was felt by The Corps that in some way Franz had disgraced it – which he would not have done if his opponent had in fact been a Jew – then members of The Corps, to redeem themselves, might feel that in this situation they had to accept a challenge even by a Jew.

I said to Minna 'But they are all mad! It would be better if they were all put in a sack, and thrown into the river.'

Minna said 'But if one of the Jewish fraternity challenges one of The Corps to a duel tonight, and if the member of The Corps who would have turned it down on account of the challenger being a Jew, cannot now because of Franz's having walked out of the *Mensur*, cannot we then perhaps challenge one of the Jewish fraternity to a duel, and they will not be able to turn us down on account of our being women.'

I said 'What?' Then – 'Minna you are mad too! You should have been a boy.'

Minna said 'I know I should have been a boy.' She hugged me.

When the Jewish fraternity came into the beer-cellar that night (they were called The Maccabees) they sat at one table and The Corps sat at theirs and they all sang sad songs; Franz leaned back with his cap on the back of his head and his pipe in front of him as if he were on a tightrope. Then The Corps sang patriotic German songs and The Maccabees sang patriotic Zionist songs, and everyone was drinking more and more beer. So The Corps, as if in response to the Zionist songs, started on one of the obscene songs that they usually did not sing until later in the evening when women were no longer present: this song was called 'The Innkeeper's Daughter' and had innumerable verses in which the sexual exploits of the daughter became ever more bizarre: each member of The Corps round the table was supposed to sing a verse which would outdo the last one in obscenity. This would usually go on until the participants passed out – as indeed would have been likely to happen to anyone trying to keep up with the innkeeper's daughter.

I said 'But Minna, we want to be different from these boys.'

Minna said 'We are different from these boys.'

I said 'Then we don't want to take all this seriously.'

Minna said 'It is the boys who do not take this seriously!' She made slashing movements with her arm.

There was one member of The Maccabees called Albrecht who was a small angry boy of great energy: it was he who seemed to be stirring himself up to challenge a member of The Corps to a duel. He was singing his Zionist song more loudly than the others; he was banging his mug down on the table so violently that bits of beer seemed to hang in the air like spittle.

I said 'But Minna, do you know how to fight a duel?'

Minna said 'I have achieved my silver medal at fencing!'

I said 'But they won't fight you.'

Minna said 'Then I will hit them over the head with one of their sticks.'

It was a convention amongst Jews that if a member of a Jewish fraternity challenged a member of a non-Jewish fraternity to a duel and the member of the non-Jewish fraternity refused the challenge, then the Jew should hit the non-Jew over the head with his stick; and then a general mêlée would be likely to ensue, in which Jews might feel that they had salvaged their honour, if not in the conventional manner.

I said 'Minna, do you know what happened when Penthesilia, Queen of the Amazons, challenged Achilles to a duel?'

Minna said 'I know very well, she tore him to pieces.'

I said 'And she ate him.'

Minna said 'Oh I would like to eat Franz!'

The contortions of the innkeeper's daughter were becoming even more outlandish (I was thinking – Songs are such obvious substitutes for sexuality!); The Maccabees had embarked on the Zionist National Anthem, the Hatikvah. (I was thinking – And what should Minna and I sing? The Lorelei? The siren-song that lured poor sailors to their doom?) Then after one of the boys at The Corps' table had sung a particularly obscene verse, Albrecht, at the Maccabees' table, jumped up and went to The Corps' table and stood to attention and said in a loud voice 'I consider such obscenity in front of ladies to be proof, if any further proof were needed, that you are dishonourable men' and he clicked his heels, as if he were a small tree being axed. The noise in the beer-cellar subsided. People were watching the boy at The Corps' table who had sung the last obscene verse: this boy seemed to be too drunk to stand up. Franz was tilted back as if on his tightrope. The boy who had sung the obscene verse at last managed to murmur 'I don't give satisfaction to Jews' – which was the formula for refusing such a challenge. So Albrecht raised his stick as if to hit the boy over the head with it. Then Minna stood up and said in a loud voice 'And we don't need you to protect ladies, thank you.' Albrecht said 'What?' I thought – Oh Minna, Minna! For a moment we all seemed stuck like flies on a fly-paper. Then Minna walked over to Albrecht and tapped him on the shoulder. He stared at Minna. The boy at The Corps' table belched. Everybody laughed. Minna said 'I feel myself insulted; can I please have your card?' This was the formula for the challenge to a duel. Albrecht said 'You?' Minna said 'Yes.' Albrecht said 'But I was trying to defend you.' Minna said 'That is why I am insulted.' Albrecht looked round at the members of The Corps, who were looking embarrassed. Albrecht said 'But, Minna, I can't fight you.' Minna said 'Why not?' Then – 'He won't fight you because you're a Jew.' Albrecht said 'But you're a woman.' Minna said 'You see?' Then she took Albrecht's stick from his hand and made as if to hit him over the head with it.

Then Franz stood up and said 'I will fight you.'

Minna said 'Me?'

Franz said 'No, Albrecht.' Then to Albrecht – 'It's me you really want to fight, isn't it?'

Albrecht said 'Yes.'

Minna said 'But what about me?'

Franz said 'All right, Minna, I will fight you too.'

Minna said 'Will you really?'

Franz stood up and came round the table. The boy who had sung the last obscene verse was trying to stand up. Franz said to him 'Will you be my second?' The boy said 'Yes.' Franz said 'Make all the arrangements for tomorrow morning.' Then he bowed in front of Albrecht. Albrecht bowed. Then Franz held out a hand to Minna. Minna said 'But I was going to fight Albrecht.' Franz said 'Please will you fight me.' He put his arm round her shoulder. Then he turned to me and said 'Will you be our second?' I thought – Oh, Franz, you have done it! Then Franz and Minna and I went out into the night.

There was a full moon: we went a short way up the path that led into the hills. There was a gate into a field: the field was on the slope between the forest and the town. We went into it. The moon made the air silvery; the grass and the trees were black. I thought –

Perhaps we have gone into a world that has been turned the right way up, from what normally goes on upside down.

Minna took off her clothes and lay on the grass. Franz sat beside her with his arms round his knees. I sat slightly apart. We looked down on the town.

Franz said 'You see why I should like the human race to be wiped out.'

I said 'You think men have to fight?'

He said 'If they are to keep their honour.'

I said 'Do they have to keep their honour?'

He said 'They have little else.'

Minna had stood and was stretching her arms above her head; then with straight legs she put her hands on the ground: it was as if she was doing obeisance to the moon.

I said 'You're a physicist; perhaps you will be able to obliterate the world soon.'

He stretched out a hand towards the lights of the town. He said as if quoting – 'I am Lazarus come from the dead.'

I lay back. I thought – Well, why should not something new be happening on this strange planet?

Franz said 'In our home village, which is near Munich, during the street-fighting that happened just after the real war, the White faction took some of the Red faction prisoners. There was one prisoner, a ringleader I suppose, who had been wounded; he was in pain, he kept on yelling; he would bang his head against a wall, trying to die. So his captors got a carpenter to build a very small cage into which they packed him so that his head was down by his knees and he could no longer bang it; he could hardly scream. He made small noises like a bird. They put him in the courtyard of the police station and people came to look at him. Sometimes people pissed on him. When they did this, he was almost peaceful.'

Minna was bent over in the light of the moon. She was like some huge queen bee, an egg. There were some cows or bulls or bullocks in the field; they were coming towards her; they were black shapes, breathing.

I thought – I will try to imagine the man in the cage.

Franz said 'But this is not really the strangest part of the story. Afterwards, when the man was dead, some of the guards, when they were drunk, would play a game in which one would crawl into the cage and some of the others would stand on top of it and piss on him. Perhaps they got some sort of peace like this. Perhaps they needed it.'

I thought – But like this, you do not get peace!

Franz shouted 'Minna!'

Minna was walking forwards, with her arms out, towards the herd of cows, or bullocks, or perhaps a bull. I thought – You mean we are all like that man in the cage? Then – It is true that the world is so awful that I would not want to have a child!

There was an enormous black animal that had come to sniff at Minna. She stood facing it, naked, with her arms by her side. I thought – Oh but there is still something that we can learn, if we are brave, we humans.

I said 'But there is a different sort of honour now. Don't we have to start again? I mean the whole human race perhaps start again – '

He said 'Can we?'

I said 'You can tell that story – '

Franz laughed and said 'Nellie!' Then he turned and shouted 'Minna!'

Minna had put out a hand as if to take hold of the horns of the cow or bullock or bull. She seemed to be talking to the animal, stroking its horns.

I said 'Don't we have to become participants in our stories?'

Minna had got hold of the horns of the cow or bullock or bull. The animal jerked its head back. Minna was pulled up and half onto its neck; she was kicking her legs as if to get up on its back; she was like someone scrabbling on a rock face. The animal tossed its head and whirled away; Minna clung on, half dragged, her feet touching the ground every now and then; she and the animal were like some sort of Catherine wheel. Franz got up and ran after her. I stayed where I was. I thought – Oh yes, to participate in our own stories, we would be like gods coming down.

Minna had fallen off the cow or bullock or bull. She was lying like a white hole cut out of the dark grass. Franz was kneeling at her head. He was like a satyr. He had taken his shirt off. With it he was dabbing at Minna's face.

I thought – They have had their duel. How could one explain this? They are the children of Achilles and Penthesilea?

There was a stampede of cows, bullocks or bulls, in the distance; black shapes rushing as if to the edge of a cliff.

I lay back. I must have slept for a time. When I woke, the moon was still full.

I had had a vision (how does one tell the difference between wakefulness and dreaming?) of Franz kneeling over Minna and Minna kneeling over Franz: they were as huge as the earth and sky: they were entwined; they were interchangeable; they made a circuit. Minna's breasts hung down; Franz's arms hung down; Minna was the earth, Franz a firmament. I thought – There are seeds falling on the ground by which we are all fed. My own head was like the sky on the ground. After a time, I slept again.

Duels fought by The Corps customarily took place at six o'clock in the morning at an inn about an hour's walk from the town. Serious duels were of course illegal, so they had to happen at this place and at this time. I could not remember exactly what arrangements had been made about the duel: it seemed that we had to be at this place the next morning. I thought – But anyway, this or that will happen. Franz and Minna were coming walking towards me across the grass. They were holding hands. They were naked. The moon had gone, and there was a thin watery light. I thought – We will see, won't we, what happens.

Franz said 'You are all right?'

I said 'Yes, I'm all right.'

I thought – The earth has been fed, and watered –

– There was that man in the cage: in the end he died.

There was a path along the edge of the forest towards the inn where the duel might be fought. We set off, Franz and Minna and I, in the half-light of dawn, in some sort of procession. Minna led the way; Franz followed; I came behind. Minna was naked; Franz had put on his trousers; I wore my clothes. I thought – We are like people carrying something sacred in a litter: some god perhaps who is ill; who has had a look at the world, and so now perhaps he will help people to die. Minna carried the branch of a pine tree in her hand; it bounced and waved as she walked, like the wings of a bird. I carried Minna's clothes. I thought – But perhaps Franz will no longer want to die.

We passed close to a farmhouse where there were the sounds of cows being milked. I thought – If people see us they will not believe us: they will think we are some sort of gods come down.

When we were close to the inn, Minna stopped and held out her hands for her clothes. She was bespattered with bits of grass and mud and smelled of dung. She put on her skirt: She did not put on her blouse. Franz went on to the inn: I followed him. There was an annexe to the inn where fraternities met and where their duels were sometimes fought: it was like a village hall, hung with arms and banners. There were a few people already there from those who had been in the beer-cellar the night before: they were sitting round the walls and were once more smoking and drinking beer. A space had been cleared in the centre of the hall. Albrecht was there; he had taken his shirt off; his chest was being bandaged ready for the duel. The boy whom Franz had asked to be his second was there; he carried two swords. Franz was already stripped to the waist, so that it was as if he had been preparing for the duel. I thought – And so what will happen when Minna comes in? Franz went up to the boy with the swords and took one of them; then he turned to the door; he seemed to be waiting for Minna. I noticed that Franz's body was also flecked with mud and grass and what smelled like dung; people in the hall were watching him. The boy who was Albrecht's second went up and talked to Franz; Franz did nothing; Albrecht watched them. There was a shaft of sunlight coming in through one of the windows of the hall: it was reddish, and there were bits of dust floating in it like stars. Franz held out his sword and seemed to touch the light. Then Minna came in: she was not wearing her blouse, so it was as if she too were ready for a duel; she went and stood in the shaft of sunlight; it was as if she were in the water of a river. Everyone in the hall had stopped talking. They were watching Minna. Minna had closed her eyes. The light splashed over her. Franz pointed his sword towards Minna; Minna turned so that it almost touched her breast; then Franz put the sword down on the ground. Minna bent to pick it up. Then she straightened and held the sword pointed to the ground.

There was a banging on the door of the hall. Someone seemed to have locked the door. Then people broke in: there were two policemen and people who seemed to be from the town; a man and a woman who looked like farmers. The policemen wore black and shiny hats: they came halfway across the hall and then stopped, staring at Minna. Minna was standing half naked in the river of light, holding the sword. I thought – Now, now, will this image rest in people's minds, when the light of the stream has gone over them? Then both Minna and Franz turned to me and held out their hands for their clothes. I gave them to them. Then people in the hall started talking. It appeared that someone from the town had seen Franz and Minna and me at night in the field; the farmer and his wife had seen us walking in our procession in the early morning. And so they had called the police because they had seen us naked;

not because we were going to fight a duel; but now, presumably, we could not fight a duel. Franz and Minna were putting their clothes on: the boys who were Franz's and Albrecht's seconds had taken charge of the swords. There was still a faint smell of grass and dung of the early morning. People kept breaking off from their talking to look at Minna. Franz went over to Albrecht and put his hands on his shoulders and bent his head: after a time Albrecht lowered his head and put a hand to the back of Franz's neck. The shaft of sunlight had turned into a rather pale thin colour like that of a dream. I thought – Well there are sometimes nuggets of gold that are found at the bottoms of rivers. There were all these people gathered around the policemen opening and shutting their mouths, but it did not seem to matter much what they were saying. I thought – We have done what we wanted to do; whatever it was; perhaps we can all now leave the theatre. Then – But oh, can this never be repeated? I waited for Minna and Franz. No one was paying much attention to us now. I thought – One day there may be no more men in cages who need to die. Eventually the police did come and question Franz and Minna; but neither they nor Franz nor Minna had much to say. I thought – Indeed about this there is not much to say: there was something of a goddess about Minna.

At the end of 1928 Husserl retired as Professor of Philosophy at Freiburg and Heidegger, who had once been a favourite pupil, took his place. Husserl had apparently expected that Heidegger would carry on his work of trying to find certainty through the so-called 'scientific' investigation of ideas; but during the time that Heidegger had been away from Freiburg he had published *Being and Time* and had become famous in his own right at least amongst students; although no one seemed able to say very clearly what the book was about. Indeed Heidegger seemed to be saying (so I gathered) that 'certainty' could not be put into words: it was to do with an attitude, a state of mind, a performance: words were good for saying what things were not; they were not good for saying what things were. I thought – Well, yes, certainly, I have come across this sort of thing before.

Heidegger was due to give his inaugural lecture at Freiburg in July 1929. (The events I have been describing took place slightly earlier in this year.) There was excitement amongst students at the prospect of this lecture: it was felt – as it had been about Einstein ten years previously – that there was something liberating about

Heidegger's vision of what was beyond the bounds of conventional thought. I said to Franz, who had tried to read *Being and Time*, 'But how will Heidegger lecture if he does not trust in words! Will he come on and be silent? Will he make noises no one understands?'

Franz said 'People seem to feel they understand. Perhaps this also says something about the nature of words.'

Bruno wrote to say that he was coming from Berlin to hear the lecture: Heidegger's fame had spread. I thought – Bruno and Franz will meet! What I feel about this cannot easily be put into words.

The auditorium of the lecture-hall was a semicircle of wooden stalls rising steeply in tiers. I thought – This is like that café-theatre in Berlin: will Heidegger's message be conveyed by coloured lights and splashing music? When he did appear he was a short, sedate-looking man with a huge head. He peered amongst the audience as if there might be someone there he might recognise – not someone he already knew, but someone (it seemed) who might understand if not his words then still what he would be saying. When he spoke his voice was lilting, almost caressing: as he looked amongst the audience he seemed to be asking – Is it you? Is it you?

What Heidegger said in his inaugural lecture (or what I imagined him to have said: I have kept my notes) was roughly this –

Science takes us to the limit of what we can know about objects: beyond science there is nothing. But this nothing is postulated by science, for how can science be aware of itself except from a standpoint of what is beyond it? Facing this nothing we experience dread: but we also experience rapture, because it is what gives us a sense of our own freedom from the tyranny of things. It also gives us the possibility of being in a knowing relation to things. Without this nothing, we would ourselves be just things.

Heidegger spoke this stuff in his quiet, melodious voice: he peered amongst his audience. It was as if the riddles that he posed were not of the kind that required answers, but of the kind that go round and round and by which things are sifted, either remaining or falling through.

After the lecture I looked for Bruno, who had come straight to the lecture-hall from the train. I wondered – Will Bruno be someone I still recognise? who has not fallen (or has fallen?) through.

When I found Bruno he seemed more guarded and watchful. He lifted me with his arms round my waist and whirled me round. I thought – He is giving himself time to see whether I have changed.

He said, quoting from the lecture ' – Nothing is that which makes possible the revelation of what is!'

I said 'Do you think it matters if one doesn't exactly know what it means?'

He said 'But of course you know what it means!'

I said 'What?'

He said 'It means nothing, that's what it means!'

One of the reasons why Bruno had come to Freiburg was because Franz and Minna and I had planned to go on a walking trip through the Black Forest and on to a castle on the shores of a lake where there was to be held a Student Congress. I had suggested to Bruno when he had telephoned me from Berlin 'Why don't you come too?' He had said 'What about your boyfriend?' I had said 'What about my boyfriend?' He had said 'I am very well, thank you.'

I had, of course, by this time slept with Franz; and Franz had slept with Minna, and once or twice I had slept with Minna. All this was in accordance with the customs of the place and time – at least amongst those students who had broken away from fraternities. But Franz was now sleeping with Minna. And I was finding it quite liberating, the uncertainty.

So I had asked Bruno to come and make up a four on this trip: but when I saw him I felt that this might have been a mistake. I thought – He will feel that I am committed to him: and have I not learned that humans are happiest when they are, as it were, nothing; on their own?

Bruno said 'What is it?'

I said 'Nothing.' I laughed.

Bruno said 'I expect you feel trapped.'

I thought I might say – Bruno, you are a genius.

Bruno said 'Don't worry. I can't wait to meet the beautiful Minna!'

I said 'Bruno, I love you! I don't feel trapped!'

Bruno said 'And Franz. The beautiful blue-eyed Franz!'

When Franz and Bruno did meet they acted charmingly, courteously, like people who might be accustomed to fighting duels. (I had heard, in fact, that Bruno had become a notable fighter of duels in Berlin.) Bruno flashed his eyes at Franz: Franz, when he held out his hand, glittered. Bruno said 'Ah you do give satisfaction to Jews!' Franz laughed and said 'Oh I am too modest!' I thought – Of course, why should they not be homosexual? Then – What will now happen if I am free?

We were in the town square by the cathedral. We were waiting for Minna. There were the stalls for the market; the spire of the huge building above. I thought – It is as if we are on a stage: perhaps I am waiting for someone to come on from outside.

When I introduced Minna to Bruno, he bowed over her hand and dabbed at it as if he were a bird. When he straightened he kept hold of Minna's hand and turned it over and looked at the palm.

Minna said 'What do you see?'

Bruno put a hand on his heart and said 'Don't ask me!'

Minna said 'Death?'

Bruno said 'My own!' He dropped Minna's hand as if it had burned him.

We set off the day after the lecture on our trip over the mountains. We each carried a rucksack, a blanket, our share of cooking equipment and food. Franz led the way with the maps: I came next; then Minna, with Bruno behind. I thought – I no longer have to imagine that I am in control: Bruno has always been something of a magician.

We went past the rock where the path went off towards the cave. I thought – But let us not go round and round: let me go on to something new.

Among the *Wandervögel* of those days there was the feeling that one could go into the mountains and become free: could look down like gods, perhaps, on people in their cooking-pots on the plains. There was a sense, certainly, of rapture: occasionally of dread. It was as if one had the chance of coming across some lost civilisation in a hidden valley; or of creating such a civilisation oneself – in which people might feel neither superior nor inferior, but in harmony with themselves. I thought – But would they not then be different from gods – who like fighting amongst themselves; who take it out on people on the plains? Then – Do humans have to be morally superior to gods?

Franz wore leather shorts, I wore a skirt, Minna wore thin cotton shorts, Bruno wore trousers. Bruno from time to time muttered under his breath as he walked behind Minna. Minna said 'What are you saying?' Bruno said 'I am making calculations about the gyrations of the heavenly spheres.'

When we got to the high ground there were narrow winding paths going up and down between trees. Routes were marked at forks or crossroads by colours dabbed on rocks or trees. I thought – We are being guided here: there are threads through the maze.

Sometimes there was a gap in the trees through which could be seen a green and fertile valley laid out as if in a painting. Red-roofed houses clustered around a church: stacks of hay were set up in fields like some primitive form of message. I thought – This is the sort of landscape that humans have put into paintings.

We found a camping-place for the night and Franz collected sticks and Bruno made the fire and Minna and I prepared food. Bruno held out his hands to the flames and talked to them in an unintelligible language. Minna said 'What do you say to the fire?'

Bruno said 'I say "Come on up! Do as I say or I'll punish you!"'

Minna said 'And does it?'

Bruno said 'If it wants to.'

Franz sat on a log beside the fire and smoked his pipe. I thought – Here, now, we know what we are: is this called nothing!

Franz took his pipe out of his mouth and said to Bruno 'Well, what did you make of Heidegger?'

Bruno said 'Ah, a direct question!'

I said 'You are allowed to answer it.'

Bruno put his hand on his heart and said 'But perhaps that is what I made of Heidegger!'

Franz and Bruno began a discussion about whether or not Heidegger, when he talked about nothing, was talking about God: but if he was, then why did he not call it God? Franz said 'It has always been correct, of course, not to mention the name of God.'

Minna took off her clothes and sat cross-legged by the fire.

Bruno said 'Minna! I am frightened!'

Minna said 'What are you frightened of?'

Bruno said 'Wolves.'

Minna said 'But there are no wolves.'

Bruno said 'I am the wolf!' Then – 'Will you sleep with me tonight?'

I said to Franz 'Do you think it would be possible to live like this? I mean not talking, but at the same time talking, about what we know.'

Franz said 'What do we know?'

I said 'Oh, nothing.'

Franz said 'In art. In poetry.'

I said 'We could live as if we were this – '

Bruno said 'Help! Minna!'

So that night Minna slept with Bruno and I lay with Franz: Franz remained stretched on his back with his hands folded across his chest; he was like the effigy of a dead crusader. Sometime in the night I awoke and there was a new moon with its single star beside it; Minna and Bruno were making love; they were like something with too short arms and legs trying to crawl across the floor of the forest.

Franz did not seem to be sleeping. I wondered if he still sometimes thought of killing himself. I thought – Things do go round and round: it is by your knowing this that you sometimes get out of the forest.

In the morning we went on in our small procession with Franz in front and myself following and Bruno and Minna behind. Bruno prodded and tickled Minna: Minna pretended not to like it and liked it. I wondered – Perhaps after all it is sad that I am not jealous?

There were clouds in the sky and sometimes gaps in the clouds where the sun shone through. I thought – Perhaps there are gods reclining on those clouds and they catch a glimpse of us every now and then and wonder if we are the sort of things that they would like to put into a painting.

Occasionally we came across other groups of *Wandervögel*; we greeted each other with cries and waves; we could hear them singing their songs before and after we could see them in the forest.

Once or twice at night round the fire we did have discussions in which words did seem to struggle to express directly what they might be meaning.

Franz told us of a conference of physicists there had been in Brussels a year ago in which questions had been raised concerning recent changes in our understanding of what could be known, or described, about the smallest particles of so-called 'matter' – about what went on inside an atom. Such questions were: Did matter in fact consist of particles or waves; were there laws to explain all occurrences or did certain phenomena happen by chance; if so, what was meant by 'chance'; did an observer inevitably influence that which he observed; was it really impossible, because of this effect of observation, to tell at the same time a particle's exact velocity and location? Each day, Franz said, Einstein would appear with the plan for an experiment which would prove the 'objective' view – which would demonstrate an occurrence which could be described apart from the observer's unavoidable manipulation. Then each evening Bohr and Heisenberg – the two other most notable physicists of the day – would retire with the outline of Einstein's experiment and by morning they would have shown that, on the contrary, the outcome of the experiment would indeed be affected by the fact of observation: it was one's choice of observation that determined, for instance, whether what one was observing was a particle or a wave. Reality remained – this was their phrase – 'a function of the experimental condition'. And all this could be demonstrated by means of the theories that Einstein himself had proposed years ago and which had since been so often vindicated. It was as a result of all this that Einstein, defeated in words but not in his present conviction, had made his famous remark – 'God does not play dice.' Franz told this story of Einstein and Bohr as if it were of some epic encounter like that between Hector and Achilles: even between good and evil. But it was not clear (of course!) just what was good and what was evil.

Minna said 'Why on earth should not God play dice?'

Bruno said 'Then why call him God, darling.'

Franz said 'You think you can tell God what he can and cannot do?'

Bruno said 'For me, I can tell God what he cannot logically do.'

Franz said 'Then for me he is not God.'

After a time Minna would turn away from these conversations and embark on her strange observances to the sun or moon. I would think – She imagines by her observances that she is influencing the sun and moon?

Then – If God plays dice, perhaps I can tonight sleep with Bruno.

Franz said to Bruno 'But you, you are someone who thinks that you can manipulate things as if you were a god.'

Bruno said 'Do you think I could manipulate things if I did not believe that there was a God?'

I said to Bruno 'Do you believe in God?'

Bruno said 'Oh Nellie, Nellie, there are very good reasons why one cannot answer direct questions about God!'

Minna said 'Pray then.'

Franz said 'To me, if God is not dead, there is no reason why he should not kill himself.'

I thought – But what might they be up to, the sun and moon, round some corner?

On about the third day of our walk we came across a group of Nazi boys: we could tell they were Nazis before we saw them because they were singing their sad song – the one about blood and doom and sacrifice and death. When we did see them they were walking in a line with their thumbs behind the buckles of their belts;

they turned to us all at the same time. I thought – They are not like birds, they are like fishes: they have managed to get back from dry land into the sea. They did their salute and called 'Heil Hitler!' I thought – There is the immediate impression that one is about to be attacked. When they saw Minna they became silent: Minna was walking without her blouse. I thought – They will not know whether to worship her or to destroy her: with luck, in their indecision, she might as a siren lure them to their doom.

I had not come across Nazis much at this time. Hitler's first attempt to get power in 1923 in Munich had failed: he had gone to jail. Afterwards not much was heard of him till the first Nazi Party rally at Nuremberg in 1927. Then I had said to my father 'But what is it that makes them different from other right-wing groups?'

My father had said 'They are the only political party who are honest about what they want.'

I had said 'What do they want?'

He had said 'To kill everyone who is not like them.'

I had said 'But what are they like?'

He had said 'They are like people who want to kill everyone who is not like them.'

I had said 'But then surely other people will kill them first.'

My father had said 'No, because they are politicians and no one believes them.'

That evening on the mountains we could hear the group of Nazis at their camp some distance away. They were playing some recording of a speech on a gramophone. There was a tiny cracked voice of someone shouting as if he were that man trapped in a cage.

Bruno said to Franz 'But if there is no God, then why should you not just bow to the will of the strongest man?'

Franz said 'That is no reason for believing in a god.'

Bruno said 'I mean, why are you not a Nazi?'

Franz said 'Because on the whole I would rather be dead.'

Bruno said 'There is nothing in wanting to be dead that would stop you being a Nazi.'

I thought – But Franz, why do you go on saying you want to be dead? It is not true! What is the point of this journey?

I watched Minna as she stirred a cooking-pot over the fire. She was like a priestess getting in touch with spirits. I thought – Perhaps those days were the best when I was in love with Trixie: then we were innocents in some Garden of Eden.

I said to Minna 'Can I sleep with Bruno tonight?'

She said 'If you like.'

I said 'I think Franz is sad.'

She said 'I don't think Franz is missing me.'

I said 'What is it then?'

Minna said 'Oh I think that Franz perhaps sees further than any of us really.'

I said 'But we were so happy! I mean, that time of the duel.'

Minna said 'I suppose he sees that we can't go on being happy.'

I wondered – You mean, he might become a Nazi?

When I told Franz that I wanted to sleep with Bruno that night he smiled and said 'You are a witch!'

Bruno raised his arm in the Nazi salute and said 'Gracious lady!'

I thought – Oh we are all going round and round in the riddle, the sieve.

When Bruno made love there was the impression of something quite impersonal happening; an operation being performed on some animal. The animal suffered with quiet eyes. I remember turning my head to the fire: I thought – I am looking for someone to hold my head; some mistress, or master.

Minna and Franz seemed to be lying together side by side like effigies of the dead crusader and his wife.

I thought – Oh I am waiting, yes, for some chance of something new to come in from outside.

The castle we were heading for where there was to be the Festival of Students and of Youth was called the Schloss Rabe: it was a medieval building mostly in ruins on a crag above a lake. There were said to be students coming here from all over Europe. There were to be performances of music and drama. Political speeches were to be taboo – speeches were to do with the noises people made in their cooking-pots on the plains. A highlight of the festival was to be a performance of Goethe's *Faust* – not only the often-performed Part I, but scenes from the almost-impossible-to-perform Part II, in which the story of Faust's pact with the Devil moves from a personal to a universal and even mystical level. The parts of Faust and Mephistopheles were to be played by two of the leading actors of the day – Kreuz and Liebermann – the former a non-Jew and the latter a Jew. It was rumoured that some particular point was going to be made about this; they were going to do some exchange of roles; the question would be put – Who was the manipulator and who was the victim? At previous performances of this production there had been angry demonstrations and even small riots outside the theatre. Politics had broken in; was it possible that there should be such taboos?

I thought – But is not the question old-fashioned, who are the manipulators and who are the victims?

The forest became more crowded as groups converged on the castle; we called out to each other like flocks of birds – for greeting or for warning. I thought – We are trying to ensure our own space, our identity: but still this does not seem to be quite what is happening. Perhaps we are more like those little bits of fungus called slime-mould that crawl together in the forest: they form a worm; this erects itself into a sort of penis; then it explodes, and little bits and pieces are scattered again in the forest.

There was one group we came across – our routes intertwining as if through a maze – which was a group of five or six boys, two of whom spoke together sometimes in English. I thought – Would it be easier to talk about the way we see and talk about things if we had another language with which to do this?

Schloss Rabe was on its crag over the lake; the village was below; there were thousands of students camping on the hills above. They were, yes, like an assembly come together for some millenium. I thought – But surely there would never be room for everybody in an ark.

We climbed amongst the groups that were like refugees or besiegers; we found a place for our camp on a piece of ground on the level but with thick undergrowth; we set about clearing it. We found that the group with the two English-speaking boys was clearing a space to one side of us. And slightly below us were the group of Nazi boys. I thought – So this is the way in which God's dice have come to rest in the forest.

Minna said to me 'For God's sake, let's you and I sleep together tonight!'

I thought – But I don't want to go back; I want to go forward.

It was in the morning when we set up our camp: the performance of *Faust* Part I was to be in the afternoon. Then there was to be an interval in which there would be time for supper: the scenes from Part II were to be done in the evening.

You remember the story of *Faust*? (Who am I talking to: you? or you?) Faust, usually taken to be representative of aspiring Western man, makes a pact with Mephistopheles, the Devil, whereby Mephistopheles will provide him with ever more extravagant experiences until such a time as he, Faust, may feel he has his heart's desire and so will call 'Stop!' And then Mephistopheles can claim Faust's soul for his own. Faust does not worry much about the chances of his calling 'Stop!' Surely there will always be more to desire, more to experience, more to learn. And anyway – if he does reach some point which he feels is perfect, then what will it matter if the Devil does claim his soul! At the back of all this is the idea that God himself encourages the pact; it is by means of the dreams that the Devil dangles in front of humans, and in response to the disasters that come upon humans as they follow these dreams, that humans are roused out of torpor and carry out God's plans for evolution. And if in the process Faust loses his soul – well, it is always up to God, is it not, to organise some deathbed salvation and so cheat the Devil.

Bruno said 'I have told you, *Faust* is profoundly immoral.'

Minna said 'Why should God be moral?'

Franz said 'Do you know what you are saying?'

I thought – Yes, I want to know what I am saying.

In the enormous courtyard of the castle a stage had been set up: it backed on to a part of the building that was still in repair: there were doorways and windows with balconies in the façade above the stage. The courtyard was crowded: the audience was to sit on the grass of a central lawn. There were one or two fraternities identifiable by the ribbons in their caps or by armbands; but for the most part people in the audience seemed to have gathered in the hope of discovering a larger identity.

In the afternoon Kreuz was to play Faust and Liebermann Mephistopheles. I suppose there have been other performances in which Faust has been portrayed as a naive and even neurotic upward-striving Aryan and Mephistopheles as a crafty and manipulative Jew, the latter being the agent of Faust's perdition but also in the end – abracadabra! – of his salvation. In this production Kreuz presented himself obviously as some prototype of a Nazi: he wore leather boots and a brown tunic belted at the waist; he had a black-and-red-and-white armband. He seemed an unpleasantly childlike man; a disaffected fraternity member. He strutted up and down; he boasted and complained. Then when he seemed to see ghosts he crouched in a corner like a rat: he looked around as if for someone's arms to run to. When Liebermann as Mephistopheles appeared, he was a huge man in a long black cloak and a wide-brimmed hat: he had his hair in ringlets. Then when he opened his cloak for Faust to

run to and be enfolded – Faust scuttling across the floor – Liebermann was wearing underneath his cloak a bulging tunic and a short
skirt and stockings, so that he seemed almost to be a parody of a
prostitute on the streets of Berlin. I thought – Well, yes, this is
clever: one does not have to say what it means! But then when Faust
and Mephistopheles were off on their journey to the seduction of
the innocent Gretchen – which Faust had stipulated as a first step to
his heart's desire – it did not seem that there was much that the
actors could do in the way of suggesting complex patterns. I
thought – Oh well, this is the same old stuff – the stuff that
audiences love and that poets love to give them – the ordinary
boring stuff about murder and self-mutilation and degradation and
then death.

Gretchen is seduced; abandoned: oh what an occasion for beautiful
performances! She finds herself pregnant; she goes mad and kills her
child. In the condemned cell she is visited by her old lover, Faust.
How purging, how satisfying it is, to watch her sweet madness: to
weep with his, Faust's, so noble, so searing remorse! The audience
was being caressed, pelted; it was being seduced or assaulted. I
thought – So what does it matter who is the Nazi and who is the
Jew? What we are witnessing is a demonstration of a universal curse;
an indiscriminate love of miserableness.

When Gretchen had been redeemed by the voice of God on high
and the audience stood and clapped, I put my head in my hands. I
thought – Oh do not let us imagine that we are gods, if gods get
pleasure from watching this sort of thing from on high! Then –
Franz is right: it is better if we are involved in some universal
catastrophe.

But Franz was standing up and clapping with the rest.

I thought – This stuff is imprisoned in our heads: we are ourselves
the cage; we cannot get out.

On the way back to our camp, Franz and Bruno discussed the
significance of Faust being played as a Nazi and Mephistopheles as
a Jew: yes, indeed, good could come out of evil: had not Jews
always known this? In the evening performance, it had been
announced, the roles would be reversed: so that in the scenes from
Part II, I wondered, might it be seen that on a higher and more
mystical level it was the wicked but ultimately self-defeated Nazis
who were goading the holy Jews on to ever more purified visions
of their proper relationship to God – after all, this had always been
God's purpose for them, no? Bruno and Franz were discussing

something like this as we walked up the hill. Minna and I did not talk much. I was trying to remember – In Part II it is the mystical vision of Helen of Troy that is conjured up for Faust in place of the mundane Gretchen: but even with Helen he does not call 'Stop!' What is it that in the end makes him (or is it only almost makes him?) call 'Stop!' to the whole damn rubbish that he loves to keep imprisoned in his head?

I thought – Helena, Eleanor: I would want to get it out; I would want you to call 'Stop!'

Back in our camp, Franz collected firewood and Bruno made the fire and Minna and I prepared food we had got earlier in the village. In the camp next door the two boys who spoke English seemed to have had a quarrel. The younger one, who was like a faun, had walked away and had come and sat with his back against a tree between his camp and ours. I thought – There is a painting like this: a girl is lying on the ground; there is a faun at her head: I have the impression that I should be part of this painting.

The other boy, who was like a large white dog, came and knelt by the boy who was like a faun. He said in English but with a German accent 'You are angry with me because of what I told you about your mother.'

The boy who had his back against the tree said 'I don't care a damn about you and my mother. What I am bored with is Faust. In fact I think you and my mother are quite like Faust.' Then he turned and looked at me.

I thought – Hullo, it is as if you remember me?

The boy said 'Oedipus is boring, Faust is boring, Mephistopheles is boring. And Nazis and Jews are boring. If we think them evil, we only encourage them. Nothing is going to change unless we think such things are boring.'

The boy who was like a dog said 'Come and have supper.'

The boy who was looking in my direction said 'Seen any good child-murders lately?'

The other boy said 'Be quiet, people will hear you.'

The boy who was looking at me said 'That is why I am speaking in English, lest people might understand and be saved.'

I thought I might say – I understand you.

The boy who was kneeling said 'You asked me to talk about your mother.'

The boy who was like a faun said 'What would be interesting would be a play about the people who are sitting and watching and loving that sort of stuff. Then at the end they could go off, yes, happy, and blow themselves up.'

I thought I might say – But it would still be boring to have to watch them blowing themselves up.

Then you said to me 'Do you understand English?'

I said 'Yes.'

After a time the boy who was like a dog stood up and went back to his fire.

You were sitting with your back against that tree. There were millions of pine-needles on the ground like forks in pathways. I thought – We can pick them up; move them this way or that. After a time you looked away.

I said 'But it would still be boring to have to watch them blowing themselves up.'

You said 'Yes.'

I said 'So what would you do?'

You said 'Something quite different, I suppose.'

You were staring in front of you as if you were expecting to be shot with your back against the tree.

I said 'What?'

You said 'I've thought it would be something to do with just what turns up.'

I said 'I've thought it would be to do with what you're talking about and what is happening, happening at the same time.'

You said 'But there would have to be some sort of code.'

I said 'Why?'

You said 'Because otherwise it would go away.'

I said 'But if you knew the code, you would know the message.'

You said 'We should know the message. We don't have a code.'

People from our two camps were calling us to come to supper. They were saying that there were only a few minutes before we would have to leave for the performance of the second part of the play.

I said 'Do you want to see the second part of *Faust*?'

You said 'No.' Then – 'I think that what is happening now and what we are talking about is the same.'

I thought – Also there is indeed this that has turned up: we are sitting beneath these trees.

I said 'What is your name?'

You said 'Max.' Then – 'What is yours?'

I said 'Eleanor.'

You said 'Helena?'
I said 'Eleanor.'
You said 'This is absurd.'
The others were saying that they were setting off to see the play: we could join them later if we liked.
We seemed to sit for a long time in silence beneath our trees.
I said 'You mean, there is some pattern in what turns up?'
You said 'I have thought sometimes that it would be like being in the inside of a painting.'
I said 'Yes, this is absurd.'
You said 'Why?'
I said 'Because I have thought that it would be like – ' Then – 'But I suppose if I say it, it will go away.'
You said 'I see.'
It was as if we were on some plane that might at any moment tip over: if I moved towards you, you might go away; if you moved towards me, I might fall.
I said 'How old are you?'
You said 'Nearly eighteen.'
'I'm nineteen.'
'You are at a university?'
'Freiburg.'
'I am going to Cambridge next year.'
'What are you studying?'
'Biology or physics.'
'I am studying medicine.'
You said 'You see, this is almost unbearable, unless there is a code.'
I said 'Unbearable for ourselves?'
You said 'Oh, and for others!'
I thought – But, I mean, we have got some sort of code.
Then – We are like two people stuck on a rock-face connected by rope: cut the rope and one of us dies; don't cut the rope and both of us may die, or live.
I said 'Are you staying here long?'
You said 'We go tomorrow.'
I said 'Will you give me your address, so that I can write to you?'
You said 'Yes, and will you give me yours?'
I said 'I will put it on a piece of paper; then you can swallow it.'
You said 'Or you can put it down the lavatory. Or in a bottle to float on the sea.'

There was the faint sound of people acting, orating, further down the valley. I thought – You mean, other people might hurt us: we might hurt ourselves?

I said 'You know that image of Plato's about the two halves of something, that look for each other?'

You said 'Yes.'

I said 'That is too obvious – '

You said 'I can't think of anything better to say.'

There was the sound of clapping from further down in the valley. I thought – Perhaps it would be easier if one of us took a short walk. Perhaps it would be easier if we were in circumstances of danger.

I said 'What happens to Faust and Helena in Part II, do you know?'

You said 'They have a child.'

I said 'What happens to the child?'

You said 'It flies too close to the sun. It falls into the fire.'

I said 'I don't think I should have a child.'

You said 'You don't think you should have a child?'

I said 'Do you?'

After a time you said 'There are enough in the world.'

You seemed to have been listening to the sounds that were coming up from the valley.

I said 'But what is it that makes Faust finally say "Stop!"?'

You said 'I thought he never did. I thought he only said "If I were to say 'Stop!' – "'

I said 'I thought it was when he was reclaiming a new bit of land from the sea.'

You said 'Well perhaps we are reclaiming a new bit of land from the sea.'

I said 'I suppose what is interesting is what Faust said to those terrible beings when he got to heaven.'

You said 'Well what shall we tell them.' Then – 'I suppose we are in heaven.'

I said 'Sh!'

We began laughing.

You left your tree and crawled towards me. It was as if you were pulling yourself along by a rope. To preserve balance, it seemed, I had to stretch out towards you. When we met, it was as if we had to become enfolded.

You said 'It's like a line in a play – "I've got to go in the morning!"'

I said 'But we might just stick it out till then.'

It was as if we were on – not exactly a tightrope: rather a pole that was balancing the earth which itself was on a tightrope: we had moved to the centre of the pole and had to stay very still; to hold on tight, or the earth would tip over.

I said 'Are you comfortable?'

You said 'Yes, very.'

I said 'Do you think this is by chance?'

You said 'Oh, I think chance might be to do with heaven.'

We got into a position like that of a circle divided into two shapes like tadpoles: these fit into each other to make the circle whole. I thought – Or the world is on the back of an elephant, the elephant is on a tortoise, the tortoise is on the sea.

I said 'I am older than you.'

You said 'I know you are older than me.'

I said 'Hold on tight.'

You said 'Or shall we go over.'

When the others came back up the hill from the valley they were having their arguments about the meaning of the scenes from *Faust*, Part II: why was Faust saved? was it just because of his ceaseless striving? And what of Helena, who had appeared and disappeared; what was the point? People were talking about these things as if there might be answers in words.

We had been lying very still. Oh yes, of course, we had from time to time used more words.

When the others were back I said 'You've got my address?'

You said 'Yes.'

I said 'And I've got yours.'

I thought – I suppose we have to go down, like angels, do we, to the cities of the plain.

Franz and Bruno and Minna had been joined by the boys who had been with you; also by a few of the Nazi boys. They all came and sat round our fire. They bobbed to and fro; they drank wine and beer.

You said 'We have to leave very early.'

I said 'That does not matter?'

You said 'No.'

The people round the fire were not paying much attention to us. I thought – We are too embarrassing: we have been into and out of the fire.

– Do not look at us and we are there: look at us and I suppose we go away.

Bruno was encouraging Minna to take off her clothes. The Nazi boys were clapping. I thought – She is like that child of Faust and Helena: she may be destroyed by the fire.

One of the Nazi boys put an arm round Franz's shoulders. Franz looked at me. Then, when I looked at him, he looked away.

You had gone back to your camp and were sitting on your own by your fire.

I thought – Oh strange and terrible world, you should not be destroyed! There are people whom you can love: who love you –

– Just let us know, every now and then, what might be an ark.

One of the Nazi boys picked a flaming stick out of the fire and held it out towards Minna. The stick seemed slightly to burn her. Minna was half naked, dancing round and round the flames.

Bruno called out 'Nellie, come and join us!'

I thought – Oh but I am happy sitting here with my head in my hands, my cage –

– Or am I a child in a pram looking up towards the leaves, the sunlight?

The next morning you and your group had gone. I did not know whether or not I had heard you leaving. I had been having a dream. We were in the courtyard of a castle. There were ladies and gentlemen on the grass. Then the ground flipped over, and there were huts and watchtowers.

I thought – The dream leaves the dreamer: what is left to the dreamer of the dream?

I had the piece of paper with your name and address on it.

That next evening there was going to be a performance of a play by Brecht. I did not know at the time much about Brecht. I had been told that he was a left-wing anarchist, that he mocked left-wing anarchists, that he was a scourge of the bourgeoisie, that the bourgeoisie were still flocking to his *Die Dreigröschenoper* which had opened in Berlin the previous year. The play of his that was going to be put on had at one time been called *Spartakus* because it had been about the Spartacist rising in 1919 in Berlin: I thus had a special interest in the play because, of course, some of my earliest memories were of this rising in Berlin. Also I wanted to see a play by Brecht because people talked about him in a way that I had come to associate with what might be life-giving: they suggested that his plays were original and disturbing without being able to say why. I thought – But you, could you not have stayed for this play by Brecht?

I tried to imagine what you might be doing. We had not yet got the image, had we, of those particles that if you do this to this one here then that happens to that one there –

I thought – I am mad to have let you go!

I went down to the castle that evening with Franz and Bruno and Minna and the Nazi boys – I was, I suppose, feeling somewhat demented: why indeed had you gone away? I thought – Should I after all commit myself to someone or something practical: to Franz or to Bruno; or to a battle with the Nazis in Berlin? But still I seemed to be part of something leading a quite separate life around me – lungs, veins, heartbeat – and from this there seemed to be some thread pulling me through the maze. I was watching myself being pulled; was my watching the thread pulling me? (Well, where were you?) I was a child left lying on the edge of a bed. I was going to a play by Brecht.

Now I must say something about this play because it was representative of something happening and being demonstrated at the same time.

Franz and Bruno and Minna and I were sitting on the grass. We were with the two Nazi boys with whom we seemed to have made friends. We were looking up at the restored façade of the castle. I was wondering about you.

At first it was difficult to know what was going on in the play: people seemed to be saying what was occurring just in the backs of their own heads; one had become accustomed, I suppose, to people in plays pretending to make sense. There was also the impression of vast and imponderable events elsewhere – but these were nevertheless of almost no importance. I had not seen a play like this before: it was like life! There was a middle-aged couple in an apartment in Berlin; they had a daughter who had been engaged to a soldier who had gone missing in the war; she was carrying on with a war profiteer. Her parents wanted her to forget her old love and marry the war profiteer. I thought – Well, I am too young to have carried on with a war profiteer, but do you not see that this is like life? (Who was I talking to? Franz? Bruno? you? Anyone who will listen?) After a time the daughter yields to the pressures of her parents and becomes engaged to the war profiteer: but just at this moment her old lover turns up (you would say – Of course!). He has been a prisoner of war (well, what were you doing in that forest?); they meet; he learns that she has become engaged to a war profiteer; he wanders off again; he acts somewhat demented; I mean you did act somewhat sad, didn't you? All this is taking place against the background of the Spartacist revolution; the rifles and machine-guns in the streets, the storming of a newspaper building. But of course the two main characters in the play are not paying much attention to this: it is boring. But then, what is not? It is for the sake of what this might be that the girl and her ex-lover have gone wandering off again: did you not say that what matters is what turns up? And in the meantime the other people in the play are carrying on seeing, saying, just what is trapped within their own heads. And Franz and Bruno and Minna and I and the Nazi boys were watching, sitting on the grass. Of course, I had not seen a play like this before! Plays were usually about people acting as if they did not know they were acting. Here everyone seemed to know this: and so it was as if they were not.

Sometimes when the girl and her ex-lover were on the stage they seemed to be searching amongst the audience and to be saying – Is it you? Is it you? Then they bumped into each other again; he learned that she was pregnant by the war profiteer; they wandered apart again. And all the time there were the machine-guns, the storming of the newspaper building, the characters like politicians appearing and disappearing in the streets. Most of these were drunk. But then why, in the end, should not the business of the girl being pregnant by the war profiteer also be boring? Oh, I had never before seen a play like this!

The Nazi boys were getting restless; perhaps this was because the whole business of politics, let alone conventional feeling, was being treated with contempt: who cares about the storming of newspaper buildings! who cares about one's girl being made pregnant by a war profiteer! The girl and her ex-lover bumped into each other again. One of the Nazi boys put his fingers in his mouth and whistled. Then the girl and her ex-lover turned and looked at him: it was as if now they might be seeing what was happening not on a stage. The girl and her ex-lover had seemed at last to be about to go off together hand in hand: what they were looking for, they said, was a bed. Almost the last line in the play was 'Now comes bed! The great, white, wide, bed!' I thought – You mean, you and I, we should simply have gone to bed? Then – This is the code: what is the message?

This was the end of the play: people in the audience were standing and shaking their fists; they were booing and whistling; several had advanced to the edge of the platform of the stage. They saw indeed that they had been treated with contempt. The cast – except for the girl and her old lover who had by now gone off hand-in-hand – had come on to the stage as if to take their bow: now they acted as if they had noticed the audience for the first time – it was just the girl and her lover who had previously looked amongst the audience. The cast reacted as if, yes, the audience might indeed be a crowd storming the castle or a newspaper building – well were they acting or were they not? Or was what was now going on on a different level off-stage. The light in one of the windows high up in the façade at the back of the stage suddenly came on: framed in the window there could be seen the girl and her lover who were facing each other with their hands on each other's shoulders; they were looking at each other tenderly: well might they be on their way to bed! People in the audience, looking up, were quiet for a moment; then this vision seemed to enrage them further. The other members of the cast were backing towards a drawbridge that was across a gap between the back of the stage and the façade; they were acting (or not) as if they were fighting a rearguard action; the mob, the audience, were beginning to climb on to the stage. I thought – Well, might it not be part of an actor's expertise to produce what is real? But to what end? A large number of the audience were now on the stage; the actors had withdrawn behind the drawbridge and were pulling it up: they were shaking their fists at the audience: I thought – Well perhaps to show things as ridiculous is real.

The audience who had arrived at the gap at the back of the stage were again looking up; the girl and her lover had moved away from one window and had appeared at another: they had half undressed: they seemed to have got even nearer to bed. The other members of the cast now appeared at windows and on balconies in the façade and began to throw down on the audience, or act as if they were throwing down – what? – arrows? boiling oil? It seemed just pieces of screwed-up paper. But no one was laughing. Franz and Minna and the Nazi boys had moved up towards the stage. I had stayed behind on the grass in the courtyard.

You know those memory theatres of the seventeenth century in which people used to act dramas to help them to try to remember what they might be about – it was difficult to remember at a time when there were so few written stories. Well, it is always difficult, perhaps, to know what one is about even when everything seems to be happening all at once; but there seemed to be something here showing this; even if it was to do just with what turns up. You said 'Hullo.' I said 'Hullo.' I mean there you were, yes, in the courtyard, having come up beside me. I said 'I thought you had gone.' You said 'But I came back.' I thought I might say – Why? But it was as if we were the man and the girl who had come across each other again outside a newspaper building. I said 'Wasn't the play wonderful?' You said 'Yes.' You had taken me by the arm. We were standing watching the façade of the castle which was like the backdrop to a theatre. You said 'This is what you meant by what you are talking about also happening?' I said 'Yes.' I thought – And you have turned up. Then – But this is what we can't talk about: so what happens now? You said 'Shall we go?' I said 'Yes, let's.' We turned to go out of the courtyard. There was all the violence behind us on the stage. You said 'I wonder if we should just go to bed.' I said 'Oh we will sometime.' You said 'Yes.' We were going out of the castle: there was the path up into the hills; there was a path down to the village. You said 'As a matter of fact, I still do have to catch a train, but I thought it vital to see you just one more time.' I said 'Yes, I do think it is vital to know that I could see you one more time.' You said 'But it is all right now?' I said 'Yes, it is. all right now.' You said 'I have missed one or two trains.' I said 'You can catch one now.'

We had begun to walk round the outside wall of the castle towards the village. We stopped underneath a wall at the side of the castle: we were somewhere beside, or at the back of, the restored façade where there were the actors besieged by the crowd; where there was the noise of banging and shouting. I thought – Oh it is the noise of people besieged in their own heads! I leaned with my back against a wall and you began kissing me. I thought – We will not stay with each other; we will not be apart; we will balance the world on its tightrope. There was an opening slightly above us in the wall of the castle; it was some sort of window; figures had appeared at it; they were leaning out. I thought – They are going to throw down confetti? rose-leaves? bags of flour? A voice said 'I wonder if you two could possibly be of some assistance?' We looked up. There was a man and woman leaning out of the window: they were wearing dressing-gowns. I thought – They are actors? Not-actors? They are gods looking down? You or I said 'What?' The man said 'There is someone in here who has been injured by a brick; also there is a child who has to catch a train.' I thought – There is someone who has been injured and – . Then – This is ridiculous. The woman said 'I wonder if you could possibly take the child, and call for a doctor in the village.' I said 'I am a medical student, perhaps I can help.' The woman said 'Perhaps you can.' You said 'And as a matter of fact I am going to the station so I can take the child.' Then – 'I know this sounds ridiculous.' The man said 'That would be very kind.' I thought – Oh well, if the world is on a tightrope, things might be likely to have to turn up. I said 'How can I get in?' The man said 'We can pull you up.' The woman said 'And we can lower the child.' You said 'Abracadabra.' I thought – Oh but one day we will be used to it. Then – But didn't we think we wouldn't have a child? The man and woman had turned from the window: they reappeared with a girl of about eight or nine. The woman said 'Can you catch her?' You said 'Yes.' The girl wore a tartan skirt and long white socks. I said 'And where is the person who has been wounded?' The man said 'He is inside.' I thought – But hurry, we must hurry: it is everything making sense that is not bearable! The child was being lowered into your arms. The woman said 'She's got her fare and she knows which train to go on.' I thought – Oh of course. I raised my arms for the man and the woman to lift me up to the window. You said 'Goodbye.' I said 'Goodbye then.' You said 'Goodbye.' Then – 'This is quite like an opera.' I said 'It is not like an opera.' You said 'Oh no, it is not like an opera.' The man and the woman were pulling me so that I could get in at the window. I said 'I'll see you then.' You said 'I'll see you.' When I looked in at the window there was a dark vaulted room with a body lying on a bed: when I looked down at you, you were standing on the pathway holding the hand of the good-looking child. I thought – We have known each other a day, we have not even been to bed, and we seem to have a child.

IV: Max

Should we not explain that such concurrences happen to everyone from time to time – as a matter of chance, of averages, on the fringes of what is ordinary. It is just that we have little capacity to recognise these things: we shy away: it is easier for us to bang our heads against what is expected, which is the walls of the cage or maze.

But, of course, if we did take note of such oddities (it would still be difficult to talk about them: one could do this by saying that one could not talk about them?) might we not find that there was growing some capacity within us as if we ourselves were a thread through the maze?

It was shortly after our time at the ruined castle that the bottom seemed to fall out of modern capitalist Western society; there was the crash on the American stock market; the dust from this drifted around the world. In Britain there were soon nearly three million unemployed: in Germany five million. It was then that these latter began to be picked up and dusted by those men in brown uniforms like vindictive nannies.

Some of the fall-out drifted to Cambridge. There was not much change in the façades of ancient academics and stately buildings: there was some new dissolution perhaps introduced into the bone.

You are right that at Cambridge we had not previously paid much attention to politics, though I remember the General Strike of 1926, which occurred during my last year at day-school. We boys were lined up and marched off in military fashion to a train which took us to help unload ships in the docks at Harwich. We took this incursion into politics as a holiday away from school: I think most middle- and upper-class people took the General Strike as the chance for a holiday away from school – what fun to be a docker or an engine-driver for a few days away from the ghastly restraints imposed on the middle and upper classes! At Harwich there were cranes and trolleys like huge toys; we larked about; we thought – So this is the grown-up world! At the far end of the quay a group of dockers came to watch us.

I did wonder – But this is politics?

In Germany, I suppose, there were people learning to sing sad songs and carry torches to bonfires.

In the autumn of 1930 I went to my father's college in Cambridge. There were the old men like bees or wasps moving in front of the façades of ancient buildings: somewhere inside were the distillations of honey or of poison from flowers. In going to the university at Cambridge I was, of course, hardly getting away from my family: I was in some sense even coming back to it, since I had been away for four years at boarding-school. I do not remember much about this time at school: it was to do with the distillations, I suppose, by which upper-middle-class Englishmen enable large parts of themselves to remain as schoolboys.

But no one gets away from their schooldays, or indeed from their families, except by what grows in the mind; and this goes on for the most part in the dark.

There is a Freudian theory that any young man who in childhood has been the undisputed favourite of his mother goes through life with the feelings of a conqueror. Well, I did not consciously want to be anything so vulgar as a conqueror: but I did imagine, yes, that I had got away from my upbringing and my family.

I felt I had been helped in this by the strange dark girl who had risen sword in hand, as it were, from the mists of that lake in the Black Forest: whom I loved; but whom I did not feel ready to take on on a mundane level.

I remember that we talked about politics, you and I: were you not closer to Communism at that time than you remember? (You imagined you had got away from your mother?) You certainly showed your antipathy to those Nazi boys: I suspected at first that you did not go down to the performance of the play in the evening because your friends had joined up with them – or was I even then being too modest? You showed some antipathy to me when I suggested that in the cannibal-race of the Western world these Nazis might play the part of scavengers, garbage-collectors, to clean the mess up. But then was not this the sort of thing that was being said by the Communist friends of your mother's?

In Cambridge before 1930, it is true, we did not know much of either Communism or Fascism. It was the fashion, I suppose, to say about Russia 'Of course, the experiment might go either this way or that.' And about Italy 'At least Mussolini makes the trains run on time.' Reactions amongst students were influenced by the contempt we had for what we saw and read of politicians at home. These seemed to be like dinosaurs already half fossilised in rock: we thought – Hurry on, ice-cap, come down from the pole.

I would say to my mother 'Freud doesn't seem too optimistic about the chances of social improvement.'

My mother would say 'Truth after all does not depend upon the chances of improvement.'

I said to my father 'But if there is no guiding principle in evolution, then why should one form of behaviour be any better than another?'

My father said 'Science and ethics belong to different worlds.'

I would think – But might not this attitude be like that of the dinosaurs just before they were caught by the cold?

But then I would think of you, my beautiful German girl: whose legs as they moved within your skirt were like the clappers of a bell; the memory of whose mouth still sometimes took me by the throat so that it was as if I could not breathe. I thought – There are connections here beyond the reach of the scientific world; sailors are lured to rocks by sirens; rocks are where fishes and humans crawl out on to a new land.

In Cambridge, young men put their heads into the sand of scrums on football fields. Old men stood and watched them as if they themselves would leap in and be blind.

Oh yes, I felt as if I were an agent in occupied territory. But what was the agency? What was it for? Who were the other agents? (Of course, you.)

Indeed one should not stay too long in the company of someone whom one feels is a fellow agent: there is such work to be done!

When I first went to my father's old college I had rooms on a staircase on which there were also the rooms of a man called Melvyn. Melvyn was a short chubby man with a round face and a high domed forehead and eyebrows that went up to a point in the middle like those of a stage devil. My rooms were above his, so that I had to pass his door when I went up the stairs. He would leave his door open when he was inside his room so that it was as if he wanted to be on show for whoever would look at him. Within this frame he would appear to be posing in various tableaux: the student at his desk; the aesthete reclining on his chaise-longue; the visionary at the window; the eccentric flat on his back on the floor with a pillow under his head. I would think – It is as if, yes, he is doing these performances because he is like one of those particles that might not exist unless someone is observing them. Then – Or is it I who make up such patterns into which people have to fit; if I did not, might I not exist?

Or – But I wonder about this, and they do not?

One morning in the middle of my first term I was going up the stairs and through Melvyn's open doorway I saw that he was lying half on and half off his chaise-longue as if he were ill; his shirt was open at the neck and half out of his trousers; one arm trailed towards the ground where an empty glass had fallen on its side. I thought – This is a tableau to which I am supposed to guess the reference: *The Death of Nelson*? *The Suicide of Chatterton*? I went on up the stairs. When I came down again some fifteen minutes later Melvyn was still in the same position. I tried to work out – Well, of course he does this to attract attention: but then don't people who try to kill themselves also do it to attract attention? I went in. I thought I might wander round his room and appear to be interested in the books that were on his shelves; then, if it were a game, I would not have appeared to have been a fool; I would not have rushed like an ambulance man into a charade.

On Melvyn's walls there were posters depicting heroic Russian workers: there were scrolls in the form of strip-cartoons illustrating the life of Lenin. I thought – Perhaps this is why I am being lured into this room, so that there can be observed my reactions to the life of Lenin. Then – But what if I am a fly; do I not want to study the life of such spiders?

There was a smell coming from Melvyn so that I was aware of him even when I had my back to him. The smell was of stale wine, unwashedness, not quite of death. I wondered – By a sense of smell, people might be tested on what they think of Lenin?

I went and stood by Melvyn. His small cherub's mouth had a slight encrustation round it. It was like the opening to a waste-pipe that had been blocked.

After a time Melvyn opened one eye and said 'Kiss me, Hardy.'

I said 'Yes, I thought of that.'

'What did you think of?'

'*The Death of Nelson.*'

He said 'England expects every man to do his duty.'

I said 'I was just passing the door of your room.'

He said 'Do you know what my nanny used to call "duty"?'

'No, what – '

He said 'After breakfast, every morning – that's what Nanny used to call "duty".'

He reached for the glass that was on its side on the floor. Then he sat up and pointed to a bottle of wine that was on a table behind him. He held out the glass. I took the bottle and poured out some wine. He drank.

I said 'Have you been to Russia?'

He said 'Why, are you a policeman?'

I said 'No, but I'd like to go there.'

He said 'You know how one loves policemen!'

I moved off round the room again. On the shelves there was a set of books bound in black leather which had no titles nor lettering on the spines. I wondered – They are pornography?

I said 'Do you have contacts in Russia?'

He said 'Oh do say you are policeman!' Then – 'You're not allowed to ask a direct question.'

I came and stood by his chaise-longue again. I looked down. I thought – I am trying to find out what is his interest in Communism: he is trying to find out whether or not I am homosexual.

There was no formal Communist organisation in Cambridge at this time: the first Communist cell was set up in 1931. But I had become interested in Communism when I had been in Germany: I had talked about it with you, my beautiful German girl. You had told me something of your early life; of your mother. Of course, I had wanted to know more.

On the other hand there was an age-old and now quite open tradition of homosexuality at Cambridge. In fact it was so unfashionable not to be homosexual that people were apt to pretend to be homosexual when they were not. I had already gathered, of course, that Melvyn was homosexual.

I sat down on the edge of Melvyn's chaise-longue. I said 'Can I have a drink?'

He said 'You come in here – you break into my room – '

I said 'You like that, do you?'

He said 'You prima donna you.'

I poured some wine into another glass. I thought – He is one of those people who like going down to the East End of London and getting themselves beaten up?

Then – This would not mean that he could not be a Communist.

I said 'I guessed *The Death of Nelson*. That means I can ask you a direct question.'

He said 'What do you want to ask?'

I said 'Are you a Communist?'

He said 'You think people tell the truth when they're asked a direct question?'

I said 'No. But you won't answer. And you have the stuff about Lenin on your walls.'

In the days that followed I saw quite a lot of Melvyn. In the evenings I would go for a drink in his room and enter into the game of Let-us-talk-wittily-in-riddles-because-then-we-need-never-feel-committed-to-whatever-has-been-said. But then I would remember – Did not we, you and I, say something about truth landing up in riddles?

Melvyn was such an obvious type of stage devil: his charm was that of Mephistopheles; he played tricks with words because the only value he recognised was that of manipulation.

I would try to remember – What was it that those beautiful earnest Germans were saying about Mephistopheles and Faust? That they are manifestations of the same person? That it is in a decadent world that dark forces get split off from a person and are put into the hands of others?

– In a healthy world one would see that they are in the hands of oneself?

Melvyn did from time to time seem to talk seriously about this interest in Communism and Marxism, but still as if he were an actor performing a serious part. An actor conventionally uses his skill so that an audience will not ask questions about reality: I thought – But we, you and I, would always want to ask questions about reality.

Melvyn would say – 'But it is quite simple. There are a few people getting big money for doing almost no work. There are many people getting almost no money for doing very hard work. It is obviously in the interests of the majority therefore to introduce a system in which people are paid for the value of their work.'

I would say 'Why?'

He would say 'Why what?'

I would say 'Do you think people are interested in choosing what would rationally be to their advantage?'

He would say 'All right, irrationality indeed has hitherto been prevalent in primitive societies – '

'But now it need not be – '

'No.'

'What if the need to have a hard time is built into human nature?'

'There is no such thing as human nature. Human beings are conditioned by the nature of their work: their system of work is not conditioned by human nature.'

'Then what about you?'

'What about me?'

'Do you think everything you do is rational?'

'Don't flatter yourself, ducky, that it is in my interest that you should give me a hard time.'

Sometimes when Melvyn was bored with the company he was in, or was drunk, he would let the conversation roll along seriously for a time and then would drag it away like one of those birds pretending to trail a broken wing so that predators should not find its nest.

He would say 'Did you know Stalin was a woman?'

Someone would say 'No.'

Then he would say something like 'At the fifteenth Party Congress, when Trotsky went to have a pee, he noticed that Stalin was in the Ladies.'

I would try to think of something to say like 'Perhaps Stalin wanted a shit.'

Melvyn would say 'Oh very good, ducky, you're learning.'

I thought – But what exactly is Melvyn's nest from which he wants such conversations to be diverted?

Then there was one evening towards the end of the first term when we were on our own and Melvyn was drunk; he had spent two days in London. He did not talk to me about what he did in

London. I would think – He has got himself tied up by guardsmen? He has been making contact with his political friends?

He said 'I want to tell you that there is nothing more disgusting than innocence, ducky.'

I said 'Who is innocent?'

He said 'You and Trotsky.'

This was shortly after the time when Trotsky had been banished by Stalin from Russia and was being blamed for most of the things that were going wrong in that country. It was only just being admitted by Communists that there was anything wrong in Russia, and there had to be a scapegoat.

I said 'Why is it innocent to talk about the millions that seem to be starving in Russia?'

He said 'I hope you are not one of those people who are starry-eyed about Russia. They have only had a year or two of their five-year plan, after all. Industrial production is up three hundred percent, electrification four hundred percent, agriculture and consumer goods – well, don't be taken in by that, they're not all starving.'

I said 'But what exactly are you saying?'

He said 'What exactly am I saying! That is what I call innocence! That is what I am saying!'

I said 'They're putting the blame on to Trotsky because they know the five-year plan is going to fail.'

Melvyn said 'Of course the five-year plan is going to fail! What on earth would happen if it succeeded: have you thought of that? You think you can transform a society by a five-year plan succeeding? You can't. It has to fail. Then people can be blamed, yes: people in Russia have to be disciplined. They have to be made to be afraid. How do you think people could be made to change if the five-year plan succeeded?'

I said 'You mean, Stalin is trying to transform human nature by making people afraid?'

'In order that there will be a society in which people need not be afraid.'

'You think you can eliminate fear by making people afraid?'

'History's not so innocent as you, ducky.'

'I don't think history's innocent.'

'Good for you.'

'You think people in Russia know what they're doing?'

'Doing what – '

144

'They know that they want the five-year plan to fail?'

'Who's said anything about the five-year plan going to fail? I've not said anything about a five-year plan going to fail!'

I said 'I see.'

He said 'You see what?'

I said 'You mean that no Russian leader could ever say, even to himself, that he wanted the five-year plan to fail, because if he did, psychologically he wouldn't be able to do what he wants, which is to embark on a reign of blame and terror.'

Melvyn said 'Didn't I say you're learning, ducky!'

I thought – Melvyn really does know more than me?

Then – But of course if one could learn to be tough and subtle with oneself, then one wouldn't need blame and terror?

I seldom talked to Melvyn about the work I was doing in Cambridge. I was studying mathematics; which was a prelude, I supposed, to specialising in physics. I do not remember what work Melvyn was doing: English? History? In spite of what seemed to be his committment to Marxism, he gave the impression of his work being of no importance. I said to him once 'But you mean Marxists, if they are serious, must have an inkling that they are engaged in something quite different from what they have to say they are doing.'

He said 'Don't be too sharp, ducky, or you'll catch yourself where it matters.'

I said 'It's quite like mathematics.'

He said 'Have fun with your mathematics, ducky!'

The most influential mathematician and theoretical physicist at Cambridge at this time was Paul Dirac: his exploratory work was held to be on a level with that of Bohr and Heisenberg on the Continent. I went to some of his lectures: he was a quiet, passionate man who spoke of things that were indeed, he seemed to suggest, just beyond one's grasp; they were like leaves, like shadows. But that there were such things as leaves and shadows meant, as it were, that there was some sun. Some of Dirac's mathematics I did not wholly understand: but in one or two publications at the time he tried to put into laymen's language some of the wider implications of what he thought he was discovering. This was quite a common activity amongst eminent scientists at this time: it was only later that they seemed to withdraw again into the fortress-jargons of their special disciplines.

What I understood Dirac to be implying was –

The laws of physics control a level of reality of which our minds by their nature cannot form an adequate picture: we deal with the world of appearances mainly through intuition. When an object we are observing is small, we cannot observe it without disturbing it, so that what we are observing is not the object but the results of the disturbance. When an object is big, we can say we observe it because the disturbance is for practical purposes negligible, but then what we are observing is inevitably to do with appearances. Two sorts of mathematics are required for a description of reality: classical mathematics, which concerns objects which are big and by means of which we can talk about cause-and-effect between them because this is how intuitively we see appearances; and a new form of mathematics which concerns objects which are small and in which we cannot talk about objective cause-and-effect because of the disturbances caused by the observer. Thus for human consciousness there is something that essentially cannot be pinned down at the heart of matter – and this is not to do with inadequacy of technique, but is built into the relationship between consciousness and language and matter. This is not to be regretted: it is a realisation necessary for understanding.

I had a friend at this time who was called Donald Hodge. Donald was older than me; he had come to Cambridge to study physics, but for the moment was trying to grapple with philosophy. Donald had orange hair and small steel spectacles of which the side-pieces were joined to points near the bottom of the rims. He and I would go for walks together by the banks of the river. In the winter the backwaters of the river became frozen so that there were the footprints of birds on the snow that lay on the surface of what had once been water. Donald and I discussed the relation between philosophy and what seemed to be being suggested by physicists.

Donald said 'But it seems to me that physicists are confused about what is the nature of language.'

I said 'But mathematics is a form of language.'

He said 'But when you say you cannot observe something but can only observe the effect of your observation – what else is it, indeed, that you ever think you are observing?'

'But a different form of mathematics is required to describe this.'

'But you make up a mathematics – '

'But you make up a language.'

Donald and I walked by the frozen water. I thought – We go

round and round: but sometimes, almost without our noticing, something gets through.

Donald had become a pupil of Ludwig Wittgenstein, who some ten years previously had become famous, at least among philosophers, with the publication of his *Tractatus Logico-Philosophicus*. This book had been concerned, primarily, to clarify what were the limits of language.

Donald said 'I mean you use words, making pictures, to describe what is otherwise indescribable.

I said 'What goes on within an atom appears to happen by chance. This is indescribable?'

Donald said 'You can describe it in mathematics – '

I said 'As a matter of probabilities.'

'But you say that Dirac seems to suggest that there are certain entities that are not describable even by numbers.'

'There are certain numbers, yes, at this level, about which it is impossible to say that one is bigger than another.'

'And you call that mathematics?'

Donald had a way of curling his upper lip beneath his nose, as if he were indicating scorn or determination.

There were footprints wandering in the snow. The footprints made patterns. I thought – Why are Donald and I walking together? It is a possibility that he is in love with me?

Then – If Donald and I are in a maze, we can see that there is some pattern.

The concluding words of Wittgenstein's *Tractatus Logico-Philosophicus* had been 'What we cannot speak about we must pass over in silence.' It was for these words above all that he, and the book, had become famous. Wittgenstein had seemed to be implying that nothing was sayable except that which was to do with reason. But he had demonstrated how narrow the area was that could be dealt with by reason.

I said to Donald '"Chance" is a word for what we cannot explain by reason. There is no reason why by some means we should not try to talk about it.'

Donald said 'By what means?'

I said 'We can look at, try to describe, the way things happen.'

I had been trying to get Donald to take me with him to one of Wittgenstein's seminars; I wanted to hear what was being said in the area that should, it had been suggested, be passed over in silence. But Donald had said that Wittgenstein insisted that his pupils should undertake a whole course of enquiry with him, that there was no sense in trying to pick up bits and pieces; it was the process itself that might be felt to be dealing with whatever it was in silence.

Donald said 'Wittgenstein would agree that philosophy is more a matter of looking than of analysis.'

I said 'When you are with him, what is the style of what you talk about?'

Donald said 'It is often as if one were finding one's way through a maze.'

It was at times like these that Donald and I were apt to walk for a certain distance in silence.

What I had learned about Wittgenstein was that he had been at Cambridge before the First World War; he had returned to his native Austria to fight in the Austrian army. It was in the trenches that he had written most of the *Tractatus Logico-Philosophicus*. In it he had tried to explain – Language constructs models of what can be called 'reality': what language cannot do is suggest what might be the connection between the structures of language and the structures of reality. But this had traditionally been a central task of philosophy. So, in a sense, Wittgenstein seemed to suggest, philosophy was over.

After the publication of the *Tractatus* Wittgenstein had himself given up philosophy; he had taught in an Austrian village school; he had designed a severely functional house for his sister in Vienna. Then at the end of the 1920s he had suddenly returned to Cambridge: he had thought that there was something more to do in philosophy.

Donald said 'But we think we can use language, yes, for the clarification of language.'

I said 'But the point is still that there is something quite different going on.'

Donald said 'What?'

I said 'Some sort of therapy.'

Donald curled his lip up under his nose.

I said 'Any success we have is to do not with reason, but aesthetics. Or even ethics. Doesn't Wittgenstein say something like that?'

Wittgenstein had written in the *Tractatus* just before his final sentence about silence – 'Anyone who understands me eventually recognises my propositions as nonsensical when he has used them to climb up beyond them. He must, so to speak, throw away the ladder . . . then he will see the world aright.'

Donald and I watched where the footprints of birds and animals had gone round and round and made patterns in the snow. I thought – Well what is a pattern? A pattern is not a thing that you can analyse. A pattern is there when you see it; but it is not just in the snow.

Donald said 'It is true that Wittgenstein is interested in aesthetics.'

I said 'Rum tiddle di um tum.'

Donald said 'And what does that mean?'

I said 'It is a song called "Footprints in the Snow".'

I had begun to have an obsession about meeting Wittgenstein. Donald said that his seminars took place in an austere room with just a table and two chairs; when students came, they had to bring their own chairs. I thought – If Donald will not take me to him, I will meet him as if by chance.

– Then I will be doing some experiment with chance?

I said to Donald 'Does Wittgenstein ever go for long walks in the snow?'

Donald said 'I don't know. What he does like doing, apparently, is to go to the cinema in the afternoon to a western film and to sit in the front row.'

I said 'Does that stop his thinking going round and round?'

Donald said 'I suppose so.'

I thought – So I might bump into Wittgenstein at a western film?

Then – But you and I, my beautiful German girl, we did not think that we would go round and round: but we were frightened?

Sometimes when I got back from these walks with Donald I would find Melvyn sitting beyond the framework of his doorway as if waiting to be looked at like a picture. He would say 'Been nuzzling with the brood of Mrs Tiggywinklestein?'

I would say 'Yes, they are doing very well, thank you.'

Melvyn would say 'Had any good silences lately?'

When I wandered into Melvyn's room I knew we would for the most part talk nonsense. I would think – Perhaps being with Melvyn is the equivalent of sitting in the front row at a western film: after a time thought stops; there is just the area in which one thing happens after another.

Then – But is not aesthetics to do with the fact that the structures of reality coincide with the structures of one's mind –

– That was what we were talking about, you and I, my beautiful German girl?

I would sit on Melvyn's chaise-longue and say something like – 'Well the crack-up of the Western world seems to be coming about quite nicely.'

And Melvyn would say – 'I don't want it to be coming along nicely: I want there to be a great many people killed.'

And I would think – In a western film a great many people get killed –

– A sorting-out; that is to do with 'aesthetics'?

Melvyn only once tried to make a pass at me. He helped me up to my room one evening when I was drunk; he sat on the edge of my bed and got me half undressed and fiddled with me for a short while. He said 'This little piggy went to market.' If I had been more sober I might have said – 'It looks more as if this little piggy's staying at home.' After a time he gave up, and left me. I thought – So you see, if you let things go, one thing happens not so badly after another.

Then – But why did I let you go, my beautiful German girl?

I was obviously still confused about sexuality at this time: I would lie on my bed and try to make my mind a blank. But images would come in: of horsemen riding across plains; of Melvyn with his cherub's mouth like sick at the edges of drains.

I would think – In physics, there are people trying to find out about an atom by breaking up its heart. (I thought – Stop thinking!) In philosophy, there are people trying to break it up to see it has no heart. (I thought – Stop thinking!)

In the outside world there were more and more ghostly figures standing unemployed on street corners. I had said to you, my beautiful German girl, 'In the end, people either will or will not destroy themselves –

– We will or will not meet each other again.'

You had said 'But which?'

We had sat facing each other with our backs against trees.

It seemed to me now that this was some form of annunciation.

So – Get up and go on!

– You think you can stop thinking?

– Oh such a situation might be aesthetic!

Melvyn had a friend called Mullen who sometimes visited him in his room. Mullen was a notable figure in Cambridge: he was tall and thin with a face like a hatchet. He strode through the streets in a long blue coachman's overcoat and a wide-brimmed hat: he seemed to expect people to get off the pavement for him. He was a poet: he was said to be writing a book about aesthetics; he was also an authority on Karl Marx. I would think – I should be cultivating people like Mullen!

– Or is it proper that I would rather, like some mad archaic god, go bumping and bouncing off walls to find my way through the maze?

Melvyn and Mullen were both members of the club, or society, known as The Apostles, the members of which felt themselves to be part of an intellectual and cultural élite. They were an apotheosis of the Cambridge tradition of it being the mark of an élite to hold everything open to question: to manipulate nihilism by sleight-of-mind. I had once said to Melvyn 'Stalin would have made a marvellous Apostle!' Melvyn had said 'But that moustache!'

I was going up my stairs one day when Melvyn called out 'Mullen wants to meet you.'

I said 'Why?'

Melvyn said 'Perhaps he thinks you're attractive, ducky.'

I thought – Perhaps I can ask him about not only Marxism but aesthetics.

I had become obsessed by the idea of liveliness residing in areas about which nothing much could be said – in physics, in philosophy; even in the way things really worked in politics. I thought – But in all these areas, there is something to do with aesthetics that might be said? I took to going at this time to the Fitzwilliam Museum to look at the paintings: I thought – Something can be looked at; found by a painter; even if it cannot be said.

In the picture gallery I became interested in two small paintings by Domenico Veneziano which hung side by side. One was of the Annunciation and was very beautiful: the Angel and Mary faced each other across a courtyard, they did not look at each other; they seemed to be intent on whatever it was in between. Behind them, and in between, there was a closed door in a garden at the back of the courtyard. The other painting depicted a group present at a miracle performed by some saint in a street: it was ugly. The people seemed to be intent on portraying dramatic emotion; as if they felt that this was required of them by some observer.

I thought – It is not exactly that this painting is ugly: it is giving some aesthetic message about what is ugly.

Then – You and I, in the Black Forest, we knew something about that first painting, that courtyard; that doorway at the back in between?

There was a day – sometime during my second term I think – when Melvyn brought Mullen to visit me in my room. I had not thought much about what they might come to visit me for: to look me over as a possible recruit for the Apostles, for homosexual purposes, possibly because Melvyn had told Mullen of my interest in Russia? Melvyn and Mullen sat on my sofa side by side; they were like two characters in a ballet – the dancing master and his pupil – and of course they were actors! Mullen wore his long blue coat with the collar turned up at the back; Melvyn had narrow trousers tapering to small pointed shoes. I sat with my chair tipped back against a wall. I thought – They have come to do an experiment with me; but why should not that which is observed cause disturbance among the observers?

'I don't think you know Mullen, do you?'

'No, how do you do.'

'How do you do.'

'Would you like some tea?'

'No, thank you.'

'A glass of sherry?'

'No, thank you.'

Melvyn and Mullen sat side by side. I thought – Well, they have cottoned on to the idea about the stylishness of silence.

Then – I wonder who, between the two of them, it is who buggers whom?

I said to Mullen 'Can I ask you about aesthetics?'

Mullen said 'Please do.'

Mullen had cold pale eyes like the water in a goldfish bowl. I thought – somewhere far inside there might be something golden swimming around.

I said 'In the Fitzwilliam Museum there are two small paintings by Domenico Veneziano: one is of the Annunciation and is very beautiful; the other is of a saint's miracle and is not. In the Annunciation, down a garden path, there is a closed door in a wall. This seems to guard some secret. What is this secret? I mean, can it ever be said?'

Melvyn and Mullen stared at me. I thought – This scene is like what I have gathered from my mother about psychoanalysis: the analyst sits in silence until the patient, out of embarrassment, makes a fool of himself. Then – But, after all, it is the patient who is being kind to the analyst.

I said 'In the other painting, of the so-called "miracle", everyone seemed to be posing dramatically for the painter. But there is nothing between them or at the back of them. There is no secret.'

After a time Melvyn said 'Ducky, Mullen's subject is fourteenth-century Russian icons.'

I said 'Do you think there are two sorts of portraits? One in which people seem to be posing for the painter, and another in which they are saying "All right I see why you have to do this."'

Melvyn and Mullen said nothing.

I said 'In religious paintings I do not think people should pose for God.'

Then after a time I said 'I see this is not the way people usually talk about fourteenth-century Russian icons.'

Melvyn said 'In that you are correct.'

Mullen said 'Melvyn tells me you are a physicist.'

I said 'Yes.'

Mullen said 'In physics, do you think there should be secrets?'

I thought – Oh good heavens, no wonder I have had to make a fool of myself!

I said 'I don't know.'

Melvyn said 'Ducky, we came to ask you if you'd like to join the local football fan club.'

I said 'What does the local football fan club do?'

Melvyn said 'It watches football.'

Mullen said 'But it should not be a political decision, whether physics has secrets?'

I said 'I suppose not.'

Melvyn said 'Time, gentlemen, please.'

Mullen said 'Perhaps we will see you at the football club.'

I said 'I hope so.'

After they had gone, I felt that I would rush out and obliterate their absurd footprints in the snow. I thought – I need your help, my beautiful German girl.

I remained in my sexual limbo at this time. There was a boy with whom I had once been in love at school: there was the fantasy that I had in some way been in love with my mother. I dreamed, but was still frightened, of girls. Sex took the form with me of what one did with one's dreams: dreams were of what one might meet again round some corner. I felt – My beautiful German girl will one day rise again sword-in-hand from a lake; she will help me to slay the dragons that entrap me in dreams; that make me feel that reality is untouchable.

Sometime after my meeting with Mullen, Melvyn caught me on the stairs and said 'Ducky, I can't quite tell into what, or not, you've put your pretty foot with Mullen!'

From this I gathered that I had been some sort of success.

I thought – But in relation to what: aesthetics? Or the local football fan club?

Then – Oh but I am bored with Melvyn's riddles! They are the posing of someone who is afraid there is no painter.

Then – We lay like a seed, you and I, beneath that tree; that might stay alive all winter.

I had one or two letters from you, my beautiful German girl. But they were like hard flashes from a sword that came up from that dark lake. Well, why do you think it was so long before we saw each other again? There is a proper fear.

Dearest Max,

Here we have some excitement because Bruno (you remember Bruno?) has been working with his professor on some of the unpublished manuscripts of Karl Marx, and they have been finding results that are, to say the least, surprising. It appears that in these manuscripts (written in Paris in 1844) Marx is by no means the materialist and anti-spiritualist that has been supposed (is 'anti-spiritualist' the word? I was taught English by my German governess, Miss Henne). Marx says it is the capitalist world that is materialist and anti-spiritualist in that its only criterion is money: it is he, Karl Marx, who works for man's spiritual liberation. This can be achieved by the recognition that a man is what he does: in his work he can be an artist.

Of course, Marx himself in later writings was somewhat responsible for the idea that he was anti-spiritualist: perhaps it was necessary for this earlier part of his work to have remained hidden?

So much of what is guarded by a prophet's followers is perverted! This has been the experience of the Christian churches, no?

Can you give me the source of your quotation about Jesus saying he teaches in parables so that people may not understand and be saved.

I have met Bertolt Brecht. He is a small man who smells. Women say they find his smell attractive. He too seems to be saying something quite different from what people think he is saying. He says he is a Marxist. Do you think it might be to protect himself (by making himself attractive?) that he smells?

Here we have been in some ferment because the Nazis obtained six and a half million votes at the last election and now are the second largest party in the Reichstag. There are still people who, like you, say that the Nazis may turn out to be something different from what they say. But if this is so, it will not be because they are clever. At the moment people don't believe them (because they themselves are stupid) when they say they want to kill Jews.

I am interested in what you say about Wittgenstein: what do people at Cambridge say of the connections between Wittgenstein and Heidegger?

There is a chance that I may come to England later this year. I am one of a group here planning to make a pilgrimage to English locations of Engels and Karl Marx. Do not laugh: if I do come to England, tell me how I can see you. I suppose our route will hardly pass through Cambridge. Could you come to London for a day?

Max, I do not know how to write this. I found your last letter very formal.

Yes, I know there are things that defeat themselves if they are said.

But you have much love from your

Elena

I walked around with this letter in a pocket next to my heart. I felt – Oh my beautiful German girl! But you know I am yours! No matter what is the business of touch, taste, smell.

Sometime in the spring (this was 1931: unemployment in England had risen to nearly three million; there was talk of the payments to the unemployed being cut) I learned that there was to be a lunch party at the house of some friends of my father's at which Wittgenstein was going to be present. I had continued to have this image of Wittgenstein as someone whom it was necessary for me to meet: it was as if he were a figure that I had to learn something from at a corner of the maze. I thought I might ask him (though I did not think I would – Can two people be together in those areas of silence: or do you have to be on your own –

– But all human relationships are not like sitting in the front row of a cinema?

I got myself invited to this lunch party through the host being a friend of my father's; I understood that Donald had not been invited. I wondered – Will he be hurt? Then – But these games people play are ridiculous.

Now that it was spring there were people in punts as Donald and I walked by the river. I said 'You say that Wittgenstein's new philosophy is to do with the games that we play. I mean, does he suggest that all language is a game?'

Donald said as if quoting ' – It is as if we are looking through spectacles and always describing the frames – '

I said 'But if we realise this – '

Donald said 'Don't you think that there would still be a game on a different level?'

Punts floated on the river. Boys with poles leaned over girls who lay in the bottoms of the punts like queen bees. I thought – But it would be a worthwhile game.

I said 'I've been invited to a lunch at which Wittgenstein is going to be present.'

Donald said 'That is impossible: Wittgenstein never goes to lunches.'

I thought – Do I mean, it would be a game in which, at the same time, one would be creating, or discovering, the conditions of the game?

Donald and I walked for some time in silence.

The party to which I had been invited took place on a bright spring day with a wind that lurked here and there round corners. Food had been set out on tables on a lawn; cushions were placed on steps going down from a small terrace. People stood with their backs to where they thought the wind might be; they turned this way and that all at once like fishes. Wittgenstein was seated in a small room inside the house: the room was crowded; there were people sitting on the floor and looking up at him as if he had been set in some niche. He was a thin, blue-eyed, curly-haired man; he seemed precisely delineated as if there was a light on the wall behind him. He wore a tweed jacket and an open-necked shirt. It seemed that although people were seeing him as if set up in a niche, he was not posing.

I thought – It is as if he were looking at the people watching him and saying: 'Is it you? Is it you?'

Then – Of course I know whom he reminds me of: Dr Kammerer!

There was a man on the floor in front of Wittgenstein asking him some boring question about aesthetics; it went on and on: I thought – Dear God, the questioner might be myself.

Then – But the question answers itself by its style, if it is to do with aesthetics.

A wind seemed to be passing over Wittgenstein's face as if the question were affecting him physically. He was holding on his lap a plate of food at an angle at which the food seemed about to fall off. When the man had finished his question Wittgenstein just said 'I don't think that is correct.' Then he looked down at his plate as if there might be entrails on it.

I thought – But if you feel you have been put in a niche like St Sebastian, can you not get up and leave the picture?

A young girl had come into the room and was standing in front of Wittgenstein; she was holding out her hand as if to take his plate. She seemed to be asking him whether he wanted any more food; but perhaps was too shy to put this into words. I knew the girl slightly: she was one of the daughters of the family who were giving the party. Wittgenstein did not seem to notice her for a time. Then he looked up and frowned and said 'What do you want?'

The girl stepped back as if she had been hit. She stumbled against the legs of the people behind her. Then she made for the door.

Someone said 'She was asking you if you wanted more food.'

Wittgenstein said 'But I haven't eaten the food I've got.'

I was standing in the doorway; as the girl went past me she seemed enraged. I thought – You mean something quite different is happening?

Wittgenstein had looked up to where I stood. I had the impression that he wanted me to do something for him.

Then – But this is ridiculous!

The girl had gone out of the house and on to the lawn. There was someone beginning to ask Wittgenstein another long and boring question. I thought I might say – All right I'll go after her. Then – This is to do with silences?

The person who was asking the question was saying – 'But are you saying that what you call "objective" is simply what happens?'

Wittgenstein, it was true, had been looking towards the door.

I left the doorway and went out on to the lawn. There were people standing holding plates with their backs to the wind; paper napkins were blowing like the tops of waves. I was looking for the girl who had held her hand out to Wittgenstein: I thought – There could be a painting of that: of a meeting, and something quite different going on. Then – How old would she be: sixteen? seventeen? Then – But what happens, I mean, if something quite different is happening.

The girl had gone to the end of the lawn where there was undergrowth beneath trees. There was a fallen willow which went halfway across a small pond or stream. The girl was climbing out on to the trunk of the tree. She had long fair hair which hung like shields on either side of her head. I thought – Her legs, yes, might almost be clappers of a bell.

I went and stood by the roots of the fallen tree. The girl was sitting on the trunk with her legs dangling above water. I said 'He didn't mean to be rude.'

The girl said 'I don't mind if he did mean to be rude. I hate this party.'

I said 'Why?'

She said 'No one says what they mean.'

I climbed out on the log and sat down slightly apart from her, facing the same way; my feet dangling above the water. I said 'It's sometimes difficult to say what you mean.'

She said 'Why?'

I said 'Because you often don't know quite what you mean.'

She seemed to think about this. She looked down into the water.

She said 'I know what I mean.'

I said 'What?'

She said 'Nothing.' Then – 'I'm Suzy.'

I said 'Yes.' Then – 'How old are you?'

She said 'Seventeen.'

'Are you still at school?'

'No.'

'What do you do then?'

'I want to go to Paris.'

I thought – Well this is what is happening: we are sitting side by side; we are looking down towards water; the light is coming through the leaves, the shadows.

I said 'What do you want to do in Paris?'

She said 'I want to study music.'

'Then why don't you go?'

'My father won't let me.'

'Why won't he?'

'He says I'm too young.'

'Have you any friends with whom you could stay in Paris?'

She looked round at me. She had a round face and a soft mouth. I thought – You mean, it is something on that other level that is happening?

Then – Of course, she is sexy.

She said 'Why are you asking me these questions?'

I said 'Have you a boyfriend?'

She said 'No.' Then – 'I had a friend at school with whose parents I could stay in Paris.'

'So it's not the money – '

'No.'

'And you can't study music here – '

'There's nothing happening in music here.'

I thought I might say – Well why not come with me to Russia: there may be something happening in music there.

It seemed that as a first step I might move along the log and put my arm around her and kiss her. I found I managed to do this. After a time she said 'That was nice!'

I thought – Dear God, and you think you can't get to Paris!

There were the people on the lawn holding their plates like gauges in which rain might be collected: in the house there was still presumably Wittgenstein in his niche. I thought – But we are being given messages, yes, as if we are in contact with gravity.

Then – But perhaps I should not be thinking of going to Russia, or to Paris: I should go to the north of England and do some work for the unemployed.

Then – Why did I think this?

I had been carrying a bottle of wine when I had come across the lawn: I had put it down by the roots of the tree. I stopped kissing Suzy and went to get the bottle. I thought – You mean, on this strange level, what you notice is just that one thing happens after another?

I noticed that Suzy's father was coming towards us across the lawn. I crawled back, with the bottle of wine, and rejoined Suzy on the tree.

Suzy said 'Does that mean you'll take me to Paris?'

I said 'I think it means something perhaps like I'll take you to Paris.'

She said 'And what does that mean?'

I said 'It means we'll see.'

Suzy and I were sitting with our arms round each other looking down into the water. We drank from the bottle of wine. Suzy's father had arrived at the roots of the tree and was watching us. I thought – Oh this might be a magic tree that will get someone or other to Paris!

Suzy's father said 'What are you two doing?'

Suzy said 'We are sitting on this tree.'

Suzy's father said 'Come back to the house.'

Suzy said 'That is my father.'

Suzy drank from the bottle of wine. I drank from the bottle of wine. I turned to offer it to Suzy's father.

There was a thick pall of smoke drifting across the garden. It was coming from some next-door garden, or perhaps from a building that was on fire. I thought I might say – Well that's nothing to do with me.

Or – We have been working on the problem of how to get Suzy to Paris.

Suzy's father said 'There's a building next door on fire.'

I thought – You mean, all this might be a part of some composition like that of a painting?

There were some firemen in metal helmets who had come on to the lawn. I thought – Or they are Greeks and Trojans –

– Or perhaps I am drunk!

The guests who had been in the house were coming out on to the lawn. They were looking at the pall of smoke, then turning away and coughing. Wittgenstein was on the lawn: he was looking up at the smoke as if he was considering its colour, its texture. I thought – Well what indeed do you make of this aesthetically?

Suzy said 'We've been talking about going to Paris.'

Her father said 'You're going to Paris?'

I stood up on the log. I was holding Suzy's hand. I thought – Indeed we are on a tightrope; do I not have to hold her hand!

Suzy's father said to me 'You're not taking her to Paris!'

I thought I might say – No, I'm going to Russia: or to work for the unemployed.

I noticed that Melvyn and Mullen had come out on to the lawn. Mullen was watching me. Melvyn was talking to Wittgenstein.

Wittgenstein was turning away as if annoyed. I thought – But indeed these images, these ideas, these people, come into my head –

– Put in a figure here: another one turns up there –

– This is reality?

People were moving off through the house, coughing.

Suzy and I walked across the lawn. I was still holding her hand. Her father followed us. Melvyn and Mullen were watching. When we were near the house Mullen said to me 'I didn't know you would be here!'

I thought I might say – Ah, you think we know anything!

Wittgenstein said 'This smoke is not poisonous.'

Suzy's father said 'How do you know?'

Wittgenstein said 'It is the smell.'

Melvyn went down on one knee and held his arms out towards Suzy and me. He said 'Beauty and the Beast!'

Suzy's father said to Suzy 'You know these people?'

The firemen seemed to be trying to clear the lawn. People were going in twos and threes towards the house holding handkerchiefs to their noses. I thought – Then there will be just our small group left in the picture.

Mullen said to me 'Have you thought about what we talked about?'

I thought – Why, what did we talk about?

I said 'Yes.'

He said 'And what do you think – '

I thought – Of physics? Of politics? I said 'It is a matter for aesthetics.'

Melvyn had put his arm round Suzy. Suzy's father was saying 'Why did you think that I said you couldn't go to Paris?'

Wittgenstein was looking at me. He said 'Thank you.' I wasn't sure if I had heard this, or if he had said it to me. Then he moved off towards the house.

I let go of Suzy's hand. I went after Wittgenstein. Then I thought – Oh, but anyway, I am drunk.

I saw that my father and mother were coming into the house from the roadway. I thought – But there are too many people in this picture! Get them out.

Wittgenstein had gone through on to the roadway where I could see that Donald was standing. I thought – Oh yes, Donald can be in this picture! Wittgenstein was now talking to Donald.

My father said to me 'I didn't know you'd be at this party.'

My mother said 'Are you all right?'

I said 'Yes, I'm all right.'

Suzy's father was pushing Melvyn out of the house. Mullen and Suzy were following; they were watching me. My mother and father were standing side by side. We had all emerged on to the roadway. Wittgenstein and Donald were going off, talking.

The smoke that had been blowing from a next-door building now seemed to be going up in a straight column into the sky.

I waved to Suzy. I thought – Oh but we had it, for a moment, exactly, didn't we, what you can't talk about, in a picture!

In the summer holidays of that year politicians went abroad to their usual watering-places while the mechanism of the capitalist world ran down; it seemed to make drooping, groaning noises like those of a clockwork gramophone. Politicians were recalled from their watering-places to see if they could get the capitalist world wound up; but it seemed that they had lost the handle, it was no longer in the nursery toy-box.

I had heard of a clergyman in the north of England who was looking for volunteers to help build, or re-build, a church hall which was to be made into a recreational centre for the use or edification of the unemployed. I thought – I can go and help build a hall for the unemployed, but will I not be doing this for my own edification?

Then – But might not the world be wound up, if everyone tried to see what was their own edification?

I bought a second-hand suit of clothes and travelled to the north of England. It had seemed that I might emerge in a different dimension. People had said – But you cannot imagine the north of England!

I might have said – But do you not carry around what you imagine in your own head?

When I got out at the railway station I seemed to be underground; the train had run into the centre of the town in cuttings and tunnels. Climbing, I emerged into an area of heavy blackened buildings – a town hall, a department store, a bank, a museum. It was as if these had been in a fire which had been put out by rain. I thought – But this is just how I have imagined the north of England!

There was a pale grey light as if the town were set on the curve of a low hill; or on the surface of a convex mirror.

I had a haversack on my back. I walked in the direction in which I imagined the river. The river was where there were the dockyards and shipbuilding yards which had once been the reason for the existence of the town.

The ground fell away from the central keep or fastness of the town hall, the department store, the bank, the museum, to where there were the dwellings and workplaces of the people that might be sacrificed, as it were, if the town were besieged. I thought – But now, what are the besiegers? they are more to do with states of mind.

I turned off the main road and went into an area of narrow streets and tall, jumbled houses. Here there were piles of refuse and splintered wood and broken carts. Men stood by the broken carts. I thought – Could not the men use the wood to mend the carts and take away the litter? Then – But of course, one is not supposed to think like this now. There were smells. I thought – Humans have lost their sense of smell: they once had a sense like that of hunting dogs, which made connections.

The men wore cloth caps and mufflers. The women had long thick skirts and shawls over their heads: some of them carried small children with dark furious eyes. There were older children in clothes and caps that were too big for them; it was as if they were involved in a game of dressing-up. It was these children who, as I walked through the streets, paid attention to me, followed me, mocked the way I walked. When I turned to them they would pretend to have been doing something different. I thought – It is this age, from five to eleven, that children still have a chance to do what they want to do.

I was on my way to the church of the clergyman who had asked for people to help build, or re-build, the recreational hall for the unemployed. He had found it difficult, apparently, to get local men and women to do this for themselves. They had felt that it would be some sort of defeat for them: they wanted work provided as part of what other people wanted to do.

I did not want to arrive at the church straightaway: I wanted to observe more of the strange landscapes in which besiegers and victims seemed reflections of states of mind.

I moved out of the narrow jostling streets into a more open area where the ground sloped down towards the river. Here there were long rows of low houses back-to-back like stitching. There were not many women and children visible here, and the men in cloth caps seemed to have been swept into groups on street corners. The windows of shops on these corners were boarded up; the walls of houses at the ends of rows were falling down. I thought – This landscape is like clothing coming apart at the seams: a shroud that has been tied too tightly over the body of the earth, our mother.

Beyond the houses was a maze of railway lines that went down towards the river. The lines were raised on posts; they were where coal must once have been carried down to ships. Now the railway was not working; there were rows of stationary trucks like bumps on the spines of skeletons. Beyond the railway lines were the shipyards with tall grey cranes that were themselves like birds become skeletons, for want of anything to feed off.

I thought – These images are of a charnel house: these images are in my mind. If I am an anthropologist come to take notes of this strange tribe, what I should be doing is taking notes of states of mind.

The railway lines were like the tracks of baby turtles that had once run down towards the sea: the birds, the cranes, the crabs, the seagulls had got them.

I thought – But one or two get through?

– Or the town hall, the department store, the bank, the museum, has burned like a volcano and the lava has pushed human beings down towards the sea –

– But it is these images in my mind that go tumbling, jostling, like a crowd running down towards a river!

I had come to the edge of an area of wasteland that lay between the houses like stitching and the delta of railway lines on their wooden pillars. Beyond the railway lines were the cranes and the river: there were no ships on the river; there were some hulks on the mud that seemed part of the land, rotting. There was a group of children playing on the wasteland: they were on top of a small hill of slag and rubble. The children were playing a game of rolling old rubber tyres down this hill; the tyres rolled and bounced and span towards the railway lines at the bottom. There was a small embankment with a wire fence on top in front of the railway lines and when the tyres reached this they leapt and whirled in the air and then flopped down like dead fishes. There was one small opening in the embankment which consisted of an archway which gave access to the area under the railway lines beyond. The children did not seem to be aiming the tyres particularly for this opening; the game seemed to be just to watch the tyres bounce and leap.

I thought – The children on that mound are like Napoleon and his marshals surveying a battlefield: they watched soldiers and cannon balls bounce and leap, flopping down like dead fishes.

– Or these children are rolling their tyres down the inner surface of the four-dimensional continuum of the universe to see what, at the end, will be the effects of light, of gravity.

There was one child who was smaller than the others who was pushing a large tyre up the hill. This child wore a cap and a coat down to its ankles. It was like a small Sisyphus just emerged from an egg, pushing its own shell up a hill.

I thought – Or this is like one of those experiments in which you bombard with particles a small aperture in a screen and it is according either to chance or to how you have set up the experiment what, if anything, gets through.

When the small child who was pushing the tyre up the hill reached the top the other children gathered round. I had sat down on my haversack at the edge of the wasteland at some distance from the hill. I thought – I will stay here and observe not only the customs of this strange tribe but myself observing –

– Out of the confusion of images, might something of myself get through?

The small child was climbing into the large tyre which the other children held for him: I mean he was getting himself wedged inside the tyre as if he were the centrepiece of a wheel. He had his head down, his knees against his chin, his arms around his knees. It was also, I suppose, as if he were within the casing of some seed; his small face peering out. Or was not this like an illustration to some sacred text – the microcosm and the macrocosm, the human within the circle, the part that is the whole. These images went spinning in my mind. Then I thought – But surely the child within the tyre cannot be rolled down the slope; those tyres went bounding, leaping, so violently: the child will die! The other children held the tyre while the small child settled himself in; then they gave the tyre a push and the tyre went off whirling, bouncing, down the slope. I thought – But the child's neck will be broken: you see why this is not possible! I stood up. I wanted to stretch out my hand against – what? – gravity? The tyre hit a projection, took off, landed, took off again. I thought – There is something so soft inside, like water bouncing against stone. This also is in my head. I picked up my haversack and began to move down the hill. The other children had turned and were running away down the far side. I thought – They know, of course, that the child in the tyre may be killed. The tyre was heading for the low embankment with the wire fence on top; there was just the one small opening through to the area beneath the railway lines beyond. I thought – So now, come on, what is it in that experiment that makes the one particle get through: the condition set by the experimenter. The tyre with the child inside made a long low leap and then disappeared, yes, through the opening in the embankment: it went out of sight in the area beneath the railway lines. I had been running; I stopped; I said – Thank you. I thought – You mean, what if that particle were a seed, with a child inside? Then – This is ridiculous. I went on. There were puddles of oily water on the wasteland in which light was reflected like rainbows. I reached the archway in the embankment and went through; there was a maze of posts carrying the railway lines above my head. I thought – So, now, what am I learning about an anthropology of the mind! The maze of posts was like some dead forest; the ruins of an ancient temple; what had the temple been used for, the sacrifice of a child? But this child had got through! And was now back in the ruined temple. And so on. I was picking my way between the posts that were like the trunks of rotting trees. I thought – It is as if they, and these images, have been a long time under water. I could not see the tyre: it had found its way, presumably, some distance into the maze. Or had it gone right over the rim of the land, and back to its origins in water. There was a small clearing within the maze; the railway lines made a loop so that there was a patch of open sky above; within this clearing there was a half-collapsed hut and two small grey-and-green bushes. I thought – This is the home of some old hermit, perhaps; or that Garden, where now these bushes are the remains of those two trees. The tyre had come to rest half propped against one of the pillars at the edge of the clearing; there was a shaft of sunlight coming down towards the hut. I thought – This clearing itself is in the shape of an egg: the tyre with the child inside is like a seed that has come in by chance, by design, from outside to that old garden, that hut like a rotting tomb. Then – Stop thinking! There was an arm hanging out from the inside of the tyre; it was a small white arm which was, yes, like some shoot not so much from a seed as into it. I said to myself again – Stop thinking! I had been thinking that if the child were dead, then people might imagine I had murdered it. I went on into the clearing. Well there it was, this strange self-risking, self-sacrificing, self-immolation of a child. I went up to the tyre and

knelt down beside it. The child was still wedged inside. Its head
was at an angle which made it seem that its neck might indeed be
broken: its knee and elbows were scraped and slightly raw. The
child's eyes were closed; it was holding its cap down by its knee; it
had dark curly hair; it was smiling. One of its cheeks was brown
and pink with dirt and blood: I wondered if I might lick it. I thought
– The child is alive! Then I realized that the child, whom I had taken
to be a boy, was in fact a girl: she was a small bright girl of eight or
nine. She had opened one eye and was smiling. I thought I might
say – Are you all right? None of this seemed, at the time, all that
extraordinary. It seemed that I should put out a hand and see if any
bones were broken; but I did not want to touch the child; I remained
squatting in front of her with my forearms on my knees. I smiled at
her. The girl moved her neck, her arms, tentatively, as if preparing
to climb out of the tyre; she was looking towards something beyond
me. I thought – Well, now, what am I going to see if I turn: some
old monster emerge from that hut that has been sleeping for a
thousand years? When I turned my head there was, yes, someone
standing by the hut; it was another child, a boy; smaller even than
the child within the tyre: this child seemed to have come out of the
hut and was standing by the two grey-and-green bushes. I thought
– Well, you mean, this is what we have been waiting for all these
centuries, these children? Then – This is ridiculous. The girl was
climbing out of the tyre; her coat was torn; she had thin arms and
legs like bones which have been picked clean. She remained
crouching. Then with her hands she made flashing, darting movements towards the child who was by the hut: it was as if she were
flicking bits of light at him; as if the bits of light might come down
on him like golden rain. Then this child came up to her and held
out his hand. He was wearing a rough brown smock to just below
his knees. I thought – Oh I see, the child who has been in the tyre is
deaf or dumb; or this other child is deaf and dumb; perhaps they
both are; that's why she makes these flashing movements with her
hands. Then – Or this silence, this scattering of light, is like the
speech, or milk, of angels. The child who had been in the tyre stood
and took the hand of the smaller child who was standing gravely by
her. She did not in fact appear to be injured. Neither child up to this
time had paid much attention to me. I thought – But that is all
right, I am an observer in this clearing in the jungle. Then the girl
who had been in the tyre did turn to me and made one or two
flicking movements towards me with a hand. I smiled; I nodded; I

shook my head. I thought – But what does it matter if I do not understand? I understand. Then the girl, laughing, held her hand in front of her hips and made one or two movements forwards and back with her finger and thumb in a circle which might have been taken, if they had not been done so laughingly, to refer to something that could be called obscene. I laughed too; I raised my hand; I shook my head. Then the girl turned away. I thought – But thank you for the offer! It was kind. The two children set off beneath the railway lines hand-in-hand. The girl stopped once more and looked back at me; she made no more flicking movements with her hands. She looked first at me, then at the hut, then at the boy; then she remained for a time looking back at me. I watched her. I thought – She is trying to make some further message. I tried to say to her – It is all right! Then I watched them go. I had sat down on my haversack in the clearing by the hut. I was thinking – Well what might indeed grow, in the mind, if there is silence: something that has been dormant for a thousand years?

The rector of St Biscop's was a sandy-haired man called Peter Reece who strode about his parish without a jacket and with what looked like bicycle clips on his shirt-sleeves, so that with these and his dog-collar and his way of walking – leaning forwards with his arms held close to his sides – it was as if he were in harness and pulling a great weight. Sometimes he would stop and look back as if the weight had slipped from him and gone rolling down a hill. He seemed to be wondering – It is my fault if people have to suffer? to die?

His parish was High Anglican; his church had a ceiling which was painted blue with golden stars; beneath it there were niches from which dapper saints looked down. Peter Reece lived on his own in the large rectory; some of the young men who came to work for him looked somewhat like the dapper saints. He lived in an attic at the top of the house and on the first floor were dormitories where the young men slept and on the ground floor were rooms where unemployed men and schoolchildren could be given free meals. Between the rectory and the church there was a piece of waste ground where there had previously been the parish hut and a tennis court; it was here that there was being built the new Recreational Hall. In this there were to be games – table tennis and snooker and whist and ludo – classes in woodwork and pottery, and lectures on current affairs in the evenings.

Peter Reece had got help from local builders to provide him with materials and there was a rich widow in the town who gave him money for expenses. But he did not get much help in this work from the unemployed themselves: they seemed to feel that they might undermine their case for what they were entitled to. So Peter Reece had asked for volunteers from Cambridge where he had recently served as an assistant priest. He then worried that his volunteers might be seen as dispensers of charity: there was a certain amount in the Bible about the virtue in the dispensing of charity, but who benefited from this virtue seemed to remain obscure.

Groups of men in cloth caps and mufflers would stand at some distance from the half-built Recreational Hall and watch us working. We thus became somewhat self-conscious in our work. I would think – Perhaps virtue resides in the embarrassment of those who are charitable? Then – What would be really charitable, of course, for the people who are watching us working, would be if we could arrange for the building to fall down.

It was difficult to make much contact with the men in cloth caps. We would try: but the more we tried, of course, the more unacceptable we became as people who were seen as doling out charity.

My first job was to transport by wheelbarrow loads of bricks to the building site from where they had been dumped by a lorry. Children would watch me: I would sometimes manage to give them a ride in the wheelbarrow. Then I got the job of manhandling bricks up to the level where two men were constructing a wall standing on planks between trestles. I thought – So here, again, might it not cheer up the watching children and the men standing on street corners if we embarked on one of those slapstick routines that play such a part in pantomimes: clowns knocking each other over with planks swinging on shoulders; builders toppling off ladders and falling head first into buckets. And after a time we might have managed to provide better recreation than that which could be provided by a hall.

Then I got the job myself of laying bricks on the top level of the wall. I had not done such work before. I thought – Ah I will not think now that the wall should fall down!

I stood on a plank on the scaffolding and took some cement on my trowel from the bucket that had been handed up to me and I flicked the cement on to the bricks that were already there and the cement seemed to go everywhere; it was like birdshit, like pollen: I thought – I am doing something that could be called building a wall? Bits, however, here and there seemed to stay in place; indeed like seeds, like pollen. I shaped the cement that had stayed on the wall and placed the new brick on top; I dropped a dab of cement in the crack and tapped at the new brick: I thought – Of course it is when you stop thinking, that something like building a wall just happens. Then there was the business of the plumbline: you dangled a piece of string with a lump of lead on the end; it went down into the depth to get the wall upright – so this was gravity! After a time the wall did seem to be building itself. I thought – Well most things living, growing, happen by themselves: you do not notice gravity?

– Gravity is people doing what they are supposed to do?

After a time, when the walls did not fall down, the groups of men who had been watching us drifted away.

I sometimes talked with Peter Reece in the evenings. We would sit in the church, which was the place where we were most likely to be alone. We would say together the service of Compline with its strange, beautiful words – 'Brethren be sober, be vigilant, for your adversary the Devil, as a roaring lion, walketh about seeking whom he may devour' – and we would talk beneath the images of dapper saints looking down.

I said 'But what is this resentment that stops people helping not just those who would help them but even themselves? It is the sort of death-wish that is talked about by Freudians such as my mother?'

Peter Reece said 'Have you thought about the parable of the Good Samaritan?'

I said 'No.'

Peter Reece said 'People think that the parable of the Good Samaritan is about the obligation for us to help our neighbours who are in trouble, but it is not only that!'

I said 'What is it then?'

Peter Reece said 'Just before Christ told this parable he had been saying that people should love their neighbours and someone had asked him "Who is my neighbour?" It was in answer to this question that Christ told the parable. And at the end he asked the questioner "So who was a neighbour to him who was in trouble?" And the answer was of course "The Good Samaritan." So the point of the parable is that we should love people who help us, not that we should love people who are in trouble. People have not seen this because they have thought – Surely it is easy to love people who help us! But it is not! It is not! It is very difficult to love people who are good to us: it is easier to imagine we are loving people we can condescend to. Perhaps it is easier still to feel at home with people who do us harm: at least they are not condescending! A burden is put on people we help: of course they feel envy and resentment! But perhaps easiest of all, yes, would be for the whole human race to be packed up.'

I said 'You mean, people choose to depend on people whose interest it is to harm them?'

Peter Reece said 'Oh I am not saying that one should not go on trying to help!'

I said 'You think that the Recreational Hall might miraculously fall down?'

Peter Reece laughed and said 'Oh I don't think they'll try to do away with us!'

There was a new radical political party that had sprung up in 1931, a local branch of which had established itself in the town. Its spokesman came to hold meetings on an open space in front of the half-built Recreational Hall. He would carry a portable platform like a prayer-desk on his back and set it up: I thought – But, of course, people pay attention to politicians because they are like clowns: they are always chucking about, and getting stuck in, buckets of cement.

This was at the time when the Labour Government of 1929–31 found itself sinking in the swamps of capitalist society: a bank in Austria had 'failed'; there was what was called a run on the pound. It was felt that the Gold Standard was something that had desperately to be clung to, like a banner floating in the waves. These events, words, were like dragons in children's fairy stories: but there, in fact, were the groups of men on street corners. I thought – We are all under the spell of dragons in the mind? The speaker from the new political party would set up his portable platform like that of a conjurer on the open space in front of the Recreational Hall.

Sometimes on a fine evening we, the people who were building the hall, would eat our supper out of doors on a trestle table; there would be food for anyone who came to ask for it – soup with meat and potatoes and bread and cheese and fruit. Children would come with cans and we would fill their cans for them to take away; not many people sat down with us to eat. I would think – But what is the terrible unattractiveness of the Good Samaritan? Is it that he is clean, he has no smell: does not love have something to do with the prevalence of smell?

The man who was making a political speech would move his

right hand up and down as if he were working a pump: words seemed to be something sloshing around inside him; he had to get them out. I wondered – Or is he working the handle of a lavatory? People are drawn to him, perhaps, like dogs to a smell.

He was saying, how could there be a world in which everyone made a profit? In a world of limited resources, one person's profit was another's deprivation. So what was necessary was for everyone to be in some sort of army; to see that in an army everyone's interests were the same.

I would think – But the interests of everyone in an army are to maim, to kill.

The speaker told of a company called National Shipbuilders Security Limited that was buying up local shipyards and then closing them down and selling them for scrap: this was an organisation formed by local capitalists to ensure that the few shipyards left in their hands would be protected and make a profit when trade improved. It was not just that shipyards were being closed temporarily during the slump; they were being dismantled so that it would be unlikely that there would ever be shipbuilding in the area again. There were tens of thousands of workers out of work now and the capitalists were making sure that there would never be such work again: all this was in order that the capitalist system should be safeguarded. The speaker reached his peroration 'My friends, are we going to stand for the behaviour of these clowns? Are we going to let ourselves be trampled on?' His audience listened to him silently. I thought – But people like watching clowns trampling on each other.

The speaker once came to join us for supper at our outdoor table after he had spoken. He was a young man with short fair hair: there seemed to be little back to his head: the skin of his face had a consistency like that of cloth. He sat with the blood-red sky of a sunset behind him. I thought – The blood has spilled on to the sky from his face, from the back of his head.

Peter Reece said 'So you are in favour of some sort of revolution.'

He said 'Oh no, we are on the side of the law, it is our opponents who are in favour of revolution.'

Peter Reece said 'But your opponents, surely, are the directors of National Shipbuilders Security.'

The man said 'Oh no, our real enemies are the Communists.'

Peter Reece said 'But the Communists seem to be saying exactly the same as you – at least with regard to the activities of National Shipbuilders Security.'

The man said 'Perhaps that is why we are enemies!' He laughed.

Peter Reece said 'Why?'

'Because we are diametrically opposed.'

'But what is the difference between you?'

'We are aiming at the highest and they at the lowest.'

'But they would say the same about you.'

'Yes.' He looked pleased.

Peter Reece said 'So it is matter of what is relative – '

The man said 'Ah, we don't hold with the Theory of Relativity!'

I said 'But you need enemies.'

He said 'Oh we have enemies all right!'

I thought – Oh yes, like the Harlequin in the pantomime, with a ladder and a plank of wood and a bucket of cement.

One evening the man was attacked on his way back to his lodgings after a speech: he was left bruised and bleeding by the roadside. Peter Reece visited him in his lodgings. I went with him. I thought – But at what point does the Good Samaritan become the enemy you need?

Peter Reece said 'But who attacked you? You think it was the Communists?'

The man said 'Oh it was the Communists all right!'

Peter Reece said 'Might it not have been people hired by National Shipbuilders Security?'

He said 'Oh I don't think they would be up to anything like that!'

He was sitting up in bed with his head and hands bandaged: his face, out of which the blood seemed to have run, seemed pleased.

Afterwards I said to Peter Reece 'I suppose that if people feel they have enemies then everything remains a game.'

Peter Reece said 'I don't want to live in a world in which people think everything is a game.'

I said 'What sort of world do you want?'

He said 'It is true, you know, that there would be no unemployment if there was a war.'

One day I took time off from the building of the Recreational Hall and went for a long walk along the line of the estuary. I started off through the area where I had seen the children playing the first day I had arrived; I hoped I might see them again. I did not know what I would do if I did; perhaps just wave; make a fluttering movement to the girl as if releasing a bird from my hands. It was a bright windy day; clouds moved like sailing ships in the sky. I had asked Peter Reece if he knew of a family whose child or children were deaf and dumb: he suggested that there might be such a family in an encampment of Gypsies that had set themselves up some distance along the estuary. This encampment was near an ancient church and the ruins of a monastery that had been founded in the seventh century: this, I had learned, was when Christianity had first come to this part of the country; it had been carried by men in small boats that blew across the sea like seeds; monks had settled and had built walls and within them had produced prayer, learning, corn, bread, fruit; they had illustrated what they were doing in exquisitely coloured manuscripts. From here further seeds had drifted across the land. I had said to Peter Reece 'Why can't you do something here like those monks of the Dark Ages?'

He had said 'Like what?'

'Pray, grow corn, illuminate manuscripts.'

'While people around starve?'

I thought I might say – What did those monks do for people who were hungry?

I did not see any signs of the children who had been rolling tyres down a hill. I had not really expected to. I thought – You do not see angels, do you, if you look for them.

I was moving past the area where there were huge cranes like the skeletons of birds; the few hulks of ships as if picked clean by vultures. I thought I might say to Peter Reece – You mean ships are needed, because they are sunk, in a war?

– And men are killed, and so men are needed, in a war?

I was moving out into an area of desolate mud-flats. I could see the squat shapes of the ancient church in the distance. It was like some resting animal. I thought – But what the monks produced in their fortress-monastery, how did it survive? Will what is produced in the banks and municipal buildings of the town survive?

– It is that which is beautiful that survives?

There was a dyke going across the mudflats towards the church; there was an embankment running alongside the dyke on which I could walk. I thought – But what was the message in the seeds that blew across the sea in small ships: there was news of – what? – the birth and then the death-no-not-death of a child?

– When those monks painted their manuscripts, they would have known that there was a message: they would properly not have quite known what the message was?

I had crossed the mudflats on the embankment of the dyke to where I could see the mounds and trees of the walls of what once must have been the monastery. And here there were, yes, children playing. There was no sign of the Gypsy encampment that Peter Reece had talked about: the children did not seem to be children I had seen before. I thought – But still, is not what I am looking for whatever will turn up. The wind had dropped so that the clouds were motionless in the sky: they were like seats, yes, from which some old gods might look down. I reached the end of the dyke and stepped over a wire fence into the area of what had once been the monastery. I thought – the monks received a messsage: it was with their hands, their eyes, that they imagined what the message was. It was difficult to see exactly what the children were doing: they were crouched in a circle, quite still, as if over something on the ground. One child seemed to have an object in its hand which it held carefully; there seemed to be a connection between this object and whatever was on the ground. The other children were watching: they all had their backs to the sky. Then as I got closer it seemed – But I know what they are doing! That child is holding a magnifying-glass in its hand: they are using it to concentrate the rays of the sun and to burn whatever it is on the ground. This was a game we had played at school – you found an ants' nest, perhaps; you chased the ants and shrivelled them up with the rays of the sun. And so you were like gods, looking so omnipotently down! I sat down on what seemed to be a fallen tombstone at some distance from the children; I watched, as I had watched the other children. I thought – But if it is children, of course, that come from seeds that are blown across the sea, still what do we learn? I stood up. The children noticed me: they turned and ran away. I thought – Oh but if I were a god I would not have minded your burning ants, would I, my children.

When I got to the place around which the children had been squatting I could still not at first see just what it was on the ground: they had been burning something, yes; there were the marks of scorching; there were things moving; they were not ants; they were not dead twigs; they were like the petals of a flower, growing. Then I realised that they were maggots. And what they were teeming on was some dead body on the ground. I thought at first that it was the body of some animal; a rat or a rabbit, perhaps. Then I saw that it was that of a child. Or rather of a foetus, at the most a newly-born child, perhaps from someone who had given birth here and had got rid of this child like a seed; and it had died, and so the children had come to burn with their glass the maggots that grew out of it. I found I could not think too much about this: I had bared my teeth: it seemed that I should just bury the dead body of the child. I looked round for something that would serve as a spade. There were some slates in a small pile of rubble by the child. I pulled at these, and there became dislodged from the pile a piece of coloured glass. The piece of glass was smooth and red and slightly convex like a small pool of blood. It seemed that the children might have been using just such a piece of glass to concentrate the rays of the sun. I used a slate to scrape at the rubble and cover the dead child. I wondered if there had been a stained-glass window here once, pieces of which had made splashes of light like blood. I succeeded in covering the child. I thought – And the maggots: oh they will live, they will die! There was one of the children at some distance from me standing at a corner of the church: it was watching me. It was somewhat like the small child who had been waiting in the clearing beneath the railway lines for the deaf-and-dumb girl who had been in the tyre: it wore a similar smock to just below its knees. I had picked up the piece of coloured glass and was looking at this; it was a strange deep red; it was very beautiful; it seemed to have retained some of the rays of the sun inside it, and not to have burned with them. The small child by the church was coming towards me; it seemed to be looking for what it might find among the stones. I thought, as I had thought before – Perhaps people will think it is to do with me, that body of a child. The child in the smock had come up to me and held out its hand: indeed, it seemed to be the boy-child that I had seen before with the girl in the tyre. I gave him the piece of blood-red glass I had been holding. The child took it, and put it in a pocket at the front of his smock. I thought – So this child collects coloured glass: to burn; to build windows with? Then – I see: but what? That seeds are being scattered like bits and pieces of light? That light does not only burn: and gods look down? And we can know this: what else need we know? That maggots sometimes grow wings and fly? The child turned away with its small piece of coloured glass.

When I got back to the rectory I found two letters which had come by the same post. One was from Melvyn. It said –

Please find out about the activities of a company called National Shipbuilders Security which is operating in your part of the world. It is run by a gang of international financiers and crypto-Fascists who are buying and dismantling temporarily out-of-work shipyards so that the effective power of the shipbuilding industry will pass to their masters, the gangsters of the United States and Japan. The active arm of the conglomerate is said to be this new so-called Radical Party. Be careful how you go! Such people would not be averse to using gangster methods to further their design.

The Prime Minister is almost certainly in their pay. His current mistress is an Austrian whose former husband was the chairman of the bank the failure of which was the direct cause of the formation of the National Government. Need I say more – as Henry VIII said when asked who was next to be beheaded.

Mullen seems temporarily to have taken leave of his senses and is interesting himself in that little girl you introduced us to at that party. I think he imagines that through her he might get some entrée to you. I suppose in the chariot position she might just be taken to be a boy.

Keep your pecker up, as the hangman said to the man he had just dropped.

The second letter was from the girl called Suzy. She said –

I have to thank you for what you have done for me as a result of our odd meeting at that party. My father has suddenly relented and says I can go to Paris. I think he is letting me do this in order to get me away from you. Someone seems to have been telling him terrible stories about you, and about those terrible people who he thinks are your friends. So I have been telling him I am madly in love with you, and so he is packing me off to Paris.

Of course, all this does make you madly interesting and I am a bit in love with you, so please get in touch with me when we both return to Cambridge.

I thought – Oh well, this is how things work, is it? Then – But there is no letter from my beautiful German girl.

Sometimes I walked with Peter Reece as he went about his business in the parish. He would go about on foot: he had a theory that people should normally go about on foot; then there might be time for things to sort themselves out.

I said 'You believe things do sort themselves out? I mean you do what you have to do, and other people do what they do; and what happens is likely to be all right?'

Peter Reece said 'What else is God?'

I said 'You mean "God" is a word for the fact that things sort themselves out, and not for the fact that there is a God.'

Peter Reece said 'What is the difference?'

We walked between rows of houses that were like stitching. The entrance to each house was through a yard at the back; at the front there were small gardens and just a footpath between them and those of the houses in the next row. Each backyard served two houses and in it there was a latrine on one side and a hut for coal on the other. I thought – It is more comfortable for people to live facing back? When Peter Reece went into the houses I usually stayed outside. I thought – As an anthropologist, I do not want to disturb these strange people.

I said to Peter Reece 'But whatever it is that happens, you could say that it was this that was being sorted out – '

Peter Reece said 'But there are some things that do not seem to be being sorted out.'

I said 'Such as – '

He said 'Love, for instance.'

I thought – He is thinking of the Good Samaritan? Of me?

– He is a bit in love with me? Then – I am mad to be so often thinking this!

Then – But perhaps love is that which gets the other stuff sorted out.

On the few occasions when I went in with Peter Reece to talk to families in their homes it seemed in fact evident that we were learning little about the families themselves; only about what they wanted to show to us. When they spoke among themselves I found it difficult to understand their dialect. I thought – But what is it that they do not show to us; what is it that goes on, as it were, behind their backyards?

I would say to them 'But what can anyone do about unemployment here if no one needs more ships? The only way in which people will want more ships will be if there is a war.'

'Oh we don't want another war.'

'So I mean, can't you do something different from building ships?'

'In this town we've always built ships.'

'Can't you change?'

'Change?'

'Yes.'

I thought – Oh this is a dialect they find hard to understand!

– They have the tombs of their ancestors behind their backyards?

Afterwards, walking home, Peter Reece would put his hand on my arm and flash his eyes and say 'You were lovely!' I would think – Well dear God, if he is a bit in love with me –

– What on earth is being sorted out?

I was waiting to hear from you, my beautiful German girl.

I had given you my address in the north of England. I had told you that it would surely not be difficult for you, with your Marxist group, to come to visit me in the place where there was the highest unemployment in England.

I tried to work out what it was that I felt about you at this time. Were you perhaps to me one of those ladies in the Middle Ages for whom knights went out to do heroic deeds: the knights could not stay except for moments with their beloved ladies, or where would be the heroic deeds?

I thought – But where are they anyway? And so, yes, I was waiting for you to visit me.

Peter Reece once said 'Have you ever been in love?'

I said 'I think so.'

He said 'I cannot imagine being loved by any human with whom one is in love.'

I thought – You mean, that is another reason for the use of the word 'God'?

Then one day there was a letter, yes, from you, my beautiful German girl. You said that you would certainly try to visit me when you came with your Marxist group to England. You added –

I have been discussing with Franz (you remember Franz?) what you say about Dirac. I am most interested in what is meant by 'chance'. Surely 'chance' is just a word for what cannot be explained by natural science. We call 'chance' what in our experiments is manifestly out of our control. But we still observe processes, patterns. One might as well use the word 'God'.

Oh I would dearly like to continue to bump into you just by chance! This would mean, Max, that we might imagine we could use the word 'God'. But then, of course, I might not bump into you! And this does not mean that I will not take care to travel to the north of England.

Do you understand what I say? No one else does.

Elena

I thought – Yes I know what you say, my beautiful German girl.

– Oh but let us be careful about the use of the word 'God'!

Then one evening soon after I had got this letter (how could I have expected you so quickly? I didn't expect you for another two or three weeks) – one evening when I had been on one of my long walks along the estuary, perhaps to look for children again or for pieces of coloured glass, I found Peter Reece waiting for me when I got back. He was standing at the foot of the scaffolding around the Hall, on which perhaps I should have been working longer hours. He looked embarrassed. I thought – Why should he be embarrassed? It is I who have been out wondering if I might see children, or angels. He said 'There have been people asking for you.'

I said 'Asking for me?'

He said 'I think it's the family of the girl you were talking about: the girl who is deaf and dumb.'

I said 'But they don't know about me!'

I thought – He is embarrassed because he has heard something awful has happened?

He said 'I think they'd like to see you.'

I said 'I haven't seen her since the first day I arrived!'

He said 'I've talked to the girl's mother.'

I said 'What did she say?'

He said 'You'd better go and see them.'

I thought – Do they think I've assaulted their daughter? Murdered some baby on that wasteland?

I said 'Is anything wrong?'

Peter Reece looked distressed. He said 'I don't know: is there?'

I thought – Or is he just jealous?

I set off that evening to the house, the whereabouts of which Peter Reece had described to me, which was where the family of the deaf-and-dumb girl lived. I was still thinking – But if it is the family of the deaf-and-dumb girl, why should they want to see me? Or rather, why should I not simply be pleased? Underneath the railway lines it was as if there had been some Annunciation. But what could they want to see me about that was not a threat? However, surely this would be better than doing something boring like continuing to try to find out about National Shipbuilders Security Limited. I was walking once more into the area of the houses that were like stitching. I was thinking – But of course, there seems to be some strange coincidence here: coincidence has to do with chance; with change? I was coming to the house of which Peter Reece had told me the number. There was the latrine on one side of the yard and the coal-shed on the other. There were no children visible as I went in. When I knocked at the door of the house it was opened by a dark thin woman in a pink flowered apron: she did look, yes, like a Gypsy. She wiped her hands on her apron. She said something in the dialect I found difficult to understand. I followed her into the kitchen which had a stove and a dresser and two rocking-chairs and a chest with a piece of carpet over it by the window. In one of the rocking-chairs there was an old woman, or man, it was difficult to tell – grey hair straggled down from a woollen cap with a bobble on the top: he or she had a large rug, or shawl, over the knees. The woman in the apron leaned with her back against the stove; the stove was out: it seemed that I was just doing what I had to be doing, I did not know what it was. I thought – You influence what you observe, all right, but what if you have no idea what it is you are observing? I said 'Father Reece said you wanted to see me.' The woman said something again in the dialect that I found difficult to understand. I thought – I can put my own interpretation on it: it will still be just this that is happening. I said 'It was your daughter I came across some time ago, was it, when she was playing by the railway lines?' I sat down on the chest which was underneath the window. There was a door at the far side of the room through to what might have been a bedroom; the woman was looking towards this door: the house seemed to have just one more room on the top floor. The woman said something which sounded like 'The lady said you might do something for her.' I did not think I could have heard this right. I did not even bother to say – What lady? I said 'Do what sort of thing for her?' The woman said 'Will you take her then?' It seemed I should say – Of course I won't take her. Then I thought – You mean, you want me to take her? I could make out less than ever what was happening. But I thought – Why should it not be all right if I don't know what is happening! The woman was looking at the old person in the rocking-chair. This person seemed to be trying to lift herself up slightly from the seat, as if she were adjusting herself on a lavatory. The woman by the stove said 'Well she can't stay here.' I thought – What do you mean, she can't stay here? The door at the back of the room opened and a man in shirtsleeves and braces came in. I said 'Hullo.' He said 'Hullo.' The woman said 'You stay out.' The man said 'I'm here.' I thought – It is not as if I were observing the situation, it is as if the situation were observing me. The man said something to the woman in the dialect that I found difficult to understand. The old person was still pushing herself up in the rocking-chair as if there were something underneath trying to get out: I thought – She is a woman, yes, and not a man: she seems to be trying to give birth. I said 'I came here because Father Reece said you wanted me to come; I understood it was something to do with your daughter.' The woman and the man were still talking between themselves. They were saying things like: 'You wanted him to take her' – 'Oh it's always me who wants things, is it!' – 'Well it is, isn't it?' – 'It was her as much as me!' – 'Your own child!' I thought – You mean, this man has been carrying on with his daughter? Then – Well that is not so strange, is it; in any old tribe. Then – You mean, they might be offering me their daughter? The woman was saying again to me 'Will you take her?' I said 'Take her where?' The woman said 'The lady told her you could get her help somewhere.' I said 'What lady?' I thought – What lady, yes, what lady? The man and woman were talking again between themselves. I thought – You mean there's something more here than even what I understand I don't understand: there is something playing like unheard, violent music. The woman was repeating 'Well she can't stay here!' Then – 'His own daughter!' The man said 'That's enough, mother, I've said I've agreed.' I said 'Who is this lady?' The man said 'The foreign lady.' I thought – This is ridiculous. I said 'What foreign lady?' The woman said 'The foreign lady who was looking for you at the same time she went up for you.' I thought – Who was looking for me? Who went up for me? The woman said 'She showed her the way.' I said 'Who showed who the way?' The woman said 'She told the foreign lady the way.' The man said 'She was asking for you.' I said 'Your daughter told the foreign lady the way?' Then – 'But I thought she couldn't speak.' The woman said 'Are you surprised after what he's done to her!' The man said 'That's enough, mother!' The woman said yet again 'His own daughter!' I thought – There is too much happening here all at once. The foreign lady: she was looking for me? The girl was looking for me too? I said 'But when was this, when did they meet, she and the foreign lady?' The woman said 'They were both there, at the rectory; they talked with Father Reece.' There was, it appeared, something stirring under the rocking-chair beneath the rug that was across the knees of the old woman. I thought – A cat or a dog? An incubus? Who would be surprised if the old woman was a witch! I said 'It is your daughter we are talking about, the one I thought couldn't speak, the young girl that I met down by the railway lines.' The man said 'She can talk when she likes.' The woman said 'The foreign lady said you might help her.' I said 'Now look, look, who is this foreign lady?' There were emerging from beneath the old person in the rocking-chair some small feet, some white bare legs, a behind in grey cotton pants. I thought – Well indeed, why shouldn't she be under the protection of some magic, this sort of angel! The girl crawled out from underneath the rug around the rocking-chair and sat crossed-legged on the floor. She smiled up at me. She was, of course, yes, my bright-eyed angel: the small girl who had gone bounding and bouncing to safety down a hill. I said 'Hello.' The girl smiled up at me. She made no movements with her hands. She had those brown-and-pink cheeks and bright black eyes: her legs were like shoots from the centre of a seed. She could have been, perhaps, nine, ten. I said 'Let's go and talk to Father Reece.' I held out my hand. Then I thought – Oh well, yes, perhaps you have been here, my beautiful German girl: is not this the sort of thing by which I shall know you have been here? The girl stood up; she took my hand. I thought – The last time I saw you, my beautiful German girl, it was by that castle and I was holding a child by the hand: and we had said that we had not wanted children! The woman was saying 'She has to be taken away from her own father!' The man was saying again 'That's enough, mother, I've said I've agreed!' I thought – Well, all right, if this is the sort of thing that goes round and round. I said to the mother and father 'We'll go; I'll let you know what happens.' The woman said 'But you'll help her?' I was holding the hand of the child. I thought – Oh but surely, my beautiful German girl, this does not mean you have come and now gone?

Then – But what if it is not bearable to live like this!

I walked through the streets holding the hand of the child.

There were bright white clouds as if gods were looking down.

The child walked beside me boldly.

When we came to the rectory Peter Reece seemed to be still standing where I had left him at the bottom of the scaffolding of the half-finished Recreational Hall. I said to him 'She was here. My friend was here. What the devil are you up to?'

Peter Reece said 'What the devil do you mean what am I up to?'

I said 'She spoke to you. My friend. A German girl.'

Peter Reece said 'I forgot. I'm sorry.'

'You couldn't have forgotten.'

'I was worried, I thought you were in some sort of trouble with the child.'

'Why should you think I was in some sort of trouble with the child?'

'She was with a group of Communists. Your friend. The German girl.'

'Where are they now?'

'They've gone.'

'Where to?'

'They went in a bus.'

'You're mad.'

'You were on one of your walks on your own. How do I know where you go when you walk on your own! I thought you were in trouble with the child.'

'Did she leave a note?'

'I'll ask.'

I said 'You don't know what you're doing.'

I was still holding the hand of the child. Peter Reece was watching me, moving from foot to foot; he seemed about to cry. I thought – Oh well, why should he not be jealous of angels.

He said 'I thought you said the child couldn't talk.'

I said 'Yes, I did.'

He said 'Well she talked to the German girl.'

I said 'She did?' Then – 'What did she say?'

'She told her where she thought you were.'

The child looked up at me brightly.

I said 'Can you find out if she left a note for me.'

Peter Reece began saying again 'I thought you might be in trouble – '

I said 'This girl is in trouble with her father.'

Peter Reece said 'Yes, I know.' Then – 'Why did your friend say you might be able to help her?'

I said 'Because I might be able to help her.'

Peter Reece said 'How?'

I said 'Will you get the note.'

While Peter Reece went off to the rectory I stood hand-in-hand with the child. I thought – Things do happen like this? If you don't expect them, but let them. Then – But you were here, this afternoon, my beautiful German girl, when I was down by the estuary, where small boats once blew like seeds on the wind, where in the mud there are bits of coloured glass. Could you not stay for me? Was there too much to be done? You said to the child 'I am sure we can do something for you' – ?

I said to the child, speaking slowly 'You do want me to help you?'

The child held my hand. She looked up at me brightly.

Peter Reece came back with the note that you had left for me.

Dearest Max,

Why are you not here? I told you I would come. The child is the only one who seems to know where I might find you. But I only have a few minutes. It was with much difficulty that I got people to call here in our bus.

Before I came here I did not know how much I wanted to see you. Now that I am here and you are not, I do! You will say 'Yes this is what happens!' Perhaps I would have stayed on if I had found you. Now I do not know what to do. I do not like your pastor.

Max, what is happening to us, do you know?

I hope you will be able to do something for the child. She said you had been good to her wherever it was you had met her: I imagined you meeting her in some forest! She wants to get away from her family. Whenever we meet, or nearly meet, you and I, there seems to be a child.

Will you telephone me before we leave London? I will tell you our address.

Max, what are we doing? I think we are mad.

With very much love from your
Nellie x x x x

I said to Peter Reece 'I will find out if legally I can do anything to help this girl. Can you see if there is a hostel run by nuns or something, where she can be looked after at least while I am away. I will go and talk to my mother about her.'

Peter Reece said 'You're going away?'

I said 'My mother will find her some school for the deaf and dumb, or whatever is wrong with her. My mother will pay. But she mustn't be made to go back to her father if she doesn't want to. Isn't that right?'

I said this to the child. She looked up at me brightly.

Peter Reece said 'How do you know your mother will pay?'

I said 'I hope your Recreational Hall falls down.'

Peter Reece said 'All right.'

I said 'You will help me find somewhere she can stay tonight?'

Peter Reece said 'I hope the whole bloody church falls down.'

I said 'You promise?'

Peter Reece said 'I've said all right!'

I thought – I don't suppose there's anything, is there, about the Good Samaritan having a girlfriend whom he missed because he was looking at something else when a bus went by.

When I got back to Cambridge, which was towards the end of that summer, I found that there was being built there a machine which, it was hoped, would 'split the atom' (this was a phrase already in journalistic use). Such a process had been achieved in embryo in 1919 when Rutherford had 'bombarded' (this was a word in both journalistic and scientific use) the nucleus of a nitrogen atom with alpha particles that emanated naturally from a radioactive substance, and lo and behold – a rabbit from a hat – out of the nucleus had popped a proton (well, I suppose words describe our attitude to whatever occurs) and the nucleus of the nitrogen atom had been changed into that of an oxygen atom, although the release of energy had been very small. But there had been a glimpse of the enormous forces that might be hidden within the atom.

The machine that was being built in Cambridge in the autumn of 1931 was more elaborate than Rutherford's toy-like apparatus of 1919; but it still had a bizarre appearance like something constructed as a prop for a modern ballet. It was like an outsize village pump crowned with a tin top hat: whoever worked it had to sit in a tea-chest lined with lead; this was to protect him from possible effects of radiation. But such was the excitement of the time that physicists did not worry much about radiation. What were to be bombarded now were the nuclei of lithium atoms – it was known that these were potentially unstable. They were to be bombarded with protons accelerated artificially to enormous speeds, so that this time there would be a man-made release of energy which, it was hoped, would be of a different order of strength from that achieved naturally by

Rutherford. But of course some of the excitement was in not exactly knowing what the effects might be: any energy released could presumably be used for either creation or destruction.

As early as 1914 H. G. Wells had published a story called 'The World Set Free' in which there had been imagined a release of power with just such ambivalent potentiality: this story had become formative of my own imagination in my childhood. Wells had described how the tapping of nuclear energy might transform the world: one lump of coal might be sufficient to drive an ocean liner across the Atlantic; nuclear-powered aeroplanes might flit in the sky like moths. He had also described how such energy could be used for destruction – or indeed how there could be interaction between destruction and creation. Atomic bombs could be built and there would thus be the threat that the human race, even the whole earth, might be destroyed: but also might it not be that the threat of such destruction would provide just the impetus that humans required to take a step forwards in evolution? On the brink of self-annihilation, they might find themselves driven to come together to formulate a system, a state of mind rather, in which there might be no more war. In Wells's story, part of the human race was in fact destroyed; but the remainder came to its senses. I wondered in 1931 – How better might humans be pushed to come to their senses?

There was the Indian god Shiva, was there not, who was the god of both creation and destruction – or rather of the interaction between the two – who danced within his circle of fire. Humans have always known – How can you have creation without destruction? Energy is just energy: it is up to humans to choose between, or to handle, the two.

When I got back to Cambridge I went to see Donald to find out what was going on. Donald had stopped doing philosophy and was back in physics: he had been encouraged to do this, he said, by Wittgenstein. I said 'When did that happen?' Donald said 'After that party.' I thought – Oh yes, at that party, there were a lot of things happening all at once!

I said to Donald 'But with this attempt to split the atom, has anyone any idea what the effects might be?'

Donald said 'Of course they wouldn't carry on with the experiment unless they thought that they had it under control.'

I said 'But they wouldn't learn anything if they had it perfectly under control.'

Donald said 'The experiments are to observe changes within an atom, not changes within human beings.'

I said 'Mightn't they be interconnected?'

Donald said 'I am a physicist now: I think philosophy is senseless.'

I went to see Melvyn: it was as if he had never left his room. His white face seemed to be made of cloth. I thought – Perhaps the bodies of politicians assume the consistency of puppets: to be successful, they have to be things that cannot change.

I said 'Have you thought how odd it is that these things should be happening in physics just at a time when old orders of things in the political world are cracking up? When there seems to be some impetus on every level for change. I mean humans will either harness new energy as a result of these crack-ups or else they can blow themselves up. Does it not make one think that there may be some connections between these apparently different orders of things – the human and the scientific?'

Melvyn said 'Ducky, who have you been reading, St John the simply Divine?'

I said 'No one in the north seemed to care very much about the activities of National Shipbuilders Security Limited: they know that if no one wants more ships then more ships can't be built. They want to make some sort of protest about this order of things: but they don't want to change it.'

Melvyn said 'Ducky, stop being an organ-grinder, and on the concrete situation start sharpening a few knives.'

I said 'As a matter of fact, I think National Shipbuilders Security Limited are thinking of building some concrete ships, then they will sink, and there won't even have to be a war.'

Melvyn said 'Darling, has anyone told you that you're becoming a bore?'

I went to see my mother as soon as I had come down from the north: my father was away on a lecture tour in Russia. I bicycled to the village which I seemed to have been away from for years: there were the walls on which I had climbed as a child; the gate through to the lawn on which I had eventually been able to beat my father at croquet. I wondered – I feel I have left childhood behind, because I am trying to look after a child?

I found my mother sitting on the seat in the bow window where I had sat with her so many times in the past: where I had rested my head on her shoulder while she read to me stories of boys going out in search of wisdom and hidden treasure, or how they had been helped by the answering of riddles. My mother had the light behind her: I thought – I usually imagine her with the light behind her: she is the Indian goddess Devi, or Kali, of creation and destruction. Then – Why is it that the goddess of creation and destruction has two names, while the god Shiva only has one? Is it because it is difficult for men to accept that with their mothers the two are one? I said 'Hullo.' My mother said 'Hullo.' I wondered – But do I mean that this makes women, mothers, more or less devious: or, of course, both?

My mother said 'Did you have a nice time?' I said 'Yes, thank you.' She said 'What did you do?' I said 'We were building this Recreational Hall, you know.' My mother said 'How sweet!'

I thought – she is angry with me because I have not visited her much this summer? She has been drinking? Or, of course, both.

I had begun to notice, as well of course as not to want to notice, that my mother had begun to drink quite heavily at this time.

She said 'And did people love you for that?'

I said 'Not particularly.'

'Did you think they would?'

I had gone up to kiss her on the cheek. When our faces were together I smelled the scent that might have been a cover-up for something different.

I thought – But of course, between mother and son, there is creation and destruction.

I said 'What I don't see is, why the working class don't start a revolution.'

I thought – But I have just been describing to Melvyn why they don't.

She said 'Well that's quite obvious, isn't it?'

'Why?'

'People don't want to die.'

'I thought Freud said they did.'

'Oh you've only been home two minutes, and you're going to get at me about Freud, are you!'

I thought – Oh yes, all conversations are for the purposes of defence or attack. I should just be making flicking movements with my hands.

I said 'As a matter of fact, I want to ask you something very important.'

She said 'Oh what is that?'

I said 'You know how Freud was struck by how many of his

patients said that they had had incestuous relationships with their parents, and then he thought that in fact they were having fantasies – '

My mother was gazing at me with a crumpled look as if there was too much weight on her from the light from the window behind her.

I said – 'Well what made Freud think that these were fantasies and not facts?'

My mother said 'The whole theory of psychoanalysis is built on the idea that they were fantasies.

I said 'But is it true?'

After a moment my mother said 'You do see what you are doing by asking me, don't you?'

I thought – She thinks I am talking about her and me?

At that moment, as so often happened at our family gatherings, the conversation had to be broken off because Watson the parlour-maid came in with tea. There were tomato sandwiches and cakes, which had been old favourites of mine since childhood; so I had to chat to Watson and thank her and tell her how glad I was to see her. I thought – How could anyone ever have thought that spoken words are to do with the imparting of information?

When Watson had gone I said to my mother 'I came across this girl in the north of England – '

My mother said 'I knew it!'

'What did you know?'

'I knew as soon as you came in that you were going to be horrible to me!'

I said 'This girl is nine or ten. She has difficulty speaking.'

My mother said 'You looked so pleased with yourself!' She laughed.

I thought – Freud did not get round to seeing that Oedipus might have wanted to give some sort of nasty shock to his mother?

I said 'This girl has been involved in an incestuous relationship with her father. It seems that this has affected her, and her ability to speak, traumatically. I wondered – this is your line of business – if you could help me do something about her.'

After a time my mother said 'Why do you think this?'

I said 'Why do I think what? That she has had some incestuous relationship with her father?'

My mother said 'My point is, what are you yourself doing when you are telling me this now?'

I thought – If my mother has been drinking, this is simply dull.

Or – If she goes on thinking I am talking about her and me, I can use this?

I said 'What do you mean, what am I doing when I am telling you this?'

She said 'It is not for me to tell you what you are doing.'

I said 'Look, I came here to talk to you about a nine-year-old girl who either is, or acts as if she is, deaf and dumb. You know special schools, don't you? You know people who are involved in child analysis?'

My mother said 'You want to rescue her from her terrible father – or mother?'

I said 'The trouble with psychoanalysis is that it is an evasion of responsibility. Analysts turn any request for help back on to a question of the motives of the person requesting it. I think this is perhaps what causes the real traumas in children: what Freud called the "death wish".'

My mother said 'I see.'

I said 'What if the people being analysed just turned all questions back on to the motives of the analyst? They would usually be too kind – or too sober.'

My mother said 'Get out.'

I said 'But these are facts, not fantasies. What are you going to do about facts?'

My mother said 'You want me to be responsible for a nine-year-old girl?'

I said 'She has to be got away from her father.'

She said 'Like you have to be got away from your mother.'

I said 'We all have to grow up. Will you help this girl?'

My mother said 'You find her attractive, do you, this nine-year-old girl?'

I said 'Did you find me attractive when I was ten?'

My mother said again 'Get out.'

As I went to the door I thought – But I have handled this badly. Then when I was going out of the room my mother called 'Come back!'

I thought – So now we are coming to something interesting in this experiment?

I said 'I'm sorry.'

She said 'What are you sorry about?'

I said 'I don't know. I wanted to say I'm sorry.'

She said 'Of course there is always something attractive about helplessness.' Then – 'But you do know now how to put the boot in, don't you!'

I had come back into the room. I thought – So here is the great goddess Devi, or Kali, dancing in her circle of fire. I said 'I just wanted to help this girl.'

My mother said 'All right I'll help you. What do you want me to do?'

I said 'Is there anything practical you can do about getting her into some special school? She is being looked after at the moment by nuns.'

My mother said 'Nuns are sometimes all right.'

I said 'Will you pay?'

She said 'Yes.'

I said 'Thank you.' Then – 'For God's sake, let's both get sloshed.'

I was standing in front of my mother. She took me by the hand and pulled me towards her. She said 'You stay away the whole summer: you come back and insult your old mother – '

I thought – Yes, this sort of thing –

I said ' – And then I turn up with a ten-year-old bride – '

She said 'You noticed I was tiddly?'

I said 'Yes.'

She said 'How brave of you to tell me!'

I said 'How brave of you to say, how brave of you to tell me – '

She said 'Ah, you see, you're quite fond of your old mother!'

There was a day when I went on my bicycle into the countryside. I was reminded of the time when, as a boy, I had gone to the ruined boathouse: there had been that itch, that pressure, like a demand to be put to the test: to suffer heroically for some phantom: to perform experiments on myself concerning the interactions between creation and destruction. This pressure was here again: I thought – So what do people do: start revolutions, win empires, sail round the globe: pull down roofs over their heads, break up orderliness within atoms. I went on the road which led to the ruined boathouse (one looks at one's childhood from time to time in order to imagine one might be free of it?) but I found that the huge country house had been demolished; there were tractors on the path going down to the lake and the boathouse; this part of my childhood was being erased. I thought – This pressure comes out somewhere, but where, if not in a ruined boathouse on a broken chair? I bicycled on to a country pub and got some beer and sat on a bench outside in the autumn sun. I thought – You mean, as we grow up, there are less harmless methods of destruction and creation? There were one or two couples in the bar of the pub; I had not paid much attention to them as I had ordered my beer. Now, looking through a window, I saw two men moving quickly and quietly to a door at the back of the bar: one of them was Mullen. The other was a short man with a round bald head wearing a brown suit. Mullen glanced in the direction of my window as he went through the door: it was as if he had seen me when I had been at the bar, and was now trying to avoid me. The other man had looked like a Russian. I thought – But of course, I would want to imagine he is a Russian! Then – But don't be taken in by this, he really might be a Russian. The two of them had gone out through the door at the back. I thought – Or are they just going to the gentlemen's lavatory, to do just whatever people like Mullen do in gentlemen's lavatories. I went through the garden round the side of the pub; there was a yard at the back, yes, with an outside lavatory; there was no one in it; there was the sound of a car starting up on the road. I was sure that Mullen must have seen me when I had ordered beer. I thought – Well, what if that other man really was a Russian, and they wanted to avoid me? You see what you want to see perhaps; but what do you know? I went round to the front of the pub. There was no car on the road. I thought – This is it, this pressure: other people than myself become involved in images, plans, of destruction and creation.

I had a letter from you, my beautiful German girl. There was the address in your neat, formal handwriting that was like something cut on stone.

Dear Max,

I could not have waited. I told you I had to return to the bus.

Your pastor did not tell me you were coming back. He suggested that you might be away some time.

The child was standing by the building when I arrived. She seemed to know who I meant when I asked for you. It seemed she had some connection with you. Yes, she spoke to me. She said she hoped to see you.

Yes, I remember how when we left each other at that castle you were going off with a child.

I did not enjoy my visit to England. I made my party come the whole way across England to see you.

I am thinking of joining the Communist Party. Here, with the danger of the Nazis, one has to be either one thing or the other. It is not good trusting any longer to chance.

No, I do not suppose I will be coming again to England. Of course, I would love to see you if you come to Germany.

I am glad that this girl you are taking an interest in is being taken care of by your mother.

I think there has to be some commitment to the struggle. I do not understand what you seem to be interested in in England. You could have telephoned me in London if you had liked.

No, I do not know the painting you refer to of a closed door at the back of a courtyard.

With love from Eleanor

I thought – Oh God damn you, my beautiful German girl!
– I did telephone you in London! But you had gone.
Then – It is true I might have telephoned earlier –
– But I will go to Germany and put things right!
At this time all these people circling round me – Peter Reece, Melvyn, Mullen, now even my beautiful German girl – seemed to want to commit themselves to something like suspending themselves from an unbreakable beam in the ceiling –
– While I, what was I, falling, falling, in empty space –
– Committing myself not to the struggle, but to chance?
There was a day not long after this time – it was just before Christmas; I had been getting somewhat depressed: I had been thinking – It is all very well, yes, to be on the look-out for this world that is said to be unobservable by the observer: the world of pure, but unknowable, chance and effect –
– But what is love; what is home? There must be something more than the suspension of disbelief, as it were, in a ruined boathouse –
There was a day when I was at Cambridge and I had been lying on my bed and becoming depressed like this, when there was a knock on my door and I said 'Come in' and someone put their head round the door whom for a second I did not recognise and then I saw that it was the girl called Suzy. She said 'Am I allowed to come in?' I said 'I don't know, are you?' She said 'I mean, what are the college rules?' I said 'Oh the college rules!' She had had her hair cut short. I said 'I was just thinking about you.' She said 'Were you?' I said 'Yes, but I didn't know it was you.' She said 'What were you thinking?'

I said 'I was wondering whether, if you came in now, we might possibly – '

She said 'Were you really?'

I said 'But if I had known it was you, you might not have come in.'

She came and sat on the edge of my bed. She was very young and pretty and healthy-looking. She said 'Half the time I don't understand what you're saying. But never mind, you seem to do the trick.'

I thought – But what's the trick?

I said 'How's Paris?'

She said 'Very well, thank you.'

'Why aren't you there?'

'I'm here for Christmas, then I'm going back.'

I said 'And what's the trick?'

'My father still thinks I'm in love with you.'

'And aren't you?'

'I don't know.'

I thought I might say – Then let's find out.

She said 'But I think I have to do a bit more to convince my father.'

I said 'Then let's do the trick.'

While we undressed she said 'You don't sound very enthusiastic.'

'I'm struck dumb.'

'That's unlike you.'

'I'm practising.'

We were like people about to go swimming from a pebbly beach. I thought – But of course, I hardly dare believe this.

She said 'I wanted to make love with someone before I went back to Paris.'

I said 'Why?'

She said 'Never mind.'

I said 'Then aren't I lucky.'

I thought – I mean, luck is when you have not imagined what you would or would not mind.

Afterwards she said 'That was nice. Thank you.'

I said 'Thank you too!'

She said 'Aren't you going to say you love me?'

'No.'

'Why not?'

'Perhaps I do, and it'll go away.'

'That means you don't.'

'No.'

'Why not?'

'I haven't said it.'

We lay like babies in a pram underneath the leaves, the shadows.

She said 'Have you got a girlfriend?'

'Yes.'

'Do you love her?'

'Yes.'

'Does that mean you don't?'

'No.'

'But you said it.'

'I said it to you.'

Then I thought – Why don't I go to Paris and settle down with this lovely English girl? I am tired of all the tricky stuff: though of course if it were not for the tricky stuff I would not be with this lovely English girl –

She said 'Why not come to Paris?'

I said 'Perhaps I will.'

'Who is your girlfriend?'

'She's German.'

'How often do you see her?'

'Not often.'

She said 'Well I'm not going to ask you why not.'

I thought – But this tricky stuff is all right, isn't it, in the end; I mean it is all right for us, my beautiful German girl?

V: Eleanor

You thought that life should be seen as if it were in the form of a painting: but you saw that aesthetics was not separate from morality?

One has to catch connections, coincidences, yes, rather than try to impose them: perhaps it is the chance of this that is created behind the closed doors of a courtyard.

I left the University of Freiburg in the summer of 1932. I went to stay for a time with my father in Heidelberg. He told me of the marvellous piece of machinery that had been built in Cambridge the previous winter and which had now succeeded in what was called 'splitting the atom'. It was indeed representative of both creation and destruction – like the alchemists' philosopher's stone, or the gold stolen by Alberich from the bottom of a river.

I said to my father 'This discovery is symbolic? It has no practical use?'

My father said 'A thing is not symbolic, usually, unless it has a practical use.'

I had wondered, yes, if I would see you again. I had for some time imagined us as figures in some modern-style fairy story – as two entities which, having once met, would never quite be separate again. But this did not make it clear that we would meet, nor did I know that such imagery was about to become scientific.

From Heidelberg I went to Berlin. I wanted to visit my mother. I had not been to Berlin for nearly two years. My mother was still an active member of the German Communist Party. I was thinking, as I told you, of joining the Communist Party myself. I wanted to be committed, all-of-a-piece. I did not want to be a particle with neither velocity nor location.

I said to my father 'I don't know when I'll see you again.'

He said 'You will give my love to your mother?'

I thought – My father has not seen my mother for – what? – four, five years? Yet there is a sense in which he does not feel separate from her.

When I arrived in Berlin there were processions of Nazis with torches in the streets. They were dead-faced, sweating men as if on their way to light some funeral pyre.

In the elections of the summer of 1932 the Nazis had become the largest single party in the Reichstag; it seemed inevitable that they would get power. No other party seemed to have the will to get power, yet still on the brink people dithered. Von Papen became Chancellor, then von Schleicher became Chancellor; what a jump in the dark it would be for Hitler to become Chancellor! People seemed to be standing on the edge of a cliff and closing their eyes and holding their noses.

Certainly the Communists did not seem to want to get power. They imagined that they had been told by Karl Marx that, before a true socialist society could be achieved, the death-throes of capitalism had to be gone through – this was an inevitability of history – and the death-throes of capitalism were represented by Fascism or Nazism. So the Nazis had to be accepted – in an 'objective' sense to be encouraged even – so that the proper historical way could be paved for the Communist revolution. In another sense, of course, the Nazis remained the enemies: in the 'concrete situation' they had to be fought in the streets. There was something slightly mad about Communists at this time; they were like archaic statues smiling and walking forwards, one side of the brain not quite letting the other know what it was doing. This was called, in the jargon, the 'dialectic'. As well as madness, of course, it could be seen as a form of esoteric knowledge like that at the heart of the philosopher's stone.

When I got to Berlin, the Communists were so reconciled to the prospect of the Nazis getting power that they were preparing to go underground. I did not know what to make of this: how can you objectively be on your way to a true revolution if you are standing smiling on the edge of a grave and are waiting to be pushed in? It did not occur to me that people might feel at home in this sort of thing.

I found my mother at work in the building behind Alexanderplatz: she was in her small office next door to where printing machinery clattered and whirred. Her desk was littered with papers, cigarette ash, dust, shavings from pencils. She was like a bird who has been trying to build a nest, and has failed.

I thought – I must have been a cuckoo in her small, fierce nest: but it was herself, and not me, that was pushed out.

She said 'Hullo.'

'Hullo.'

'Is that fancy dress you are wearing?'

'No, it's a skirt I bought when I was in England last year.'

'It makes you look like a child.'

I thought – You do not want me to look like a child? You do not want to hear about my visit to England last year?

I said 'I wondered if you had any work for me here.'

She said 'Work for you here?'

'For the Party.'

'You want to join the Party?'

'Yes.'

My mother had a cigarette which she was trying to keep alight on a small metal tray on her desk. She worked at it, puffing, then put it down carefully on the tray; then she coughed and watched it roll off on to her papers.

'We can't pay you, you know.'

'I know. I've got a little money from Father.'

'You've got money from your father?'

'Yes.'

My mother had got this habit, which I had not noticed in her before, of repeating what I had just said in the form of a question. I thought – This is what people do when they feel they have to protect themselves: when one side of the brain feels itself threatened by the other?

I said 'It doesn't matter if you haven't got work for me here. I can go and stay with Bruno, who is living in something called the Rosa Luxemburg Block.'

My mother said 'Bruno is living in the Rosa Luxemburg Block?'

My mother had a photograph of Rosa Luxemburg on her desk.

Rosa Luxemburg was the bright-eyed, slightly crooked-nosed lady that I had know as a child; she had come to our apartment, had held me to her breast, then had been hit on the head and thrown into a canal. In the photograph she was wearing one of her flowered hats. I wondered – Did one side of her head have time to know, suddenly, what the other was suffering?

My mother said 'You're seeing Bruno?'

I said 'Yes.'

'You should be careful.'

'You know he's now a member of the Party?'

'We're having a certain amount of trouble with the people in that block.'

I thought I might say – You're having a certain amount of trouble with the people in that block?

My mother managed at that moment to catch the attention of a man who was passing in the passage with his arms full of papers: she spoke to him; he stood still, and as if long-suffering, with the papers in his arms. I thought – This is like those times in our apartment in Cranachstrasse when Helga the parlourmaid came into the dining-room and whatever of interest might be being said had to stop: it was as if servants were censors between one side of the brain and the other. Now instead of servants it seemed that my mother for this purpose had her cough, her cigarettes, and just any comrade in the passage who happened to be passing with his arms full of papers. After a time my mother stopped talking and the man went on.

Mother said 'Sorry – ?'

I said 'As a matter of fact Bruno has been doing some very interesting work for the Party: he has been involved in the editing of some of the early manuscripts of Karl Marx. Do you know about these early manuscripts of Karl Marx?'

My mother was chewing the inside of her lips and looking at the photograph of Rosa Luxemburg; it was as if she were carrying on a conversation with Rosa Luxemburg just inside her head.

I said 'These early manuscripts seem to be very interesting because they are saying that true socialism, or Communism, is not to do with argument, with reason, which is often playing with words, but with the work one does with one's hands. I mean a person has a sense of the aesthetic value of himself only in relation to the work that he is doing with his hands – '   .

My mother began coughing and her cigarette rolled off its tray on to her papers: she began beating at her papers, and ash flew over her desk. I thought – To create a diversion, she might be a bird that would set fire to its nest.

I said 'And what is interesting is that this idea in Karl Marx is almost exactly the same as what Heidegger has been saying, who has now been taken up by the Nazis. Do you think it is because of this that – '

My mother said 'This is what Bruno has been telling you?'

I had been going to say – Is it because of this that we are not taking our opposition to the Nazis seriously? But I thought – If I say that I will be playing tricks with words.

The man with his arms full of papers came back along the passage. He paused by the door and looked in at my mother as if to see whether he was needed.

I said 'No, someone else told me that.'

My mother said 'Who?'

I said 'Franz.'

My mother pulled a piece of paper towards her and rummaged about on her desk; she looked through the door but the man with the papers had gone.

My mother said 'Franz is a Nazi.'

I said 'Apparently.'

'And Bruno's family are Social Fascists.'

'They're Social Democrats.'

'Socialists who are not with the Party can be called Social Fascists.'

I said 'They're Jews!'

I thought – But I must be careful here: though surely there is a way in which to talk of such things without tricks.

I remembered of course the argument that, in an 'objective' sense, Communists should feel more hostile to the Social Democrats than to the Nazis because Social Democrats appeared to be trying to delay the death-throes of capitalism and so were making it difficult for true Communism to arise from Fascism's ashes. I thought – But surely you can see the ugliness of the trick that calls left-wing Jews Social Fascists!

My mother seemed to be having a conversation inside her mouth with the photograph of Rosa Luxemburg.

I said 'But I don't see the point of this playing about with words. We may think it's inevitable that the Nazis will get power, all right;

but shouldn't we be fighting them for the sake of what will come after?'

My mother said 'Bruno says it is inevitable that the Nazis will get power?'

'No, I thought it was the kind of thing you were saying.'

'I never said it!'

'But you're preparing to go underground – '

'Do you know how many of our people have been killed in the streets?'

I thought – But either this conversation is mad, or is it in fact a good dialectical trick that one side of the Party's brain should not admit to the other that the Nazis should get power?

I said 'But surely it's important, on some level, to admit to yourself at least what you're doing; to give a hint perhaps to other people that you know – '

My mother said 'I don't know what you're talking about.'

I said 'I see.'

I thought – It may be that I am a child in all this: but what is this style that has no regard for a child –

My mother said 'Perhaps it would be useful, after all, to have someone in the Rosa Luxemburg Block. You can let me know what the people with Bruno are doing.'

I said 'Why, what are they doing?'

She said again, as if it were a phrase in which she had been rehearsed 'We're having a certain amount of trouble with the people in that block.'

I thought – You want me to be a spy?

I said 'You mean, you think there may be spies or traitors in that block?'

My mother said 'Have I said anything about spies and traitors?'

When I was out in the street I thought – Perhaps, after all, this is normal in politics: you have to make out you do not know what you are, so that when things go wrong it can be believed that you have not known what you were doing –

– Otherwise you could not bear it?

– But things will come round, in the end, on the curve of the universe; and they either will or will not hit you on the back of the head.

In the streets of Berlin there was something of the same atmosphere as there had been when I was a child: a sense of aftermath, of premonition, of things in suspension here and now. When I had been a child there had been the impression of enormous events round some corner: these had manifested themselves only perhaps when the soldiers going out through the Brandenburg Gate had turned and fired on the crowd. But now there were these lines of Nazis coming marching from around their corners: it was as if they were the urgent heralds, harbingers, of enormous events to be unveiled; they had none of the tricks or innocence of people who did not know what they were doing; with their sweating faces and flaming torches they were simply people out to light funeral pyres.

I thought – Or they are like long lines of shit, these Brownshirts, churning in someone's insides –

– Will not the inevitability of natural history mean that they will have to dump themselves as muck on the world outside?

That evening when I left my mother I made my way to the Rosa Luxemburg Block. This was a workers' tenement building now occupied mostly by left-wing students and intellectuals – 'intellectual' being a word to describe any Party member not of working-class origins. People gather together according to type at times of crisis, and it was true that in the summer there had been dozens, even hundreds of Party members killed in street fights with the Nazis. But people in the Rosa Luxemburg Block seemed to be far more conscious of their own danger than, for instance, the people in the building where my mother worked: they sheltered behind barricaded doors and shuttered windows. I wondered – Is this because as 'intellectuals' they are more frightened or more in the forefront of the street-fighting with the Nazis? Or is it just that it has traditionally been the role of intellectuals to be picked on by both sides as potential enemies or traitors; so indeed there might be reason for their apprehension of danger?

When I first arrived at the Block I was taken into a guardroom at the side of the barricaded front door: there was a girl sitting on a mattress on the floor cleaning a rifle; a man and a woman were keeping watch through slits in the boarded-up window. I was made to stand in the middle of the room while I was questioned by a man in a Trotsky-style cap: the others pretended not to notice I was there. I thought – But these people are like actors; they are acting what they have learned from films about people keeping watch through slits in the window; they have had to learn to act, because they are not working class.

The man with the cap said 'You are looking for Bruno?'

'Yes.'

'You have information that Bruno is here?'

I said 'I have a letter from Bruno. He suggested I might join him.'

I held out to the man in the cap a letter that I had had from Bruno when I had been with my father in Heidelberg. Before he took the letter the man looked as if for instructions at the girl who was sitting on a mattress on the floor cleaning the rifle. The girl did not look up. After a time the man took the letter.

I thought – It might have been a better shot, in a film, if the girl had leaned forwards in a disinterested manner and put a drop more oil on the rag with which she was cleaning the rifle.

I said 'And perhaps you know my mother: I have just come from her.'

I told them my mother's name and the name of the building behind Alexanderplatz.

The man in the cloth cap said 'You have just come from your mother in Alexanderplatz?'

I waited while he read Bruno's letter. I thought – It might have been a mistake to mention my mother. Then – But these people are not professionals: they may simply be having difficulty with their scripts.

I said 'Is there some trouble between you and the people at Alexanderplatz?'

The man with the Trotsky cap said 'Your mother told you that?'

I wanted to say – But there is no script! There is no stage! We are all at the edge of a cliff!

After a time the man with the cap sent the woman by the window to find Bruno. The girl with the rifle took the woman's place by the window. The man with the cap sat down on the mattress. I leaned with my back against a wall. I thought – All right, in such situations we have to be actors, but should we not also be writers of our scripts?

Then – But how can I truly work with these people!

The woman who had been by the window came back into the room and was followed by Bruno. When Bruno saw me he at first pretended not to know who I was; he gazed around blankly. I wanted to say – But Bruno, you will have us shot! Then he seemed to recognise me suddenly: he put a hand up over his eyes; he backed away to the opposite wall with his other hand groping behind him.

He said as if he were obviously quoting ' – Have I yet eyes to see? Now in my soul doth beauty's source reveal its rich outpouring – '

I said 'Stop it, Bruno.'

He said 'That's the password! Right!' Then he came and put his arms around me.

I said 'When Faust says "Stop!" – it's the password?'

Bruno looked at the man with the Trotsky cap. He said 'You see?'

Bruno held me at arm's length. He had grown thinner and more pale. He had dark rings round his eyes, as if tiredness had got lodged there like dirt against a grating. I thought – And within his huge soft eyes there is something like fingers groping through with a message.

He said 'We have to be careful! There are traitors everywhere: spies! That's the official Party line!'

I thought – Bruno, you can't get away with this!

The man in the Trotsky cap watched us. Then I thought – But this style – this is the message that Bruno is carrying?

I went to live with Bruno in the Rosa Luxemburg Block. This was at the end of October 1932. Few people in the Block had any sort of work at this time: there were six million unemployed in Germany. Food and fuel had to be scrounged: it was difficult not to act as if one were some sort of outlaw. I thought – Indeed, perhaps it is reasonable for people to feel themselves on the edge of a cliff and not caring too much about who pushes them over.

But then in new elections in November the Nazis actually lost seats in the Reichstag; the Communists gained: it seemed that at last the country had realised that it might not have to jump or be pushed. But still – what on earth were people to do if they did not now go over a cliff: wander for ever in lost multitudes in a desert?

When I first moved in to the Rosa Luxemburg Block the inhabitants were organised into cells of about twenty people: this was for the purposes of administration and defence. Then after a time we were split further into cells of just five or six people: the point of this, it was explained, was that if we did have to go underground then only the leader of each cell would know the identities of the other four or five in his cell and only he would have contact with a Party member higher up in the heirarchy; this was in order that, if anyone was taken prisoner by the Nazis, it would be difficult for him or her to betray more than a few of their colleagues.

I said to Bruno 'But why is all this happening just when the Nazis have lost seats in the Reichstag and the Communists have gained? I mean why are we preparing to go underground now?'

Bruno said 'But think what a terrible betrayal of history it will be for Communists if the Nazis go on losing seats in the Reichstag! Of course we will want to hide our heads in shame underground!'

I said 'But what is the point of our being split into cells of five or six people so that we can't betray each other? We all know each other in the Rosa Luxemburg Block!'

He said 'That's why I pretended not to know you when I first saw you.'

'Why?'

'I was practising.'

'Practising what?'

He said 'Oh it takes a lot of practice to know you're an actor: to pretend not to know what you do know, to be able to be what you are.'

Bruno and I began by being in the same larger cell: then we were split up, and had to move into an all-female and an all-male dormitory at opposite ends of the building.

I said 'You mean, practising how to stay alive – '

Bruno said 'Oh but you mustn't say that! Think of the Party line!'

I said 'You're the one who seems to want to get us shot – '

He said 'In the dialectic perhaps: not in the concrete situation.'

Bruno and I did manage to sleep together from time to time. He would come along to my dormitory at night and would put his head in at the door and say 'I have the password' and one of the three or four other girls would say 'What?' and Bruno would say something like 'Workers of the world unite!' or 'Has anyone lost their chains?' One or two of the girls would laugh; one or two did not. I would think – But Bruno, Bruno, you think in the end jokes may keep us alive?

I once said 'But I wanted something to commit myself to!'

Bruno acted as if he were someone like my mother 'You wanted something to commit yourself to?'

I said 'Everyone already seems to think we're traitors, you and I.'

Bruno said 'With everyone lined up, as you say, at the edge of a cliff, who are traitors – '

I said 'Then shouldn't we get out?'

Bruno said 'Where would we go?' Then – 'Anywhere else, how could we even make jokes!'

The group of cells of which I was a member met once a week to be given instruction by a cell leader on the current Party line, or to hear a lecture on Marxist-Leninist theory by someone higher in the hierarchy. We were told of the manoeuvrings that were going on in the Reichstag between the Nationalists and the Nazis and the Communists and the Social Democrats: in theory it might be supposed that there was common ground between the former two on the one hand and the latter two on the other: but in the concrete situation, of course, we knew according to the iron laws of history that it was in the interests of the first three often to combine against the Social Democrats. I thought – But of course, the point of this sort of language is that the brain becomes paralysed.

– But you mean, if we know the danger of the brain becoming paralysed we might learn how to tip-toe along these high-wire Party lines of words?

I said to Bruno 'You mean, if you know language has almost nothing to do with truth, this knowledge might be some form of truth?'

Bruno said 'Sh!'

I said 'But how could you ever communicate – '

Bruno looked at me with reproachful eyes. He said 'Nellie!'

I said 'Yes, I see.'

Part of the political activity we were engaged in in the Block was the distribution of the pamphlets and newspapers that were written and printed by the group working with my mother. We would pick up the bundles in a car from the building behind Alexanderplatz and dump them at various points through the city. Once or twice in the summer our cars had been ambushed and attacked; we now travelled with two or three men with truncheons or even guns on the front seat and the running-boards. I had some part in these activities because I had bought a small second-hand car with some of the money from my father, and this car was sometimes borrowed for these operations. I was not allowed to go on these expeditions myself. I protested about this. I thought – But of course, the most satisfactory position might be to protest and still not to be allowed to go on the expeditions.

However – What if in fact the situation is that Bruno and I are not trusted?'

Bruno said 'Wasn't it you who told me the legend that there are seven just Jews who, without knowing the existence of each other – probably without knowing their nature themselves – keep the sanity of the world intact?'

I thought – Perhaps it is true that I don't really know Bruno.

Bruno said 'I know what you're thinking!'

I thought – It would be necessary for such people not to know each other, or else they would feel absurd.

Then – But all this is an image; for what might keep one's own sanity intact.

One day a grenade was thrown into the back of one of our cars that was distributing newspapers; three of our people were injured; one later died. The injured were carried into a room at the back of the guardroom of the Rosa Luxemburg Block and I, because of my medical training, was put to look after them. I had not trained as a surgeon: I had to dig out splinters of metal from the arms, the face. I thought – Now will they trust me? Then – But feelings here are not to do with trust. They are to do with what people need for their identity and location.

Heidegger had suggested that life becomes authentic when lived in the presence of death: I thought – But this means living in the presence of one's own likely death: in the presence of other people's one just puts up defences.

I said to Bruno 'But the idea of those seven just Jews is perhaps a metaphor for what it might be right for everyone to feel: otherwise they would feel absurd.'

Bruno said 'I wonder what's happened to old Franz.'

I said 'Franz is a Nazi.'

Bruno said 'What, and not even a Jew?'

I had not tried to get in touch with Franz since I had come to Berlin: it was from my father that I had heard he had become something of a Nazi. He had been working in the physics department of the University of Berlin. I used to wonder – Will he meet Einstein? Or has be become like one of those absurd people on the stage of that theatre who Einstein so mockingly applauded.

I said to Bruno 'But do you think it would matter if one or two of such people appeared to be on different sides? I mean, would not one or two almost have to appear to be on different sides because one of the points would be that sides do not matter.'

Bruno said 'Oh but sides do matter!'

I said 'What people do on them matters.'

Bruno said 'Isn't that the same?'

I said 'Not necessarily.' Then 'I'd like to find out from Franz what's going on in physics.'

Bruno said 'Oh that's good – yes – I'd like to find out from Franz what's going on in physics – !'

In retaliation for the grenade that had been thrown into the back of our car one of our groups had fired shots at some Nazis who were sticking posters on a wall. In retaliation for this a car-load of Nazis with a machine-gun came past our Block one evening and fired through the windows; none of us was hurt; and in fact the Nazis' car broke down at the end of the street, but we were too frightened, behind our barricaded walls, to sally out in pursuit. Afterwards we were ashamed of this – so there was a meeting of cell leaders in the Block and it was decided that this time we should make a large-scale effort at retaliation. It was difficult to get near the barrack-like buildings where the Nazi Brownshirts lived because these were well guarded: it was decided that an attack should be made on one of the clubs, or cafés, where the Nazis congregated in the evenings.

I said to Bruno 'Do you ever get frightened?'

Bruno said 'Do I ever get frightened!'

I said 'Is that why we can't get out?'

Bruno said 'Oh I see: the test is, to stay where we're frightened?'

The plan for retaliation was that two or three of our group should climb up on to the roof of a certain café building and should drop a grenade or a home-made bomb through a skylight on to the company below. It was known that Nazis frequented this club or café; it was also known that it was some sort of brothel. A car was needed for the approach to the club and for the getaway. I was asked if I would lend my car: it was also suggested that Bruno should drive it.

I said to Bruno 'But other people like playing these games: you're no good at them!'

Bruno said 'Oh yes, we're on the side of reality.'

I said 'I mean, why do you think they've chosen you?'

He said, 'You mean, I might not be able to get up at the end of the third act?'

I had imagined that I would not be involved in the raid on the café-brothel just as I had not been involved with the uses to which my car had been put before. But now the chairman of the Retaliatory Strike Committee came to me and said that there was a job for me to do. He looked away towards the door. I thought – He is waiting for a diversion like someone coming past with an armful of papers.

Then – But why indeed are they taking so much trouble this time for both Bruno and me to be involved?

It appeared that the job that had been worked out for me was to dress up as a streetwalker or prostitute and to hang about in the street outside the café-club so that I could be some kind of liaison between the people on the roof and the getaway car which would be round some corner. Because the club was also a brothel, this in theory might seem to make sense: but in fact it did not, for why should someone pretending to be a prostitute outside a brothel be any less likely to be picked up and questioned than anyone else? When I mentioned this the eyes of the chairman again drifted away. I thought – He would not mind if Bruno and I were picked up and questioned?

When I began to tell Bruno my doubts about dressing up as a prostitute he said 'Anyway, it's a transvestite brothel.'

I said 'Bruno, how do you know?'

Bruno said 'A joke!'

I thought – Bruno, you think you can do anything with jokes!

Bruno and I joined the other members of the Retaliatory Strike Committee round a table on which there was a sketch-map spread out of the streets in the area of the brothel. I thought – Now we are officers in a dug-out scene in a film about the Great War: where do these images come from; where are they going? Is it that there are wars and so we have these images, or that our minds have these images and so there are wars?

There did not seem to be any sense in there being a liaison between the waiting car and the people on the roof – except that it completed some design on the map. The chairman of the Committee had small steel spectacles and a drooping moustache; he waved a pencil above the map. I thought – He is conjuring up a vision of heroes; of people who on paper have identity and location.

Then – Why did those people in the Great War not get out? Because if the war was in everyone's mind, there was nowhere for them to go?

– But just by seeing this, Bruno and I think we can get out?

It seemed that I should visit my mother before I went on the raid: I might not see her again; I felt I might get some hold on what on earth I was up to. My mother was in her two-roomed apartment at the top of the building in which she worked; she shared these rooms with a woman friend who had once also been a friend of Rosa Luxemburg. I had wondered – Do my mother and this woman make love? Then – What does it mean if one has no difficulty in imagining one's mother and a woman making love –

– That there is nothing about which one is caring?

My mother was propped up in bed with a shawl around her: she said that she had a feverish headache. She had often said she had a feverish headache when I had been a child. I wondered – Does she now understand any more what she is protecting herself against?

The woman who had also been a friend of Rosa Luxemburg's was not there. I thought I might say – I would not mind, you know, if she were.

I told my mother about the raid. I said 'But it doesn't make much sense. We're going to drop a bomb through the skylight of a brothel.'

I waited for my mother to say – You are going to drop a bomb through the skylight of a brothel?

She wrapped her shawl around her and rocked backwards and forwards. She said 'Your father never had much time for brothels.'

I thought – She has in fact gone mad? Then – She is plotting something like a witch?

I said 'I suppose it's dangerous.'

She said 'I blame Bruno.'

'You blame Bruno what for?'

'For getting you into this.'

'For getting me into what?'

She said 'He took you once before to a brothel.'

I thought – There is something purposeful in this madness. Then – Who told her that: my father?

I cooked a meal for my mother on a gas-ring in a corner of her bedroom. She tried to insist that she did not want anything to eat. She hugged her shawl around her. I thought – But this may be the last time I will see you, my mother!

I said 'Why have you got it in for Bruno?'

She said 'I never liked him. His parents were snobs.'

'You talk about him as if he might be a spy.'

She said 'Yes.' Then – 'Probably it's because you're my daughter.'

I thought – But if you can see that, can't you see everything?

– I mean, isn't everything all right?

I sat on the edge of her bed and ate sausages and beans I had cooked for her: she still would not eat anything. I thought I might say to Bruno – She does understand: but perhaps she has been in too long to want to get out.

Then – Of course I am trying to defend my mother.

I said 'Why can't we let the Nazis just get on with it, whatever it is, if we think they're anyway going to pull the roof down on their heads?'

My mother said 'You still have to go through with it.'

I said 'Even if you die?'

My mother said 'You think you achieve anything without being ready to die?'

I thought – All right. Then – But you shouldn't be saying this to your daughter, O my mother!

Before I left her I said 'You won't tell anyone that I've told you about the raid, will you: we're not supposed to have told anyone.'

My mother said 'You think I'm a spy? Did Bruno say that?'

I thought – God damn! And I thought everything might be all right.

I said 'Goodbye.'

She said 'Goodbye.'

Walking through streets I thought – Oh mothers, what is it about mothers? We are tied to them as if by some terrible rope to the centre of the earth: we cut the rope and we go flying off through the universe; we do not cut the rope and our life-blood runs backwards like that of a baby left lying on the edge of a bed.

I had an almost physical sensation of being pulled in different directions at once: an arm here, a leg there: perhaps I would disintegrate: perhaps there would be a mad confident voice repeating my cries as questions as I fell through the universe.

Back in the Rosa Luxemburg Block preparations were going ahead for the raid. The home-made bomb was like a children's toy with bits of bottles and wires. I sat on the edge of my bed and prepared the clothes I had to dress up in. I said to myself, as if I were my own mother – Take care, my little one.

I said to Bruno 'What is it about Jewish mothers?'

Bruno said 'Oh they have a very important message about life!'

I said 'What?'

Bruno said 'If you sick it up for breakfast, you'll have it back for tea.'

I thought – But what we are doing here is evil: I think good may come out of evil –

– But it is not good to dwell on thinking like this.

You know the style in which streetwalkers in Berlin dressed at that time – high heels, short tight skirt, furs round shoulders like a life-belt; you've seen the paintings and anyway I've told you – well why was this supposed to be attractive? There must have been some cord dragging people back to an area of phantoms. When the time came for the raid we dressed up in the room behind the guardroom; this was where the people who had been wounded had lain; we were putting ourselves in a position to get wounded; there were these cords, tie-ups, in the brain. We were soldiers going off for a raid in war: well, why do soldiers do it? They do not hate the enemy: they like to dress up in plumes, furs, breastplates. But if humans had not liked playing soldiers, how would they have survived? I mean how would they have fought against mammoths, bears, tigers – except in some sort of ecstasy, with the feathers of dead birds in their hair? I was dressed up in my ghastly tart's uniform for the parade or raid; the others were in black – bombers, burglars, hung with the tools of their trade. And now it was too late to turn back; we ourselves were like bombs ticking with little mechanisms inside us; sooner or later we would go off; tamper with the mechanism and all of us would die, let it go and perhaps one or two would live. And then wake up and find ourselves in some cold new world on the edge of a bed. Bruno and I did not look at each other much. He had put on a jacket like that of a chauffeur. I thought – But in my small car, who would have a chauffeur! We went out into the street; we piled into the car. I thought – Of course, we are on our way to a fancy-dress party. It suddenly did seem, with clarity, that I saw what we were doing: we were some sort of children doing what Mummy was telling us; we could not get out of going to the party because we would be alone and too much in the cold. But what was Mummy? Mummy was what in our minds we were tied to. But was I not now also myself looking down? We drove through streets. I wanted to say again – Hullo my little one! It's all right, my darling! We stopped the car a block or two from the café. We got out. Bruno was to wait with the car unless something untoward occurred – a gang of Nazis turned up, for instance – in which case he was to drive round the block to find me and I was to signal to the people on the roof. Or if something went wrong on the roof the people could signal to me, and I could pass the message on to Bruno: then we could all make our own way home. Sometimes this made sense: sometimes it was ridiculous. I thought – Does this depend on whether you look on it from the point of view of a child or a mother? Then – But could not the child help the mother to see that this is ridiculous?

I was on my own now: the others had gone on ahead. I was playing the part of a streetwalker. Of course it was in my interest to play the part quite well or I might be caught; so here I was, high heels, furs, cold air coming in between; clip-clopping on the pavement. So this was being in the presence of death! Looking down on myself as if from the edge of a bed; a tart dressed up to help drop a bomb through the skylight of a brothel. And just because I could see this did I think I could say – Hullo, hullo, my little one! The three people who were to climb up on to the roof had gone off down an alleyway. They had been like schoolboys, indeed, with satchels over their shoulders. I thought – But I must be careful; I do want, after all, to live? I came to the street where there was the back entrance to the café-brothel. The street was empty as most streets were in Berlin at night at this time: there was too much violence; though the violence would also go on, of course, indoors, in torture-cellars, brothels. I went and stood in the doorway of a courtyard from which I could see the back of the building across the road. There was a parapet at the level of the roof at which, if things went to plan, the raiders might briefly appear and indicate any message to be transmitted. I thought – Well, what might we learn from knowing that this is ridiculous, my little one. There was the sound of a car at the end of the street. I thought – Well, either it is Bruno or it is not: in either event, I am a tart in this doorway. The car came towards me down the road. It was my car and Bruno was driving. Bruno was staring straight ahead: he seemed to be smiling. I thought – He is getting out; he is one of those mad archaic statues. Then – I know, but how do I know, that something has gone wrong: Bruno is telling me but, of course, he cannot be seen to be telling me. I stayed where I was in the doorway. Bruno had not looked at me. There were people running in the wake of the car, chasing it; they were calling out; they were, yes, a group of Nazis. When they got close to me they slowed to a walk; there were five or six boys; they were talking and laughing. One of them saw me and stopped: the others went on towards the back door of the café-brothel. I thought – But we never discussed what happens to me if I am simply approached as a tart: even for Bruno and me, that was a joke we did not think of talking about. The boy who had not gone on with the others was coming towards me: he had taken off his cap and held it in his hand; he had fair hair; he wore a Brownshirt uniform. I thought – But he is quite like Franz. I had been thinking, had I not, quite recently, of getting in touch with Franz. I had thought he might be able to tell me something of importance. The other Nazi boys had gone in through the back door of the café; they had called out mockingly to the one who was now standing in front of me. One of the raiders at this point appeared at the parapet on the rooftop; he was looking in my direction: I thought – Well, you will get the message, won't you? Is it or is it not just that I am being picked up as a tart. The boy who was like Franz said 'Hullo.' I said 'Hullo.' I was standing in the shadows of the doorway. He said 'Have you got a light?' I said 'Yes.' He pulled out a cigarette-case that seemed to be made of silver; he offered me a cigarette. I took one. Then I had to say 'I'm sorry, I haven't got a light.' He said 'Oh that's all right!' I thought – Oh well, yes, this is all right, isn't it? He pulled out a lighter and lit my cigarette. Then he lit his own. He was a good-looking boy, not so tall as Franz, but with a lean face and clear skin. We blew smoke about. The raider on the roof had disappeared from the parapet. The boy who was like Franz said 'Don't go in there.' He made a gesture with his head to the back door of the café-brothel. I said 'Why not?' He said 'There's going to be trouble.' I said 'Trouble?' He said 'A raid.' I thought – Oh dear God, yes, there is some sort of message here! The boy and I stood close to each other; we blew smoke about. After a time I said 'How do you know?' He said 'We've had a tip-off.' I thought – Well a tart might say, mightn't she, 'What sort of tip-off?' The boy had taken me by the arm and was trying to move me into the light of a street-lamp. I tried to resist. Then I thought – But I have to try to get information, don't I? I let the Nazi boy move me into the light of a street-lamp and I stared up at him. After a time I said 'What sort of tip-off?' He said 'What do you do?' I said 'What?' Then 'Oh, anything.' He said 'Anything?' I said 'Yes.' He was this good-looking boy dressed up in a Brownshirt uniform: he was staring at me. I thought – Well, somewhere or other he is a child on the edge of a bed. He said 'Do you do English lessons?' I thought – English lessons? Then – Oh English lessons, yes. Then – Would you know what 'English lessons' are, my beautiful English boy! I said 'If you like.' He said 'You are beautiful.' I thought – Dear God, is this the message, that they like to be given English lessons, these terrible, beautiful Nazi boys? Then – But should I not thus be able to find out what I need to know? There was an explosion from somewhere inside the café-brothel; bits of glass fell out into the street. Someone started screaming. The Nazi boy said 'I must go, but can I see you?' I said 'Yes.' He said 'Where?' I said 'Here.' He had not stopped looking at me when there had been the explosion. He said 'Can I really?' He put his head down meekly in front of my shoulders. I thought – Oh you are a child all right; you were lain over the edge of a bed by your mother? I put my hand on his arm and held it firmly. I said 'Who was it who gave you the tip-off?' He said 'Why do you want to know?' I said 'Just tell me!' He said 'It was one of their own people.' I said 'Who?' He said 'I don't know.' After a time I said 'All right, you can go.' Then I put my hand up and touched his cheek. He seemed transfixed. I moved away. I thought – So after all, this is not ridiculous?

There was the arrangement that if anything went wrong with the plans we would make our own ways back to the Rosa Luxemburg Block. The Nazi boy did not try to stop me as I walked away: I did not think that he would. I thought – Oh but I have heard stories about how Nazis like to be treated like that: to be beaten, shat on –

– Perhaps that's why they like to get people with mops and pails out on to the streets –

– To compensate for wanting this to happen to themselves?

I was a tart clumping along the pavement in high-heeled shoes. Bruno had come past in the car like a mad archaic statue.

But who had given the tip-off: Bruno might be suspected?

But it was Bruno who had nearly been caught! Or was he in fact just getting away –

And it was myself who had been seen talking to a Brownshirt in a doorway.

I thought – You mean, we all might like being beaten; being shat on –

– What else are we up to?

When I got back to the Rosa Luxemburg Block I found all the others had got back too. The raid had been a success – I mean the bomb had been dropped through the skylight of the brothel; it was likely that Nazis had been injured, even killed. I thought – So what would be the point if I told the story of a tip-off? Would it not just seem that I was out to cause trouble –

– It would be just to myself or Bruno that I would be causing pain?

The people in the Rosa Luxemburg Block were excited, yes: they were on the look-out through cracks in barricaded doors and windows: the enemy might come at any moment! I thought – I do not need to complicate their game.

Bruno's story was that the gang of Nazi boys had come running up where he was in the car; he had had to get away to avoid them.

My story was that I had managed to distract the attention of the Nazi boys while the raiding party was on the roof. I thought – Well, if I make myself into something of a heroine, is not this a point of the game?

Bruno stayed in the dormitory at the other end of the building: for a night or two he did not come to see me. So I went to him and found him lying on his back on his bed. I said 'We came through.' He said 'Yes.' I said 'One of the Nazi boys told me that they had had some sort of tip-off.'

Bruno said 'What Nazi boy?'

I said 'The one I told you about: who spoke to me in the doorway.'

Bruno said 'For God's sake, what were you two doing talking about a tip-off?'

I thought – You don't mean, for God's sake, that you think I might be a traitor?

Bruno lay on his back with his hands folded. I thought – But perhaps he knows (or is he acting?) that it was him, after all, that someone was out to get.

I left Bruno. I thought – That Nazi boy had such sad blue eyes! He had been quite like Franz. I wondered – Well why should I not see Franz; if he can give me information; and if everyone is thinking anyway that everyone else is a traitor?

One of the results of the raid was that it was decided that it was no longer safe for me to go about in my car. So the Block Central Committee took it over.

At Christmastime I telephoned Franz at his home. He was not there. I left a message saying that I would telephone again. I could not ask him to telephone me, because I was at the Rosa Luxemburg Block.

I thought – Traitors may be those who wish to break up old dead forms of alignment: people on the side of life want to break up old alignments: but there is a difference.

I felt cold and sad. Bruno continued to seem not to want to talk to me. I thought – Perhaps he is in touch with something with which he does not want to involve me.

When I telephoned Franz's home again I found that he had left a message to say that if I telephoned when he was out would I meet him at such a time on such a day for coffee at the Adlon Hotel. I thought – The Adlon Hotel! Shall I dress up as one of those so much higher-class tarts, O my father.

I thought – But it was Bruno who said 'I wonder what's happened to old Franz', as if there might be some virtue to be found in this.

For my meeting with Franz I wore a white shirt and the tartan kilt that I had got in England: I thought – This makes me look like the sort of girl who might be the friend of a Nazi.

On my way through the streets I felt again – But if I am a spy I want to understand how things work: I am an agent for understanding in hostile territory.

In the hallway of the Adlon Hotel there were a lot of foreigners; they seemed alert, watchful. I thought – They have come on the chance of seeing terrible events round some corner. There were a few Nazis standing about bright-eyed, glowing: I thought – It is as if they are about to be flogged.

There were none of the financiers with cigars and women with acorn hats that I remembered from the times when I had come here with my father. I wondered – Where are they now? Looking through cracks in the shutters of guardrooms; wielding burning cigarette-ends in brothels?

There seemed to be something sexual, yes, in the excitement of the foreigners and Nazis in the hotel, at the prospect perhaps of seeing something unnameable happening round a corner.

I could not at first see Franz. There was a boy with fair hair in a Brownshirt uniform whom I imagined for a moment might be Franz: or he might be the boy with whom there had been that air of excitement in that doorway –

Franz was half hidden behind a pillar by the staircase. He had been watching me. When I saw him, for a time he did not move. Then he came over and said 'I thought you might not recognise me.'

I said 'Why not?'

He said 'You might have thought I had changed.'

I thought – But I do think you have changed!

We went to a table and ordered coffee and cakes and ices. Franz was paler and more thin. He wore a grey double-breasted suit in the lapel of which was a small swastika badge. When I looked at it he said 'I could have taken it off.'

I said 'I might have put my badge on.'

He said 'What is yours?'

I said 'Oh, the hammer and sickle. The Star of David.'

He said 'That one's different.'

I said 'Why?'

He looked away across the room. Then he said in a quiet voice as if quoting ' – But on a dark night can you tell the difference – '

Then he turned and looked into my eyes as if he was searching for something there. I thought – For whatever might be behind the closed door of a courtyard –

He said 'You remember what we used to say about power?'

I said 'What?'

He said 'That all ganging together, alignment, is self-destructive.'

I said 'I see.'

I was wondering how there might be described the atmosphere in the hallway of the hotel: it was as if people were on their toes, were on their way to becoming slightly elevated with tension. This was the sexuality of fakirs who lie on hot coals; who cut themselves with knives and there are no marks of wounds in the morning.

I thought – There have been rumours that Hitler might even now be being made Chancellor?

Franz had looked away around the room. When he talked he seemed to be talking to no one in particular; as if he did not mind whether or not, or by whom, his words might be picked up; as if it were likely that they would fall on stony ground.

He said 'You remember I used to say "I do not think it is worth living if the world goes on like this: there is either blindness or such disgust!" Well, why should the world go on? At least things will have very nearly to die, before they change.'

I thought – There are dark rings around Franz's eyes as there are around Bruno's; bits of exhaustion that have got stuck in a grating in a stream.

Then – But are there such rings round mine? Is this a badge that we share?

I said 'That is why you're a Nazi?'

Franz said 'Ever since the Enlightenment, men have thought that they could dominate the world: they've wanted to dominate it by reason. But no one has had the courage, yet, really to try. The Nazis want to try. Well, we'll see what will happen.'

I said 'But Nazis are nothing to do with reason!'

Franz said 'What do you think reason in action is? If things get in your way, remove them.'

I said 'But the way the Nazis are on is nothing to do with reason!'

Franz said 'But that is on a different level from technique. Of course, the way they are on might be to do with destruction.'

There was a group of Jewish businessmen coming down the

stairs. At least, I thought they were Jewish businessmen because they were like those men who, years ago, had been in the Adlon Hotel when I had come with my father. They wore black jackets and striped trousers: they carried document-cases under their arms. I thought – Or this is the way the mind works; we just call them Jewish businessmen; these images get stuck like flotsam against a grating.

Then – But these businessmen must know that this is the way the mind works: why do they choose to be seen like this? Where are the rings of knowing around their eyes!

Then Franz said 'Are you still in touch with that English friend of yours?'

I said 'Yes, I sometimes hear from him.'

Franz said 'Could you put me in touch with him? He is a physicist, isn't he? I'd very much like to ask him some questions.'

I said 'Yes, I'll give you his address.' I thought – But is that why you wanted to see me?

After a time Franz said 'You remember how Heidegger used to say that human life is only lived authentically when one is aware of the presence of death; that without this, there is only the impoverished rubbish of materialism. Well, what happens when you know that power is self-destructive? What, after all, might it be that is killed?'

The group of businessmen had gone to a table in the lounge. They were sorting out papers and replacing them in their document cases: they were not talking. They seemed both aware and unaware that in the lounge and hallway of the Adlon Hotel there had fallen a slight hush: that people were watching them. It was as if the lights in the auditorium of a theatre were going down: a curtain going up. I thought – They can hardly fail to know that they are on some sort of stage!

Franz said 'If the human race does not learn to look at the business of death it will not be a viable species: there will have been too much self-deception. And how else do we learn except through catastrophe? What is evolution?'

I said 'You mean, you think the Nazis might look at the business of what has to die? But they will be more than self-destructive!'

Franz said 'Do you know what work in physics your friend has been doing in England?'

Franz and I were sitting in the lounge of the Adlon Hotel. We were eating our cakes and ices. I thought – But we ourselves are just off the stage: is it as if we are prompters?

Then – It was I myself who wanted to ask Franz about physics!

The group of businessmen who might be Jewish were standing round a formation of chairs and a table in the lounge: they were facing inwards; they seemed to be posing for an illustration. I thought – Oh they are still like that image I used to have years ago of the General Theory of Relativity: a group of people stand facing inwards and what each one sees comes round and hits him on the back of the head.

Franz said 'The head of my department was granted an interview with Hitler the other day. He wanted to make some protest about what seems to be the attitude of the Nazis towards the Jewish academics and especially scientists. Nazis have been saying that if they get power they will turn Jewish academics out of the universities and even out of the country. The head of my department wanted to tell Hitler what a disaster it would be if this policy was carried out; much of the research work in chemistry and physics is being done by Jews; the industrial and indeed even military strength of the country might depend on this work. And Hitler seemed to hear him. I mean he seemed to hear the words – this was the head of my department's description of him – but it was as if he heard something quite different in the way of meaning. It was as if Hitler was getting – the head of my department did not quite know how to describe this – some almost sensuous pleasure from the words; he went up and down on his toes; he seemed to be glowing. And then, when the head of my department had finished, Hitler came over to him and put a hand on his arm and said in a voice that was almost caressing – this is exactly what he said, it makes one's mind go numb – "There are greater things than victory: more terrible things than death."'

There was a group of Brownshirts by the porter's desk in the hallway of the hotel. They were watching the businessmen who might be Jewish in the lounge. The Brownshirts had their feet apart and their stomachs pressed forwards and their thumbs in their belts as if they were peeing. I thought – Oh God, all right, they are showing that they like being peed on.

Franz said 'What do you make of that?'

I said 'I see.'

Franz said 'The head of my department said that Hitler seemed to have no smell.'

I said 'Do you mean that the Nazis might bring about a change in the world, like devils are supposed to do?'

He said 'A change for the better?'

I said 'Is that what you can't ever say?' Then – 'I have sometimes thought that people like us, you and I, by being observers, might be carriers of what might come after.'

The businessmen were moving towards the door into the street. They had to move past the group of Brownshirts. The hush in the hall had slackened; now it intensified again. As the businessmen went past the Brownshirts one of the latter broke off from his group and followed; he crouched at the knees and let his arms hang down like an ape; he made a grunting noise; then he returned to his group and laughed. One of the businessmen who seemed to be Jewish stopped and turned. I thought – Oh but will not someone kindly go and piss on that Brownshirt if it comforts him!

Franz was looking at me. He said 'Carriers of what?'

I said 'You're not watching.'

Franz said 'I am.'

I said 'Of what we know but can't of course say or even quite see.'

The crowd in the hallway of the hotel had been both watching and trying to seem not to watch the scene going on between the Brownshirts and the businessmen. I thought – But what is the use, for God's sake, in such a situation, of what you can't say or even quite see?

Franz had been looking at the scene in the hallway of the hotel. He said 'You mean, all this is boring.'

I thought – Boring!

The businessman who had turned was still watching the group of Brownshirts. The Brownshirt who had mocked him had now turned and faced him – his thumbs in his belt and his stomach pushed forwards. I thought – But do you not want it to die, this that is boring!

Franz stood up and went over to the Brownshirt and clicked his heels and bowed; then he took out of his pocket a card which he held out to the Brownshirt. After a time, the Brownshirt took it. He smiled somewhat sheepishly. Then Franz went to the door of the hotel into the street and held it open for the group of Jewish businessmen. He bowed to them slightly. The Brownshirts watched him.

I wanted to shout – Oh Franz, I do love you!

As the group of businessmen who seemed to be Jewish went out of the door each one of them bowed to Franz; Franz acknowledged them. When Franz came back past the Brownshirts he stood to attention and clicked his heels again. He seemed to be waiting for some reaction. Then one of the Brownshirts laughed. Then they all began laughing. I wanted to say – But Franz, Franz, be careful; they may kill you!

When Franz came back to my table he said 'Terrible people.'

I said 'Franz, I will do anything for you!'

He said 'Will you come upstairs with me?'

I said 'Yes.'

He said 'I've got a room.' Then 'Of course, I staged this whole scene. I knew I would have to do more than just book a room to get you.'

When we were in Franz's room, somewhere at the top of the hotel, Franz hugged me and buried his face in my hair. He said 'Carriers of what, of what! Let me carry you, let me carry me – '

I said 'Do you know the story of Judith and Holofernes?'

Franz said 'Oh for God's sake, do I know the story of Judith and Holofernes!' Then – 'Please, if you want to, chop my head off.'

After we had made love, I had thought – There was a time, once, when I thought that Franz was like a dead crusader –

Franz said 'Do you ever see Bruno?'

I said 'Yes, I see Bruno.'

Franz said 'Tell him to get out.' Franz's face was still buried in my hair. Then he said 'You and Bruno and your mother should get out.'

I thought – How extraordinary to throw in my mother!

Then – But oh Franz, you would not get out!

This was Christmas 1932: a month before Hitler became Chancellor. There were the processions sweating through the streets at night; columns of Brownshirts like a demonstration of intestines with shit. The news in the papers was of the comings and goings at the Chancellery and the President's Palace: photographs were of ugly men like insects on the steps of public buildings. I thought – These are rituals so that life may go on: they are nothing to do with what sort of life might be worth going on with.

In the Rosa Luxemburg Block we waited and watched behind our barricaded doors and windows. I thought – But perhaps I am like a tick waiting to drop onto the hide of whatever strange animal comes lumbering by; to burrow into its bloodstream; to feed off its guts through a long winter.

Or – Life might be worthwhile so long as we can have these images?

I said to Bruno 'I saw Franz the other day.'

Bruno said 'Good old Franz, how is he?'

'He calls himself, but I don't think he really is, a Nazi.'

'I know.'

'He said you and I, we should get out.'

Bruno said 'Good old Franz, is he getting out?'

We had a lecture in the Block one day from a girl who had just come back from Russia. She told us of the miraculous things that were being done under the five-year plan: how dams and power stations were being built; how after only three and a half years of the plan, the Soviet Union now could hold its own against any industrial nation in the world. I thought – But how would one know whether or not such stories are true: or has it really to be accepted that truth is no more than the effect that is made on listeners?

I was sitting next to Bruno. Bruno gazed back at the lecturer with his huge troubled eyes. I wished I had remembered to tell Franz what Bruno had said – 'In a society lined up at the edge of a cliff, who are the traitors?'

But then – Who are the agents of evolution?

After a time the lecturer glared at her audience and said 'You may have seen stories in the Fascist press about conditions on the agricultural front. These stories are lies; but it is necessary to face squarely in the spirit of revolutionary self-criticism the fact that attempts have been made by opportunist elements, yes, to sabotage heroic efforts on the agricultural front. Crops have been burned and cattle have been killed by criminally sectarian peasants or Kulaks rather than that their produce should be provided for the town. So be warned, comrades! The price of freedom is eternal vigilance!'

Bruno clapped loudly and said 'Bravo!'

I thought – For God's sake, Bruno –

Then – There was that lecture years ago at which my father and I saw Einstein clapping and mocking –

At the end of the lecture there was an opportunity for discussion. Bruno stood up and frowned accusingly at the lecturer.

I thought – But Bruno, do you want us to survive?

Bruno said 'Should we not pay more concrete tribute to the

foresight of Comrade Stalin in ensuring that there has been this failure in the five-year plan – '

I whispered 'Sit down, Bruno – '

Bruno said ' – for otherwise how could saboteurs and criminals be weeded out!'

Bruno sat down. After a time the lecturer said 'But there has been no failure in the five-year plan.'

Bruno said 'Are you saying that it is not Fascist revisionism to deny that for criminals to be weeded out there shall be revolutionary self-criticism?' He glared round the room with his eyebrows raised. No one looked at him.

I thought – Bruno, I suppose this might be one way of getting out!

Bruno leaned back with his hands in his pockets and closed his eyes.

I thought – What about my arranging a meeting at the Adlon Hotel between Bruno and Franz and me – and you, my English boy?

One day Bruno and I went by bus and on foot to the cold and windy lake where, eight or nine years before, Bruno and Trixie and I had come to row and walk between trees and lie on pine-needles and play at making love. Here we had discovered some world of love; we had been like seeds, had germinated within ourselves something that seemed to have a life of its own. Bruno and I went to re-visit Kleist's grave: houses had been built in the area so that the tomb was now in a space between gardens; there were empty bottles and bits of cardboard within the fence around the grave. On the stone there was the message – 'He lived and sang and suffered in hard and sorrowful times: he sought death on this spot and found immortality.'

Bruno and I stood looking at the grave holding hands. I thought – We humans, yes, are like old bottles and cardboard containers; what do we contain; what is our immortality?

I said 'Kleist did not have to kill himself.'

Bruno said 'Perhaps he did not see the bits of himself that would go floating like messages in bottles on the sea.'

I said 'But they are so beautiful!'

Bruno said 'Don't cry.'

Bruno put his arms around me. He was a fragile, rather top-heavy figure with a huge head. I thought – Perhaps we are both like those creatures that are born before their time.

Bruno said 'Do you know the story of Josephus?'

I thought – Of course I know the story of Josephus! Then – I have forgotten it. Then – Stories, of course, are what are immortal.

Bruno and I walked around the lake. We had our arms round each other. He said –

'Josephus was a general in the Jewish army in AD 67. The Jews were fighting the Romans; Josephus found himself and his army besieged in a town called Jotapata. The situation was hopeless: Josephus wanted to surrender; he was told by the Romans that his life would be spared. But the other Jewish elders, with whom he was sheltering in a cellar, refused to consider this: they insisted that he, and they, should die, together with the rest of the townspeople, although Josephus told them that if they surrendered he could probably get some sort of terms for all of them. So it was arranged that those in the cellar should kill one another, drawing lots to see who should kill who, and then the last man should kill himself. But it seems that Josephus managed to fix the lots so that he and another man were the last two left alive, and then he and this man agreed to surrender to the Romans.'

I said 'And what happened then?'

Bruno said 'The townspeople were killed; Josephus went to live in Rome, and wrote the history of the Jewish war, including this story.'

I said 'And how did he manage to fix the lots?'

Bruno said 'Josephus has always been regarded as a grotesque traitor by the Jews: he is what Judas Iscariot is to the Christians.'

I said 'How did he manage to fix the lots?'

Bruno said 'No one knows. Perhaps he was one of the seven just men.'

I said 'I suppose he what might be called cheated.'

Then he said 'Nellie, I love you, but I can't make love to you any more!'

I said 'Oh I think that is all right.'

I thought – There are other ways in which we might be immortal.

In Berlin I found a letter from you, from England, which had been sent to a poste-restante address because I had not wanted to give you the address of the Rosa Luxemburg Block. I had written to you to say that Franz wanted to get in touch with you: I thought he wanted to talk to you about physics. I had said that I hoped that one day we all might meet. I had told you that in February I hoped to be going skiing; I had added 'Why don't you come too?'

In your letter you said –

226

Dearest Eleanor,

As it happens (can you believe this!) I am tomorrow going skiing with my friend called Hans (do you remember? he was the one who thought that Mephistopheles should be played by a twelve-year-old boy). Hans's family have a chalet somewhere in the mountains of southern Germany. I will find out the address and put it at the end of this letter. And where will you be?

Perhaps we will bump into each other like two of those particles which, if they have bumped into each other once, may never be quite not as if bumping into each other again.

Yes, indeed I would like to talk to Franz about physics. Shall I come to Berlin after skiing?

Do you know about these particles? People have become interested in them here. You remember the problem: how do you measure objectively what a particle is up to when what you measure is just the effect of your measuring? Well someone here has got an idea. Why not take two particles that have bumped into one another once (by a castle in the Black Forest, for instance) and if you know all about this meeting, and you measure what one of the particles is doing now, then although your measurements of this one will be affected by your measuring, you will be able to work out from these and from your knowledge of the effects of the original meeting, what the second particle will be doing – and this won't be affected by your measuring because it won't be it that's being measured – and so can this be called 'objective'? No, of course this doesn't make sense. Having measured the one, then if by doing this you are finding out anything about the other at all, you are affecting it.

So where are you now? Why should anyone want anything to be called 'objective'?

I am thinking of taking up biology.

Or that pseudo-science, whatever it is, by which the future is foretold by studying the cracks in heated bones.

I am dispirited. I do not know how to find you. You did not tell me where you were going skiing in your letter.

Love from Max

You had put no address at the end of this letter. I thought – You are angry with me? Well why should you not be, if I did not give you my address: but how could I, when I was suggesting that you meet Franz?

The envelope that the letter arrived in did look as if it might have been tampered with. I thought – But at least not by the people in the Rosa Luxemburg Block.

Then – But if you are angry with me, cannot I, even from hundreds of miles away, make you better?

I went skiing. I was on my own. I was in southern Germany. In the mountains there were these shapes, bumps, curves, that I sped down. I thought – All right, yes, these slopes are like that image of the pitted inner surface of a sphere: the four-dimensional space-time continuum of the universe. Such an image might not be a metaphor for scientific reality; science may be a metaphor for the reality of such an image. So – Who said that? My father? You? I am confusing you with my father, my mad angry English boy?

Then – Or perhaps your letter is telling me that you have a new English girlfriend.

I loved the mountains: I seemed to be in touch, indeed, with what was called 'gravity'. I was pulled: there was a force pulling: because of this I myself could steer – this way or that. But the bumps, shapes, curves, told me which way to choose. It seemed that one day, of course, I might go over the rim of the universe.

And so, at last, find what might be called 'objectivity'?

Of course your experiment made no sense! If the particles had anything to do with one another, then affecting the one would of course be affecting the other.

I thought – But if with enough style, elegance, on these mountains, one remains upright –

– With another there would be the same force by which the one might survive?

By the time I got back to Berlin Hitler had become Chancellor. There seemed to be some sort of hiatus, gap, in the streets. People had been holding their noses and had now toppled over: they were falling, falling.

I found that Bruno was not at the Rosa Luxemburg Block. People said that he had left. He had left no note for me. I thought – It is impossible for him to have gone and left no note for me! People in the Block said that he had just gone out one evening and had not returned. They seemed to suggest – Perhaps because Hitler has become Chancellor. I said 'What – ?' Their eyes slid away. He has got out? Gone over? This was not worth saying. I thought I might say to them – 'Bruno might have wanted to survive; it is you who have wanted to betray him.'

I thought I should ask my mother if she knew what might have happened to Bruno. Then – When I am in trouble, I still go to my mother?

In the streets the Nazis were setting up loudspeakers on street corners. Lamp-posts were hung with wires: they were like the umbilical cords of whales. I thought – These people are arranging so that they will be forever tied to their mad shouting Nazi mother; with luck, their lifeblood will run back to their destruction.

My mother was in her office with the machinery whirring next door and her cough and cigarette smoke rising up like spirits to torment her. There were people burning what seemed to be documents in the basement; the smoke from this too came up to plague my mother. It was as if she were some witch at a stake above a fire: I thought – Perhaps witches want to be pissed on to help them with the fire.

I said 'I wondered if you might have heard anything about what has happened to Bruno.'

'You think I might have heard something about Bruno?'

'He's disappeared.'

'So I hear.'

'Then you have!'

'What?'

'Heard.'

'I haven't said anything about knowing what's happened.'

I thought – But I can feel my own lifeblood running back! I will die if I don't get out, O my mother!

I said 'I saw Franz the other day. He said we should get out, you and I.'

'You have been in touch with Franz?'

'I went to have tea with him at the Adlon Hotel. I thought I might learn something from him, and I did.'

'You go to see Franz and you ask me if I know why Bruno has disappeared!'

She looked so pleased, my mother. I thought – But I do not need to be tied to a stake and pissed on by you, my mother!

I said 'Bruno wouldn't have gone of his own accord without telling me. You were all suspicious of him. Why?'

She said 'Didn't we have reason to be suspicious of him?'

I thought – Do you have reason to be suspicious of me?

Then – There are myths, in fact, about daughters wanting to kill their mothers: Electra, Clytemnestra. But Electra had to get her brother to do it for her: perhaps women know that they only tighten the cord by wanting to kill their mothers.

I said 'You were always suspicious of people in the Rosa Luxemburg Block! They were suspicious of Bruno. They were suspicious of you. You all live on suspicion. Without it, you might have time to fight the Nazis!'

My mother rocked backwards and forwards in her chair.

I said 'You don't really think Bruno and I had contact with the Nazis?'

My mother said 'You've just admitted that you had tea with Franz.'

I said 'That is unforgivable.'

I thought – But of course I should never had told her about my seeing Franz!

Then – Dear God, perhaps I should never had told her about the raid on the café-brothel.

As I went out of the door my mother shouted after me 'He was never any good for you!'

I thought – Don't give me that stuff now: the caring mother!

Then – This is not ridiculous, it is evil –

– You think it might even have been my mother who was responsible for the tip-off?

As I walked through the streets it seemed, yes, that my lifeblood was draining away. I thought – But in so far as it is her blood that has run through me, let it run back to her destruction!

The streets were hung with wires like entrails.

I thought – Will I always be that child lying on the edge of a bed while people tend to the dying earth, its mother?

– Oh cut the cord: tie the liberating knot! Can the child do this itself? It can re-create its own blood, from that of its mother.

I found myself walking in the direction of the Adlon Hotel. I suppose I was going there on the chance of seeing Franz. Of course I knew that there was almost no chance of seeing Franz – he had taken that room in the hotel only for one day – but then, what is this operation of chance? You put yourself in the way of it. I wanted to see Franz because I wanted to ask him about Bruno: also I needed a friend. Then coming along Unter den Linden there was a squad of motorcycle outriders and behind them a car and in the car, Hitler. It was an open car, although this was in the middle of winter; it was as if Hitler had to be on show, as if he were some sort of dummy. I mean a perfect dummy, all-of-a-piece, to be admired. Well, humans are not all-of-a-piece, are they? Hitler was like something made of cloth, waxed and polished; you can walk all round a dummy and examine it. Human beings react: but a dummy is an object. I thought – But what is this waxed dummy for? It is some huge candle to light an ultimate bonfire? It is something into which pins are stuck, to make humanity suffer?

Hitler whisked past in his car. I thought – Or perhaps he will go round and round like a Catherine wheel until he goes out and is dumped on someone else's bonfire.

Franz, of course, was not in the Adlon Hotel. I walked straight through and out of the side door into Wilhelmstrasse. I thought – You have to go on putting yourself in the way of chances if you want to survive.

Then – But why didn't you come to Berlin instead of going skiing –

– It is you I am so often talking to, isn't it, my English boy?

There had been more Nazis than before in the hallway of the hotel. They were on their toes, almost taking off; they were balloons about to be lifted by hot air.

– But might not sparks from bonfires burst them on their way round the universe?

I was summoned to appear before the Central Committee of the Rosa Luxemburg Block. There were eight men and women behind a table in the basement. They were coughing and smoking and trying to see that their cigarettes did not roll off the small metal trays on the table. I thought – There are children's games like this: you hold a small box in front of you and you have to steer a silver ball along grooves and see that it does not fall through holes.

They said 'We wish you to tell us what you know about Bruno.'

'I know nothing about Bruno. He's disappeared.'

'He left you no message?'

'No.'

'That is unusual?'

'Yes. I have been trying to make my own enquiries.'

The chief interrogator was a woman who wore small steel spectacles like Trotsky. I thought – Has she not heard that Trotsky has fallen through a small hole in the board of this game in Russia?

She said 'What enquiries?'

'I have been to talk with my mother.'

'We have information that you had a contact at the Adlon Hotel.'

'Contact?'

'You do not deny it?'

'I do not deny what?'

'That you met a Nazi official at the Adlon Hotel.'

I thought – I was followed?

Or – Only my mother knew I met Franz at the Adlon Hotel!

I said 'I met an old friend of mine called Franz at the Adlon Hotel.'

'You do not deny that he is a Nazi?'

'He is nothing official. And anyway that was before Bruno disappeared – '

'Yes?'

'Franz and I have been friends since childhood. This has nothing to do with Bruno.'

'You say Bruno and you and this man called Franz have all been friends since childhood?'

I thought – I am doing this all wrong.

Then – But certainly it is only my mother who could have known that Franz and Bruno and I have been friends since childhood.

– Help me, Josephus, to get out!

The woman in the Trotsky spectacles said 'Begin again. You went to see this man in the Adlon Hotel.'

I said 'Don't you think that it is in the interests of the Party to gain information? Did my mother not tell you, or did she not know, the terms on which I went to see my friend in the Adlon Hotel? Don't you think it would be to your advantage to make further analysis before you question my objectivity?'

The woman with the Trotsky spectacles picked up her cigarette and drew on it heavily and seemed to be balancing smoke like small silver balls in her head.

I thought – This is dangerous: but if words have ceased to mean what people think they mean, might one not still use them to survive?

The woman with the spectacles said 'We will question you further. You will not leave the Block.'

I thought – But now, should I not catch any chance to get out?

It seemed that I should make my own bonfire of the documents and bits and pieces of my life – the few possessions I carried around with me. I took my suitcase down to the basement where there was a furnace and I emptied the contents on to the ground; my bits and pieces lay there like those old bones, or entrails, yes, by which people used to think that from the past or present they could tell the future. There were letters from my father: I came across a sentence which said 'You must not be surprised at your mother's antipathy to Bruno: you are her daughter. Though it is odd, I agree, her admiration for Franz.' The date on the letter was three years ago. I thought – So patterns are there, yes, if you see them, like cracks in bones; but how can one tell from these about the future?

There was a letter from my old girlfriend Trixie which began 'No, I don't think it is interesting that you and Bruno are Jews and I am not: I think this sort of thing is boring.'

There was a letter from you from the previous winter –

Humans are containers to be put on a bonfire? Right! But why should not the message they carry be: What infinite care has been taken to make them such beautiful containers!

It is persons, containers, after all, that either live or die.

The care now might be to develop a sense to do with the appreciation of chance.

I put in a satchel the letters I had had from Franz, Bruno, Trixie, my father and yourself; the rest I put on the bonfire.

I thought – But these seeds that I will carry round with me will be in some pouch, some pod; and one day they may burst over an indifferent multitude?

I did not want to stay indoors behind barricaded doors and windows as did other members of the Block but I had nowhere to go except on the circuit I had fixed in my mind – to the building where my mother lived, then on round the north side of Unter den Linden to the area of the Adlon Hotel, then back to the Block. I wondered – In some way I imagine I am looking for Bruno? Or Franz? I might bump into something if I keep moving round and round.

I paid no attention to the orders of the Committee that I should not leave the Block. I thought – It is when you let yourself be lined up, when people know where you are, that you are self-destructive.

Then – Oh but why should one bump into anything except oneself as one goes round and round!

One evening I set off on my usual round: it was after dark, at the end of February. I did not really want to see my mother: I had told myself I wanted nothing to do with my mother ever again. I thought – So what am I trying to do: seeing what flowers might have been put on a grave? There had continued to be the hush, the

233

expectancy, in the streets – as if people even now were waiting for the enormous events round some corner. There are paintings like this: that show menace in half-deserted streets. I had gone some way towards Alexanderplatz when lorries came whirring towards me from around some corner; they carried Brownshirts; the Brownshirts were not leaning over the sides of the lorries laughing and jeering as they had used to do when they were on a raid, they were sitting in rows facing inwards like dummies with spikes up their arses. I thought – So the time has come when they want to be perfect, all-of-a-piece. I stood in a doorway while they went past. They were going in the direction of the Rosa Luxemburg Block. I thought – They are going there to arrest people? Then – I have already got rid of my bits and pieces. Then – This is all that I feel about people in the Block? I went on through the dark streets. I thought – But I have got out, and perhaps Bruno has got out; now indeed people in the Block will think that Bruno or I have betrayed them: though why should they need anyone to betray them, when they seem to have the need to betray themselves? I was making my way towards Alexanderplatz. I was sorry that I had not got my few letters, or satchel of seeds, with me: I thought – They will be scattered; but who can tell on what ground? Somewhere to the west there was a red glow above the rooftops: the hour was too late for it to be sunset. I thought – What, the great big bonfire? Then – This is ridiculous. There were some more lorries going along a street across the top of the one in which I was walking: they, too, seemed to be carrying Brownshirts. I thought – So they might be going to arrest the people with my mother. Then – But if I am alone, should I expect to survive? I went on towards Alexanderplatz. I think perhaps I was too cold, with a feeling of too much urgency, to be frightened. I thought – But I see why people might not want to survive. I was trying to keep to the shadows. I imagined – If my mother has been arrested what must I do: rush towards her crying Mother! Mother!; flop about as if on a stage until I am arrested too? Then there will be no one to get up at the end of the third act – and indeed, are we not at home in blood and death and destruction. So how will there be preserved anything that is immortal? I thought I could go down a side-street and round a block or two and so get to a vantage point opposite the building where my mother lived: from there I might see without being seen – indeed was I not now like an agent in occupied territory? But in that case what would I be being a traitor to: is it not as an agent for oneself that one has the chance of being immortal? From the bottom of an alleyway, in the shadows of which I could see without being seen, there was the front of the building facing me in which my mother lived and worked; lorries were parked outside it; Brownshirts were standing around the lorries. The windows of the building were lighted so that it was like the backdrop to a stage: I thought – But I have seen this before – where? – in that courtyard of the ruined castle: they were playing Faust, yes, about what good can come out of evil: then there was that play by Brecht in which two people were wandering through a town in which there is a bloody revolution; they meet, wander away, meet again; and so there are patterns. Through the lighted windows of the building I could catch glimpses of Brownshirts swarming like invading ants; they were capturing files, stores, secrets; they appeared beyond the windows here and there with their arms full of papers. I thought – And now my mother will feel justified in her feelings about betrayal! Then – But surely I should be thinking of something more useful. The inhabitants of the building were being led out in ones and twos to the waiting lorries; they were being held by the arms; some were protesting; some were half-collapsed between Brownshirts. I thought – But I cannot be just an observer of this: can I not get at least some message through to a suffering world. There was still the red glow above the rooftops. I thought – Dear God, but what are the images I have myself harboured about this: about bodies being carried to the bonfire. I saw my mother being led out into the street between two Brownshirts; she was like a doll; she had her head down. I had an image – She has been hit on the head like Rosa Luxemburg. Then – Oh but now must I not rush out and be heard to cry Mother! Mother! What else can I do, even if I get myself arrested: did I imagine that I could escape the bonfire? I began walking across the road towards my mother. My mother was dangling like some out-of-use puppet between the arms of two Brownshirts. She looked so small: she was like some bird caught on a hook: I was being pulled by some line from my insides towards her. Or was it that my mother and I were two climbers fastened together by rope on a rockface; she had fallen; either one of us would die or, unless I cut the rope, both of us would. But still, was there not something practical to be done? I went up to one of the Brownshirts who was holding my mother and I said 'Where are you taking them?' My mother still had her head down so that I could not see her face. I could see – Nothing. I said to the

Brownshirt 'That much you can tell me!' He had a rough, wet face like the inside of a rubber ball. I thought – Perhaps I should smile and put a hand up and touch his face: then – Probably he is homosexual. I was standing quite close to my mother. She did not lift her head up. The Brownshirt whom I had spoken to said 'You get out of here.' I thought – My mother may still think I am betraying her: or by not acknowledging me, is she trying to help me? The other Brownshirt said 'The Reichstag's burning.' I said 'The Reichstag's burning?' I thought – I am acting like my mother. My mother still would not look at me. The two Brownshirts lifted and pushed her into the back of one of the lorries. I said loudly 'I will find my father and perhaps he will be able to do something.' When she was in the back of the lorry my mother did turn and look at me: the hair on one side of her head was slightly matted; she frowned, as if she wanted me to go. I was holding my hands against my stomach and I opened my mouth: it was as if, after all, I might scream. There were more people being led out of the building and brought to the back of the lorries. I thought – After all, my mother must love me! One of the Brownshirts stretched out a hand as if to grab me. I said 'She is my mother!' I thought – Well I have said that: what more can I do? I turned and began to walk away. I thought the Brownshirt would come after me. He did not. They were pushing people on to the lorries. I thought – But this is no trick: I am just walking away from my mother. Then – Is this just everything I have ever been or done? But I am going over the rim of the world to where there might be no gravity.

I had begun to walk in the direction of the Adlon Hotel. This was my usual round. I thought I could try to find Franz: I would telephone my father: what else was there to do? There was nothing, nothing. Then – At least I will see the Reichstag burning! There were indeed sparks like souls flying up over rooftops. I was walking through streets, keeping away from the sound of lorries. I wondered if the Reichstag had been set on fire by some of the people in the Rosa Luxemburg Block; or by those with my mother, and so they were being put on to lorries. But I had gone forwards, in some sort of style, hadn't I, crying Mother! Mother! But had I not cut the cord? and now was I seeing what happens when there is no gravity. There is indeed nothing, nothing; you are just falling. My father had said once (or was it you?) that the only emotions worth having are ecstasy and despair. I thought – Well yes, but there is also a terror at this nothing. I was walking towards the Reichstag and every now and then I could glimpse the outline of the huge dome which was lit like the mantle of a gaslamp; I thought – Indeed it might be some message: we are dying! I had wanted to arrange a meeting between you and me and Franz and Bruno at the Adlon Hotel. I was walking in the direction of the Adlon Hotel. I thought – But you used to have an image of the whole world burning; or will these sparks settle down like light that comes from a painting? I was moving along streets on the north side of Unter den Linden. There were people in the streets now moving in the same direction as me: they were going to watch the bonfire. I thought – What you and Franz and Bruno and I would have talked about is physics: the transmutations that might go on in an atom; in the sun; some secret like that behind the closed door in a courtyard. Or that which connects this particle to that across the universe. I had reached a place from which, if I was to get to the Adlon Hotel, I had to go down and cross Unter den Linden; there were sure to be lorries with Brownshirts there: I thought – With one great leap – what? – there can be mutation? On each side of Unter den Linden there were, yes, lines of police and Brownshirts: crowds were piling up; they were settling to watch the bonfire. I could see it quite clearly now; the whole of the enormous building was on fire. I thought – It is a construction like a nest: what monster will arise from the ashes? It did not seem possible to get across the road: I had pushed my way through the crowd and was standing at the back of the line of Brownshirts. I thought – And anyway, why do I want to get to the Adlon Hotel? Because there is nothing else to do? Because I used go there with my father; with Franz? Because if there is nothing, you find yourself drawn to where you have once or twice felt at home? I said to one of the Brownshirts 'Can you help me get through to the Adlon Hotel? It is urgent.' He too had a round rough face like the inside of a rubber ball. He looked at me and then looked away: I thought – Dear God, are they all homosexual? There were cars going past in the road with motorcycle outriders: it seemed that this might be Hitler, being carried home to a bonfire. A policeman turned to me and said 'You want to get to the Adlon Hotel?' I said 'Yes please.' The policeman took hold of me by the arm as if to help me; then the Brownshirt spoke to him and he let go. I thought – Well, what trick did Josephus do: his people were homosexuals? Then I saw you on the other side of the road. I mean I saw you beneath the trees in the middle of Unter den Linden. I was sure it was you. I

had not seen you for three or four years. You were talking to a
Brownshirt.

I thought – Well dear God, on what strange planet have we
landed!

The Brownshirt you were talking to was holding a card or
document; you were leaning by his shoulder and pointing to it;
there was an intensity about this scene, as if you were figures in a
painting. I thought – The document is your passport? Then you
looked up and saw me. Or it was as if you had already seen me:
you looked so pleased. You waved. The Brownshirt looked up
from the document he was holding; then he beckoned to the
Brownshirt who was with me on my side of the road. This
Brownshirt took hold of me by the arm and said 'Wait.' There were
cars coming along Unter den Linden. I thought – You arrange
things like this on this strange planet? When there was a gap in the
traffic the Brownshirt gave me a push and I began running. I
thought – So after all, you mean, one or two get through? I ran to
the space where there were trees in the middle of the road. Then –
But these things are in the mind: they are in the outside world too?
When I got to where you were standing you took me in your arms.
I thought – Ah well, this is like a painting. Then you said 'He found
you!' I thought I might say – Who found me? You talk about
yourself like this on this strange planet? Or about God? The
Brownshirt who was beside you was giving you back the document
he had been holding; it was your passport; he smiled and saluted. I
thought – Oh but you are not all homosexuals on this planet! You
seemed so much more confident and grown-up; you had your hair
in a fringe like a Roman Emperor. I said 'Who found me?' You said
'Your father.' I thought I might say – My father? Then – This is
some code for the sake of the Brownshirts on this planet? We began
walking across the far side of the road towards the Adlon Hotel.
You had your arm around me. I said 'But what are you doing here?'
You stopped and held me at arm's length and stared at me. I thought
– All right, all right, you know I do love you! You said 'Didn't you
get my letter?' I said 'No.' Then – 'What letter?' You said 'The
letter that told you I would be here: I sent it to the address given me
by Franz.' You took me by the arm and we went on towards the
entrance to the Adlon Hotel. We pushed our way through the
crowd, who were watching the bonfire. You did not seem to be
interested in the fire. I thought – But if you sent a letter to the Rosa
Luxemburg Block, yes, they might have taken it and opened it.

Then you said again 'You haven't seen your father? So how did you know we'd be here?' You said this quietly as if it were something not really to be heard, let alone answered. I wanted to say – But I didn't know you would be here! We went on and up the steps and into the Adlon Hotel. I said 'But what is this about my father? He is in Heidelberg.' You said 'No, he came to get you.' There was a crowd in the hallway of the Adlon Hotel: they were standing with bright smiles and talking excitedly about the bonfire. I thought – But you, haven't you come to get me? You were standing on tip-toe looking round the lounge of the hotel. Then we sat down at a table. You held my hand; you gazed at me. I thought – Well, why didn't you come before? You said 'You didn't get my letter and you didn't get your father's letter.' I said 'No.' You didn't even say this time – 'Then how on earth are you here?' I thought I might say – But I have always been coming here: with my father, with Franz: it is you who need the explanation. We were sitting facing each other in the hotel with our knees almost touching; there were the things like the bonfire going on elsewhere: I thought – But it is we ourselves who are the enormous events! You said 'I've been in touch with Franz: I think he got in touch with your father.' I said 'Have you seen my father?' You said 'Yes.' I thought – What things go on on this strange planet! I said 'I think the people with whom I have been living must have been intercepting my letters.' You said 'You've got to get out.' I thought I might say – Yes, I've got to get out. I said 'My mother has been arrested.' You said 'I see.' You were looking round the lounge of the hotel as if you might tell the future from bits of bone and entrails. The lounge of the hotel was like a railway station. Then I saw Franz coming towards us through the lounge. Franz was wearing his grey suit with the swastika badge in the buttonhole. He came up to us and said 'Oh you've found her.' You said 'Yes, we've found her.' Franz said to me 'Why weren't you here?' You said 'She never got our letters.' Franz said 'I see.' He didn't even bother to say – Then how did she know we were here? He looked away across the hallway. I thought I might say – You mean, you and Franz and my father have all come to rescue me? You said 'Hurry; we must hurry.' I said 'But where is my father?' Franz had sat down at our table; we three were facing each other; it was as if the events were unimportant elsewhere. Franz said 'He went to look for you at the Rosa Luxemburg Block.' I said 'Is he coming back here?' Franz said 'Yes.' Then I said 'But we can't leave my mother.' You said 'Her mother has been arrested.'

There was a clatter and a roar from the crowd outside: I thought –
Perhaps the roof of the Reichstag has fallen in: perhaps Hitler has
turned up and has at last managed to get himself put on a bonfire.
Franz said 'Yes, they're rounding up the Communists. You've got to
get out.' I said 'Where do you think one can get out to?' You said
'Switzerland.' I said 'Switzerland!' I thought – This is ridiculous.
Franz said 'I understand your father has relations in Switzerland.' I
thought – But this is not possible; it is happening too quickly. We
were sitting round the table in the lounge of the Adlon Hotel. Franz
was looking towards the side entrance to the hotel which led out into
Wilhelmstrasse. There was a group of high-up Nazis by the door who
were talking and looking towards us across the lounge. I thought –
But what are we waiting for: my father? Then – Things do not seem
to get filtered, on this strange planet. I said 'How are we going to get
to Switzerland?' You said 'I'm taking you.' I imagined that you were
talking about me and my father. I thought – That is extraordinarily
kind! I said 'But what about my mother.' You said 'Franz can try to
find out about your mother.' I thought – But could we be together,
for a time, you and I, in Switzerland? I said 'But we can't go
without my mother.' Franz said to you 'You didn't tell her about
Bruno?' You said nothing. There was a noise from loudspeakers
out in Pariser Platz; it was the sound of a voice hugely amplified; it
was like someone being sick, like someone's insides being torn out.
I said 'What about Bruno?' I was thinking – I am indeed like those
Jews, with Josephus, in that town called Jotapata; but I do not want
to be trapped in a cellar of the mind. The loudspeakers in the square
outside seemed to be saying that the Reichstag had been set on fire
by the Communists, the enemies of the state; they would be weeded
out and ruthlessly punished. I thought – Oh but why couldn't those
people in Jotapata get out; they had guilt about their mothers? You
stood up. You said again 'We must go.' I thought – Dear God, will
I really have to act. We can't go! Franz said 'Your father had a letter
from your mother about Bruno.' I said 'My father had a letter from
my mother about Bruno?' I thought – Now listen! I must listen!
You sat down. You looked round the lounge. I thought – But you
will promise, won't you, to get me out? I said 'What did my mother
say about Bruno?' Franz said 'She said she thought that Bruno
wasn't suitable for you and she hoped that what she had done was
right.' I said 'Why, what has she done?' I thought – You mean, she
did betray Bruno? The loudspeakers were going on and on in the
Pariser Platz: I thought – Oh for God's sake, why does not whoever

it is being sick never quite get his insides all torn out! Franz said 'She told your people in the Rosa Luxemburg Block that she thought Bruno was a Nazi spy.' I thought – She might as well have told them that I was a Nazi spy! Then – But you mean, so Bruno got out? Bruno was betrayed in turn by the people in the Block and handed over to the Nazis? I stood up. Franz said 'Bruno has been arrested.' I said 'But why, if he was said to be a spy?' Franz said 'But he wasn't.' I said 'Oh no.' Franz said 'So now you must get out.' We had all stood up. We were going to the door of the hotel which led into Wilhelmstrasse. I thought – So you mean, all this has happened so that I can get out? You said to me 'Have you got papers? A student's card? A passport?' Franz said 'I will do what I can about Bruno.' I said 'But what about my father?' Franz said 'He went to look for you in the Rosa Luxemburg Block.' I said 'My papers are in the Rosa Luxemburg Block.' Franz said to you 'Perhaps at the frontier you can say that she's your girlfriend.' You said 'Oh at the frontier I can say we're married!' We went out through the door into Wilhelmstrasse. I saw my father coming towards us on the pavement. He was carrying my satchel. I mean, this was the satchel in which there were all the bits and pieces of my life: my papers and letters. I thought I might act putting my hand over my eyes, as if I could not bear this. My father looked so pleased. I wondered – You mean, this is the sort of thing behind the closed door in that courtyard! When my father came up he said 'You've found her!' We stood on the pavement like one of those groups in a painting. My father looked older and more frail; his hair was brushed up above his forehead as if he were like sparks on their way to heaven. I took my satchel. I said 'How did you get it?' He said 'I've been to the Rosa Luxemburg Block.' I said 'They are being arrested?' My father put his arms around me and I put my head against his chest. We were standing on the pavement of Wilhelmstrasse as we had done so many years ago when crowds had rushed past us laughing to the Brandenburg Gate and then had been shot. Franz said 'She knows about her mother and Bruno.' My father said 'Oh, so then you will go, you will be all right.' But I thought I still had to say – 'But I don't know if we can just leave my mother!' My father said 'I'm not going to leave her.' I said 'But you're coming to Switzerland.' My father said 'No, I'm staying here; it is you who are going to Switzerland.' I said 'Why?' My father said 'Because I am her husband and you are her child.'

Then I began to cry. Oh God, this terrible world! With me on the edge of a bed and arms so harsh and tender. My father said 'Don't cry.' I thought – But I may not see you again. My father said 'My brother has everything ready for you in Switzerland.'

We were standing on the pavement of Wilhelmstrasse. My father and I had taken our arms from around each other. There were not so many people in the street: from here one could not see the fire. There were a few police and Brownshirts looking up to the sky. Franz said 'Where's your car?' You said 'Round the corner.'

I said to my father 'Thank you for my satchel.'

He said 'Oh that's all right.'

You and Franz had moved off a little way down the street. You were saying 'I will let you know of any developments in England.' Franz was saying 'And I will let you know of any developments here.' I thought – You mean, much of this time you have been talking about physics? I put my head up and kissed my father. I said 'Goodbye.' He said 'Goodbye.'

I went and joined you and Franz; I did not look back. I thought – My father and I may be able, in the future, to transmit some sort of messages.

Then – I will get used to things on this strange planet.

Franz was talking to one of the Brownshirts. He gestured to you and to me as if for us to go across the road. I thought – But to Franz I have not even said goodbye! I waved at him. I thought – But I will see Franz again.

You and I went arm in arm across the road. There were police and Brownshirts in front of the Chancellery. You said 'If anyone stops us we had better speak English.' I said in English 'Where is your car?' You said 'It's extraordinary how well you speak English!' I thought I might say – Oh yes, as you know, that is because I had a governess called Miss Henne. We were going along Wilhelmstrasse away from the fire. After a time we turned down a side-street. There was a small car with British number-plates on it. I said 'I once had a car.' You said 'Oh what happened to it?' I thought – You mean, we are talking as if we are on a stage? We do this when we are in occupied territory: when there has been too much going on? You opened the door of the car for me; you went round to the other side and got into the driving seat. You said 'Perhaps we can say that you are pregnant.' I thought – Why on earth should we say that I am pregnant? Then – Oh I see, you mean when we get to the frontier. I said 'That'll take days.' Then – 'I mean, to get to the frontier.' You said 'It'll take all night.' I thought I might say – Oh yes, we can be laughing! You said 'Can I stay with you for a few days in Switzerland?' I said 'Yes, you can stay with me for a few days in Switzerland.' You said 'Thank you very much.' I opened my mouth as if I might cry. You said 'After that, I'm afraid I've got to get back to Cambridge.' I thought – Oh but we can't do better than this, with so much going on! You said 'Don't cry.' I thought I might say – I'm not crying, I'm laughing. Then I found myself saying 'I wanted to ask you, what did happen to that child?' You said 'What child?' I thought – What indeed! The one on the edge of the bed? The one at the back of that ruined castle? The one with whom I might in some way be pregnant? I said 'The one who was deaf and dumb.' You said 'Ah, her.' You drove for a time in silence. Then you said 'But you said she did seem to hear you; and she spoke.' I said 'Yes.' You said 'That's important, because no one else heard her speak.' I was going to say as I had said to you before – She told me where to find you! But then I was crying too much – for myself, for my parents, for you and me. I thought – But there is the voice of that girl, isn't there, that can he heard though people said she couldn't speak, going round the universe.

VI: Max

It is difficult to write about love: I mean to live in the presence of it. You can run towards it and perhaps bump into it and you can watch it running away: but when it is there it is like two people coming face to face on a tightrope; they have to keep moving or they will fall; they would like to pass into, through, one another; at moments this is possible! But then it is not. How much more easy it is, more natural, to be like a leaf and live and fall.

What I remember about our three days in Switzerland is – Let us touch wood or this may die: hold our breath or we will fall. For three days we did this: how much longer without breathing can love stay alive? But if you do manage this then it is only yourselves, and not love, that will fall.

I remember you literally on a mountain path like this: you were my brave dark girl whom I wanted to be possessed by and whom I wanted to possess: we had been walking with our arms around one another; the path became too narrow for us to remain side by side. We had to separate; you let go and looked at me with such funny sadness! I thought – But anything might be possible: I might step over the edge of the mountain and we would still be balanced, joined; you would be part of the earth, and I would fly.

You said ' – *Mon joli bourgeois à la petite tache humide – !*'

I said 'What is that?'

You said '*The Magic Mountain.*'

I thought – I will read it when you are gone.

I said ' – On this mountain path there is a stone, a gateway, a spider; everything has happened eternally before and will happen eternally again – '

You said 'Oh I know that!'

I thought – For these messages, there has to be some code.

There were the moments at night when we were one: this is the experience; then afterwards one is on one's own. You looked back, I suppose, at your past life; your lost family, your friends. Then again you might need me to hold you. I wanted to say – We will always be one: we will be like two of those particles –

You said 'Would you really choose to live every moment of your life again?'

I said 'If one were ready to say that, then perhaps one would not have to.'

You said 'I want to say it.'

I said 'Then our lives may be good enough.'

When the time came for me to take you to your uncle, or cousins, or whoever they were, in Zurich, they were calm, grave men in knickerbockers like gardeners. In becoming separated from you there was a terrible violation like a seed-pod being torn apart: my head and heart were being split, crushed: I thought – It is necessary, I know, to put oneself into the hands of gardeners: knowing this does not alter the pain of having to grow.

Your uncle sat behind his desk with catalogues to do with his business of chemical fertilisers. He said to you 'You now want to study psychology? We no longer know if it is psychology or alchemy that we have here at the university in Zurich!'

You said 'Psychology or anthropology, it will be the same.'

Your uncle said to me 'And what will you do?' He had found it difficult sometimes to acknowledge that I was there.

I said 'At Cambridge I will take my degree in physics, then I want to change to biology.'

He said 'Why?'

'In physics we don't seem to be finding out about the nature of the world, we seem to be finding out about the nature of the equipment we're using.'

'And in biology?'

I said 'Well, in biology I suppose things either do or do not stay alive.'

You and I went for a last walk through the town. I remember the lake on the edge of which the turrets of the town appeared like sandcastles. I said 'You're sure I have to go back? You have to stay here?'

You said 'Aren't you sure?'

I said 'It's pride to think that one can alter the world!'

You said 'Isn't it pride to think that one shouldn't?'

Your uncle and cousins came on to the steps to see me off. I thought – At the last moment, there might be something like a war; a bomb going off.

I said 'Even if something is unique, it can be repeated.'

You said 'Repeat it then.'

I said 'Goodbye.'

You said 'I'll see you.'

When I got back to Cambridge there were the people like shadows moving against the walls of ancient buildings. I had to go to see the head of my college because I had missed a part of the winter term. I said 'I'll take my degree: but then I'd like to change from physics.'

The head of my college was a small bald man with eyebrows that were like the wings of a bee. His room was lined with books; he walked up and down and glanced at the backs of them from time to time as if they were flowers.

He said 'What do you want to change to?'

I said 'I wondered if I could combine physics with biology.'

'Why would you want to do that?'

I thought I might say – Why does not everyone want to do that?

I said 'It seems that in the connections between the two there might be some sort of objectivity.'

He walked up and down. I thought – He has, yes, made of his life a sort of honeycomb from flowers.

I said 'In physics you manipulate what you see or you can't see it. In biology you at least know you are part of the nature you are studying.'

The head of my college said 'You don't think that what you see is conditioned by the physical properties of the brain?' I could not tell whether or not he was being hostile. Then he said 'Are you interested in religion?'

I said 'No.'

'Can you read German?'

'Yes.'

'Have a look at this.' He took down from his shelves a German translation of a book by Kierkegaard, of whom I had not at that time heard.

I said 'Thanks.'

He said 'Let me have it back sometime.'

I said 'I will.'

I went to see my father, who was behind his desk on which were piles of catalogues and periodicals to do with plants. I said 'The trouble is, people keep the subjects they study in separate compartments. So how are you ever in contact with the whole?'

My father said 'Your mother tells me that you've got a girl in Germany.'

I said 'She's had to get out of Germany.'

My father said 'Is she a Jew?'

I said 'Yes.'

My father said 'They cause a lot of trouble.'

I wondered – Do people know why they are embarrassed when they use the word 'Jew'?

I said 'I suppose they feel they have some destiny.'

My father said 'You see in that some contact with the whole?'

I said 'I wondered if I might go and study in Russia for a time. They seem to be doing there some experiment with reality.'

My father said 'I suppose if you get shot in the back of the head, you can call that reality.'

There were two Russian scientists I came across during my years at Cambridge: one was a physicist called Kapitsa; the other was a biologist called Vavilov.

Kapitsa was an impressive, sparkling man with a large oval head like one of the sculptures in polished metal that were fashionable at the time. He came from an aristocratic Russian family and had survived the revolution because of his talent as a student for physics; he had come to Cambridge in 1921 as part of a Russian scientific delegation. Then he had been allowed to stay on as a pupil of Rutherford's – allowed by both the Cambridge and the Russian authorities. I had thought – He is someone who is able to move from one compartment to another; who has had to learn a trick or two in order to stay alive.

In Cambridge he had started a club called the Kapitsa Club in which scientists and others could meet and indulge in speculation and fantasy no matter how apparently absurd: I had been told about this by Donald, who had been taken to one of the meetings. I had said 'You mean, old ideas have to be broken up before new ones can come alive?' Donald had said 'Oh everyone likes a bit of nonsense every now and then.'

In the summer of 1933 I met Kapitsa at one of Melvyn's parties. I thought suddenly – He is not, is he, the man whom I saw Mullen with at that pub outside Cambridge, when they pretended not to see me?

At the party Kapitsa laughed and joked and was a centre of attention. Once, when he was talking with Melvyn, he looked across the room towards me and pulled the corners of his mouth down like a clown. I thought – No, he is not that man who was with Mullen; but still, it is as if he might know me.

Melvyn came across the room to me. He said 'I've been telling Kapitsa that you want to do post-graduate work in Russia.'

I said 'Oh I didn't really want you to ask him!'

Melvyn said 'It's all right, ducky, he won't make a pass. He'll just want to get you to sell some secrets to Russia.'

I waited till Melvyn had left me and then I went over to Kapitsa. He was, as it happened, now standing with Mullen. I thought – The impression that I have known Kapitsa before is some trick of the mind?

I said to him 'Melvyn says you might help me to get some post-graduate work in Russia.'

He said 'You are a physicist?'

I said 'Yes, but after my degree I want to do biology.'

'Why?'

'I want to see how the two are connected.'

Kapitsa laughed. He said 'You want to see how power and love are connected?'

I said 'Yes.'

He said 'Ah, you may learn that in Holy Mother Russia!'

I did not know what to say to this. Kapitsa seemed to be laughing at a joke within himself. I thought – It is as if he is seeing something in the future?

I said 'I was in Germany last winter: everyone there seemed so confident, all-of-a-piece; striding forwards like mad archaic statues.'

Kapitsa said 'In Russia they are not confident.'

Mullen said 'Is that necessarily a bad thing?'

Mullen was like a ghost waiting for its cue to come out of a cupboard.

I said 'But are the stories about Russia true?'

This was the time when stories about conditions in Russia were filtering through to England: there had been famine caused by the enforced collectivisation of agriculture; during the enforcement thousands of peasants had been shot.

Kapitsa said 'You're a physicist, not yet a biologist: who can say what stories are or are not true?'

I said 'Old ground has to be broken up, before something new can grow?'

Kapitsa said 'The pelican tears with her beak at her breast so that there shall be enough sustenance for her children – that is an image of Holy Mother Russia!'

I thought – He is a trickster: a survivor –

– He will be too careful of himself to get me work in Russia.

The other eminent Russian scientist I had met during these years was the biologist Vavilov who was a friend of my father's. Vavilov was of an opposite type to that of Kapitsa; he was a serious-looking man with thick wavy hair parted in the middle so that he was like a ship making heavy weather in rough sea. He travelled round the world collecting specimens of plants for the Biological Institute in Leningrad and the Academy of Agricultural Sciences in Odessa. He sometimes used to stay with us when he visited Cambridge. One weekend at this time when I went home I found my father and Vavilov on the lawn under the mulberry tree. I thought – It is because they do not look like tricksters that they look like conspirators.

My father said 'I've been telling Vavilov that you want to give up the study of things that cannot be said to exist by using methods that are admitted not to refer to what they talk about, and return to the land of the living.'

I said 'Kapitsa says that biology is to do with love and physics is to do with power.'

Vavilov said 'Kapitsa said that?'

My father said 'You've met Kapitsa?'

I thought – But of course real conspirators would not look like conspirators.

I said to Vavilov 'I wondered if you might be able to help me get post-graduate work in Russia.'

Vavilov said 'I have told your father that I might be able to get you a place in the Academy of Agricultural Sciences at Odessa.'

I thought – Vavilov, if he is kind to me, might not be a survivor?

My father said 'Vavilov has been telling me of the weird and wonderful work that is being done in Odessa. There is a man there who claims to make two ears of wheat grow where only one grew before: who thinks he can pass on by inheritance this acquired characteristic.'

Vavilov said 'The results are still under investigation.' He looked anxious.

My father said 'How long will it be before he is exposed?'

I thought – But my father does not realise that it is Vavilov who might be exposed.

I said 'My father and I have never quite agreed about what might be called the passing-on of acquired characteristics: perhaps that is because we are father and son.'

My father looked put out. I thought – But what is the point of being a biologist if one does not see that it may be jokes that help one to survive.

My father said 'Max once tried to repeat one of Kammerer's experiments with salamanders.'

Vavilov said 'Ah, and what did you find?'

I said 'I wondered in how large an area one might look for what one might find: perhaps the experiment was to do with love.'

Neither Vavilov nor my father seemed to see the point of this. I thought – Ah, but perhaps I am learning to be a trickster.

I got my degree in the summer of 1933: there was a delay before I could get a place at Odessa. During the year I lingered on in Cambridge I tried to find out what I could about what was going on in Russia. There had been Stalin's five-year plan for industrialisation which had begun in 1929; this was said to have been completed in 1932. Steel output was up by 300%; electrification by 400% – but what did these figures mean? Why should they refer to anything? Why should they not just be figures worked out by men in white coats sitting in front of lots of paper – not even screens and dials. There were, yes, the enormous dams visited by tourists; the rivers diverted; the festoons of wires stretching across the countryside. But where did the wires go: perhaps they ran out into a desert.

There were the stories of starvation and mass murder, but also the attempts at justification: the demand for food had increased greatly as a result of the growth of the population of the towns; it was this that had led necessarily to the enforced collectivisation of agriculture; it was when peasants had hoarded their produce that there had been some shootings; of course there had had to be some break-up of traditional ways of life. But then also there were the official stories of triumphant peasants riding across vast plains on tractors and waving their caps in the air; workers with a new strain of hope where none had been before. I thought – But why should not all these sets of stories be true? Just as, if one looks at light in one way it can be said to be waves; in another, particles –

– And it is not true, anyway, that old ground has to be broken up – and so on.

My mother was away through much of that summer and autumn; she was taking a further step in her psychoanalytical training in America. She did not spend much time with my father now. I thought – With everything you learn, you also learn to be alone –

– What work are you doing in Zurich now, my brave dark German girl?

When my mother came back from America she seemed older and more calm. She moved about the house with her hands folded in front of her. I thought – She has stopped drinking? She has come to terms with some young lover? Then – She has come to terms with me?

She had a way of appearing to think before she spoke and then saying something that seemed designed to keep one slightly under her spell. She said 'How odd that you don't want to be with your girlfriend in Zurich! Are you sure you're not running away by staying at home?'

I said 'I'm trying to get to Russia!'

She said 'But not succeeding!'

I thought – But that is grotesque! Then – Anyway, you don't seem to be getting very far in setting yourself up as an analyst.

I said 'Aren't you supposed to be jealous of my girlfriend in Zurich?'

My mother said 'How can I be if you are not with her?'

I thought – Well, that's quite clever.

I did nothing much of importance in Cambridge during this year. I learned some Russian: I spent time working in the laboratory under Kapitsa; we were examining the properties of liquid helium. But I had lost much of my interest in physics temporarily. I thought – What indeed if they are connected to nothing, these switches and dials?

I once said to Kapitsa 'But why does no one seem to be interested in finding out more about this power at the centre of the atom – what might be a practical use?'

Kapitsa said 'People only find, you know, what they want to find.'

'People don't want power?'

'Oh, they want power they can handle!'

I thought – But is it not a power which they cannot handle that would be to do with change?

I said 'H. G. Wells wrote a story years ago about the making of an atomic bomb. This had results that were so hideous that it eventually brought peace to the world.'

Kapitsa said 'Can you give me the reference of this story?'

Often I had thought about going to Zurich. But I had to work, and you had to work; and I remembered what you had said about our three days. You had said 'I cannot do more than this now: I am still the German child of my father and my mother: I have to stay here and wait and see.' And I had thought – I must not press things: they will come round again. If I press, nothing either new or old may grow.

Also, I suppose, I was still frightened – not of having too little but (as you would say) of taking on too much.

Also from time to time I was carrying on with the girl called Suzy. (There are not many things I have not wanted to tell you concerning these years!)

During that winter I did write to you to say that I was thinking of coming out to Zurich. Then before I posted it I had a letter from you –

I cannot stay in this place. It is only just over the border from Freiburg, Heidelberg. I did cross the border secretly one night; my father sent me back. He said I would be arrested: I am known as one of a gang responsible for killing Nazis. And I suppose I would endanger my father if I went back. He says my mother is in some prison-camp near Munich. But if I cannot go home I do not want to stay here. I do not like these people. They are quite right, perhaps, to say we have brought the Nazis on ourselves.

I have been offered work with a group of anthropologists who are going to the interior of West Africa: I have agreed to go with them; I have to sign on for two years. They are leaving next week.

Oh Max, I am so sorry, but what can I do? I have such hatred. I cannot settle here. I cannot come to England as I have not the proper papers.

I will probably be gone by the time you get this letter. You will not save me this time: I have so longed for you to come here! But you have been right not to come. I have felt so destructive, I would have destroyed what we have had together. My only pleasure about Europe has become the prospect of people killing each other. I sometimes feel this about my mother. I cannot stay here thinking things like this.

I would mind if they killed you! They cannot kill the time we have had together. This I suppose was the best of my life. You do believe it will come round again.

I will let you know where I am. Let me know if you go to Russia. You may find something there but I do not think that it will be what you expect. We are both trying to learn in our different ways, I suppose, how to survive.

I thought – But dear God, to survive you first have to die?

– Or is it that the thing in oneself that throws such chances away has to die?

In the summer of 1934 there were two incidents that seemed to increase the sense of threat in Europe. The first was the murder by Hitler of Röhm, one of his oldest colleagues, together with several hundred Brownshirts of whom Röhm was the leader. Hitler had done this, it was said, to placate the army, which he now needed more than Röhm. Then shortly after this the news came through that Kapitsa, who had gone on his annual holiday and then to a conference in Russia, had been detained against his will and was not being allowed to come back to Cambridge. I thought – But perhaps the pelican is trying to look after its own breast: what if Russia becomes interested in the sort of power that might be locked up in the heart of the atom?

My father said 'Well, now it's out of the question that you should go to Russia!'

I thought I might say, as if I were acting – I didn't know you cared!

I said 'I'm not Kapitsa.'

My father said 'Presumably you're enough of a physicist for them to want to keep you. Also you're my son.'

I thought – We might both be flattered if they kept me?

I said 'I might be able to find out something about Kapitsa. He might quite want to stay in Russia. He might be making out that he doesn't want to stay to get more out of the people in Cambridge.'

My father said 'Why do you say that?'

I said 'Anyway, I'll be under Vavilov's protection in Russia.'

My father said 'They'll do away with Vavilov if they want to, those Russians.'

I thought – But it might be interesting to try to look at what they want?

My mother floated about the house as if it were she who were being martyred. I said to her 'But why aren't you showing more emotion about my going to Russia? Why aren't you rolling about on the floor and yelling, as in an opera?'

My mother said gravely 'I have spent enough time, goodness knows, trying to stop myself reaching a condition in which I am rolling about on the floor.'

I thought – Well, that's quite witty!

I said 'It might be more jolly for me if you were rolling about.'

She said 'That's your problem.' She put a hand up and touched my cheek. Then she took her hand away quickly. She said 'We can't have everything we want, you know.'

I thought – It helps you to survive, if you are witty?

When the time came for me to set out for Odessa I travelled by train to Marseilles and then caught a boat. I was thinking – no, not thinking! – I was trying to say to myself – Listen; watch; see what happens, one thing after another.

This was the first time I had felt, really, that I was getting away from home. When I was in Marseilles I wondered – Boats go from here to West Africa?

Odessa was a large modern city that seemed to be flourishing. (I thought – So what had I expected?) There were wide streets with buses and trams; heavy stone buildings not so different from Berlin, Paris, Manchester. There were men in cloth caps and old women with shawls over their heads; young women in hats like acorns. What I had known previously about Odessa was that it was where Trotsky had been to school. Trotsky believed in permanent revolution – that you could not build a socialist state unless the rest of the world was becoming socialist too: socialism was a sort of purity that had to be guarded from corruption. It seemed that Trotsky had been defeated because people did not want to become pure; they wanted to be what they were, to be tethered to the earth and corrupted. They needed some iron to be put into their souls, or how would they know what to do? Stalin was the man of iron: he was at home with the corruption of power. But then in what sense would this be revolution?

I thought – Stop thinking! How do you stop thinking?

The family that I was going to stay with were called Platov: the father was a lecturer in zoology at the Academy of Sciences: he was a friend of Vavilov's and had corresponded with my father. The mother was of German extraction so that the family spoke German; I would thus be able to converse with them fairly easily, although one of the purposes of my visit was that I should learn Russian. The Platovs lived in an apartment block, the outside of which was decorated with heavy stone scrolls and pediments and balconies. Inside there were lampshades with fringes; red velvet cushions with black tassles. I thought – One's expectations are to do with needs of the mind: do people in Russia have images of people starving in Berlin, Paris, Manchester?

Then – Life in fact goes on in nests; hurricanes blow over them.

There was a son, Kolya, who was slightly younger than I; and a daughter, Mitzi, who was slightly older. The father was a tall thin man with a pointed beard: the mother was a short bulging woman with a tight waist that made her like an hour-glass. She bounced slightly as she walked: she wore a long skirt so that one could not see her legs. I thought – You mean, I am still interested in mothers?

When I arrived, Mitzi and Kolya welcomed me politely. Then Mitzi giggled and went out of the room. I thought – What does that mean? Then – Can I not make it what I want it to mean?

We sat round a dinner-table on high-backed carved wooden chairs. Mr Platov made formal conversation as if there were servants in the room: Mrs Platov stood at the sideboard and ladled out soup or stew. The children looked down at their plates as if embarrassed. I thought – Perhaps if there are no servants there are still secret police in the next-door room so that we can have polite conversation.

Mr Platov said to me 'So you wish to go to lectures at the biology department of our Academy of Sciences? There is much interesting work being done in the biology department of our Academy!'

I said 'Ah yes, the fame of your Professor Lysenko has spread to England.'

Mr Platov said to his wife at the sideboard 'A little more seasoning in the stew, do you think?'

I said 'Are Professor Lysenko's theories taken seriously in Odessa?'

Mr Platov said 'Indeed Professor Lysenko's theories are taken seriously in Odessa!' He held his knife and fork on either side of his plate as if they were implements to hold something burning. He said 'Is that not right, Kolya?'

Kolya said 'What?'

Mr Platov said 'Professor Lysenko's theories are taken seriously in Odessa.'

Kolya said 'I don't know.'

Mitzi said 'Kolya is a poet.'

I said 'Oh.'

Kolya said 'I am not.'

Mitzi giggled.

I thought – If I were an anthropologist I would make a note: human motives are equally incomprehensible in Berlin, Cambridge, Odessa.

The lectures I hoped to go to at the Academy of Sciences, about the subject of which I had tried to find out more before I had left England, were to do with the claims of the biologist called Lysenko whom Vavilov had been talking about in Cambridge. It was he who was being hailed as the leader of a new breed of Soviet scientists – who could make two ears of wheat grow where previously there had only been one; who saw his task – in emulation, as it were, of what Marx had said about history – as not just to describe nature but to change it. I had talked more to my father about this: I had said 'Is it possible that a new strain of wheat might be found if it were badly enough needed?' My father had said 'It is possible that a new strain of Soviet scientists might be found if it is badly enough needed.'

It seemed that what had happened was that when the shortage of food had been most severe, the Soviet government had called on scientists to discover a more productive strain of wheat – not just to discover circumstances by which wheat growing would become more productive, but to create a type of wheat in which this characteristic would be passed on genetically. Orthodox biologists had explained: but this cannot be done to order; a new strain of wheat will depend on a chance mutation; this can be looked for and perhaps caught and then can be encouraged, but this will take patience, time; what is the meaning of 'chance' if we think we can summon it to order?

It was then that Stalin himself had apparently replied (might this not have been a joke? was it inconceivable that Stalin might be a joker?) that the task of a Marxist scientist was not to describe nature but to change it.

And so just then there had turned up this scientist called Lysenko who claimed to have come across an improved strain of wheat, indeed by chance – he happened to have dropped a bag of winter-wheat seed in water one day and then had thrown it away in the snow because he had thought it would be useless. And this his father had happened to pick up by mistake and had sown the seed the following spring and, lo and behold! – a rabbit from a hat – out had popped two ears of wheat where one had grown before; and this new strain was one whose characteristics – yes! – could be passed on genetically. No evidence was put forward for this: it seemed that it was sufficient evidence that Marx might be thought to have suggested it. And so now all Soviet farmers had to do in order to save themselves and the country from famine was to dip their bags of winter seed into water and then throw them into snow –

I had said to my father 'All right, this new breed of Soviet scientist has in fact popped up: but what will happen when it is found that what they claim is not passed on genetically?'

My father had said 'Why should they ever find this? Isn't it this that I was saying to Vavilov – in a Soviet system it is necessary not for something to work, but to find someone to say that whatever is wanted works – '

I had thought – But what an amazing experiment! To find out what happens when you say something happens, quite irrespective of whether it does or not –

– Would not this be a real test of reality being a function of the experimental condition?

Now, sitting round the dinner-table with the Platov family who were like actors on a stage keeping up appearances in front of an audience or secret police, I thought –

– There may in fact be people in the wings waiting to kill them if they do not conform to the terms of the experimental condition!

I went with Kolya to attend the lectures at the Academy of Sciences. I sat at the back of the lecture-hall which was very cold and I did not understand much of what the lecturer was saying. I thought – But if words have so little to do with meaning, what does it matter if I do not understand what a lecturer is saying? Here we all are in our overcoats and quilted jackets and caps with flaps that come down over our ears: we are like bags of winter-wheat seed dumped in the snow: indeed what is interesting is what will happen when, as it were, we are sown in spring – or what will happen if nothing happens in the spring – some ground will have been broken up, something one day may grow –

– Might not Lysenko in fact just be saying – If an old strain is broken up, how can you know what will grow?

I would walk back with Kolya from the Academy of Sciences. There were markets in the streets selling second-hand clothing and bits of old furniture. The atmosphere did not seem so different from the town in the north of England where I had been three years ago: there was even less food; but the atmosphere was somewhat more lively. I thought – It is within the mind that old patterns are being broken up –

I said to Kolya 'But do you yourself think that Comrade Lysenko's theories will work?'

Kolya said as if quoting ' – If there is a passionate desire, then every goal can be reached, every objective overcome – '

I said 'That sounds like a poem.'

He said 'It is.'

I said 'Did you write it?'

He said 'No, Comrade Stalin wrote it.' Then he ran on ahead and kicked at a stone, or did a little dance, in the street.

I said 'Comrade Stalin is a poet?'

He said 'In Russia we are all poets!'

I thought – A poet crosses out a word here, a sentence there –

– Might a poet not see people as no more precious than words?

I said 'Have you heard of an Austrian biologist called Kammerer?'

Kolya said 'Oh yes, there was a film about Kammerer. He was on his way to take up an important position at the Academy in Moscow, when he was murdered by reactionary Fascist academics and priests.'

I said 'He was?'

Kolya said 'You didn't know?' He did a small entrechat half on and half off the pavement.

I said 'He thought he had discovered something about the inheritance of acquired characteristics.'

Kolya said 'You see?'

I thought – It is because no one knows whether people mean what they say or not that ballet is so popular in Russia?

In the apartment I shared a room with Kolya. Kolya was a red-headed boy with eyes set close together. When we got ready for bed at night we each acted as if we were conscious of the other watching. I thought – But this is not homosexuality; it is in the style of a play by Brecht: we are trying to pass some message about being conscious that messages are being transmitted.

Then again – Stop thinking!

Mitzi was a strong round-faced girl who was training to become a champion discus-thrower. In the evenings she would change into a white blouse and white shorts and do exercises in her room. I thought – With Mitzi, indeed, it might be possible to stop thinking: to be held in her strong hand and whirled round and round and sent spinning through the universe.

I began to look for opportunities to waylay Mitzi: I was some-times able to walk with her to the Academy of Sciences where she was studying metallurgy. When the cold weather came she dressed in a long coat with a fur collar and a fur hat and muff. I thought – She is like a girl in Dostoevsky: not one of those demure girls, but one of the ones who get men's heads spinning round on platters –

I said to Mitzi 'You like dancing? We could go and dance!'

She said 'Oh I used to love dancing, but I now fear it is not good for the physique.'

I said 'But of course it is good for the physique! Has not Comrade Stalin said "Let all the discus-throwers dance!"'

She said 'Comrade Stalin has said that?'

I said 'It is in one of his poems.'

When I said things like this Mitzi would stop and stand at the edge of the pavement and look across the road as if she were waiting for a gap in the traffic.

I thought – But if reality is a function of the experimental condition –

– Am I really trying to get Mitzi into bed?

I said 'Mitzi, but we can talk, no one can hear us here! Or if they do, you can always say that you were being kind to me, in order to get me sent to Siberia!'

Occasionally I got Mitzi to smile. She would then walk for a time with her arm through mine. She would say 'Why are you not serious? It is your way in England never to be serious?'

I said 'But it is you who are not serious!'

She said 'Me?'

I said 'The things you will not talk about. The things you will not even listen to – '

Mitzi began to take her arm away from mine.

I said loudly 'For instance, the magnificently improved production of wheat – !'

Mitzi put her hands over her ears and ran across the road.

Then I thought – But perhaps it is they who know some things are too serious to be within the range of talk –

– And I am protecting myself from Mitzi by talking like this?

– Why do I not say just – Let's make love!

Once I caught up with her after she had run away and I said 'Oh Mitzi, all the things going on in your country may be all right for all I know. I mean the theories of Comrade Lysenko, the failures in the production of wheat. I mean, of course, it may be true that old patterns have to be broken up; then what lovely things may grow! I'm not saying you're wrong, I'm saying you may be right! I mean, I'm saying that for all I know Comrade Stalin may be right – '

I was holding Mitzi's arm. She was staring at me belligerently as if by will she could make me do whatever she wanted me to do –

I thought – But I am trying to say just – Let's make love!

This was a time – the winter of 1934/35 – when what became known later as the Terror had not yet got under way in Stalin's Russia; but there had been the stories of senseless killings as well as those of famine on and off for years. However, not long after I had arrived in Russia there was the assassination of Kirov, the Bolshevik Party leader in Leningrad, and this was seen later as the starting-point for the Terror. Kirov was murdered by a mentally unstable dissident; this dissident, Nikolaev, could have been working on his own or he might have been one of a group; but the point was that in the Soviet system he could be said to have been working with anyone – so that anyone could be said to be responsible for the murder of the Party leader, Kirov. And how useful this could be for someone who wanted to get rid of enemies! The precedent for this sort of thing was the Nazis' use of the Reichstag fire, when a mentally unstable dissident had given Hitler the chance to get rid of anyone he chose. Now Kirov's assassination was being used by Stalin to arrest and put on trial Zinoviev and Kamenev, two of his oldest colleagues – and the precedent for this, of course, was Hitler's killing of Röhm. I thought – Well, indeed, there are patterns here that become established in the mind: but dictators, of course, are too stupid to see that they are parts of patterns of mind –

Then – It is because of you, my beautiful German girl, that I find it so difficult to get involved with Mitzi!

I went on trying to talk to Kolya. I said 'But I see that for a

Communist society to work, old loyalties have to be broken up. But why can't you just say this – '

Kolya sometimes spoke with passion. 'Why should you say anything? What do you think you have to say? You people in the West make an idol of words! You think that once you have said something you have achieved it.'

I thought – Yes, I know that.

I said 'All right, there may be things better not said. But does anyone know this at the top? I mean, does anyone know what's happening? If there's no one – '

Kolya said 'You think you can know what is happening? What is happening? Tell me!'

I said 'All right, people are being shot without reason – '

He said 'How do you know?'

I said 'You can look.'

He said 'Do you look at every battlefield? Do you find somewhere where people do not die?'

I thought – Kolya has learned something that I have not?

– But I used to know once that it is impossible with some experiments to limit the area in which one might look for reasons or results.

Kolya said 'What do you think human beings are! Look to actions, not to words.'

I thought – Kolya is saying, like Kapitsa: Look at the paradoxes in Holy Mother Russia!

Then – I am using you as an excuse, my beautiful German girl, for not getting involved with Mitzi?

One afternoon when I thought I was alone in the apartment (I would sit on my bed with my Russian textbooks on my knees and wrapped against the cold like a kidnap victim), and so could get on with what seemed to be my business of dreaming about Mitzi (I would think – But are not good Communist girls supposed to be easily available in Russia?), I heard a noise in the dining-room as if someone were moving quietly, not wishing to be heard. I got up and went out into the passage surreptitiously because I too did not want to be heard (I had been thinking – I know it is my own fault that I get no further than dreams with Mitzi: I must be more resolute, cunning: why do I see everything as an experiment to see what will happen?) and through the open door of the dining-room I saw Mrs Platov standing by the sideboard. She was holding a bottle dangling from her hand. She had her back to me and was quite still; she herself seemed to be in a dream. I thought – so perhaps now I will see what people here do when they think they are not being seen; when they show not what they talk about, but what they are in themselves. Then – But of course I have an image in my mind of a middle-aged mother with a bottle in her hand: I do not have to come all this way to learn about that, O my mother! There was a thin silver light coming into the room from snow outside; this lit up glints in bottles and glasses on the sideboard. I thought – But this is something archetypal: a Dutch interior perhaps? A Vermeer? Then Mrs Platov held the bottle behind her; the bottle seemed to be empty; it had been of vodka: then she began to lift up her skirt at the back. I thought – Good heavens, is that what they do in Russia? Then – If Mrs Platov sees me I can say I have come to mend the pianola. There was a pianola that was broken in the dining-room, and I had for some time been hoping to mend it. Mrs Platov seemed to be wearing nothing underneath her skirt. She began to walk, waddling somewhat, to the far end of the dining-room table with her skirt still raised and the bottle held against her at her back; then she turned and began to lower herself on to the chair on which she usually sat at the end of the table. In this position she was now facing me, who was just beyond the open door. I could not tell whether or not she saw me; she seemed to become frozen, either in some sort of trance, or perhaps under the impression that if she stayed still enough she might be invisible. I thought – But of course, she wants to be like one of those toys that sit with spikes up inside them; who thus stare straight ahead and do not see anything, hear anything; indeed, yes, they would want to be this sort of thing in Russia. It seemed that if I moved then Mrs Platov might have to notice me beyond the doorway, so I stood still: I thought – You mean, it is thus that visitors who come to Russia have to make out that they do not hear anything, see anything. Or I thought I might say to Mrs Platov – But I don't mind if you are on the bottle! Ha ha! I mean I don't mind if you are this literally. Then – Perhaps it is this that is peculiar about Russia: they do things literally; they don't use metaphors. After a time, Mrs Platov seemed to see me; she was crouching, half sitting, as if getting down on a lavatory. I said 'I thought I might try to mend the pianola!' I smiled and waved, and moved away. It seemed to me that I had thought of something very clever here – I mean about metaphors; about pianolas – though I could not quite explain to myself why. When I got back to my room I was less than ever able to work, and was having even more violent day-dreams about Mitzi. I thought – Dear God, is it not I who bring together metaphors and reality; but do not seem to manage for one to be comforting the other.

When snow came to the streets, Kolya and I and some other boys would have snowball fights on our way home from the Academy: Kolya fought with a bright-eyed energy; he would try to put snow down the back of my neck.

Mitzi did more of her training in her room; in her white blouse and white cotton shorts she pushed and pulled at strings and bits of elastic. I thought – Perhaps Melvyn is right and Stalin is a woman: people want to be stretched and pulled and flung like plates and discuses round the universe.

I bought a bottle of my own vodka and sat with it in my room. I thought – But you are not frightened of reality, of life, my beautiful German girl!

Mitzi moved some of her equipment in to the dining-room to have more space. I thought that this was now the time for me to try to mend the pianola.

The pianola was a magical machine with bellows and cogwheels and cylinders and chains and pipes with little valves that went up and down. Mitzi lay on her back with her weights on her feet and her hands above her head holding bits of elastic attached to the wall. She would raise and lower the top half of her body with lungs blowing and limbs straining and little bits of muscle going up and down. I thought – Mitzi is the eternal spirit of the pianola! I have come to help these chains and cogwheels: to hold them in my hands.

When Mitzi rested I said 'Would you like some vodka?'

She said 'How are you getting on with that pianola?'

I said '*Regarde la symétrie merveilleuse de l'édifice humain! Les épaules et les hanches et les mamelons fleurissants de part et d'autre sur la poitrine; le nombril au milieu dans la mollesse du ventre; le sexe obscure entre les cuisses –* '

She said 'What's that?'

I said 'It's in a book called *The Magic Mountain* that was recommended to me by a friend.'

'Can you rub on some of that here?'

'Rub on some of that there?'

'Yes.'

I had been holding out to her the vodka bottle. She took a swig from it, then handed it back. I had knelt down beside her. Her feet were still under weights; she was leaning on her hands behind her by the bits of elastic fastened to the wall.

I thought – Dear God, now magic stand me in good stead!

Mitzi said 'Comrade Stalin says vodka is good for the muscles, no?'

I said 'Comrade Stalin says vodka is good for the muscles, yes!'

I rubbed some of the vodka on to the calves of her legs. I thought – Lucky old pianola! We pedal away: we send out music?

Mitzi lay back and went on with her exercises. I continued to kneel. The muscles in her arms and legs stood out; it was as if her white blouse and shorts were like some old skin that she was trying to shake off. I thought – There, there, I can help! I put my hand on the place on her shorts where there seemed to be the centre of the struggle going on. I thought – Yes, this is gravity.

When Mitzi rested again she held out her hand for the vodka bottle. I gave it to her and she put her head back and held it to her mouth. I could see the liquid going like a sword down her throat. Then she seemed to hold some of the liquid in her mouth. She put a hand to the back of my head and pulled me to her. She kissed me and opened my mouth with her tongue and shot the vodka from her mouth inside me. This was indeed like a sword going into me; it had, as it were, to emerge somewhere. Nothing quite so violent had happened to me before: I began to pull and tear at Mitzi's clothes; Mitzi herself became quite passive. I got her blouse off quite easily: but her shorts – her shorts seemed to be made of sailcloth; have you tried to tear sailcloth? I mean in a high wind. I did not try to get her shorts down over her feet because her feet were attached to the weights and this seemed to be some sort of bonus. So I wrenched and pummelled at her shorts; I put my knee against her and heaved. Mitzi leaned on her elbows and opened her mouth and put her head back. I seemed to be making the most tremendous love to Mitzi. I might have thought – So what indeed are the connections between love and power! Mitzi was reaching up towards me as if we were on some rock-face; she was scratching at me with her fingers; I rent her shorts; she seemed to like this; it was as if both of us had to fall, or neither of us would. We did and did not fall; we got where we wanted. Of course there was violence, hurting: how could there not be? So forgive me, my beautiful German girl: with us, you and me, there had been, is, no hurting.

264

But things have to be let out, aired, do they not? There has to be some practice on a rock-face.

Some days later I received a letter from West Africa, which said –

Alaba, Dahomey, West Africa
February 25th 1935 (St Walburga's Day)

My Angel,

Here we have been learning the language of this strange tribe (as you would say). Have you found anyone in Russia yet? I mean someone who is good enough so that the world may not have to be destroyed.

In the capital of this country, not many miles away, not more than a few generations ago, there was a king who grew rich and fat through selling slaves to European traders. The slaves were captured in wars with neighbouring tribes; the traders paid for them with elegant dinner-services and guns. The slaves were kept in cages like shopping baskets. The trade with Europeans was in fact incidental to the taking of slaves: what the slaves were most needed for was what was called the 'feeding of the king's people'.

There are beautifully written descriptions of this by European travellers just after the time when the slave-trade had been stopped. The captives in their baskets were dressed in clean white robes and had tall caps like those of dunces on their heads; they were carried to the edge of the high wooden platform on which the king and visiting dignitaries were enthroned. The king made a speech to the multitude below – he said that once more the time had come for him to feed his people – then one by one the victims were tipped out of their baskets on to the crowd, who tore them to pieces. And the pieces were fed to the dogs.

Well, what have you found, my loved one, in Russia? Should not the world be destroyed?

When the French took over this country in 1894 the elite troops who fought them were women – archeresses, blunderbusseresses, razor-women. When the French got into the city there were also ladies of the bedchamber in plumed hats and satins and silks. Such beautiful descriptions have been written of this! Such beautiful artefacts to illustrate it have been made. Oh Max, I do not see why the human race should go on!

Rudi tells me that this is St Walburga's Day. St Walburga was a Christian saint of the eighth century AD who founded the first community for both men and women.

The Italians here say that Mussolini will invade Abyssinia. Shall we go, you and I, and fight against Mussolini; become blunderbussers and razor-women; put a few European heads on spikes?

If one felt that there was a cause worth fighting for, one might not think one were mad, but in fact one would be, because one would think one were sane.

Descriptions, artefacts, of evil things to do with change – do you think these could be beautiful?

Oh Max, let us do an experiment with space, with time. Let us say that we will meet in the not-too-far future – we don't know where or when, perhaps we will not say too much even that we have this plan – but let us say we will thus meet and then we will watch, and listen; and perhaps we will be two of those particles who having bumped into each other once (or twice!) in some way are always connected and so we will know the process by which we meet again. Did you have as a child those drawings in Christmas crackers on which there were trails of gunpowder which you lit and they moved as if by magic and then met and this was the mysterious explosion?

If you wanted to imagine a meeting-place where you from Russia and me from Africa might properly meet, where would you say?

Don't tell me!

It would be the process of finding out that would be proper. I have always thought that after this it might be possible to live together.

Keep in touch with me from your strange tribe.

With all my love

Eleanor

I found myself trying to imagine – Who is Rudi?

My life as a student went on through that long winter; I sat at the back of lecture-halls; I tried to protect myself against the cold. I felt it had been a mistake to come to Russia: I had learned little – except from Mitzi. But Mitzi, after a period of doing her exercises at home, as it were, went back to her old friends.

I thought about going home, but I felt that I should endure till spring – for self-respect, and anyway what would I find at home? I heard that my friend Suzy was engaged to be married. I was not sure what I meant by 'self-respect': but I thought – Yes, if one has lost one's way, one might still learn from a process in the dark.

I moved among the ice-floes of students: I kept my eyes down, the flaps of my fur cap over my ears. I explained to myself – The whole of Russia is, has been for years, frozen: there is nothing to learn here until it can be seen what seeds have lain dormant and come up in the spring. People appeared to be paralysed by the impression of being listened to from behind walls: somewhere off-stage, it seemed, were slave-kings on their thrones. To stay alive (but this was what I was learning?) you watched yourself carefully; you looked for signs of a path; the rest was boring.

My fellow students studied, play-acted, sang; sometimes danced. I thought – All this is a code: it is not direct language.

– Some people are shot: some get sent to Siberia. But when has life not depended on what is random?

Occasionally I found myself with Mitzi in the afternoons. Then there were, yes, the impressions of exertion, risk, machinery, music, vodka, power.

I thought – But these things, with Mitzi and Suzy, are possible because they are little: with my German girl things are too much.

Much of the time I sat on my bed in my room with my knees up. I sometimes wrote poetry. I wanted to tell you – Occasionally it may be possible to make beautiful descriptions of terrible things to do with change: perhaps this is what goes on behind the closed door in a courtyard.

I began to think that I might give up the work I had been trying to do – both in physics and biology. In both, people seemed to be seeing whatever they wanted to see: and the sufferings of the tribe, the feeding of the people, went on.

I had come to Russia because I had thought – Here will be people struggling with predicaments that are real: there will be suffering; but at least they will be looking not just at what they want to see. Now, it seemed – But the propensity for humans to see what they want to see is endless: people will have to stop being human for them to be in touch with what might be called 'reality'.

In particular, at the Academy of Sciences there was the following of Lysenko. It had become known that Lysenko had been publicly applauded by Stalin; it was decreed officially that there should be Lysenko's treatment of wheat. It was no use scientists like Vavilov saying that this did not in fact work – that there was no evidence of increased yields let alone the inheritance of such acquired characteristics. Stalin had proclaimed – In the dialectical unity of theory and practice, theory must guide practice. And so if anyone questioned the theories of Lysenko it was they, and not the failed wheat seed, who were in danger of being dumped on the bonfire.

I thought – But just this might be the reality that is required by the experimental condition?

I had come to Russia acknowledging that old ground had to be broken up; not asking too many questions about what might come after. Now Lysenko and Stalin seemed to have this attitude themselves. I thought – So why should not deathliness be the experimental condition? Have we not agreed that humans as they are are not viable?

Then – But I should get out into the countryside and see the actual conditions.

I would lie with my head underneath the bedclothes and try to practise justification – But I always knew that it might be in quite a different area that something new might grow. Then – Words are used to justify anything –

– A million or two dead children?

I tried to work. I tried to stop thinking. I thought – For God's sake, other people manage to stop thinking.

Then – It is old patterns in my own mind that are being broken up: you think something lively there may grow?

– Einstein may be right: it is not bearable that reality should be no more than a function of the experimental condition!

– But why should reality be bearable to humans?

Then – Am not I becoming paralysed like other people in Russia?

– Why indeed should not humanity be wiped out!

I saw Vavilov briefly when he came to Odessa: he seemed reluctant to see me at all. I thought – Because I, being a foreigner, might endanger him: because he might endanger me? A persecution seemed to be underway against Vavilov and the rational scientists like him: they were being called bourgeois, formalistic, metaphysical. I thought – Ah, but it is metaphysical to be human! (What was it you called me on that path on our magic mountain – '*Joli bourgeois à la petite tache humide*'?) When I saw him, Vavilov seemed to want to caution me about my seeing him.

I had a letter from my father giving me news of Kapitsa. Kapitsa had for some months refused to work with the Russians: now he had relented, and had asked the Cambridge authorities to send him the equipment in his old laboratory. The Cambridge authorities were looking favourably on this request: of course there should be no national barriers against the dissemination of scientific knowledge! My father suggested that it might be useful if I could get personally any news of Kapitsa. He added 'People here may be a bit naive about what they call "scientific knowledge".'

I thought – You mean, Kapitsa from time to time interested himself in things other than the superfluidity of low-temperature helium –

– Kapitsa is a trickster?

– Scientific knowledge can of course blow the world up?

– This is the reality. These are the real experimental conditions.

I saw Lysenko once or twice at the Academy of Sciences. He was a small furtive man with a cigarette usually hanging out of his mouth; he dressed ostentatiously as a peasant. It was said that in the summer he went around in bare feet – that as a scientist he believed not so much in the efficacy of laboratory experiment as in the feel of the ground that comes up through bare feet. I thought – Well, a peasant might feel from the ground things to do with birth and death –

– But it could not be beautiful, this so-called 'feeding of a people'.

News came from Moscow that Zinoviev and Kamenev had been sent to prison for what was said to be their responsibility for the Kirov murder. It was argued that, because the murderer was a dissident and Zinoviev and Kamenev had from time to time shown dissidence within the Party, then logically and objectively they were accessories to the murder. Zinoviev and Kamenev themselves seemed to agree about this. I continued to try to talk to Kolya. I said 'But what is happening is that words are being used to justify anything: anything, that is, that anyone in power wants.'

Kolya said 'Are not words always used like this?'

I said 'Are they? I'm trying to find out.'

Then Kolya looked embarrassed and even furtive and said 'I've been meaning to ask you: are there any openings for Russian students of biology in Cambridge?'

I thought – You mean you trust me? You want me to trust you?

– Or you are playing a trick on me? You see!

I said 'I will find out.'

There was a day on which spring seemed to come to Odessa; the snow melted; drops hung on the ends of trees. I began to make enquiries about going home via Moscow and Leningrad. When I announced that I might be leaving, not only Kolya but Mitzi became more attentive to me. I thought – But it's too late, isn't it, to try to guess what things really mean. Mitzi had been going out with a tall thin boy with small steel spectacles and a pointed beard; now she came home to me more often in the afternoons. I thought – This may be genuine: she may want something from me: what's the difference? If there are no answers, why go through the questions of what things might mean? I began to think that, after all, I might stay longer in Russia. There were stories about how in summer everyone, boys and girls, ran down to bathe naked in the Black Sea.

Mitzi and the boy with small steel spectacles were planning some picnic, or expedition, they would be going on with a gang of their friends. It was not clear if I was to be included in this. There was chatter; then the usual secrecy. It was an expedition of a kind that they had apparently made before. I thought – But if no one cares what things might mean, why have secrecy?

I said to Mitzi 'Well, am I coming on this picnic or not?'

She said 'Do you want to come?'

'Do you want me to?'

'You may not like it.'

'Why not?'

'It is on Walpurgis Night. Do you know about Walpurgis Night?'

I said 'St Walpurga was a Christian saint in the eighth century AD. She founded the first community for both men and women.'

Mitzi said 'I do not think that can be correct.'

I said 'Mitzi, come away with me and live in a community for one man and one woman!'

She said 'Why are you always joking? It is boring.'

I thought – Perhaps they have some great orgy in the forest.

Kolya, it appeared, was refusing to come on this picnic: I heard him and Mitzi having an angry argument in her room. I thought – Perhaps I should have been taking Kolya more seriously?

I said to him 'What is it about this picnic?'

He said 'You think you will find some answers to your questions in the forest?'

I said 'Is there something you don't want me to find?'

He said 'Look, will you remember what I said about Cambridge – '

I thought again – Oh but how do I know you are not just evading my question!

– There will probably be terrible devastation in the countryside: I have felt myself a coward not to have looked before –

– Must I worry about Cambridge?

There had been few signs of famine in the town. Occasionally there were ragged people searching among dustbins: this was not all that different from scenes in the north of England, though in Odessa it seemed that such people were rounded up at night and taken away. But then there were gangs of children, like those of Gypsies, who lurked around street corners; if one approached them they ran away. I had heard stories of these children before I came to Russia: they were called *besprezornii*; they were orphans – first of the revolution and of the civil war, now of the enforced collectivisation and the famine. Their parents had died or had been carried off to Siberia; the children formed gangs to keep themselves alive. They came into towns to scavenge and to steal at night; they lived in the forest.

I thought – We seem to become involved with children, you and I, in spite of what we say –

– What is it about children: the kingdom of heaven? the chance to survive?

The day for the picnic was the last day of April; we were to stay out all night. Mitzi gathered provisions; Mr and Mrs Platov seemed as usual to be taking care not to be aware of what was happening. We had been told by the boy with steel spectacles, who was called Igor, and who seemed to be the leader of the expedition, that each participant was expected to bring a supply of food and vodka.

I thought – Oh perhaps we will plunge into icy water and roll about in the snow! And so old patterns will be broken up and two-headed wheat will grow.

On the day of the picnic we met at the railway station; there were about twenty of us; each had a blanket and a store of provisions and vodka. It was a pale grey day. We began to drink the vodka as soon as we were on the train. I thought – Oh yes, I will chase Mitzi through the forest and I will flick at her with birch twigs; Mitzi, if she is feeling generous, will flick at me. Then – But I must remember to look out of the window and take note of what is happening in the great and terrible world outside. There were hills with white dotted houses; later a grey and level plain. I thought –

In the countryside it is still as if you are on a stage; the sky is the audience looking down.

The boys passed round the vodka bottles and made jokes: most of the jokes I did not understand. One of the girls demurred about drinking from a bottle and a boy went down on his knees imploring her. A contest was held to see who could drink while being held upside down. I thought – Oh yes, there will be bacchanals; fauns and centaurs will prance and lumber in the forest. Then, looking out of the window – There is nothing growing on this grey and sterile plain: a dragon has come and has left dust and bones behind it.

Once when one of the girls continued to refuse to drink Igor held her arms and another boy held her head and a third boy poured the liquid down her throat. Mitzi watched me. I thought – You mean, you think I may be shocked by this environment?

– But in orgies one gets pleasure from degradation, especially one's own, does one not?

As well as drinking we seemed to be eating all the food. I did not understand this. The plan was that we should stay out all night.

I thought – We will go hunting?

One of the boys carried a coil of rope over his shoulders. Most of them carried sticks.

I had not asked many questions about the expedition. I thought that if I had I might not have been allowed to go.

When we reached our destination we spilled out on to the station platform acting, it seemed, even more drunk than we were. The platform was on an embankment above the flat, bare landscape; there was a line of forest in the distance. There were no buildings on the platform: we were the only people who had got out of the train. There was a village slightly below – a jumble of huts, some with thatched roofs and some with flat roofs made of mud. At the far end of the platform was a group of people who seemed to have been waiting for anyone who might get out of the train: they seemed very old; they were dressed in rags. Some were bent; most had their feet wrapped in cloth; they were like figures specially drawn to illustrate, yes, famine. I thought – But one cannot just say 'famine'! I bared my teeth. I could not think what else to do. Mitzi and another girl had wrapped up in old newspapers some scraps of food left over from the train; they now walked towards the figures at the end of the platform and when they were not too close but not too far away they tossed the bundles of newspapers towards the figures and then turned and ran back; the bundles burst and scraps of food were scattered. I thought – Dear God, I see, do I, why we had to eat most of the food on the train. The figures at the end of the platform scuttled and scrambled for the food. Before this they had not moved: I thought – Dear God, they know the rules, do they, of feeding time at the zoo? Then – But why is it not us that they are tearing with their hands? Mitzi and the other girl looked pleased. I thought – But what am I feeling: nothing? except – Is it not better that there should rather than should not be feeding times at a zoo?

Igor raised his arms and jumped off the platform on to the slope that ran down to the village. He acted as if he were an aeroplane, or suddenly scared; the others acted as if they were scared; we tumbled and slid down the slope; by the time we reached the village we had managed to be laughing. The figures behind us on the platform were smoothing out the bits of old newspaper carefully. I thought – They will use them for clothes. Then – In most parts of the world there are people like this.

The village seemed to be deserted. Through the doorways of hovels there were visible occasionally lengths of rags that might be bodies on beds; the whites of eyes above bundles in corners. I thought – Of course, in such an environment the mind goes numb: the brain reacts easily only to what it has been accustomed to.

Mitzi took me by the hand. I thought – I have passed the first test; I have not acted like a moralist. I have seen – There are different predicaments for different strange tribes?

Then – But what about that thing about a person losing his life in order to find it?

We were walking along a track that went out from the village. On either side was barren land that seemed once to have been ploughed. Now there was nothing but grey tufts of grass like diseased and flattened hair. The line of the forest was like a wall in the distance. I thought – Well, walls guard secrets.

Forests in Germany are so dramatic; so picturesque! In them we had walked as if in a well-loved fairy story. Here the wall of the forest was like the end of the human world: it seemed that there might be simply a drop behind it.

Sometimes we sang as we walked. We sang in quick bursts, like gunfire. The jokes had stopped. We picked our way among puddles. The sky seemed to press down on the backs of our necks. I thought – The gods are sitting on clouds like sofas in which the springs have gone. Then – This is the sort of landscape that Kapitsa meant by Holy Mother Russia?

We were heading for the nearest line of trees. It seemed to be getting no nearer: then it loomed up abruptly. I wondered – There will be deer, bears, in this strange forest? We sat in a group at the edge; we passed round the vodka bottles. There were a few seedlings round us where the forest was spreading. Trees seem to whisper when you do not listen; you turn to them and there is just a rustling.

Igor spoke to our group in some dialect I did not understand. I thought – But I am here to observe: speech anyway often obscures understanding. Two of the boys got up and went off along the side of the forest. I thought – They are scouts? They are looking for a way to break into this strange territory?

Mitzi came and sat on my lap and kissed me. We squirted bits of fire, sword, vodka, down each others' throats. I thought – I am being softened, broken up, to enter unknown territory.

Then – Oh I understand why these people do not want to answer too many questions!

There was a thin afternoon sun. We dozed on the grass. The vodka seemed to make time stretch eternally in front and behind. Igor watched in the direction in which the two boys had gone. I had long since given up wanting to understand what was happening. I wondered – So what is reality if ignorance is the experimental condition?

The two boys came back slowly along the edge of the forest. They were like snails, like ants, at the bottom of a wainscot. They spoke to Igor in the dialect I did not understand. Mitzi turned to me and put a finger to her lips. I thought – It is all right, I do not understand! I took Mitzi's finger and put it to my lips. It smelled of sweat or shit. I thought – Dear God, let us go into the forest.

Igor was getting us to spread in a line along the edge of the trees. I thought I might say to Mitzi – This is some sort of hunt? There are paintings like this: of stags and dogs and horses; of beautiful people with plumes prancing between trees. Mitzi and I stood hand in hand facing the forest. Some of the others had gone off in the direction in which the scouts had gone; the rest went off in the other direction along the lines of trees. I thought – Those are the beaters, these are the trappers, yes: but what is the quarry? Deer? Surely in this barren and starving landscape there are no more deer? And we have no guns; not even bows and arrows. There was the boy who carried the coil of rope. I thought – Perhaps a bear? But bears do not live within the walls of such flat forests. Then – Perhaps it is just that we have drunk too much vodka.

People often have to get drunk before they go hunting, do they not?

All the others except Mitzi and I had gone into the forest. Mitzi was still holding me by the hand. Mitzi had strong brown arms; a soft mouth and white teeth. I thought – Perhaps Mitzi and I are the quarry: we will be caught and tied to a tree. Then – Or perhaps it is just I, yes, who will be the victim; Mitzi will lead me to the tree.

There was a sudden whooping and shouting within the forest; Mitzi ran forwards, pulling me with her. The whooping was the sort of noise that hunters make: I thought – They do it as a foretaste of the noises that will later by made by their victims. There were a few clear spaces between trees; then undergrowth. Mitzi plunged straight through; sticks snapped like brittle bones. I felt I did not want to go hunting; I wanted to sit with Mitzi beneath a tree. I was still carrying a bottle of vodka. I thought I might fall, and pretend to twist my ankle, and play games of swords and victims with Mitzi.

There were shapes ahead of us moving between trees.

They were not rabbits or hares: they were too big. They were too squat and scurrying for deer. They might be wild boar? But they seemed to have arms and legs. They could not be monkeys! Then I realised that they were children.

I stopped. Mitzi stopped. We were at arms' length distance. I thought – Oh she is watching, yes, to see what I will do: so this is the experiment?

I said 'They're children.'

'Yes.'

'What do you do with them?'

Mitzi did not answer. She let go of my hand. She stood watching me.

I thought – You eat them? You hurt them? You abuse them? You tie them to a tree?

Then – You want to catch them because they are free?

I had forgotten about these children – the *besprezornii*. I knew they had camps in the forest.

It seemed that what we had been doing was sending out scouts to find out where these children were; and now we were hunting them, rounding them up; and they were trying to get through. I thought – Dear God, let us be drunk enough, and then they will get through.

One came towards us through the undergrowth and Mitzi made a grab at it; she was lithe and strong; the child was a ragged and flailing thing like tumbleweed. It slithered past Mitzi's legs as if blown by the wind; it got through. Mitzi almost fell; for a moment she was ugly. I thought – What is beautiful is what gets through?

Mitzi watched me. Then she went on ahead of me through the forest.

I followed. Mitzi held her arms out and occasionally made howling noises. I thought – So what is this experiment: to eat of forbidden fruit?

– But it is we who are like gods hunting in the forest!

Members of our group, from different directions, were coming together. It appeared that two children had been caught. One looked like a boy: he was very dirty and in some way misshapen; he was being held half off the ground with his arms behind his back. I thought – This is a position, yes, of someone being tortured.

The other child was a girl. She was being carried horizontally by Igor with one hand over her nose and mouth and the other arm between her legs underneath her: it was as if she were a puppet and he had his arm inside her. I thought – Dear God, it is because of this I think she is a girl? Then – I may not be able to bear this.

We went in a column through the forest – members of our tribe carrying our victims. I thought – Well is there or is there not someone watching. Then – You watch, and you know you enter into the experiment?

Remember, we had drunk a lot of vodka.

We came to a clearing which seemed to have been where the children had camped: there were a few shelters made with sticks and leaves and earth. There were the remains of fires. On the edge of the clearing, at the foot of a large tree, was a shelter bigger than the rest. I thought – Well, here I am. Then – If I am a god, it is a god who has come to eat the forbidden fruit of the tree?

We sat in a circle and passed round a vodka bottle. The children, the girl and the boy, had been stood in the middle of the circle. They had had their hands tied behind their backs; the hands of each were tied to those of the other. The children were about eleven or twelve: the girl was taller than the boy. The boy was misshapen because he had a crooked leg; he seemed to hang from the hands of the girl: every now and then he pulled at her as if trying to fall. The girl was quite still, composed: she stared ahead of her intently. She had long legs that emerged from her rags like twigs. I thought – Why was she caught: she could have got through? Then – She has something to show to this terrible tribe of gods?

Igor went into the circle with the children. He carried a stick. He spoke in the dialect that I did not understand. He hit at the ground with his stick.

I thought – There are witchdoctors who make patterns on the ground with sticks, to try to tell the future.

The girl had such matted hair that it was difficult to see her face. Her rags had been pulled and twisted so that one could see bits of her body. Her body was brown like a nut. I thought – Indeed she and the boy are like Adam and Eve in the Garden of Eden –

– Oh have some contempt for that vengeful God!

Mitzi put up a hand and stroked my face. I pushed her hand away. I thought – God shits on the world: poor bugger, he has to shit somewhere?

Igor was drawing two parallel lines on the ground. He spoke to the children: he spoke to us. He seemed to be saying that we should form two parallel lines on the ground: the children would be in between. I thought – Well, indeed there are images of this: humans are made to run, stumble, between parallel lines; on either side are judges, gods; they get pleasure from hurting; parallel lines never meet.

Then – But there are also paintings of this: of saints with seraphic faces on the grid or riddle, and the sad hideous faces of the people on either side.

The boy and girl were like the two halves of something that had not yet quite separated: of a seed; of Siamese twins: or the boy, hanging from the hands of the girl, was like a shrivelled fruit, or testicle, about to fall –

– And the girl, what knowledge was she carrying so secretly?

Mitzi said to me 'They come into the town. They obey no laws. They steal.'

I thought I might say – They demonstrate that humans are morally superior to gods –

– You envy them?

Igor had got us to move into the two parallel lines. The children were at one end of the lines. Igor seemed to be waiting for the children to move. The children did nothing. They were facing the same way, looking in the direction of the far end of the lines beyond which there was the large shelter at the edge of the clearing. Igor raised his stick. Most of the boys in the two lines were carrying sticks. I wondered if the children were deaf and dumb. I thought – I must do something. Then – Remember me, I pray thee –

Then – Oh but I am supposed to be morally superior to God!

I stood up. Mitzi took hold of one of my legs, as if to stop me. I thought – Of course, I could always kick her teeth in.

I went and stood beside the girl-child, who was at one end of the two lines of boys and girls and was watching the shelter on the edge of the clearing. It was as if she were waiting for something to emerge from this. After a time, such was the intensity of her concentration, that it seemed that something might emerge: I thought – Some guardian of this young tribe? What indeed might have guarded those children from that savage God in Eden! I remained standing by the child. After a time Igor lowered his stick. He looked, as I was looking, in the direction in which the girl was looking. Then he said something in the dialect that I did not understand. The girl answered him. I did not understand what the girl said. I thought – She is not deaf and dumb: she speaks when there is something to say. Then – That shelter is like the closed door at the back of a courtyard.

I said to Igor, and then to Mitzi, 'What did she say?'

Mitzi said 'Sh!' She put a finger to her lips.

Then she said 'She said she sometimes speaks to them.'

I said 'Who speaks to who?'

Igor went across the clearing towards the shelter; he bent down at some distance from it and tried to look in. The shelter had been made of sticks arranged around the roots of a split and hollow trunk of a tree. There was a low triangular opening at the front. I thought – Like some womb; tomb –

Igor went down on his knees and crawled to the opening of the shelter: he put his head in; then the top half of his body. I thought – He is like one of those figures being swallowed by a seed-pod in a Bosch painting of hell. Then Igor jerked back from the shelter as if he had been struck; he sat on the ground holding a hand to his mouth. Then he scrambled away. Mitzi called out to him: he answered, holding his hand to his mouth. I said to Mitzi 'What did he say?'

Mitzi said 'A snake.'

I said 'A snake?'

Mitzi said 'He says it bit him.'

I thought – It is a snake that sometimes speaks to them?

The two children had not moved. The boy was still hanging from the hands of the girl. I thought – For goodness' sake, fall and free her.

Mitzi was getting up and going over to Igor. Mitzi looked drunk and overblown; she swayed. She knelt down by Igor at the far side of the clearing. I said to no one in particular 'What does the snake say?'

Igor was holding his wrist. Mitzi took hold of his hand. Some of the others in the two lines of our group had lain back; they had their eyes closed; they were clutching their bottles of vodka. It was suddenly as if everyone had lost interest in what they had been doing.

I thought – Well, go to sleep: there are paintings of this.

I went towards the shelter; it was getting dark; I did not think that I would see much inside. I squatted down at some distance from the shelter as Igor had done. Then I went forwards on my hands and knees. I thought – What did I mean, it is as if the sky were coming down?

When I got close to the shelter there seemed to be a shape of something large inside. It filled the interior of the shelter; it might have been a seated figure; it might have been an image fashioned from mud or clay. There was something bright like an eye halfway up it. I thought – That is the eye of the snake? When I put my head in at the opening something struck me lightly, almost caressingly, on my forehead. I jerked back; but then stopped; for what I had been imagining inside the shelter turned into something quite different. There was no enormous shape, not even mud or clay: these had been shadows: there were just the huge roots of the tree with holes and hollows between them. In one of the hollows was a white stone; it was this that had seemed to be the eye of the snake; it was held like a baby in the arms of the tree. I thought – You mean, this whole setting is what sometimes seems to speak to the children? What had touched me gently on the forehead was, when I looked up, a small toy aeroplane made of tin; or it might have been the cut-out image of a bird; it was suspended from the roof by a length of trailing creeper. I thought – Or this is what speaks? Or what touches you? Or what goes between? I backed out of the shelter. I thought I might go back and try to make sense of what I had seen. Then I thought – But there is no sense: why should it not just be – I have seen what I have seen. Mitzi was kneeling by Igor in the clearing. Most of the rest of our group were lying in positions like people overcome by sleep or drink. The two children were still tied with rope. I thought – Oh yes, they are climbers on a rock-face! I went to the children and pulled at the rope to untie it. No one tried to stop me. There were lice, or fleas, or anyway things moving, in the girl's hair. I thought – Or lights, fireflies; or the eggs of snakes. Then – She will send these like devils into the world: to spread plague? chance? redemption?

I said to the girl in as clear Russian as I could 'What is it that speaks to you? What does it say?'

The girl spoke in the dialect I did not understand.

Mitzi called 'She says it's told her not to say.'

I thought – Yes, that's what they're usually told.

Then – The girl's mouth is like a seed-pod that has been broken open by someone's foot on the ground.

When I had untied the rope from the boy, he scuttled into the undergrowth. The girl stayed where she was. She held one of her wrists with the other hand. She looked at me. I thought – She will now do that flicking gesture like creating stars with her hands? That so-called obscene gesture in front of her?

I smiled at her. I picked up some of the remains of our food, to offer it to her.

She looked as if she had nothing more to say.

Night was coming down. It was cold. The figures on the ground had half wrapped themselves in blankets. Mitzi was with Igor. The girl went to the shelter at the far side of the clearing and looked in. I found a bottle that still had some vodka in it and I sat with my back against a tree. I thought – Well what were we going to do with those children: anything? nothing? Then – It was Adam's first wife Lilith who had devils in her hair; who felt equal to Adam; who was ignored by God, so she went and sat on a rock and sent devils out to haunt us; well some of these might have been the fruit of a forbidden tree? The girl at the far side of the clearing was doing something to the dust around the shelter: she was smoothing it like a gardener. I thought – So what was there behind the closed door in that courtyard: a snake, an aeroplane, a bird; the tree of life? Then – What do these images mean: they mean what you make of them. I finished what there was of my vodka. One or two of the others of our group had gone to the shelter and had looked in gingerly. I thought – They will see what they want to see: they will not be able to talk about it. They came back to their blankets and wrapped themselves like children. I thought – One thing happens after another; why do I think anything more than this?

I woke in the middle of the night and was very cold. I thought – And I thought I had discovered the secret of the universe! Then – But it will be somewhere, that coming together of bits and pieces.

In the morning the girl had gone. The shelter that had been like a shrine had been half pulled over. Neither the white stone nor the piece of tin like a toy aeroplane or bird were there.

We did not talk much on our journey back to the town. Most of us, presumably, felt very ill. I thought I might say once more to Mitzi – But what was it that spoke to them? What did it say?

Then I thought – But what would it mean, what Mitzi had to say?

When we got back to the apartment we found Mr and Mrs Platov in a state of alarm because Kolya had gone out the previous evening and had not come back: they had thought he must have joined us in the forest. But then two men from the Academy had come looking for him in the morning: they had asked questions about him which made Mr and Mrs Platov feel that he might be in serious trouble. But when it was found that Kolya had not been with us, it seemed that no one had any more to say. I thought – I should have paid more attention to Kolya! Then – But perhaps after all I did what was necessary: I did tell him it might be possible for him to get to Cambridge.

I felt I wanted to go to bed and put my head underneath the bedclothes; but it seemed that there would be too much going on.

When the time came for me to begin my journey home I made arrangements to travel via Moscow and Leningrad: partly I wanted to see the sights; partly I still wondered if I might make contact with Kapitsa. I had had a letter from my old tutor in Cambridge that seemed to suggest that they would like more information about Kapitsa before they made the final arrangements to sell the contents of his laboratory to Russia. This part of the letter was in an amateur code; I had had to do my own deciphering. The code was to do with Peter Pan (Kapitsa's Christian name was Peter) and Captain Hook and the crocodile. I thought – Stalin is Captain Hook? Stalin is the crocodile? Kapitsa's old boss in Cambridge, Rutherford, had in fact been known as the Crocodile; but did not the crocodile eat Captain Hook? I thought – It is stupid, this code: I can make up the message?

When I arrived in Moscow I stayed in the huge hostel for foreign students across the river from the Kremlin. I went to the Institute of Physical Problems and enquired if they knew the whereabouts of Dr Kapitsa. There was a woman behind the desk who did not at first seem to understand what I was saying; then I understood her to say that she had not heard of Dr Kapitsa; then she seemed to be saying that Dr Kapitsa was now head of the Institute of Physical Problems. I thought – This is ridiculous. I said 'In that case, can I see him?' The woman did not seem to understand. We were about to go back to the beginning when a man came out of a side room and said that I should leave my name and the address of where I was staying. I wrote my name on a blank sheet of paper. The man took it. I thought – Of course, now he can write anything he wants above my signature on the piece of paper, and make out I have made a confession.

I had not known that Moscow would be so beautiful. Red Square in the summer sun was like a plane representing the curve of the universe: St Basil's Cathedral was a vegetable growth from strange seeds fallen from the sky. I thought – What will Kapitsa be trying to find: the big bang that may be the end, as well as the beginning, of the experimental condition?

– But the knowing that this might be so: this might be a reality?

– From this sort of knowing something new might grow?

It was the beginning of the tourist season in Moscow: I wondered if I might bump into people whom I knew. I remembered that Wittgenstein was travelling that year in Russia: I once imagined I saw Melvyn chatting to a good-looking soldier in Red Square. I did in fact come across a group of Cambridge economists, some of whom I knew; I hid behind one of the Kremlin's mediaeval walls. I thought – Tourists in Russia are like those travellers in Europe in the eighteenth century who were always bumping into each other; there were so few of them that coincidences were likely to occur.

I thought – Chance can be helped, I suppose, by paying attention to statistics –

– One can put oneself in the way of the experimental condition.

One of the sights I wanted to see in Moscow were pictures by the painter Andrei Rublev. Andrei Rublev had lived around AD 1400 at a time of much savagery and destruction in Russia. The legend about him was that he had been trained by a painter but then had become so numbed by the horrors he saw that he had been unable to paint; then sometime later he became a monk and painted pictures of serene, adoring angels. I had been told this by Mullen before I had left England. I now regretted that I could not remember details of what Mullen had told me. I had made a note – the Trinity Sergiyev Monastery. I imagined that this must be where his paintings were. I seemed to remember Mullen saying that this monastery was in or just outside Moscow. But when I made enquiries from the woman behind the desk in the tourist office in the hostel, she made out – inevitably – that she could not understand me. The Trinity Sergiyev Monastery? Andrei Rublev? I thought – The monastery has been pulled down, Rublev's name expunged from history, because in whose interests is it to have pictures of adoring angels?

I began to have an obsession about getting to see these paintings by Andrei Rublev: I felt I had to see them to confirm something I was on the edge of understanding about Russia. There were special tourist taxis. I asked the drivers if they would take me to the Trinity Sergiyev Monastery. The drivers looked blank: they called to other drivers. I thought – But if I am arrested I can say that they did not understand me!

After a time I found the driver of a horse-driven carriage, who, when I spoke to him, showed no signs of my existing at all. I thought – Perhaps he is deaf and dumb? I went on saying 'Trinity Sergiyev Monastery. Andrei Rublev.' I thought – But perhaps he will in fact get me there, if he is deaf and dumb.

The driver put a hand out and opened the door of the carriage. I thought – Oh he is my fairy godmother! Then – Or perhaps he will take me to the police station.

The carriage rattled and shook. It was an old four-wheeler. It went slowly round the back of Red Square and then in a direction towards where we had begun. I thought – We are shaking off pursuers? We ourselves will shake to pieces first. We stopped outside a large modern official-looking building that might indeed have been a police station. I supposed this could be what they called a monastery: but with fourteenth-century frescoes on the walls?

I said 'The Trinity Sergiyev Monastery?'

The driver said 'Andrei Rublev.'

I said 'But this is the Trinity Sergiyev Monastery?'

The driver said 'Andrei Rublev.'

I thought – If we go on like this long enough, I suppose, walls may fall down.

Or – Andrei Rublev might be the name of a chief of police?

There were steps up to double doors. The driver stretched back a hand from his seat and opened the door of the carriage. I got out. Before I could ask about payment he drove away. I thought – He felt he was in danger? Then – There is always danger in magic!

I went up the steps of the official-looking building. Inside there was, inevitably, an old lady sitting behind a desk. I went up to her and said 'Is this the Trinity Sergiyev Monastery?' The old woman said 'The museum's closed.' I said 'I want to see the paintings of Andrei Rublev!' The old woman said 'The museum's closed.' I thought – So this does seem to be a museum! And she has not said that there are not paintings here by Andrei Rublev!

There was a stone staircase going up from the back of the entrance hall to a landing on the first floor. Here two people were walking and talking; they were moving behind a balustrade like targets in a fun-fair shooting-range. I thought – But I recognise them! Then – But I am always thinking I recognise people in Moscow. But at least I could tell the old woman they are my friends. I began to go past the old woman towards the staircase. She got up from behind her desk and came after me. I stopped and waved a hand and said 'They are my friends!' The old woman paused. I thought – Well it has seemed that there is some magic! The old woman went back behind her desk. I went up the stairs. The two men who had been on the landing were now out of sight. I thought – I mean, if I have enough passion to see paintings by Andrei Rublev, then perhaps, as Stalin said, every goal can be reached, every obstacle overcome.

At the top of the flight of stairs I was on the landing but I had to choose which way to turn – either the direction in which the two figures had gone, so that it might seem to the old woman that they were my friends, or in the opposite direction to avoid them. I went neither this way nor that but through a doorway straight ahead: the building did seem to be a museum, or picture gallery. However, there were step-ladders and planks as if paintings were being put up or put away. I wondered – How will I recognise a painting by Andrei Rublev? Then – But if I do not, why am I here?

I had gone into a room in which there were some dull nineteenth-century paintings; in a further room there were paintings which seemed to have been done in the early years of the revolution. I thought – Come on, come on, I know what I am looking for. Then I heard someone talking in English.

I said to myself – But I know that voice! Then – I said he was a friend!

The voice I recognised – which belonged to one of the men whom I had thought I recognised walking and talking on the landing – was that of Mullen. The other man had seemed to be, yes, the bald-headed Russian-looking man whom I had once seen with Mullen in the pub outside Cambridge. Even then they had seemed to be like conspirators; spies; I had imagined that the man with the bald head might even be Kapitsa. In the pub they had made out that they had not seen me; they had gone out of a back door. I had thought then – But of course it is part of their game, to pretend not to recognise me!

I thought now – But this is not a game! Or will I go round a corner and find that indeed they are just shadows in my imagination?

Mullen's voice, and that of the other man, who was also speaking English, were coming from a smaller room somewhere to my right. They must have got there by another route from the landing. I thought – I can still go back. Then – But it was Mullen who told me about the paintings of Andrei Rublev!

I walked into the smaller room in which there was Mullen and, yes, the man with the bald head with whom I had seen him in the pub in England. For a moment, of course, because I was out of context for him, Mullen did not seem to recognise me: I thought – But they, the two of them, are now not out of context for me: they are still like spies or conspirators.

They were standing in front of paintings, most of which seemed to be of angels.

Then when Mullen did recognise me I thought for a moment – He is frightened: he will think I have been following him. Then – What are angels; they are to do with coincidence?

I said 'Hello.' Mullen said nothing.

After a time the other man put his hand on Mullen's arm and said something in a low voice that I could not hear. Then he walked out of the room with his back to me.

Mullen said 'You've found me.'

I thought – Well, yes, I see what you mean, I've found you.

Mullen put his hand on my arm. He said 'How are you?' He looked round. He said 'How did you get here?' Then 'We can talk here.'

I said 'I was trying to get to see paintings by Andrei Rublev.'

He said 'You were trying to get to see paintings by Andrei Rublev?'

I said 'Yes.'

He said 'Here there's a painting by Andrei Rublev.'

I said 'I thought I recognised you at the top of the stairs.'

He said 'I see.'

Mullen was a tall, gaunt figure who might have been some sort of monk. He might have gone wandering across Russia seeing horrors; might he from these have imagined pictures of serene, adoring angels?

I said 'I thought the paintings were in a monastery, but the taxi brought me here.'

Mullen said 'No one told you I was here?'

I said 'No.'

Mullen said 'But it was I who told you about Andrei Rublev!'

I said 'Yes.'

Mullen smiled. He said 'What a coincidence!'

I thought – He may know the code! But what is the message?

Mullen turned away towards a painting that was on the wall behind him. He murmured 'I thought you were somewhere in the Ukraine.'

I said 'I was.' Then – 'I wondered about Kapitsa.'

Mullen said 'You wondered about Kapitsa.'

I said 'Yes.' Then I became aware of the painting on the wall behind Mullen.

Do you know this painting by Andrei Rublev? It is called *The Old Testament Trinity*. It was one of the paintings of which I had seen a reproduction before I left England. It is of the three angels that came to tell Abraham and Sarah that, even though they were about a hundred years old, they would have a child. The three angels are said to be God the Father, God the Son and God the Holy Ghost. They are all three much the same; they are neither male nor female; they are all young and beautiful. They sit round a table, on which there is a bowl; and behind them is a tree, and what seems to be the entrance to a courtyard. The three angels, though separate, seem to be held together by a common inner absorption – by the fact that this seems to give them control over the spaces between. I thought – They are serene, but they are not exactly adoring: they know too much to be adoring: what they are in contact with is themselves.

Mullen said 'What did you want to know about Kapitsa?'

I said 'How he is.'

Mullen said 'He is all right.'

I said 'He is not being held against his will?'

Mullen said 'No.'

I thought – It is difficult to get away from this picture, to concentrate on Mullen: I will try to become part of the spaces that the angels have under control.

Mullen said 'You were working for a time with Kapitsa.'

I said 'Yes.'

Mullen said 'What work was he doing then?'

I said 'Research into the superfluidity of low-temperature helium.'

When one was at some distance from the painting, the faces of the angels seemed to be grave and sorrowing: then when one stepped close to them their faces – especially the face of the angel on the right – seemed to smile.

Mullen said 'Was he?'

I said 'Yes.'

Mullen said 'I see.'

I said 'What is the significance of the three angels that came to Abraham?'

Mullen said 'I think it was that unless there was this child born to Abraham then the human race would find it difficult with any dignity to carry on.'

There were other paintings in the room besides *The Old Testament Trinity*: I did not know whether or not they were by Andrei Rublev. There was one in which the Virgin seemed to be lying on a bed with a dark tent-like shape above her; within this space the figure of Christ seemed to be holding the toy image of a child. I thought – But this is the image that there seemed to be in that shelter in the forest! At the top of the painting there were angels like small aeroplanes or birds.

Mullen said 'I am going to put a proposition to you.'

I said 'What?'

He said 'That you have not seen me here. That you have not seen anyone I have been talking to, now or then.'

I thought – You mean, this is like an experiment?

I said 'What work is Kapitsa doing now in Moscow?'

Mullen said 'You have agreed that it is important that scientific knowledge should be disseminated.'

I said 'There are people starving in Russia. There are people being shot.'

Mullen said 'I know.'

I had come back to the painting of the Old Testament Trinity. I thought – It is the figure of the Holy Ghost, on the right, that seems to be smiling?

Mullen said 'I might be able to arrange for you to see Kapitsa.'

I said 'Would you say that knowledge should be disseminated to the Nazis?'

Mullen said 'I see.' Then 'I don't know.' Then after a time 'No.'

I said 'What do you think is special about this picture?'

Mullen did not look at the picture. He continued watching me. He said 'There are deaths and deaths. There are some which are just deaths, and some through which other things come alive.'

I said 'And you think you can tell which is which?'

Mullen said nothing. Then he said 'I am asking nothing of you. All that I am asking is that you shall say nothing.'

I thought suddenly – You can tell what is death and what is life-giving in a painting.

I said 'This painting is about love.'

Mullen said 'When I saw Kapitsa, he said that in this country he felt loved.' Then – 'You liked Kapitsa?'

I turned away from the picture. I thought – I suppose Mullen could have me eliminated. I suppose Mullen himself might be eliminated since he is talking to me here.

I said 'I once asked Kapitsa why other people did not seem interested in the power that might be obtainable at the heart of the atom.'

Mullen said 'And what did he say?'

'He said "People are only interested in a power they can handle."'

Mullen said 'But that is the point!'

I said 'What?'

For the first time that I had been with him, Mullen looked at the picture. He said 'What if people had to become interested in a power that they feel they might not be able to handle?'

I thought – Oh yes, there might be change.

I said 'I once talked to Kapitsa about the connection between love and power. He said "We don't confuse them in Holy Mother Russia."'

Mullen said 'What else did he say?'

I said 'I don't remember.' Then 'I think myself that the connection would be something aesthetic.'

I suddenly felt very tired. I thought – I must get away and think. Then – No, not think: is not everything of importance what one feels one cannot handle?

I had begun to move with Mullen towards the head of the stairs. I said 'No, I won't say anything about having seen you in Russia. Why should I?'

Mullen said 'Thanks.'

I said 'What was that other picture I looked at: the one in which the Virgin Mary seems to be lying on a bed and Christ is in a dark space holding a toy child above her?'

Mullen said 'That is her soul.'

I said 'Her soul!'

Mullen said 'It is a common image in Russia.'

I thought – Is that which speaks? Which says what you can't say; what you can't handle.'

I said 'And that other picture – the one I love – is it the angel on the right that is the Holy Ghost?'

Mullen said 'Why do you say that?'

I said 'Because it looks sad when you are far away: but when you get close it is smiling.'

TWO
So what do we do

VII   1: Eleanor

From where I sit I can look on the jumbled huts of this village: some have thatched roofs and some have flat roofs made of mud: the whole construction is like a maze, or the model of a brain.

During the year we have been in West Africa we have recorded and tabulated the mechanisms by which is maintained the stability of this strange tribe – the kinship structures, descent groups, property systems, customs concerning marriage and divorce. We have asked questions and listened for answers. When answers have come they have been to do with sorting, classifying, rejecting anomalies, making patterns: this is what words do: thus is maintained stability of mind. We have not asked – What are we doing here recording and classifying the customs of a society? Might we not simply be exercising the customs of our minds? To ask this would be to step back from the protective mechanisms of our own tribe: it would be to risk, perhaps, stability of mind.

But as we – you and I – have said before, might there not be an anthropology in which the observer is seen as part of what he observes: in which his observing is taken into account as affecting what he observes? If it is by not asking such questions that stability is maintained, then by asking them might there not be some anthropology to do with change? If we stand back from the part of ourselves that is part of what we see – between these two parts of ourselves might there not be freedom for change?

Something like this was in a letter that I wrote to you, Max, when I had been in West Africa a year. I did not send it – perhaps because I did not know where you were; perhaps I got tired of playing with these questions. Consciousness can look at itself: but if you pull at anything's roots, how can it grow?

In this village in which we were recording and tabulating property structures and co-operative institutions we were like ticks with our heads just under the skin of the tribe; but it was the sense of our own identity and importance, it seemed, that thus might grow. So I would think, yes – Stop thinking! Then there might be a chance for something quite different to grow.

The leader of our group was Rudi. Rudi was a German. He liked to walk about almost naked in the hot sun; he had a lean golden body like that of a sacred cow. I think Rudi liked to see himself as something sacred: how better to achieve this than by being the leader of an anthropological expedition in a primitive village? Rudi liked to question people; he did not like to be questioned himself; he was fed answers as if they were propitiations to some awkward god. Rudi seemed to be thus satisfied, with his golden Buddha-body in the hot sun.

Then there was Trudi (Gertrude), Rudi's girlfriend. Trudi was a thick-set dark-haired girl who was the correlator of our notes and lists, the formulator of diagrams and statistics. Trudi would sit in the doorway of their hut and Rudi would bring to her the bits of information he had been fed with round the village; he would regurgitate them to her like a mother bird at its nest. Trudi would receive them and set about digesting them; Rudi would wander off again on his rounds in the village.

Then there was Stefan, our photographer, who was Swiss: he was thin and elfin with hair brushed forward on his forehead. Stefan had a passion for trying to photograph people without their knowing that they were being photographed: perhaps he thought that by this something might be observed apart from the effects of the observer. He would stand here or there festooned with equipment; he would pretend to be interested in the top of a tree; then, as if adjusting a belt, he would take a photograph of something behind his back. I would think – But he is taking photographs of what happens in a village when a photographer stands and pretends to be adjusting his belt: a really interesting photograph would include the photographer doing this.

I was the fourth member of the expedition. Well, what was I doing as a member of this strange tribe? Escaping what was happening in Germany, yes: acting out what we seemed to have agreed, you and I – that each has to learn how to stay alive in his own way, in what are always strange societies.

I would sometimes say to Rudi 'But what is the point of your asking questions if they do not include questions about yourself doing this?'

– Or to Trudi 'Should not one of your diagrams be one of a hand drawing a hand that is drawing the first hand – '

– Or to Stefan 'You think you might be like God, trying to show that things can exist without him in a garden?'

But then I said to myself – I call this an anthropology of change? This playing with words; risking getting myself thrown out of my tribe, my stability of mind.

It was Rudi's job to collect information about social structures and institutions. I took on myself the job of trying to find out about the tribe's religion. This of course is an area in which it is always difficult for people to make sense with words.

On one level there were the religious rituals: these were to do with sacrifice; they could be explained without too much difficulty. Sacrifice is to do with the maintenance of stability; if you want something out of a system you have to put something back in; humans imagine that gods require payment just as they do themselves. There had once been human sacrifices in this tribe: now sacrifices were made in the form of corn or oil; occasionally of animals.

On the level of trying to describe what the tribal god was, words were more difficult. Definitions slid away; images flipped over on to their opposites. The supreme deity of the tribe was like the two halves of a single nut: these were male/female, sun/moon, power/ love. It was by such paradoxes that, again, there seemed to be maintained stability. Paradoxes were like the two ends of a horizontal pole by which a tightrope walker keeps himself upright. But what was this tightrope deity: an idea? a mechanism?

The levels of ritual sacrifice and paradoxical dogma were, it seemed to me, like the levels in the Christian religion represented by God the Father and God the Son: but what, as usual, of God the Holy Ghost? It is true that there is seldom anything said about this.

But this is the level at which the whole religious business might be seen to be operative to the advantage of humans.

Outside the perimeter wall of the village, and outside each family compound within, there was a small hut like a doll's house placed on stilts. These huts contained wooden figures with drooping breasts and wooden models of penises; they were the homes of a divinity that was to do with the individual rather than the tribe – that dealt not with questions of stability and balancing but with occasions when there was a need for practical and personal choice. People approached this divinity when they felt themselves confused or stuck in their personal life; when they were up against a brick wall and did not know how to get through; when they needed help to decide this or that. This deity was called Legba. Words used about or by Legba were in the form of stories and legends; he was a joker, a trickster; he often indulged in sexual excess. But the point of the stories about him or from him did not seen to be in fact to give personal advice: they were often comic; their aim seemed to be to show the absurdity of predicaments. They appeared to encourage people to free themselves from set expectations; to have a more humorous and ironical attitude to themselves and life – and by this means perhaps to be helped to practical solutions. The likelihood of making a right choice, that is, seemed to depend on a person's ability to look somewhat ironically at himself.

I thought – In rituals and dogma you find mechanisms to satisfy your own self-protective manipulations –

– The Holy Ghost is the experience that it is to your advantage to lay yourself open to chance?

There were certain specialists in the tribe to whom individuals went when they were faced with practical predicaments; when they wished to be helped to find the right attitude to choice. An individual could however, if he wished, learn such a process himself.

The specialist magician sat in the dust and held sixteen palm-nuts in his right hand. He made a swoop at these nuts and scooped them up with his left hand. If there was one nut left in his right hand he made a double stroke in the dust in front of him; if there were two nuts left in his right hand he made a single stroke in the dust; if there were more than two nuts, or none, then he made no mark and did the swoop again. When he had done this often enough to have eight single or double strokes in the dust this formed a master sign which referred to one set of a body of sayings and legends which were known to the experts of the tribe. There were 256 possible sets of sayings, and from the one which had turned up you could take as being relevant to your predicament whatever piece of advice or warning that you liked: there was at least the impression that this had come in from outside; or perhaps you were helped to see the absurdity of your manipulations and thus of your predicament.

I said to Rudi 'Of course it is not exactly that you are put in touch with cosmic forces of the universe; but it might be that there are forces within you by which, if old patterns of mind are broken up, something different might occur.'

Rudi said 'And these forces might be in contact with the cosmic forces of the universe?'

I said 'Well, you would have to look and see; you would never know, would you?'

Rudi went off like a beautiful bronze cow through the village.

When we had first come to West Africa Rudi had been sleeping with Trudi. Then, after a time, he had begun sleeping with me. I had thought – In the predicament of fighting to survive, what is my responsibility? Then – We are making patterns in the dust: palm-nuts are being flipped from one hand to the other.

Trudi became ill. She lay on top of her blankets on her camp-bed and shook. I thought – She is like a container for dice: she thinks that thus she can effect the way Rudi falls one way rather than the another.

Rudi said 'It is malaria.'

I said 'Perhaps it is something to do with you and me.'

Trudi said 'It is nothing to do with Rudi and you!'

I said 'Have you taken your quinine?'

But Rudi went back to sleeping with Trudi because she was ill; he seemed to feel safe with someone who was helpless. I thought – No, this is not to do with the cosmic forces of the universe.

Stefan was the one I often felt most at ease with at this time. Stefan was homosexual; he was in love with Rudi. He would follow Rudi round the village and take photographs of him while Rudi pretended he did not know he was being photographed; he would, however, adopt the sort of poses he knew were attractive to Stefan. The children of the village would follow Stefan round in the hope that he would let them look through the viewfinder of his camera, which he did when he was not photographing Rudi.

Stefan said to me 'You are right! Someone should do an anthropology of us anthropologists.'

I said 'None of us really want to break up our own patterns. You want to go on being able to take photographs of Rudi; Rudi and Trudi feel secure if Trudi is ill in bed; and I am all right, I suppose, as long as I can say "Look, we don't want to break up our own patterns!"'

Stefan said 'You think I don't want to go to bed with Rudi?'

I said 'I think you like being like St Sebastian, shot through with arrows.'

Stefan said 'Oh my dear, what do you think they felt like, those arrows?'

I thought – What we need is an anthropology to do with learning.

There was one old man of the tribe who could speak French quite well: he was one of the experts in the processes of divination. I would go and sit in front of him and he would cast his palm-nuts from one hand to the other; he would make his marks on the ground. He would say 'You are going on a journey but you will not know your destination.' I thought – You mean, how would I find out where I wanted to be going if I knew my destination? Or – This journey will be in the mind.

I once said to the old man 'I think I've worked out a way of talking about what happens in the process of divination: there can be no learning, evolution, without the operation of chance. You can't by definition say much about chance; but you can show that you see that it's this that you learn from.'

The old man rocked backwards and forwards as if he were in pain.

I said 'In divination you are saying "Look at what you call chance!", and then see if there are not connections between what is in yourself and what happens in the outside world.'

The old man said 'You will meet a snake on your journey.'

I said 'Will I be helped by this snake?'

The old man said 'You will come to a place where animals will seem to know more than humans.'

I thought – It might be that place, wherever it is, where we planned to meet, you and I, on this journey.

I loved much of my time in the forest. There were the tall stately trees, the quiet way in which people went about their business, the impression that they were just within hearing distance of enormous events elsewhere. The tribe had lost much of its energy; it seemed to be coming to the end of one cycle of life; perhaps it missed the feeding by the king of his people. I thought – Oh it is in Europe, now, that primitive tribes are being fed with human sacrifice!

Mussolini had succeeded in conquering Abyssinia. Then Hitler marched into the Rhineland. I had a letter from my father in which he said that he had had no news of my mother for some time.

With the vision of what was happening in Europe we ourselves seemed to lose heart in our group, our expedition. This was the spring of 1936; we had contracted to stay in Africa till the end of the year. But we had all begun to feel – What are we doing here with this dying tribe: why are we not making a study of what is happening at home, where mad kings still feed slaves to their adoring peoples?

Or I sometimes thought – Oh I should return like a wild-eyed goddess of death riding a white horse above a battlefield!

Rudi began to spend less and less time gathering information in the village; he travelled around the countryside in our truck making a collection of tribal artefacts. Some of these artefacts were very beautiful – embroidered hangings, headdresses of ivory and shells, elaborately carved and inlaid ceremonial maces and thrones. Rudi claimed that he was still gathering information as an anthropologist; but he did not trouble to deny that he planned to take his collection back to Europe to try to sell it at a great profit. He and Stefan quarrelled about this; Stefan said that such objects should not be taken out of the counry, or at least if they were they should be donated to a museum. Rudi said 'What will be the point of museums, if there is a war in Europe?' Stefan said 'What will be the point of anything else, if there is a war in Europe?'

Trudi shouted at Stefan 'You are jealous because Rudi is sleeping with me and not you!'

Stefan said 'He isn't sleeping with you, dearie, he's sleeping with Nellie.'

Trudi said 'You are degenerate! There will be no more people like you in the new Europe!'

Rudi said to me 'You see why people don't like looking at themselves.'

I said 'I don't see why there shouldn't be a war in Europe.'

Trudi got up from, then went back to, her bed of malaria: Rudi went to and fro between Trudi and me. Once, when Trudi had got better and Rudi was sleeping with me, Stefan found Trudi filling up with water the bottle from which she took her daily dose of quinine.

I said to Stefan 'You see, it's true that we none of us want to get well. We are like the people of Europe; we are in thrall to sacred cows like Rudi and Hitler; we put water in our quinine in order to stay in thrall.'

Stefan said 'You're a Jew: you know what you're saying?'

I said 'Oh but Jews are supposed to know about things like this.'

Stefan once said to me 'If you feel like that, do you really want to go home?'

I said 'I can't go home. I haven't got the right papers.'

Stefan said 'So what are you going to do?'

I thought – I will consult my friend the wise old man of the tribe; get him to cast palm-nuts from one hand to the other.

There was a day when the recurrences of Trudi's fever became so frequent that Rudi announced that he was going to drive her to the hospital on the coast. Also he could make enquiries about shipping ourselves and his collection of artefacts back to Europe.

Stefan said to me 'You know what he's going to do? He will go with Trudi and the truck and all the loot to the capital, and then he will get the loot and the two of them shipped home by boat.'

I said to Rudi 'Stefan says you and Trudi are going to go to the capital and get on a boat with the loot, and leave us dumped here.'

Rudi said 'How do you know I'm not going to dump Trudi by the side of the road, and then there'll be all the more for me and you?'

I said to Trudi 'Will you be all right?'

Trudi said 'Oh I know how you'd love to be going with Rudi to the coast!'

I thought – We think we protect ourselves, amuse ourselves, with all this rubbish.

Our truck was an old American four-wheel drive. Stefan was our mechanic: he used to fuss over the truck as if he were getting it ready for a show. I thought – Without Stefan, Rudi and Trudi may not even get to the coast.

I said to Stefan 'Can't you arrange it so that the truck won't start. Then sometime later you and I can drive it with the loot across the Sahara.'

Stefan said 'You think we'd have a chance of getting across the Sahara?'

I thought – Well where can I go? I cannot stay here.

Then – The Sahara is a word for the journey I have to go on in reality? In my mind?

Rudi and Trudi set off for the coast. They had all Rudi's collection in the back of the truck. Rudi had promised to return. He had continued to explain that he wanted to get rid of Trudi: that he did not trust her to keep quiet about the loot.

I thought – For chance to have its proper effect, it is right not to worry too much about palm-nuts landing this way rather than another?

Stefan and I tidied our camp and made preparations for leaving when Rudi got back. I sometimes thought – But why did we not insist on all of us going with Rudi and Trudi to the coast? Then – But there is no point in my going to the coast if my passport is not valid.

I said to Stefan 'If we were driving across the Sahara, you and I, and the truck broke down, and it was a question of either saving yourself, or both of us dying if you stayed with me, you'd save just yourself, surely, wouldn't you?'

Stefan said 'But we're not going across the Sahara!'

I said 'But if we were.'

Stefan said 'It would be no good, darling, even if you do sometimes behave quite like a boy.'

After a week Rudi returned on his own with the truck from the coast. He said that after consultation with doctors, Trudi had agreed to be put on a boat going to Marseilles. Stefan said 'I expect the truth is that the customs stopped you taking the stuff out of the country.' Rudi said 'Yes, as a matter of fact the customs won't let us take the stuff out of the country.' I said 'Did you dump Trudi by the side of the road?' Rudi said 'What about us driving with the stuff across the Sahara.'

Stefan said 'Are you mad?'

I said 'We were just talking about driving across the Sahara!'

It was in fact not all that difficult to drive across the Sahara in a good truck at this time: the first crossings had been made in the 1920s; recently there had been a rally of ordinary touring cars in which all those taking part had got across. Now there was a track maintained by a French company and even a service by bus. I wanted to go on this journey not only because I would not then have to worry about my passport till I was nearer to Europe, but also because I would be engaged in the sort of activity that would make it easy to stop thinking about the distant future at all.

Rudi said 'If we get to Spanish Morocco I know someone there who will help us cross the straits into Spain. And then there will be people who will buy the stuff, or who will help us to sell it. And we should not have trouble with customs, or papers, going across the Sahara.'

Stefan said 'The route is closed at this time of year.'

Rudi said 'We do not yet know if the route is closed at this time of year.'

Stefan said 'You have to have special permission.'

Rudi said 'Then I will get special permission.'

Stefan said 'I'm not going.'

Rudi said 'Whoever does not come will not have a share of the loot.'

Rudi had brought letters with him back from the coast. There was no letter from my father. There was one from my uncle, which said that he had not heard from my father for some time, so that now there was as much cause to worry about my father as about my mother.

Stefan said 'Nellie! Tell him! Be sensible!'

I said 'My mother's disappeared, and now my father.'

Rudi said 'So you will come?'

Stefan said 'And disappear yourself in the Sahara!'

I thought – Yes indeed, perhaps I want to disappear in the Sahara.

We packed up our camp and told the people of the village that we were going. We said it was possible that we would be back. Our plan was to go to Gao, which was some 500 miles away on the river Niger, and there we would find out more about the crossing of the Sahara. I said to Rudi 'But we can't go without Stefan: it will all depend on his doing the right things with the truck.'

Rudi said 'I'll let him think I've got hold of some diamonds and they are in the truck, and it's because I don't want to be caught with these that I want to go across the Sahara.

I said 'Have you got diamonds in the truck?'

Rudi said 'It's quite easy to pick up diamonds very cheap at the mines near the coast.'

I thought – Oh, and perhaps you did dump Trudi by the side of the road!

I went to see my friend the wise old man of the village. He sat in the dust and rocked backwards and forwards; he made cooing noises; he did not cast palm-nuts from one hand to the other. I said 'What do you see? Is it good? Is it bad?'

He said after a time 'Where is this place you want to go?'

I said 'But I don't know where I want to go!'

He said 'There is somewhere, I see it, where you want to go.'

I said 'Describe it.'

He said 'It is a place under a mountain. There is a gateway. You will know it when you see it.'

We arranged Rudi's load of loot so that there was room for a person to lie in the back of the truck. We could pick up the necessary extra supplies in Gao. Stefan seemed now to be in two minds about coming. He said to me 'You know Rudi says he's got some diamonds in the back of the truck: it's true you can pick them up very cheaply on the coast.'

I said 'Why don't you tell Rudi that you'll come if he lets you bugger him?'

Stefan said 'Because I want Rudi to bugger me.'

I was not making much sense of what was happening at the time; certainly old ground was being broken up. I could not think much about the news about my mother and father; there was an emptiness inside me which, it seemed, terror might rush in to fill. But there also seemed to be a thread by which I was being pulled across the Sahara; by which I might survive.

I thought – I might play this thread; I might be played by it; I mean, as if I or at the other end of it, were a fish.

With my conscious mind I worked out – If I get to Spain, I might get to – not Germany, no; not Switzerland; but to England?

However, I was not getting any letters from you at this time.

One night Rudi went into Stefan's hut and spent the night there. I thought – So Rudi will get Stefan to come with us across the Sahara; and then there will be no reason why we should not survive.

In the morning Stefan and Rudi both looked happy: Stefan said he had agreed to come with us as far as Gao. The people of the village came to see us off. I said to my friend the wise old man 'Wish me luck!' When the wise old man smiled his teeth were like megalithic stones.

I wondered – But there is this place to which he thinks I want to go?

The road to Gao was of a kind over which we had often driven before – a rough track over sand and stones that suddenly went into a swamp or over ridges of rock like a washboard. Occasionally we got stuck in the sand and had to put down wood or matting; we sat by the side of the road and mended punctures. Stefan fussed around his truck as if he were a mother bird with an enormous cuckoo: I thought – Do cuckoos fly across the Sahara? We may indeed have to be some sort of mutant.

At Gao there was a camel market where the huge strange animals lay in the dust as if their bodies were just under water and their heads were like periscopes. I sat in the shadow of a wall and made drawings of them. I thought – By what chance did the first camel learn that it had a hump in which there was enough food for it to get across a desert?

Then – I am that hand that is drawing a hand that is drawing itself.

Rudi had gone off to find out about the regulations for crossing the Sahara. Stefan was showing the viewfinder of his camera to a crowd of children. I was trying to explain to myself – But I have to find out about my father: what else can I do except go across this desert?

Rudi came back and said that the season for crossing the Sahara had just closed: conditions became too hot in the summer. Also the rainy season was about to begin in the area around Gao, which might make the roads impassable on the first stage of the journey.

I said 'But how can it be too hot if the rainy season is just starting?'

Rudi said 'Exactly.'

I said 'And the crossing's been closed only one or two days!'

Stefan said 'You're not still thinking of going?'

Rudi said that during the winter months the crossing by trucks and even ordinary cars was relatively simple; if all went well, the journey could take as little as three or four days. Drivers had to get permission from the French authorities and to leave details of the timing of their journey, and to deposit a sum of money so that they could be rescued in case of breakdown. But now, of course, there would be no breakdown service because the season was over.

I said 'So there's no point even in waiting for permission.'

Rudi said 'Quite.'

I said 'And there certainly wouldn't be any customs or immigration authorities if no one is crossing the Sahara!'

Stefan said 'You are all mad, you Germans. You want to destroy yourselves.'

I thought – Well, it is true that there is a state of mind in which one does not care much if one lives or dies: how else could homeless mutants ever get from one side of a desert to another?

Stefan said 'Anyway, you'll never get across the Sahara without me.'

Rudi said 'You won't get any of the diamonds.'

Stefan said 'Show me.'

Rudi said 'Don't you trust me?'

That night we drove a short way out of the town and camped under palm trees. Rudi went into the back of the truck with Stefan. I lay and looked at the stars. I thought – What made humans think that there are patterns among stars: there is the Plough, there is Orion –

– Am I Aquarius the water-carrier about to cross a desert?

Stefan came to me and said 'Rudi really has got some diamonds.'

I said 'He hasn't shown them to me.'

Stefan looked shifty. I thought – Does this mean Rudi really has got some diamonds, or now should I not trust Stefan as well as Rudi?

Stefan laughed and said 'Perhaps he will dump both of us by the side of the road!'

Sometime in the middle of the night Stefan and Rudi had a fight. They were like two spiders at one another's throats: silhouettes like imagined constellations of stars. Then they fell to the ground and there was the sound of Rudi laughing and Stefan making whooping noises of pleasure or of pain.

I though – A mutant would of course be living in an environment that seemed mad and hostile to it: then either itself, or the others, would survive.

In the morning Rudi said 'Stefan is coming with us as far as the first depot. This is the stretch of road where there might be rain. After that, we will see what the prospect is before any of us go on.'

Neither Rudi nor Stefan would quite look at me. I thought – But of course, it would be just me who it would be in their interests to dump by the side of the road.

I said 'But if rain makes the road impassable, then we won't be able to turn back.'

Rudi said 'But if there's rain, we'll have plenty of water.'

Stefan said 'Look here, do you want me to come or not?'

I thought – Rudi might always have been homosexual?

We went into town in the truck to get spare parts and provisions. Stefan got special tyres and extra cans for petrol and water. He fussed around his truck like someone in love. I thought – But I have always known that Rudi, being seen as somewhat godlike, was also a devil.

Rudi said 'There's a second depot halfway across where we can

fill up with petrol and water. But before that, of course, we may
have turned back.'

Stefan said 'But we will have enough petrol and water to get us
across.'

I thought – But what is this image I have of God like a fisherman
at the other side of the Sahara; would not the line, the hook, appear
like the work of some devil?

We set off on our journey into the desert sometime before dawn.
We planned to travel mainly at night when the heat was not too
great. Rudi and Stefan sat in the front of the truck: I lay on the bed
we had made at the back. Because of the extra load of cans we were
carrying I was up near the canvas roof. I thought – This is like a
tomb: or that hump of the camel in which it did not yet know it
had stored its food.

When the sun came up the landscape was yellow and grey with
scattered trees with a black line around them as if they were on the
point of bursting into flames. The road was at first no different
from those we were accustomed to: it followed the line of the river,
then turned off over a stony wasteland with low bushes and
occasionally the dried-up beds of what might at times be shallow
lakes. But in my hump, or tomb, I did not notice much of the
landscape: I listened to the sounds of the engine, felt the bumps of
the wheels on the road as if they were blood, heartbeats.

When we got to the first depot there were palm trees and a
concrete building and dozens of empty oildrums; but there was no
one to ask about the further crossing of the desert. It was very hot
although it was not yet midday. Rudi said 'We'll stay till evening
and then we'll go on.' Stefan said 'I'm not going on.' Rudi said
'Then how are you getting back?' Stefan said 'You Nazi bastard.'
Rudi said 'Start walking, twinkletoes.'

It seemed to me worth saying 'We've got to stick together, or we
won't get across.'

I thought – But it would have had to watch the other animals
dying, that first camel that got across a desert?

Rudi and I lay in the shadow of the concrete building. The
shadow got smaller and smaller so that it was as if we were being
pushed off a ledge. Stefan went off into the desert to look for some
sign of human habitation. I said 'He shouldn't be out in the sun.'
Rudi said 'That's his problem.' I said 'Surely it's ours.' Rudi called
'Stefan!'

When Stefan returned he was wobbling his head and staggering;

he drank a lot of water; then he lay down under the truck. When the sun was low on the horizon Rudi and I ate some food. We pulled at Stefan but he would not sit up. Rudi said 'He's pretending.' I said 'With any luck.' We helped Stefan on to the bed in the back of the truck.

I said 'What are the chances of there being petrol and water at the next depot?'

Rudi said 'Stefan swore that we had enough water and petrol for the journey.'

I said to Stefan 'Is that true?'

Stefan said nothing.

I thought – Stefan may want us all to die, just to prove that after all he was right about the journey.

Rudi said to me 'It was you who said we had to have him on this journey!'

I thought – Why on earth should men survive, if they are like Rudi and Stefan?

I said 'I'll drive.'

Rudi said 'Why?'

I said 'Because it will be easier for me if I do.'

There was a time during that night when I thought – But driving is so beautiful! It was possible to see the track ahead by the light of the moon; by the markers on tall poles at the side of the way which were like ghostly sentinels. It was often necessary to go fast because the corrugations on the surface of the track shook one like dice if one went slowly: if one went fast the truck seemed to take off, to plane, to fly. I thought – So one becomes like a speedboat or a bird; it is possible to transmute the earth and fire of the desert into water, air.

Once we had a puncture by which an inner tube was destroyed. Rudi and I changed the wheel while Stefan still lay in the back of the truck. I said 'How many tyres have we got and how many innertubes?' Rudi said 'If you drive so fast all our tyres will be destroyed.' Stefan said 'That's not true.' Rudi said 'I thought you were dying.'

There was a time when I had to go slow because the sand became thicker. Then there were thoughts that bounced and rattled through my mind – If it is 400 miles to the next depot and we use up petrol at so many miles to the gallon if we go fast, and at so many miles to the gallon if we go slow, and we have so many gallons in the back of the truck, then if one puts those figures over these figures –

dear God, is it on this sort of thing that it depends whether or not we survive? And the same with water – We have got just so much water for ourselves, for the car, in the heat of the day, in the cool of the night: but what of the chance of breakdown, the unforeseen eventuality, the lion, as it were, in the desert? But it was to expose us to this sort of thing, wasn't it, that was the point of the journey? Such thoughts went round and round: the wheels of the car went round and round. There was a way in which one's mind could become part of the mechanism of the car: one's hands on the steering-wheel, one's feet on the controls, one's mind in touch with the tyres on the earth – might one not be in touch with what controlled the shape of the world, like gravity?

Rudi and I took turns driving through the night. I was happier when I was driving. When Rudi drove he seemed to treat the track, the desert, like an enemy.

I said 'Why are the stars always in the same position in the sky?'

Rudi said 'I don't know, are they?'

I said 'In astrology, the world is now moving out of the age of Pisces, the fishes, and into the age of Aquarius, the water-carrier. Perhaps we in this truck are the carriers of fishes, or the eggs of fishes, in our water-jar, across the desert.'

Rudi said 'We've got one dead fish in the back of this truck.'

I thought – Of course the ordeal would have to be in the outside world, on this journey.

When the sun came up the heat made it seem that there was water in front of us across the road; we were driving as if into a sea that was always moving just away from us. I thought – We are like the children of Israel imagining that we are going across the Red Sea. There were other effects of mirage: sometimes it was as if there were a whole caravan of camels in the not too far distance beneath palm trees. Once or twice I felt this must be real. I said to Rudi 'Is a mirage just a hallucination of the mind, or is it in fact the result of there being a real grove of palm trees far away from which light is refracted?'

Rudi said 'What's the difference.'

I thought – I suppose the difference might be between a state of mind by which you might live and one by which you might die.

We stopped during the greatest heat of the day at a place within sight of mountains, but there was no shade; Rudi and I fixed up a shelter at the side of the truck from some of the ornamental hangings. I sponged Stefan's face and gave him water. His forehead was very hot. I wondered – Oh God, are the kindnesses people do to others always for the sake of themselves?

There is a way of lying by which areas of skin are not touched by one's clothing: then in the gap between the burning heat and one's sweat, refrigeration can take place. I thought – This cooling by fire, these feedbacks between earth, air, fire, water: these are miracles?

I said 'Dinosaurs were able to live in the desert because their huge areas of horny skin made them successful mechanisms for refrigeration. No one knows exactly why dinosaurs became extinct.'

Rudi said nothing.

After a time Stefan raised his head and said 'Perhaps they got tired of being mechanisms for refrigeration.'

I thought – That's witty.

I dozed on and off through the day. Once I saw Stefan refilling his water-bottle quietly from one of the cans. I thought – In the end, Stefan will want to get across the desert.

The next night was the one in which I became frightened. We were travelling now almost continuously over sand: when we got stuck the wheels went round and it was as if they were mechanisms not for going forwards but simply for digging their own graves. Rudi seemed to have less and less energy when we worked under the wheels with the spade and pieces of matting. I thought I might say – Stefan, you can get up now, you have proved your point: we shouldn't have gone on this journey.

When the sun came up we were still a hundred miles or so from the depot which was our halfway point and at which we had been told there would be petrol and water. I had stopped trying to work out – So many miles at so many miles to the gallon. I found I did not want even to ask – If we do not find petrol and water, you are sure we have enough to survive? I was perhaps frightened of an answer. I wanted to say – Please help us.

After we had stopped for some food, Rudi went and lay down by Stefan in the back of the truck. Stefan sat up and looked at Rudi. He said 'Not so much the master-race now, are we.'

I said 'Do men want to die?'

Stefan said 'I'll do some driving.'

Stefan looked under the bonnet of the truck and did this or that to the engine. He checked the tyres. He seemed to have recovered now that Rudi seemed ill. I thought – Well one would never know, would one, what those chances or forces were that got that first camel across a desert.

When Stefan drove he drove even faster than I had driven. He charged at the soft sand like a bull, as if the bumps of sand were a matador. I thought – But how many have to die, dear God: does a bull ever get through?

Rudi lay in the back of the truck as if he were now suffering from heat-stroke.

I thought – Matadors would have to become extinct, before a bull got through?

I sometimes did not quite know whether or not I had been sleeping.

In the heat of the day it was as if we were ancient sailors coming to the edge of a world that was, as they had imagined it, flat: in front of them was a waterfall; beyond it, nothing. I thought – But what would the sailors have thought when they found themselves going on and on round the world: this is a miracle?

By midday we were on the look-out for the depot at which there should be petrol and water. There were palm trees and a building with a veranda; these were on the edge of a lake; then this of course was a mirage. Then looming up there was what seemed to be a fleet of huge swans; then these became bumps on the back of a sea-monster; then they seemed to be the tops of buses rising up out of the lake. I thought – They are waiting to carry off the spirits of dead travellers, these ghostly buses.

When we got close to them they were, indeed, yes, the bodies of old buses that had been dumped in the sand; they were like megalithic stones. I said to Stefan 'What is this?' Stefan said 'This is the depot.' I said 'But the buses.' Stefan said 'In them passengers spend the night, in bunks, when they are on their bus-trip in the winter across the Sahara.'

Stefan got out of the truck and went round the old buses banging on the doors: he pulled one open and looked inside: then he went on to the next. I thought – He's sweating too much: he is using up too much water.

He said 'There's no one here.'

I said 'Is there petrol and water?'

Stefan said 'I don't know.'

I said 'But we have got enough if there isn't?'

Stefan said nothing.

Rudi sat up in the back of the truck and said 'You murderer.'

Stefan said 'You've been driving too slowly.'

Rudi said 'You use up more petrol when you drive quickly.'

Stefan said 'Anyway, it was you who said that here we would find petrol and water.'

Rudi began to crawl out of the back of the truck. Stefan began to run away and he stumbled over a stone and Rudi caught him and he and Stefan began to fight again like a spider and a scorpion in the desert. I thought – Dear God, but it should be like this that things become extinct!

I took from the truck one of Rudi's ornamental hangings and I covered my head and body with it. I thought – Perhaps I will become a perfect refrigerating machine – like the earth itself, with its visions of water in the desert.

I went round the buses but there was no one there; so I walked a short way beyond them into the desert. I thought – Either I will die quickly, or there must be somewhere where they store petrol and water. The ground was like the hot coals that fakirs walk on. I thought – But they do not go very far, fakirs. Then – Oh where are those transmutations of earth, air, fire, water!

There was a pile of rocks and a pole with a marker on it a short distance into the desert. On one side of the pile there was an iron door let into the rocks. I thought – Well yes, it is like a tomb: or a store for water and petrol. I pulled on the door but it would not open: it was locked, and wedged with sand. I did not know if Rudi and Stefan would be able to open it. I thought – Perhaps they will have already killed each other, fighting like tiny dinosaurs in the desert.

I felt feverish and weak. There was a wind getting up which was suddenly making, yes, the air like fire. We had not experienced a sandstorm before. I sat with my back against the locked door in the shelter of the pile of stones. Bits of earth and fire began to hit against my face. I wondered – How long does it take to die in the desert?

– Oh I am outside that tomb, but the stone has not yet been rolled away, in that garden.

The sandstorm made clouds in which there were strange swirls of golden light. I found it difficult to breath: I covered my face with my cloak and I still found it difficult. It seemed that I should remain very still. I thought – There are fakirs who can stay alive for three days in a tomb!

I tried not to think, because thinking was to do with helplessness and fear. But to whom do you pray? I wondered – Should not prayer be valid, when your throat is so dry that you cannot speak?

There was a figure in a black robe standing in front of me in the golden cloud: I mean, it seemed I imagined that there was a figure in a black robe standing in front of me in the cloud of sand: I thought – Well what is the difference! I had made a small opening in my cloak for my eyes. The figure was that of a man, with just an opening in his black robe for his eyes. I tried to say something but my throat was too dry. I waited to see if he would go away. He did not.

He seemed to be gesturing for me to stand. I thought – But he is wearing a black robe, not white. Then – This is ridiculous.

I realised that he was telling me to move to one side, which I did; then he took a stone and scraped at the sand in front of the iron door. Then he took a large key from beneath his robe and with it he unlocked the door. He held the door open for me to go through. Inside it was dark. I went in and he followed me; he closed the door and propped it with a stone. After a time the man struck a match and lit a small oil-lamp on a shelf: we were in a half-underground chamber built of stones that did contain, yes, a number of drums of the kind which might hold petrol and water. The man in the black robe squatted with his back against one of the drums. I sat opposite him while he watched me and the wind made a howling noise outside. I thought – At the moment we have nothing to do except shelter from the storm.

Then – It was always likely that halfway across the desert there would be a store: but a storeman? Anyway, what is a miracle –

– I am sheltering in this tomb, or womb –

– Thank you, whatever it is that has got me this far across the desert.

I went to sleep for a time in the underground store, or hump, or womb. The storm made clattering and shrieking noises outside like witches. I do not know how long I slept or dreamed. When I awoke the man in the black robe did not seem to have moved: he was watching me.

I thought – He could, indeed, do anything he likes with me.

– What else are the conditions, to make prayer valid?

Outside, the wind seemed to have gone down.

I said in French 'I am with two companions. We have a truck. We need petrol and water.'

The man stood up and held out his hand to me.

When I touched him, I thought – But I did not think you were not real!

When we went out of the shelter the wind had gone and there was the lesser heat of the evening. We found Rudi and Stefan lying in the back of the truck: the truck was littered with sand. Rudi said 'I think I've killed him.' I said 'Have you?' Rudi said 'He accused me of taking water.' Stefan said 'He did take water.' Rudi said 'I didn't.' Stefan sat up; he had some sort of bandage round his head. I thought – If men have to die, it will be because they did not see that they were ridiculous.

Rudi and Stefan went with the man in the black robe and took our empty cans to fetch petrol and water. I sat and watched the darkness coming down like a flood to put out fire. I thought – At the time of Noah, the earth might have longed for water!

Rudi and Stefan and the man in the black robe made several journeys with the cans. Rudi said to me 'Where did you find him?'

I said 'He just turned up.'

Stefan said 'I told you there would be petrol and water.'

Rudi said 'You didn't.'

When we had filled enough cans Rudi offered the man in the black robe money. The man would not take it. He spoke in a French that we found difficult to understand. We made out that he wanted us to take him the rest of the way with us on our journey.

Rudi said 'Our load is too heavy already!'

Stefan said 'And we don't know where he's come from.'

I said 'He's saved our lives. If we don't take him, I expect he'll kill us.'

When I said this the man smiled at me.

I do not remember much of the rest of our journey across the desert: the man in the black robe travelled with us. It was another 300 miles or so to where there was a main depot. The man in the black robe sat in the back of the truck; he propped himself up by the tailboard. He did not seem to sleep: he spent much of the time watching me. When we got stuck in the sand it was he who got out and dug us out again. I felt he was my guardian angel. I did not worry much more about the desert.

The main depot was a village, a small settlement. It had a post office and even a hotel; it was the end of the proper desert. We had to wait there while we sent for a new tyre and new inner tubes; also there was some question of our being in trouble with the French authorities for having crossed the desert out of season and without permission. But no one seemed to be interested in my lack of a valid passport. And I thought – I have come through!

The man in the black robe saw us into the hotel: this was like a giant toy fort. Then he went away. Sometimes he would turn up again in the evenings and would sit in the hall of the hotel. I thought – He is keeping an eye on me.

I sent a telegram to my cousins in Switzerland asking them to telegraph news to me both here and at the poste restante in the town on the coast of Spanish Morocco to which we were heading. This town was called Melilla.

Rudi and Stefan shared a room in the hotel. They seemed not to want to be with me. I thought – They are either buggering each other or watching to see that one or the other doesn't go off with any diamonds – or both. Certainly, I no longer want to be with them.

I would walk each day to the local oasis and would make drawings of the camels, the children, the goats, the trees. I thought – There is a point to that drawing of the hand drawing a hand that is drawing itself; we make the way in which we see the world; I know this now; should I not include this knowledge in my representations?

The children and the palm trees and the camels by the water were so beautiful. I would think – And I am grateful! I will never quite give honour to ugliness again.

Sometimes in the village I came across the man in the black robe. I smiled: he smiled at me. I thought – Well it was indeed odd how you just turned up in the desert!

There was a day when the truck was ready for us to go on with our journey to the Mediterranean. The French official who was based in the hotel said that we were to report to the immigration and customs authorities on the frontier with Spanish Morocco.

Then Rudi said 'Stefan's not coming with us.'

I said 'Why not?'

He said 'He thinks we'll be arrested at the frontier – that you may be arrested for having no passport. He thinks they'll take the loot.'

I said 'I'll go and talk to him.'

Rudi said 'No. He's gone to find out about buses.'

I said 'I'll say goodbye.'

Rudi said 'No. I've given him his share of the loot.'

I thought – I do not believe any of this: they are hatching some plot: they might even, to get rid of me, get me arrested –

– Or Rudi has already got rid of Stefan?

– But should I explain: I don't care about any of this!

I wanted to say goodbye to the man in the black robe, but I could not find him.

I thought – He will pop up again, if he wants to?

It was a journey of another three days to the coast. Rudi sometimes tried to give explanations – 'We might have a bit of trouble at the frontier, yes, but I have friends in Spanish Morocco who will help us!' 'It is a shame about Stefan, but Stefan never had his heart in our plans, did he?' And so on. I thought – But I can tell now about such words; they go round and round like the wheels of a truck stuck in sand: with luck, they dig their own graves.

Then – But it might be that Stefan has stayed behind to guard the diamonds; so that if I am detained, they will still be safe with their loot?

Then – But I am a water-carrier crossing a desert: I am not carrying Rudi and Stefan.

Rudi and I did not sleep with each other on the way to the coast: we arrived at inns late at night and lay separately and went on early in the morning.

On the third day we came to the frontier of French territory with Spanish Morocco; I happened to be driving. Rudi said 'If they won't let you through, because of your papers, I will go on and I will get my friend to do what he can for you in Melilla.'

I said 'I see.'

Rudi said 'I don't see really what else we can do.'

I thought – Rudi, you have taught me about people like you.

The frontier post was a building like a small barracks just off the road. There was no one outside it. The frontier barrier was raised. From inside the building there was the voice of someone talking on the wireless.

I thought – Oh, there will be men bent over the wireless listening to sounds that with luck will go round and hit them on the backs of their own heads.

I said 'I'm going on.'

Rudi said 'You can't go on.'

I thought – You really want me arrested?

I put the truck into gear and drove on. No one tried to stop me. I drove fast, because I thought Rudi might make a grab at me. I knew that the frontier was not far from the sea.

I thought – Oh I am like one of those baby turtles on their run down over the sand –

– They think they will be safe in the sea?

I drove for about an hour. Rudi was silent. Then we were coming down through groves of cork trees. I could see the sea. I slowed down because it was so beautiful.

Rudi pulled on the handbrake and switched off the engine. He said 'Now get out.'

I could see that there were some soldiers some distance in front of us on the road.

I said 'Why?'

He said 'Because I don't want to be caught with you if you don't have the right papers.'

The soldiers were wearing blue tunics and baggy white trousers and red fezzes: some were standing and some were sitting on the road. I thought – Now help me, you crabs and seagulls that look out for baby turtles as they run towards the sea.

Rudi was throwing my haversack out on to the road.

I said 'Rudi, God damn you to hell!'

I got out of the truck because I wanted to be rid of Rudi and I had very nearly reached the sea.

Rudi started the truck and drove it slowly towards the soldiers. A soldier raised his hand. Rudi stopped. The soldiers gathered round the truck. I was some distance behind the truck, on the road. I thought – These soldiers do not seem to be so different from my man in the black robe!

I saw that there was a party of officers in khaki uniforms in a hollow just off the road; they had been having what seemed to be a picnic under the trees. There was a long table, at one end of which an older officer was standing and making a speech: at the other end a younger officer was being held by the arms by two soldiers in fezzes. The scene reminded me of some painting – one of those paintings of prisoners being shot in war. The soldiers round the truck on the road had opened the door and they seemed to be telling Rudi to get out: Rudi seemed to be showing them his papers. I had sat down on my haversack at the side of the road above the hollow. I was thinking – Oh I may still be that first camel that survived across a desert! In the group beneath the trees the older officer at the end of the table had stopped speaking; the younger officer who was held by the arms was being taken and placed with his back against a tree. I thought – It is, indeed, as if he is about to be shot. Then – Do I not care? But if this were a painting, in what way would I care? The older officer moved along the length of the table and he stood in front of the young officer who was being held against the tree. Then he did the Fascist salute. The man against the tree shouted something in Spanish. Then the older officer took a pistol from his belt and shot the man in the head. I mean the man against the tree turned his head sideways and the older officer put his pistol to his head and shot him. The two soldiers in fezzes ducked as if they were being showered with hail. Then the truck on the road started up. I supposed Rudi panicked – he seemed to be trying to force his way through the group of soldiers in front. Or perhaps his foot had slipped on the clutch – the truck heaved and jerked – anyway, one of the soldiers raised his rifle and fired a shot into the back of the truck. The truck went off the road and bounced down in the direction of the group of officers; it came to rest against a tree. The body of the man who had been shot was slipping down against a tree like a snake or like a skin being shed by a snake. The truck in which Rudi and Stefan and I had travelled across the Sahara was steaming, like something that has been skinned and propped against a tree. I thought – Well, there is still no reason why I should not get through to the sea.

VII   2: Max

It began to seem to many people in 1936 that there would sooner or later be war in Europe: the Nazis marched into the demilitarized zone of the Rhineland; inside Germany the laws which deprived Jews of German citizenship were being put into effect – concentration camps were filling up. In England a general election had just been won overwhelmingly by a National Government on a programme of disarmament and peace.

When I got back to England in the summer of 1935, I had been seven months in Russia: I felt that I understood now something of both Russia and Germany – even of the differences between them. Just what these were, I found difficult to put into words. In both there was much evil: but some evil seems to be to do with the way evolution is going and some does not. This does not make the former any less evil on a human level: and God save humans from the evolutionary plans, as it were, of gods.

In England most of the people I knew looked favourably on Stalin's Russia: news of the brutally enforced collectivisation and the famine did not alter their views. They would say 'Of course there is a cost in such a grand experiment!' I would say 'But still, just what do you think is being learned from this experiment?' Many people I did not know looked tolerantly on Hitler's Germany:

they would say 'Of course there is a cost in such a grand experiment!' I said to myself – The difference is in taste, touch, smell. Then – But can one really tell the way in which evolution is going?

There seemed to be no doubt about the way in which Hitler thought history should go: ten years previously he had written in *Mein Kampf* that Germany should attack Russia to make more room for Germans; also that Germany should get rid of its Jews. People did not quite say about this – What a grand experiment! But they chose simply not to read or to talk about *Mein Kampf*. I thought – It is this refusal to look at what is under one's nose that is evil on any level?

About Russia it was true that there was the grand hope – the classless society, the spread of worldwide socialism. But still, people did not want to look at what was under their noses. I thought – Evil should not just be accepted, even if it is to do with the way in which history is going.

I had been due to go back to my Cambridge college in the autumn of 1935: there had been talk of my being offered a junior fellowship. But I did not want to go back to Cambridge. I did not know what I wanted to do. I felt at this time that I should do something like go on some great pilgrimage.

I did not much want to continue with the excursion I had made into biology: I could not get people in England interested in the psychology of the business of Lysenko. They said 'But of course he is a charlatan!' I said 'Yes, of course: but why is it that people give their allegiance to charlatans?' People said 'That is not a matter for biology.' I said 'But might not it be part of why people are taken in by charlatans – this separation of subjects into different compartments, for instance biology and psychology?'

In the Cambridge physics laboratory there was a lessening of the excitement of a few years previously: there was now not so much talk of the possibility of harnessing the enormous power potentially available in the atom. In fact it had been pronounced by pundits that this would be impossible. The work going on was of the analytical kind in which I had been involved a year earlier with Kapitsa. I said to people 'But Kapitsa was always interested in something more than this sort of work: I expect he is interested in something more now in Russia.' People said 'What evidence have you for this?' I said 'What sort of evidence do you want? You remember Kapitsa!'

I had promised Mullen not to say anything about my meeting

and conversation with him in Moscow, but it seemed that anything I said would anyway not be taken seriously.

However, there were some extraordinarily interesting speculations in theoretical physics going on at this time, although these were not talked much about amongst Cambridge physicists. They had their reputations as hard-headed experimentalists to maintain: perhaps also they were reacting to their abandonment by the fanciful Kapitsa.

You remember how Einstein had tried to show that the Complementarity and Uncertainty Principles of Bohr and Heisenberg were not complete statements about reality: that there must be some way of understanding reality apart from its dependence on the observer. And so he, Einstein, had suggested an experiment in which the behaviour of one particle – its location and momentum – might be described 'objectively' by measuring the behaviour of another particle with which it had once interacted; for although the location and momentum of this other particle would be affected by the acts of measuring, those of the first particle would not and so there might in theory be calculated the 'objective' behaviour of this first particle from the information given by the measurement of the second and from information available from the original interaction. To deny this would be to imply that the act of measuring the second particle would somehow affect the first particle now quite separate from it; and this would imply some magical action-at-a-distance which no reasonable definition of reality, Einstein claimed, would permit. But then in turn Bohr and Heisenberg claimed that this was indeed just what their sort of definition of reality permitted! And not only permitted, but also forced to be recognised if any sense was to be made from what was observed and from what could be worked out mathematically.

Argument about this had gone on between the continents of Europe and America (Einstein was by this time living in America). Then towards the end of 1935 there had been published a paper by Schrödinger that was intended to support Einstein by reducing to absurdity the way of looking at things proposed by Bohr and Heisenberg – in particular their proposition that an event cannot in fact be said to exist until it is observed: that before this it exists only as a matter of potentialities. Supposing, Schrödinger said, you take a box and put inside it a cat, a phial of poison gas, a lump of radioactive material and a radiation detector which is set up so that if there is an emission of a particle from the lump of material through radioactive decay then the phial of poison gas will be broken and the cat will die; but if there is no emission the cat will live. And supposing, Schrödinger said, the timing of the experiment is fixed so that there is a fifty-fifty chance that there will be or will not be the emission of a particle while the cat is in the box (radioactive decay occurs by chance – for physicists this had become a definition of 'chance': whether or not a particle is emitted within a certain time was held to be predictable only as a potentiality, a matter of statistics). Well, according to Bohr and Heisenberg, the potentialities for the emission of a particle and for the non-emission of a particle exist side by side; they exist side by side in the box, as it were, until an observer opens the box and looks inside: only then can one or another eventuality be said to have occurred or to occur. It was not just that the observer would not know what had happened inside the box until he looked inside, but that neither one thing nor the other would in fact have happened until an observer looked inside: the two potentialities would have existed together in the box and it would be the act of the observer looking in that would be the occasion of one or the other to have happened or to happen. This was supposed to demonstrate the absurdity of Bohr and Heisenberg's position. In this experiment, which became known as that of Schrödinger's Cat, it was, according to Bohr and Heisenberg, the act of observation that was the occasion of the cat being alive or dead: until then the cat itself (like the emission of the particle) existed in a state of suspended animation, as it were; its state was a matter of potentialities; it was both or neither alive/dead. And so this potentially alive/dead cat – was not this indeed an absurdity! But the question remained: why should not reality be absurd?

I tried to talk with my father and mother about this. I explained 'But this is only the beginning of the riddles that you get on to in this area. There is then the question: but what if the cat itself in the box can be said to observe, as it were, the emission or non-emission of a particle through radioactive decay – I mean, should not the cat be able to observe whether itself is alive or dead? Or what if you put an experimental physicist inside the box: how difficult would it be for him – ha ha – to observe whether he was alive or dead – '

My father said 'But have you not put your finger on the nub of this matter, which is that these people are not serious?'

I said 'But they are. They are trying to describe things which seem to them to be deadly serious, but which are taken by most people, of course, as frivolous.'

My mother said 'You mean, people who make these speculations may have some special need to go on in this way?'

I said 'According to their observations and to the mathematics, the whole universe may have a need to go on in this way – and perhaps a need for us to understand it, if we are not to blow it up.'

My father and mother faced each other across the dining-room table. I thought – They are waiting for Watson the parlourmaid to come in to make something frivolous of the situation, like Schrödinger looking into his cat's box.

Then – But people must know that there are levels at which reality does seriously seem ridiculous?

There was a girl I had met at Cambridge about this time (you will not mind if I write about this: I will suggest it is ridiculous!) who was called Caroline. Caroline was a tall blonde girl with a baby face; she had long legs and a thin body with amazing protuberances in front and behind; she was like a barb, a hook, a fluke. (You know the definitions of a fluke? It is a parasitic worm that gets its teeth into the livers of sheep; it is that part of an anchor which holds a ship to the bed of the sea; it is a piece of random good fortune that falls on one out of the sky: well does not language show how some things are ridiculous?) Caroline was a girl who lodged in my inside: God knows she must have seen me as a sheep.

Caroline came from an aristocratic county family: she appeared in Cambridge at some May Week balls. (No, I cannot remember what year! Did my meeting Caroline in fact stop me coming out to Germany, to Switzerland? And why should I be anxious about writing about this now: have you not been writing about your affairs that were ridiculous?) Caroline appeared at some May Week balls and caused a slight social sensation: she wore a khaki shirt and skirt and a red beret during the day; and even in evening dress – a high collar and long sleeves – she looked like a stern figure on a revolutionary poster, pouting and heroic; pointing the way in which history is going. Then when one got close there was the soft English face; the terrible demandingness of the innocent and bold and young. When she was introduced to people she would stand with her hands clasped in front of her or occasionally she would do briefly a clenched-fist salute. I would think – Like someone holding a sea-shell to their ear. When I had first come across Caroline she had seemed to be unapproachably surrounded by men. I had thought – A Lilith on her rock guarded by the bodies of half-drowned sailors. Then when I got back from Russia it seemed – Well, I might now be more of a siren myself, might I not: a lure to innocent so-called Communist maidens.

At some party in a tent in which there were thousands of bottles of champagne, men in white ties and tails like sea-horses, women with straps over their shoulders like pack-mules –

– And I was thinking – A tent which is indeed like Schrödinger's cat's box: how would anyone here know whether they were alive or dead? –

– At this party Caroline came swimming towards me from her rock and when she was close there were her red mouth and white teeth like a wound that had already been made by a hook and I thought – Dear God, who indeed is the caught and who is the catcher: but let me indeed be thus suspended between life and death –

She said 'You've been to Russia!'

I said 'Yes.'

She said 'How ever did you get back!'

I said 'By boat.'

She said 'I mean, how could you bear to?'

I said 'Oh I see.'

When I danced with Caroline there was her body like a probe, a proboscis; her barbs were at my heart, guts, liver. I thought – Are fishes in some sort of ecstasy? When we kissed we seemed to be putting hooks in, pulling them out of, each other's mouths.

She said 'If I had known you were going to Russia, I would have asked if I could have come with you!'

'If I go to Russia again, will you come with me?'

'Are you going to Russia again?'

'No. But for you, I would go anywhere.'

'I only want to go to Russia.'

I used to meet Caroline at parties. We did not exactly make or not make love: this was the convention of the time. We stood propped behind doorways; we floundered in the backs of cars or taxis; indeed like Schrödinger's cat we remained in lengthy states of suspended consummation. I thought – But by this we keep things going? It is not simply a matter of convention.

Sometimes Caroline would say 'No no!' And I would say 'Why not?' And once she said 'Because I do not think of you like that!' I said 'What do you think of me like?' She said 'Like St George.' I thought – Poor old George! Then – But even he might have realised that something would be over, once he had killed his dragon.

For much of the time, of course, it was I who was protecting myself. The convention was: if things went too far, I might have to marry Caroline. I thought – But I could always pretend to go mad, to become ill, to die, before I married Caroline.

That winter and spring when I was with Caroline I used to talk much of the time: I suppose this was to protect myself. I pressed a button, as it were, and out came old gramophone records on the mechanism of my mind. I thought – Talk is a way of keeping up suspended animation.

'You do not imagine, do you, that life is pleasant in Russia? Of course, old ground has to be broken up before something new can grow –

'It is significant, surely, that Dostoevsky has never been banned by the Party! Except, of course, that they do not understand what he says –

'Bolsheviks have their hope, their aim, which is the true socialist society: but in the meantime, of course, there are simply the leaders and the led – '

Caroline would say 'You are very cynical about Russia!'

I would say 'Does not Marxism–Leninism thrive on a spirit of revolutionary self-criticism?'

I would think – Perhaps it is by Caroline that I will have to be carried off, broken up, before something new can grow.

I sometimes talked with my old friend Donald about this. Donald was anxious about my involvement with Caroline, not because she was a Communist – almost everyone we knew at Cambridge at that time was sympathetic to Communism – but because he disapproved of the way in which Caroline's brand of left-wing activity also seemed to involve her with fashionable drunks and jazz musicians. Donald's idea of left-wing politics was to be a member of innumerable committees.

Donald and I went walking along the reaches of the river where a few years ago we had been discussing Wittgenstein's problems about how to talk about what could or could not be said. Donald was now doing post-graduate work in physics. He said 'A girl like that – she'll have your guts for garters.'

I thought – Ah, my guts wound round Caroline's legs, with roses!

I said 'But what else is this sort of love? Is it not some larva of a tapeworm that lies about in shit; then it is eaten by a pig and bores its way through the intestinal wall; then lodges in the ham of the pig – oh the beautiful ham of a pig! – which is eaten by man so that indeed the larva hatches out and becomes a tapeworm with its teeth in the man's guts and there it stays with its tail hanging out of his arse, as it were, and every now and then dropping more eggs to hatch in the shit – '

Donald said 'I am not sure if you have got the biotic interaction quite right.'

I said ' – And all you can do in the end is to blast it out with – what? – gunpowder?'

Donald said 'Ah, the question of why men go to war!'

When she was in London Caroline lived with an aunt by marriage called Mrs Fortescue who had a house in Fitzroy Square. Mrs Fortescue was a society hostess for the kind of so-called 'bohemian' people who lived around Fitzroy Square. From a distance Mrs Fortescue looked neat and elaborate like a matador, as sometimes did her niece Caroline; then when you got close she seemed to be sewn up here and there like a picador's horse.

In the spring of 1936 I moved to London myself and took a room in an apartment block at the other end of Charlotte Street from Fitzroy Square. My friend Melvyn lived in this block: it had an outside iron staircase and iron-grating landings. I was supposed to be doing some post-graduate work at University College: I had just enough money from an aunt who had died to enable me to live without earning much for about a year. Melvyn showed his concern about my obsession with Caroline.

'But my dear fellow, I can give you an address, much cheaper, if you really want things like that.'

'Like what?'

'Like being buggered about by a frightful little tight-arsed bitch. Getting yourself pissed on. Things like that.'

I thought I might say – You make it sound so exciting! I said 'Why do you see her like that?'

Melvyn said 'Ducky, when you really want to know, I'll tell you.'

I thought – But what are you, Melvyn (what perhaps is anyone?), except a frightful little tight-arsed bitch?

Melvyn at the time was living with a fair-haired boy called Cecil who would appear in a Blackshirt uniform every now and then. When I called in on Melvyn he would usually send Cecil out of the room on some errand – to buy cigarettes or bottles of wine. The only conversations I ever heard Melvyn and Cecil having together were about what happened to their cigarettes or to the change from money that Melvyn had given him for wine. I thought – But don't people know that they like being buggered about by their loved ones; arguing about things like cigarettes and change from bottles of wine?

I said to Melvyn 'Why don't you ever ask me about my time in Russia?'

He said 'Because I don't want to hear it, ducky.'

'Why not?'

'Because either it might be true, or you and I play tricks on one another, ducky.'

I thought – You mean, at this moment of history, on the objective level, you don't want to become interested in hearing what might be true?

The relationship between Melvyn and Cecil was particularly odd at this time because it had just become official Communist policy for Communists to see Fascists as the main political enemy: until recently there had still been the idea that it was somehow necessary to tolerate Fascists as representatives of the death-throes of capitalism. But now, with the continuing successes of the Nazis and their persecution of Communists, word had gone out from Moscow that hostility to Nazism must be unequivocal: alliances against it should be made with Social Democrats who had previously been seen as perverters of the true and inevitable revolution. These were the days of the left-wing and anti-Fascist Popular Front. I thought – But Melvyn would not be an innocent in his relationship with Cecil: he wants some cover for whatever are his real activities. Or he just gets pleasure from there being such conjectures about him?

I said 'But this is the interesting question: why do you and I play tricks?'

He said 'Well, why do you?'

I said 'I suppose because I want to keep alternatives open: I want to see what happens.'

He said 'That's not why I play tricks.'

I thought I might say – Well, why do you? Then – But is this one of the things that I do not want to hear?

Sometimes when I was with Melvyn he seemed to be on the point of stopping our banter; of telling me something of importance; of deciding not to get drunk on the cheap wine that Cecil brought back to the flat. I thought – But what could he tell me that in some way I do not already know? And anyway, I do not want to be in any real relationship with Melvyn, just as I do not want to be in a real relationship with anyone just now, not even with Caroline. Does it not suit all of us at times like this to be in some suspended animation with our tricks; like that ingenious cat, not really alive nor dead –

I said 'Well, you might be living with a Fascist boy as some sort of cover: you might not want to be thought too much of a Communist just now when they seem to be making practical sense of their politics; when they might want you to work for them under cover.'

Melvyn said 'But it isn't I who've changed, ducky, I've always been serious. And there's still that to be said for Fascists, they're serious; they're not just a load of Mrs Fortescue's rich shits.'

I said 'But that's what you would say, isn't it, even if you were a Communist spy.'

Sometimes Melvyn looked at me with a sort of love. I thought – And that was the impression I had from Mullen when we were in front of that painting of the Old Testament Trinity in Moscow.

I said 'But you must see, don't you, that it doesn't seem to me to matter, to be serious, whether or not you're a Communist spy.'

Then Melvyn said 'Well, that's your cover, ducky, with Mrs Fortescue's rich shits.'

Melvyn had once been a favourite of Mrs Fortescue's, but she no longer invited him to her parties because he had been caught making love to her footman in the lift. Melvyn used to tell me stories about the private lives of the people whom Mrs Fortescue had at her parties: there was a junior minister who liked dressing up as a chambermaid and being seduced in suburban hotels; there was a newspaper columnist who liked to take the job of a public lavatory attendant at weekends. I had no means of knowing whether or not these stories were true. I thought – But this is the point; what is the point of asking what is or is not true?

Melvyn said 'And you know what The Infant Fortescue's speciality is, don't you?'

I said 'What?'

Melvyn said 'She has little balloons of scented farts which she lets off in bed.'

I said 'Caroline has little balloons of scented farts which she lets off in bed?'

Melvyn said 'No, you fool, her aunt is The Infant Fortescue!'

I said 'And what is Caroline's speciality?'

He said 'Ah, I don't think you're yet ready to know that, ducky.'

I thought – Ah, who would want Caroline's farts to be scented in bed!

I used to meet Caroline in a pub halfway up Charlotte Street. I had thought at first that one of my tasks might be to lure her away from her aunt, because it was through her, obviously, that she met other men; then I seemed to be trying to lure Caroline to get me invited to Mrs Fortescue's parties. Caroline would come into the pub wearing a silvery summer dress; she was one of those metal fishes flashing through the water with a hook in its tail. I would think – Dear God, but is it not the point to put up some sort of fight when one has swallowed this bait?

I said 'Why do you have to hang about with your aunt's friends in Fitzroy Square? What is a good Communist doing with *canaille* like that?'

Caroline said 'As a matter of fact, most of my aunt's friends are staunch supporters of the Popular Front.'

I said 'Everyone jumps on the bandwagon: then hoopla! everyone on the bandwagon suddenly gets shot. That's what I liked about Russia. You never knew whether you were watching a triumphal procession or a tumbril.'

Caroline had a way of leaning forwards with her mouth open as if she were inviting me to do something with a hook. She said 'Is that what your friend Melvyn says?'

I said 'Melvyn never pretends to do anything other than play tricks.'

Caroline said 'My aunt says, would you like to come to one of her parties. And she says you can bring Melvyn, yes.'

I tried to work out – Your aunt has instructed you to get Melvyn back? It is you who for some reason want to meet Melvyn?

I said 'Somewhere, I have read, there are people who do not play tricks, who try to get at the truth: there are pockets of ideal communal societies. But these are not to do with Communists, they are run by anarchists: Communists have from the beginning been committed to tricks. But anarchists believe that societies work if you just tell the truth: if you trust one another.'

I thought – So where are you now, my beautiful German girl?

Caroline said 'Where are these people?'

I said 'In Spain.'

Caroline said 'Spain!'

I said 'Come with me to Spain!'

I thought – Dear God, will I one day stop doing tricks?

Caroline leant forwards and said 'You bring Melvyn to my aunt's party. She wants to ask him whether or not it is true he is a Fascist.'

I thought – This is boring.

There was an evening when I went with Melvyn on an expedition to the East End of London. I had imagined that this was where Melvyn picked up his boys – where he got himself buggered or beaten up or whatever. But Melvyn announced that he was going to a political meeting. I wondered – On what side will be this political meeting – for his cover: for the cover of his cover? Melvyn wore brown riding-boots and pale brown breeches and the sort of smock that might be worn for ju-jitsu or indeed by a Russian peasant. I thought – Or perhaps after all he is more like the actor-manager of a theatrical company on tour. We went by Underground to the East End; there was to be a march by Fascists through a predominantly Jewish area. I thought – Of course, Cecil will be one of the marchers. Melvyn and I lined up with some counter-demonstrators at the side of the road. When the Fascists arrived they were a column of rather undernourished-looking men; they marched firmly; Melvyn and the people around us shook their fists and jeered. When Cecil went past Melvyn jumped up and down with the others and shouted. 'Thuggery buggery Fascists and war!' One could not tell who, if anyone, he was mocking. Cecil did not look round, but he seemed to be aware of Melvyn. Melvyn seemed happy. I wondered – So which came first, politics or sexuality? When the column of Blackshirts had gone past there was left behind at the side of the road a man selling Fascist newspapers; he was set upon by some of the crowd; he was pushed to the ground and kicked; he curled up in the position of a foetus. Melvyn started across the road as if to join in or help him; then stopped and looked in the direction in which the marchers had gone. From here there came running some Blackshirts. The men who had been punching the man on the ground began to run; one of them was caught by the Blackshirts and he was pushed to the ground and punched and kicked; he curled up in the position of a foetus. Then Melvyn ran forwards and started hitting at the backs of the Blackshirts: after a time they turned on him and he fell to the ground and curled up. I had begun to move towards him but then I stopped. I thought –

Well, what can one say about this: it is cheaper than having to pay for it?

Afterwards Melvyn went into a public lavatory to clean himself up. He chatted with the attendant. I thought – This is where he has to pay for his boys?

He said to me 'You were a fat lot of good, ducky.'

I said 'You seemed to be getting the sort of thing you wanted.'

Melvyn said 'You're so blunt you'll give yourself piles, ducky.'

The kicking and punching that Melvyn had received seemed to have left no marks on him. I thought – It is true that in ecstasy the body neither is lacerated nor bleeds?

Once at about this time I went to see a psychoanalyst friend of my mother's. He was a large man with a beard of the kind that makes you wonder what he might want to hide about his face. I sat on a chair while his couch waited like a coffin beside me. I said 'I don't seem to want to do anything. Also I'm obsessed by this girl. Of course I want to go to bed with her, but it seems that I'm afraid that if I do she'll hurt me.'

The analyst said 'And you think it odd that you don't want to be hurt by her?'

I said 'You think it's sensible to want to go on being obsessed by her?'

After a time the analyst said 'It seems to me that what this girl represents to you is your mother. You feel that you will be hurt because she is the hostile breast – the breast that you were helpless with in front of your mother. You need the breast and so you cannot get away from her; but it is your fear of incest that prevents you wanting to go to bed with her, just as you would fear to go to bed with your mother.'

I said 'But I have been to bed with my mother.'

The analyst began to blush. Through his dark hair and thin beard, he was like a sunset in a forest.

I said 'I mean, in a way. But that was a long time ago.'

I thought – Perhaps this analyst is upset because he is in love with my mother?

Much of the time I lay in bed. I read: I wrote some poetry, as I had done in Russia. I thought – Well, what is the difference between here and in Russia? I read some Freud; some Melanie Klein. I thought – Everyone has a death-wish in their own particular way: in this present society a death-wish seems to take the form of an allegiance to Fascism, Communism; indeed those could be said to be the devouring breasts of a mother. Then – So what about me: what happens when you know that in a way you have a death-wish; that in a way you have been to bed with your mother? What are you frightened of – who is devouring whom?

Melvyn would come and sit on the end of my bed. Once he had the mark of a rope, or burns, at his wrist and neck. I thought – Cecil has been tying him up; like his mother?

I said 'My friend Caroline has asked us both to one of Mrs Fortescue's parties.'

Melvyn said 'Ah, the good Mrs Fortescue wants to take the mothballs out of her pissoir.'

I said 'You said you would tell what is Caroline's speciality.'

He said 'You really want to know?' Then – 'On a dark night can you tell the difference?'

I said 'Let me work it out. A dark night. Something she likes that cannot be seen. Oh, she likes to go to bed with black men!'

Melvyn said 'You're so sharp, ducky, you'll circumcise yourself.'

I said 'Is there anyone special?'

He said 'A trombonist.'

I said 'Why a trombonist?'

He shouted 'For God's sake, ducky, how do I know why a trombonist?'

I thought – But what a chance to have said something witty!

There was a party, then, one hot evening in July at Mrs Fortescue's house to which both Melvyn and I went. There were the sort of people there whom I seemed to take as my natural enemies: Conservative politicians, left-wing intellectuals, professional dinner-party wits. I thought – What, no black trombonist? In Mrs Fortescue's crowded drawing-room people seemed to be pressed into odd shapes as if they were fishes at the bottom of an ocean. They talked and talked: they talked politics: I thought – They talk to keep the pressure out; to keep themselves inflated. I wedged myself into a corner like some old octopus. I thought – Well, I will talk too: I will squirt out my old gramophone records at anyone who approaches me.

'But politicians don't want power, they want an enemy; politics is a game, how can you have a game without an enemy? Politicians have to say that they want power because this is part of the game: but what they really like is for other people to have power and then they can attack them and have a game. People who really want power want something very secret. Then they don't get beaten.'

Caroline said 'Don't you want power?'

I said 'Even if I did, I'd say I didn't, wouldn't I?'

Caroline went off and talked to someone I recognised as a young Conservative MP. He was like some small, neat sea-horse; sticking out in front and behind.

I thought – What I need, I think, is to go on a journey across a desert.

There was a man who came and stood close in front of me as I talked. It did not seem that anyone in the room was listening to other people's talk; they were letting it bounce off them so that they could talk themselves. I was saying –

'Communists are like the cat in Schrödinger's box; do you know about Schrödinger's box? Communists are waiting to see whether they are alive or dead, then they will know which way to jump. I suppose they think that they will know this when Hitler opens the box and looks inside: until then they are in a state of suspended animation; they have no one to beat up except themselves.'

I had been churning out this sort of stuff when the man standing in front of me took a card from his pocket and handed it to me and said 'Come and see me in my office.' Then he moved away. I tried to put the card in my pocket, but it kept sliding down the outside as if my fingers were slipping on rock.

Caroline came up to me excitedly and said 'Do you know who that was?'

I said 'No.'

She said 'The editor.'

I said 'What editor?' Then – 'Not the editor of the *Deep-Sea Fisherman's Gazette*, who wrote the authoritative work on the species Black Trombonist?'

Caroline said 'Do you know how boring you are when you are drunk?'

I said 'I am preparing to go on a journey across a desert.'

A tall dark man who looked like a Moor had come into the room. I thought – Dear God, is he the trombonist? But he is rather the sort of man who might be standing at an oasis under a palm tree. People were gathering round him as if he were one of those messengers who come on stage in a Greek play with news of enormous events elsewhere. I heard him saying 'At Ceuta, yes; and Melilla.'

People were saying 'Where are they?'

He said 'In Spanish Morocco.'

He sat in a chair and people sat on the floor at his feet. I thought – He is a ju-ju man, a magician, who has a vision of the future to tell: who pokes about amongst cracked bones in the dust.

He was saying 'That's where the rising seems to have begun. But it's now spread to the mainland.'

I thought – Spanish Morocco is somewhere I might head for, to a desert?

Caroline was sitting at the feet of the man who looked like a Moor. Then after a time she came back to me and said 'Don't you think you should go home?'

I said 'I'm planning to go on a pilgrimage across a desert.'

She said 'You've said that six times.'

I said 'And on the seventh, it might come true.'

I do not remember how I got home. I woke up in the middle of the night and thought – But I have destroyed my relationship with Caroline! Then – Good! Then – But perhaps I will be able to persuade her that I was talking in some sort of code all the time.

Oh there was much excitement, yes, amongst our circle of friends – our circle of about half a mile radius from Fitzroy Square – much excitement about the outbreak of the Spanish Civil War! The rebellion had indeed started, the papers said the next day, with a military rising at Melilla in Spanish Morocco: it seemed to have started slightly prematurely there because officers feared that their plans might have been betrayed: the next day there were risings or attempts at risings by the army against the socialist government in most of the large towns on mainland Spain. Our circle round Fitzroy Square was excited because this could be seen unequivocally as a right-wing Fascist rebellion against a democratically elected Popular Front government: and there was even perhaps something that might be done about it since it was taking place in the almost fairy-tale country of Spain. Regarding recent Fascist aggressions – Hitler's march into the Rhineland; Mussolini's invasion of Abyssinia – what could there be done about these from Fitzroy Square? And for this sort of politics it had been necessary, had it not, to wait to hear the line from Moscow: and the line from Moscow had been so equivocal!

The morning after Mrs Fortescue's party, Caroline came to visit me in my room. She had not done this before. She said 'Had you really an idea of what was going to happen in Spain? I mean, the way you were talking to the editor!'

I said 'I'm afraid I was very drunk last night.'

She said 'I don't suppose you were as drunk as you made out!'
I said 'Who is this editor?'
'He wants to see you.'
'What about?'
'Something you said must have impressed him last night.'
It appeared that the man who had given me his card at the party was the editor of *The Crucible*, an extremist left-wing Popular Front magazine. He had told Caroline that he had been interested in what I had been saying about the nature and tactics of power – about the way in which Communists were waiting for Fascists to see which way to jump. He had seemed to think that I was commending this. He would like me, he apparently had said, to write for his magazine.

I thought – So this might be a way for me and Caroline to go to Spain!

I said 'It all depends on what's really going on in Spain.'

She said 'There's been a Fascist uprising against a Popular Front government.'

I said 'But what's really interesting in Spain is what advantage all this might be to the anarchists.'

She said 'You and your anarchists!'

I thought – But I must pick the right time to say again 'Let's go to Spain!'

I had, it was true, been trying to find out more about anarchists. They were people who had said simply – Things must be destroyed before anything new can grow. The modern anarchist movement had been founded by Bakunin in the nineteenth centry; Bakunin had wished to do away with all forms of state control; he had thought that society would be orderly if people were left to themselves. By advocating this he had of course become an anathema to both Fascists and Communists. He had coined a slogan 'The passion for destruction is also the creative passion.' I thought – Yes, but when you know this, on what level, in what style, are things creative when they are left to themselves?

I said to Caroline 'The only place where Bakunin's ideas have been put into effect is Spain. His ideas were promulgated by disciples who couldn't speak a word of Spanish, and they were understood and received rapturously by people who couldn't speak a word of anything else. It was like the Holy Ghost.'

Caroline said 'Why was it like the Holy Ghost?'

I said 'After Pentecost, Christianity spread like wildfire because no one understood a word of what the disciples were saying.'

Caroline said 'I never know when you are serious.'

I said 'Come with me to Spain!'

Caroline was sitting on my bed. My bed was littered with books and papers about anarchism: there was also a book about pilgrimages in the Middle Ages. I had got the idea that a pilgrimage might be representative of a journey across a desert.

Caroline said 'But there's a war in Spain.'

I said 'But don't you want to have a look at the real war between Communism and Fascism? Or do you just want to go on talking like those bums in Fitzroy Square?'

Caroline picked up the book on pilgrimages in the Middle Ages. One of the pilgrimages was to Santiago de Compostela in Spain: people used to travel there usually on foot from all over Europe; they seemed often to have done this to get away from conditions of boredom and madness at home.

Caroline said 'What are you doing!'

I said 'Feeling your behind.'

She said 'Not now!'

I shouted 'When then?'

She said 'You are clever! You know I'd adore to go to Spain!'

I thought – At Pentecost, did the disciples ever understand what they were doing?

When I told Melvyn about the editor of *The Crucible* who wanted to see me and possibly to write for him, I imagined Melvyn's mind flicking like a lizard's tongue that darts out to catch flies. He said 'You watch out, ducky, or he'll get you sent to Spain.'

I said 'But you know I want to go to Spain!'

He said 'You want to get killed? That's what they'd really like to happen to you in Spain.'

I said 'Why?'

He said 'To be a martyr. To be killed by the Fascists. A fine young Englishman! Good publicity.'

I thought – But then they might send Caroline too: think of the publicity!

Melvyn said 'If you want it, it could be arranged.'

I said 'You could arrange two journalists' passes for me and Caroline to get to Spain?'

I thought – And then we could be real lovers! Who of course have always liked getting themselves martyred.

Then – But what does it mean, that Melvyn thinks he's someone who can get such things arranged?

335

Most of the people in our circle around Fitzroy Square were organising petitions, putting out declarations, attending protest meetings in support of the government in Spain. No one was yet showing much sign of going there. I thought – Oh, but this could be a real reason for going! When I next saw Caroline I said to her 'Well do you or don't you despise these people who talk and never do anything? They are like those primitive organisms whose mouths are the same as their anuses.'

She said 'Are you serious about going to Spain?'

I said 'I don't know if I want to fight. I want to see what's happening. All this talk is rubbish unless one can see what is happening. Even though, I suppose, one might still only see what one likes.'

Caroline said 'You don't want to fight?'

I said 'If I could see what was happening, I might fight.'

Caroline said 'I would do anything for someone who fights!'

I had stopped trying to find out what Caroline did when she was not with me in the evenings: I sometimes imagined her with the black trombonist; sometimes with the young Tory MP; sometimes with the dark man like Othello. I thought – The more I worry about this the more I pull the hook deeper –

– But we would be together in Spain!

I went to see my father and mother to tell them that I was thinking of going to Spain. I thought I would put it to them that I had planned, quite apart from the war, to go on some trip, perhaps on a pilgrimage to Santiago de Compostela. If they thought me mad I could say – But it is my vision of myself as mad that I am trying to get away from.

My mother was sitting with her back to the light in the bow window of the drawing-room. I thought – This is how I shall always remember her: her face in shadow; the sun as if behind some entrance to a cave.

I said 'I'm thinking of going to Spain.'

She said 'Are you going with that communist German girlfriend?'

I said 'No, I may be going with a communist English girlfriend.'

My mother said 'Well what, as an English mother, am I supposed to do? Shall I get Watson to make you some of your favourite cucumber sandwiches?'

I thought – How extraordinary that my mother always asks about my communist German girlfriend!

I said 'I don't really want to fight. But I want to see more of what this sort of politics is about. One can't just go on talking.'

My mother said 'Nowadays you never talk to me.'

I said 'Oh Mummy, let's have the cucumber sandwiches!'

At some stage in the afternoon my mother began to cry. She said 'I've never been any good for you!' I said 'Of course you've been good for me!' She said 'Do you love me?' I said 'Yes, but we know all this!' She said 'Yes, but let's go on talking about it for a while.' I put my arm round her and she took refuge under my wing. I thought – It is good that my mother and I are all right.

Then my mother said 'What about that other girl: Nellie – '

I said 'Why do you always go on about Nellie?'

My mother said 'No, I don't mean your German girl. I mean Nellie. You know, Nellie.'

I said 'Oh well, still, why do you bring her up now?'

Nellie was the name of the tiny deaf-and-dumb girl I had tried to do something about years ago in the north of England. (I mean, it is odd, yes, that Nellie was the name by which you, my love, were sometimes called and by which I often called you.) My mother had got Nellie, the young Nellie, into a special school run by nuns, and was paying for her there. I was always meaning to go and visit Nellie: I did not know why I found it so difficult to do this. I had sometimes wondered – Is it on account of the same instinct, not quite to be put into words, which prevented me from visiting my other beautiful Nellie? The fear that something might not be too little, but too much? I thought now – My mother thinks that her question about Nellie might influence my going or not going to Spain?

I said 'I'll see her when I get back.'

My mother said 'Yes, you see her when you get back.'

I thought – My mother is suddenly mysterious, or is she in pain? Rocking backwards and forwards like a witchdoctor above dust.

When my father came home from Cambridge he seemed suddenly very old; he walked with a stick. I thought – What was that riddle put to Oedipus by the Sphinx about old men having sticks: what is it that has three legs in the evening? But Oedipus had killed his father. My mother said 'Max is going to Spain.' My father said 'Why is he going to Spain?' My mother said 'He's thinking of going on some sort of pilgrimage.' My father said 'Then he'll need a sleeping-bag and a pistol.'

337

I thought – Why have I ever thought that my father and mother were not all right?

My father went out of the room moving slowly, as if by clockwork. I thought – He and my mother are like those figures on the base of a clock that come out and tell you the time and the state of the weather; but time for them is running out. When my father came back he was carrying a revolver-type pistol. He said 'It belonged to your grandfather and then your uncle: don't lose it.' I said 'Thank you very much.' I thought – If the worst comes to the worst I can always put it to the roof of my mouth. My father said 'Where is the sleeping-bag?' My mother said 'What sleeping-bag?' My father said 'The nice double bag in which we used to go camping.' My mother said 'I don't remember a sleeping-bag.' My father said 'Oh no, you were too busy running through the woods.' I thought – Perhaps I can go off to war now, because my mother and father are all right.

I said 'Goodbye then.'

They said 'Goodbye.'

At the end, of course, I thought I might cry.

Then – But it is as if I am being pulled along on a hook: one thing happening after another.

When I got back to the block of flats in London it was at night and Melvyn's door was open and he was sitting up in bed fully dressed. He looked shifty. I thought – He is waiting for Cecil to come and hang him up in the clothes' cupboard?

He said 'Biddle wants to see you.' Biddle was the name of the editor of *The Crucible*.

I said 'Now?'

Melvyn said 'Oh he can't wait for you, ducky.'

I said 'Oh I thought you meant at night, dressed up as a spy, with a false moustache and dark glasses.'

I wondered – But it is true that Melvyn has this influence with Biddle? That he might want to get me tied up in this business like he seems to want to get tied up by Cecil?

In my room it did seem that someone might have been going through my belongings. I thought – And indeed it might have been Melvyn who originally got Biddle interested in seeing me: then – But this is boring.

Next morning I went to Biddle's office in a block near Holborn. On the ground floor there was a printing press which churned out left-wing pamphlets. Biddle's office was cold, although we were in the heat of summer: it was as if he sat in a grate in which a damp fire had failed to light. There were bundles of papers going brown at the edges; cigarette-ash was scattered on his desk. Biddle was a big man who gave the impression of having a hand up inside him like a glove-puppet. I thought – We are all of us creatures to which one thing happens after another: but knowing this is not one of the things that happens after another.

I said 'Melvyn says that you might be able to get me accredited as a journalist in Spain.'

He said 'Melvyn says that I might be able to get you accredited as a journalist in Spain?'

I thought I might say – I know you have to talk like this: I've been to Russia.

I said 'I thought you might want martyrs.'

He said 'Now just a minute! Hold it! Begin again.'

After a conversation that seemed to go on for hours with very little of what was meant being said, Biddle agreed to provide me with a press card and a letter I could use in an emergency in Spain saying that I represented the Party. In return I would send him dispatches from Barcelona. He said that he could give me very little money in advance, and I had to sign a paper agreeing that he would not be responsible if I got into trouble. I said 'And oh yes, did Melvyn tell you, can I have a card for an assistant.'

He said 'Can you have a card for an assistant?'

I said 'It's for Caroline, you know, Caroline. Think of the publicity if both of us became martyrs!'

He said 'You think we want you to become martyrs?'

When I got back to my apartment block with its outside iron staircase and the landings like those of a fire-escape, there was a groaning and scraping noise coming from Melvyn's room. I knocked on the door and waited and then pushed and went in. Melvyn was sitting tied to a chair. He was naked and gagged. I said 'Do you want to be untied?' He nodded. I said 'It is interesting, this; it is one of the situations in which one could not tell what you really wanted.'

Melvyn rubbed his wrists and neck. He said 'That little bugger went out to get cigarettes.'

I said 'What sort of contacts have you got with Biddle?'

Melvyn said 'You've been to see Biddle?'

I said 'Unless you tell me what are your contacts with Biddle, I will tie you up again and burn you with cigarettes.'

Melvyn said 'Ducky, so you don't want to know what my contacts are with Biddle!'

I sat on Melvyn's bed while he walked up and down. He was a short fat figure with thin legs: he had a mottled body like a Harlequin. After a time he said 'Look, I have got something to tell you.'

I said 'I know. I don't want to know.'

He said 'Why not?'

I said 'Because it's boring. And anyway, what means would I have of knowing whether or not to believe you?'

He said 'That I'm a spy?'

I said 'Yes.'

I thought – That Cretan who said he was a liar, if he had said he was telling the truth, would one or would one not have believed him?

Melvyn came and stood in front of me. I thought – But this is like some dreadful offering – a stringy old cock, to be sacrificed on an altar.

He said 'You're the only person I love, you know.'

That evening there was another large party in Fitzroy Square; it was in aid of raising funds for the loyalist cause in Spain. The party was out of doors, centred on the grass plot in the middle of the Square: there were lotteries and hoop-la stalls and girls in flowered hats with collecting boxes; tables where you could hand in old clothes and trinkets for Spain. I walked up the street with Melvyn and for a moment he held my hand. He said 'Take care of yourself.' I said 'I will.'

I thought – With any luck Caroline won't turn up tonight; and then I won't be going with her to Spain.

– But oh my God, do I or don't I want Caroline to come with me to Spain!

The windows of Mrs Fortescue's house were lighted and uncurtained. There were people moving in the drawing-room and the bedrooms; there were people leaning out of the windows looking at the crowd in the square below. I thought – This is like that façade of the ruined castle in Germany; some demonstration is going on about the farce of most human behaviour; about the knowledge that there may be something different going on elsewhere.

There was the young Conservative MP whom Caroline had shown an interest in; there was the tall dark man like a Moor. I could not see Caroline. I thought – At least in Spain there will be nothing to be jealous of; all this will seem truly to have been a pantomime, and I will have got out of the theatre.

The man like a Moor was leaning out of one of the windows of Mrs Fortescue's house; he held a megaphone; he seemed about to make a speech. The young Conservative MP appeared at another window and leaned out and blew one or two kisses to the crowd.

Melvyn said 'That boy's quite attractive.' He seemed to be referring to the Conservative MP. He went off towards the house.

There was a black band playing on a platform set up in the square. People were standing round as if not quite knowing whether or not to dance on the grass. I thought – Dear God, is that the black trombonist?

I saw Caroline talking to someone at the back of the platform. Then when she saw me she came running across the grass. She said 'Is it true that we're off to Barcelona?'

I said 'How did you hear?' Then – 'You'll come?'

She said 'Yes!'

I said 'That's wonderful!'

Then she said 'Even if the war is over by the time we get there, in Barcelona there will be the Workers' Olympic Games.'

I thought – Dear God, the Workers' Olympic Games: the black trombonist will be playing?

The man at the window with a megaphone had begun to make a speech. He was saying how we must all give generously to the loyalist cause in Spain. The young Conservative MP at the next window had put on a false Hitler moustache and was giving the Nazi salute. People were laughing. I thought – Oh get on with it then, great kings: hurry and feed your peoples.

I said to Caroline 'I've got you a journalists' card.'

Caroline said 'You are so wonderful!'

I said 'Can you be ready to start tomorrow morning?'

She said 'Yes. When and where?'

I said 'Midday. Victoria Station.'

She said 'I love you.'

At the window out of which the young Conservative MP was leaning, the top sash suddenly came down on him like a guillotine; he was trapped at the waist. He made a face of alarm and flung his arms out. I thought – He is like Petrouchka. Then he began to hit backwards with his hands at the bottom of the window.

Caroline said 'Where's Melvyn?'

I said 'I think perhaps he's behind that young Conservative MP at the window, buggering him.'

Caroline said 'You know I'll sleep with you once we're out of England.'

Caroline and I stood in hand looking up at the façade of Mrs Fortescue's house.

I said 'I'll get a room at the Paris Ritz.'

Caroline turned and kissed me.

I wondered – But how did she know it was all fixed up about Spain? And why does she ask about Melvyn?

Then – But why should I not trust this, one thing happening after another.

VII   3: Eleanor

The truck in which Rudi and I had travelled across the Sahara had
gone bounding off the road with Rudi at the wheel and had come
to rest against a tree: the body of the young officer who had been
shot in the head had slid like a snake down the trunk of a tree and
was lying like a cast-off skin at the bottom. These trees were in an
olive grove in which the group of Spanish officers had been having
what looked like a picnic. Above them, on the road, were soldiers
in their baggy white trousers and fezz-type hats. The scene was like
one of those paintings in which rural harmony is disturbed by the
sudden appearance of some old god: the god demands that festivity
shall be paid for by sacrifice.

I was standing at the edge of the road looking down at the scene.
A young man in white overalls was coming up towards me through
the trees. He seemed to be part neither of the group of officers nor
of the soldiers on the road: in his white overalls he was like some
technician taking care of machinery. Or he was like some angel, or
a devil dressed up as an angel: I thought – This is what devils do, so
what is the difference. He had fair hair: he smiled at me. I thought
– He looks like a German: perhaps I have known him? Perhaps he is
one of the young Nazis that used to be with Franz in Berlin? But
whatever he is now, let me use him; use him.

343

Soldiers had gone to the truck which Rudi had driven into the tree; then they stood back as if they were afraid of its catching fire. The older officer who had shot the young officer in the head was bending down and tearing things off the lapels and shoulders of the young officer's uniform: then he looked up and shouted orders at the soldiers who were by the truck with Rudi. The soldiers went to the truck again and pulled out Rudi. Rudi was collapsed as if he might be dead; he was at least unconscious; a shot had been fired into the back of the truck as Rudi had tried to drive off down the road. I found that I did not care much whether Rudi was alive or dead. The young man in white overalls had come up to me and he said in German 'You are German, are you?' I said 'Yes.' He said 'What are you doing here?' I thought – He might be the young Nazi I went into the alleyway with the night we made the raid on the brothel in Berlin? Then – But of course, he would know I was German because he would have heard me and Rudi shouting at each other just before Rudi drove off down the road. I said 'I'm trying to get to Spain.' The soldiers were laying Rudi on the ground; he was making a groaning noise; he seemed to be unconscious. Some other soldiers were picking up by the shoulders and heels the body of the young officer who had been shot. I thought – They are laying out the bodies like those of game-birds at a shoot. The man in white overalls said to me 'Do you know him?' I thought – You mean, do I know Rudi? Then – You mean, you saw me climbing out of the truck higher up the road so you think Rudi might just have been giving me a lift? The man in white overalls was looking at my legs. I was wearing shorts. I thought – Well why should I say that I know Rudi? Rudi was trying to betray me, dump me by the side of the road: this man in white overalls will believe what he wants to believe; why should I say anything?

Soldiers were poking about in the back of the truck; they were lifting out and holding up some of the artefacts that Rudi had collected or stolen. I thought – And I too might have been shot, probably arrested, if Rudi had not told me to get out of the truck: so this is luck! Then – Use it; use it. The man in white overalls said 'You want to get to Spain?' I said 'Yes.' The soldiers round the truck were talking excitedly. The man in white overalls said 'Wait here.' He turned to go down into the grove of olive trees. Then he called back to me 'Do you speak Spanish?' I said 'No.' He smiled. I thought – Oh well, I will be to him one of those German girls who go striding over mountains and through forests wearing shorts; he will want me to go with him to Spain.

I sat on my haversack on the side of the road. I thought – Well, indeed, on what strange planet have I landed –

– You watch, and one thing happens after another?

The man in white overalls was talking to the older Spanish officer; the officer shouted at the soldiers who had been rummaging in the back of the truck; the soldiers came to him carrying one or two of Rudi's artefacts. I thought – But should I be going down and taking an interest in Rudi, even if I do not know him? I left my haversack at the side of the road and went down into the olive grove and knelt by Rudi. He was breathing quite easily; he did not seem hurt seriously; there was a bump on his forehead; he had concussion. I thought – I have felt his pulse, his forehead; should I not be looking through his pockets? The Spanish officers by the table where they had been having their picnic were watching me. In Rudi's pockets were his passport, cigarettes, some papers: round his neck was a chain at the end of which was a small leather pouch. The pouch was of the kind that might have contained tobacco. When I felt it, it seemed to contain small stones. I thought – You mean, after all, Rudi was carrying diamonds? Then – So what shall I do, leave them? Put them in my pocket? For if I don't the soldiers will find them. I was sitting on my heels in the grove of olive trees. The man in white overalls and the older Spanish officer were watching me. I put the small leather pouch in my pocket. Then I held out Rudi's passport and papers to the man in white overalls and the Spanish officer. I said in German 'Will you be able to get him to hospital?' The man in overalls translated this for the older officer who had taken Rudi's passport and was looking through it: he nodded. I thought – Well, that is all right then: one thing happens after another.

The soldiers were putting back the artefacts that they had taken from the truck. Rudi was being lifted on to some sort of stretcher. The man in white overalls said 'You don't want to stay with him?' I said 'No.' The man said 'He may have to answer a few questions about the contents of that truck.'

I said 'What will they do to him?'

The man said 'Perhaps I will have some influence.' He smiled. Then – 'One man's misfortune is another man's good luck!'

I thought – Yes, I can smile back at him.

The body of the young officer who had been shot was also being put on a stretcher. His stretcher and the one with Rudi on it were being carried up towards the road. The soldiers were fastening down the back flap of the truck. Other soldiers were packing up the table on which the officers had been having their picnic. I thought – It is as if I were an actress on a stage: but there are quite different events going on outside the theatre?

The man in white overalls said 'All this will be over in a few days.'

I said 'What?'

He said 'They are having a small amount of trouble in Spain.'

There had been the unmanned customs post at the frontier; the impression of men huddled round a wireless. The news might have been, yes, of some sort of war: of men being shot in cork or olive groves as one made one's way down to the sea.

The man in overalls and I had walked back to the road. I picked up my haversack. He tried to take it from me. At first I demurred: then I let him carry it. I thought – Indeed, make use of what turns up, on this strange planet.

He said 'You are not interested in what is happening in Spain?'

I said 'I thought perhaps you would not want to tell me, if I was.'

He laughed. Then he stopped and held out his hand and said 'My name is Heinrich.'

I took his hand and said 'My name is Eleanor.'

He said 'Helena?'

I said 'Yes, Helena.'

He laughed and said 'Heinrich and Helena! You have read *Faust*?' We walked on down the road. Then he said 'No, you do not ask me what I am doing and I do not ask you what you are doing, Heinrich and Helena, on our way to Spain!'

There were some cars and trucks parked slightly further down the road. Heinrich went ahead of me and opened the door of a small open car. He put my haversack in the back. I thought – We are in some film, perhaps, of people picking each other up in small open cars in Spanish Morocco.

Then – I do not care even that I did not say goodbye to Rudi?

– But I will be saving, will I not, his diamonds; and so perhaps him?

Heinrich and I sat side by side in the small car. We drove through olive groves down towards the sea.

I said 'I wonder if you could kindly stop off at the poste restante in the town, I am expecting a letter or a telegram from my father.'

He said 'Your father is in Germany?'

I said 'Yes.'

He said 'There is a military government taking over in Spain.'

I said 'I see.'

I thought – Do I see? Then – But the point of the journey I am on is to find out where I am going.

On the outskirts of the town of Melilla there were mud-coloured hovels with occasional walls of white; they were like cardboard cartons that had been discarded and were used for toys. There were almost no people in the streets. Towards the centre of the town there were rows of buildings with brown arcades and arches. I thought – There are paintings like this: of arches and stuffed dummies in empty streets: they seem to indicate enormous events round some corner.

We came to a small square with a large stone building along one side. Heinrich stopped. He said 'I think this is the Post Office.' There were still no people in the square: this might not be unusual, because it was in the heat of the afternoon. The door of the Post Office was ajar. I said 'I will only be a minute.' He said 'I will stay here.' I thought – Am I doing this because I think there will in fact be a message from my father, or is it because this is just one of the things that seems to have to happen after another?

I went up the steps of the official-looking building. There was a large iron doorway half open and half closed at top. Inside it was dark; there were counters with metal grilles above; the building did seem to be a Post Office, but one from which all signs of humans had been taken away. I thought – It is as if there has been some catastrophe, and I am one of the few people left alive. I went round in the half-dark looking for what might be the counter of the poste restante; behind one of the counters there was a construction consisting of pigeon-holes in which there were letters. I thought – The pigeons have left their droppings, even if they have flown away. It was not difficult to climb over the counter and the grille to get at the letters: I seemed to be watching myself doing this. I thought – Oh I think I am a survivor, do I? One of those baby turtles who think they will be safe in the sea. When I was over the grille I lowered myself onto the far side of the counter. There was what seemed to be a dead body on the floor. It was dark behind the counter so that I could not see clearly. But it did not seem to be particularly odd that there was a dead body on the floor. I had to stand with my feet on either side of it to reach to the piles of letters in the pigeon-holes. I took the pile in the pigeon-hole marked 'A' and I went through the letters: there was, yes, a letter to me in the handwriting of my uncle: there was nothing from my father. I thought – Perhaps it will be easier, in the proximity of a dead body, to deal with whatever news I will receive from my uncle.

I sat on the counter with my legs hanging down to read the letter. My uncle said that he hoped I had got his telegram to the town on the edge of the desert. (I had not got this telegram. I thought – Rudi and Stefan might have taken it?) He said that he, my uncle, had no real news for me other than that for which his telegram had tried to prepare me: my father had been arrested and no further news was obtainable about him; he had been arrested because he had made some public protest about my mother. Nothing had been heard about my mother for some time; it was probable that she was dead. My uncle advised me not to return to Germany: indeed he said he felt strongly that it would be unwise for me to return to anywhere in Europe – Hitler had occupied the Rhineland, had I heard? And who knew where Hitler would strike next! In fact my uncle advised me to make my way somehow to South Africa, where there would be many good people to befriend me. He enclosed, he said, one or two addresses. But with regard to himself and his family, I would surely see that it was in my own best interests not to return to Switzerland! I thought – You mean there are Jews in South Africa who might befriend me and you yourself in Switzerland do not want to be encumbered with a Jewish relation? I was sitting in the half-dark Post Office with my feet hanging down over the dead body. I thought – Well, piss on you, shit on you, uncles and cousins: if I were a God, yes, I would want to scatter around the world as many dead human bodies as possible. Then – O my father! O my mother! I put my head back and opened my mouth as if I would scream; but I did not scream; there was some quite silent pain as if I were a fish and my insides were now finally being dragged out. I thought – So it is for this that I have been dragged across a desert: gutted: but if I have no insides perhaps I will still be able to ride across a battlefield like a goddess; to look down on dead bodies like shit.

I folded the letter and put it in my pocket. In my pocket I felt the pouch containing what might be diamonds. I opened the pouch and it did contain, yes, what seemed to be small uncut diamonds. I closed the pouch and put it back in my pocket. Then I thought that my uncle's letter should not be found on me, so I crumpled it and dropped it among other debris behind the counter.

Out in the square there was the small open car; the man called Heinrich standing beside it. He had been joined by another man in white overalls; also by two men in Spanish uniforms with dark blue caps with tassles. I thought – But does it not seem that with such emptiness, such despair, I have power on this strange planet?

I crossed the road from the Post Office building. The light was blinding. Heinrich said 'Did you get what you wanted?'

I said 'Yes, thank you.'

Heinrich said 'No bad news, I hope?'

I said nothing.

Then Heinrich said 'I have been asking these gentlemen about how you may help me get to Spain.'

I was standing by the car. I thought – But I thought it was all arranged, that you were going to help me get to Spain.

I said 'How are we going?'

Heinrich said 'By boat.'

One of the men in uniform talked in Spanish. Then the other said in German 'May I ask one question?'

Heinrich said 'Yes.'

The man in uniform said to me 'What was your business in Morocco?'

I said 'I was working as an anthropologist in French territory south of the Sahara.'

The man said 'South of the Sahara?'

I said 'Yes, I crossed the Sahara.' I waited. I thought – Well, is not this the way to get to Spain?

They all laughed. The second man in white overalls put his hand on his heart and said to me 'Would it not be more comfortable for you to fly with me!' Heinrich said 'It would not!'

I thought – The two men in white overalls are Germans: they are going by boat, they are flying aeroplanes, to Spain?

One of the men in uniform spoke to the other in Spanish. I thought – Of course, what I have to do is to give the impression that there is nothing to worry about; that everything is for the best in the best of all possible worlds.

From somewhere at the back of the Post Office building there was the sound of firing. The other three men moved into the shelter of some arches. Heinrich and I got into the car. I thought – Oh yes, all this sort sort of thing is easier, if there is the sound of firing.

Heinrich and I drove in what seemed to be the direction of the harbour. Heinrich said 'I have a job to do and I need one helper.'

I said 'Good.'

He said 'You trust me?'

I thought I might say – I am someone who wants to kill the people who have probably killed my mother and who might kill my father –

I said 'Don't you trust me?'

He said 'So we ask no more questions, right?'

I said 'Right.'

He said 'Oh, and your friend, yes, has been taken to hospital.'

I thought – You have guessed that I was travelling with Rudi?

We were coming down towards what seemed to be the harbour. There were some soldiers at the gates. Heinrich spoke to them in Spanish. The soldiers opened the gates. In the harbour there were fishing-boats, and against a jetty on the far side some naval boats like a row of kitchen implements. Beyond the fishing-boats at the jetty along which we were driving there was a motor boat of the kind in which people might go for pleasure trips around the Mediterranean. Heinrich stopped the car beside the boat: it had a central wheelhouse and a flat deck in front and what seemed to be cabins in front and behind.

Heinrich said 'Would you like something to eat? To drink?'

I said 'I'd like a glass of water.'

Heinrich spoke in Spanish to a man who was in the wheelhouse of the boat. The man went into a cabin and came out with a glass of water. He brought it to the car, and handed it to me.

Heinrich said 'There is nothing else that you would like?'

I said 'No, thank you.'

He said 'We start at nightfall.'

I said 'Good.'

He said 'Where do you come from in Germany?'

I got out of the car. I took my haversack. I said 'Berlin.' Then – 'I'll be waiting at the end of the jetty.'

He laughed and said 'I have not met someone like you before!'

I thought – He is happy to be with me: he is like someone who has been challenged to a duel.

At the end of the jetty there was a view to the open sea. The stonework was very hot: it shimmered like water. I thought – If I could make the sea burn, I would, and I would turn the land to dust, O my father, O my mother.

Sometime towards the evening, trucks came along on the jetty behind me. They stopped by the boat where Heinrich had left the car. There were wooden crates on the trucks: some Moorish men got out of the trucks and began to unload the crates and carry them on to the boat. Heinrich came out from the boat and looked up the jetty towards me. I sat with my back to him and looked out across the sea. I thought – I suppose in the crates there are – what? – guns, spare parts for tanks, for aeroplanes –

– Would it not indeed be better if the human race were destroyed?

At some stage in the afternoon or evening the Spaniard from the boat came towards me along the jetty carrying a tray on which there was food and a bottle of wine. I was sitting with my legs over the edge of the jetty and my back against a bollard. I thought – Oh well, why should this not be a pleasure trip across the Mediterranean? War has often been a pleasure for humans by which they are destroyed.

Sometime after nightfall we set off, Heinrich and I, on our trip across the Mediterranean. With us on the boat were the Spaniard who had brought me food and water and another Spaniard who acted as a mechanic. The crates from the trucks had been tied down on the decks in front and behind. There was writing stamped on the crates that had for the most part been scratched or chiselled out; the writing seemed originally to have been in German. I thought – Well why am I doing this: am I mad? But what does it matter, if the human race deserves to be wiped out.

For the first part of the night I sat in the bows with my feet hanging over the water. Now that we were moving it was easier to let my thoughts go: perhaps after all I might not be mad: sanity might depend on bouncing like this over rushing water. So – Let my imagination go: thus I might keep my balance. What had happened to my father, to my mother: were they starved? Were they tortured? Were they tied to chairs with their hands behind their backs? And their legs spread like the water through which the prow of the boat was cutting. What were human beings for: where were they going? I was going to Spain – to kill? To get my revenge for my father and my mother? Who was that Jewish woman, Judith, who went into the camp of the enemy and chopped off the head of their captain, Holofernes? I was going to Spain because I had nowhere else to go. Europe was some sort of home: but I had no home: in this strange territory, I just did one thing after another. What had they thought, felt, my father and my mother? Had they despaired? Had it seemed that their lives had been worthwhile?

What did I think, feel? I was their only child. I had wanted to move on from them – to be like the prow of a ship bouncing above water.

– What better could one do, perhaps, than to go for the heart of the enemy –

– Carried, as if by gravity, like Judith, for some high purpose? At least for one killing to be followed by another.

Sometime in the night Heinrich came to me and said 'Can I show you how to steer?'

I said 'Yes.'

He said 'Can I sleep with you?'

I said nothing.

He took me to the wheelhouse and showed me how to steer by the compass. He said 'There may be other boats on the look-out for us.'

I stood at the wheel and watched the compass which was a disc that floated in counterpoint to the boat: when the boat rolled to one side the disc rolled to the other; it was attached to a force independent of that of the boat: this of course was gravity! The disc was suspended at a single point in the middle. I thought – If I could thus be balanced, suspended, on or from a point at the centre, might I not be in touch with the forces of the universe?

There was that story by Kleist of the puppet-maker who said that puppets and gods were viable but that humans were not, because they had become separated from a line going to their centre –

– The line by which they were connected to the forces of the universe.

One of the Spaniards stood in the bows looking out for other boats. The other slept in the rear cabin.

Heinrich stood by me for a time: then he went and lay down in the front cabin.

I thought – Riding through the night, I might be that figure of death above a battlefield.

Sometime in the night Heinrich came and took the wheel from me. I went and lay in the front cabin. I thought – He will come to lie with me now, or not: what is the difference.

When I awoke it was daylight and the engines of the boat had been shut off; we were drifting. When I came out into the sun Heinrich was looking at charts and the two Spaniards were each side of the boat looking out and listening. There was the sound of water, insistently, like the fingers of things perhaps waiting to be born.

Heinrich said 'Did you sleep?'

I said 'Yes.'

He said 'I'll come down in a moment to the cabin.'

I took one of the charts that Heinrich had been studying with me into the cabin. I found the port of Melilla, which was about a hundred miles east of the straits between Spanish Morocco and Gibraltar; these straits were only a dozen or so miles across. We were waiting, I supposed, to go through the straits after nightfall. It had seemed that we might be in sight of land on our left; but when I looked carefully this seemed to be a mirage. I thought – But do I really think I may be able to avenge you, O my father: my mother.

Heinrich came down into the cabin and said politely 'You are sure you do not mind?'

I said 'No.'

I thought – Oh but Heinrich is not the equivalent of Holofernes.

He said 'It was not because of this that I asked you to come with me to Spain.'

I said 'What was it then?'

After a time he said 'Are you human?'

We lay in the hot cabin; the door was closed and the curtains drawn: it might have been a tomb. It was as if there were some ritual I had to go through, some sacrifice to be made – for all the terrible people who carry the spare parts of tanks or aeroplanes across seas; to a million or two dead sperms; to the bodies of baby turtles or children. Perhaps this sexuality was always some sort of line, yes, going down to the centre of the earth. I thought – But none of this, yet, is what really matters: I am the egg: I can remain inviolate: perhaps one day I can say – This or that gets through.

Afterwards Heinrich said 'That was all right?'

I said 'Yes, that was all right.'

He said 'Who was that princess, in an opera, of whom no one knew the name?'

I said 'It wasn't a princess, it was the prince.'

He said 'What was it then about the princess?'

I said 'She chopped up her lovers.'

After Heinrich had left me I tried to remember what I knew about what had been happening recently in Spain. There had been a left-wing government, then a right-wing government, then a left-wing government again. People had said 'This cannot go on!' Men here and there had stood up and shouted and banged their fists on tables. This I remembered from the time before I had gone to West

Africa: little news had reached us later. We had met a Frenchman who had talked about anarchism in Spain: Spain was almost the only country, he had said, in which anarchism had taken root. I had thought – That might be a good reason to go to Spain!

In the wheelhouse Heinrich was looking very happy. He seemed almost to dance. The two Spaniards were looking glum. Heinrich said 'Of course you are not human, you are a water-goddess: I knew that from the first time I saw you!'

I said 'When we get to Spain, will you give me a gun?'

He said 'A gun!'

I said 'I won't shoot you, I promise.'

We drifted most of that day. We listened. Once we had to start the engines to keep away from land. I dozed. But the pain and despair would come in, like random flies, to haunt me.

I thought – But I might yet be able to come on my white horse with my sword in my hand, O my father, my mother.

When it was dark we started the engines and went fast; we had to get through the straits at night. I sat in the bows again with my feet hanging over the water. Now that we were moving – the bottom of the boat hitting against the sea – it seemed that it was possible to see bits of my life in waves; in some sort of pattern. First there had been my mother's friends who used to come to our apartment in the days of Rosa Luxemburg – the men with their moustaches and pince-nez and the stiff wing collars at their throats like knives; the women with their flowered hats like plates on the poles of jugglers. In my imagination I saw these moving fast, in and out of our apartment, as if in a speeded-up film – the bottom of the boat banging against the water – the men and women being hit on the backs of their heads with rifle butts; popping up again, like some eternal Punch and Judy; and orating, always orating. Then there had been the boys at the university with everything except their faces bandaged; just their childish faces to be cut and sewn up again like cheeses. Then there were the people in Berlin who had betrayed Bruno: then Rudi and Stefan in the desert fighting. I thought – Could not the human race just get this sort of thing over and done with quickly instead of having to endure it through millions and millions of years; could they not hurry on to a true revolution? To life on another planet? Or yes, of course, to a final entropy? We were rushing through the straits like a stone skimming on water. But might we not consciously one day be able to make contact every thousand minutes, days, not only years, with whatever was necessary for evolution? There were lights in the distance on our right; these would be from Gibraltar; on our left, in the dark, was the Spanish–Moroccan port of Ceuta. These rocks had once been known as the Pillars of Hercules – the end of the known world. Had it been only Hercules who was strong enough to get beyond the edge of the known world – into some dimension from which he could look down and see life as a whole, with some pattern, on this odd planet? There was the memory of my father coming up to me in the street by the Adlon Hotel; he was wearing his black overcoat with the fur collar and a grey Homburg hat: he held out his arms to me and I ran to him. Then there was my mother being bundled into the back of that truck – . In the boat now we seemed to be moving slower. I thought – At the edge of the known world do memories slow down, become solid, like an experience that approaches the speed of light? Then there was the memory of you in your car parked in a side-street; we had sat side by side; this had been the edge of the known world? I had said (why had I said this?) 'Whatever happened to that girl who was deaf and dumb?' You had said 'She sometimes speaks now.' I thought – Do images become one with that which is universal? There is a sort of bang, like that of glass breaking, and then you are through?

For a time I steered the boat again: when I turned the wheel the compass went this way or that; I was connected to gravity. Heinrich stood in the bows and looked out; the two Spaniards sat facing each other in the cabin at the back and rolled cigarettes. I thought – They are frightened. Then – Why should they not be frightened? Fear is perhaps what you experience when you do not feel that there is any force pulling you across a sea, a desert.

Towards the end of the night I lay in the cabin. I thought – Or we are those seeds in a seed-pod being shaken like dice: it would seem to be chance whether or not the human race is destroyed –

– But you had said to me 'Let us meet at some point in space, in time' –

– Which will be in relation to what we are, but also to our ability to let us be taken to where we are going?

I prayed – Please let me sleep: please let me rearrange these bits and pieces in my mind so that when I wake I can look down, as if from a cloud, and see what it is that has been rolled on to a table.

Sometime during the morning of the second day – I had slept

355

late: on what journeys does one go in sleep! Is it not sometimes as if one had been carried in the jar of a water-carrier across a desert –

Sometime during the morning of the second day I emerged from the cabin and there was bright sunlight outside: I had expected to see – an endless grey sea? The cataract at the edge of the known world? The lost continent of Atlantis? We were moving quietly between the banks of a river. The banks were high and the land must have been flat on either side because one could see nothing beyond the banks; it was as if this world were just a channel, a way through. A man and a donkey were walking on top of one of the banks: they were in silhouette; a sort of target. I thought – Perhaps beyond the edge of the known world objects are seen as what they are, as symbols. I did not know about this river: Heinrich had not mentioned it. It was a river of the underworld? The river up which fishes go to breed in the place where they were born? Heinrich was at the wheel; the two Spaniards were at either side of the boat looking out. Or were we still a seed, a sperm – oh not a sperm! – was not I the egg: why should it not be I who say that this or that gets through? We were moving slowly between the banks of the river. A barge came down the stream towards us; a man with a straw hat stood in the stern; he had a neat round head but under the shadow of his hat he seemed to have no face; he was like a diagram. Occasionally there was a break in the banks of the river and the hovels of a village toppled towards the water; men and women stood quietly watching the boat go past. They were demonstrating – what? – we come from the nursery toy-box: one false move and we know we may all be put back! What is it, after all, that holds the universe together: does not room have to be made by humans killing one another? Oh let all the pieces be shaken and rolled out again on to the table.

Heinrich had given me some white overalls to wear, of the same kind as his and those of the other German in Melilla. Heinrich put an arm around me: we stood together at the wheel. I thought – We are both angels of death in our white uniforms coming to the place where humans breed up this river.

Towards the evening of this second day we were approaching a town. I had learned the name of this town: I had looked at Heinrich's maps in the cabin. The town was Seville; the river was the Guadalquivir; at its mouth had been the port of Cadiz, which we had passed while I had been sleeping. Maps consist of lines, planes, words; we look at maps and think we find out what is happening.

There were the backs of houses with gardens coming down to the river. Then around a bend were huge cranes like birds – I mean, these were the huge metal constructions, cranes, with wires hanging from their beaks like worms: it was as if they might once have been birds; they were like skeletons, fossils. There were no signs of humans in the gardens nor amongst the cranes by the river. I thought – Perhaps there has already been some false move on the part of the universe, or the human race, and it has been wiped out; we will be picking our way, as angels of death, around the bodies on a battlefield. Then – But all this is in the mind, looking down: will not the mind itself be destroyed by a false move of the universe? Or will it be able to look and say – Oh what good husbandry, all these dead bodies to feed the earth!

By the cranes were cargo ships and sea-going barges: they were all deserted. I wondered – If I look away, then look back again, quickly, might I see beings that otherwise do not seem to be there? I was still at the wheel; Heinrich went down into the forward cabin and from a locker took out a gun; it was a sort of sub-machine gun with a magazine hanging down like a horse's penis. Heinrich squatted in the wheelhouse trying to keep the gun out of sight. The two Spaniards squatted on either side of the wheelhouse trying to keep out of sight. I thought – They want me at the wheel because I will appear to be innocent? Then – We are trying to be one of those particles with either no velocity or no location.

Heinrich had told me to proceed slowly up the river. We were approaching a bridge. There were shapes behind the ironwork balustrade of the bridge; they might be human. If they were they might have guns. I thought – But indeed, it matters that these images are not just in the mind! Heinrich and the two Spaniards went slithering about on the floor of the wheelhouse. As we went under the bridge I did not look at what might be the shapes behind the balustrade: I thought – In these circumstances I could not make of them just what I would like! There was a sensation again of my insides being dragged out. I thought – Well, if I am a fish, I am about to be landed.

Ahead of us, beyond the bridge, on the left-hand side of the river, there was the façade of a row of rather elegant houses that was like – oh yes! – the backdrop to a stage set. On the other side of the river, on the right, was a quay of a different kind from that to which the cranes and cargo boats had been tied: this was the sort of quay where yachts and pleasure boats might come to rest after an elegant trip round the Mediterranean. I thought – Well, angels of death would be on a pleasure boat, wouldn't they? There were, in fact, a yacht and a paddle-steamer moored: there was still no sign of life either on the boats or on the quayside.

Heinrich took the wheel and spoke to the Spaniards; he seemed to be giving them orders which they were reluctant to obey. We were moving in towards the quayside. One of the Spaniards crept to the front of the boat holding a rope; the boat bumped against a tyre hung over the edge of the stonework. The Spaniard jumped out and looped the rope round a bollard. It was as if he were still trying to keep out of sight. He could be seen from anywhere on the quayside or from the houses across the river, but there was, in fact, at the back of the quayside a high stone wall which blocked off what was presumably the town on this side of the river; only sky could be seen beyond a balustrade at the top of this wall. I thought – But one is exposed to the sky?

I said to Heinrich 'Can I have my gun?'

Heinrich said 'You must stay here.'

I said 'You said I could have a gun.'

Heinrich said 'You will be shot if you are caught with a gun.'

I thought I might say – I don't mind, so long as I can shoot people first –

– This or that gets through.

The second Spaniard was tying the back of the boat to a bollard; then both Spaniards remained squatting on their haunches on the quayside. Heinrich climbed out of the boat and walked across cobbles towards the high wall at the back of the quay. He carried his gun. I thought – Well, they can shoot him. There was a ramp with steps going diagonally up the wall to a gap in the balustrade at the top. Heinrich went up the ramp. He was a small figure in white overalls moving against stonework. I thought – He is brave: he is one of those absurd toy figures like Siegfried. When he was at the top of the ramp he slowed and peered through the gap in the balustrade: there was, presumably, some sort of roadway between the top of the wall and where the houses began on this side of the river. Then Heinrich moved out of sight beyond the balustrade. The two Spaniards left the quayside and went into their cabin and sat and began to roll cigarettes. I thought – But I do not want to stay here: if I am caught with the Spaniards I will be shot; and I will have been no sort of angel, not even of death –

– What would be a right sort of angel? Someone who can be

killed – like Siegfried, like someone on a fun-fair shooting-range –
and come alive again after the last act?

I tried to work out – Everything is so quiet here because we are
in some sort of no man's land: the insurgents, whoever they are, are
on one side of the river, and the government forces are on the other.

– So might I not be some sort of dice rolled out on to no man's
land? On my own, could I not be a particle that could choose its
velocity and location?

I climbed out on to the quayside. There were the cobbles
stretching to the high wall at the back. The wall was about twenty
feet high. The ramp went up diagonally to the gap in the balustrade.
I was wearing the white overalls that Heinrich had given me. It
seemed that there might be an audience watching me from the
houses across the river. I thought – Perhaps all in white I will seem
to be the Virgin Mary –

– Come down on a barren hillside to give, oh yes, just this
message to children –

– 'Tell me one or two good reasons why the human race should
not be destroyed.'

I was going across the quayside on the cobbles. To my left there
was a bridge further up the river. Across this bridge I saw figures in
white shirts running: they were crouching, moving in spurts; they
were carrying what seemed to be rifles. I thought – Well of course
people enjoy such scenes in films; they know they are watching
shadows; but what of this sun? I was approaching the ramp with
steps up the wall. The figures in white shirts had crossed the bridge
and had moved out of sight into the part of the town to which I
was heading. I thought – I will climb the ramp and sit on the top
step so that I can see over but still be sheltered from what is beyond.
And behind me, the other side of the river – perhaps that will be
like the fourth wall of a stage: people in an audience don't shoot
people on a stage; and if people on a stage shoot each other, then oh
don't they get up after the last act –

I got to the top of the ramp and looked beyond the gap in the
balustrade. There was, yes, a roadway which was deserted: there
was a white Moorish-style building at the far side. This building
had windows decorated with arches and pillars and wrought-iron
balconies: on the ground floor the doors and windows were boarded
up. I sat on the top step of the ramp with my head just above the
level of the roadway. The figures in white shirts would be somewhere in the town beyond. I thought – I will rest here, like the

Virgin Mary, until there are some children to whom I may elaborate my message –

 – 'It can be as if we are on a stage-set, children: we look down on ourselves and on this level we are not shot; or we may be able to get up again even if we are.'

One of the windows in the white Moorish-style house across the roadway suddenly opened and a figure in a khaki shirt and a dark blue cap appeared: he seemed propelled against the ironwork railing of the balcony; he flung his arms out; he seemed about to make a speech. Then he just yelled. I thought – Well, people who make speeches do sometimes just yell, don't they? From within or behind the building there was the sound of firing. The man who had emerged from the window seemed to be dragged back in. I thought – He is a missile in a blow-pipe: or perhaps Petrouchka, about to have his insides strewn on the pavement. Then the man came hurtling out of the window again and this time went right over the ironwork of the balcony; he was in the air for a moment and then landed, with no bounce, on the pavement. There were shadowy figures in white shirts in the room behind. The man on the pavement had become flattened like something soft and he did not seem able to regain his shape; he lay half on his side with his arms underneath him. One or two men in white shirts appeared on the balcony; they looked down on him as if he were a crowd. Then suddenly there were men in khaki and dark blue caps emerging or bursting from several of the first- or second-floor windows of the Moorish-style building; they were jumping into the street; they were escaping; they were falling and rolling over and then running on across the roadway. It was as if the first man in khaki had been a herald, a shot from a starting pistol, for this race across the roadway. I thought – Dear God, a race of huge prehistoric turtles down towards the sea! I had been sheltering at the top of the ramp beneath the level of the road; now it seemed that the opening to the ramp was the only easy way for the men in khaki to get to the river. So I had to move up and out of their way on to the pavement beyond the balustrade: I wondered – Oh this is dry land, yes: and this is fear? There were more and more men in white shirts appearing at the windows and on the balconies of the Moorish-style building; some of them carried rifles; they were raising them and aiming them at the men in khaki who were running away across the road. The men in khaki had dark, enrapt faces as they went past. I thought – But they are like dancers; they cannot look at what they are doing:

is this fear? One or two of the men in khaki were hit by shots fired by the men in white shirts in the building; they fell and rolled over and held on to a leg or an arm. I thought – I must not move too fast or I will appear to be running; I must not move too slowly or I will be swept away by the runners; I must find the right speed to appear not to exist, to have velocity but no location. I was heading to where there was a large heap of stones and a workmen's hut at the edge of the pavement; here it seemed the road was being mended; I thought I might find shelter by the pile of stones. Some of the men with white shirts were having trouble with their rifles; they banged the butts on the stonework of the balconies; one of the rifles went off and seemed to shoot one of the men in the head. I thought – Oh how lucky, yes; that is like the universe: shots go round and shoot you in your own head. Some of the men in khaki when they reached the balustrade jumped straight over the wall and down the long drop to the quayside; one or two stayed where they had landed and rolled over holding an arm or a leg; but most were trying to crowd through the gap at the top of the ramp where I had been sitting. There they were being shot quite easily by the men in white shirts in the building. I was making my way to the pile of stones at the roadside as if I were treading on hot coals; lifting my feet up as if this might help me keep out of the way of bullets. I wanted to cry – But I do not want to be a dancer in this mad human ballet!

There were windows now being opened in the elegant houses across the river; figures were appearing there on balconies; some carried rifles; they raised them and seemed to be aiming at what was happening across the river. The doors on the ground floor of the Moorish-style house were being broken open from inside and now men in white shirts were erupting into the road; then they paused, as if they might not, after all, know what they were doing; as if they had not expected to find themselves on a stage. There was firing now from the people across the river: they were firing on the men in white shirts: or was it that they, with the men in white shirts, were both firing at the men in khaki who had now got down to the river? It was difficult to tell: I thought – Well, of course, it is often difficult to tell what on earth is happening in a ballet. There were just these successive lines of men bursting through doors and windows, leaping, cavorting; rolling over, clutching an arm or leg: *Prince Igor* perhaps? *Sheherazade*? Well, who cares to work out what is happening in a ballet: it is just the sort of thing people like, isn't it? There was a man in khaki who had got on to the boat in which

Heinrich and I had crossed the straits: he was confronted by one of the Spaniards: the Spaniard and the man in khaki seemed to take hold of one another and dance: it was a stilted *pas de deux*: they fell into the water. I thought – The comedy is usually awful in a ballet. The other Spaniard had jumped into the water and was swimming away. Some of the men in white shirts had reached the balustrade and were firing down at the men in khaki on the quayside; there were several on their backs and holding their feet in their hands. Up to now I had been sheltering at the side of the heap of stones away from the Moorish-style house across the road; but now, with what seemed to be the firing from the houses across the river, I was exposed on this side too: I thought – But what part can I properly play if I cannot get out of this absurd and terrifying ballet? It seemed that I might crawl into the workmen's hut that was like a sentry-box at the base of the pile of stones; there perhaps I might pose as the Virgin Mary. I thought – Well, all that business of the Virgin Mary in her grotto – that is like a ballet?

I made my way round the pile of stones. Quite close to me was the man in khaki who had been the first to jump, or to be propelled, out of a window; he had dragged himself towards the pile of stones. He was lying on his back and holding a foot; he seemed to be trying to get it into his mouth, like a baby. I had reached my workmen's hut or grotto and was squatting there; he turned and looked at me. I thought – Shall I stand with one hand across my breast and smile faintly like the Virgin Mary? Or is that Venus? Or what is the difference: whatever will be suitable for this poor bugger? There was a man in a white shirt coming towards this man in the road; the man in the white shirt held a rifle delicately like a flower. I thought – He is like some terrible interior decorator coming to rearrange a vase. He took hold of the man in khaki by the hair; then he looked up at me. I was, yes, in my niche, like the Virgin Mary. I thought – You mean this might be some offering? Some sacrifice? Then – You think I might make any difference? The man in the white shirt held his rifle to the head of the man in khaki; then he shot him. I jerked. The head disintegrated on to the pavement. I thought – Oh, like old petals, yes. Then – For God's sake, this sort of thing is always happening. Then – Could I have made any difference? And would it not be proper for me now, in this role, just to say – Oh do please go on with your games of killing yourselves, my children: what a meet and proper sacrifice of blood and flowers! Then the man in the white shirt began hopping up and down holding one foot. I thought – With luck, yes, he has managed to shoot himself too; or he has been shot by the people across the river; or perhaps he is just doing whatever step he is supposed to do in this ballet. Then – Dear God, yes, what is the difference. Then there was yet another lot of men appearing at the doors and windows of the Moorish-style house; these men wore baggy trousers and fezz-type hats: I thought – Aha, perhaps at last I know where we are in this god-awful performance! These are the men who were on the road by the officers' picnic in Morocco: have they been ferried across the straits in the men in white overalls' aeroplane? Or do they just go round and round and in and out of wings like a stage army? These men were now firing at the men in white shirts on the road who were now in turn leaping over the balustrade in order to get down to the river. I thought – But dear God, this is boring; is that why I am crying? Because there is such a sad, limited number of things that humans can do in war or in a ballet – like that old king feeding his people? So what can we do if we can watch ourselves watching such a ballet: get up and leave the theatre? The man in the white shirt who had shot the man in khaki and who had also seemed to shoot himself in the foot had now sat down and had begun to scream; there was a man in baggy trousers coming towards him. I was thinking – Well yes, but what about the poor old audience, will not they too soon need to be put out of their misery? The man in baggy trousers took hold of the man in the white shirt by the hair; he pulled his head back; he looked at me. I thought – Please go ahead, do, have we not had all this before: and while you're at it let's have a few scenes of people being flayed alive, boiled in oil, et cetera, shall we? As there so often are for the edification of humans on the walls of sacred buildings. The man in baggy trousers held a knife to the man in the white shirt's throat: I thought – Indeed, for the glory of God; in honour of the Blessed Virgin Mary! The man in baggy trousers drew the knife across the man in the white shirt's throat. It seemed, again, as if my own inside was being drawn out; I had opened my mouth to scream; there was a peculiar soundlessness; I think I was trying to say – Oh yes, please, dear God, either you want the human race to be wiped out, or will you go yourself and jump into the river.

Then shortly after this there was the sound of an engine on the road behind me; then a bang like a small clap of thunder. There was the impression of smoke: a puff of dust appeared on the façade of the elegant houses across the river. The man in baggy trousers who had cut the throat of the man in the white shirt was staring at something behind me as if he had seen a vision. I thought – Oh well, what has happened now, some god has in fact come down? Some old queen in a stage chariot perhaps, camping it up as Zeus or Apollo? The noise of the engine grew louder; then there appeared round the side of the heap of stones a contraption that was indeed like some stage chariot: it seemed to be made out of huge saucepans and a kettle; the spout of the kettle was a gun which slightly smoked. It was, I suppose, a small tank or armoured car. I thought – Or perhaps the fire-brigade come to tell us at last that we can leave the theatre. The top half of a man was sticking out of the turret; he wore a blue cap with a tassle. I thought – Or perhaps this is a representation of the person being boiled in oil; people did maintain their sang-froid in such circumstances, didn't they? The appearance of this armoured car seemed to have cleared the roadway; everyone was now either back in the Moorish-type house or was running and jumping into the river. I thought – Well, perhaps at least this may be the interval; we can have a cup of tea; the armoured car is like a kettle, isn't it, ha ha. Then – But how can anything about war be called serious? I saw Heinrich walking in the roadway behind the armoured car; he was looking over the balustrade at our boat; the boat was still moored by the quayside but there was now no one on it. There were a lot of heads of men swimming in the river. They were indeed like turtles: one could not tell whether they wore white shirts or khaki. Then Heinrich saw me by my pile of stones. I had crawled from my grotto and was sitting with my arms round my knees. He said 'You!' Then – 'Are you all right?' He came and knelt in front of me. He said 'Thank God!' He put his head down on my knees. I thought – Oh yes, you can do this to the Virgin Mary. The soldiers in fezzes and baggy trousers were still firing from the balustrade down at the heads in the water. There was another enormous explosion from the armoured car; then everyone stopped firing. They ducked and turned and watched the armoured car. The man whose top half was sticking up out of the turret seemed to be in pain. I thought – Perhaps he has injured himself with the recoil of the gun; perhaps he is in ecstasy, having shot himself and brought his suffering to some apotheosis. Heinrich said to me 'And you didn't even have a gun!' I said 'I didn't seem to need one.' Heinrich held out to me a small delicately inlaid pistol. I took it. I thought – But I can't go through anything like this again! Then – But with a gun, yes, the Blessed Virgin Mary might not have to wait for humans to destroy themselves, but get the whole thing over quicker.

VII   4: Max

You felt that the Spanish Civil War was being laid on for your
benefit? That there were these particular corners, bumps, to guide
you as you went through the maze?

But there are always coincidences: always what turns up. There
is a pattern because there is the ability to see patterns. It is through
seeing this ability that we create our way through the maze.

So let's look at what happened. The Spanish Civil War began on
17 July 1936 with the rebellion of middle-rank army officers in the
port of Melilla in Spanish Morocco. It was there that the rebels
learned that their plans had been betrayed and so had to act
prematurely: the next day there was the rising in Seville and other
garrison towns in Spain. The rebels gained only a tenuous hold on
Seville until the evening of the 19th when, yes, there arrived a small
detachment of Moorish troops by plane from Morocco. With these
troops the rebels were able to cross the river and take control of the
working-class district of Triana. There is no official record of
Germans being involved in the transportation of these troops:
German backing for the rebel General Franco officially began a
week later when Junkers transport planes were sent from Germany
to Morocco. But there are contradictory reports about the nature of
the air-lift on the 19th; mercenaries of several nationalities were

known to be in the area, but of course any German mercenaries would have wanted to keep their presence secret.

History is put together from what people want to say or to remember: but how little of what is written seems to do with what an individual on the spot has experienced! History for the most part is made up from the public professions of politicians, but politicians are not primarily concerned with truth, so history becomes a statistical amalgam of special pleadings.

You seem to be saying that the actual experience of an individual in war is that he or she is being put to a personal test –

– Do I live or die: does it matter if I live or die.

This is a common experience. But when we see it, should we not see more about why there are wars?

I reached the frontier at the opposite side of Spain some two or three weeks after you: I had travelled down through France with Caroline. There is a sense in which my experiences up till now had had little in common with yours: my mother and father had not been abducted, murdered: they were framed in my memory within a bow window against a background of green lawns and hoops for croquet. But for some time I had felt close to wanting to die, or at least not to go on being human. I felt disgust with the society in which I found myself; this disgust was increased by my own participation in it.

I had wondered – But why do I imagine that the predicament of being human is made more propitious by being able to glimpse it?

I had arrived with Caroline at the Spanish frontier town of Port Bou; we had travelled through France by train; we had spent an afternoon in Paris where we had gone to a cheap hotel. There Caroline had kept her part of the bargain in this adventure of going to the Spanish Civil War: she had undressed and lain on the bed; had turned her head from side to side as if avoiding bullets. She had said 'I'm so sorry!' I had said 'But it's all right!' What more, after all, had I wanted – than to be able to crawl over the beautiful no man's land of Caroline's body and to stick my flags in, as it were, here and there to signify a victory.

Afterwards, it is true, you ask yourself what you have been doing; finding yourself crawling, as it were, out of something like a shell-hole.

I thought – But there will be other victories (will they be worth it?) when we get to Spain.

At Port Bou we had come out of a tunnel; railway lines stretched into the distance. We had not known, Caroline and I, just what we would find when we reached Spain. There had been reports in the papers in England of the frontier being closed; of refugees fighting to get out; of foreign journalists being turned back; of foreigners being welcomed in. There had been fewer and fewer people on the train during the last stages of our journey. Now that we had arrived, those that were left were struggling with their luggage along a strangely empty platform.

Caroline said 'Well, here we are.'

I said 'You do want to go on?'

She said 'Yes, don't you?'

I said 'What about finding a nice hotel room in Port Bou?'

I thought – Of course, she will think I am joking.

Then – But is not this sort of love some personal test: do not young men correlate making love and war?

There were buildings at the end of the platform which was where the immigration and customs offices seemed to be. There nothing much was happening: a small crowd of travellers had gathered in front of a counter; they held out their papers to the people behind the counter who took them and held them and turned them this way and that. The people in front of the counter seemed to be Spaniards returning home; the men directly behind the counter were in dark green uniforms; then beyond them were men and women in workmen's overalls carrying guns. These seemed deliberately to be taking no notice of what was going on at the counter: they leaned against walls; they did things with cigarettes; they walked to and fro sedately. I thought – They are demonstrating the real nature of power: power is held by people who can afford to make out that they are not interested in what is happening; who carry guns, and who pass the time doing elaborate things with cigarettes.

Caroline said 'Go on.'

I said 'Go on what?'

She said 'Show them our passports, and the letter which says that we are accredited journalists on the right side.'

I said 'For God's sake, we don't yet know what exactly is the right side.'

From the newspapers in London it had seemed that the rebellion of the generals had succeeded in large areas in the west and in the south of Spain: but elsewhere it had been defeated, most decisively in Madrid and Barcelona, and indeed in the whole of Catalonia on the borders of which we now were. But on the day we had left England there had been reports that in Barcelona, to which we were heading, the question of who held power was far from clear: the rebel soldiers had been defeated by civilians, but those who had taken over were not necessarily under the control of the socialist government in Madrid. Anarchists, or rather anarchy, seemed to have taken over; and anarchists (as I had learned) were the enemies not only of Fascist soldiers but of any central socialist or Communist government as well.

I was standing at the back of the small crowd of Spaniards at the immigration counter. I thought – If I stand here long enough, making out that I have not much interest in what is happening, then perhaps I will be seen as representing some sort of power.

Caroline said 'Are you afraid?'

I said 'Oh how can you ask me if I'm afraid!' Then – 'The point about not rushing in is that if we do we may provoke a reaction, all right; the opposite of what we intend.'

I pushed my way through the crowd of Spaniards and placed on the counter in front of one of the men in green uniform Caroline's and my passports and press cards and the letter which accredited us as journalists working for the extremist left-wing newspaper in England. This letter was in English, with a Spanish translation. The man in uniform glanced at these documents briefly and then ignored them. I picked the letter and passport up and banged them on the counter; I said something in the primitive Spanish that I had been learning with Caroline on the train. The man picked the papers up and banged them back at me; he said something in a dialect that I did not understand. Than he said in French that no foreigners were being allowed into Spain.

Caroline, who had come up beside me, said 'Oh I'm sorry!'

I thought – Why do you say you are sorry? Then – Why should I care if I am not allowed with Caroline into Spain.

I stayed where I was at the counter. I gazed over the heads of the people in the space behind. I thought – But I am interested in this purely technical problem: what is the nature of the power that would get me and Caroline into Spain?

There was a young man in overalls in the area behind the counter: he was carrying a shotgun: he was showing an interest in Caroline. Caroline was looking beautiful. With her blonde hair and long legs she stood out from the crowd like a mountain antelope on a plain.

I thought – But, of course, it will be Caroline that will get us into

Spain: she is to do with power: have I not always imagined that Caroline would be useful in Spain?

Caroline said 'What are you going to do?'

I said 'I'm not going to do anything.'

Caroline said 'I sometimes think you don't really want to get to Spain.'

After a time the man in overalls with the shotgun came up to the counter and looked at our passports without appearing to be interested in what he was doing: then he picked up the translation of our letter and read it; then he said something to the man in green uniform in the dialect that I did not understand. The man in uniform started talking loudly at him and waving his arms. The man in overalls watched him quietly, holding his gun. Then the man in uniform turned back to the counter and the man in overalls took up our documents and beckoned to me and Caroline. Caroline and I made our way through the crowd to the space behind the counter. The man took us through to a bench against the wall. He explained to us in a mixture of careful Spanish and French that the orders were, yes, that no foreigners should be allowed into Spain; but he had authority, in exceptional circumstances, to allow in some foreigners. While he spoke he watched Caroline. Caroline said 'You are so kind!' She looked at him from beneath dark lashes, from her blue eyes. The man went to look for a rubber stamp with which to stamp our passports. I thought – Perhaps I myself will be got rid of, shot, before I even get to Spain.

The man in overalls came back and told us that there was a train leaving for Barcelona that afternoon. He watched Caroline while she asked him a few questions about Spain. Then a man appeared at a door who wore knee-breeches and a military-style cap; he did not carry a gun; he carried a stick. I thought – He is on an even higher level of power. He watched the man in overalls, who after a time left us and went back to his role of appearing unconcerned at the back of the room.

I said to Caroline 'Perhaps there's just time to go to a hotel room in Port Bou.'

Caroline said 'Is that all you ever think about?'

I said 'There are always connections between making love and war. I think it's to do with wanting to break things up; for something different to occur.

The train started later that afternoon. On the way to Barcelona it stopped several times at village stations; men in uniform got on to examine papers; somewhere behind them were groups of people in overalls carrying guns. The people in overalls watched and yet did not appear quite to be watching the people in uniform. I thought – Is it that in anarchism no one can be trusted? Or is it that everyone has a stake in trusting that everyone can be trusted – so what is the difference? The men in uniform flicked through the pages of our passports: sometimes a person in overalls was summoned to look at the translation of our letter. I thought – Oh power, what is power? Is it just the chance to act as if you had power?

Our compartment filled up as we got further into Spain. People carried food; wineskins were passed round; for the most part the talk was in the dialect we did not understand. There was one old man who spoke French. Caroline smiled conspiratorially; she held on to my arm; she shot glances here and there from beneath dark lashes, from her blue eyes. The journey lasted all night: this was our second night in a train. I thought – Perhaps, after all, what I want from Caroline is her being beside me and clinging to me for safety on trains at night: ah, but then when the train stops I will be crawling out over her beautiful body again as if it were a no man's land and I will be thinking – What is love! What is power!

We learned something of the progress of the war from the old man who spoke French. Barcelona was in the hands of the people, yes: no, not the anarchists nor the socialists nor the Communists but the people! Did we not understand what was the people? The rebels had been killed, rich people had been killed, priests and nuns had been killed – oh yes, it was necessary for nuns and priests to have been killed! Did we not know what nuns and priests kept up their skirts? The old man said something in the dialect I did not understand. An old woman who was sitting next to him laughed and slapped his hand. The old man said 'Armaments!' Caroline put her tongue between her teeth and shot her glances here and there. I thought – She wants to be desirable to all men: this is what to her is making love. Or – Her desire is to be a girl on a white horse riding across a battlefield.

Caroline said 'You've cheered up.'

I said 'I'm drunk.'

She said 'There's no need to get drunk.'

I said 'Young men going off to war, to make love, often get drunk.' Caroline took her head away from my shoulder. I said 'Caroline, it's you that I love!'

At the ticket barrier in Barcelona there were groups who seemed to be examining peoples faces and even clothes rather than asking for tickets – no one in fact had required us to buy tickets. I was wearing grey flannel trousers and an open-necked shirt; Caroline was wearing a dark grey skirt and a pink blouse. I thought I might say – It's all right, comrades, I know we don't look working class! But don't be taken in by that, we're really not working class –

Outside in the street there were no taxis but there were horse-drawn carriages. Caroline said 'We can't go riding in a carriage!' So we walked, carrying our suitcases. People offered to carry them, but we refused. Caroline said 'I've never been in a city run by the workers before!' I said 'I don't suppose workers have ever wanted to run a city before.' Caroline stopped and shouted 'Look here, why have you come to Spain?' I said 'Caroline, you know I make jokes: shouldn't one make jokes in Spain?'

There were trams and buses running but they were filled with people who seemed to be just travelling round and round, hanging on to the outsides and smiling and waving. They seemed to be saying – Look at us, we are in a position now to go just round and round as if at a fair! There were a few cars; these for the most part had large white letters painted on their windows and windscreens so that it seemed it would be difficult for the drivers to see where they were going.

When we came to the main avenue, the Ramblas, there were thousands of people promenading – men and women with guns marching arm in arm and calling out and singing. It was as if they too were just demonstrating – Look, we are now able to be demonstrating! I thought – But it is also as if they are being blown by a wind: leaves being gathered for a bonfire.

Caroline said 'Isn't this exciting!'

I said 'Yes, it is.' Then I shouted 'Yes, it is exciting, it is exciting!' I did a little dance on the pavement.

At the hotel to which we had been directed by people on the train there was a man on top of a ladder trying to raise a banner to the lintel above the entrance door; he held a piece of rope with his arms stretched above his head; on the banner there were capital letters and exclamation marks in black paint. The other end of the rope was in loops on the steps of the hotel; standing among the loops was a man in overalls with a gun. Caroline went to talk to this man and at the same time the man on the ladder began pulling on the rope, so that the man with the gun felt the rope tightening around his feet and he gave a tug at it and the man on the ladder nearly fell off. I said to Caroline 'Sorry, what?' Caroline said 'What are you laughing at, another joke?' I said 'Caroline, I would never have got here without you, I am so grateful.' She said 'This hotel has been requisitioned.'

We were directed to another hotel which was, we were assured, one specifically designated for foreigners. I thought – Hotels that are specifically designated for foreigners are ones in which one can make love in the afternoons?

When I said this to Caroline she said 'But we've only just arrived!'

I said 'We may not have any more chances. Tomorrow I may die.'

She said 'Yes, that's true.'

We were shown to a small room which looked out over rooftops. I thought – One makes love because one wants to: one suffers love because of a political duty: there is, yes, a difference. Caroline lay on the bed naked in the attitude of someone listening to a national or rather an international anthem. I thought – The point is, is it, that I do at least have these victories?

Caroline said 'I'm sorry, I'm not much good.'

I said 'It's me who's not much good!' Then – 'You once said that you thought of me like St George.'

She said 'I think I think of you more like Jesus Christ.'

I said 'Jesus Christ!'

She said 'But I did think I would like making love!'

I tried to work this out. I thought – But now, anyway, it is impossible to go on making love. I said 'Let's go out and get drunk.'

She said 'I thought you already were drunk.'

I said 'That was last night.' Then – 'Jesus Christ didn't seem to mind having a drink.'

There was a café next door to the hotel of a kind, it seemed, that might have been designated for foreigners to have drinks in. There was an enclosure with tables in the central area of the avenue where people were promenading: the café itself was across the roadway and the pavement. Most of the tables in the enclosure were full, except one at which only one man was sitting. He was a man with a thin sallow face and the sort of moustache that seems to have been drawn on by a pencil. There were two empty chairs at this table. Beyond him, in the promenade, people went past with their chanting and shouting. I thought – It is as if a space has been left around him because he has been designated as a pariah, a victim –

– Or is he some sort of decoy: a goat left tethered to lure other animals into a clearing?

Caroline asked him in her bad Spanish if he minded if we sat at his table. He looked at her as if he were trying to tell her something more than that he did not understand what she was saying.

People at neighbouring tables were watching us and yet making out that they were not quite watching us. I thought – After all it may just be that everyone is drunk in this strange landscape –

– Except that in this café no one in fact is drinking?

We sat at the man's table. We observed the scene. After a time Caroline said 'I know what you're thinking.'

I said 'What?'

She said 'That in a worker's state how disgraceful it is that there are not waiters to serve you!'

I said 'I'll go and get something at the bar.'

She said 'I don't suppose that there'll be anyone serving even at the bar.'

I thought – Well, Jesus Christ would have done some miracle, wouldn't he?

I went across the road and into the café building. There was no one by the bar; there were bottles on shelves behind a metal grille at the back. The grille was padlocked. I thought – But I need a drink in order to feel sober, in this anarchist landscape.

A man came out from a side door by the bar. He was carrying a shotgun. He pointed the gun at me and began shouting in Spanish. I smiled and pointed to the bottles behind the grille. I said in my bad Spanish that I would like to buy a bottle of wine; I held out one of the pound notes that I was carrying. The man took the pound note and turned it this way and that as if it were a passport; then he handed it back to me. He pulled at the padlock; he looked round; then he gestured to me to stand back and he raised his gun and fired a shot in the direction of the padlock. Several bottles on the shelves behind the grille disintegrated. The man went to the grille and pulled at the padlock; it seemed to be still intact. I got a jug from the counter in front of the bar and collected what I could of the liquid that was running off the shelves and through the grille and down towards the floor. The man watched me. I collected almost a jugful of liquid which was the colour of dried blood. I found some glasses and I offered a glass of the liquid to the man with the gun. He took it, and we clinked glasses. I said 'Thank you.' I thought – Well, do you call that a miracle?

When I got back to Caroline in the enclosure in the central area of the promenade she said 'What was that?'

I said 'Someone took a shot at the bar.'

She said 'At the barman?'

I said 'No, at the bar.'

The man with the thin moustache who had not spoken before said in English with a strong accent 'They have already shot the barman.'

We talked with the man with the moustache while the people at the other tables both did and did not watch us. Caroline asked him about the situation in Barcelona: she told him she was a journalist. The man said 'Ah, in my time I was a journalist: now I am simply a loyal servant of the state!' Caroline said 'But who exactly now, in Barcelona, is the state?' The man reached for my jug of dark brown liquid. I gave him a glass. He said 'The people, the people, they are the state.'

I said 'Can you tell us something about the fighting at the time when the rebellion was defeated?'

He said 'What rebellion?'

I said 'The rebellion of the Fascist generals.'

He said 'Oh that rebellion.'

I thought – He is acting like someone under sentence of death: he has seen this sort of thing in gangster films?

But it was true that the people at nearby tables were maintaining the empty space around us; keeping us under some sort of surveillance.

Caroline asked the man questions about the burning of churches and the killing of nuns and priests. The man said 'And the killing of horses: don't forget the horses!' Caroline said 'Why the killing of horses?' The man said loudly 'Don't you think they deserved it, the Fascist horses?' Caroline looked away as if she were bored. The man watched her out of yellow eyes.

I filled up my glass with some more of the dark brown liquid. I filled up the glass of the man with yellow eyes. I said to him 'But what about the war: the war now against the Fascists?'

The man said 'What war now against the Fascists?'

I said 'The armies of General Franco and General Mola: what is being done to oppose them?'

The man said 'They are a long way away. Why should anything be done to oppose them?'

I said 'But where is the front?'

The man said 'There is no front.' He leaned forwards. He said 'You can take a taxi, now, and go anywhere you want in Spain. You could drive, if you wished, all the way to Santiago de Compostela.'

I said 'To Santiago de Compostela!'

The man said 'Right across Spain.'

I said 'But I was thinking, as a matter of fact, of going to Santiago de Compostela!'

Caroline said 'Oh do shut up!'

I said to Caroline 'That was the place to which people went on pilgrimages.'

Caroline said 'Don't you feel any obligations to your job?'

Caroline asked the man questions about the CNT, the UGT, the POUM – the letters that were painted on banners and on the windscreens of cars. The man was saying – 'Oh they are the anarchists, yes, they are very good; they are the socialists, yes, they are very good; they are the Trotskyites, ah, people say they are Trotskyites, but they are all against the Fascists, no?' Caroline said 'And what about the Communists?' The man suddenly smiled at her with bright white teeth; then he drew a finger across his throat. I said 'Oh the Communists, yes, they are very good!' Caroline said to me 'Look here, why don't you take a walk?'

I said 'That is what people say in gangster films.'

I had been wanting, in fact, to go for a walk on my own; to use my eyes; to stop talking. I had a street-map that I had brought with me from England; I could go for a walk in the old part of the town. I thought – I do not trust words: indeed, not my own words! Why do journalists ever think they can trust words? Then – But don't people who use their eyes also usually see only what they want to see?

Caroline was saying to the man 'But surely, with the Popular Front, the days are over when Communists might have thought Social Democrats or anarchists would be a threat in the struggle against Fascism – '

I said 'I'll see you back at the hotel.'

I crossed the wide avenue and moved into an area of tall, closely packed buildings. Here there were fewer people in the streets: there was a clutter like that in the back areas of a theatre: it was out in front in the wide avenues that people walked round and round like a stage army shouting and raising their fists. In the narrow alleyways there was litter; there were indeed one or two dead horses; there were barricades or the remains of barricades; there were churches, the insides of which had been burned. There was a smell that got worse as I went deeper into the old part of the town. I was thinking – This rotten world: these terrible human beings: oh Caroline, now that we have made love, once, twice, is it true that I should now leave you: that I should go on?

There was one church that had been burned and its religious images had been pulled out into the street: they had been set up in some sort of tableau. There was the Virgin Mary on her back and a crucified Christ on top of her: Christ's body was torn and bleeding; Mary peeped out demurely from beneath his armpit. I thought – Dear God, is this what love is like; what gods see when they look down – on me and Caroline? There were some coffins that had been broken and propped on their ends; bits of rag and bones were tumbling out. The coffins had been set round the central figures of Christ and the Virgin as if they were boxes at a theatre. I thought – Well dear God, yes, there are such peep-shows. Pigeons were flying down and pecking around the recumbent figures; there were what appeared to be communion wafers scattered like confetti over the figures on the ground. Children were darting in trying to catch the pigeons; the pigeons were flying away with bits of wafer in their mouths. On the tops of blackened pediments the pigeons tried to swallow the wafers; crumbs like dust in sunlight floated down. I thought – Well, what does this mean? Then – What do you mean 'What does it mean?' It doesn't mean anything.

Or – Why should I not now go off on a pilgrimage to Santiago de Compostela?

A group of children had gathered and were watching me. They said something to me in the dialect I did not understand. One of the children, a boy, made a circle with his finger and thumb and moved his hand up and down in the gesture which seemed to suggest an offer of sexual gratification. I thought – For me? With reference to Christ and the Virgin Mary? Then – But this was the gesture that the angelic girl called Nellie made to me years ago! I smiled and shook my head. I thought – But there are these bumps that recur, are there, at the corners of a maze?

One of the pigeons flew away with what looked like a piece of Christ's loin-cloth in its beak. I thought – Oh build a nest with it, yes, on whatever land may appear after the deluge –

– With the image of Christ and the Virgin Mary making love;

with these images that are their own meanings, from which some new Spirit might be born.

Then – This has nothing to do with me and Caroline –

– But my beautiful German girl?

I walked further on into the dark part of the town. There were bundles covered by blankets that might have been bodies in doorways. The group of children had followed me. I thought – They might rob me: they might pass signals ahead for me to be waylaid and killed. Then – But for what have I wanted to come to this dark and foetid part of the town? I have wanted to see what there might be at the centre of this maze.

You remember that book, *The Magic Mountain*, that you told me about on our mountainside in Switzerland – how its hero, when lost in the snow, lies down and has a dream (how could you not remember this!): he dreams that he is on a beach where beautiful people walk serenely hand in hand; he wonders what enables them to be so beautiful and serene; he notices that every now and then they glance in a direction over sand-dunes; he goes in this direction in which there seems to be that to which they give honour; he comes to a temple in which old hags are dismembering a child. And it seems to be in awareness of this that the people on the beach are so beautiful and composed. Moving within the narrow and stinking streets I was reminded of this. I thought – But those people striding up and down in the wide avenues; they do not imagine they are beautiful and composed?

I had come to a place where the alleyway I was in opened out into a small dank yard scattered with refuse; an opening at the far end was blocked by a barricade; on the barricade there was what looked like the head and skin of a donkey. I thought – Dear God, a donkey. Then – The donkey that carried Christ into the dark centre of Jerusalem? The children had come to the edge of the yard behind me. The boy again made the gesture with his finger and thumb in a circle. A girl pointed to where there were some steps going down to a low archway at the side of the yard. I thought – You mean, just, that this is an area in which there are brothels? The temples, perhaps, in which hags dismantle a child? Then – But having come this far, I should at least make sure I have glimpsed what there is in this maze.

I went down the steps to a dank underground passage. There was an arch with a metal-studded door in a wall. I thought – But such images are also in the mind: where do they come from; where are they going? One of the children went past me and called through the door. After a time a figure in a smock the colour of ashes opened the door – a woman or a man, I couldn't tell. The figure had a heavy round face and long thin hair. I thought – An old hag, yes: but what are these images doing here? This is the real world; this is hell? The figure opened the door; beckoned for me to come in. The children spoke in the dialect I did not understand. I moved to where I could see through the doorway. I thought – I can still run, get away; the real horror is not to die but to be caught and kept alive – this would be hell – like someone in an iron casing, or in a cage on the wall of a municipal building. Within a room that was a sort of cellar there were two of the heavy androgynous figures: it did seem, yes, that they were women. I thought – Well, all right, but what of a child? Then – But this is ridiculous. At the back of the cellar there was an alcove with a curtain across it; one of the women went to the alcove and put her hand on the curtain; she looked at me; she waited; I smiled, and shook my head. Do you remember how in Madam Tussaud's, in the Chamber of Horrors, there used to be a waxwork which was supposed to be so horrific that it had to be placed behind a curtain; you could pull the curtain back if you liked – well, of course you liked – and then there was a man hanging from a meat-hook through his middle: well, not exactly a child. And not the sort of thing on a hook, do you think, that might have pulled one across a desert, to the dark centre of a town? The woman pulled a side of the curtain back. Inside – I could not quite see – there was something that might have been a waxwork, certainly; it was dressed in the habit, the cowl, of a monk. I thought – Oh well, people do have pornographic images about priests, monks, dead bodies propped up in coffins, don't they? Of course these are ridiculous! But they are what people like? Then the woman held out her hand as if for money. I thought – Well, I am not going to give you money! Then – But what if this is not a waxwork but one of those figures that are in fact alive; that cannot die; that are kept in tiny cages? I could not see the face beneath the cowl. Then the woman put a hand on the lower half of the habit of the monk and pulled it back. There was inside – inside the inner curtain that covered the monk, as it were – what seemed to be a white, soft, somewhat hairy male human body. It had such large, life-like genitals: how could it be a waxwork! Its genitals even semed slightly out of proportion to the rest of its body, like those of a new-born baby. I thought – So does this or does it not mean that it is alive?

The woman had gone to the side of the alcove and was turning the handle of what seemed to be a rack or winch; something was tightening round the throat of the figure in the alcove; I could not quite see – I felt as if there were something tightening around my own throat. I found myself standing on one leg – but the figure in the alcove seemed to be getting an erection. I thought – This is impossible: it is some trick: you wind a handle and a dummy gets a rise: you pay your penny for a peep-show on a pier. Then I thought – But this, in fact, is what happens to someone who is hanged, garotted: am I not myself supposed to know about this? I went further into the cellar and tried to see underneath the cowl of the figure in the alcove; I put a hand out; there was something both hard and soft at the throat. I thought – I am reaching through into another dimension; through the wall of the cave into – oh – the clockwork tawdriness of hell! The body seemed to be a corpse: I was sure it was a corpse. I took my hand away. I thought – So what are they demonstrating; asking for money in demonstrating: that this is war? That dead men or monks still get erections in hell? I found that I had my teeth bared. I was shaking. I thought – Some child in myself is being dismembered.

One of the old women was coming towards me; she had her hand out; when I turned to the door the children hung on to my clothes. I pulled some cigarettes out of my pocket and scattered them on the floor. The two old women and the children went after them. I got out into the passage. I thought – But dead bodies do not react like that! Then – But of course, it was worked by some wire.

Then – But should I not go back to make sure?

I went up the steps from the passageway into the yard. I walked through alleyways back towards the more crowded part of the town. I thought – What was meant by the harrowing of hell –

– What is important that I learn from this?

I did not want to go back to the café to find Caroline. It did not seem, really, that I wanted to go back to anywhere I had ever been before.

I thought – All right, all right, the noose tightens round one's throat –

– The umbilical cord –

– Of course one wants to make love; to make war –

– God must have seen that, at humans' birth, there is some hell.

I avoided the café and went to the hotel room: Caroline was not there. I tried to wash the hand with which I had touched the figure or corpse. The tap above the basin did not work. I thought – Dear God, to get clear, what does one do? If one's hand offend thee, cut the wrists, cut it off –

– The figure in the alcove had been getting such a lifelike erection!

– It is I who am trapped?

The images, the messages, were piling up: what attention should I pay to them? I lay on the bed. There was the roar of the crowd on the promenade outside.

I thought – Cannot these images be put back in my head; the cord round the throat unwound, and used as a thread to guide me through the maze?

– Of course I should go on a pilgrimage –

– My beautiful German girl, where are you!

Caroline had not returned to the hotel by the evening, so I went out to look for her at the café. The crowds were thicker than ever in the promenade. I thought – They are all wound up like clockwork toys by some old woman in an alcove –

– Put them back in the toybox?

Caroline was not in the café.

The sallow-faced man who spoke English was still there. He seemed hardly to have shifted his position. By now there had been cleared an even larger space around him. I thought – Perhaps he has been here for days: perhaps he thinks that if he stays in a public place, then no one will carry him off and put him in a cage with a wire down through his throat to his genitals.

I sat in the chair that I had sat in some hours ago. I said to the sallow-faced man 'Have you seen the girl who was with me here this afternoon? You were talking to her. You remember?'

The man seemed to hear but not to see me. I thought – Perhaps he has already been blinded. The jug in which I had collected the dark brown liquid was still on the table and was empty. The man said 'Sit down.'

I said 'It is important that I find her.'

The man said 'Do you speak Russian?'

I said 'Yes.'

He said in Russian 'You do?' Then 'I am Russian.'

I said 'I see.'

He said in English 'Can I tell you something?'

The table at which we sat was at the edge of the enclosure in the promenade. The people were marching up and down singing and shouting just outside.

The man said 'The human race is involved in a suicide pact.'

I said 'I agree.'

He said 'Do you know how a suicide pact works?'

I said 'Yes.'

He said 'Each person draws a lot for one person to kill another until there is only one person left. Then that person kills himself.'

I said 'But suppose he does not.'

He said 'What?'

I said 'There's a story about that.'

The man put a finger to his lips and looked round as if we might be overheard. Then he said 'I am talking about God.'

I said 'You were telling me how to get to Santiago de Compostela.'

He said 'St Francis of Assisi once set out for Santiago de Compostela.'

I said 'Did he?'

He said 'Yes.' Then – 'He never got there.'

I said 'Why not?'

Two Englishmen had come to sit at the next table. I was sure that they were English because they wore white shirts and grey flannel trousers: also one of them I thought I recognised from Cambridge. The other was a young man with a hard-soft face like a boxer.

The Russian said 'That girl will betray you.'

I said 'Why do you say that?'

He said 'Because she has betrayed me.'

I thought – You mean you had time to go with her to a hotel room?

The Englishman at the next table whom I thought I recognised from Cambridge took a pipe out of his mouth and said to me 'Excuse me, but I have been asked to advise you that it is not wise for you to be seen sitting with the person at that table.'

I said 'Why not?'

He said 'Because there's going to be a spot of trouble.'

I looked round and saw Caroline amongst the crowd in the central promenade of the avenue. She was standing with a group of men in overalls who carried weapons that looked like sub-machine guns and were festooned with bandoliers. There was a large man with a black beard standing by Caroline; he had an arm around her. She was looking in the direction of the enclosure of tables; when I looked at her, she looked away. I thought – But should I care if she is betraying me?

The Russian man said 'People feel safe if others die; that is why there is a suicide pact.'

I said 'People feel safest if they themselves die; that is why there is a suicide pact.'

The Englishman, leaning over, said 'Ah, you were talking of the story of Josephus.'

The Russian man said 'That is a story about how to survive.'

Caroline was looking at me. She said something to the large man with the beard. The man with the beard was looking at me. I thought – But they are talking about the sallow-faced Russian man: their victim, the pariah.

Then – Well, indeed, how does one survive.

I said 'Josephus fixed the lots.'

The Englishman said 'Yes, but how?'

The Russian man said 'He did some trick.'

I said 'He must have had some luck too.'

The Englishman said 'Oh yes, he must have had some luck too!'

The other Englishman, the one who looked like a boxer, said to me 'Don't I recognise you? Have you come here for the Workers' Olympic Games?'

I thought I might say – You mean there really is, now, in Barcelona, something called the Workers' Olympic Games?

I said 'In a sense, yes.'

He said 'What's your event?'

I said 'The long jump.'

Caroline was coming through the crowd towards me. I thought – Oh Caroline, I'm so terribly sorry I have brought you here!

The Englishman with the pipe said to me 'Watch out that you aren't for the high jump.'

Caroline had come up to the railing round the enclosure just inside which was the table at which I was sitting. She looked so out of place: vulnerable, yet inviolable. I thought – Like an angel of death. She said 'Oh darling, I've been so anxious! I've been looking for you everywhere!'

I said 'I've been in the hotel.'

She said 'But I went to the hotel!'

I thought I might say – Then have we all three been in the hotel. The man with the beard was watching us.

Then Caroline said quietly 'Come away. You mustn't be seen with that man at the table.'

I thought – Who says so: the man with the beard?

I said 'Did you tell those people what he had been saying to us earlier?'

Caroline blushed. She stood slightly back from the railing round the enclosure. She said 'No, of course not!' Then – 'Why shouldn't I?'

The man with the beard was talking to the group of men with bandoliers. Two of the men started to move in the direction of our table.

I turned to the Russian man and said 'What do you think he did?'

He said 'Who?'

I said 'Josephus.'

The Englishman at the next table said 'Oh, Josephus!'

The Russian man had his back to where the two men with bandoliers were approaching. He leaned forwards with his hands on his knees. He said 'Did he tell the truth? Did he tell lies?'

The Englishman at the next table said 'Do you know the paradox of the Cretan?'

I said 'The one who said all Cretans were liars – ?'

The Englishman said 'So he could do what he wanted.' Then – 'It is all a matter of timing.'

The Russian man got up and bowed. He began to make his way through the enclosure of tables away from the promenade and towards the roadway. People cleared a slight path for him. I thought – You mean people can now see others coming to get him: so this is a matter of timing?

Then – Just this, and then that, is happening.

The second Englishman, who was like a boxer, said 'That man is a spy.'

The two men with bandoliers had changed direction and were going round the edge of the enclosure as if to cut off the Russian man who had gone through the crowd. The crowd seemed to be making it slightly difficult for the two men to follow him. I held my hand up as if for a waiter. The two men paused, and looked towards the table.

Caroline was looking at me belligerently. She said 'He certainly talked like a spy!'

I thought I might say – But don't be taken in by that –

I said 'You did betray him!'

The man with the beard had come up to the enclosure. He put his arm round Caroline again. I thought – They really have been to a hotel? He began to talk to me in the language that I did not understand. A small crowd had paused in their promenade and had gathered behind him at the railing round the enclosure. With him were several more men with bandoliers.

I said to the Englishman 'Do you understand this language?'

The Englishman said 'You are being told what an honour it is for an Englishman to come out and join the struggle against Fascism.'

I said 'But there doesn't seem to be much of a struggle against Fascism.'

The Englishman said 'But you see what I meant, when I said you might be better to prepare for the high jump.'

I thought – Yes, that was witty. We both began laughing.

The man with the beard stopped talking.

I said to Caroline 'Where did you pick him up?'

Caroline said 'Buenaventura? We were looking for you in the hotel.'

There was a burst of firing from somewhere in the direction of the café. I thought – Either the men with bandoliers have caught the Russian and have shot him, or perhaps he has escaped and they are trying to get a drink from behind the bar.

Caroline said 'He will be enormously useful for us, darling! He'll arrange interviews! Don't you think I'm clever! He's got a column going out before morning!'

I thought I might say – And will you be on the end of his column before morning?

Caroline said 'Why are you laughing?'

I said 'Where is his column going to?'

Caroline said 'I think towards Huesca.'

I said to the Englishman 'Is Huesca in the general direction, do you know, of Santiago de Compostela?'

The Englishman said 'Yes, I think certainly Huesca is in the general direction of Santiago de Compostela.'

There was a disturbance going on on the pavement in front of the café. There was a figure running through the crowd. I could not see if the figure was the Russian. I could not see what had happened to the two men with bandoliers.

I said to Caroline 'Will you ask your friend if I can be on his column that is going out before morning?'

Caroline said 'Oh you are wonderful! You are so brave! Then I can stay behind and do the interviews here.'

The Englishman said to me 'I think perhaps you'd better start training for the pole vault.'

There was a man being led through the crowd by one of the men with bandoliers: they were coming from the direction of the café across the pavement. The man was not the Russian; he was a smaller man with a paler face, but he had the same sort of pencil-thin moustache. I thought – The Russian has indeed been able to perform some trick: he has got them to arrest the wrong man?

Then – But I have no means by which to work out – nor indeed to falsify – what is happening in this strange country.

I said to the Englishman 'I think I know you. Aren't you from Cambridge?'

He said 'Yes. I remember you at a party. You were sitting on a tree with your feet over a pond.'

I said 'Oh yes, I was with Suzy. Do you know Suzy?'

He said 'Yes, I'm married to her.'

I said 'You're married to her!'

He said 'Yes, and I've always been very grateful to you. She says you altered her life.'

I thought – How did I alter her life? Then – So that's all right.

The man who had been led up to the railing round the enclosure was being made to kneel by one of the men with bandoliers: he was looking up beseechingly at the man with the beard who had his arm around Caroline. Caroline was leaning half-heartedly away from the man with the beard; her mouth was open; she was like a shining fish in the claws of a crab. I thought – But this is the sort of thing you like, O Caroline: you will be all right?

The Englishman said 'Can I ask you something?'

I said 'Yes.'

'Did you sleep with her?'

'Who?'

'My wife. Suzy.'

I said 'No, of course not!'

He said 'I just wondered.' Then – 'So that's all right.'

I thought I might have said – When she slept with me, she altered my life.

One of the men with bandoliers had handed to the man with the black beard a small pouch or wallet made of leather: this seemed to have been taken from the man with the thin moustache. The man with the beard put his arms underneath Caroline and carried her over the railings that were round the enclosure; he sat on the chair which the Russian man had left and placed Caroline on his lap.

Then he untied the tape round the wallet. Caroline shot at me glances from beneath her dark lashes, from her blue eyes.

The Englishman said to me 'You're in physics, aren't you?'

I said 'Yes.'

He said 'Have you heard this theory about the nucleus of an atom being held together by some force like the surface tension that holds together a drop of water?'

I said 'No, I haven't heard that.'

I thought – So you mean, if you took an unstable nucleus and bombarded it –

The man with the beard was spreading out on the table the contents of the leather pouch. The contents were jewellery – bracelets and rings and watches: a few cut and uncut stones, and pearls. The man with the beard held up one of the bracelets against his wrist. Then he turned to the people who were outside the enclosure watching him and he threw the bracelet high over the heads of the crowd. People raised their heads and hands as if to reach for a star. Then the man with the beard raised his sub-machine gun and fired a burst into the air. People in the crowd ducked slightly; then straightened and watched the man with the beard. The bracelet landed somewhere behind them. No one went after it.

Caroline said to me 'He sent one of his men to talk to me when I was talking to that Frenchman! He wanted to warn us so that we should not get into any trouble!'

I said 'He wasn't a Frenchman, he was a Russian.'

Caroline said 'Oh all right, a Russian then!'

The man with the beard turned to the man with the thin moustache who was kneeling on the other side of the railing and took what looked like an uncut diamond between his finger and thumb and held it out towards the man's face. I thought – It is, I suppose, yes, as if they were on either side of an altar rail. The man with the beard said something in the language that I did not understand. One of the men with a rifle dug the kneeling man in the ribs; the man opened his mouth; the man with the beard put the diamond on his tongue. The man who was kneeling stayed with his mouth open. Then the man with bandoliers put his hands round the kneeling man's face; the man struggled; the crowd laughed and cheered. After a time the kneeling man seemed to have swallowed the diamond. Then the bearded man spoke to the man with bandoliers who lifted the kneeling man and turned him round and seemed to hand him over to the crowd. People in the crowd took him, laughing, and led him away. I thought – And what will they do now? Tear him to pieces? Disembowel him to get at the diamond? So here, indeed, is a dismemberment; a feeding of the people.

Caroline said to me 'You do see what a wonderful chance it will be for us! You going out on the column, and me talking to Buenaventura here. What a story!'

I said to the Englishman 'Who is this Buenaventura?'

The Englishman said 'It's true that he is one of the few local leaders who are doing any fighting. He has this column that goes out into the countryside.'

I said 'Can you ask him where his column is starting from – the one that goes out before morning?'

The Englishman said 'It seems to me that the story you'll be getting will be that of David and Bathsheba.'

The man with the beard was offering Caroline one of the pearls. He was holding it in front of her mouth to put it on her tongue. Caroline was shaking her head and smiling. The man was saying something in the language that I did not understand.

The Englishman had been talking to one of the men with bandoliers. He said to me 'He says you can go with them now if you want to, and he will show you where they're starting from before morning.'

I said 'Was the story of David and Bathsheba the one where King David arranges for Bathsheba's husband to go into the front line and be killed so that he could get her?

The Englishman said 'Yes.'

Caroline said to the Englishman 'Can you tell me what he is saying?'

The Englishman said to her 'He is saying that the story of David and Bathsheba – '

Caroline said 'I mean Buenaventura.'

The Englishman listened to the man with the beard for a time, and then said to Caroline 'He is telling you that if you swallow this pearl, then that will be a surety that he will look after you for two days and two nights, until your husband returns.'

Caroline suddenly took the pearl from the hand of the man with the beard and put it on her tongue and seemed to swallow it; then she looked at me as if belligerently.

I said 'It will come out in your shit.'

She said 'Then you can look for it when you come back.'

I thought Dear God, yes, what a thing to come back for. Then –
But what if I have had enough of all this –

I said to the Englishman 'What was the name of the husband in
that story?'

The Englishman said 'Bathsheba's husband?'

I said 'Yes.'

He said 'Uriah.'

I said 'What is your subject at Cambridge?'

He said 'I am an anthropologist, interested in the nature of
stories.'

I thought – But we make up stories! Then – But might not Uriah,
like a pearl, have gone right through his story, and come out at the
other end of all this shit?

VII   5: Eleanor

Yes, I quite wanted to die: but then there was the fantasy – Can I not do something useful before I go?

What a god-like chance you have if you do not mind if you die! Take one or two murderers with you as you go.

When I had learned of the arrest of my father and the probable death of my mother I had not had much time to plan what to do: it had been a question, yes, of do I live or do I die. But then, in this state of hardly caring, what dramatic figures, smiling and pointing, popped up at the corners of the maze!

In Seville I had come through: there were all the dead bodies around me on the quay. The boat was intact. To Heinrich and the people with him I thus became some sort of heroine. Heinrich hugged me on the quayside and said 'Without you we could not have got through!' But it was these people, it seemed, who were allied to those responsible for what had happened to my father and my mother. Heinrich had given me a gun. I said 'Can you show me how to work this gun?'

You do know the story of Judith (do you not!) – the beautiful Jewish girl who gets herself taken into the camp of the Assyrians when the Assyrians are about to break into her home town and massacre the inhabitants; and then, when Holofernes the Captain of the Assyrians plans to make love to her but gets drunk instead, she takes down his sword and chops his head off. And thus she is the saviour of her people. Well, my fantasies did not extend to my becoming the saviour of my people; but I thought – Certainly circumstances seem to have turned out so that I am in the camp of the enemy: might I not be able to do something truly useful before I go?

– And Judith herself in the end did not even have to go.

When I was with Heinrich on the roadway by the pile of stones I found I had difficulty in walking. I said 'I think I have been wounded in the foot.'

He said 'You are Achilles!'

I thought – No, not Achilles, but Penthesilea, Queen of the Amazons, who fought Achilles and chopped him to pieces.

I was able to walk, with an arm round Heinrich, from the river to somewhere near the centre of Seville; the main part of the fighting seemed to have moved to the far side of the river. Where we walked there were men in dark blue shirts running through the streets; men with jackets and ties carrying shotguns; men hanging on to the outsides of cars like the claws of crabs. I thought – Oh I have known this scene before! In the streets of Berlin: but then it was more like a carnival, at least around the Adlon Hotel. The white overalls that Heinrich and I wore seemed to give us some immunity. Men in blue shirts were kicking at the doors of the buildings; they were breaking windows with their rifle-butts; people were being led out with their hands in the air. Occasionally they were not even taken round corners before they were shot. They were shot in the back of the head; they fell forward with such violence that it was as if they were being hurled towards hell. Heinrich said 'Don't look!' I thought – Why should I not look? Have not such images been with me since childhood: of mad archaic people smashing in the backs of heads and then turning and posing as if for a photograph –

– And then with luck, their bullets go right round the universe and hit their own heads.

There was an enormous cathedral squatting on the town like a toad. There was a tower above it with bells that swung and whirled like a poisoned tongue.

I thought – If I were God I would want to destroy the human race, yes; but I would want them to take me with them as they went.

At the back of the cathedral there were narrow streets painted white: this was an old part of town, with pretty courtyards and grilles over windows hung with baskets of flowers. I do not remember much about this particular stage of my journey: I suppose I was tired; perhaps I was becoming feverish from my wound. I did not know how I had got this wound; it was a cut, a throbbing in my foot: there had been firing almost at random to and fro across the river: perhaps some ricochet had hit me when the man in the white shirt had shot his own foot. I thought – It has all seemed a bit of a mirage, this part of the journey. We came to an ancient white house with a coat of arms above the doorway: in the coat of arms there was a man in a shirt leaning on a sword: I thought – Well, indeed I might be Judith entering the camp of the Assyrians. Heinrich led me through to a cool white courtyard where we were greeted by a large fair-haired woman wearing white. Heinrich spoke to her in German: she answered in German. They took me to a room with a bed in it: they looked at my wound. It was a small wound on the arch of my foot above the instep. My overalls had blood spattered on them – perhaps from the man whose throat had been cut just in front of me. The woman was saying that she would take care of me; Heinrich said that he had to go. She and he stood in the doorway for a time; she laid her head on his shoulder and she seemed to be crying. It did not seem to matter that I did not understand most of what was happening: I was Judith being prepared by the handmaidens of the Assyrians.

When the woman helped me to undress she said 'What a heroine you have been!'

I said 'You are German?'

She said 'Yes.'

I thought – Wake me up, will you, for my assignation with Holofernes.

There were several days, I suppose, when I was indeed feverish; I remember almost nothing of this part of my journey. I lay in a room in which there was a picture of the Virgin Mary on her throne; a crucifix with a torn and bleeding Jesus. I think I translated even these into images of Judith and Holofernes – Mary immaculate beside her chopped-up son. My foot went septic for a time; it swelled; the fair-haired woman put on disinfectant and bandages. The bells of the cathedral banged like a battering-ram against my head. I thought – The poison in my foot is trying to get out, to get in: it is all over the town, like spores from the tongue of that poisonous toad.

The tall fair-haired woman would come and sit with me on my bed in the evenings. Bit by bit I learned something of her story. I thought – People make up their stories: but this is the point? They either are, or are not, threads through the maze.

The woman was called Walburga (such a name! yet was it not on St Walburga's Day that I wrote to you from West Africa?). Walburga was the daughter of an aristocratic Prussian family; she had been brought up with horses and dogs on a bleak northern plain; she had been sent to Munich to complete her education. There she had fallen in love with a Nazi and they had become engaged; her family had disapproved because he was a Nazi; then he had been shot in the purges associated with Röhm. There were rumours that he had been homosexual. To escape all this Walburga had come to Spain. After a time she had become engaged to the younger son of a Spanish aristocratic family; but then this fiancé had disappeared shortly before the rising in Seville. He had been last seen riding on his horse on a bridge across the river; it was thought that he might have been captured and was being held to ransom by the people across the river, but when nothing was heard of him it was feared that he had been killed. The rest of the ex-fiancé's family were away in the north in San Sebastian, where they always went at this time of year. So when the civil war started they were cut off, and Walburga found herself alone in the rambling old house in Seville. Heinrich had been a friend of both her family and that of her fiancé. Was it not lucky, Walburga said, that when I turned up I had her to look after me: and she had me to look after! She did not know what she would have done, she said, if she had had to stay any longer in Seville on her own.

I thought – Lucky for you, lucky for me: but does not luck go its own way?

Walburga was a pale thick-set girl with a face like a Greek hero: she was now in her middle or late twenties. Her body, as was then the custom amongst her sort of people, was strapped into a tight brassière and corset. I thought – Her lovers have been Nazis and aristocrats: they like her to be in armour, do they, so that they will be protected.

When nursing me Walburga struggled rather inconsequentially with sponges, towels, bowls of water. Sometimes her left hand did not seem quite to know what her right hand was doing. But she showed no interest in talking about politics. I thought – Her sort of people are becoming extinct: or is she trying to learn to become a survivor?

She said 'Tell me – no don't tell me! – about yourself. It is so much more exciting if I know nothing about you!'

I said 'I was a medical student once.'

She said 'You were a medical student once!' She put her head down on my knees. She wailed 'What you must think of me!'

I said 'You're doing very well.'

It seemed that when she made out that she was embarrassed, she could have an opportunity to hug me. I thought – It is all part of her charm, her heavy aristocratic charm, to make out that she does not quite know what she is doing.

Heinrich came to visit me. He was staying at the airfield some way out of the town. He sat on the edge of my bed. He said 'And how are you getting on with the beautiful Walburga?

I thought – You think she is beautiful?

I said 'Very well. I am lucky.'

He said 'The family of her fiancé is one of the richest in Spain.'

I thought – That is why you think she is beautiful?

Then – Dear God, I am jealous about Heinrich and Walburga?

Then – But the point of my relationship with these people is that they might take me to wherever it is I want to go.

There was a day when the poison retreated and I was able to put my foot to the ground. I went walking on crutches with Walburga helping me. We went along pale hot passages and around inner courtyards. There was sometimes the sound of firing from the streets outside. I said 'Is the fighting still going on?' Walburga said 'I don't think there's much fighting now in Seville.' I said 'They're shooting prisoners?' She said 'I'm afraid that's just the way they do things in Spain.'

I said 'And in Germany?'

We sat on a stone bench at the side of the courtyard where there was a fountain playing. She said 'I told you, the first man I was engaged to was shot in Germany.'

I said 'I'm sorry.'

She said 'I do not know whether or not he deserved to be.'

I thought – But why don't you know? Then – But do I think I would know?

We sat near the edge of the shade trying to keep our feet out of the hot sun. Between the arches of the courtyard there were flowers that hung on walls in tiny cages.

I said 'It seems very beautiful, this part of the town. I didn't like the bit between the cathedral and the river.'

She said 'Yes, it is odd, isn't it.'

I said 'What is odd?'

She said 'This was once the Jewish part of town.'

I thought – Ah, come on now, Judith; you knew you were in the camp of the Assyrians!

I said 'It is no longer the Jewish part of town?'

She said 'Oh no, they were turned out.'

'When?'

'In the fifteenth century.'

'Oh I see.'

I had had some idea of Walburga's fiancé's family turning them out a year or two ago. I thought – If this was so, what would I have done?

Then Walburga said 'So practical, the Spanish! But where did the Jews go? To poor old Germany!'

I thought – These people carry their ignorance and self-protection around like a disease. Then – Oh well, I can always take Walburga with me as I go.

I imagined some ancestor of mine in the fifteenth century perhaps being the proprietor of this beautiful white courtyard: then there was the vision of my mother being bundled into the back of a truck in Alexanderplatz.

I said 'Were all the Jews turned out?'

She said 'Oh no, quite a number I think were converted and became Christians.'

I said 'And they were accepted?'

She said 'Oh I think they were accepted. But then, of course, like that they can be more dangerous than ever!'

I thought – And that is what I want! To become more dangerous than ever.

I had a quite vivid vision at this time of myself, when I had recovered from my wound, being taken by Walburga or Heinrich perhaps to some great gathering of high-up Nazi or Fascist dignitaries – in a ballroom; in some huge public stadium – and I would make my way up to the podium through an enrapt crowd – perhaps it was even me they were applauding on account of my heroic defence of the boat on the river! – and then I would take my pistol from my bag – no, not bag, because I would be wearing my white overalls like an angel – I would take my pistol from my pocket and in front of me there would be the grinning face of someone like Goering or Goebbels or even Hitler; and I would shoot –

Walburga said 'What are you thinking?'

I said 'Did any of them fight – those Jews?'

She said 'Oh no, I don't think they do, do you?'

I said 'Perhaps they feel too superior to fight!'

Walburga said 'Superior?'

I thought – Why do none of these people wonder whether I am a Jew –

– They see only what they want to see?

I got up on my crutches and walked away.

There was a time when I was able to walk on my own. I went exploring in the house that might have once belonged to Jews and now belonged to Walburga's fiancé's family. Walburga watched me. I thought – She is like a dog left behind while its mistress goes for a walk.

– It is true that Jews are most dangerous when they are in the camp of the enemy?

Along white corridors and up steps I came across a library. This consisted mainly of old books in Spanish, but there was a section of books in German, and some of these were to do with history and theology and some were to do with Jews.

I thought – These books might have been dumped here mysteriously for me at this corner of the maze – by my own Jewish ancestors? By Walburga's Nazi or aristocratic lover?

There were a few modern anti-Semitic tracts of the kind I had been accustomed to seeing in Germany – cartoons of hook-nosed Jewish men ravishing Aryan girls; of Jewish children being suckled by pigs. I thought – Oh well, how terrible for Christians to be so cowardly and afraid. Then – I am trying to understand you, O my father, O my mother.

There was an academic book concerned with the expulsion of Jews from Spain at the end of the fifteenth century. Just before this there had been serious debates between Christians and Jews about their differences. Christians had argued: Jews are people who have known the truth but have denied it; it is this denial of the incarnation of God that has put them beyond the human pale. Jews had argued: but look what you Christians have done with your absurd ideas of truth! You have invented a tortured and murdered God and so what do you expect, other than to be torturing and murdering among yourselves! So the Inquisition had taken Jews and tortured and murdered them, and turned them out of Spain.

And now in the streets of Seville there were the bells of the cathedral and the sounds of prisoners being shot.

There was also a modern book by a Jew which said: yes, but what did Jews expect once they had been told that they had some special destiny? History, of course, is to do with killings and counter-killings; with who comes out on top. But Jews are a people who have been taken out of history; they are in a special relationship with eternity; and so for them what do these killings and counter-killings matter? Jews can look down on them from their own proper dimension; and in this respect it is as if they are always on top.

I thought – You mean I can look down on what has happened to my father and my mother: you call this on top?

Then – But indeed I have always thought that Jews should remain somewhat secret: then they can do what they have to do; thus they can be on top!

There was a day when I was well enough to go out of the house; Walburga said 'I will take you to the gardens.' She added 'Please!' We went out into the hot sun that crossed a small square to where there was a narrow door beneath an arcade. Walburga produced a key. We went into what seemed to be a whole old world of a garden: there were palm trees and orange trees and tall trees with leaves like feathers; there were beds of roses and flowers with dark blue heads like small explosions. Paths ran between low hedges in geometrical patterns; at the intersection of each path there was a fountain; each fountain had different marble and ironwork and tiles. The water kept the air cool; the trees shaded the paths; it was as if this was a garden in which one could walk for ever. I thought – It is not like a maze, the point of which is to get to the centre: this is just where people walk round and round. So – Is it from a place like this that people have to go out to fight battles? Battles are the other side of the coin, from just walking round and round.

I said to Walburga 'What have you got against Jews?'

She said 'They drag everything down to a materialist level.'

I said 'But that is what they say about Christians: and they think of themselves as being in a special relation to God.'

Walburga said 'Then what a God!'

I said 'But when you look at Christians, what a God!'

I thought – But perhaps neither people who have to call themselves 'Jews' nor people who have to call themselves 'Christians' are in fact in relation to God: such labelling is to do with words going round and round: it is to do with battles, with people having to know where they are, with people banging their heads against a maze's walls. It is not to do with a person looking for the thread that will take him or her to the centre of the maze; where there might be God; where there would be no names.

There was in fact a small maze in the middle of the gardens: it was made out of untended cypress trees; there were gaps in the walls, where trees had died. It was not difficult to push a way through towards the centre: but then, being exposed, there did not seem to be a centre there.

I thought – A proper Jew would not go on about being a Jew: she or he would hold the thread; why make it possible for it to be taken away?

– Except, of course, how much easier to let it be taken away!

Walburga had come with me into the maze. She said 'I don't mind, you know.'

I said 'You don't mind what?'

She said 'Whatever you are! Whatever you say!' She looked at me as if she were on the point of tears.

I thought – You're trying to tell me that you know I'm a Jew?

– But you think this makes things easier, if you say that you don't mind?

There was a day when General Franco was said to have landed in Seville. I did not know much about General Franco: he had apparently been the head of the army in Africa: he had flown in from Morocco. The general who had led the uprising in Seville was called Queipo de Llano. When Walburga or Heinrich talked of Queipo de Llano they usually smiled: it seemed that he was a joker, an oddity, something like Don Quixote. Out of all the characters in European mythology I have most disliked Don Quixote: he has seemed to me to epitomise the dreadful uproariousness with which Christians try to deal with their obsessions about degradation and death. When Walburga and Heinrich talked about General Franco they did not smile. I thought – Then do I mean that I might prefer Torquemada to Don Quixote?

Heinrich came from the airfield and sat on the edge of my bed. He looked at me with hot eyes. He said 'How long do you think it will be before we are able – '

I said 'Able to what – '

He said 'Oh – travel up with Walburga to the north!'

Walburga had told me that there was about to be some conjunction between the Nationalist armies of the south and those of the north: General Franco would soon be marching up from Seville to meet General Mola.

I said 'We can make love now if you like.'

He said 'You are an angel!'

He was, as usual, very cool, controlled, mechanical. I thought – Well it is true that by doing this I am getting closer to the heart of the enemy.

Heinrich said 'Walburga is right about the conjunction of the armies of the north and south. The only serious opposition seems to be at Badajoz.'

I said 'What's happening at Badajoz?'

He said 'There has to be some fighting or the troops get bored.'

I said 'Doesn't the shooting of prisoners stop them getting bored?'

He frowned and said 'As a German, I don't approve of everything they are doing here, you know.'

I thought – Well, dear God, as a German, do you approve of everything they are doing at home?

Heinrich said 'As a matter of fact I have got bored. I have asked if I can be attached to a unit at the front.'

I said 'Why?'

He said 'You like risks, don't you? You like seeing for yourself what's going on?'

I thought – We think that makes things all right?

There was a day when there was a big gathering in the square by the town hall in Seville: it was said that the Monarchist flag was going to be unfurled. There was no question of the restoration of the monarchy: it was just apparently thought that people would like to see this flag unfurled. General Franco was going to make a speech. Walburga, of course, planned to be in the square. She said 'I don't suppose you'll want to come!' I thought I might say – Why do you think I won't want to come? Don't you think I might pull out my pistol and shoot someone in the square?

– But what is the difference, indeed, between fantasy and reality.

In the space in front of the town hall there was a crowd of men in uniform: men in blue shirts; men and women in smart clothes as if they were now indeed out for some carnival. The town hall was a Renaissance building with a central balcony: it was hung with flags and banners. I thought – Oh well, there will be some Punch and Judy show: figures will pop up here and there and shout and yell; there will be delectation, feeding, for the attendant multitude.

The first speaker was Franco: he was a small dapper man who flung his arm up in a Fascist salute and jerked his hips forward as if he were being propelled to the edge of the balcony from behind. I thought – Dear God, perhaps he will be like that man in the Moorish house by the river who went right over and landed on the pavement. As Franco made his speech he paused every now and then and jerked his hips and did the Fascist salute. One of the banners at the side of the balcony was that of the Spanish Falangists – the men in blue shirts – and the emblem on the banner was a bundle of splayed arrows held together by a yoke. I thought – Perhaps when General Franco jerks his hips forwards he is having one of those arrows stuck up his behind. He shouted like most orators do; there was a microphone that sometimes seemed to work and sometimes did not; the noise came and went like the yelling of a baby. After a time a piece of rolled-up cloth was brought out and General Franco began to kiss and to cuddle it. I thought – Perhaps it is one of those pieces of cloth that are given to babies as substitute mothers to stop them screaming. Franco unfurled the piece of cloth and shook it out over the edge of the balcony and then the crowd began to shout and yell: it was a red and yellow piece of cloth which I supposed was the Monarchist flag. Franco seemed to shake out crumbs from it on to the multitude below. I thought – Well, for God's sake, yes, feed your people. Franco kept on bending down and kissing the flag; then straightening and jerking his arm up. I thought – Well, indeed, what do babies in the crowd want from their mothers? To be told that it is acceptable to have things stuck up their behinds?

Walburga was shouting and yelling and jerking her arm up. I thought – What did her Nazi lover do: pour boiling castor oil up her behind?

The next speaker was Queipo de Llano: he was a tall stringy figure with limbs and a face that seemed to belong to a corpse: he was the man on the meat-hook, the metal going up through his throat. When he spoke it was evident that he was drunk; he tottered and swayed; his words got stuck at the back of his throat; the crowd laughed and cheered. When he embraced the flag he almost did manage to project himself over the balcony; General Franco stepped forward to restrain him. I thought – Perhaps the two of them will have a tug-of-war over the flag – as babies might do over a substitute mother. And in the meantime more and more prisoners will be being shot in the streets – for the feeding of the multitude. Queipo de Llano was indeed like Don Quixote: a puppet trying to jerk at its own strings. And then the multitude could laugh, as people were killed in the streets.

Walburga laughed and cheered. I thought – Her Spanish fiancé, the one that disappeared, was he hung up on a cross, before he could make love?

The third speaker I had not heard of before: he was a slight figure with an eye-patch and only one arm: he wore a fore-and-aft military cap and had close-cropped hair; his face was curiously beautiful, like a skull inlaid with jewels. He came to the edge of the balcony and looked over at the crowd. I thought – But of course, all these powerful people are not so much kings as victims themselves: this one with so many bits of him shot away – what a business to keep him alive! – he is the man kept in a cage on the wall of a municipal building. When he started shouting it was even possible for me with my limited Spanish to understand what he was saying because he used such simple slogans: the crowd shouted these back to him as if they were giving responses to versicles in a church. He shouted 'Down with Socialists! Down with Intellectuals! Down with the Reds!' He waited for the crowd to give him back his echo. Then – 'Down with Freemasons! Down with Jews!' I thought – But I might be the only Jew in Seville! This is ridiculous. Then he shouted 'Long live the Flag! Long live Spain!' He was a small dapper figure screaming and yelling as if from his cage. Then – 'Long live Death!' This got the biggest response of all from the crowd. I thought – Well, of course, this poor mutilated man, it is understandable that he wants death. Then – But have not I, at times, as if I were part of this crowd, said that I wanted death?

Walburga was pushing her hips forward and shouting 'Long live Death!'

I thought – Well, indeed, there might be hope for the world after all with all these Christians screaming and asking for death.

I was carrying my pistol in a pocket of my white overalls. I thought – So I might give them what they want, these terrible people: then – But why should I: babies can't always be given what they want –

– And besides, it looks as if they'll get it for themselves.

– And have I not said that Jews should be able to stay alive on some quite different level?

Soon after this ceremony in the square it was reported that the road to the north had indeed been opened: the armies of General Franco and General Mola had met. Walburga could now in theory make her way to her ex-fiancé's family in San Sebastian. But she seemed reluctant to do this. She came and sat on my bed. She examined my wounded foot. I said 'It's better now.' She said 'We have to make sure.' I thought – She does not want to go to the north because she thinks she may have to leave me.

– But what is it that in fact I want to do: on any level?

One evening Walburga came back from a visit to Queipo de Llano's headquarters and she shot at me glances that were almost coquettish from beneath her pale lashes, from her somewhat nondescript eyes.

She said 'You know what I would like to do?'

I said 'What?'

'I have a plan.'

When Walburga leaned and put her face close to mine there was an impression of something slightly ill.

She said 'We could run a first-aid station, you and I. Or even a small hospital. You with your medical training and I with mine.'

I said 'You've had medical training?'

She said 'I did a first-aid course in nineteen thirty-two when there was the threat of a Communist take-over in Germany.'

I said 'There was the threat of a Communist take-over in Germany?'

I thought – I am talking like my mother.

She said 'It looks as if there'll still be fighting in the north. Then that would be a way of our staying together!'

I thought – Yes, at least in the north I will be nearer home –

– But what do I mean by 'home'?

I said 'If we ran a hospital, would we be allowed to take in prisoners?'

Walburga said 'You and your prisoners!' She put her arms around me. She said 'For you, I promise, we will take in any number of silly old prisoners!'

I wondered – What is this thing I have about prisoners?

Heinrich returned from his expedition to the front. When he came to see me he was not calm and controlled as he usually was; there was some heat inside him; a glow like that of phosphorus. He said almost immediately 'Can we make love?' He did not usually say this. I told him that I had my period. This seemed almost to fan the slow fire inside him; he said this did not matter; we must make love. I thought – He is like this because he has been at the fighting? I mean, because – do I really mean this? – that he has a taste for blood? I agreed that we could make love. I suppose it would not have been in my interests not to – I might depend on Heinrich to help to get me to the north. But there seemed to be more to it than this: is there not always! Perhaps I felt – All right, you have been fighting: do you think that I, as Queen of the Amazons, will stand back from my own blood? Or is there just something catching about Heinrich's sort of desire? Anyway, this was the first time with Heinrich that I enoyed making love: perhaps it was the first time with anyone that I had made this sort of love – I mean what might be called an animal sort of love, except that animals do not in fact behave like this: how briefly and bumpingly do animals make love! Like people trying to tie up shoelaces in the rain. Animals, of course, do make love when the female is on heat, but this is when she can conceive. When it is as if a human female is on heat she does not conceive; is this why there has been a taboo on this timing of love? Yet in the human way of dissembling about taboos, we call an animal form of love this open-mouthed, piss-licking, savaging sort of love. Well, humans are the only species that kill for pleasure, aren't they? So of course they might get pleasure from this sort of love! There is that question that is supposed to strike terror into men's hearts: 'Would you drink from a cup of a woman's menstrual blood?' But as we, you and I, have so often said 'What scares humans is not what is too little, but too much.'

Heinrich and I lay on the bed while the light from criss-crossed shutters made patterns on our bodies like a grid, a riddle, on which we had perhaps been burned –

– The riddle being: what is salvation, and what is damnation, in the tasting of blood?

– If I am Penthesilia, Queen of the Amazons, should I not kill Heinrich, since it is probable that he is a Nazi?

– Or if I don't believe this, then what am I doing here?

After a time Heinrich said 'They shot a lot of people in Badajoz.'

I said 'They've been shooting a lot of people here.'

He said 'No, but it was different in Badajoz.'

I thought – Why, because you were part of it?

He said 'People enjoyed it.'

I said 'They enjoy it here.'

He said 'Why are people like this? It was like seeing how many rabbits you can get before they go down their holes: like clearing all the pieces off a board to win a game.'

I said 'Then if you saw this, couldn't you stop?'

He said 'Yes, I can stop.'

I thought – But it might be to get people to say this sort of thing that I am here?

Walburga collected equipment for the first-aid station that she hoped to set up in the north: she found two ex-novices from a nunnery who had been trained as nurses. I thought – Well, I can always find a way to leave her in the north. Then – But if there are other things to do than to kill, the place to do them might still be in the camp of the enemy?

Walburga had received a bundle of English newspapers sent to her from Gibraltar: in one of them was the news of the fighting – what the paper called a 'massacre' – at Badajoz. There had been more than a thousand people shot in the bullring; many of them had been women and children; the ground had run with blood.

Walburga, who was reading another newspaper, said 'Look what the Communists are doing to each other in Russia!'

I said 'Look what the Fascists are doing in Badajoz!'

Walburga looked over my shoulder. She said 'That's Communist propaganda.'

I said 'Oh but I believe, you see, what they are doing to each other in Russia!'

Looking over Walburga's shoulder I read that in Moscow there had been the opening of the trial of Zinoviev and Kamenev who had once been two of Stalin's closest colleagues. They were accused of plotting to murder Stalin; they had both pleaded guilty and confessed. In the dock it did not seem that they had been coerced or maltreated: the reporter did not know what to make of this. He wondered – In whose interests could it be for Stalin's colleagues to say publicly that they had plotted to murder Stalin if they had not? How could it be in Stalin's interest to publicise this absurd comment on his administration if it were not true! The reporter concluded that the evidence probably had to be accepted as it stood, because nothing else made sense.

I said 'But when has politics ever made sense? Of course people want to make sacrifices for what is stronger than themselves: of course the Party seems stronger to those who love it: and if the Party needs scapegoats – what is more demanding than death?'

Walburga said 'Rubbish!'

I said 'But you yourself stood in that square and shouted "Long live Death!"'

Walburga began to blush.

I thought – But if I go on like this, might I not be colluding in my own death?

Just before we started out for the north, Walburga made a point of going to Mass: this was in one of the side-chapels of the cathedral. I went with her: I thought – Should I not check up on the customs of this strange tribe? Above the altar was a painting of the Assumption of the Virgin Mary: I could not remember what this event was supposed to imply – had the Virgin never died; had she been whisked up in a cloud on her way to burial; was there just, as there had been before, an empty tomb? The ceremony of the unfurling of the flag had been on the feast of the Assumption of the Blessed Virgin Mary. I wondered – So is that nicely painted piece of cloth a virgin-mother substitute: is that being whisked up to heaven? Walburga knelt at the altar-rail and looked up with such adoring, beseeching eyes. When the wafer was put on her tongue she clasped her stomach as if she were swallowing some quite painless hook. I thought – It is symbols that have become trapped in the cages of our minds; it is they, and not the killings, that should be out in the streets.

When the time came for us to leave Seville it was decided that we should go by train: the line was said to be clear up to Burgos in the north. We packed the first-aid equipment that Walburga had collected: we waited with our two Spanish nurses. I wondered – But now, in this senseless situation, what is my sort of faith –

– I am still on some sort of hook: there is a line outside on which I walk as if on a tightrope –

– All this is a patterning like gravity?

On our journey to the north there were delays and breakdowns on the train: we were in a compartment with civilians who wore their smartest clothes to show that they were not workers. At first there was a lot of talk but then in the heat of the day it dwindled: we were stuck on an embankment above a dry and dusty plain. The talk consisted of the sort of rumours that there had been in Seville: Madrid was about to surrender; a troopship containing Russian soldiers had been sunk off the east coast; the socialist President of the Republic had caught a venereal disease from a monkey. I thought – Surely at some stage people realise that what they believe is what they want to believe –

– Or is this too terrifying, if one is stuck up like a target on a dry and dusty shooting-range.

Walburga said 'General Queipo de Llano has promised that within a week he will be drinking a bottle of port in his club in Madrid!'

A man in a white suit said 'He will certainly enjoy a bottle of port in his club in Madrid!'

People rocked with laughter. I thought – This is ridiculous.

We were told to get out of the train at a place called Caceres: this was 150 miles north of Seville, but no more than a third of the way up Spain. It appeared that the line was, after all, not yet clear to the north; the armies of the south had turned east to march upon Madrid. But General Franco himself, we were told, was going to make his headquarters in Caceres. As Walburga and I made our way on foot from the railway station into the town, I thought – Dear God, but what is this patterning I am involved in: I will now be literally in a headquarters of the camp of the enemy!

General Franco in fact came past us in a car from the airfield while we were walking with our baggage on a handcart. He was a neat figure like one of those seated toys that are held steady by spikes up their arses. We were like refugees. I thought – Why do refugees imagine that there is nothing they can do?

The centre of Caceres was an old walled town; there were steps up to a ceremonial gate; armed guards stood on the threshold. General Franco had set up his headquarters within the old town: Walburga was told that we could have accommodation there too.

I thought – When Judith felt that she was involved in some patterning, would she not sometimes have wished to be simply a refugee?

The old town of Caceres consisted of austere and beautiful small fortress-palaces set close together on a hill. They had been built at a time when Caceres was in the forefront of the battles of Christians against the Moors. Now the élite troops of the Christian General Franco were Moors.

I thought – But what difference does it make if the symbols are out in the streets; what is fidelity, what is betrayal; for someone on a tightrope above them, what is gravity?

– Where is the pole by which one balances: which tells the left hand what the right hand is doing?

Walburga and I were given rooms in a sixteenth-century building, part of which was the outside wall: we were told that we could set up our first-aid station here for the time being. I said to Walburga 'But now we will not be able to get to the north!' Walburga said 'I promise I will get you home!' She put her arms around me and her head against my neck. I thought – But have I not told her that I have no home –

– That I am a Wandering Jew?

Walburga and I were told that this golden-stone house in which we lodged was on the site of what had been, centuries ago, the chapter-house of the founders of the Order of Santiago – a group of knights in the Middle Ages whose task had been to protect pilgrims on their way to Santiago de Compostela.

This meant very little to me at the time. I thought just – Knights, I suppose, are like pilgrims, like Jews: they are not supposed to have an earthly home.

Then – What was that story about the Seven Just Jews that my father used to tell me, in whose hands is supposed to reside the preservation of the world –

– They would not have a home!

I do not imagine I was making much sense at this time. I had been ill. When I was not indulging in fantasy, I was apt to become frightened.

I thought – This is what happens when you set yourself up on a tightrope?

– Oh gravity, what big claws you've got!

Walburga and I set out our beds and hospital equipment in a cool, vaulted room; at first no casualties came to us. I went for walks between the austere, golden-stone walls of the palaces of Caceres; the sun made shadows with the sharpness of knives. I thought – A tightrope-walker is one of those fakirs who tread on knives –

– What might it mean that one should try to love one's enemies?

Then – How on earth did they think they were helping those pilgrims to Santiago, those knights 500 miles away in Caceres?

There was an afternoon when I came back from my walk and found Walburga in my room; she was sitting on my bed; she had opened my haversack and was holding a bundle of letters in her hand. Many of these letters were from you. Oh yes, I carried with me the letters I had had from you – *mon petit pèlerin avec la tache humide*! Walburga seemed stricken: she hardly looked up as I came in. I thought – Well now, will she not have to betray me? She will have found out that I have been a Communist: she knows I am a Jew: and so what am I up to in the camp of the Assyrians? I took the letters from her hand. I thought – But she has not found my gun?

Walburga said 'I'm so sorry!'

I said 'What are you sorry about?'

She said 'I know I shouldn't have done this! Will you ever forgive me?'

When I put my letters back in my haversack I felt, and found, my gun.

Walburga said 'Who is this person you are in love with in England?'

I thought – Who indeed is this person I am in love with in England!

She said 'I'm so terribly in love with you, you know.'

I thought I might say – Yes, I know.

Then – In love, you only know what you want to know; you will not have noticed what it does not suit you to know?

I took out again from my haversack one of your letters. It was the one about everything being connected to everything else: how what is happening to a particle here affects what is happening to a particle there, once they have been together.

Walburga said 'I have never known anything like this! It tears you to pieces.'

I said 'Then I'm sorry too.'

She said 'What have you got to be sorry for? You are an angel. Without you, I do not know what would have become of me.'

I thought – Then that's all right.

The old town of Caceres gradually filled with the personnel and paraphernalia of a headquarters staff: more Germans arrived; Italian pilots and technicians established themselves at the airfield just outside the town. A few casualties came to our first-aid station suffering from dysentery; there were a few officers who had been wounded in the fighting on the road to Madrid. We worked under a Spanish doctor who was part of Franco's entourage. But we were sent few ordinary soldiers, no Moors, and of course no prisoners.

I thought – This obsession I have about the tending of prisoners: is it just that the killing of prisoners is the part of the fighting that I have seen?

– Or like the Knights of the Order of Santiago, I have to justify why I am here?

Walburga did not speak to me again about the letters that she had read. I thought – Is it love, gravity –
– Which connects everything to everything else?

There was a day when the usual comings and going in the town increased dramatically: it was said that high-up dignitaries were due to arrive from Germany – possibly Goering or Goebbels or even Hitler himself (such are rumours in wartime) – to give a blessing to Franco. So squads of soldiers in baggy trousers rehearsed in the small square in front of the headquarters palace: men in blue shirts practised flinging their arms up in salutes as if they were having arrows stuck up their behinds. I thought – Oh well, I can lurk in the shadows of the square; imagine myself on a knife-edge; imagine myself with a knife –
– Then, when the high-up dignitaries arrive, I can leap out from my shadow, down from my tightrope, my knife or my pistol in my hand, and say –
– No, not say; just shoot; one or two in the back of the head; so that their faces go down on to the pavement as if they were already on their way to hell, and will not come round the universe again –
– Then blow my own brains out –
– But am I not supposed to be operating on some quite different level?

Walburga was told that the high-up dignitaries were two colonels from the German and Italian intelligence services: they were coming to assure General Franco, yes, that from now on he would be being supported officially by Germany and Italy. When the two dignitaries arrived by car I did not in fact get into the square in front of the headquarters until just after they had arrived: they were figures in dark-grey and light-grey uniforms disappearing up the steps of the headquarters palace. I thought – Oh hard luck, Judith! Then – I am behaving as if all this were some schoolgirls' game of hockey. Then – But what on earth are the connections between fantasy and reality –
– If I do not try to make some gesture now, is not everything I have been doing here not only ridiculous but evil?
– There is no reason why it should not be ridiculous –
– But evil?

Walburga had become excited when the German and Italian colonels had arrived: she went about singing snatches of Wagner's *Götterdämmerung*. I thought – Well, for God's sake, in *Götterdämmerung* the whole bloody Noah's Ark goes to the bottom of the river –

– What more could a would-be Judith hope for than that?

Walburga said 'The war will soon be over! And then we will go home together.'

I said 'I've told you I can't go home. I haven't got a passport.'

She said 'Oh we will be able to get you papers!'

I thought – Who are 'we'? Then – But how can you not want to know about me what in the end you will have to know –

– It cannot always be easier not to know what is happening!

There was an evening when there was to be a reception in honour of the German and Italian colonels: Walburga had been invited. I dreamed that I might get her to get me invited so that then at last I could march up on to the steps of a dais and pull out my gun –

But did I imagine that this was reality?

Walburga said 'What are you wearing?'

I said 'What am I wearing for what?'

She said 'This reception.' Then – 'Of course you're coming!'

I thought I might say – Well, I need something loose, you see, in which to hide my pistol.

– But indeed has it not been bizarre how events seem to have conspired to make this pattern!

The reception took place in the fortress-palace that was the Nationalist headquarters. There was a doorway with a coat of arms above it: soldiers with rifles stood on the steps. I had in fact put my pistol in a handbag that Walburga had lent me: this seemed to be the least I could do: I hardly believed, I suppose, that I would use it. I thought – And if I am searched, I may be arrested, and that will be the end of my predicament. No one stopped or searched me. Inside there was an arcade like a cloister round a central courtyard with a fountain: the dignitaries and special guests were in a room just off the cloister. I was wearing a plain black dress that Walburga had procured for me: I thought – Oh well, they are always in mourning for something or other in Spain. In the cloisters there were men in white gloves coming round with glasses of champagne. I thought – Perhaps after all, at the last moment, Walburga will come to her senses and denounce me; and then I will be shot, which after all is what at one time I thought I wanted.

Walburga said 'Shall we try to get ourselves introduced to the General?'

I thought – This is ridiculous: what reality do I want; do I trust?

I began to have a feeling that this was the sort of scene in which I had been before (this is some trick of the brain? some unit of memory splitting? nothing to do with two of those particles which once they have been together are in some sense always connected – !). I mean, I asked myself these questions then: I ask you them now. I imagined that I was in some scene like that in the courtyard of that castle: a mountain path with a stone, a gateway, a lion, a spider –

I said to Walburga 'Who is that man: the one who is talking to the General?'

She said 'Why do you ask?'

I said 'I feel I might know him.'

I thought – Of course I don't know him!

She said 'I think he came with the German colonel.'

I thought – It is just that one has such imaginings when things seem to be happening on a different level.

Walburga and I went into the high vaulted room in which the dignitaries were standing not quite on a dais. Walburga went ahead: I stayed by the door. The people in the room were of a kind that was particularly hateful to me: I mean, they were men as if with arrows stuck into them but with no air coming out; no water, no fire, nothing; just solid bodies in uniform punctured but immune and distended. The room was like some wound in which poison was pulsating. I thought – Well, what does one do: keep the pus in; squirt it out? Might it not indeed be easier in the end to do what Jews have so often done in such circumstances: put the gun to their own heads –

A man had come up to me where I was standing; he was bowing and clicking his heels. He was the large florid-faced man I had seen talking with Franco: he had combed-back hair; he wore a well-cut pale grey suit: I thought – Oh yes, he would be one of the entourage of the German colonel. He said to me in German 'What are you doing here?' I thought – I both know him and don't know him. Then he said 'Looking down on us like an exterminating angel!'

I said 'How did you know I was German?'

He said 'Your fame has travelled with you, you see.'

I said 'What fame?'

He said 'You cross deserts; you drive boats between Scylla and Charybdis; you are a friend of the beautiful Walburga!'

He had put out an arm as if to guide me further into the room – towards where there was a group of high-up dignitaries. I thought – Dear God, you want me to be put to the test?

Then – All right, whatever happens happens.

Then the German man said 'When was the last time you saw Trixie?'

I thought – When was the last time I saw Trixie?

Then – Dear God, this is the test?

– I am alive: it is not my business who might be dead –

– All this has been going on on quite a different level?

I had stopped. The man had moved slightly ahead of me. He now turned and looked down on me. He had a huge, somewhat flat face like the façade of a building with lighted windows.

I said 'Who are you?'

He said 'I'm Trixie's husband.'

I said 'Trixie's husband.'

He said 'Yes.'

I said 'How did you know who I was?'

He said 'Trixie of course has often spoken of you. She has a photograph of you on her desk.'

I thought – Was Trixie's husband not a Nazi? Was he something in the Foreign Office? I have not seen Trixie for – how many years.

Then I found myself saying – 'Trixie and I used to go on expeditions to Kleist's grave.'

He said 'Yes, I know about that.' Then – 'And you were all three going to go on your separate journeys round the world; and then into the Garden of Eden again by the back way.'

I felt that I was going to cry. The man's face seemed to be dissolving so that I could see right through its façade into whatever was going on in quiet rooms behind.

He said 'Trixie has a message for you.'

I said 'What?'

He said 'She tried to get hold of you, but we didn't know where you were. And now you turn up here.'

I said 'What is the message?'

He said 'Bruno is all right.'

I said 'Bruno is all right?'

He said 'Yes.'

I said 'How is he all right?'

He said 'He was in prison for a time, but now he is not.'

I said 'Did Trixie help get him out? Did you?'

He said 'I don't think one asks that sort of question.'

I said 'No, I don't think one asks that sort of question.'

He said 'He is in England.'

I said 'In England!'

I thought – But I cannot bear this: is it this that is not too little but too much?

The man said 'I have to go away tomorrow. Will you be all right?'

I said 'Yes, I'll be all right.'

He said 'I had no idea, of course, before I came, that I would find you here.'

I said 'You have no idea how important this has been for me. It is meeting you now, here, that has made me feel that I will be all right.'

He said 'You know, don't you, that each of us now has to some extent the other in their power.'

I said 'Yes.'

He said 'Trixie loved you very much.'

I said 'And I love Trixie very much.'

The man looked down. It seemed that he might be looking at my handbag, which I was clutching against my middle. He said 'I don't ask you what you think you are doing here.'

I said 'I am doing nothing that would be of interest to anyone else here.'

He said 'I will give your love to Trixie.'

I said 'And give it to yourself too.'

VII   6: Max

Well, here is another fantasy: how, in a latter-day catastrophe or deluge, might it happen for oneself and for those whom one cares about to become the denizens of some Noah's Ark?

This question is more to do with reality in these days of the Bomb: but at the time about which we are writing such questions were no less haunting, if more indistinct – how can an individual stay sane in an insane society? If he opts out, in relation to what does he stay sane?

I had come to Spain partly in deference to the tradition that young men go to war to escape from dead-ends at home: in war either one becomes literally dead or there is the chance of the feeling – Look! I have come through! At home I had come to dead-ends in my work and in my relationship with Caroline; both, however much at the heart of things, seemed trivial; but then, what did not? I imagined – Matters of life and death in war should not seem trivial! But then, in Barcelona, it seemed that they did.

In Barcelona the battle against the rebel generals had been won quickly; the task was then seen as being to establish the workers' revolution. But in practice this was demonstrated by workers splitting themselves into separate containments, from each of which people could look out contemptuously at those in others. But this was what, it seemed to me, humans had always been doing – in their commitments to tribes, armies, classes, nations – so where was the revolution? Workers were just repeating patterns that humans seemed to feel were required in order to gain and maintain social identity.

There were the UGT, the CNT, the PSUC, the POUM – socialists, anarchists, Stalinists, Trotskyites. These took over large hotels in the centre of Barcelona; they barricaded themselves in; they made sorties, strutting and shouting. They were like those aristocratic families in towns in Italy in the fourteenth century who built for themselves taller and taller towers; after a time the towers overbalanced and fell. It was true that in Barcelona the anarchists were in the majority and thus in some sense in power; but in what sense could anarchists in fact be in power? They repudiated the whole concept of political power; they recognised its triviality and self-destructiveness. But then, in what practical sense could a revolution be said to be being established?

Beyond my recognition that I was coming to Spain to escape from dead-ends at home there had been my genuine interest in anarchism. I had thought – Of course anarchists are right to see the self-destructiveness and trivialities of power, but might there not be some level from which it would be possible not contemptuously to look down? Anarchists had seen themselves as the destroyers of moribund patterns and institutions; they had not seen it as their task to specify what new actual patterns should take their place. This, they felt, was the task of forces of nature – which would be free to perform their task once humans were freed from their cages. Here in Barcelona all this seemed to be being put to the test. But the questions remained: what in fact happens when humans are freed from their traps? What indeed are the ways in which nature takes its course!

I thought – Might not humans be able to reach a level from which they could look down on the violences of so-called 'nature'.

When I came to Barcelona bringing Caroline with me I had explained to myself – All right, we know, do we not, the failure of young men in fact to get away from what they have left behind at home by going to war: they carry around with them in their heads the images of their upbringing, loved ones, mothers: there is enough about this in poems, in legends, God knows; in fact, young men seem to become more than ever in thrall to their loved ones when they are away at war; it seems to be just because of their dreams of them that they justify killing and dying. Now I had brought Caroline with me and so might there be an argument to justify this –

– All right, you carry your dead-ends, your loved ones, with you to war; then might there not be some dying or killing of old dreams on a proper level?

– This might be the level from which one would not mind seeing nature taking its course?

I do not know exactly when I began to take seriously the idea of a pilgrimage to Santiago de Compostela; I had read of this in books at home: it seemed to me that in the Middle Ages pilgrimages had been used as sensible substitutes for war – I mean, they had been non-destructive ways for people to get away from dead-ends. And there had indeed been dangers in those days attendant on going on a pilgrimage: pilgrims, unarmed, were often set upon by robbers; they were taken hostage by infidels and had bits chopped off them and sent with demands for ransom to loved ones; and sometimes the loved ones had paid, and sometimes they had not. There had been, at a place called Caceres, I had read, an order of knights whose vocation was the protection of pilgrims to Santiago. In all this there was the pattern of a person being put to the test – of choosing that he or she should be put to the test – which is what I had begun to think was anyway at the back of the pattern of young men rushing off to war: this was basically the desire to break up oneself and the ruts around one so that something new might grow. People who did the actual fighting had always, it seemed, seen war as mainly a personal test: feelings about the enemy were tempered by the knowledge that they too – the enemy fighters – were involved in a personal test: it was only the people on both sides at home – the politicians and generals – who seemed to need to hate the enemy and thought that the point of war was just that the enemy should be destroyed and nothing new need grow. But it was just these people that one was getting away from when one went away to war. And so on a pilgrimage one would be choosing just to be exposed; it would be this that would be being put to the test.

In Paris, Barcelona, I had made love with Caroline. I thought – Once, twice, and am I freed? This is what is called letting nature go its own way?

In the café in Barcelona Caroline had sat on the bearded man's knee. I had thought – What do you do about what might be jealousy; this is part of the test?

Oh yes, and in Barcelona there was the workers' revolution; the groups strutting in the streets: they looked at each other with contempt: how to deal with this – this would be part of the test.

The Russian man in the café had told me that I could go all the way across Spain to Santiago in a taxi if I liked: there was no front line: factions in the countryside had barricaded themselves into towns and villages just as they had barricaded themselves into hotels in the centre of Barcelona. He had suggested that there was no real fighting; no real war –

– And yet the bearded man had a column going out in the general direction of Santiago!

So what a chance not only for a journalist to find a story away from dead-ends –

– But to see what the nature of this test might really be like?

And by the end of the evening I was also, of course, very drunk. The man with the beard had produced bottles of whisky: Caroline had come and sat on my knee.

I said to Caroline 'You will be all right?'

Caroline said 'It's to you I should be saying, you will be all right!'

There is usually a genuine excitement too, I suppose, about going off to war: the feeling – Now I will really be free, with no commitments except those of putting one foot in front of another –

– As if on a tightrope: in co-operation with gravity?

I do not remember much about getting from the café to the place where the trucks for the expedition were drawn up. I remember being given some overalls by the man with bandoliers who had been put in charge of me; also a blanket, and a couple of mess-tins and an old and rather rusty rifle. I wondered if I should have the rifle since I was supposed to be a journalist: but then – How grand to have a rifle! I remember going to the hotel where I had been with Caroline and picking up some soap and a razor and a toothbrush. I wondered – Might it not be too bourgeois to have soap and a razor and a toothbrush: or might in fact these be my credentials as a journalist? Then it seemed that I just had to find somewhere to lie down. While I was saying goodbye to Caroline I both had tears in my eyes and was wondering if I were going to be sick. I thought – If only she had not made friends with the man with the black beard! But then I would not be able to be lying down in the back of this truck.

I managed to sleep through much of the night, though after the truck started we were shaken about like dice. Bits of metal hit against my shoulders, hips, head. At moments when I woke I thought – Dear God, old patterns are surely being broken up! I tried to reassure myself – Those people did say, didn't they, that we would be back in Barcelona in two or three days?

When I awoke properly from whatever strange journeys I had been on in my dreams (well, what does happen in dreams? those odd encounters, conjunctions, recognitions; they are like messages scattered on the wind) – when I awoke properly the truck was stationary and there was pain in my head and a terrible dryness in my throat and mouth; it seemed as if I had been dragged face-down across a desert. I thought – Or I am a fish on the bottom of some terrible fisherman's boat; the air is too dry to breathe; I must get hold of some water or I will die. For a time I felt too paralysed to put my head out from beneath the blanket that was covering me: I thought – Dear God, why did I get so drunk last night; where have I come to; do I really want to die? Then the pain in my head was such that I had to get water. When I did put my head out from the blanket it appeared that I was now the only person in the back of the truck; there had been many during the night. We must have travelled a long way. I crawled to the end of the truck and lifted a flap and looked out on to the light; on to a strange landscape.

We were in what seemed to be a square in a village; the houses round the square were like hovels or only half built; there was one completed structure on the right which seemed to be an official building. Ahead of me there was an open side to the square beyond which the ground fell away so that it was as if the village was on table-land at the top of a mountain. On the left, at the opposite side of the square to the official-looking building, there was an armoured car; a group of men in overalls were standing round it carrying rifles: it seemed that these must be the people who had been with me in the trucks during the night. The armoured car was made of sheets of metal like stuff hung on a clothes-line; it had a turret with a gun sticking out like the spout of a kettle. There was a man in military uniform and with a large moustache half out of the lid of this structure; he was like someone being boiled; he was shouting and gesticulating at the men in blue overalls and they were shouting and gesticulating back at him. Beside the truck out of which I was looking there were four or five trucks which presumably belonged to our column; these were drawn up at the end of the square opposite to where the ground fell away. The armoured car had letters painted on it in white which were different from the letters which were painted on our trucks. I thought – I suppose everyone is having an argument about these letters. Then – But I must drink some water.

At one side of the square just in front of the official-looking building there was what looked like a well. I was almost sure it was a well – it was a circular stone structure with a canopy of the kind which might contain a windlass and a rope; why should it be a mirage? I got out of the truck and started to move across the dusty square. Two men wearing uniform jackets and brown corduroy trousers came out of the official-looking building; they carried between them what seemed to be a dead body; they took the body to the well and leaned it against the rim. I thought – Dear God, they are going to put the body down the well before I can have a drink: isn't there a nursery rhyme about this? I got to the well myself and there was a rope going down so that it seemed that there should be a bucket on the end of it; in order to see better I put my head down below the level of the rim; then I thought I was going to be sick – so what would be the difference if they threw the body down the well? I began to turn the handle of the windlass: the man with the large moustache on the armoured car began to shout at the two men with corduroy trousers who were by the well and they began to shout back at him: I thought – With any luck, this argument will go on for two or three minutes so that I will have had time to have a drink. Then I saw that the bucket that I was raising had holes in it; water was pouring out; I would have to begin again and raise the bucket more quickly. The two men in corduroy trousers had lifted the dead body so that it teetered on the rim of the well. Have you ever tried to fill an empty bucket with water at the bottom of a well? You have to drop it upturned, at an angle, or else it will not fill. I was bouncing the bucket up and down; the two men in corduroy trousers seemed about to push the body over: I thought – But if they do it may knock the bucket off the end of the rope and then I will never to able to have a drink! Or perhaps it might make a splash that will help fill the bucket with water. Then – This is ridiculous. I did manage to drop the bucket so that it filled. I was pulling it up hand over hand and as I pulled the men in corduroy trousers pushed the body down the well. But because I was pulling the bucket up so fast it was swinging from side to side and the body missed it. I thought – Well, thank you, thank you. Some of the men in overalls were now running towards the well from across the square; I thought that they might still try to stop me having my drink. I had got the bucket to the top and was lifting it to my face when there was an enormous explosion from the direction of the armoured car. Water was still pouring out of the holes in the bucket and I could raise it above my head and so get one of the streams of water pouring into my mouth. I thought – Well, yes, indeed, what a chancy business! Like walking on a tightrope across Niagara. The men in overalls who had been running across the square had dropped to the ground when there had been the explosion from the armoured car, so I was able to finish my drink: I wanted to say again – Thank you. After a time I was able to put the bucket down on the rim of the well and scoop up what was left of the water with my hands. The two men in corduroy trousers were squatting behind the rim of the well. The man with the moustache who was sticking up out of the armoured car was making a yelling noise as if he had been injured. I thought – Well, here we are: what is the style of this strange country?

We were in this village which seemed to be on the top of a hill. There did not appear to be any people in the village except the men in overalls and the men in corduroy trousers and the man in the armoured car and myself. There were some pigs nosing about in the rubble; a dog or two in the shadows. I thought – Oh well, I can construct from these data what has happened. The men in corduroy trousers are with the man in the armoured car and they were in the village before us and cleared it or shot the inhabitants and they were putting bodies down the well perhaps to poison it, to make the village uninhabitable; then we arrived in our trucks and wanted to inhabit it; then the gun in the armoured car went off and it seems to have injured the man in the turret – but I have had my drink of water.

Then – There might have been bodies already down the well?

– What on earth was the point of that nursery rhyme!

The attention of the people in blue overalls had now turned from the well to whatever it was that had happened in the armoured car. The man with the big moustache seemed to by trying to heave himself out of the turret; some of the men in blue overalls had climbed up and were helping him; there was a faint screaming noise coming from further inside the armoured car. I thought – This is like a grandfather clock winding itself up to strike: hickory dickory dock –

– It is to show how ridiculous human behaviour is, that is the point of nursery rhymes?

I thought that I would go and sit in the shade at the corner of the square. I was glad that I had had a drink of water even if there had been bodies down the well. What might I die of: typhoid? Dysentery? When I looked in at the entrance to the official-looking building I saw that there were, yes, what seemed to be corpses laid out in rows; I did not want to look too closely; or perhaps I should. I wondered – All right, this has been a personal test: but what happens if one is in the presence of unequivocal evil? I found a place where I could sit at the side of the square. I thought – But what I should like now, would be a drink of wine.

Some of the men in overalls had wine-skins at their belts. I thought – How drunk must I have been last night not to have got a wine-skin at my belt! Then – Oh but should this be what people think about when they are in the presence of evil?

The village square that I was in was surrounded on three sides by the buildings that seemed to have had their tops knocked off by the closeness perhaps of the bright and burning sky. I thought – Perhaps this is the top of that tower that humans were once building up to heaven; but why did the gods confuse their language so that they could not finish it? Perhaps the gods wanted to continue to look down and be entertained by humans playing their games with evil – murder, farce, tragedy – but this is what humans enjoy on their own ground, so why should they have been trying to get to heaven?

The village square was indeed like a stage with the fourth side dropping away to mist and mountains where a god-like audience might sit. I thought – Or is it that humans need gods to justify their own ghastly productions.

– Silence might have been the language that humans had when they were succeeding in building their tower up to heaven?

A man in blue overalls was coming towards me across the square. He carried a wine-skin. He had large dark eyes and a soft mouth. He knelt down in front of me and offered me his wine-skin. I thought – He is an angel. I had a drink of wine. I smiled and nodded and tried to convey to him – You are an angel! He had bright white teeth when he smiled. I thought – He is like a bite that has been taken out of an apple.

Because it was hot, and because I now had had my drink of wine, I half-dozed, half-watched the scene around me, and continued to dream. I thought – Well, it is true, isn't it, that the imagination is liberated from conventional patterns by war: poets write poems; Wittgenstein wrote the *Tractatus* in 1917 while in the trenches –

– People are thus liberated by that temple containing the dismembered bodies of children?

The men around, or on top of, the armoured car were pulling what looked like a body out of the lid. The man with the moustache was lying on his back on the ground and holding his leg as if he were a baby. I thought – Something must have been wrong with the recoil of the gun in the turret: or did the shot go right round the world and hit the people who had fired it in the leg or the back of the head?

There was something that the Englishman in the café in Barcelona had said to me the previous evening. He had said 'Have you heard about this latest theory in physics?'

They were lowering the body from the armoured car.

I thought – But what an almost unimaginable series of coincidences has brought me on this journey!

What the Englishman had said had sparked off an idea I had previously had at Cambridge.

The Englishman had said – Supposing the force that holds the nucleus of an atom together is like the surface tension that holds together a drop of water. Now the accepted view at Cambridge had always been quite different – that the nucleus of an atom was hard like glass, so that even if penetrating particles like neutrons were fired at it then only chips, as it were, would be knocked off: this process could give one information about the composition of a nucleus but there would be no significant release of energy, which could only take place if the nucleus split into something like two halves – in which case the two parts, being of the same electric charge, would indeed fly apart with comparatively enormous force. But the conventional view had been that it was not credible that the forces which held a nucleus together could be overcome in this way; and even in so far as they might be, the energy released would still be on a microcosmic scale unless some way could be found to turn the splitting and release into some form of geometrical progression.

I was sitting at the side of the square with my legs in the hot sun. I had once thought – But why should there not be a form of geometrical progression? I thought now – What I need is a pencil and a piece of paper to try to work on the mathematics. I then realised – I was too drunk last night even to have brought with me a pencil and a piece of paper. Then – But what on earth could I write even if I had them?

The body from the armoured car was being laid out on the ground at the far side of the square. I thought – But what if it is increasingly obvious that the human race does not want to survive?

There had already been experiments in Cambridge of firing neutrons at the nucleus of a heavy atom such as that of uranium: uranium atoms seemed to be inherently unstable: when neutrons were absorbed by them no one seemed quite able to understand what occurred. The nucleus was transmuted, but it was not clear into what. However if, as the Englishman in the café had suggested, an unstable nucleus was held together by no more than a tension like that which held together a drop of water, and it was hit by a neutron, then indeed why should it not split into something like two halves and the two halves fly apart; and had it not already been observed that if one neutron were absorbed by a nucleus then others were apt to be pushed out –

I was sitting in the sun at the side of the square. I was feeling as if my head might split. I had a bad hangover: there were all these ideas like neutrons coming in from outside. I thought – But at least I can go round a corner and be sick.

– If one neutron not only split a nucleus so that the two halves flew apart but also other neutrons were forced out –

– Then why should not these hit the nuclei of the other atoms so that indeed there might be some geometrical progression such as in chemistry is called a 'chain reaction' –

– Until there was a release of enormous energy that either could be controlled –

– Or the human race might be wiped out?

It seemed that, indeed, I would have to be sick. There was the hot sun; the wine that I had drunk. I thought – Perhaps also it will be a relief, being sick, from these ideas exploding in my head like a geometrical progression.

I went round a corner and there were some tiny blue flowers among the stones. I was sick. I thought – Poor tiny blue flowers! Would a god not want to save them, if he were finally sick on to the world?

On the way back to my comfortable corner in the square I looked again into the official-looking building that was like a charnel-house. There were bodies piled up: many had not even been laid out in rows. People look so wrinkled when they are dead: like seeds. There were flies feeding on dried blood. I thought – I do not see why God should spare humans; they are not beautiful enough: let him be sick: but this might feed the seeds?

I sat again at my place at the side of the square. The men in blue overalls and the men in corduroy trousers and the man with the big moustache were now all going off in a procession across the square; they carried the body of the man who seemed to have somehow managed to get himself injured in the armoured car. I thought – He was one of the people who killed the people in the official-looking building?

Then – What might be the terrible play that is being performed on this mountain for the delectation of gods – *Hamlet*? the *Oresteia*? 'Jack and Jill'?

I took another drink from the wine-skin that the man like an angel had left with me. I wondered – But if I have had a vision of the possible ending of the universe –

– Should I not really try to find a pencil and paper to see if the mathematics works?

In the days that followed (it was said that we were waiting for the man with the beard to join us from Barcelona: I thought – Why should the man with the beard join us from Barcelona; is he not with Caroline?) – in the days that followed, the man with the big moustache and the two men in corduroy trousers eventually left the village in their armoured car; we stayed on. We buried some of the bodies that were in the official-looking building; some we threw over a cliff. We began to prepare primitive defenceworks just outside the village but then gave up, because this job was too obviously boring. What did not seem boring for most of my companions was to sit in groups and shout and argue in the shade at the sides of the square.

I sometimes did go looking for a pencil and paper, but it did not seem possible that I would find these in the rubble of the village. I thought – Perhaps it is better if my moments of illumination lead a quiet life of their own in my head.

I lived and ate and slept in a small bare room pockmarked where there had been bullets. There were five or six men with me who had been in the trucks; they spoke amongst themselves in the dialect that I did not understand: when I spoke Spanish they often did not understand me. I thought – Perhaps it is because I live in some sort of silence that these ideas are free to come in and out of my head. Whatever furniture there had been in the hovel had been taken out and burned; we slept on blankets on straw on the ground. It was very hot. I learned from what conversations I could manage what had in fact happened in the village: most of the original villagers had been so-called Fascists and they had killed the Republicans; then some or other group of Republicans had come with their armoured car and had killed the Fascists; then we had come – and so on. I thought – But I know all this; this is indeed the sort of subject of much human entertainment. Every now and then I was caught up by the vision that had occurred to me in the square; some catastrophe might be about to happen; did or did not humans deserve to be wiped out; should I see myself as being in any different position?

In our bare room people gradually became ill with some sort of dysentery; they held their stomachs; they lay with their knees up by their chins. I thought – But they are catching what I should be catching; or do you think that I was made immune by drinking what was probably the contaminated water of the well? We carried our water now from a spring down the hill. After my hangover of the first day I remained quite well. Sometimes I observed my companions watching me as if I might be some Jonah. I tried to remember what happened to Jonah: he was thrown overboard from a ship; he was swallowed by a whale; he was spewed out on to dry land; he sat in the shade of something called a 'gourd'. Well, what was a gourd. As I sat with my legs out in front of me in my corner of the hot square I thought – For God's sake, I need a gourd.

Or – Perhaps it was this seeing things in terms of stories, or of stories about stories, that was the language of the people who were getting their tower up to heaven.

Sometimes I walked round the village from which whoever might have been left alive of the inhabitants seemed to have fled. We caught and ate pigs: the dogs and cats kept to the shadows. There was a church in which a bonfire had been made of the fixtures and fittings. On the stone walls there were frescoes: the largest of these was to do with hell. There were the usual scenes of humans impaled on forks; of humans being piled up like furniture and burned. I thought – What would happen if humans just admitted that this sort of thing gave them pleasure? Then might there not be some proper battle – in the mind – looking down on the question of what might or might not be changed –

– This looking might be a proper pleasure, on another level?

There was a terrible smell in the village: flies with bright green bodies fed like devils off the corpses of goats, horses, cows. We had given up trying to bury the corpses of animals. In the hovels people lay and held their stomachs and writhed. I thought – We have arranged thus to be in hell: to be anywhere else takes too much trouble?

– But those tiny blue flowers like moments of illumination – do they not live in this rubble? Fed by my sick?

Slowly a few old women came back into the village. They took no notice of us and we took little notice of them. They, like the dogs, kept to the shadows.

I thought – An illumination about terror: this would be an illumination about the nature of change?

After a time I did manage to find a pencil and some paper in the rubble of the church; so it seemed that I would now have to make an effort to write something down.

I sat in my comfortable place at the side of the square. I found I did not want to try to do the mathematics concerning the possible end of the universe: I was not up to it; and what would be the point? It might be more profitable to do my job as a war reporter of describing to readers what war was like – here we are sitting in the sun: somewhere or other are dead bodies – ding dong bell pussy's in the well; Jack fell down and broke his crown; down will come baby, cradle and all; and so on.

I looked down at my blank sheet of paper.

One of the men had found a wireless in the village that worked. The wireless had been set up on a window-ledge on the opposite side of the square. It was like an idol in its niche; it poured out a terrible sound like the noises that people might make if they were being tortured or being sick. Sometimes there was music: but even the music seemed designed to cover up shouts of people somewhere behind – the sounds of the universe collapsing into chaos.

This noise besieged my head: it made it difficult for thoughts to come in. I thought – It was such noise that prevented people from getting up to heaven.

There was another idea that had come to me at Cambridge that I was trying to remember –

But then I would wonder – How on earth have I got here? Sitting on the edge of a hot square in Spain; being battered by mad and ghostly yells and music; with almost no communication with the outside world, so that just by this there might be such ideas coming in: by what almost unimaginable series of coincidences –

The noise of the wireless suddenly stopped. The people at the far side of the square had switched it off because they seemed to be about to hold some meeting.

The idea that had come to me in Cambridge, and that was now again coming to me here, was –

How in the course of evolution was it that there had been so many almost unimaginable coincidences? This had always been a problem for biologists – how could a mechanism such as an eye, for instance, that depended on myriad coincidental interactions of parts, be said to be formed out of random mutation and natural selection? Biologists had dealt with this question by saying that once the process had started then the huge amount of time involved and the huge amount of possible chances ensured that indeed there could naturally be evolution by these means – from the production of life out of matter to the production of consciousness out of life. It was physicists who were apt to say – Yes, all right, but what started the whole process; and more importantly, what continues to hold it together: what indeed is this concept of process – why is there order and not simply chaos? It is, indeed, by a process of almost unimaginable coincidences (physicists said) that out of primordial energy even an atom is formed, a molecule is held together; that such a delicate balance of bits and pieces is kept that there is life and the maintenance of life. Of course, if all this is assumed then evolution might follow naturally: it might even be natural if in time consciousness evolved –

– But still, for there to be the process to have the consciousness to say this, what unimaginable coincidences!

There was a dog sniffing at my feet. I was sitting with my pencil and paper on my knee. My paper was blank. I thought – What am I to put down: a hand that is drawing a hand that is drawing itself –

Another idea was coming to me.

It is a fact that this is a universe that has produced consciousness. But do we not also say, we physicists, that it is consciousness that in some way produces the universe: I mean produces what we see of the universe – this or that – and of what else indeed can we say is the universe? I mean – If what happens is in fact ordered by what we observe – by our act of observation – then of course the universe has evolved conscious beings that can observe, or how can it be what it is? What it is is the result of consciousness. I stared at my blank piece of paper. I thought – I am one of those mad people who wake up in the middle of the night and think they have solved the riddle of the universe.

The committee of men at the other side of the square were sitting in a semi-circle underneath the now silent wireless in its niche, their god. Sometimes they glanced across the square at me. I thought – They are discussing me. Then – Of course I think they are discussing me. Then – I must get this straight. I wrote down –

> The universe is such that it produces us who observe:
> We are such that we produce the universe by observing:
> It is thus that what is, is –
> We and the universe are a mutually creating organism.

I thought – Indeed, there is potency in the image of the hand that draws a hand that is drawing itself!

– How many more illuminations can I bear, before I am carried off screaming and yelling –

– Or will there be able to be in the mind some sort of mutation?

I was sure that the group on the other side of the square were talking about me. I thought – They will, of course, want to kill me; there is something monstrous in my head: do not mutations always get killed?

I thought – Let it go now: guard it.

I had in fact made little attempt to make friends with the people in my group: the barrier of language had made this difficult, and anyway it had not seemed that this was what I was here for. I had thought – I want to try to look down on all this objectively. Then, from time to time – But dear God, why should they not want to kill me?

The exceptions to the objects of my attitude were two men whom I found myself singling out in my mind and caring about because they seemed to be in some relationship with me on a level at which I hoped to find myself. One was the man with a soft mouth and huge dark eyes who had given me the wine-skin on the day we had arrived and who had seemed like an angel: the other was a boy who, through his aloofness and attitude of apparent self-absorption, I had seen as being somewhat like myself.

I was sitting in the shade at the side of the square. I felt that I should look once more to see how that illumination was getting on in my head –

If the universe is produced by an observer who asks this question –

And has produced the observer who asks the question –

Would not the required mutation be just the ability to live with this realisation?

Quick! My pencil and paper –

Then – But before there can be the conditions in which such a mutation can live, would there not have to be some sort of catastrophe?

My friend who was like an angel was coming towards me across the square. He was coming from the group of men who were in a semi-circle like a committee. He stood in front of me. I thought – But just a minute! I have one or two more things to write down about the nature of the universe. My pencil hovered above the paper like a bird. It was as if in my head an explosion had left just a white light. I wrote – There should be some Noah's Ark in the mind, if there are to be held the results of all these almost unimaginable coincidences –

– In the mind: in the outside world?

I tried to listen to what my friend like an angel was saying.

Then – But has this not indeed something to do with my other illumination about a potentially universally destructive bomb? It may be something like knowledge of this that may make it possible, necessary even, for the other sort of illumination about the self-creativeness of consciousness to be held: no not even to be held – to take off, like some new species of monstrous but life-giving bird –

It did not seem necessary to write this down.

Then – Oh but indeed there are these coincidences!

My friend who was like an angel seemed to be telling me that my presence was required by the gathering on the other side of the square.

I said 'Just a minute!'

I wanted to write – But the mutation will have to be produced first, or the universe may explode and take any potential mutation along with it.

The man like an angel pulled my arm.

I thought – All right, all right.

– Will it not be a relief for me to have to stop thinking; to deal with the committee across the square.

The committee was what had come to be in charge of our group in the continued absence of the man with the beard. At the head of it were two or three clean-shaven men that I could distinguish from the other members of the group, though I could not easily distinguish them one from the other. Almost the whole group seemed to be assembled at the far side of the square. They sat in a semi-circle beneath the window-ledge on which the wireless was enthroned like a tribal god. I thought – But if they have to keep their god silent in order to hear me speak, then will I not have a chance to produce some order out of chaos?

I sat on the ground in front of them. They watched me. I thought – I could draw patterns in the dust.

One of the clean-shaven men began to talk. He did not talk to me but to the group to whom he was always talking, though he did speak in some sort of Spanish that I could just understand. He said that many of the group could not understand what I was doing with them: could I explain why I should not be treated as a spy?

The boy who I imagined was like me sat slightly apart: the man who was like an angel looked down at the dust. I thought – Oh come on now, how about the children of light being as cunning as the children of darkness!

I said – But of course they knew exactly what I was doing with them! I had come at the invitation of their leader in Barcelona. I was composing reports about the nature of war, of the fight against Fascism; had they not seen me sitting at the side of the square with my pencil and paper on my knee? I spoke in what little Spanish I knew; then I went off into French, even a few Spanish-sounding words in English. They looked at me as if they both did, and did not, understand what I was saying. I said 'In the battle of anarchism against Fascism does not every anarchist have to fight in his own way: what else is anarchism? Anarchism is to do with truth! Each person has his own truth! The evidence for this can now be presented scientifically! They were anarchists, I was an anarchist, we were all anarchists! Long live anarchy!' I mixed in even a bit of German with my primitive Spanish and schoolboy French: what seemed to be effective with my audience was the repetition of words to do with anarchy. I thought – So what a coincidence, indeed, that this word is understandable in almost any language. When I finished, there was silence for a time and then some half-hearted laughter. Then the boy whom I had thought was like me got up and switched on the wireless. Someone patted me on the shoulder. I thought – So it is all right? Then – If all language is gibberish, and I have spoken gibberish, then in some sense I have spoken truly?

Then – Dear God, didn't those disciples after Pentecost talk gibberish, and everyone thought that they understood what they were saying?

– And what they understood, could in no other way have been said?

It was that evening, I think, that a message arrived from the man with the beard in Barcelona; the messenger said that he had been trying to find us for three days, but he had no maps. We said we had no maps. The messenger said we were in the wrong place. We said how could he tell if none of us had any maps? And so on. I thought – People are happy with words just because of the noise; it protects their heads; in silence truth might come in, which is frightening. The message from the man with the beard was that we were to carry out a reconnaissance raid behind the enemy lines – or, rather, we were to find out where were what might be called enemy lines – and then we were to return to Barcelona. There was no message to me from Caroline. I thought – But of course there would be no message to me from Caroline! Then – But I cannot go back to Barcelona, I must go on.

I had not worked out what I might do if the column ever succeeded in going into battle. Since my first night with it the chance of battle had seemed unlikely: I had imagined that we would sit around in the village until the time came to go back to Barcelona. But now – Would I fight, if I wanted to go on? Would I carry my rifle? Or would I just trail along with my pencil and paper? There had always been some part of me that had wanted to fight – to fight and to get it over with, to have the experience of whatever it was by which young men felt they had to be put to the test – to do it just this once and then I might not have to do it again. But after fighting, what? I had never really wanted to go back: I had always wanted to go on. I thought again now – Might it not really be possible in some way to go on a pilgrimage to Santiago de Compostela? Would not this be a test on some quite different level?

There had been a time, yes, when I had thought that it might be worth fighting for anarchism; but there seemed no military way of doing this. In military terms it seemed that Fascism or Communism, being fashioned for imposition, would always win.

On some other level, however –

– A pilgrimage? A bomb?

When the time came for us to get into the trucks I still had not made up my mind what to do if there was any fighting: I thought – Just with this open mind, I imagine coincidences will rise up and guard me? We got into the trucks: I carried my rifle: it seemed silly not to. We set off in the early morning. I do not think I was more frightened than I had been from time to time since we arrived in the village. And it is always pleasant, is it not, on a fine clear morning to be off on some journey. There were still arguments about maps; someone had drawn his own map on a piece of paper. I thought – But this is like the hand drawing a hand drawing itself.

We bumped down the hill from the village; we rattled and shook along rough roads. Sometimes we passed other villages on the tops of hills: sometimes groups of people with rifles and shotguns stopped us in a village and we shouted and gesticulated for a while and then everyone became quiet while people looked at the self-drawn map. We picked up a guide who said he knew where we should be going and he came with us for a time; but then we were shouting and gesticulating at him and we put him down. We stopped in a village in the middle of the day and found food and lay in the shadows of the trucks; we picked up another guide and went more slowly along a wide valley with grey-green mountains in the distance. Towards evening we stopped and were silent. I thought – You mean, this silence is to do with war?

In the valley in which we had stopped there was a slight rise ahead with a gap through which the road went snaking. We got out of our trucks and sat at the side of the road. We smoked. The leaders of the committee gathered around the map. One or two people practised firing their rifles into the air. I thought – Should I practise firing my rifle into the air? Then the members of the committee round the map were shouting and gesticulating and saying that we should not be making so much noise. I thought – I suppose I can always refuse to go on. Then after a time there was a tearing noise in the sky – it was as if the sky were made of paper and were being rent in two – and then a loud crash and a blast of smoke in a field to one side of us. It seemed that we were being shelled.

We had none of us, I think, been shelled before; people ran hither and thither; some ran back to the trucks. The shells were coming from somewhere on our left and going over and landing in the field on our right. We tried to follow the sound with our eyes, as if it were a rainbow.

It seemed to be decided that we should go forward on foot. I thought – Now this is the test? I will have to go on. Or – You think there has been a rainbow?

We set off up the road towards the gap in the ridge ahead; I was towards the back of our group; I carried my rifle: I thought – Oh well, fear is like treading on the rainbow of a tightrope, tra la la. As we approached the gap in the ridge I was afraid that we might come into sight of wherever it was that the shells were coming from on the left; then when we got to the gap there was in front of us a scene that might have been an illustration to a fairy story. There was a rocky landscape and the road winding up into mountains on a spur of which was a castle: the castle was high and square and surrounded by a wall at the corners of which were round turrets: it was the sort of castle in which some ogre might live and a princess be imprisoned. The shells that were being fired were not coming from the area of the castle; they were coming from what seemed to be a village in the distance on our left. We had stopped when we saw the view beyond the ridge; now we spread out and began to run forward. I thought – But it is much too far to the castle! We had not gone far when a machine-gun opened up: I thought – God damn, what am I doing here! Do you know what it is like when a machine-gun fires at you? There are the cracks of the bullets as they pass you by (you would hear nothing if they hit you): then slightly later there are the sounds of the shots as they are fired; this is because bullets travel faster than sound so you hear them as they pass you before you hear the sound of them being fired, which becomes like an echo. I did not know this at the time: for a moment it even seemed that it might be one of our own machine-guns that was firing from behind, over our heads, and was hitting something in front: then I thought just – All this is happening too quickly: indeed there has been some change, flip-over, on to a different level. Then – Dear God, what of your rainbow! Ahead of us there was a hut, or hovel, by the side of the road; it seemed that our aim should be to get quickly to the shelter of the hovel; then I worked out that this was, in fact, where the machine-gun bullets were coming from. I had run on some way towards the hovel by this time; then I was able to get down behind some stones. Most of the people in my group had got down some distance behind me. I thought – Oh dear God, forgive me and pray for me now, and for a time when I will be no longer mad. One of our men behind me was screaming – it seemed that he had been hit in the leg – then I saw that it was the boy whom I had thought was like myself. He was sitting up and holding one leg and rocking backwards and forwards. I thought – Please God, let me never do this sort of thing again! We were in this barren landscape with the castle on its rock ahead of us and the road going up to it like a snake. The machine-gun had stopped firing: the boy was screaming for help. I thought – Well, go and help him, someone, can't you? Then – You mean, me? Then one of the leaders of our group, one of the clean-shaven men, shot him. I mean, this man who was in charge of the boy raised his rifle and aimed at the boy and shot him. I supposed that he wanted to stop him screaming. I thought – Perhaps this is happening, after all, too slowly. Now the clean-shaven man was shouting at me; he seemed to be telling me to go on towards the hovel; he was pointing his rifle at me: I thought – But of course I am not going to go on towards the hovel! Then – But if I don't, he will shoot me. I put my head down towards the ground. There were some tiny stones like crystals; like blue flowers.

I thought – Oh I am Uriah, yes: but that other man, what was his name, how did he get out of his suicide pact?

Then my friend who was like an angel ran up and lay down beside me; he was looking at me and smiling. He had a soft wide mouth and white teeth. The two of us were some way ahead of the others because we had got down behind better stones. Some of the others had got up and were now running back in the direction of the trucks: it seemed that they were being fired on from the village on the left; one or two of them fell; then from the village there were people running as if to cut them off from the trucks. I thought – So what is the difference: you go back, you go on –

– I had imagined, after all, that this would be some quite personal test.

The man who was like an angel got up from beside me and started running forward. I thought – Oh God damn, why do I deserve this; I have chosen? Been chosen? You are joking! I got up and followed my friend who was running forward. I did not think that there was anything better to do; I felt that if I went back I would certainly be shot. My friend was running up the slope towards the hovel. I thought – If we can get to the hovel without the machine-gun firing again then we might get through. I did not know what I meant by 'through'. Of course it was likely to be true that there were gaps in the front line: of course there is no way for baby turtles to go except through.

Then the machine-gun in the hovel began firing again. It might have been firing at myself and the man who was like an angel; it might have been firing at the men in our group who were running back towards the trucks. The man who was like an angel was quite close to the hovel now; he reached a wall at the side; the machine-gun was firing out of an opening at the front. I thought – Well now, let this be the once-and-for-all test: then – And I thought I had a choice! When I reached the hovel the man like an angel smiled at me; he had white teeth and bright black eyes. Then he went to the front of the hovel. The machine-gun stopped firing. There was the sound of a single shot. Then the machine-gun began firing again. My friend who was like an angel came blown back round the corner like something lifted by a wind, like feathers from a bird, like seeds; he seemed to be shedding bits and pieces of light. Then the machine-gun stopped firing. I went to the back of the hovel and there was an opening through which I could see the machine-gun, which was like the exhaust pipe of a lorry, and there was the body of one man lying across it and another man was holding the machine-gun and looking cautiously out of the opening at the front. I began to work the bolt of my rifle but my hands were shaking, and then I realised that I already had a bullet in the breach of my rifle; all I had to do was to get the safety-catch off. I pushed and pushed at the safety-catch with my thumb: I thought – Dear God, you mean it is already off? Then the man by the window turned and saw me and he began to turn the machine-gun round at me; I did not know if I should shoot him while he was still turning the machine-gun round: time seemed to have become solid, like something to do with the speed of light. Then I shot him. I was glad, afterwards, that I had at least waited for him to turn round; this is what you are taught, isn't it? And he had killed my friend. But I wanted to say – I'm so sorry, sorry. I had shot him somewhere in the chest. I was trying to work the bolt of my rifle to get another bullet into the breach. I did this. Then I went into the hovel, where the man had sat down. I took a pistol from the holster of the man who was lying across the machine-gun; this man appeared to be dead. I looked out of the window at the front of the hovel and there was still firing going on in the direction of the trucks; there were some shells going over; there was, or was not, the sound of the engines of the trucks starting up. There were no signs of the rest of my group; it seemed that they must have retreated at least beyond the rise in the ground. But the body of my friend was dead; quite dead. It had been made quite flimsy by machine-gun bullets from close range. I thought – So what does it mean, one or two get through? There was a part of me that seemed to have died and now found itself alive. I thought – Or flipped over on to another level.

I did not know if the man whom I had shot was dying; I put some sacking under his head and gave him a drink of water. He seemed to be grateful for this. I thought I heard in the distance the trucks driving away. After a time everything was quiet. The man I had shot had stopped groaning; he seemed to be unconscious. There was no more firing from the direction of the village; even no more shells. I thought – My group will now be on their way back to Barcelona.

Then – I had hoped that myself and the man who was like an angel and the boy who I thought was like me would have all got through.

It was becoming dark. Darkness comes quickly in this country. I thought – I will wait and see if there is any moon, or no moon, and then I will go on. I will go in the direction of the castle.

I took the bullets out of my rifle and the pistol; I laid the rifle and pistol by the man that I had shot; I threw the bullets away. I had a box of matches with which I burned the letter I carried from the left-wing editor in England. I kept the card accrediting me as a journalist.

I wondered if I should take off my overalls, but I was wearing almost nothing underneath. I thought – But people might have gone almost naked on a pilgrimage to Santiago de Compostela?

There were some more pieces of sacking in a corner of the hovel. I took off my overalls and put the largest piece of sacking over my head and shoulders. I thought – I need a stick: pilgrims had sticks, didn't they? When I looked out of the front of the hovel I thought I saw what might be lights approaching from the direction of the village.

I went out to the back of the hovel and began walking up the hill in the direction of the castle. I did not think I should run. It seemed – Everything should happen in due order: to trust this is part of the test.

– What did they hope they might find, those pilgrims, those particles separated and yet connected, wandering on paths of light –

– They are frightened: they are in a strange country –

– They are hopeful: they are a mutation?

VII 7: Eleanor

My journey to the north of Spain? Yes, from time to time I saw this as a matter of coincidences.

One sees what one wants to see; but what one wants to see appears to be there anyway. Does one's seeing make it more active?

You suggest that out of innumerable potentialities it may be by the act of attention that a single one is made potent; that out of the wave, the energy, comes the particular, life.

But this act of attention is able to look at itself; it is in the doing or not doing of this that there is a choice?

I did not stay long in Caceres after the visit of the German and Italian colonels. There were not many casualties coming to us from the fighting on the road to Madrid. Walburga and I managed to get ourselves and our hospital sent to the north because there fighting was expected and because of Walburga's connection with her fiancé's family who were believed to be in San Sebastian, which was still in the government's hands. But in Pamplona we met the British Consul from San Sebastian who had come to Pamplona for the festival and had been caught by the Nationalist rebellion which had been successful in Pamplona, and he told Walburga that he had information that her fiancé's family had escaped over the border into France. So Walburga lost interest in going to San Sebastian, and in fact there did not seem to be any fighting there, so it was arranged that we should go east to the Aragon front where there was said to be about to be an enemy attack on Huesca.

Yes, why indeed should there be some coincidences rather than others.

In Pamplona it was as if people were still celebrating the festival: there were parties and drinking in bars at night; dancing to the gramophone in private houses. I set out to make friends with the British Consul. He was a sandy-haired man who wore a panama hat and drank a glass of brandy at breakfast.

I said 'Is it possible to get to England?'

He said 'If you have a valid passport.'

I said 'I have friends in England.'

He said 'You do not have a passport?'

I had become accustomed to what I saw as my role of being an agent in hostile territory; I had no papers and no home. But I was no longer in a situation in which I wanted to die. This change was due largely to my meeting with Trixie's husband in Caceres. I had thought, of course – What a coincidence! But also – They too, he and Trixie, are in some sense agents in hostile territory; might this not be what all humans are properly? sometimes such a situation is not dangerous; sometimes it is.

Also I had given up the romantic idea that it was my task to kill some enemy celebrity: was this not an idea characteristic of the enemy? And would they not in time manage to kill themselves?

I had watched them in Seville where they had been like infants clutching at flags representing their mothers; they had cried 'Long live Death!'

I had thought – One should survive, if one has a message, and not feel guilt about surviving: survival seems always to be at enormous cost: as with seeds, the million or two dead children.

I said to the British Consul 'No, I do not have a valid passport. And I can't go back to Germany.'

Walburga said 'She has a boyfriend in England.'

I thought I might say – I do not have a boyfriend in England!

The Consul said 'Then the position is potentially not insuperable.'

At the back of my mind at this time was perhaps also what I had read and thought about in Seville concerning Jews. When the Jews had been a nation they had felt that they had a special task concerning the salvation of the world; then they had been scattered – indeed like seeds – and thus they found themselves (it seemed to me) in a position to carry out whatever had been their vision. But then, in hostile territory, they seemed to have lost the idea of their task of salvation; and seeds had lain dormant for 2000 years.

Walburga said to the Consul 'You will help her?'

The Consul said to me 'You are in touch with this boyfriend?'

Walburga said to me 'But of course what I want is for you to go on being with me here!'

I thought – No, I am not in touch with this boyfriend. Then – But I would have to think that?

From Pamplona, eventually, we went to the Aragon front. We travelled over rough roads to within a few miles of where the front was supposed to be; we set up our hospital in the ruins of a monastery called San Juan de la Peña. I had thought *peña* meant sorrow, but I found that it meant a rock. I thought – Such signposts are at the corners of the maze.

San Juan de la Peña is a monastery which was built originally in the tenth century on the ledge of a mountain under an enormous overhanging cliff. This monastery was damaged by fire. A new monastery was built in the seventeenth century on the plateau on the top of the mountain. Both monasteries by the time of the Civil War were partly in ruins. When we arrived there was a discussion – should we set up our hospital in the old monastery under the cliff, which would be cramped and dark but where we might be safe from bombardment, or should we set it up in the buildings on the bright tree-encircled plateau above, where it would be open to the sun and sky?

I thought – How do you learn from symbols: you expose yourself: you stay hidden?

A party of monks arrived at the deserted buildings of San Juan de la Peña at almost the same time as we; they had fled from their monastery which was in territory taken over by anarchists in the east. The discussions became elaborate – would it be more suitable for us, or the monks, to be on the top of the mountain, or hidden? I said to Walburga 'But if we are attacked or shelled we could always move down to the lower monastery.' She said 'But what about the monks?' I thought – You mean we would all rather die, than be under the same roof?

Then – But what matters is that this is one of the most beautiful places I have ever been in!

The upper monastery – which was where, in fact, we did set up our hospital in rooms of the old hostel – was built of gold-red brick:

there was a huge baroque church: all this was in a setting of grass which was kept green by the fall of dew. Beyond the grass was a forest of tall dark trees that stretched into the air like antennae; they seemed to be listening, yes, for any messages that might come from elsewhere. In the lower monastery far below there was a Romanesque cloister which was open to the air and yet covered by the overhanging cliff: on the capitals of the pillars there were sculptured scenes from the Old and New Testaments which were unlike other religious sculptures I had ever seen, in that they portrayed humans who were neither saintly nor demonic but who seemed to observe the peculiar situations they were in with serene and wide-eyed irony.

I thought – The trees above are listening for messages –

– These sculptures are seeds underground waiting for rain from the sky to be reborn.

Amongst the group of monks who made their homes in the dormitories of the old monastery under the cliff was one who had introduced himself as Anselmo: he was much younger than the others and did not have the air of being a monk. I thought – Or is he too obviously an agent in hostile territory? When there had been the argument about who should set themselves up where – and I had said to Walburga in German 'Oh it would never do for monks and nurses to be under the same roof!' – Anselmo, looking at me, had said in German 'It would certainly be distracting.' I had said 'I'm sorry, I did not think you understood German.' He had said to Walburga 'St Walburga was the abbess of a monastery in the eighth century which contained both monks and nuns.' I had said 'And that is how Walpurgis Night got its name.'

Anselmo had said 'Is that so?'

I had thought – I am flirting with Anselmo?

Since leaving Caceres I had found it increasingly difficult to be on good terms with Walburga: she would watch me with dog-like eyes; when I went for walks on my own she would be waiting for my return. Sometimes she came and sat on my bed at night and put her arms around me. I tried not to mind this. I thought – There would be some cost, wouldn't there, in being in hostile territory –

– In loving one's enemies: or whatever is the business of salvation?

We settled with our two nurses in the hostel in the buildings at the top of the mountain: we had helpers who came from the village each day; we had the promise of a doctor who would come out when needed from the local town of Jaca. At first we still had few patients; then there were casualties from a nearby village when some children had found an unexploded bomb in a field and had carried it in triumph to the village where it had exploded. There was a child with no hands and almost no face. The doctor from Jaca operated sometimes with a cigar in his mouth. The ash fell as if on newly ploughed fields. I thought – Oh these symbols: what is it I think I am looking for!

I went for walks in the woods. The sun above the trees made the air seem brittle. It was as if the trees were trying to reach through and listen for something in another dimension.

Anselmo would sometimes come up from the monastery under the cliff: he said he came up to visit the wounded in our hospital. He had a young boy's face and a tonsure that was so neat that it was like a halo. Once he came up with an old monk who was carrying the sacrament to the child who was dying. He broke away to join me where I was sitting by the façade of the huge baroque church.

He said 'You are not a Catholic?'

'No.'

'You believe in the free association of men and women!'

'No, I think you're right, it is distracting.'

'Distracting from what?'

'The need to make sense of things.'

I had stood up and began to move off in the direction in which I usually went in my walks. He walked beside me. I thought – You think you recognise, but of course cannot show that you recognise, another agent in hostile territory.

Anselmo said 'You believe you can make sense of things?'

'Yes.'

'How?'

'I suppose to find out that is part of the search.'

We went in our walk past the place where a steep and rocky path went down from the upper plateau to the lower monastery. We were heading to where the path we were on ran along the edge of the cliff. There was a legend, I had been told by Walburga, that the monastery had originally been founded in the tenth century when a young nobleman had been galloping his horse by this cliff and his horse had gone over but the rider had been miraculously saved by an overhanging tree; so the young nobleman had become a holy hermit in the hollow under the cliff near where his horse had landed.

I had thought – How odd that the monastery was first built near where the horse landed!

Anselmo said 'You know the legend about the founding of the monastery?'

I said 'Yes.'

He said 'There is another legend: that this monastery was once where the Holy Grail was kept. Did you know?'

I said 'I thought the Grail was supposed to have been found somewhere in England.'

He said 'No, it was taken from Jerusalem to Rome; and then it was sent here for safe-keeping by St Lawrence when he was martyred. St Lawrence was a native of Huesca.'

I thought – Why do these coincidences keep making me think of England?

Anselmo and I had come in our walk to the edge of the cliff. We stopped there. Anselmo held his hands inside the sleeves of his jacket. He smiled at me. I thought – He is like one of those knowing, ironic figures on the capitals of the pillars of the cloister. Then – He is attractive.

I went to the edge of the cliff and looked over. I thought – Perhaps the horse is a symbol for sexuality which falls –

– And lands among those figures in the cloister, who look after it?

Anselmo said 'In the early version of the legend it is Perceval who goes in search of the Grail because he is the innocent, the holy fool. He is the one who can persevere in the search, because he is immune to the temptations of women.'

I said 'And in later versions?'

Anselmo said 'It is Galahad who finds the Grail. He is not an innocent; he is the son of Lancelot and Guinevere: he too has renounced women, but consciously.'

I said 'Galahad was a Jew.'

Anselmo said 'I don't think that is correct.' He had come up close behind me. Now he seemed put out. He walked up and down by the edge of the cliff.

I thought – Oh well, who are you? Then – We are both being put to the test.

I said 'The name Galahad comes from Gilead which is the name of a place in the Old Testament.'

He said 'How do you know these things?'

I said 'And the Holy Grail, the chalice, is the symbol for a woman.'

He laughed and came back to me and put his hands on my shoulders. He said 'All right!' Then – 'But the woman is the Virgin Mary, the Mother of God.'

I said 'But that too is a symbol. I mean, on a higher level.'

He said 'You and your symbols!' Then – 'You think your search is like that of Galahad the Jew?'

He rocked me backwards and forwards. I thought he was going to kiss me. Then he turned to walk back quickly in the direction of the monastery. When he had gone some distance he turned and said 'Don't you want to be helped?' Then he went on.

I thought – Dear God, what did he mean by that?

Walburga went off to Pamplona in our truck to get supplies for the hospital: I was left in charge of our patients and the two nurses and the helpers who came up from the village each day. We had some more wounded in now from the fighting around Zaragoza. There was a man with a head wound who had to be held if he was to be prevented from further battering his head against a wall: I had to decide whether or not he should be tied down. I watched while others did this. I thought – I can see why one does not want to be both responsible and conscious, like a god.

One of our main tasks was simply to wash people. When they arrived they were usually caked with dirt and blood and were a feeding-ground for lice and fleas. Sometimes when we washed them we got through to the bone. I thought – Does one ever in the end have the choice to live or to die?

When I walked in the woods it was as if the sky was so close that my head might go through and light would fall down on me like bits and pieces of glass –

– Like those cosmic seeds or particles which, you used to say, are always falling down upon the world –

– For its destruction and creation?

One afternoon I walked down the steep and rocky path to the lower monastery under the cliff. I wondered – What will it be like not to feel so exposed? Also, of course, I thought I might see Anselmo.

In the cloister there were the extraordinary sculptures on the tops of pillars: these were to do with the creation of the world, with working in the Garden, with the performing of miracles. I thought – The beings who are doing all this are watching themselves doing it: they are both men and god-like. The sculptor had given them huge round eyes. I thought – It is by these that they see themselves; also themselves in relation to the universe.

There was an archway at one side of the cloister that was in Moorish rather than in Romanesque style. On the stones that formed the arch there was an inscription that appeared to be in Latin but was in a strange primitive script. I tried to decipher this. The inscription began on one side of the arch with 'Through this door' and ended on the other with something about 'the laws of God'. I thought – Indeed, but what are the laws of God?

Anselmo had come up beside me. I imagined – He is a black cat, and I am his witch.

I said 'Do you know what that inscription round the doorway says?'

Anselmo translated ' "Through this door there is a way to heaven, for whichever one of the faithful learns to connect faith to the laws of God." '

I thought – You mean, this might be that doorway for which you go right round the world and into the Garden of Eden again by the back way?

Then – But was there not some plan for us, I mean you and I, to meet here? I mean, at the back door to the Garden of Eden.

I said to Anselmo 'Yes, but what are the laws of God.'

Anselmo and I gazed at the inscription. He said 'I have been trying to make enquiries about the connection between Galahad and Gilead.'

I said 'Have you?'

Anselmo said 'Gilead was the place where Jacob was forced to stop by Laban when Jacob had absconded with his, Laban's, daughters. Also Rachel, Jacob's wife and Laban's daughter, had stolen her father's household gods, but Jacob did not know this.'

I said 'Oh yes?'

He said 'When Rachel's father asked her if she had taken his household gods, she lied.'

I said 'Ah.'

He said 'I have been catching up with your symbols, you see. Women seem quite often to want to dissimulate in the Old Testament.'

I thought – The plan about a meeting was in those letters we wrote, you and I, when I was in Africa and you were in Russia.

Anselmo said 'If I asked you about yourself, would you tell me?'

444

I said 'I think symbols, legends tell us about the way the world works.'

He said 'Which is what?'

I said 'What do you want to know about me? For things to work, don't you have to find them out for yourself?'

I had turned back into the cloister. On the tops of the pillars there were also figures of strange, benign animals and birds: they were like creatures that were able perhaps naturally to watch themselves and their relation to the universe; creatures that had not yet been born.

I thought – They are hopeful monsters!

Then – You and I, we talked about these?

I said to Anselmo 'I suppose those women of the Old Testament felt themselves responsible for a higher good: so in what sense was this dissimulation?'

He said 'You feel like that?'

I said 'Don't you?'

Anselmo was standing behind me. I thought – He will put his arm around me. Or – He knows I am an enemy agent? A Jew?

He said 'Gilead means "the place of witness".'

I said 'Witness of the higher good?'

He said 'Do you know what *peña* means? I mean, in San Juan de la Peña – '

I said 'I thought it meant a rock.'

He said 'It also means a circle of friends.'

I said 'A circle of friends!'

When I turned to him he put his arms around me. He kissed me. I thought – Oh but this circle of friends: they do know each other! Do they know what they do?

Then – But does anyone know more than that they are doing it! Not what it is that they do?

After a time Anselmo, as usual, hurried away.

Anselmo and I behaved rather formally to each other for a time. Walburga came back from Pamplona. She did not have much news of the war. The advance on the road to Madrid had been re-directed towards Toledo. It was hoped that San Sebastian would be surrendered without a fight. Walburga said 'So it seems that, after all, we may not be doing much good up here! We may have to go back to the south.'

I said 'But we have only just got here!'

Walburga said 'I know you want to get to England!' Then – 'Have you been seeing Anselmo?'

I thought – But why should not Anselmo, whoever he is, help me; if all this is to do with a circle of friends?

Then – But how will it help me to be here near to the northern front, near the French frontier, if I still have no papers?

I said 'Who is Anselmo?'

Walburga said 'You have noticed that he is not a monk?'

I said 'Do you know him?'

Walburga was watching me. She said 'Perhaps he is someone who feels he might not be popular either on one side or on the other.'

I thought – She is talking about me.

I said 'But I can't get to England! And where else can I go?'

She said 'I will look after you.'

I thought – And we can live like nuns in this monastery?

One of the stories Anselmo had told me about the monastery was that St Francis of Assisi had come this way in the thirteenth century on a pilgrimage to Santiago; he had travelled on foot through Languedoc in France and had crossed the Pyrenees by the road down to our local town of Jaca. Almost nothing was known of his journey after this: there was a legend that in Spain he had almost immediately fallen ill. Anselmo had said 'I like to think that he might have fallen ill here, at San Juan de la Peña: then one might indeed feel one was within a circle of friends!' I had thought – But it might be possible for me to cross the mountains illegally into France?

I said to Walburga 'I know you will look after me! But I can't stay here for ever. And I can't go back to Germany. And what would I do in France?'

She said 'Why can't you stay here?' Then – 'What would you do in England?'

I thought – Oh England, England! Then – It is because she is jealous, that she is looking at me so strangely?

There had been some only half-hidden excitement, or anxiety, about Walburga, since she had returned from Pamplona.

Then she said 'What did you want to do when you joined us in Seville? You looked so fierce? As if you wanted to kill someone!'

I said 'Not you!'

She said 'Who then?'

I thought – Who has she been talking to in Pamplona?

I said 'My mother died in a camp in Germany. My father has been arrested.'

She said, 'I see.' Then – 'I'm so sorry.'

I thought – But why am I telling her this now: something is happening on quite a different level?

I said 'But now I don't want to kill anyone.'

Then she said 'This friend of yours from England, is he fighting for the Reds?'

I said 'My friend in England fighting for the Reds?'

I thought – What has happened is that she has gone mad. Then – But I am talking like my mother.

She said 'I met that British Consul in Pamplona.'

I said 'You met that British Consul – ' Then – 'Of course my friend in England is not fighting for the Reds!'

She said 'Of course not, no.'

I thought – There is too much coming in. It is my own head that has broken, into a different dimension.

Walburga said 'I just wondered if that was why you wanted to be here, that's all.'

I took to going down most afternoons to the cloister in the lower monastery; under the cliff I felt more sheltered from the encroaching sky. I took a sketchbook and pencil that Walburga had got for me in Pamplona; I wanted to make drawings of the figures on the tops of the pillars – of the humans with huge heads and wondering eyes: of the creatures that seemed as if they were mutants waiting to be born. I thought – Here we all are, under the earth, perhaps, like seeds, like a circle of friends, like hopeful monsters. Who? You and I. Well what are you doing now? What does it mean that Walburga appears to have gone mad?

Then – Of course, I cannot think too much about this.

Anselmo came to watch me while I sketched. For the most part he did not speak, yet it was as if he might have something to tell me. One day when I was trying to make a careful copy of the Latin inscription in the strange script around the archway he said –

'There are almost identical inscriptions on other doorways in this vicinity: one in the church in the village down the hill and one in the cathedral in Jaca. There is also one in a castle at some short distance to the south of here.'

I said 'This doorway reminds me of a legend that used to mean much to me: about how in order to get back into the Garden of Eden you have to go right round the world and in at the back way.'

He said 'There is no Garden of Eden!'

I said 'This is a gateway: you carry the garden inside you.'

He said 'Do you?'

I said 'Why did St Francis not go on with his pilgrimage to Santiago: why did he turn back?'

'I told you, he became ill.'

'Was this illness before or after he got the stigmata?'

'I think before.'

I said 'I don't think one should turn back. I think one should go on. Look at what's happened to the stigmata: to Christ's circle of friends!'

I made plans to borrow a horse so that I could go and have a look at the doorways in the church in the village and in the cathedral in Jaca. I thought – Then I might also have a look at the road to the frontier to France.

Walburga said 'Why do you want a horse?'

I said 'I'd like to go and look at these doorways Anselmo has told me about. Then apparently there's another somewhere in a castle to the south.'

Walburga said 'You know about that castle?' She sat down as if she were somewhat bemused. I thought – Why do people act as if something quite different were happening round some corner?

There was a farmer who came up to tend to his sheep on the plateau by the hostel: he agreed to lend me his horse. I told him that I wanted to go to the village down the hill and to Jaca: then another day I might try and go to a castle in the south. When I described this to him he said 'But that is two days' ride!' I thought – It is as if no one wants me to go to this castle: is it this that is round some corner?

I said 'All right I'll only go to the village and to Jaca!'

When I did go on my journey I did not find much of interest in the two doorways I looked at: I could not quite understand why I had come. I went a short way up the road towards France. I thought – But it is no good my thinking I can get into France: there is something pulling me as if I were on a tightrope –

– Something like gravity?

When I got back to the road by the lower monastery I found Anselmo sitting on the edge of the rock that supported the cloister. He was not wearing his monk's habit: he was wearing a dark blue shirt and dark blue trousers. He jumped down into the road and took hold of my horse. He seemed excited. He said 'Did you find what you wanted?'

I said 'Yes, thank you.'

He said 'I thought you might have tried to escape!'

I shouted 'I keep telling everyone that I have nowhere to go!'

Perhaps it was because I was in a dark part of the forest, in the gorge below the level of the lower monastery – or perhaps it was because of Anselmo's change of clothes which made him look young and full of energy – but I had an impression, then, that I suddenly understood what was happening; I mean I did not really know what this was, but I felt it was right, whatever was happening.

Anselmo stretched up to lift me off my horse. I said 'So after all you're a Fascist!'

He said 'I am in more trouble with the Fascists than you will ever be!'

I said 'That is impossible.'

He said 'Well, we know about you now.'

Perhaps my feeling of things being all right had something to do with an impression that I sometimes had when I was by the lower monastery – that it was like outbuildings of that castle in the forest where we had watched that play – the play about two people wandering in a town in which there was some sort of revolution going on –

I said 'You've been talking to Walburga.'

He said 'Perhaps now you will find your Holy Grail!'

I said 'What does that mean?'

He said 'Oh you have said, haven't you, we have to find things out for ourselves!'

Anselmo kissed me. I thought – But of course I cannot think too much about what might be happening.

When I got to the upper monastery I found Walburga sitting outside the hostel in the evening sun. It was, as usual, as if she had been waiting for me. She watched me half smiling as I came up. I thought – She is herself, now, like one of those sculptures, those seeds, on the pillars of the cloister; knowing and ironical –

She said 'I've got something to tell you!'

I said 'You've been talking to Anselmo.'

I sat down beside her: I thought – But why do people look so pleased: it is I who seem to be mad: who feel myself being led towards some secret behind the closed door in a courtyard.

She said 'I've heard again from the British Consul in Pamplona.'

I said 'Oh yes.'

She said 'He says there is an Englishman being held prisoner in that castle near here that you have talked about. He has been caught fighting for the Republicans.'

I thought – Now wait quietly.

She said 'He apparently has the same name as that boyfriend of yours in England.'

I thought – You know the name of my boyfriend in England?

Then – Oh yes, it was on the back of the envelopes of those letters you read in Caceres.

Then – But this is not possible!

She said 'You are not interested?'

I was thinking – But I must not think too much –

– We had planned to meet somewhere such as here!

She said 'You've been so interested in that castle!'

I thought I might say – But if he has been fighting, and has been taken prisoner, has he not been shot?

She said 'He apparently says he's a journalist.' Then – 'Now perhaps you will have a chance to help your prisoners!'

I thought – Oh but there is terror, as well as glory, beyond that courtyard!

I said 'Can I borrow the truck in the morning?'

She said 'Yes.'

I said 'Thank you.'

She said 'And as far as I can make out, you're a friend of a friend of mine called Franz.'

I said 'You're a friend of Franz?'

I thought – But there is too much, too much, yes, coming in: I must hold myself looking down, or ahead, very carefully; as if I were being led towards whatever it is beyond that doorway.

She said 'So you see, I was not wrong, when I felt from the first that I loved you!'

One of the things I had been worrying about at this time was that I had begun to think I was pregnant. My period had not come: the last time I had made love was over a month ago with Heinrich in Seville; that was when we had made love as if in blood, exulting, like Achilles and Penthesilea. But because it was when I had had my period how could I be pregnant? However, I thought now – This might just be the time when I would be caught by a devil!

That night I could not sleep. I thought – But perhaps I will be too late: perhaps by morning they will have shot you!

I tried to work out – But all this cannot be true! Then – I cannot think! Then – There is nothing that I can do before morning.

Then – Human responsibility is both bearable, and not.

– I have got to do everything in due order, or it will not be true.

During the night I went out into the forest where the moon seemed to be making solid bars of light; the trees were like empty spaces in between. It was as if I wanted to make of myself some sort of offering on this grid, this riddle; for all the pain and chances and wonder of the world; for what might be possible. I thought – Then something may remain on the surface and something may fall through: transmuted, on to another level.

Because the moon was making seem so solid the bars of light, I did not watch where I was treading; suddenly, in my walk, I did fall through – into some crevasse, some pit; I had stepped on what had seemed to be a solid slat of light and now my own body, more solid, was falling; was being torn, broken, by branches. I thought – Perhaps I have gone over the cliff and after all I will die! Or will there be some miracle and I will be saved and it will be my horse, as it were, that will die. Then I came up against something hard, violent, that checked my fall; I was being held up by thorns; if I moved the thorns would go in deeper: I thought – But why should I not move and be in pain? Then I would be held more safely. I was wearing a thin nightdress. I thought – So somewhere am I looking down on myself like one of those wide-eyed sculptures in the cloister. There were some clouds, quite still, through a gap in the trees above me; they were in the shape of two people sitting at a table; the people were playing some game. I thought – So old gods might think they are playing a game with me – as one of the endless bits of the universe. Then – I am a child who has fallen off the edge of a bed; but have they abandoned me? They have freed me: and now I am being held up by thorns and branches. And then it seemed that of course I could go on, I should climb up on any pain; the thorns being a ladder. When in ecstasy, is it not true, the body neither lacerates nor bleeds. Then the shapes of the clouds seemed to reach down to me. I thought – All right, you old hags, with your claws, be a ladder! Then – Thank you, thank you, for your helping talons. I found I could in fact climb out from whatever it was, the crevasse, the pit, quite easily. Then when I was out on the floor of the forest looking down I thought – That was where I have been:

this is where I am now; as if I am one of those seeds, come alive, from the pillars of the cloister.

I found that I was bleeding from inside, as well as outside, from the wounds of the thorns. I thought – So what you have got rid of is my past, my blockage; you old gods, you hags of the forest.

I got to my room in the hostel and washed my wounds. It would soon be morning.

I thought – When there is too much coming in, I must learn to be quiet.

In the morning I put on the white overalls in which I had crossed the straits so that I should look something like an angel. I found Walburga and made arrangements to take the truck for the day. Walburga said 'What have you done to your face?' I said 'I scratched it.' She said 'How?' I thought I might say – They are scavengers, garbage-collectors, those old hags in the forest.

I said 'Have you got any document I can show: any sort of official letter?'

She said 'I've got the letter from the Nationalist Headquarters in Burgos which gives me authority to set up a hospital in San Juan de la Peña.'

I said 'That might do.'

Walburga said 'Anselmo will help. He seems to have cleared himself with the authorities.'

I said 'Who is Anselmo?'

Walburga said 'He thinks it possible that there might be some exchange of prisoners.'

I do not remember much about the journey to the castle: it was about fifty miles: it took two hours. There were wooded hills, green and gold fields, then barren rocky mountains and dust. For a time there was a river. It seemed – This might be the road we had been on an infinite number of times before, would be on an infinite number of times again: it was a path on which it was my business to travel as on a line, to remain upright, but not to ask where I was going.

I came to the road that you have described: there was the gap in the hills and the road like a snake; the castle perched on its rock in the distance. Yes, it was like something in a fairy story. And it did not seem to be something that, if I looked away, it would disappear.

Does one ever get used to living in a world like this? Where it seems that nothing is quite without meaning – such as putting one foot in front of another.

There was an area of dust in front of the outside walls of the castle and sentries who were young men in blue shirts with rifles and bandoliers. They moved to and fro as if without any purpose: they were like members of the chorus of an opera. I thought – But there is no music: of course one can see that such people make no sense if there is no music.

I left the truck and spoke to the sentries in Spanish at which I had become by now quite practised. I said that I had authorisation from the Commander in Chief in Burgos to visit the English prisoner that they were holding; I was an official at the hospital at San Juan de la Peña. The sentries acted as if they did not understand me. I thought – They make out they do not understand me because there is no music?

After a time a man came out of a door in the walls from what seemed to be a guardroom or gatehouse. He wore a dark blue shirt and a red beret. I showed him the letter that I had been given by Walburga. I thought – Dear God, these people will one day have to learn to live without their castanets and twanging. I looked up to the high walls of the central keep of the castle: there were towers with loopholes through which arrows could once have been shot. My letter had official stamps on it, one of which was the representation of a castle with round towers. I thought – You mean, one should be one's own music –

Then – This is like that castle in the Black Forest?

Another man in a red beret came out of the gatehouse. He looked at the letter. He said 'But this says nothing about the English prisoner.'

I thought – At least there is an English prisoner.

I said 'I am authorised, if necessary, to take him to the hospital at San Juan de la Peña.

The man said 'He is not ill.'

I thought – So that is all right. Or it might mean that he is ill?

The two men in berets talked between themselves. They seemed to be discussing a call that they had received earlier on the telephone. I thought – Now let me listen to silence, as if it were music.

One of the men in berets went back into the gatehouse. The other man had folded the letter and handed it to him. He said 'You are German?'

I said 'Yes.'

He held out his hand – we shook hands. He said 'You want the English prisoner?' He laughed.

I thought – Oh yes, but he is seeing me as something of an angel, all in white, on this strange planet.

The man who had gone back into the gatehouse reappeared at the main doorway in the outside walls, which he was opening; he beckoned for me to come through. I thought – Is there anything else I should be doing? Inside the walls there was a rocky forecourt and a ramp up to the central keep; people in various states of raggedness sat with their backs against stones; they wandered to and fro like the chorus of an opera; there was a group playing a game with a ball made out of what seemed to be bits of old cloth. I thought – This is a limbo where seeds lie in wait: where one or two continue through?

You were sitting with your back against the pillar of an arched window in the wall of the main structure of the castle; you were holding a pencil and a piece of paper on your knee. You were turning the pencil over and over. I thought – Yes, you are like one of those figures on the pillars in the cloister; you are being your own music. Then – Well, here I am: have we not been at this place an infinite number of times before; will we not be at this place an infinite number of times again –

But when you looked up, it seemed that the light might break, it was so fragile!

I said 'It's all right! I knew you were here!'

I knelt down in front of you.

When you had looked up and seen me you had not shown any very obvious surprise. You became very still. You had stopped turning the pencil over and over on your knee.

I said 'The people I am with heard about you! They told me you were here!'

I suppose I was afraid that you might think you were mad. You watched me. You were very thin. I thought – But you know how things can be real, in this strange territory?

I wanted to say to you – You remember how we have had experiences of something like this: in that castle; on that path on the side of the mountain –

When you spoke it was as if you had to dig down deep to get to the mechanisms of speech.

You said 'Dear God, I did not think that you could know that I was here.'

I said 'I'm working in a hospital at a monastery called San Juan de la Peña.'

You said 'I was in Barcelona.'

I said 'Yes, I know.'

I thought – But of course I didn't know!

You said 'Then I thought I'd try to get to Santiago de Compostela.' You laughed.

I said 'Santiago de Compostela!'

You said 'I wanted to go on a pilgrimage.'

I thought – How like you! Then – But you do know, don't you, that we planned to meet somewhere like here.

I had sat down in front of you. It was as if there were bits and pieces of light falling between us on to the dust.

I said 'I crossed the Sahara.'

You said 'The Sahara!'

I said 'Yes.' Then – 'I've come to get you.'

You said 'You do know, don't you, that we – ' Then – 'No.' Then – 'Well, we are here.'

One of the men in red berets had gone past us up the ramp into the main keep of the castle; he had been carrying my letter. There were men in blue shirts by the guardroom looking in our direction. I thought – If we remain quite still, they may see us as figures in a painting?

I said 'Will they let you go?'

You said 'I don't know.'

I said 'No, I don't know.' Then – 'What will it depend on?'

You said 'What do you think?'

You were wearing a vest, and what looked like a piece of old sacking round your middle. You had no shoes. You had a beard.

I said 'When you came to Berlin, you got me.'

You said 'If I get out of here, will you come back with me to England?'

I said 'Yes.'

You said 'Will you marry me?'

I said 'Yes.'

You said 'Thank God.'

I said 'But I haven't got any papers.'

You said 'Then thank God you haven't got any papers.'

I said 'Why?'

You said 'Because then you will marry me.'

I thought – Oh dear God, yes, this is like being within a painting: this is being whatever is music.

The men in blue shirts at the far side of the courtyard had disappeared through the door into the gatehouse.

I said 'I won't be a trouble.'

You said 'But we will be together?'

I said 'Of course we'll be together!'

You smiled and said 'One never knows.'

I said 'I wasn't going to say "One never knows"!'

You said 'I don't know if I can bear this.'

There was a figure in the habit of a monk who had appeared briefly at the inside doorway into the gatehouse. He seemed to be looking at us and yet trying to keep out of sight. I thought – It is Anselmo?

I said 'I know what I want to do: I mean, when we get back to England.'

You said 'I know what I want to do when we get back to England.'

I said 'What?'

You said 'I'll tell you.'

The man in the red beret came back down the ramp from the main keep of the castle. He came up to you and spoke in a dialect I did not understand. You answered him. You did not look at me. Then he looked towards the gatehouse. Then he went back up the ramp.

I said 'Have they treated you quite well?'

You said 'I fought them; they don't know: did you know?'

I said 'I thought you were a journalist.'

You said 'Yes, I was a journalist.' Then – 'That man said I was lucky to have friends.'

I said 'Were they going to shoot you?'

It was hot in the rocky forecourt. I thought – Perhaps it would be easier, after all, for us both to be shot: then we would always be what we are now here: we would be these bits and pieces of light.

You said 'What is the work that you want to do in England?'

I said 'It's about coincidences.'

You said 'Coincidences!'

I said 'Why?'

You said 'Because I want to do some work on coincidences!'

I said 'What a coincidence!'

When you laughed it was as if you were crying.

The man in the red beret had come out again on to the ramp. He made a gesture for us to come to him. I stood up. You seemed to stand with difficulty. You had to hold a piece of sacking around your middle. The man led the way, with us following him, down the ramp.

We waited outside the inner door to the gatehouse. You were looking down towards the ground. I thought – You are thinking that we have to be careful, or it might break, this structuring of the universe.

Within the gatehouse there was further talk between the men in red berets. I could just see the arm and the shoulder of the man in a monk's habit. It seemed important that I should not exactly know whether or not it was Anselmo: it was as if we, all three of us, might be agents in hostile territory.

I said 'I think there's a chance that you might be being exchanged for a prisoner on the other side.'

You said 'Yes, there was a time when I thought I might be shot; then I tried to explain that I was a pilgrim.'

One of the men in red berets came out from the gatehouse and talked to you in the dialect I did not understand. He smiled. Then another man came out and handed you your passport and wallet; then a razor and a bar of soap. You laughed. You shook hands with the two men. I thought – But coincidences are not miracles: miracles are when you do not see –

I had got out of the hot sun into the shade: I thought – But I do not know how to finish that sentence.

Then – If that man is Anselmo, he will know that I thank him?

The door was opened for us to go out through the walls round the castle. In the area of dust outside there was the truck where I had left it; close to it was a primitive motorcycle of a kind that the monks from the monastery sometimes used. I thought – I suppose one does not see what one is not fitted to see.

We walked across the dust, you and I, away from the castle. I thought – You do not look back: this is one of the things we have learned? Things can disappear, turn to stone, if you look back.

You said 'You can drive?'

I said 'Of course I can drive!'

You said 'Well, I couldn't drive.'

When we were in the truck and on the road we did not speak for a time. I thought – If nothing of importance can be said, will we ever speak again?

I said 'What is this work that you want to do about coincidences?'

You said 'How the world is held together; how there is not chaos.'

I said 'I want to do the same thing, but about mind.'

You said 'Oh it is all about mind!'

I thought – What we mean is that if I turn this wheel to the right then the truck will turn to the right and will not just fly to pieces?

I said 'Oh yes, there was something I wanted to ask you about that castle – '

You said 'What?'

I said 'Was there a Moorish-style doorway, anywhere in the castle, with an inscription round it in Latin, in a funny script?'

You said 'I don't know.' Then – 'I think so.'

We were coming to the place on the road where it ran beside the river. I had noticed on my outward journey that there were dams for irrigation that collected water into pools. I had thought then – We might stop by one of these on the way back, and bathe.

You said 'Why do you ask that?'

I said for what seemed to be for both of us the hundredth time 'I don't think I'm going to be able to bear this.'

You said 'Oh yes you are.'

I turned the wheel of the truck and we went off the road and rolled across hard-baked earth and stones and came to rest by the side of one of the pools in the river. I thought – Perhaps things will be easier if we bathe; if we do whatever people are supposed to as some sort of baptism in a river.

You climbed out of the truck stiffly. I thought – Perhaps you are wounded: I could have been asking you about things like that.

You went to the river and knelt down by the water and washed. You took off your vest and then your piece of sacking. You were so thin that your bones were like wounds within your flesh.

You said 'You crossed the Sahara? You crossed the straits to Spain? You became a nurse in a monastery near here?'

I said 'Yes.'

You said 'I see.'

I said 'And what did you do?'

You said 'I came to Barcelona because I wanted to have a look. Then I fought once, but never again.'

I said 'You felt you were on a pilgrimage?'

You said 'As if I were on a tightrope: on a hook.'

I had left the truck. I knelt by the water at some distance from you. I took my shirt off. I washed. I felt you watching me.

I said 'I fell into a thorn bush.'

You said 'The things you do.'

The river was within a bowl of hills. The sky seemed so close that it was as if a hand might come down; or one could move between earth and sky on a ladder.

I said 'There's a doorway with an inscription in this monastery where I've been living and I was told that there was a doorway with the same inscription in your castle. It was this that made me first think of coming to the castle – I mean, before I knew you might be there.'

You said 'I suppose there might be several such doorways in Spain.'

I said 'It seemed to be that doorway, you know, by which one got back into the Garden of Eden.'

You said again 'Well, here we are.'

You came and sat by me. I sat with my hands around my knees. We were looking out at the water, side by side.

I said 'Of course I can bear this! But I don't think I can have children.'

You said 'Why not?'

I said nothing.

You said 'I suppose you will want to look after the world.' Then – 'We will have some sort of children.'

There was a huge dragonfly flitting above the surface of the water. I thought – But I did not think that there were dragonflies at this time of year. Then – Perhaps it too is a hopeful monster.

I said 'You know those things you told me about – that are born before their time.'

You said 'Oh yes.'

I said 'Perhaps they're what we can't talk about, you and I.'

You said 'We can try.'

I said 'Can a British Consul marry us?'

You said 'I think so, yes.'

I said 'We can talk about that.'

You said 'Oh we can talk about that!'

I said 'I know one in Pamplona.'

You lay down on your back and looked at the sun.

I thought – We will go back to the monastery; we will see Walburga; Anselmo will either have returned or not, or he may have never been away –

– How amazing are dragonflies! They live for such a short time: yet they lay seeds, eggs, and so go on –

459

You said 'Do you feel that there is some sort of task to be done?'
I said 'Yes, I feel that there is something urgent to be done.'
I thought – Oh we will scatter seeds, which will be our children, who will be as lucky as we have been, and go on.

VIII: Max

Between 1936 and 1939 the politics of Europe went freewheeling downhill towards hell; at first slowly, then ever faster. At the beginning of this time it was still possible to imagine that the Nazi experiment, after the violence attendant initially on any revolutionary movement, might become more staid: during 1938 there was the annexation of Austria and of a large part of Czechoslovakia, but even then it could just rationally be argued that this was a gathering-in of Germans to their homeland; then suddenly it was seen that the situation was in runaway, out of control. The Germans were carried along by an impression of their own omnipotence; their opponents, having let them get away with so much, began to feel shame. At the end of 1938 there was in Germany the first openly and deliberately state-organised pogrom against Jews: synagogues were burned and victims were killed in the streets. It seemed that one was no longer in the province of politics, but of witches and demons.

Between 1936 and the end of 1938 not much happened about the Bomb. There had been glimpses years ago of a strange conjunction of terror and hope – of an ultimate weapon which, after an initial demonstration of catastrophe, might put an end to the way in which human politics ran out of control: there might be held in front of

461

the eyes at the top of the hill, as it were, a vision of annihilation at the bottom. But recently there seemed to have been a paralysis in physics just as there was in politics – an inability to face up to hope perhaps because of despair at the chance of final horror.

The neutron had been discovered in the early Thirties: it had soon been seen that this would be a more effective particle than those used hitherto for penetrating the nucleus of an atom. In 1936 it had been seen, separately, that the bits and pieces of a nucleus were held together by a force similar to that which held together a drop of water; and that if this force were overcome, and a splitting took place into roughly equal parts, then these, being of the same electrical charge, would fly apart with enormous energy. But the two insights or bits of information were not put together: there did not seem to be the mathematics by which to do this – nor perhaps the urgency. Physicists continued to view the bombardment of nuclei by neutrons as a means of just knocking out small bits and pieces from a nucleus in order to discover what an atom might consist of: it was still not a serious proposition that a nucleus might be split into anything like two. Although for certain theoretical purposes it might be imagined that a nucleus had properties like those of a drop of water, in practice it was accepted that a nucleus was as hard as glass: to think otherwise – might this indeed not lead to imagining the possible disintegration of the universe?

During 1937 the Spanish Civil War meandered on. By the end of the year it could be seen by anyone who chose to look that it was not so much a holy war of the Left against Fascism (or indeed vice versa) as a ground on which various groupings or individuals could work out particular obsessions or escape from or indeed even welcome dead-ends. Stalinists cared more about killing Trotskyites than killing Fascists; Trotskyites and anarchists could make experiments and at least come to heroic ends with their faith still intact. Fascists went into battle singing boldly and clearly that they were on their way to meet their bride who was Death. Few people of goodwill maintained hope during these years beyond the idea that it might be the extremists who achieved self-destruction.

About Russia up till the middle of 1936 it had been possible to argue that there might be sense even in the widespread slaughter and starvation: might not the landowning peasants have had to be defeated in pursuit of the ideal of agricultural collectivisation; were not purges amongst the bureaucracy necessary in order to make the system more effective? Then in July 1936 – almost exactly coincident (yes!) with the start of the Spanish Civil War – there was the first of the public trials for treason of top-level Soviet dignitaries: Zinoviev and Kamenev were taken from prison and put on show for their lives. They themselves confessed to having been for years active enemies of the state: they had organised sabotage, they had been the agents of hostile powers; they agreed – of course they deserved to be shot! They were followed in similar trials during the next three years by most of those who had exercised top-level power in Russia since the revolution – two-thirds of the Party Central Committee, half of the delegates to the 1934 Party Congress, 25,000 army officers including most of the senior generals, a million or so more anonymous bureaucrats. By the end of this time, those who had been the public accusers at the beginning were themselves being shot. The mystery in all this was: why was the history of a system's degradation, whether true or untrue, being so much publicised? Why should people be made to, or be willing to, confess to such self-destruction? There seemed to be being enacted eagerly a ghastly parody of the way in which human politics was running downhill out of control. But then, what could there be of parody about the catastrophe at the bottom.

I said to you 'Do you think that on some level Communists know what they are doing: they still think that out of the self-destruction something new will grow? And it is the Nazis who talk about the heroism of death and yet are not subtle enough even to see in this the likelihood of self-destruction, who will rush on down the slope to simple disaster at the bottom.'

You said 'Communists will not have worked out anything consciously.'

I said 'But still, something in their ideology may work for them?'

You said 'I'm sure that Germans, before they can begin again, will have to reach rock bottom.'

And for us – my angel, my sweet love – we had those two years! While Europe trundled or rushed down its slope we were on our tightrope on our one-wheeled bicycle: you on my shoulders with your legs around my neck; our arms out in the shape of a cross; the crowd below shouting 'Hurrah!' 'Oopla!' 'Upsadaisy!' We had been married, you and I, yes, by that British Consul in Pamplona. It had not been difficult to get out of Spain: you had your friends; I had our passport. Together we had our sense of tasks to be done, if there was to be larger-scale hope of liveliness and renewal.

In England I took up physics again and went to work for my old

463

friend Donald Hodge who was now in charge of a section of the physics department in a university in the north of England. With makeshift equipment and little money he was trying to find out what went on in the nucleus of an atom. I had had my vision of potential creativity or destruction on that mountain-top in Spain; but of course evidence depended on painstaking experiment and mathematics. My ideas did not seem so sensible, nor their possible effects so desirable, in the calm atmosphere of the scientific establishment at home. However, what seemed vital was that the Nazis should not be the first to make a Bomb.

We settled, you and I, in two rooms in a boarding-house on the outskirts of the town. We were very happy. I thought – But could not we, with our particular story, be involved in some experiment to find out what goes on at the heart of being human?

I said 'The real race, do you think, is between people or forces intent on self-destruction, and the chance of being able to begin to stop it because one can see what is happening?'

You said 'You mean for thousands of years people have just liked war?'

I said 'But now, with the chance of this Bomb, people surely won't like what they may be able to imagine.'

You said 'You mean, it is necessary that at this time there should be discovered this explosive force in the nucleus of the atom, to give a chance to a change in people's minds.'

I said 'Necessary, I suppose, for continued existence.'

I thought – Minds, matter, flying apart, coming together again –

For some renewal, yes, of what might be called 'spirit'.

You said 'But how odd, the idea that by seeing something one might stop it!'

I said 'But there's been for some time the idea that by seeing things we affect them. And there's that other crazy vision I had in Spain – that we are in some sense part of a self-creating universe.'

You said 'Well you and I, before we could begin again, had very nearly to hit rock bottom.'

I went out to work in the laboratory each day: you went to work in the university library. You were pursuing a line of enquiry you had embarked on in Zurich – about the rituals people go through in order to try to view from a higher level, to correlate, the outside and inside worlds: about the ways in which a situation might be influenced by an attempt to come to terms with it. When we came home in the evenings, you and I, we sat side by side in front of a small coal fire; we held out our hands to the flames. This is how I see us at this time: as if in a painting, yes: two things that have been apart and have come together; and are even demonstrating that in some sense, in so far as they are agents in a larger context, they are together all the time.

I said 'Are we lucky or did we work for it – '

You said 'You can't talk about what is the difference.'

I said 'That is what you are doing in your work?'

You said 'This is happiness.' Then – 'But don't you find it difficult to talk about what you are actually doing in your work?'

The laboratory to which I went each day was in a long stone building on top of a hill: it looked out over a dark landscape striped with grey houses. My work was to do with seeing what happened when the nuclei of a heavy element such as uranium or thorium were bombarded with neutrons. Now indeed it might be thought odd what I was actually doing. There was a small glass phial that I had to fill with a radioactive material that emitted neutrons; this material was usually in the form of a radon gas which had to be caught in the phial by means of condensation; this could take place when the closed end of the phial was dipped into liquid air which lowered the temperature to 200 degrees below zero. I could then direct the gas into the phial from its radium source so that it condensed on the walls; then I had to melt the open end of the phial to seal the glass. With such cold at one end and heat at the other there was a danger that if the task were done too quickly the glass would break; but if it were done too slowly then the condensed liquid might evaporate again and escape; so this was a performance indeed requiring skill: hoopla! abracadabra! The small sealed phial had then to be fixed within a larger glass tube so that the assembly could be handled without too much danger of radiation; then this apparatus had to be taken quickly into another room – quickly because the radioactive life of the material was short; into another room because the material to be bombarded had to be kept clear of any stray radiation during the assembly of what was to bombard it. In this other room the material to be irradiated was packed in special containers; the packing consisted of some material that might slow the neutrons down so that they might be caught and absorbed by the target-material more easily; into this container was put the phial which would emit the irradiating neutrons. These materials were left in the container for this or that length of time: then the phial containing the irradiating material was removed and the material which, it was hoped, had been made radioactive was taken to yet another room to be tested for just what particles, if any, were being emitted. This test was carried out by means of Geiger-counters placed in the proximity of the irradiated material: the Geiger-counters themselves were gas-filled tubes with electrically charged wires strung inside: if any electrically charged particles from the irradiated and now (it was hoped) irradiating material entered these tubes then the gas inside them was affected so that electrons were released from it and were drawn to the wire with the effect of causing a change in the pulse of the electric current; this change was converted by an amplifier into a sound like a click, or it was shown in the form of a jump in a line of light on a screen. It was these clicks or jumps that were showing us what went on in the nucleus of an atom.

And so – for minutes, days, months – by listening to noises like those of old bones being cast out on the ground; by watching for bumps like those in a snake swallowing a mouse; by such rituals one felt one might be discovering the basic stuff of the universe – the ways in which humans might be able to use the secrets of the universe, or blow it up. I would think – Ah well, at least in so far as we are able to look at the style of this process by which scientists hope to understand the secrets of the universe, this is an interesting experiment!

There were innumerable variations which could be played with these games – in the type and strength of the neutron-emitting material; in the substance to be irradiated; in the type of packing by which the neutrons might be slowed down; in the spacings and duration of the experiment. Also, indeed, there were variations in the state of mind of an observer – who might sometimes be enthralled; might sometimes at the end of a long day find himself wondering – Well, if this is the way in which humans think they get into contact with the basic stuff of the universe, why shouldn't they blow themselves up? But then again – Is it not the state of mind of seeing that the observer in some way orders what he observes that might preserve the universe?

When I came home to you in the evenings you would be sitting with your hands held out to the fire: you would say 'But these little bits and pieces you say you are dealing with in these experiments – atoms, nuclei, particles, whatever – you do not in fact know what it is that exists?'

'Exactly.'

'What you see, hear, touch, are little clicks that come out of an amplifier; lines and bumps on a screen – '

'Right.'

'But because, according to science, you have to ask what causes these bumps and clicks, and because you have to give names to what you say are causing them, you make up atoms, nuclei, particles, neutrons – '

I said 'But what else do we do anyway with our sense-impressions?'

When you held out your hands to the fire you were like a being that is at home within flames.

You said 'What do you really think?'

I said 'It's often fairly ridiculous when you look at what you actually do: you do have the impression that you are engaged in some ritual for the sake of something quite different.'

You said 'Such as what is behind the shadows in that cave.'

I said 'If there is energy, constancy, then there is a sun. You know the sun, even if you see only what it does or doesn't light up.'

When we were together thus in the evenings, you and I, it was, yes, as if we were held by a force as strong and brittle as light; as gentle and vulnerable as that which forms a drop of water; so delicate that a shaft from outside might break us; so indestructible that we would still be together even if we were at different parts of the universe. I thought – What joy, even with the chance of the universe blowing up!

You said 'Human activities are games: words are toys – '

'For the sake of what – '

'This.'

I said 'You see, one can say this much about it!'

The line of enquiry that you were pursuing at this time was to do with psychological implications of mediaeval and sixteenth- and seventeenth-century alchemy. Alchemists had talked as if they were concerned with the physical transformation of matter, but they had hardly ever talked about what they actually did, and from this it seemed that they themselves might have felt that there was something different going on. You said 'They were trying to examine ways in which there might be connections between the inside and outside worlds: but they couldn't talk about these much or they disappeared, or they occurred in individual instances, and thus were not to do with science, which depends on instances that are repeatable and with the statistics you get from these.'

I said 'They were coincidences.'

You said 'If you like.'

I said 'What sort of thing in fact did they say?'

You said 'Oh something like "Take a phial of an arcane substance such as mercury; entice darkness into it and seal the phial by fire. From this watch the dragon, half-serpent and half-bird, emerge. This will be the spirit imprisoned in matter; from its liberation, there can be the marriage of opposites – the spirit and the stone."'

I said 'Quite like we physicists.'

You said 'But alchemists seemed to know that they were using a code.'

I said 'But in physics there might in fact be a big bang at the end.'

You said 'Perhaps alchemists were talking about the sort of things that might follow from a big bang.'

I said 'Perhaps they were talking about us.'

When we carried on like this in the evenings it was, yes, as if we might be in contact with something quite different going on: with some parts of ourselves that were beyond the walls of a cave; that were burning, without being consumed, in a hot sun.

You said 'Oh I do love you.'

I said 'I love you too.'

I thought I might say – You are particles of light: I am the crests of waves.

– This room, this fireplace, you and I, will always be: whatever lives or dies in the sun.

There came a time when I felt that I should take you to visit my parents. I had telephoned them when I had got back from Spain: I had told them I had married my German girl. It was evident that they had not much liked the idea of this: you were, after all, not only a German but (though of course this was not said) also a Jew. I said to you 'They think you married me in order to get a passport.' You said, 'Well, I did marry you in order to get a passport.' I said 'Oh yes, of course, so you did.'

We went by train to Cambridge: we walked from the station. Here were the bits and pieces of the cocoon out of which I was born: the shop that sold sweets, the village post office, the stream in which there could be races with floating sticks. You walked with your long strides as if you had been trained like a camel to cover vast distances. I thought – A camel or a cloud; or an angel riding a horse across a battlefield.

My mother and father were in the room with the bow window

468

beyond which were the lawn, the croquet hoops, the red-brick walls. They had been playing cards: they were themselves like cards lying face up on a table, waiting to be picked up for a new game. I said 'This is Nellie, Eleanor; she saved my life, I told you; I was about to be shot.' My mother said 'I can't remember, what was it they were going to shoot you for?' My father said 'We could have sent the car for you to the station.'

I thought – Now tread carefully amongst these old bones, these bumps of childhood: remember that there is something different going on in the sun.

My mother would not look at me. She sat very upright during lunch. She watched you and my father at the other end of the table. You were saying 'Yes, we met in Spain. We had planned to meet, you see. I mean, we had planned to meet somewhere, but we didn't know that it would be Spain.'

My father said 'You mean it was by chance.'

You said 'Max needed to get out of prison. I needed a passport. Yes, it was by chance.'

My mother said 'But anyway, I don't understand, weren't you working for the other side?'

You said 'Yes, it was odd how it happened, wasn't it?'

I said 'She was saving lives.'

My father said 'People nowadays don't seem to know which side they are on in politics.'

My mother said 'And of course no one talks about love.'

My mother was beside me at the other end of the table. She did not eat. I thought – Perhaps she is on the bottle again: or perhaps as a practising analyst she knows about jealousy but not how to use it.

I said 'Yes, it seems to be very difficult to talk about love.'

She said 'Oh it is if you don't have it.'

I said to her 'Did we, you and I, talk about love?'

My mother rang a little bell on the table. A servant came in. This servant was a stranger.

I thought – And my mother is a stranger: whatever we used to be, she and I, is now perhaps in little bits of light in another part of the universe; like Mrs Elgin the cook and Watson the parlourmaid.

– And there are you, my angel, as if flying over rooftops; looking for marks on the doorposts and lintels of this or that house, for who shall be preserved and who shall be scattered in bits and pieces.

After lunch we walked, you and I, on the lawn. I held your hand. You were trembling. You said 'Will I have to come here again?'

I said 'No, you won't have to come here again.'

You said 'You see what they are, parents and children!'

I said 'There are enough in the world: we will find enough children.'

I thought – And perhaps we will pick them up, your children, and carry them out of Egypt.

When we went back to the house my father was waiting for us by the french windows. He said 'Your mother has a headache.'

I said 'Shall I go up to her?'

He said 'No, I don't think that would be wise.'

I said 'Shall we go then?'

He said 'I appreciate your bringing Eleanor here.'

I thought – Perhaps this is the way that mothers, if they are analysts, have to wean their children.

There were things I was not understanding in the experiments I was doing in my work: it was difficult to tell if, in fact, atoms were being split, and if there were any signs of the geometrical progression that might lead to a Bomb. There were certainly transmutations taking place that were the results of neutrons being absorbed into the nuclei of a heavy element; this absorption disturbed particles already there which were then emitted; the element was thus transmuted into one of a somewhat different number or weight (the atomic number of an element being the number of positively charged protons its nucleus is said to contain; its atomic weight being the number of protons together with neutrons); but it was often difficult to tell just what the element had been transmuted into. This classification had to be done chemically: the chemical analysis of an atom depends on the number of electrons it can be said to have in its outer orbits or shells; it is these that make the chemical combinations by which it is tested. However, the atoms of barium and radium, although the former is of almost half the latter's atomic number and weight, have an identical number of electrons in their outer shells; so that in practice it is difficult to distinguish atoms of radium from those of barium. In our laboratory neither Donald Hodge nor I were expert chemists. Sometimes the calculations that one of us made and passed to the other – all arising from the little clicks and bumps of light – made no sense. I would think – But don't we then just make up new names for things that seem to make no sense?

Donald said 'It looks like barium, it sounds like barium, but don't be taken in by that –'

I said 'You insist that it must be radium?'

We had been irradiating an element with an atomic number and weight very close to those of radium. If, in fact, this had been transmuted into barium this could mean that the atom had indeed been split; but it was easier to see it as having undergone the slight transformation into radium, because orthodox opinion still held that as a result of the bombardment of a nucleus only small bits and pieces would be chipped off.

I said 'But you know Bohr's theory that, in fact, the force which holds a nucleus together is like that which holds together a drop of water – '

Donald said 'Or fairies at the bottom of the garden.'

I said 'But why not?'

He said 'You theorists would see a dragon at the heart of the philosopher's stone.'

I thought – But of course what you can't accept is that if what we are getting is in fact barium and even with the chance of a chain reaction –

– That would indeed release the dragon from the philosopher's stone!

Donald sometimes came up to see us in the evenings; he would join us in a chair round the fire. Donald had become more sceptical with age: he was still a bachelor: he was uneasy in the presence of women. He would assume funny voices; do his trick of curling his top lip up underneath his nose.

You said 'But what would be the conditions that would make you believe that it was barium?'

Donald said 'The mathematics.'

You said 'And you can't get the mathematics.'

Donald said 'No.'

You said 'Perhaps you don't want the mathematics.'

Donald poked at the fire. I thought – But we, you and I, do we want the dragon?'

I thought – Donald will be needing to make a joke of all this. I said 'But if mathematics is a description of a function of your mind – '

Donald said 'Then is it in my mind that the earth goes round the sun.' He mimed putting a telescope to a blind eye. He said in an upper-class voice 'I say, isn't that an eye that I see out there?'

You said to him, as if you were taking what he said seriously 'But doesn't the earth go round the sun?'

I said to Donald 'But it's you who say that it must be the instruments that are wrong – '

Donald said 'Do you know the story of the frog in the saucepan of water?'

You said 'No.'

I thought – But Donald, you do really know what we are trying to talk about: I mean, if it were barium; about the dragon in the stone.

Donald said 'If you put a frog in a saucepan of water, and then raise the temperature of the water very slowly so that there is no decisive moment at which the frog will know that it should jump, then it will boil to death.'

You said 'Is that true?'

Donald jumped up and flapped his elbows up and down. He said 'Me no wantee boil to deathee!' Then he went to the door. He said 'A bedtime story, children.'

After Donald had gone, you said 'You don't all have to protect yourselves by pretending to be mad scientists.'

I said 'That's right. But I've got you.'

When I lay with you at night we were either face to face with my arms around you so that it was as if what I held were glowing patterns of light: or when you turned with your back to me we fitted into one another like the yin and yang of the universe. Then after a time when you turned again there would be no separate parts of us; my mind had gone out; we were the whole. Then some image might come in – This frog is about to boil! Dear God, this red-hot saucepan is the sun! Jump! What a miraculous universe!

We were some salamander, perfect in the flames.

In the laboratory Donald and I gave up the experiments which presented us with problems for which we could not or would not find answers: we went back to a different and more boring line of checking results obtained by others. I wondered – So where is our task? Our mission? What are we doing, you and I? Then – But there is still the interesting question of what I think I am doing watching for little clicks and bumps of light: what, indeed, in general do humans think they are doing?

In the evenings when I came back to you we would not talk much now about what we had done during the day. I thought – These bumps and clicks: either there is, or is not, something growing elsewhere.

We began to read English and German literature to each other in the evenings. (You said 'Not French.' I said 'Why not French?' You said ' Oh all right, but the French seem to use words as if they say everything.') We read Shakespeare, Milton, Goethe, Kleist. I said 'What things are seems to depend on an act of recognition: but one seems almost to have to give up hoping for this before it occurs.'

You said 'You go on a journey.'

I said 'You know you're going; you don't know where you're going, or how would you be discovering?'

Time passed, or perhaps seemed to stand still, in this routine: it was in the coming round again that there seemed to be a present. So of course why should we want anything to come in from outside to break us up, we bits and pieces of a nucleus! I thought – Oh but how can there be creation, even of what we are now, if there is not some breaking up?

And what was happening in the outside world during 1937? In Spain and Russia Trotskyites and anarchists were being murdered: in Germany Hitler gathered his generals round him and plotted for war. In England there was the visit of the New Zealand cricket team: what quiet clicks, what pleasant bumps of light! I thought – And for us what a miracle that we should be undergoing no further violent change; but being, for the moment, just as we are!

You said 'What was this vision that you had in Spain?'

I said 'That consciousness creates things: but for us to become used to this, we have to become used to some breaking up, re-forming, breaking up, of ourselves.'

You said 'Do you want that?'

I said 'Want!' Then – 'It is too paradoxical for us to talk about want.'

Sometime early in 1938 Donald Hodge set about rebuilding and re-equipping the laboratory: I was encouraged to take a holiday. I said 'We can go to London.' You said 'Yes.' I said 'I suppose this is the sort of thing I'm talking about.' You said 'I've been thinking for ages that I must try and find out what has happened to Bruno.' I said 'But you don't think I want to go to London!' You said 'Then I suppose that's all right.'

I arranged for us to stay in the rooms of my old friend Melvyn: Melvyn would be away; he said that he would be on some expedition to Spain. It was in this building that I had lived two years ago. I wondered – Will there be anything from that old outside world coming in?

I said 'What shall I do while you are out looking for Bruno?'

You said 'I hope you will cease to exist.'

I said 'But we will be connected!'

You said 'Then that's all right.'

In London we went to cinemas and exhibitions. The films were for the most part about people being together, going apart, coming together again: I thought – Well what else is a story? Then – But no one gets the point. In the exhibitions the most interesting paintings were those in which people and things seemed to be being split up into little bits and pieces of light. I thought – But the point is that we, the people watching, can know this; and so we are not split up. I said to you 'It's not as if I want to be with anyone except you.' You said 'It's not as if I want to be with anyone except you.' I thought – Well, that's all right.

I said 'How will you find Bruno?'

You said 'I can't write to Trixie and her husband; it might be dangerous for them.'

I said 'Can't you write in code?'

You said 'They would still have to answer.' Then – 'Perhaps I can do something like cast palm-nuts from one hand to the other.'

There was a committee that provided aid for refugees from Nazi Germany; you found their address and made enquiries. They said they had no knowledge of Bruno. You also tried to find out what you could about your father.

You said 'There's no news except from my cousins that he's in a camp.'

I said 'There's nothing you can do.'

You said 'I should have tried to do something before.'

I thought – I suppose I should have found out long ago what happened to Caroline.

There was a day when Melvyn arrived back unexpectedly from Spain. Or perhaps he had never been to Spain: I thought – Of course, he has just been waiting round some corner so that he can break in on us in bed. We were, in fact, in bed, and making love. Melvyn's eyebrows had become so pointed that they were indeed like those of a devil. He said 'You two! See me in my study after prayers.'

I said 'How was Spain?'

He said 'Very hot, Spain.'

I said 'This is Helena.'

He said 'Darling, you've got the face, but I'd take the thousand ships.'

I thought – The Devil becomes a bore: but he was necessary to do whatever it was in the Garden of Eden?

You said 'How do you do.'

Melvyn said 'Fairly straightforwardly in the morning, ducky.'

I said 'I don't suppose you've even been to Spain!'

He said 'You two were clever to have got out when you did.'

You said 'Why?'

Melvyn said 'Franco's going to win.'

I said 'Whose side are you on at the moment, the Russians or the Germans?'

Melvyn said to you 'Oh but have I heard some stories about you!'

You got out of bed to dress. Melvyn watched you.

He said 'I've always thought that one is given a much easier time by one's enemies than by one's friends.'

I said 'Oh very true.'

When you were dressed you said 'I'll go and look for Bruno.'

I thought – You won't let Melvyn hurt us, will you?

Melvyn said 'I do think Hitler's doing the most tremendous job, you know: getting rid of all those nice clever unmentionables who could help him.'

You said to me 'I'll see you.'

Melvyn said 'Those naughty Aryan boys can't boil a cup of tea!'

I said 'Eleanor's father and mother have disappeared in concentration camps.'

You said to me 'It's all right.'

I thought – The Devil, or Melvyn, must be in some sort of despair –

– He will get us out of our Garden of Eden, to look for Bruno?

Melvyn and I went to a pub. It was a pub where I had sometimes gone with Caroline. I thought – Is there not some weird Middle Eastern sect in which the Devil is considered a saint, for having got Adam and Eve moving on from their Garden of Eden?

Melvyn was saying to whoever would listen to him in the pub – 'Of course Stalin doesn't want the Reds to win the war in Spain. What he wants to do is persecute Trotskyites. He's got his problems at home: he has to say they're caused by Trotskyites. Who cares about Spain? Hitler, too, wants the war to go on: what a chance to try out weapons! And for the rest – oh what an opportunity to act a bit of caring! If you think anyone outside Spain wants the war to end, you're a child – one who'll end up like one of those orphans of the children's crusade.'

I thought – My angel, take care, will you, how you cross the road: look to left and right; remember, if you want me, perhaps I will know?

Melvyn said 'People with power always want to wipe out heretics rather than infidels: if power is kept pure, then infidels wipe out themselves.'

I said 'So why be in politics at all – that of the Germans or the Russians?'

Melvyn said 'Do you know about this children's crusade? There are a lot of children in Europe left over from Stalin's burning of the heretics, and so they are being sold into slavery in Spain.'

I said 'I was going on a pilgrimage to Santiago de Compostela.'

Melvyn said 'I like the idea of your wife getting herself on to the wrong side. That was clever.'

I thought – But Melvyn, if you're so clever, don't you know that you should know more, or nothing?

There were some people at the bar of the pub whom I recognised from meeting them two years ago with Caroline. They were talking about the prospects of war if Hitler moved into Austria: would Austria fight; would Britain and France recognise their obligations. Melvyn went to fetch beer and got into a conversation with them. I thought – But if human life is a matter of style, of means rather than of ends –

– Do I imagine that means just turn up for me?

After a time I followed Melvyn to the bar. I thought – Where are you now, my angel, my loved one.

Melvyn was saying 'The more success Hitler has the more he'll get rid of those terribly useful Jews. And those pretty Aryan boys couldn't boil a cup of pee.'

Then one of the men at the bar, whom I had met when I had been with Caroline, said to me 'There was a chap in here asking about you the other day.'

I said 'Oh was there?'

He said 'A German chap. He heard someone talking about you and Caroline.'

I thought I might say – Do you know what's happened to Caroline?

I said 'Who was he?'

He said 'Working at the university. A philosopher. Got out of Germany a year or two ago. One of them. Said he knew you.'

I said 'Was he called Bruno?'

The man said 'Can't remember his name.'

I thought – Do I really think that things work like this?

I said 'Do you know what's happened to Caroline? I heard she was back from Spain.'

He said 'She's around. Why not call her?'

I thought – But you and I, so we are all right, my angel, my loved one.

Melvyn was saying to someone at the bar 'But I am a secret agent, didn't you know?'

Someone was saying, 'No, I didn't.'

Someone else said 'But how can you be a secret agent if you do not keep it secret?'

Melvyn said 'Good thinking!'

I said 'I'm going.'

Melvyn said 'Stop that man! He's a Nazi agent!'

Out in the street there were placards announcing news of Hitler's latest threats against Austria, of this or that statesman's journeys between London, Vienna, Berchtesgaden. I bought a paper and sat in a café. I thought – Well, here we are, my angel: out on a mystery tour from the Garden of Eden.

There was news of the latest trial in Russia. Some high-up Soviet dignitary had confessed to crimes that he could not possibly have committed; then in court he had denied his confession; then the next day he had confirmed it again. The newspaper reporter speculated – was this the only way in practice he could make a protest? Or was the whole to-and-fro business a put-up job by the prosecution to give verisimilitude to the ludicrous business of confession? I thought – But the point is, this is all at random, it is chaos.

There was also an item about some minor official on trial who was accused of arranging the distribution of thousands of tons of deliberately poisoned wheat-seed in Odessa. The official was called I. A. Platov. I thought – Might those be the initials of Mitzi's father? Not of Kolya.

Then – If things are random, is it not possible to avoid them?

– But what is surprising about these events in Berchtesgaden, Vienna, Moscow, is not that they happen, but that anything different ever happens –

– Would it not be a miracle if Kolya got to Cambridge!

I saw your face looking in through the café window. I had chosen the café because it was opposite the building where Melvyn had rooms, but I had not expected you to come back before evening. You came in and said 'I didn't think you would be here.' I said 'No, I didn't think you would be here.' You said 'I've missed you.' I said 'I've missed you too.' You said 'Now we can have lunch.' I said 'Yes, I'm starving.'

Then I said 'I think I may have news of Bruno.'

You said 'Oh.'

I said 'He may be at the university.'

'What university?'

'London. You could make enquiries at the central office building.'

You said 'You want me to find Bruno!'

I said 'I don't want you to find Bruno!'

You said 'Oh no, it does not matter what we want, I suppose.'

I said 'Someone told me when I was having a drink in a pub with my horrible friend Melvyn.'

I thought – Those terrible people in Moscow, Vienna, Berchtesgaden – they get what they want?

After lunch you went to the university to make enquiries about Bruno. I went back to Melvyn's rooms and lay on the bed. I felt lost and sad. I thought – Human beings are required to be something too difficult if they are to create, to break things up, to create. After a time I went to Melvyn's desk and opened it and on the top of a pile of letters – placed there, it seemed, so that anyone who opened the desk would immediately see it – was a letter from Caroline to Melvyn which had been written, I could tell, a year and a half ago from Barcelona. It began –

You wouldn't believe it, but M. has gone off to the front! Oh what a relief! He was becoming such a bore. You'd like my new friend, though. Do you remember what you once said about some boy? – Wherever you kiss him, it's like kissing his beard.

I put the letter back and closed the desk. I thought – Well, I was sad and depressed anyway –

– What do you do, fart at the Devil?

– But I have known that long ago I should have made some contact with Caroline.

I tried to remember the telephone number of Caroline's aunt: I found it in the telephone book. I got through, and asked if Caroline was there. Caroline's aunt said 'She'll be back this evening.' I tried to explain to myself what I was doing. I thought – Explanations are ridiculous.

Then – It is knowing that things are ridiculous, that will get us round and round the world on our journeys from and to the Garden of Eden?

I skimmed through some of the volumes of Melvyn's pornographic library. I thought – All this pain, this violence, it is what kills people; without it they would not survive?

When you came back in the evening you were with Bruno: I was sitting at the window looking out. You both seemed so young; you came skipping down the pavement – you with your long legs and hips like a pestle and mortar; like one of those animals down from the skies. I thought – It is when I have been away from you that I can see you once more like this; pounding at my heart from anywhere in the universe.

You said 'You remember Bruno?'

I said 'I remember Bruno!'

Bruno said 'You were the character in that play by Brecht who wandered on to the stage and stole our darling daughter Elena!'

I said 'It took me some time.'

Bruno said 'Ah, the timing is not our business.'

I thought – You and Bruno and Trixie, when you were young, when you visited Kleist's grave, you knew what was your business?

I said 'You're teaching philosophy?'

Bruno said 'No one has heard of Heidegger in this happy country! And now I learn from Wittgenstein that there is nothing anyway to be said.'

I said 'But there are still beautiful ways of saying this.'

Bruno said 'Ah that is why Heidegger has become silent!'

You were looking so pleased, with your hands clasped in front of you, like a mother proud of her children.

I said 'You two go out by yourselves to dinner tonight.'

You said 'You come too!'

I said 'No, you have a lot to talk about.'

Bruno said, 'Sir, are you casting aspersions on my dishonour?'

When you and Bruno had gone – talking, talking; skipping on the pavement as if on hot coals in a game that fakirs or children play – I rang up Caroline's aunt's house and this time Caroline answered the telephone and I said 'This is Lazarus come from the dead, come back to tell you all; I shall tell you all.' Caroline said 'Good God,

I'm not talking to you!' I said 'Meet you behind the gasworks, twenty minutes.' This was a phrase I had used when years ago we were arranging to meet in the pub. I rang off. I thought – Well, this may not work. Then – But after all it is quite fun. And what was that other phrase – Shall we sin, that grace may abound?

– And the answer was God forbid!

In the pub there were one or two of the people who had been there that morning. When Caroline came in she looked much more grown-up and assured. I thought – Well God, if you want to, forbid! She said 'I'm really not going to talk to you!' I said 'You mean, we can skip the preliminaries?' She said 'I thought you were dead.' I said 'I very nearly was.' She said 'Then we were told that you'd gone over to the Fascists.' I said 'I think your friend with the beard wanted to have me shot.' She said 'Well, you've perked up, haven't you!'

I wanted to send some message to you – Don't worry, this is all right, my angel, my loved one.

I said to Caroline 'I should have got in touch with you before, but I did hear from Melvyn that you were all right.'

Caroline said 'Melvyn says that you're now with some Fascist tart holed up in the north.'

I said 'She's not a Fascist tart, she's an agent in occupied territory.'
She said 'She is?'

I said 'She saved me when I was going to be shot; I mean, not by your friend, but by the other side.'

Caroline said 'It doesn't seem you were very popular.' Then 'But I never believe anything you say, you see.'

I said 'But you were all right?'

Caroline told me how she had made a great success of her reporting from Barcelona in the early days of the Civil War; her reports had been taken up by a national newspaper in England. She had come home, had gone out to Spain again in 1937, had been in Barcelona for the fighting between Stalinists and Trotskyites. She had, in fact, got a scoop because she had been with her boyfriend, the man with the beard, when he had been arrested by Stalinists. While Caroline talked she leaned towards me and I found that I was leaning slightly away from her: it was as if she were wearing scent to cover up some quite different smell.

I said 'Then you're on your way to becoming a top-class journalist.'

She said 'I am a top-class journalist!'

I said 'That's good.'

She said 'When you can't think of anything else to say, you always say "That's good"!'

I thought – Well, that's quite witty.

She told me a little about her life in Barcelona with Buenaventura, the man with the beard. I watched her mouth as she talked. I thought – People feed on the violence of war as they feed on Melvyn's pornography; then they spew it out again, chewed, like sick, to feed others.

Caroline was saying 'He did the most fantastic things with the co-operatives, he got them working round the clock.'

I said 'Did he hang little tassles on them?'

She said 'On what?'

I said 'The co-operatives.'

She said 'You are disgusting!' Then 'I'm not going to stay with you if you're still like that!'

I thought – Then good, it will be – God forbid.

She said 'And anyway what about you and Spooks?'

I said 'Why do you call her Spooks?'

She said 'Melvyn calls her Spooks.'

I said 'Do you still see Melvyn?'

She said 'Now don't start that again!' Then – 'Do you and she roll about in the snow in the frozen north?'

Caroline and I got rather drunk. I told her a fanciful version of the story of the battle I had been involved in in Spain – And there was this castle! And there was I like Jack on the beanstalk! I felt, as I listened to myself – But I am making myself sick. I found that I did not tell her of my shooting of the man with the machine-gun. I thought – This is not because I am ashamed: it is too heartfelt to be brought up as sick.

She said 'All right, let's go back to Auntie's.'

I thought – You mean, you want to make love at Auntie's?

Then – Well God, come on then –

Caroline put her head on my shoulder. She said 'As a matter of fact, I think he did want you shot!'

I said 'Who?' I thought – But you can't say that!

She said 'Buenaventura!' She giggled.

I felt I had to get out of the pub. On our way out we passed a group of people by the door. One of them was Mullen. I had not seen Mullen since I had been with him in the picture gallery in Moscow. There he had stood with his back to the painting of the three Old Testament angels: he had been like a shadow against networks of light. He looked at me now, as he had looked at me then, with his sad yellow eyes. I thought – Perhaps he will not want to recognise me: perhaps he is once more waiting for that bald Russian man with whom he was in the picture gallery in Moscow, in the pub outside Cambridge. Here he was with a group of people I did not know.

I said 'Hullo.'

Mullen said 'Hullo.' Then – 'I heard you'd been in Spain.'

Caroline said 'I've spent much more time than him in Spain!'

Mullen said to me 'And now I hear that you're working at some university in the north.'

I said 'Yes.'

Mullen said 'I wonder if you would like to have lunch with me sometime.'

I said 'I would.'

Caroline said 'What about me?'

I said to Mullen 'How's Kapitsa?'

Mullen looked at me with his almost expressionless eyes.

I said 'But, in fact, I've got to get back to the north tomorrow.'

Caroline said 'You're going back tomorrow?'

I thought – Why did I say that? Then – Yes, I see.

Caroline said 'Well, I'm not going with you to Auntie's if you're going back to Spooks tomorrow!'

I thought I might say – All right, God, thank you.

Mullen said 'You won't stay and have a drink?'

Caroline said 'I will!'

Mullen said 'I was talking to him.'

Caroline said 'Oh you two, have a nice bugger!' She went back to the bar and seemed to be ordering herself a drink.

I said 'Goodbye.' I seemed to be talking both to Mullen and to Caroline. I went out of the pub. I thought – Mullen is my guardian devil?

I was lying on the bed in the room we had borrowed from Melvyn when you got back from your evening with Bruno. I was still feeling very sad. You looked tired. I said 'How was Bruno!' You said 'He was all right.' I said 'I met Mullen.' You said 'Who is Mullen?' I said 'He's the one, you know, who really is a Russian spy.' You said 'Bruno thinks that my father may be alive.'

I said 'Why does he think that?'

You said 'Because he says they're not killing people other than Jews.'

I said 'So what will you do?'

You said 'Bruno will find out what he can. Then I'll see.'

I said 'Let's go home tomorrow.'

You said 'Yes, let's go home tomorrow.' Then – 'Oh God, let's very nearly blow up the world, but not quite.'

When we got back to our home in the north I found Donald Hodge's laboratory equipped with new and more elaborate devices. There were Geiger-counters encased in lead to guard against stray radiation; amplifiers connected to recording machines which had numbers showing on dials. We embarked on yet another series of experiments to check the results of the experiments of others. I sat and made notes of the numbers that appeared on the dials. I thought, as I had thought before – But we are trying to achieve two things here: one is to understand what might be going on in the nucleus of an atom; the other is to understand what is meant by understanding; and in this, of course, we are doing an experiment with mind. That which experiments is in a sense the same as that which is experimented on; but to understand understanding – would there not have to be developed some further level of mind? Perhaps it is just this for which I am waiting in front of these switches and dials – for some stray seed to be encouraged by this I that is watching and to be nurtured in this strange world of mind.

I said to you 'But those old alchemists of yours – did they feel they had to change what it was to be human?'

You said 'I suppose they wanted to know what it might be to be gods.'

I said 'So humans couldn't blame any more what they called "gods".'

You said, 'If you succeed in what you are doing in your work, I suppose we won't have anyone to blame except ourselves.'

I found it increasingly difficult to talk to Donald Hodge about our work. He took up rugby football and cricket: he played these passionately: I thought – He finds it easier to knock around these simple bumps and clicks and balls.

I said to you 'Gods made such terrible things occur.'

You said 'You think we can't make terrible things occur?'

I said 'Chip away at the stone – '

You said 'We can still call "gods" the knowing that there is shape inside.'

I had a letter from Peter Reece, the clergyman I had stayed with years ago in the derelict town in the north. He gave me news of Nellie – the deaf-and-dumb girl whom my mother and I had befriended, whom I had first come across when she had gone bounding down the hill in her tyre. Nellie had been at the school for handicapped children run by nuns. Peter Reece wrote to say that Nellie was about to be inducted as a novice into the order of nuns; she had asked especially if I might be present at the ceremony. Peter Reece had sent his letter to my parents' house: he had not known where I was; nor, of course, that I was married.

I said to you 'That time when we missed each other in the north of England – '

You said 'Yes.'

I said 'And then I turned up in Berlin two years later at the time of the Reichstag fire – '

You said 'Yes?'

I said 'I suppose if I had not missed you that time in the north, then I might not have turned up just when it was necessary for you to get out of Berlin; and we might never have had our three days together – or this, or anything.'

You said 'You think you can't say that?'

I thought – Or you can say it about anything.

During the last six or seven years I had often thought I should visit Nellie: I had put it off, I did not quite know why. I had sometimes written to her: I had got letters back in a meticulous, childlike hand. She told me news of her school: the work and the gossip: she had said – I do not suppose this will interest you. In later years she had ended her letters with 'With love from yours in Christ.' I thought now – Well, yes, but what does this mean: some shaping within the stone?

I said to you 'But if we ever have to go apart from each other again, do you think that this time we will have to leave so much to chance, or can we not make our own arrangements to come together?'

You said 'You think we will have to go apart?'

I said 'No.'

You said 'We have been together, yes, for nearly two years.'

I wrote to Peter Reece to say that you and I would both come to Nellie's induction. I wrote to Nellie to say that you and I were married. I said to you 'I wonder if she will remember you.' You said 'Of course she will remember me!' I said 'You only met her once.' You said 'So how often did you meet her?' I said 'Oh yes, I see.'

We went by train to Nellie's ceremony. It was a grey cold day. We travelled to the landscape of mudflats and the estuary of the river – to where seeds, in the shape of humans, had once blown across the sea in small boats.

I said 'I don't see why there shouldn't be a world of coincidences as well as a world of cause and effect; why "gods" shouldn't be a word for our knowing this and trusting it.'

You said 'Put ourselves in the way of it? Of knowing what to do?'

I said 'Two years is not such a long time!'

You said 'We've been so lucky!'

We got out at the station to which I had come years ago; from which I had walked with my haversack down towards the river; where had been the derelict railway lines like the trails of dying animals dragging their way towards the sea. Here Nellie, the child Nellie, had gone rolling and bouncing like a seed; there had been a barrier like the edge of the known world; she had got through.

You said 'Don't be sad.'

I said 'Things are so frightening!'

You said 'I suppose you loved her.'

We got a bus from the bridge over the river to Nellie's convent which was some way out of the town. There were the mudflats; there were the ruins of the monastery built by men who had arrived in boats like acorn-cups; there the children had played with their burning-glass in the sun. I thought – The monks brought their own light, which was like fire.

I said 'It's things as they really are, that get you through?'

You said 'If you love them.'

The convent, which was next to the nun's school, was a grey stone building set back from the road: traffic struggled past like a retreating army. There was a bell that was worked by a chain near the door; when I pulled it a bit of the chain came away in my hand. A young nun came to the door and saw the chain in my hand and began to laugh. I said 'I'm terribly sorry!' The nun took us through to a room with cream-coloured walls and a large mahogany table on which there were cups and saucers and an urn; we were offered tea or coffee. The nun seemed always to be on the edge of laughter: as if what an extraordinary business it was to be offering tea or coffee! There were four or five other couples in the room; it seemed that these were parents or relatives of other would-be novices to be inducted. Neither Nellie's mother nor father was there.

I thought – We, you and I, are Nellie's mother and father?

– It is because this is like one of those Shakespearian recognition scenes that I seem to be on the edge of tears?

The time came for us to be taken through to a chapel at the back of the building. We were placed in a gallery below which were rows of nuns like shadows. I thought – They see that they are shadows on the walls of a cave; they get out into the sun when they are praying? Three would-be novices were led in and knelt at the altar-rail: even in their habits and seen from the back I thought I could tell which one was Nellie. I thought I might say – Ah, we know each other, we are agents in hostile territory! An old priest moved to and fro beyond the altar-rail. I thought – This is a ceremony that has been performed thousands of times before, will be performed thousands of times again: could there be evidence that it holds the world together?

You were kneeling beside me. It seemed that it might be we, you and I, who were again being married; who were to be sent out into the world, of course together, but on our own in so far as we were agents in hostile territory.

I wanted to say to Nellie – Give us your blessing.

After the ceremony we went back into the cream-walled room where cakes and sandwiches had been added to the cups and urns. The nun who had welcomed us had been joined by others; several of them seemed to be on the edge of laughter. I thought – The people who landed here centuries ago in their acorn boats; what made them survive, what did they hear, was it laughter?

When Nellie, the young Nellie, came in, I saw I had been right, yes, that it was she: such an open, clever face; such bright dark eyes. It was as if she would always be close to laughter – in her black habit scattering bits and pieces of light. She greeted, and was greeted by, people near the door: they conversed with her in deaf-and-dumb language; they seemed to be sprinkling each other with drops of light. Then she looked across the room at you and me. I thought – Oh why have I not been here before! Because this would have been not too little, but too much? Nellie became quite still; she clasped her hands in front of her: I thought – There are, indeed, paintings like this: of the recognition of what seems to be too much. She came towards us across the room. I held out both my hands to her; she took these and placed them on her shoulders. She was quite a small girl; pale; like something that has had to grow a long way towards the light. I thought I might say – I did not know if you would remember me! I said 'Nellie, I am so glad to see you, we have come to give you our love.' Nellie, looking at me, put a hand against my throat. I said 'This is my wife, Eleanor.' After a time Nellie said in a voice that was like bird-song coming from a roof 'Yes, I know.' She turned to you and you put your arms round each other and kissed. Then Nellie stood back and said something to an older nun who had come up to her, using her hands. The older nun said 'She says that every day she has prayed for you.' Nellie said quickly in the voice that seemed to come from the sky 'For you both.' The older nun laughed and said 'And of course will continue to pray for you.' Then we all started laughing. It was as if we might have to hold on to each other. I thought – Oh dear God, you see why I could not have come here before; I would have been burned up by this sun.

It continued to be almost unbearable, this sense of pleasure to be in the presence of Nellie. I thought – It was not exactly silence, that language, when they were building their tower up to heaven.

What is it, this energy that is light?

On the way back in the train I said to you 'When you spoke to her, all those years ago, what did you say she said to you?'

You said 'She told me where you were.'

I thought – Where was I? Then – I was already one of those bits and pieces of light?

This was in the spring of 1938 – after Hitler's Nazis had marched into Austria, at the beginning of his threats against Czechoslovakia, halfway down Europe's runaway descent towards hell. In the laboratory we were getting nowhere with our work; it was as if we knew we would get nowhere, we were waiting for something from outside to come in. There were rumours that people in Berlin were on the edge of a breakthrough. I thought – If there is to be the risk of total destruction, then there will perhaps be an equally great need for light.

In the summer Bruno came to stay with us. He was hollow-eyed, Jewish, full of energy. He said 'If Hitler marches into Czechoslovakia, then at last there will be war!'

I said 'But do you know what may happen if there is a war? I mean, what they might be discovering in Germany?'

Bruno said 'Can't you find out from Franz – you remember old

Franz – what they are doing, how far they have got, in Germany? He's up to his neck in that sort of work.'

You said 'Yes, perhaps I will try to make contact with Franz: and he might have news of my father.'

I thought – Pray for us, Nellie, will you? We may be off to some sort of war.

Melvyn came up to stay with us: he overlapped with Bruno for one night. He said 'You Jews, it's you who are going to discover how to get us all blown up! Why don't you do what you usually do to prove your moral superiority?'

Bruno said 'Which is what?'

Melvyn said 'Get just yourselves blown up.'

Bruno said 'Oh don't worry, we'll doubtless do that.'

People began to fill sandbags and dig trenches in the parks. Hitler was appearing on newsreels at Berchtesgaden like a strict governess showing men in striped trousers in and out of her study. Melvyn said 'You know what he's supposed to like having done to him, don't you?'

Bruno said 'Yes.'

Melvyn said 'But think of having to do it!'

You said 'Perhaps we will.'

Then in September there was the agreement at Munich between England, France, Germany and Italy by which a large part of Czechoslovakia was handed over to Germany without a fight; there were cheering crowds at railway stations and at airports. But the sandbags were not emptied; trenches were not filled in. Very soon it seemed that there was some shame at the celebrations; a knowledge that, after all, there would be war.

You said 'Perhaps I should go to Zurich before it is too late and find out what I can about my father.'

I said 'Yes, you've always wanted to go back to Zurich.'

You shouted 'Don't say it like that!'

I said 'I'm not saying it like that!' Then – 'And perhaps you'll be able to talk to Franz.'

We continued to cling to each other, you and I – in our bed; in our room in front of the fire. These were our rocks in a cold sea. I thought – But if we go apart, we can send each other messages, like those mythical sea-birds that can build nests on the waters of a cold sea.

You said 'You think we can only do what we have to do, become active, if we are sometimes in a practical sense separate?'

488

I said 'I have not said that!'

You said 'Of course you have not said that!'

I thought – And then from time to time we can have again those Shakespearian recognition scenes, miracle scenes; and at least will not have become fused, without energy, like ordinary ghastly married couples.

Sometime before Christmas I paid my annual visit to my father and my mother. I went on my own. I said to you 'Goodbye!' Then – 'Oh no, you never much liked opera.'

You said 'Meet you behind the gasworks – or whatever is that strange place that you say.'

I found my mother, upright, in her seat by the window. I thought – This is how she will appear, having been dug out of the ashes in a thousand years. She said 'I'm sorry I was horrible the last time you were here.' I said 'Oh that's all right.' Then – 'I thought psycho-analysts were usually awful to their children.' She said 'Yes, why is that, do you think?' I said 'I suppose it's to try to help them get away.' She said 'How kind!' I said 'Yes, but it only works if it's conscious, and then you can't really do it, can you?'

When I found my father in his study he seemed old, as if ash were already falling from factory chimneys on to snow. He said 'What are you doing for Christmas? Or don't you have Christmas any more?'

I thought I might say – Oh no, we eat babies.

I said 'I always find it frightening, Christmas: all those babies being killed: and such celebration!'

My father said 'I suppose it's like the production of any new species.'

I thought – Well, what I have learned from you is some sort of irony, my father and my mother: thank you: let it stand me in good stead.

I went to see Mullen at Cambridge. He had not been in touch with me since the time I had been with Caroline in the London pub. He was in the same building in the college in which he had been an undergraduate years ago. I said 'You never got in touch with me so I thought I'd get in touch with you: but what inferences you will draw from this!'

He said 'What news have you of our friend Kapitsa?'

I said 'I have no news of Kapitsa. I was going to ask you.'

Mullen was a long thin figure who seemed to be bent into his chair in the shape of a hook. He said 'Sherry?' Then – 'Your wife was a Party member, was she not?'

I said 'That was a long time ago.'

He said 'And then she was a nurse with the Nationalists in Spain.'

I said 'The things we have to do, in our different ways!'

He said 'You asked me a question a long time ago.'

'What was that?'

He said 'What is the essential difference between Communism and Nazism – when they both seem so similar in their ruthlessness and in their manipulation of power.'

'And what did you say?'

'What I say now is that Communists, for all their brutalities and stupidities, are on the side of life; whereas Nazis – as they say so explicitly themselves – are on the side of death.'

I said 'What about these people in Moscow now who say they deserve to die?'

He said 'But you know the answer to that.' Then – 'Why shouldn't they want to die?'

When Mullen smiled he had large yellow teeth which seemed to have been stained perhaps by drops running down from his eyes.

I said 'What you really want to know is, whether anyone is getting anywhere here with this business of radioactivity.'

He said 'Yes.'

I said 'We're getting nowhere. Kapitsa might be getting somewhere. There are stories that they might be getting near to a breakthrough in Germany. That was what I wanted to talk to you about.'

Mullen said 'Why do you say that Kapitsa might be getting somewhere?'

I said 'Because he has the imagination, he would want to succeed, he would not want everything he cared about to be destroyed.'

Mullen spread himself in his chair as if he were trying to make himself more anonymous, like a linen cover. He said 'You agree that it would be a disaster if such technology was developed by the Nazis.'

I said 'How far has Kapitsa got? Don't you know?'

He said 'Would you tell me if you got anywhere here in the future?'

I said 'I'd say what I thought was right so long as I'd made no undertaking not to. I wouldn't do anything explicitly for a foreign power.'

He said 'You wouldn't tell the Nazis?'

I said 'Of course I wouldn't tell the Nazis!'

He said 'And you wouldn't tell me.'

I said 'Oh I'm just going through the motions of what I think is right! What does it matter if you have nothing to tell me about Kapitsa?'

For Christmas that year we went, you and I, to Holy Island, or Lindisfarne – a piece of land off the Northumberland coast stuck out like an antenna into the sea. I had wanted to go there because it was one of the places to which, centuries ago, people had been blown across the dark sea in little boats; they had landed, had put down roots; they had built monasteries and places of light: where had they come from, where were they going? We stayed in a boarding-house, you and I. We were the only guests. I thought – Here we are, on these mudflats: there is plenty of room at the inn.

There was a Nativity scene set up in the village church: Mary and Joseph and the shepherds and the child were all looking at an empty space on the ground just outside the framework of the setting. I thought – It is as if there had been some sort of nest there: the bird has flown.

You said 'I used to think how important it was that there should be a reconciliation between Christians and Jews.'

I said 'And don't you think that now?'

You said 'I think we're always parts of the same thing.'

There was a walk across fields to huge sand-dunes and a beach to which it seemed only birds ever came; they hurried on wet sand with their reflections underneath them. I thought – It might be they who carry strange seeds in their crops; from these seeds, when they drop them, a new race of men might grow. Where would they have come from, where would they be going? There was a hard rain driving in from the sea. Donald Hodge had gone for Christmas across the sea to Germany, then Denmark. He had gone there in response to rumours about what might be about to be revealed of the secrets of the atom. Perhaps was it from this that a strange new race of men might spring – as it was supposed to have done that first Christmas years ago, but not quite: the seeds for 2000 years having remained dormant as if under snow. I said to you 'I don't think it has ever really been seen, the point of that story.' You said 'The point is, what is a story?' I said 'Perhaps something the effect of which, in spite of its not being seen, grows.'

At night it was so cold that it was as if spray were breaking over us where we clung to each other on our rock, and all the devils that had been sent out into the world were rushing back to us for warmth, for protection.

It was just after Christmas that I got a telegram from Donald Hodge asking me to return home urgently; he said something of great importance had occurred of which he could not tell me in a telegram. I thought – Oh indeed, some parturition? Some projected slaughter of innocents? Then – What we need, perhaps, is a story about stories.

– Once upon a time, children, when it came to be necessary to eat the fruit of that second tree of Life –

We left Holy Island, you and I, and went back to the laboratory. There we learned the story of what had actually happened across the sea that Christmas. I thought – It would be a technical problem, certainly, to put it into words.

Once upon a time, children, there were two scientists who were working in a laboratory in Berlin. One was called Otto Hahn and the other Lise Meitner. One was a chemist and one was a physicist; one was a man and one was a woman; one was a Gentile and the other was a Jew. They had been working together for many years to try to understand the secrets of the atom. Then in the summer of 1938 their partnership was broken up: Lise Meitner, an Austrian Jew, was forced to leave Austria/Germany: she went to Sweden to be an exile in a foreign country. Otto Hahn stayed behind in the laboratory in Berlin; he carried on with the experiments. He had been the one to set up and tabulate the experiments; Lise Meitner had been the one to try to understand what they might mean. Otto Hahn found that now more than ever the experiments made no sense: the nuclei of uranium seemed to be being transmuted into the nuclei of a much lighter element; and what understanding was there for this? There had, of course, been the theory that the nucleus of an atom might be held together like a drop of water; but although it could conceivably be imagined that a drop of water might split into two almost equal parts, there was still no mathematics to explain how this might occur; and what could be said scientifically about what could not be represented by mathematics? Otto Hahn wrote to Lise Meitner to tell her of the results of his experiments: she was, after all, the one who might be able to explain them, even if in exile. This was Christmas, 1938. Then Lise Meitner was joined in Sweden by her nephew, Otto Frisch: Otto Frisch was also an exile; also a physicist and a Jew. On Christmas Eve Lise Meitner and Otto Frisch went for a walk by the sea. There was snow on the ground: would this have reminded them of that very first Christmas years ago? Lise Meitner told Otto Frisch of the results of the experiments in Berlin: of the uranium nucleus that seemed to transmute itself into much lighter parts. They knew, of course, that if this were true (what a miracle!) – if the uranium nucleus were split into anything like two – then these parts, being of the same electrical charge, would repel each other with enormous force: then indeed there would be released energy locked up in the heart of an atom – a force for terrible creation or destruction. Lise Meitner and Otto Frisch sat down in the snow: by the waters of a cold grey Babylon they – what? – held pencils and pieces of paper on their knees; they worked on the mathematics. The mathematics for once – perhaps it was the cold; perhaps it was the urgency of being in exile – did not seem too difficult. The internal charges within the unstable nucleus of an uranium atom were such that it was likely on its own to be on the point of overcoming the surface tension that held it together anyway: for it to split into two might after all indeed take no more than the impact of a neutron. And then – if the nucleus of a uranium atom did in fact split into the two much lighter nuclei of a barium and a krypton atom, which was what Otto Hahn was suggesting – then indeed there would be the violent repulsion and the release of force. But still – where was it, as it were, that the energy for this force came from? For in mathematics something does not come out of nothing. Then it was worked out – since the sum of the weights of barium and krypton nuclei are slightly less than the weight of a single uranium nucleus, some mass must have been lost in the process; and so what could have happened to this mass except that it must have been transformed into energy? The formula by which mass was transformed into energy was known. Lise Meitner and Otto Frisch sat with their pencils and bits of paper on their knees. And so, yes – abracadabra! – it was seen that the mass that had been lost in the fission process was, when transformed, almost precisely the amount of energy which would be involved in the two new nuclei repelling each other with enormous force; and it was indeed exactly the amount of energy (though this was not seen till slightly later) – if it could be supposed that as part of the explosion were emitted also two or three loose neutrons – which, if suitably controlled, might then, of course, be used for the exploding of further uranium nuclei – and so on – in geometrical progression or chain reaction to whatever strength of explosion might be required. And what sort of explosion might be imagined to be required – for creation or destruction – by two such exiles in a strange country on a cold Christmas Eve?

You said 'That is a good story.' Then – 'Yes, it should be true.'

I said 'It is not all that far from what I imagined in Spain.'

Donald Hodge said 'The day after Christmas, Otto Frisch travelled to Copenhagen to see Niels Bohr. And Niels Bohr said "But what fools we have been, not to have seen this before!"'

I said 'Oh but how would it have been proper for us to have seen it before!'

You said 'How long will it take?'

Donald said 'It will take time to handle, if indeed it can be handled at all – time, and a great deal of money, and work, and imagination.'

I said 'Then that's all right.'

Donald said 'What is?'

I said 'I think imagination is on our side.'

Donald said 'And, with luck, money.'

You said 'But time?'

It was not long after this that Hitler marched into what was left of Czechoslovakia; then began to make threatening noises against Poland. I thought – It is obvious what is in runaway: what else but a coincidence like this might be imagined to be in control!

I said 'We always knew that there was something urgent to be done.'

You said 'I don't think this makes it easier to separate from each other.'

In the summer, you set off for Zurich: to find what news you could about your father; to try to make contact with Franz, to find out what was happening in Germany about a Bomb; perhaps to pursue the course of study that you had embarked on years ago – the one concerning the connections between coincidence, the workings of the imagination, and fact.

I said 'You will be careful.'

You said 'And write to me every day.'

I said 'Meet you on top of the gasworks, twenty minutes.'

IX: Eleanor/Max/ Eleanor

I am sitting by this lake with a pencil and notebook on my knee.

You are – Walking through a wood? Watching for bumps and bars of light? Testing. Testing.

Gasthof Friedrich, Kusnacht, Zurich See
August 29th 1939

My Angel,

It looks as though there will be war – so that humans can bear the burden of their contradictions?

Having learned to distinguish between good and evil; having also learned that learning, evolution, goodness, take place as a result of trial and error and enormous waste –

– Why should not they be destined for waste?

What logic, what comfort, on this strange planet!

Testing. Practising.

This is a way to get through to you, my angel?

Here the summer term has ended. The Wise Old Man and his Witch's Coven have all gone over the hill.

By this I mean – Professor Jung has completed his seminars on the 'Spiritual Exercises of St Ignatius Loyola', and the conference at

Ascona this year is on 'The Symbolism of Rebirth in the Religions of All Times and Places'.

These metaphors! They remind us that language is no more than a shot at reality.

– In reality, am I in touch with you?

I have been told of an experiment in which you take a mother and a child cat, separate them, then if you kill the child cat, for instance in Australia, the mother cat, in Europe, attached to suitable recording instruments, will show signs of instantaneous distress.

I am sad. I am lonely.

You are happy?

I sit on a jetty and look out across the lake. I imagine rising up out of the water a hand with a sword with a message on it –

– You call this reality?

There is no more news from my cousins about my father. He was in Sachsenhausen concentration camp in 1936; he remained there till probably early this year; then he was let out. He is now said to be working for the government.

Why did the Nazis let him out? Does he know what he is doing? Does he expect me to know?

Might we not both be in danger if I, his errant daughter, try to make contact with him?

Practising. Testing.

In the years before 1936 he had become known for his outspokenness in defence of Jews: it was for this, presumably, that he was arrested. He was also becoming known for his work on the philosophical and even political implications of modern science. For this (as well as for the other accomplishment) he had gained the respect of many different kinds of scientists. So the government might well have thought that he could be useful to them in the run-up to war; and his wife, my mother, a Jewess, was now dead.

There might be good or bad reasons for his not getting in touch with me. There might be good or bad reasons for my not having got in touch with him. He might be ashamed: or he might be something more rare on this strange planet.

He might have some design. He might know that I would know what he is doing. To take responsibility on oneself – to expect others to take responsibility on themselves – this is to go against the dependence on others that is taken to be social responsibility on this sad planet.

So what are the techniques – if we do not accept that the human race should destroy itself?

Practising.

The seminars we have been engaged in this last term have been to do with how one might, as an individual, get in touch with some operational level of this so-called 'reality'. There are Eastern techniques for this; but these are apt to encourage a mystical turning away from the world rather than a dealing with it. There are Christian techniques; but with these one puts oneself into the hands of a religious authority, and why should such hands be any more to do with reality than one's own? Jung and his coven of witches here advocate what they call 'active imagination' – you let consciousness go, and then messages come in from an unconscious that is said to be universal. But why should such a game between consciousness and unconsciousness be to do with reality? It seems to me that anything called 'reality' would have to be a to and fro between oneself and the outside world – at least between oneself and that which has the appearance of an outside world. I mean, if you let the barriers that form the defence of your personality go, then the messages that pop up will be in the form of actual events, juxtapositions, recognitions.

I am trying to write my thesis about this. When I am not sitting at the end of this jetty and trying to imagine what you are doing, I am by the window in my room which has a view over the jetty where I have been sitting. You have said – It is necessary to have a way of looking down on oneself. I can say from here – Why, there I was at the end of the jetty! How interesting that I am lonely and sometimes frightened!

Do you think this is possible?

Seeing a pattern is on a different level from what is frightened or frightening? Testing.

I am wondering if I can bring into my thesis something about our experiences in Spain: I was here; you were there: what can one say about connections? An appreciation of these would be aesthetic. The state of mind required, looking back, was not to plan, not to try to sort out: but to listen, and carry on, and discover.

Should I go myself into Germany now? There is not much time if there is to be war.

I have tried to get in touch with Franz. I have tried to get in touch with Walburga. Walburga, as you know, is a friend of Franz. They are both away. I have not thought it proper to try to get in touch directly with my father.

We know there are patterns because there is our experience of what is aesthetic. But knowing this involves us in more than knowing that the patterns are there. What do we do, as part of a pattern?

What should I do now? In the humdrum world, what is moral?

The one thing that I have not done which I have thought I should do (looking down on myself) is to try to get in touch with Stefan or even Rudi (you remember Stefan and Rudi? the people with whom I went across the Sahara). Stefan is a Swiss: I know his home is somewhere near Zurich. Rudi came from southern Germany. I have not wanted to get in touch with them because after the dramas in North Africa I did not think that they would want to see me; nor did I want to see them. Also I thought that there might still be some trouble for us all with the authorities. Up to now I have felt myself protected by my new passport.

But – morally, should I not get in touch with Stefan or Rudi? To find out how they are? Also I have something of their property.

But what would this have to do with any pattern we have imagined?

Testing. Testing.

With anything aesthetic or moral, however, one knows not what will emerge: only the means; not even the connections.

So I will go out now and see what might be done.

See you behind the gasworks, forty minutes?

Bodensee
August 30th 1939

My Angel,

I went to the polytechnic, but they had no news of Stefan or Rudi: they had an address, however, for Stefan on the shores of the Bodensee. So I have come here. I have found where Stefan lives, and have left a message for him to meet me. I don't know why I am doing this. It is true that I owe something to him and Rudi.

I am in a café and am sitting looking out across this lake on the other side of which is Germany. Is this why I have come here? To put myself close to what you physicists call 'potentialities'?

I feel as if I have put myself into one of those experiments of which you physicists are fond: will this or that potentiality become

498

actual. But as we know – does this not depend on the conditions chosen by the experimenter?

Talking to you. Talking to myself. Experimenting.

Later.

I was sitting in the café writing this to you in my notebook when Stefan turned up. He looked awful; he had pale gold hair; one eye seemed to be bigger than the other. He said 'I hear you were looking for me.' I said 'Oh Stefan, how nice to see you!' He said 'We thought you were dead.' I said 'I wanted to find out what happened to you!' He said 'Well, here I am.' He sat down at my table. He seemed aggrieved: perhaps he was frightened of what I would want. It seemed that he had succeeded in turning his face into a mask. I thought – Well, this was always one of his potentialities. I said 'But what happened to you? I mean, in Morocco?' He said 'I came on later in the bus.' I said 'Did you find Rudi?' He said 'Of course I found Rudi!' I said 'He was in hospital?' He said 'I picked up both Rudi and the truck.' I said 'Oh Stefan, you are clever!' Then – 'Rudi was all right?'

I thought – One of my potentialities perhaps must be to wear a mask.

He said 'Yes, Rudi's all right.' Then – 'But what about you?'

I tried to tell Stefan the story about how I had got to Spain. But this came out wrong; I could not make it sound anything but chaotic. And Stefan was not interested; both he and I seemed to be waiting for something quite different.

He told me more about himself and Rudi in Morocco. He had come across in the bus the scene of what he called the 'accident'; he had learned where Rudi was in hospital; they had been told that I had been taken off by soldiers. In hospital Rudi had recovered from concussion; he and Stefan had retrieved the truck and what was left of the contents and then, because of the war in Spain, they had got to the French port of Oran and had taken a boat to France. I found that I was not much interested in this story either: I was thinking – Oh, but what makes anyone interested in this sort of stuff?

Stefan was saying 'We got hardly anything for the contents of the truck: it scarcely covered our expenses.' I said 'Oh what a shame!' I thought – He is giving reasons, I suppose, why none of the proceeds should come to me: then – But this is still not what is concerning him. Then he said 'Rudi wants to see you.' I said 'Is Rudi here?' He said 'He's not here now, but he's coming tomorrow.' I said 'I suppose I know why he wants to see me.' Stefan said 'You know why he wants to see you?' I was feeling ill. I thought – Oh but I can see why this might not be boring.

You remember the diamonds that Rudi had been carrying when he ran the truck into a tree; that I had found when he was unconscious; that I had been carrying around with me in their small leather pouch ever since. Of course, it was likely that I had been reluctant to see Rudi or Stefan simply because I had not wanted to tell them (or to lie to them?) about these diamonds: but this was also why I had felt I had to see them now. But now I had begun to feel ill. It seemed that I was being waylaid by a business that had nothing to do with what I was properly involved in; that I must get it over with quickly. I thought – But at least I have kept the diamonds safely. Then – But it is diamonds that are boring: they are part of a pattern of self-destruction. Then Stefan said 'Rudi has been keeping a letter that was sent to you.'

I said 'A letter?'

He said 'It came to the polytechnic some time ago. They gave it to me, and I gave it to Rudi. We didn't know what had happened to you.'

I said 'What sort of letter?'

Stefan said 'Rudi will bring it with him when he comes tomorrow.'

I thought – You mean, he will give me the letter if I give him the diamonds? This is the point of this business?

I said 'You're sure he'll bring it?'

Stefan said 'Yes.' Then – 'The reason why I was travelling on the bus in Morocco, you know, was because I didn't agree with what Rudi was doing.'

I said 'I'm awfully sorry, I'm feeling ill, I must go and lie down.'

Stefan said 'But you'll be here lunchtime tomorrow?'

I am writing this in my room in the *Gasthaus* where I can look out across the lake towards Germany. A letter addressed to the poly-technic might well be from my father: so was this why I had made efforts to see Stefan or Rudi? You see how this is difficult. The way in which I am feeling ill is that waves seem to be breaking into my head; a white light coming down; you know the feeling.

Rudi must want to see me because I have the diamonds? And how else would I have ever heard of this letter! Would I have wanted to see Rudi if I had not had the diamonds? The speculations are fruitless. What a style to have to learn, to be in a pattern with what is happening.

Testing. Testing.

Oh how interesting that I am feeling ill!

The gasworks may blow up, twenty minutes.

I have been to the landlady downstairs and asked her if I could use her telephone. I wanted to talk to you, but there was no chance of a line to England. I suppose everyone is talking about something boring like war. So I booked personal calls once more to Franz and to Walburga in Germany. One goes on, does one, casting lines, lifelines, over the water.

Don't you think we might settle down, one day, you and I, on the edge of some beautiful painted desert?

You remember when you said – There is no mathematical reason why messages should not come to us from the future –

– It is just difficult to imagine how we might be able to recognise these.

Practising.

The landlady came to tell me that one of my calls had got through: I hoped it was to Franz: it was to Walburga.

Walburga said 'How marvellous to hear your voice! I cannot wait to see you! Where are you?'

'I am just the other side of the Bodensee.'

'Then I am coming!'

'Tell me, have you any news of Franz?'

'Why do you ask that?'

'It is important that I get in touch with him.'

'Always Franz! But I will find out.'

'But do come tomorrow! I am longing to see you.'

'Where shall we meet?'

'At the Café Miramar, Romanshorn; it is on the lake. I will be there at lunchtime.'

'I will be there!'

I am now back in my room: I do not know what is happening: there are these waves coming in.

Do you think Walburga will have found where Franz is? Do you think I should try to see Franz? Do you think Rudi will bring the letter? Do you think it will be from my father?

Should I have asked Walburga to find out about my father?

I still am not used to this: testing!

Do tell me what you are doing.

I imagine you, yes, walking in a wood. You come to a cottage in which a beautiful girl is imprisoned. I cry out to warn you – This is a witch! My cry goes round the world like that of the kitten to its mother. You say to me – But it is children, not witches, who are imprisoned!

This is what the witches here call 'active imagination'.

Bodensee

August 31st 1939

My Angel,

I went to the café today. There we were acting like people in masks. It does seem, does it not, that war will be declared.

Rudi was like someone whose mask has grown out from the inside: a skeleton become a shell: a lobster: a glove-puppet.

I said 'Oh Rudi! How good to see you! I am so glad you are all right! I had such guilt about leaving you!'

This is my mask – of Legba, the trickster?

Rudi said 'I imagined those people gave you no option but to leave me!'

'Oh yes, that's right!'

'I'm glad you say so.'

Stefan had come to the café with Rudi. I thought – Of course, they are living together: like the two Ugly Sisters.

I said 'Stefan says you've got a letter for me.'

'I've got something to ask you first.'

'Oh I know!'

'I understand why you ran away: why you never got in touch with us.'

'Have you got my letter?'

'Stefan says you may know what happened to some property of mine – '

'Have you got my letter?'

Rudi took a letter out of his pocket and held it up in front of him. I could see that the name on the envelope was, yes, in the handwriting of my father. There was a different writing for the address. I was not sure I recognised this.

Rudi said 'Did you take –

I said 'You always said there weren't any diamonds.'

He said 'Do you want your letter?'

I leaned forwards to take the letter. Rudi held it away. I said 'Yes,

I've got the diamonds. The soldiers would have got them if I hadn't taken them first.'

He said 'You've got them here?'

I said 'No, but I can get them. You can have your share.'

I saw Walburga coming towards us along the promenade by the lake. When she saw me she began to run. She was like a Valkyrie; like an actress playing both a Valkyrie and her horse.

Walburga shouted 'My darling! My precious! What a feast for the eyes!' She hugged and kissed me.

Stefan took the letter out of Rudi's hand and held it out to me. The handwriting of my name, yes, was that of my father: the writing of the address seemed to be Franz's. I thought – But that indeed is not possible! Then – Stop thinking. Walburga leaned back with her hands on my shoulders. She said 'Let me see you!' Rudi was watching us from across the table.

I was holding the letter from my father. I said 'This is Walburga. This is Rudi. Stefan.'

Rudi said to Walburga 'Can you please go away. We are discussing important business.'

Walburga said 'Elena has told me about you two! You are the idiots who tried to kill my precious in the Sahara!'

I found that in the presence of the others I was not wanting to open the letter. I felt that wild devils or angels might fly out.

I said to Walburga 'Did you find out about Franz?'

She said 'Yes.'

I said 'Where is he?'

She said 'Aren't you pleased to see me?'

Rudi said 'What do you mean, we can have our share?'

I said to Walburga 'Yes, it's lovely to see you.' I said to Rudi 'I mean, you two can have your share of the diamonds.'

Walburga said 'Franz is not far from here.'

Rudi said 'When?'

Walburga said 'He's in that house, you know, his family have got in the Black Forest.'

I thought – Yes, I went there once.

Stefan said 'Where are they?'

I said to Stefan 'They're with my things at Kusnacht.' I said to Walburga 'Have you got a car?'

Walburga said 'I left it on the other side of the lake.'

I said 'Could you get it?'

Walburga said 'If you like.'

I said 'That's very good of you.'
I thought – Now, I will open the letter.
Rudi said 'Will you pay attention!'
I said 'This letter is from my father.'

My beloved Leni,
　　I saw your mother briefly before she died.
　　When I was arrested I asked if I could be detained in Sachsen-hausen Camp because this was where, I believed, she was. My request was laughed at. Then I was told that it might be granted if I was classified as a Jew. I said that this was agreeable to me.
　　In Sachsenhausen men and women were housed separately but I managed to catch several glimpses of your mother. I am almost certain she saw me and knew who I was. There were good reasons perhaps for her not to show too much that she recognised me. When she no longer appeared, I made enquiries, and I was told that she had been taken to the prison hospital. Later I was told that she had died. I think this information was reliable.
　　I wanted to tell you this, my beloved Leni, because now we must look to the future. Will you understand what I mean. The age of sacrifice is over. There has to be, I believe there is, a new dispensation.
　　The children of light will have to be as wise as serpents: wiser than the children of darkness.
　　I believe I have a means of getting this letter to Franz.
　　Will you trust –
　　　　Your ever loving, ever trusting,
　　　　　　　　　　Father

When I had finished reading this letter I folded it and put it in my pocket. It was as if I were still standing where I had been standing before but the world had flipped over, and on again, in a circle. I had been, briefly, in the presence of huts, watchtowers; now I was again with ladies and gentlemen in their masks.
I said to Walburga 'Can I borrow your car?'
She said 'What do you want it for?'
I said 'I've got to see Franz. To find out about my father.'
She said 'Now you mustn't be angry with your father!'
Rudi said 'Will you please answer our questions.'
I said 'You can have the diamonds when I get back.'
Rudi said 'I want them now.'

Walburga said 'You two ought to be in jail.'

Rudi was sitting, Walburga and Stefan and I were standing, at the table in the café. I thought – Oh but I will be once more on a journey in the Black Forest!

Stefan said 'But you may not come back.'

Walburga said 'Can I come too?'

I said 'No, I think I must go alone.'

I thought – But indeed I may not be able to get back!

Rudi said 'How do we trust you?'

Walburga said 'All right, I'll fetch the car.'

I said to Walburga 'Has my father been working with Franz?'

Walburga said 'You know he's been working for the government?'

I thought – But of course I trust you, of course you can trust me, and all that is happening, O my father!

That was at lunchtime. Since then I have been writing this in the *Gasthaus*. Walburga will be back here by midnight. I will set off in the morning. Or will the war have started? So how, in fact, will I get back. I will leave this notebook in my suitcase addressed to you. Something of me will get back – to my angel in England!

Take care of yourself, my beloved.

I think I glimpse how things work: will we ever be able to describe this?

Thank you for being more to me that what I am to myself.

Sit on the gasworks: keep them warm for me.

★　★　★

Tollington Park, Norfolk
August 1939

My darling Eleanor, my Angel,

This is the enormous country house we have been evacuated to: I think I am supposed not to tell you where it is.

Donald is here, and some of the people from Cambridge. The idea is that we will be away from the likelihood of bombs. What irony!

Please take care. Please don't go into Germany; and come home, if war seems certain.

I am supposed to say nothing of the work we are doing here. I will write to you in this notebook.

We have imagined that we might send each other messages, you

505

and I: of course, there would be no means of describing exactly what these were.

Practising.

This is an enormous country house in the baroque style. It consists of a central block and two wings. The central block has been empty, which is where we are to set up our laboratory. In one of the wings lives a very old lady who is the owner of the house: she was supposed to have moved out when we arrived, but then she became too ill, and so she stays on with a cook and two nurses. No one sees her.

I have a room on the top floor of the opposite wing. From my window I look out across parkland. The landscape is very beautiful: there are sheep and groups of deer dotted here and there; the trees stand out from the paler green like things that contain their own shadows. It is like a landscape into which man has not yet come.

In fact, this is a part of the country where some of the earliest traces of humans have been found: primitive humans settled here not because the soil was good but because it was poor – and so did not encourage predators. And just under the ground there were flints, which humans could mine and so make weapons to keep out what predators there were. Oh humans have to use cunning in the face of adversity!

To be cunning, to be wise, humans of course have had to get out of the Garden of Eden.

Near to this house there is being built an enormous army camp: the uncluttered landscape is seen as providing a perfect training ground for soldiers. And the soldiers might be useful in protecting us scientists, I suppose, from anyone who might be jealous of our chance to destroy the world – or of giving it a chance of survival.

As a matter of fact it is now thought that our work may take several years: a particular uranium isotope has to be separated if there is to be a chain reaction. And this, as Donald has always said, will require complex engineering and much money. To find a moderator to slow the reactions down we are beginning to experiment with both graphite and heavy water: but it is difficult to make the former sufficiently pure, and almost no supplies are available for the latter. So there are still many who say that the thing can't be done: in which case who cares – so long as it can't be done by Nazis. But there are other ways of destruction; there may not be other ways for survival.

Perhaps you will have been able to see Franz? The Nazis are the only people I can imagine who might be glad to blow up themselves along with everyone else: what could be more glorious than such a *Götterdämmerung*! But if we learn to look at and live with the implications of such a Bomb, self-destruction might seem less glorious.

The Russians have seemed not to mind killing or being killed: but they have not made out that there is much glory in destruction and self-destruction.

Is there any news about your father?

I sit at my window here and try to imagine what you are doing. I see you on the edge of your lake: perhaps a bird comes flying across; perhaps it has a message in its mouth, like the twig of a tree.

What do you think that Tree of Life looked like that those people never came across in their Garden of Eden?

A young girl has come to stay with the old lady in the opposite wing of the house. She is the old lady's granddaughter. She comes wandering on to the stone-flagged terrace in front of the house – past the orangery, the antique bowling-alley, a huge ornamental fountain. She has long fair hair. Of course, I have invested her with the lineaments of a fairy story! She is like someone in exile from a future country. So can I tell you this? Do you remember the idea that there is no mathematical reason why messages should not exist from the future as well as from the past; it is our structuring in accordance with time that would prevent us from recognising these.

This girl also reminds me of myself that summer, years ago, when I was at home and had nothing to do; my school had burned down; I used to go out on my bicycle to look for lost landscapes, lost gardens. I found a lake and a ruined boathouse. This was the summer when I tried to make a perfect setting for my salamanders. This was not to show the possibility of the inheritance of acquired characteristics – God forbid! – but to see whether from a setting that was aesthetic something new and beautiful might grow – something like a visitor from the future, do you think? This was the sort of experiment, I imagined, that had been performed successfully by Kammerer. So I collected my ferns and crystals, my rare alpine plants, my white sand and coloured stones. And in the event I achieved – but how did I know what I had achieved? – I glimpsed, yes, that something beautiful had grown; but I hardly stayed to check; I had to go back to school; or did I not really want to check? Was not what I had wanted to achieve just such a glimpse of something beautiful? And if I had stayed to check might it not have gone; was it not safer in my mind, whatever it was – something secret, even sacred. Or perhaps, after all, I had just imagined it! Who wants the responsibility, after all, to have brought to birth something new, something beautiful: what a lifetime would be needed to look after it! How much easier to have done what was expected: to have gone back to school. Certainly no one else seemed to want to know, let alone to nurture them – my hopeful monsters!

Perhaps they and their offspring lived: perhaps they all went into the dustbin.

Now, I would wish to have the chance to look after something like them.

But what would this mean?

In those days I had at least loved enough to have brought an offspring into existence: though in reality, of course, the birth could have had quite natural genetic causes. But still, what a miracle!

Here our equipment has not yet arrived. So I have time to sit at my window and let my thoughts go on journeys.

Donald is playing croquet with some of the men from Cambridge on the lawn.

I am thinking –

If it is radioactivity that at random causes a mutation – and this has become part of the definition both of a mutation and of what is called 'random' –

– And if it is consciousness that brings into existence a particular activity out of potentialities that I suppose could be called 'random' –

– Then why should not a state of consciousness be the environment that might favour a mutation?

This lives: that dies –

I loved my salamanders.

And I can write this stuff to you, my angel, because for reasons of what is called 'security' it may never be posted.

Testing. Testing.

I shall go for a walk in this aesthetic landscape.

September 1st 1939

There is a track that goes down from the house through the park and over a hill and then on and on through this strange landscape until it reaches a cluster of houses, a miniature village, all uninhabited: this is where people who worked on the estate must once have lived; they were moved out, I suppose, in preparation for the area becoming a playground for soldiers; or perhaps they had left earlier, such has been the state of farming recently in England. I had not walked as far as this before. I found the place faintly alarming. The impression from ruined houses is of the impermanence of humans; of the way in which humans play with fire, burn themselves, blow themselves up; of the way in which humans will one day be no more.

I also had the impression that I had been in this place before, or perhaps that I would come here again: there is a theory that this is to do with some split in the memory system of the brain. But what sparks this off in the outside world? We understand very little about memory systems; and indeed what do we understand of the outside world except what comes in through the brain. And there are those areas of the brain for which we seem to have no present use: well, might they not be waiting for some understanding of – what does it mean, the question 'Have I not been here before?' the pattern 'Might I not come here again?'

There was a path going down from this derelict village into a small dell with trees. The path was overgrown with nettles but a way had been made recently by someone trampling through. Now it is true that on a previous occasion I had noticed from my window in the house the girl with fair hair walking this way over the hill: it had seemed that she might be on her way to some rendezvous – with a lover? But was she not too young? Or she might simply have wanted, as I had done years ago in the ruined boathouse, to be alone. But then – had there not also been those intimations of death, of self-destruction, in the ruined boathouse! And had not this girl seemed to be as I had felt myself to be then, an exile in a foreign country? And was not this deserted village now heavy with an air of the impermanence of humans; of death.

The path through the nettles led down into the dell. I went down this path and into an area of trees; in the middle of this there was a clearing. In the clearing there was a very small and low thatched cottage: it was, yes, like something in a fairy story. Across the roof of the cottage had fallen a large branch of a tree; the cottage was like an animal in a trap with its back broken. The path through nettles went from the edge of the clearing to the door of the cottage. The door was half open and half off its hinges. It seemed that there might be someone inside. I stood underneath a tree at the edge of the clearing. It was as if I might be waiting for – what? – something from the past? The future?

The girl came out from the cottage. She carried a saw in her hand. The saw was one of those that are shaped like a bow. She went to the end of the large branch that had fallen across the cottage, to where the lesser branches of the tree rested on the ground. She began to climb up into the branches. She wore a dress with a short yellow skirt. I had the impression that she might have seen me where I was standing at the edge of the clearing. She climbed till she reached the main branch of the tree then crawled along this and sat astride the ridge of the roof of the cottage. Then she began to saw at the thick branch. After a time her saw got stuck. She pulled, but failed to get it loose. Then she looked at me.

I said 'Can I help you?'

She said 'Can you?'

I walked across the glade. I said 'You may have to saw from underneath, since the pressure from the branches on the ground is such that if you saw from the top the saw may always get stuck.'

She said 'How can I saw from underneath when the saw is now stuck and, anyway, the tree is resting on the roof?'

I said 'That's true.'

When I got close I saw that there was a second saw stuck in the main trunk of the tree close to the first.

The girl said 'What I should have done, I see now, after the first saw had got stuck, was to saw further away from the roof from underneath with the second, but I did not see this at the time.'

I said 'Yes.'

She said 'So what shall we do now?'

I looked round on the ground. I thought – She said 'we'. I said 'What we can do is to look for a suitable lever which we can put under the branch where it's on the roof, then I can raise the tree so that the pressure will be taken off the saws and you can free them, and then we can use them to cut the branches which are on the ground and the pressure will be such that we may not even have to cut the main branch from underneath.'

She said 'But can you find a suitable lever?'

I said 'I don't know.' Then – 'And anyway, the lever might go through the roof.'

She said 'So what are you going to do?'

I climbed up the branches of the tree. I pulled at the saws but they would not come out. I sat facing the girl on the ridge of the roof. I thought – It is as if we are on the back of an elephant, which is on the back of a tortoise, which is on the back of the sea.

I said 'What I will do is to try to get my back underneath the tree and raise it so that like this the pressure is taken off and then you can free the saws.'

She said 'Like Atlas.'

I said 'Yes, like Atlas.'

She said 'But what if you go through the roof?'

I said 'That is the sort of risk you have to take in this business.'

I got my back underneath the main branch of the tree. I was on my hands and knees on the sloping roof; I was like some strange female animal. I thought – You see, perhaps I am giving birth.

– To what? At least, to some sort of language like that of those people who were building a tower to heaven?

I said 'Now!'

She said 'There!'

I said 'And now the other saw.'

She said 'Got it!'

I lowered the branch of the tree and crawled backwards. We sat side by side, the girl and I, facing the same way, on the ridge of the roof, our legs hanging down.

She said 'I've seen you at the house.'

I said 'Yes, I've seen you.'

She said 'What work are you supposed to be doing?'

I said 'We're not supposed to tell.'

She said 'Well, I'm supposed not to tell what I'm doing here.'

I said 'The work I've been doing up to now, which is not secret, has been to do with discovering what might be a suitable moderator for the irradiation of uranium so that a nucleus might split and produce further neutrons.'

She said 'I just couldn't bear to see this cottage with its back broken.'

I said 'I see.'

She said 'Is that all you're doing?'

I said 'The rest is difficult to explain.'

She said 'Yes, the rest is difficult to explain.'

Holding one of the saws, she slid down the sloping thatch of the roof and landed on the ground. She was like a child going down a slide at a fairground. Then she walked with the saw round the branches of the tree that were pressed against the ground.

She said 'Did you say we should cut these branches?'

I said 'Yes.'

'And then we can saw more easily the main bit on the roof?'

'Yes.'

She said 'Isn't it lucky then that we have two saws.'

I took the other saw and slid down to the ground. I went to the far side of the tree from where she stood. We both began sawing the minor branches.

I wanted to describe this to you: to say – This scene is to do with those who might be our children.

She said 'I wanted to build a home. But, of course, I know I'll never live here.'

I said 'Why won't you live here?'

She said 'Of course I can't!' Then – 'But you don't think it's odd, that I want to build such a home?'

I said 'I once did an experiment with salamanders. I wanted to produce a perfect environment for them so that they would produce an offspring, a mutation, that would be different.'

I could see her face peering at me through the branches. She had stopped sawing. We had cut through quite a lot of the branches that had been resting on the ground, so that the main branch of the tree was becoming cleared.

She said 'How did you know?'

I said 'How did I know what?'

She came round to my side of the tree. Together we looked at what were left of the smaller branches.

I said 'We can now try cutting it again at the top.'

She said 'And was it?'

I said 'What?'

She said 'Different.'

I said 'Oh yes. But I couldn't really tell. I had to go back to school.'

She said 'And didn't you have anyone to help you?'

I said 'No.'

She said 'Then aren't I lucky.'

At first I didn't know what she meant. Then I thought I might cry.

She had begun to climb up again on to the roof of the cottage.

I went and looked in through the doorway. The floor of the cottage seemed to have been swept and the walls and ceiling brushed down; the grate was clean with sticks in it ready for a fire. There was a table with one leg almost off and two rickety chairs; these had been scrubbed; there was a pile of bracken as if for a bed in one corner, and on a table a vase of exotic-looking lilies.

It was quite like something I might have made for my salamanders; or like that room, perhaps, where you and I sat in front of the fire.

There was the sound of sawing from the roof. Bits of dust and rubble drifted down.

I went out of the cottage and round to the back where there was the heaviest part of the fallen branch. The girl on the roof was sawing just past the ridge, so that the top part of the tree would fall at the front of the cottage and the heaviest part at the back. I said 'I'll catch this part at the back, then it won't damage the cottage.'

She said 'Thank you.'

When the branch where she was sawing cracked it was difficult to support the heavy end of the branch and swing it round; I got it somehow into my hands; I staggered about like someone tossing a caber.

The girl watched me from the roof. She said 'Do you often do things like this?'

I said 'I'm practising.'

She said 'For what?' Then – 'Would you like a cup of tea?'

I said 'Yes, please.'

She slid off the roof. I got rid of the branch of the tree, and went into the cottage. She was lighting the fire. I took a chair and sat in it.

She said 'I'm pregnant. Did you know?'

I said 'No.'

She left the fire and went through to the back where there seemed to be a larder. From there came the sounds of utensils and crockery being moved about.

I said 'Where are your parents?'

She said 'They're abroad.'

'And you're living with your grandmother.'

'I'm staying with my grandmother.'

'Are you still at school?'

'Yes.'

'How old are you.'

'Nearly seventeen.'

She came in from the larder carrying a kettle. She knelt down in front of the fire; she blew on it; she put the kettle on the flames.

I said 'Does anyone else know?'

'No.'

'You haven't told the father?'

'There isn't any father.'

She left the grate and went back into the larder. I took a stick and poked at the fire to make it burn properly. She called out 'And I don't think I'm the Virgin Mary!'

I thought I might say – Then who do you think you are?

She came back into the room. She said 'I wanted to make something like a home, yes; what did you call it, an "environment" –'

She had brought in a teapot and a mug. She stood by the fire, watching it.

I said 'You want your child to be different.'

She said 'I think the grown-up world is mad. People seem to want to die, to kill. They seem to get people strung up, to get themselves strung up, like Jesus. That's why I wouldn't want to be the Virgin Mary.'

I said 'What can people do to you? I mean, about the child.'

It took some time for the kettle to boil. We watched it.

She said 'They can't make me get rid of it. They can make me something called a "ward of court". Then perhaps when it's born they can try to take it away from me.'

I thought – So you are building some sort of nest; here, and in your mind.

I said 'Why don't you tell the father?'

She said 'Because it wasn't his fault.'

I said 'Who said it was anyone's fault!'

I thought I saw her smile. She went back into the larder.

She said 'Anyway, I love him too much. I don't want to ruin his career.'

I shouted 'God damn it, why should it ruin his career?'

She said 'Milk? Sugar?'

I said 'Yes, please.'

When she came back into the room she was certainly smiling. She said 'I'm afraid I've got only one cup.'

I said 'Thank you.'

I thought – Will it do good if I manage to have tears?

She stood with her back to the grate, facing me. Her yellow skirt was embroidered with flowers. It was torn in several places.

She said 'All right, I don't want to blackmail him into marrying me. I want him to be free.'

I said 'If you tell him, you will not be blackmailing him into marrying you.'

She said 'How do you know?'

I said 'I know.'

She said 'How will I ever know he loves me?'

I shouted 'Oh of course you know he loves you!'

She said 'You're mad.'

She made some tea in the teapot. She poured the tea into the mug. She offered me milk and sugar. I took them: I said 'Thank you.' I drank. Then I offered her the mug.

I said 'It's the grown-up world that you think is mad. You're building this house. You want things to be different.'

She said 'Are you married?'

I said 'Yes.'

'Where is your wife?'

'In Switzerland.'

'Why?'

'Because she has work to do there.'

'Do you love her?'

'Yes.'

Then she said 'Well, why do you think I don't tell him?'

I said 'What people like you and I are frightened of is to have not too little but too much. It's easier, as you said, to be strung up.'

She said 'What's the alternative?'

I said 'This.'

I looked up to the ceiling where the ridge-beam had been cracked by the branch falling on the roof.

She said 'Don't we need a prop for that roof?'

She went out into the glade in front of the cottage. I tried to send a message to you – This is all right, my angel: you will be all right? The girl came in dragging a branch that we had cut off and I sawed it to the right size and trimmed it of its lesser branches and then we put the narrower end against the cracked ridge-beam of the ceiling and the other end at an angle on the floor.

She said 'Can you tell me – what is a mutation?'

I said 'It is a new sort of being that happens as a matter of luck. What you can do for it, which is not a matter of luck, is to make an environment that you would wish for whatever turns up. This is what you have been doing. You love your baby.'

She said 'In my imagination.'

I said 'In fact.'

She said 'I told you I was lucky.'

We got hold of the bottom end of the prop and heaved; I kicked it so that the top end pressed against the ridge-beam; then I got hold of another piece of wood and banged the bottom of the prop with it while the girl pulled and the prop gradually became upright and the ridge-beam was raised so that it became level and dust and rubble drifted down like bits of light.

She said 'You mean, this is some sort of practice?'

I said 'Yes.'

She got a broom that seemed to have been made of twigs from the glade; she swept up the dust and rubble that had fallen to the floor; she tidied the tea-things that were round the grate; she made sure that the fire was safe; then she stood and looked round the room.

I said 'You see, you have made this place; now you can carry it in your head.'

She said 'Is that what you do?'

I said 'Yes.'

She said 'All right, I'll tell him. I expect he'll marry me.'

I thought – This place, this afternoon, exist as if they were a painting.

She said 'Did you hear what I said?'

I said 'Yes.' She took the jug of milk and poured a little of it into the vase of lilies.

She said 'If my baby is a girl I am going to call her Lilia.'

I said 'Why?'

She said 'Because lilies are the flowers that grow at this time of year.'

★ ★ ★

Gasthof Friedrich, Zurich See
September 2nd 1939

My Angel,

The fact that I am writing this means that I am alive –

That I am alive means that this is what the universe is like –

You are taking care of yourself?

I got Walburga's car. I set off early in the morning. There was news on the wireless coming through about the German invasion of Poland. There was almost no one in the streets. People were huddled round their wirelesses. It seemed that I might have just one or two days before Britain and Germany declared war.

Walburga had tried again to come with me. She had said 'Why not?' I had said 'Because then it wouldn't work.' I suppose it will always be impossible to explain this.

At the Swiss frontier the man who looked at my passport said 'You are sure you want to go into Germany at this time?' I said 'I have to find my father.' He stamped my passport.

On the German side of the frontier the man said 'You are sure you want to come into Germany at this time?' I said 'I will only be here for one or two days.' He stamped my passport.

The men in the customs house were huddled round their wirelesses. It was a scene like that in Morocco on the day when there was the first news of the war in Spain.

Here there had been rumours that if Germany attacked Poland, and if France and Great Britain declared war on Germany in accordance with treaty obligations, then Germany might attack France through Switzerland in order to avoid the defences of the Maginot Line. But there was hardly any traffic on the roads: no troops, no cheering. It was as if everyone was turned inwards in groups round wirelesses, waiting for news of war perhaps to go round the universe and hit them on the backs of their heads.

It was fifty miles from the frontier to the village above which Franz's family had their house. I had been there once before when Franz and I had gone wandering like birds in the forest. Then some time later I had met you, and we had been like those two people in that play wandering but also looking for each other in a town in which there was already war.

Bruno had said 'Germans split themselves into Mephistopheles and Faust: the one is deep enough to know that good can come out of evil, the other is too shallow to take responsibility for this knowledge.'

You had said 'I do not want to be like Faust.'

I had said 'Faust needed someone to save him.'

Franz had said 'I am like Faust!'

I drove up into the mountains. I stopped in the village to ask someone the way. There was a voice on the wireless coming through half-closed shutters; it told of the extent of the German advance into Poland. I found that I did not want to talk to anyone to ask them the way.

It was not difficult to find Franz's house; there was only one road up from the back of the village. I recognised the driveway. The house was a long single-storey building with plate-glass windows and a view over the top of the forest. There was a car parked at the side of the building which might have belonged to Franz or to some other member of his family. I left my car and went to the front of the house and looked in through one of the huge windows. There were signs of someone having recently been in the sitting-room: the cushions of the sofa had the imprint of a body; there were an ashtray and a glass and an empty bottle on the floor. There is something alarming about looking through a window into a room where humans have been recently but are no longer; what is the need for them to have been there at all.

I rang the bell by the front door. Behind me was the enormous expanse of the forest. A large black dog appeared from round a far corner of the house. Mephistopheles first appeared in the guise of a black dog, did he not? This dog was one of those that appear to be so embarrassed at the presence of humans that they can hardly move: it smiled and squirmed and dragged the back half of its body along the ground. But it was also behaving as dogs do when they want you to follow them. It seemed that there was no one in the house. I thought – Dogs behave like this when something terrible has happened to their masters in a forest.

I followed the dog past the far end of the house and into the trees. The forest was like that on the upper plateau of San Juan de la Peña at the place where the horse but not its rider had gone over the cliff. Or there was that mountain path in Switzerland where you and I had stopped in our walk – do we not often come to this place? – where there had been a rock, a butterfly, a cobweb, a tree. Or, indeed, before this there was the cave in a wood to which I had followed Franz and he had indeed seemed to be practising some self-destruction. The black dog snorted and slithered like a snake in front of me. Ahead, through the trees, in a small clearing which did seem to be, yes, on the edge of a cliff, I saw Franz sitting to one side of the path with his back against a tree. He was holding a shotgun between his knees; the barrel went up past his face. The black dog went up to him; it seemed to be laughing or crying. Franz gave no signs of seeing me. I went to him and said 'Hullo, Franz.' He still did not look at me. I said 'I've come to ask you if you know about my father.' When he looked round it was as if he had experienced some sort of dying.

I said 'I understand that you've been in touch with my father.'
He said 'Who told you that?'
I said 'Walburga.'

He said 'Oh yes, Walburga.'

'And you forwarded to me a letter from my father.'

'That was a long time ago.'

'Can you tell me what he is doing now? And I also, yes, wanted to talk to you.'

I had squatted in front of Franz. He was wearing one of those hats that have a feather from the tail of a bird sticking up on the crown. His once handsome face was like something plucked and hung in a larder.

He said 'He's said to be working for the Nazis.'

I said 'Do you believe that?'

'Why, is it important?'

'Of course it is.'

'Is there anything I could say, that you would necessarily believe?'

Franz seemed to yawn. He made stretching movements with his neck as if he were trying to loosen something from around it. I thought – He was thinking of shooting himself.

I said 'What work are you doing now?'

'I am doing nothing.'

'Are you working for the Nazis?'

'No.'

I said 'You were doing the same sort of work as Max, my husband, is doing in physics.'

Franz tried to laugh: or he sneezed; there was a sound like that of dice being rattled in his throat. He said 'Ah, about that, what can you believe!' Then he sat up and looked around the clearing. It was as if he were acting waking up and noticing where he was for the first time. He said 'But you shouldn't be here! The war's started.'

I said 'I know.'

'Then why have you come?'

'I wanted to talk to you, I told you, as well as find out about my father.'

Franz pressed his knuckles into his eyes. His face was so thin that it was as if his eyes might be pushed out. Then he said as if he were acting again or quoting ' – You cannot know the message without the code: how can you know the code without the message – '

I said 'Don't you know the message?'

He said 'That was a quotation from your father's book: he's had it published, did you know?'

I said 'Which one?'

Franz said 'Yes, I've been doing the same sort of physics as, I suppose, your husband has.' Then – 'Your father's book is on the relationship between language and scientific enquiry.'

I said 'Oh that one.'

Franz said as if quoting again ' – Truth is what occurs: the telling of it can make it something different – '

I said 'And they let him publish that?'

'Who?'

'The Nazis.'

Franz seemed to laugh again with dice rattling in his throat. He said 'Oh in your father's system there is some autonomy for the will.' Then – 'And, of course, they are very stupid.'

Franz put his gun down with the barrel pointing away from him. The black dog, which had been at his feet, wriggled out of the line of fire.

I said 'What else did he have to do? I mean, to get this job.'

Franz seemed to quote again ' – Truth is protected by masks: it can be sensed in the recognition of this – '

I said 'That's my father?'

Franz said 'No, that's me.'

I said 'Then why should I not know what to believe, in talking to you?'

Franz leaned forwards and tickled the ribs of the black dog. He said 'Your father has been put in charge of a department at the Institute which correlates the activities of other scientific departments. He has no direct powers. He is useful because he can get people to work for him who otherwise might be reluctant.'

I said 'Did he have to repudiate my mother?'

'Your mother's dead.'

'I know.'

'And you were in another country.'

I said 'So now what will he be able to do? I mean, you and he, what will you be able to do?'

Franz picked up the gun and held it with the ends of the barrels under his chin. The dog stood facing him with its back arched, its teeth bared.

Franz said 'I do not want to be a traitor to my country.'

I said 'In what way would you be a traitor to your country?'

Franz said 'There are certain circumstances, it is true, in which a patriot might not want his country to be a hundred percent successful in an area of scientific enquiry over which its wartime leaders would wish to take control.'

I said again 'So what will you do?'

He said 'Ask your father.'

I said 'I'm asking you.'

Franz made a sound like an air-gun going off; like air being let out of a balloon. He took the gun away from under his chin and held it upright in front of him pointing into the air: he bowed his head down in front of it.

He said 'Of course one can always do nothing: I mean, try to see that nothing occurs.'

I said 'Yes, nothing: that was what I was going to ask you.'

He said 'You have not been in touch with your father? He has not been in touch with you?'

I said 'No.'

He said 'Then how did you know?' Then he said quickly, as if to stop my answering this question – 'Oh how did you know, how does one ever know, that is the question.'

I thought I might say – But Franz, we have known each other so long, of course you and I both do and don't know!

Then – We have known this ever since that time of the Reichstag fire in Berlin.

Franz stood up. He brushed at his clothes. He was wearing knee-breeches and a short corduroy jacket. The dog heaved about in front of him. He said 'Come to the house.' He set off along the path through the forest. I followed him. It seemed that it might be easier to talk now that he had his back to me. He said 'What exactly is the work that your Max is doing in England?'

I said 'You know more about it than I do.'

He said 'I've been working in the laboratory in Berlin.'

I said 'And you can go back there?'

He stopped and turned and wagged a finger at me. I looked at the ground and poked a toe amongst the pine-needles, acting as if I were contrite. Then we went on through the forest.

I said 'Were you thinking of shooting yourself?'

He said 'Oh I've always been thinking of shooting myself, as you know!' Then he laughed and said 'That's something that one can talk about!'

When we got to the house we went in and there was heavy wooden furniture and photographs in frames: thick green-and-yellow curtains framing the darker green of the forest. Franz picked up the glass and bottle and ashtray from the floor. He went to a desk and rummaged through its drawers. He said 'We used to talk about its being aesthetic, what can't be talked about, you remember?'

I said 'Yes.'

He said as if quoting ' – How do I trust you: how do you trust me – '

I said 'Yes.'

Franz seemed to find what he was looking for in the desk. He held a bit of paper in front of him, reading.

He said 'Not something moral?'

I said 'Oh of course something moral.'

Franz said 'This is the statement that your father made after he had been released from detention; before it was announced that he was to return to the department at the Institute.'

I said 'I see.'

He said 'How do you tell what is moral?'

I said 'Can't you tell by the style?'

Franz handed me the piece of paper on which there was pasted a press-cutting. At the bottom of the cutting there was a photograph of my father. I skipped a few paragraphs which did not seem to be interesting; then I read –

I myself am of Aryan descent. My late wife was Jewish. While my wife was still alive I made no statement on this Jewish question. Now, however, I feel free to say that in my opinion all adult human beings – except those suffering from mental incapacity – have to believe that they are responsible for themselves. To suggest otherwise is to suggest that certain persons are not human. This statement about responsibility, of course, I believe applies to the Jewish people.

I laughed and said 'Well dear God, how awful, but this is all right!'

I handed the piece of paper back to Franz. He said 'You recognise the style?'

I said 'My father used to say, as a matter of fact, that Jews were somewhat like gods.'

Franz said 'And gods, to be operative, have to be somewhat hidden: that is what you have come to say?'

He put the piece of paper back in the desk. He closed the drawer.

I said 'Yes.' Then – 'And you will be all right?'

He said 'Ah, what you want of a poor mortal!'

He walked round the room. It was as if we, and indeed the whole room, were balanced precariously on a tightrope.

I said 'I don't think they're getting anywhere very quickly in England.'

He said 'Oh well, indeed, why should we be getting anywhere quickly in Berlin.'

I said 'It's very good of you.'

He said 'Have you noticed how embarrassing scientific words are – "heavy water"; "isotope" – they are not aesthetic!'

I said 'It's the context.'

Franz came and put his hands on my shoulders. He said 'But you must escape! My Little Red Riding Hood: come to visit her grandmother wolf in the forest!'

I said 'That is aesthetic!'

Franz left me and walked round the room again. It was as if there were a crowd somewhere watching us. He said, as if he were an actor rehearsing a speech –

'– Of course, from our point of view, even if there were the knowledge how eventually to build such a weapon, what a waste of time! There are more pressing tasks! What would be the need for such an effort if the war is going to be over in months if not weeks –'

I said 'That sort of thing.' Then – 'And, as you say, the Nazis are unimaginative.'

He acted – 'Oh I did not say that!' Then he stood still and looked at me. He said 'You believe this?'

I said 'What?'

He said 'That good may come out of what might be called betrayal –'

I said 'But we've always known that one can't say much about this.'

He walked round the room again. He murmured as if quoting ' – Huts, watchtowers: ladies and gentlemen on the grass – ' Then he stood by the window looking out.

After a time I said 'So you will go back to Berlin?'

He said 'And you'll go back to your husband.'

I said 'I'll tell him I saw you.'

Franz said 'As a matter of fact I do see something of your father. We sometimes have tea together at the Adlon Hotel.'

I said 'Tell him you've seen me.'

Franz said 'What on earth shall I say?'

I said 'He'll know.' Then – 'Tell him that to humans gods have always seemed morally ambiguous.'

Franz said 'Ah, it would be a help, like gods, to have no country!'

He went to the wireless and turned it on. There was a voice buzzing like a trapped fly: it gave the latest news of the advance into Poland. Franz twiddled a knob and then there was a sad voice in French talking like a stone falling through space; it was saying that unless Germany set about withdrawing its troops from Poland forthwith then the French and British governments would fulfil their treaty obligations to Poland and so France and Great Britain would be at war with Germany. Undertakings had been given about this: there was a deadline the following day. Franz switched off the wireless. He said 'So what undertakings have we given. You have got what you came for?'

I said 'Yes.'

Franz said as if quoting ' – We are to be actors in this drama – '

I said 'We are actors anyway – '

Franz said ' – In what Nietzsche called "The great hundred-act play reserved for the next two centuries in Europe" – '

I finished the quotation ' – "the most terrible, the most questionable, the most hopeful of all plays" – '

Franz said 'We may just die of the absurdity.'

I said 'Oh we die anyway. What use might we make of the absurdity.'

Franz came and put his hands on my shoulders again. He said 'You make me believe this!' Then – 'Goodbye, my little one.'

I said 'Goodbye.' I put up a hand and touched his face.

Then Franz put his head back as if he were listening. I could hear no noise. But then he said, as if he were acting now specifically for the benefit of some audience ' – Oh we disgusting little band of brothers, who think we can manipulate – '

Then I heard, yes, a car arriving in the drive outside.

He said 'Quickly, once more. I can talk with your father?'

Yes.'

'What shall I tell him from you?'

'Give him my love.'

'Is that all?'

'And my love to you.'

'And what will you tell your husband?'

'What we've said.'

'But we've said nothing.'

'And he'll say nothing.'

'Yes.'

There were the sounds of the doors of a car slamming on the drive outside. It did seem suddenly, yes, that there might be people coming to arrest us: even perhaps that Franz might have summoned them. I thought – One never completely knows in this strange territory.

Franz made a noise like the black dog sneezing.

He said ' – A mountain path, a stone, a bird – ' Then – 'And my love to both of you.'

There was a banging on the front door. Franz went to open it. A man in army uniform came in. He was followed by two men in SS uniform. When the man in army uniform saw me he stopped. The two SS men remained by the door.

Franz held out his arms to the man in army uniform. He said 'Hans!'

The man called Hans took hold of Franz by the arms. He said 'My old friend!' Then looking at me but speaking to Franz – 'We have come to make sure you get to Berlin!'

Franz laughed and said 'Am I under arrest?'

The man called Hans laughed and said 'We have come to ensure your safety!'

I thought – But I can tell the style: they know they are actors.

Franz turned to me and said 'You remember Hans.' Then to Hans 'Eleanor. Frau Ackerman.'

Hans put his hand on his heart and said 'Frau Ackerman! For how many years was I in love with Frau Ackerman!'

Franz said 'Hans met us in the forest. You remember? He was with Max. All those years ago!'

I said 'Oh yes, of course I remember!'

Hans said 'How is Max?'

I said 'He's very well, thank you.'

Franz said 'Hans is one of my colleagues at the Institute.'

I thought – Yes, I see! Then – But there are the two SS men standing by the door.

Then – Oh dear God, now let us give beautiful performances!

Hans walked round the room. He had been holding a hat under his arm; he took it in one hand and he flapped it against the palm of the other. He said 'Max was an extraordinary little boy! He was more interested in biology than physics at that time. He did an experiment with salamanders.'

I said 'Oh yes, he told me about the experiment with salamanders.'

Franz said 'What was that?'

Franz had been tidying the room as if in preparation for leaving. I thought – Oh please God, let me go home!

Hans said 'As I remember it, he tried to encourage some mutation, or the emergence of what had been a potentiality, by a rearrangement of the environment.'

I said 'Of the aesthetic environment.'

Hans said 'Ah, the aesthetic environment!' He stopped by me. He said 'Is that correct?'

I said 'Or the moral environment.'

Hans said 'The moral environment. The mental environment.' He watched me. Then he turned to the two SS men by the door and said 'We will go in two or three minutes.'

Franz said 'I am ready. I have my luggage in the hall.'

Franz had tidied the room and put his gun away. He had the dog on a lead. Hans and I were by the window.

Hans said to me 'And where will you be going?'

I said 'To Switzerland.'

He said 'Max used to call them "hopeful monsters".'

I said 'I know.'

Hans turned to Franz. He said 'But in fact, if such things were to live, how would you know them? They would have to have very few distinguishing marks, or others would know to destroy them.'

Franz said 'One of their distinguishing marks might be that they would not want to destroy.'

Hans said 'Oh they would not want to destroy themselves.'

I said 'I'll go now.'

Hans said 'Give my love to Max.'

I said 'I will.'

Hans said 'What was that phrase Max used to say "Meet you behind the gasworks, twenty minutes" – '

I said 'He said that then? I mean, to you?'

Hans laughed. He said 'Yes.' He went to the door. Then he said 'And what was that other thing he used to say: "Flowers are the flowers that grow at this time of year."'

I said 'I've never heard him say that.'

Hans said 'I suppose he meant – everything happens in the right order, if you let it.'

I said 'You have to have luck.'
Hans said 'Oh don't you think we're lucky?'
Franz said 'I don't know when we'll see each other again.'
I said 'We'll see what flowers grow.'

X

The correlator (as it were) of these stories uncovered the traces of the lives of his friends Eleanor and Max over later years; but it was as if they themselves chose not to record any more details after the outbreak of war in September 1939. Up to this time the overall pattern of their story (so they seem to have been saying) had been one of trying to learn how to deal with the patterns of the self-destructive society they were part of – how to see these clearly, how to try to become not destructive themselves, and by this to be doing what they could for society. Beyond this one of the requirements they seemed to have learned was that a too open demonstration of any success might result in the disappearance of whatever it was that had been glimpsed or touched on.

So far as Max was concerned (the correlator of these stories, the writer of this postscript, did not try to put together this account of what had meant so much to him until some forty years after the events heretofore described) – Max carried on with his scientific work during the 1939–45 war; he was exempted from military service because of the national importance of this work; he himself used to say that he felt he had done enough about war personally when he had been in Spain. For two years he worked in nuclear physics in the country house to the north-east of Cambridge to which he had been evacuated: then when America entered the war he crossed the Atlantic with other British physicists and joined in what became known as the Manhattan Project. He stayed in America till the first practice Bomb was exploded in the Nevada desert in July 1945; then he resigned from the project, saying that it seemed to him that the necessary work had been done. He stayed long enough to argue that a demonstration Bomb should be exploded in an uninhabited area and observers from as many countries as possible should be invited to attend; only after this should consideration be given to a Bomb being dropped on a still persistent enemy. By the time the two Bombs were dropped on Japan in August 1945 Max was in New York trying to get a boat back to England. For a time he came under the suspicion of the American security services and was taken in for questioning. Under interrogation (Max himself used to tell this story) he said that personally and from a military point of view he felt relieved that the Bombs had been dropped on Japan since it was likely that this had shortened the war by months if not years, also it would serve as a ghastly warning for the future: it was as a scientist that he felt that it was his responsibility to make a protest. When his interrogators argued that there was no sense in his suggesting that there should be different moralities for different individuals or groups or indeed within the same person, Max replied that, on the contrary, he was convinced that for a proper working of society such an attitude of mind was essential; courses of action could only be said to be right if there had been a genuine interplay of what indeed might be conflicting moral inclinations. Moreover, it was some such complexity of mind within an individual that was necessary if there was to be the existence of the Bomb without the use of the Bomb – a situation which he, Max, saw as being likely to be necessary for the human race if it was to survive or evolve; human nature having evidently such a propensity for evil that with all the technological advances it was only the existence of something so shocking as the Bomb that would prevent the evil from going into runaway, out of control. While he was explaining these ideas to his interrogators, Max used to say, they seemed to understand him and even have some sympathy with him: but after he had gone they must have felt that he had tricked them, for they had him back for further questioning. This sort of thing became typical of what was apt to happen to Max: as he developed and formulated his ideas he intrigued but also alienated people by the unexpectedness of his thinking; he seemed to be saying that experience could be best dealt with not so much by reason as by a style – a style of mind involving trust in a connection between it and an organising spirit in the outside world.

Regarding the Germans and their building or rather not building of the Bomb – much of the story is well known. The Germans had been months ahead in theoretical work in 1939; then after the outbreak of war not much in practice was done. The British and American authorities did not know this at the time, so that the driving force behind the enormous resources eventually provided in America for the production of the Bomb continued to be the fear, as it had been from the beginning, that the Nazis would get the Bomb first and would use it if not to conquer the world then to blow up everyone including themselves. Without the impetus of this fear, Allied scientists and governments might never have embarked on the doubtful and expensive enterprise of building the Bomb. And when they did, the skills they used were those of refugees from Nazi Germany who in other circumstances might have been working in their homeland – so this indeed was an example, Max used to say, of the Nazis scattering the seeds of their own destruction. When British and American observers entered Germany at the end of the war they were amazed to find that although much work had been done on the production of nuclear energy for peacetime purposes, almost nothing had been done about a Bomb. There were, of course, some straightforward explanations for this. At the beginning of the war it had indeed been thought that the military conquest of Europe could be achieved so quickly that there would be no sense in Germany diverting resources from the production of tanks and aeroplanes to such a long-term risky project – especially one about which, to Nazi fanatics, there had always been a whiff of 'Jewish physics'. Then towards the end of the war the Nazi hierarchy seemed anyway to have become less interested in winning the war than in the killing, before defeat, of the maximum number of Jews. This had begun to seem to some top Nazis even a justification for the war – and by this time it was too late to embark upon a project that might otherwise have seemed attractive to them: that of killing, before defeat, the maximum number of everyone. But with regard to the middle years of the war there were strange stories that began to come to light – of chances missed, of experiments wrongly reported, of false trails laid and followed. So it did seem sometimes, yes, that there might have been a hidden conspiracy, conscious or half-conscious, to do with the Nazis not getting the Bomb.

How much Franz, and Eleanor's father Professor Anders, might have had to do with this, can, by the nature of the case, never be known. The nature of the case was, as Eleanor and Franz had recognised in their conversation on the first day of the war, that to be effective it had to remain secret; both at the time, for obvious reasons, but also later, because of the participants' sense of self-responsibility. (This was a good example, Eleanor used to say, of the way in which certain attitudes and effects cannot be talked about without the loss of their virtues.) Some shelvings of important information and false trails laid during these years could be explained by the interdepartmental rivalry that always existed in the gangster style of the Nazi regime (yet another example of the Nazis allowing to take root the seeds of their own destruction); some occurrences might indeed have been the result of psychological blockages in men responsible enough to fear the prospect of a Nazi Bomb yet too loyal in a traditional sense to take responsibility for deliberately preventing this. But there was evidence of delays and diversions that were uncanny if they were not intended. There was one experiment to do with testing the suitability of graphite as a moderator for irradiating neutrons that was wrongly recorded or interpreted so that the Germans abandoned the line of research which was in fact the one that led the Americans to success; there was a report on the feasibility of the use of plutonium as a fissionable material that was locked away in a safe. Nothing, of course, could be proved about what might have been deliberate: what would constitute proof? Max, looking back, used to say 'The hand of God, of chance, of responsible humans, of a universal unconscious – how could you tell the difference?' And nothing could be asked of Eleanor's father or of Franz after the war: Eleanor's father died, probably by his own hand, after being suspected of implication in the plot against Hitler which failed in July 1944; Franz, having been in a reserved occupation for much of the war, took up arms at the very end and was killed fighting against the Russians on the outskirts of Berlin. Hans survived; and after the war remained in friendly contact with Max. But he would talk little about the war years: he would say just 'What is odd, in human affairs, about things being uncanny?'

Regarding the Russians – there is evidence that they, possibly under the guidance of Kapitsa, were quite far ahead in research into the Bomb by 1945: they were helped comparatively little by the spying that Max had been unwilling to be part of. Max's friend Kolya, from Odessa, did eventually find his way to Cambridge, in the 1940s: but he too did not like to become involved in fruitless speculation.

With regard to Eleanor – when she rejoined Max in England in the autumn of 1939 (she used to maintain that she could not remember what exactly in the end had happened in the matter of Rudi and Stefan and the diamonds, because the subject was too boring and was it not the job of memory to get rid of stuff that was boring? but to those who knew her it seemed obvious that she had given what was not her share of the diamonds back) – when Eleanor got back to England in 1939 she stayed with Max for a time in a village near the country house to the north-east of Cambridge where he was working. (It was Eleanor who used to tell the story of what happened to the girl with fair hair: she did marry the child's father, who was an undergraduate at Cambridge; he later joined the army and was sent abroad and the girl spent much of the war alone with her child, who was indeed a girl called Lilia.) Eleanor and Max took a room in the village and there Eleanor began to write her first book, which was some sort of history or meditation on the history of the Jews: it was never published in its original form. Eleanor had had the subject in mind, I suppose, ever since she had been in Spain: something of the substance of the first version of the book can be gleaned perhaps from what she wrote later of her time in Spain.

Eleanor had had the vision of the Jewish and Christian versions of history as being essentially not contradictory: Jews were a chosen people, to be sure – this was their own conviction, thus could be explained the destructive jealousies of the people around them. Their 'chosenness' could be understood in the sense of their being endowed, genetically even, with some special trait: this could be seen as a gift of God just as well as a result of chance. The special trait of the Jews, Eleanor argued, was to do with their ability originally to hold a view of humans both as entities subject to laws of cause and effect but also as agents, components, in the working-out of a larger pattern. Those who were not endowed with this trait – who had no vision of 'God' or 'chance' in fact working out a pattern – of course felt a threat from those who had: this was a characteristic of evolution: those who possessed a special trait might supersede, if circumstances favoured them, those who did not. But, having thus been endowed with a special trait, it seemed that Jews had not been endowed at the same time with a gift for creating circumstances in which it could flourish – and this too was a characteristic of evolution, that a coincidence of chances, gifts, is required for successful adaptation to be achieved. The Jews, that is, with their faculty for seeing a pattern for themselves and through this for the things around them, yet had little ability to prevail over nor indeed to live at peace with their neighbours. And their neighbours, of course, without the ability to see any pattern (if it could be so called) except that of one organism flourishing at the expense of another, were apt to set out to disprove the claims of 'chosenness' by the Jews by turning on them every now and then and killing them or carrying them into captivity. This was indeed the Jews' own view of their history and mythology. This had at one time been particularised into the expectation of a Messiah – the coming of the Messiah would be the circumstances in which their facility which had been potential could become actual; what had hitherto been a predicament could become a triumph.

But then when either the Messiah did not come (the Jewish version) or did come and was not recognised by Jews (the Christian version) there occurred what might have been expected to occur according to either interpretation – the Jews were scattered throughout the world. Either they were being punished for apparently not being sufficiently worthy of a Messiah, or they were being punished for not recognising a Messiah when he came. But also might they not have been scattered (this was Eleanor's interpretation) in a way that had nothing to do with punishment but be part of a required pattern whether or not a Messiah had come: might they not have been scattered, that is, as seeds, so that their special trait – their view of the working-out of a pattern – might have had a chance to take root around the world. But as things were, everyone seemed stuck within a cycle of hopelessness or vengeance: Jews with their faculty for seeing that there was some design for the world but still without the ability to find much of a part in it for themselves except through suffering; Christians with their taking over of the triumphal Messianic idea but still without a faculty for trusting any pattern except that of so-called 'victory' by the elimination of one thing by another. Neither Jews nor Christians in their formal protestations seemed to have the attitude of mind to see their responsibilities as agents of self-creation within a larger pattern – a trust that, by attending with care to means, ends would look after themselves. Christians had glimpsed something of this with their doctrine of the

Holy Spirit: but having noted the potential power of such a trust, they had not been able to say much about it.

In the first draft of her book it seems that Eleanor wrote that the Jewish people might have to undergo some extreme form of suffering before they could see that there had been enough of this and they could once more feel themselves as active agents in their destiny – as agents even in the destiny of others – in the way of imparting knowledge of the frightening interplay, beauty even, between triumph and suffering in events' patterning. But Eleanor wrote the first draft in the early days of the war before the extemities of actual Jewish suffering were known: later, when stories of horror began to filter through from occupied Europe, Eleanor put aside the first version of her book, with its view of the efficacy of suffering, and concentrated on what might be a direct and practical connection between this and the chance of the creation of a state of Israel: she became, that is, an increasingly ardent and optimistic Zionist. She did not mind the shelving of her book: she knew, as Max had done, that even in what might be true about the working-out of patterns, there are some things best recognised in silence.

Eleanor had been with Max when he had first gone to America: they had had their home, for a time, on the edge of a painted desert. She had been writing: he had been working on the Bomb: they had, as always, been happy together. But how was it possible in such circumstances to settle down without anxiety? So when Max still had work of importance to do but Eleanor had put her book aside, she went off on her own for a time to be an active worker in the cause of Zionism; she managed to get to Palestine, where she became part of an organisation that helped Jews to get out of occupied Europe. Max encouraged her in this: he said 'In marriage, why should it not be life-giving to be sometimes apart: what else is pattern?' Eleanor stayed in Palestine long enough to see success in her work but also the dangers inherent in Zionism – that the very reaction to suffering might go into chauvinistic runaway, out of control; that only by stepping back from memories of suffering might there be a coming to terms with the necessity to live at peace with neighbours. She would say 'Indeed, what else is pattern.'

During the years that followed, Eleanor and Max were sometimes together, sometimes apart: but always, they said, they felt them-selves together – as partners, that is, in the working-out of some design, under the guidance of what turned up. They evolved an ironic style of talking about their love and their marriage: sometimes they made jokes; sometimes they talked with great seriousness: usually they left spaces through which a listener or observer had to make his or her own way. What they seemed to be saying about marriage was that if there was disjunction there was no liveliness and if there was fusion there was no liveliness: liveliness depended on openness; on an energy going between.

Over the years, in fact, they each of them became increasingly involved with their own threads through the maze: they had sadness, difficulties in maintaining the vision and hopes they had had for themselves; but friends did not easily see signs of such uncertainty, which seemed peripheral to so much energy. Max, after an unproductive period in England just after the war, was offered a research fellowship in Canada: he was to be allowed to enquire into an area which had increasingly come to engross him – the borderline between physics and biology. When Eleanor returned from Palestine she stayed with Max in England for a time: then she went back to West Africa to complete the anthropological study she had planned when she had been there before going to Spain – on the possibility of an anthropology in which the anthropologist recognised his part in what he observed. To those who knew Max and Eleanor during these years it was true that there often seemed to be few conventional signs of their being married: Max from time to time had relationships with other women; Eleanor in her travels was likely to join up with someone she liked. But there was always the impression that in some crucial sense they trusted they were together; that it was this surety that gave them the freedom to go their own ways. Those who became fond of them sometimes protested about this. The girl called Lilia once said to Max 'You treat Eleanor as if she were God!' Max replied (with irony of course) 'Yes, it has been said that successful relationships depend on a third person, God.'

When Eleanor came back from West Africa she spent some time writing a long essay on marriage: she took as her anthropological field of study, as it were, European literature. In literature, she suggested, marriage was seen first as an end to be aimed at but then as something boring and even deathly when achieved: what seemed to be almost impossible to write about (or indeed to experience) was marriage as a successfully going concern. Of course, Eleanor argued, humans do get taken over by an exciting drive for surety and when this is achieved it is apt to seem second-rate: but what might happen if people just recognised this? Could there not be a going concern on some quite different level – one from which it could be seen that a drive for security, when achieved, might then have to be turned to a drive for freedom, for the spark of liveliness to be maintained; and vice versa; and so on: this level being to do with a recognition of pattern. It is a contrasting to and fro, like that of a heart-beat, that is life-giving: one strand on its own, pursued to an end, of course is deathly. This was the first anthropological-type essay that Eleanor published. Max wrote to her – But who, except you and I, will understand this business of to-and-fro; of levels?

Max himself tried to make more of the matter of levels: he wrote papers which introduced the concept into most of the lines of research he was engaged in at the time. In physics, for instance, there had for long been the conundrums posed by quantum theory – light could be said to consist of either particles or waves according to the condition of the experiment – but this was a conundrum only when one was talking on the level of what was light. On the level of the viewer – the setter-up of the conditions of the experiment – there was no conundrum, Max argued, but simply a matter of choice: shall I set up this condition or that? And so the question on this level was what were conditions of mind. And indeed quantum theory allowed that it was mind, consciousness, working as it were on a higher level, that produced on a lower level the effects of choice – it was through the intrusion of consciousness that Schrödinger's cat, for instance, became actually rather than potentially dead or alive. And so should it not be one of the tasks of physicists not only to be trying to understand the nature of the outside world, but to be trying to understand the nature of understanding – the understanding by which the outside world in some sense seems to be organised.

In biology, Max continued to be interested in the recurring problems of how order had evolved and continued to evolve out of 'chance'; how chaos was organised into shape and then how shape and pattern were maintained. Once the whole process was under way evolution could perhaps be explained by the mechanisms of natural selection: but how did the whole process exist? What was the provenance of shape and pattern? If in physics there was a sense in which this or that occurrence was brought about by observation, by an activity of mind, then why should this not be the case in biological evolution – with regard to both the creation and perpetuation of forms, and to the possible emergence at least of new forms of understanding. At the heart of the disciplines of both biology and physics, Max argued, there was an area about which not much could scientifically be said: scientific language was a tool of consciousness when it looked at the outside world; it was not one much fitted to the process of consciousness looking at itself. Perhaps what was needed here was some language that was only too ready to recognise its own limitation; some self-mocking style – ah, look at consciousness looking at itself!

Max got as far as he could with these ideas: he wrote his papers in which he tried to keep to a scientific style: this became increasingly difficult. It seemed to him that the area into which he was moving was now not so much one of science as of philosophy. He gave up his job in Canada and returned to England; although by now somewhat middle-aged, he embarked on a study of philosophy in London. He pursued especially a line of enquiry into the concept of levels of language that had been introduced by Russell and Whitehead before the First World War in order to rescue logical systems from self-contradiction. There were various paradoxes that had threatened to invalidate the consistency of logical systems ('These terrible vandals, paradoxes,' Max used to say, 'ploughing up the fallow ground of moribund systems!') – the paradox of the Cretan who said that all Cretans were liars, the paradox of the barber who said he shaved everyone in the village who did not shave himself, the paradox of whether the class of classes that are not members of themselves is or is not a member of itself. (Max used to say 'Oh of course they are farcical, these paradoxes, these routines of clowns, breaking up logical systems!') Russell had argued that sense could only be made of such paradoxes if it was seen that language was being used on two different levels – one to talk about things or events and the other to talk about one's talking about these. If one did not recognise this difference then there was contradiction: if one did, then there was the recognition of movement between the two – an oscillation in time, a pattern. But then there might be the question: From what level did one recognise the operation of such patterning? There might be an endless regression of levels: it was this prospect that seemed to be objected to by philosophers. But – Max concluded – what was important here was not the number of possible levels but the use of language to describe the fact that the mind moved between them: it was by means of a style that would embrace such movement that there could be intimated what otherwise could not be said.

Max's first book was a collection of his papers in physics and biology and philosophy: at the centre of each there were the questions: 'Is it consciousness that forms structures?' 'What is pattern?', 'Is not life that which is held, moves, across levels, between poles?' He suggested that scientific and philosophical language may not indeed be fitted to deal with these questions but might not a suitable language be what is called 'aesthetic'? It was at this place in his book that Max seemed to lose many of his readers. People had become accustomed to physicists hinting at the existence of what could not be described logically, but Max seemed to be claiming some special verity for aesthetics.

When Max returned to England at the end of the 1950s he became involved almost immediately again in controversies concerning the Bomb. At the end of the war he had achieved some notoriety for first having helped to construct the Bomb and then having disassociated himself from the dropping of it – and now there was not only the Atomic but the Hydrogen Bomb. In England, Max was approached by the Campaign for Nuclear Disarmament; he went to their first large-scale rally in Trafalgar Square; he found himself joining their protest march to Aldermaston which was where components for the British Bomb were said to be being made. On the road near Maidenhead he was spotted by a journalist who knew him: he was carrying a pole which supported one end of a banner which proclaimed 'Let's Go Back to Bows and Arrows': carrying the pole at the other end was a pretty girl. The journalist wrote the story in his paper the next day with a headline – 'British Physicist Renews Anti-Nuclear Attack with Arrows'. By the time the march reached Aldermaston Max was marching with the banner folded and his arm round the girl; there was a posse of reporters waiting for him by the side of the road. Max explained – He had a great respect, yes, for the aims and especially the sprit of people in CND but he did not agree with them, no: he was still glad that the Bomb existed on account of the depravity of human nature; it was only through something like the existence of the Bomb that human nature might be kept within bounds or even change. Then why, he was asked, had he been carrying a banner which advocated a return to bows and arrows? Because, Max said, he had wished to be of assistance to people to whom he felt friendly. He was asked by reporters – Was this a responsible attitude for a physicist in a matter of such importance? Indeed, Max said, just as it had seemed to him sensible years ago to have helped in the construction of the Bomb and then to have protested against its use in war, so now it seemed sensible to show sympathy with the good people of CND even though he was doubtful about their aims: what mattered in such a business was to distinguish between means and ends: if each person practised what he or she thought was right and recognised the obligations of others to do this, then ends could be left to themselves. In fact this was just the sort of attitude that might be required for, and indeed exemplify, a proper change in human nature, Max went on – but by this time most of his audience had drifted away. One or two papers the next day printed a photograph of Max leaning so heavily on the pretty girl that it was as if he were having to be propped up. A month or two later Eleanor came across a copy of one of these papers in Borneo: she sent Max a postcard saying – Indeed who but you and I would understand this business of levels!

Eleanor had gone to Borneo after West Africa. In her profession as anthropologist she was still pursuing the idea that had come to her during her first period in Africa – the question of how there could be a form of anthropology that was not just to do with the recording of events and processes but which would include a consideration of the function of the recorder in organising them into systems. An anthropologist was the filter through which events and systems came to mind; yet anthropologists wrote as if they themselves did not exist. Eleanor's first published book was a collection of essays mainly about her time as an anthropologist. On one level the book was a straightforward tabulation of ethnographic facts; on another there was the arrangement of these facts to give the picture of a culture; both these levels were in the area of traditional anthropology. But then on a third level (Max wrote to her – 'This is our level!') Eleanor tried to speculate on her own activity as picker of facts and recogniser of patterns: what as an operator was she doing: was it not a characteristic of life, this forming and recognising of patterns? To understand living systems, perhaps one had to understand what one was doing in trying to understand living systems: they themselves were of the same nature as the activity of mind. It was by this that from what otherwise seemed to be at random there was produced orderliness: and to have a vision of one's own role in this would one not have to have an experience like the appreciation of what is called 'aesthetic'? At this point, to many of Eleanor's readers, she seemed to be dabbling in the occult. Her book was published at much the same time as Max had published his. Max wrote to her – 'And you hadn't even read

539

my book!' Eleanor replied – 'But of course I didn't have to: and of course I will read your book!'

Eleanor left Borneo and was with Max again in England for a time; then she went back to Zurich to complete her training to be a qualified analytical psychologist. She wanted, I suppose, to find out more about mind. She had already done her years of training as a medical student, and then her psychological studies in Zurich. She became one of the acolytes around Jung during his last years: she was in Zurich when he died. Then she left the entourage that had formed round him and came back to London: one of the things she had learned, she said, was that a prophet's teaching was likely to be distorted by his disciples organising themselves into something like a church after his death. This was a difficult time for Eleanor; she had disagreements with many of her friends. But the best form of promulgation for a prophet's ideas, she said, was, as always, for seeds to become scattered.

Eleanor wrote a short book about Jung's alchemical studies: this book was an elaboration of her thesis of 1939. Towards the end of his life Jung had become obsessed with alchemy: alchemists, he suggested, had used materials and material symbols but in fact they were trying to deal with states of mind. Eleanor elaborated on this: it had been necessary, she said, for alchemists to have spoken in riddles about what they were doing because what they were dealing with were processes rather than states – and the experience of a process had necessarily to be that of a journey in the dark. A too well-lit imaginative idea of what was happening would result in an end being assumed and thus the function of a process being destroyed – this function being a search, a testing, a trying-out of this or that, in recognition of the necessity that one should learn to learn for oneself. If an end was clear then there would be no process but a following of what was given; and from this, what could be learned for oneself? What was required of every organism if it was to develop or even survive was to learn to be flexible, to deal with whatever unexpectedly turned up: of what help in such practisings would be journeys in the light! The business of learning to learn as opposed to learning to follow a line would be learning on a higher level: a level of openness and testing on which there might be furtherance of life.

Eleanor did not settle down to earn her living as an analytical psychologist straightaway: she continued to travel; she obtained grants from universities and academic foundations for her work abroad. She and Max continued, in their different disciplines, to echo and interweave with one another – about the business of levels, of patterning, of the way in which by the recognition of such structuring there were made possible what otherwise seemed to be impossibilities about life. Max persevered in the areas of his scientific disciplines: he toyed with the idea that had first come to him on the mountain-top in Spain – Granted that in some sense the observer brings into existence that which he observes (there are potentialities from which he chooses) then indeed what should be the criteria by which he chooses; should not these indeed be called 'aesthetic', since he appears to act like an artist – trying out, testing, this or that? Why are scientists in their experimenting so reluctant to recognise their creative role? At the same time Eleanor noted how even writers in modern literature carried on as if people like themselves did not exist: they wrote of people who were helpless or comic victims: they did not write of people, that is, who were able to recognise and deal in patterns. And thus there was a contradiction in their work: the helplessness that they wrote about was belied by the skill of their performances: their description of other people's despair seemed to offer a successful protection perhaps against their own and that of others, but why could they not even try to write about the implications of this? At this point in her essay, however, Eleanor seemed suddenly to change tack: she said –

But of course it might be self-defeating to write too openly about such protection; this would be on a different level from that of telling a story. As with the old alchemists, to achieve what one wants there probably has to be some secrecy; but if there is a code, then still it might be recognised that there is a message!

Eleanor and Max saw quite a lot of each other during these years (the mid-1960s). Eleanor was setting herself up as a psychoanalyst in London: Max had been given a professorship at the university in the north of England where he and Eleanor had been before the war. He and she travelled to and fro; they went on holidays together; they spent some time trekking in the Himalayas. In later years they talked with great animation of this time: they were never quite at ease, it seemed, in justifying their many separations. Eleanor would say 'But think of the self-satisfaction in settling down!' Max would say 'But you sometimes get tired of being on a tightrope.'

They were both now becoming recognised names in the academic and scientific world: it was as a cyberneticist that Max had gained his professorship in the north of England. Cybernetics was a field coming into fashion at this time: it was defined as 'the study of systems of communication and control'. Max said 'I was a cyberneticist long before the word was invented.' Eleanor said 'No wonder no one knew what you were trying to say!'

Max's commitment to cybernetics arose from his interest in patterns of interaction and control. Living organisms regulate themselves by maintaining a steady state in the face of changes in the environment; they heal and restore themselves in response to pressures and damage; they ensure consistency of form even when they reproduce themselves. In this they resemble a thermostat, which performs a function of maintaining a temperature within limits. This mechanical function is on one level; on another is the business of setting the dial, which is performed by humans. It is on this human level of consciousness that oscillations are apt to get out of control: there are dashings between extremes – wars, obsessions, self-destructions – a snowballing effect so that the human psyche, and thus human societies, are often like engines without a governor, so of course eventually they are likely to fuse or blow themselves up. At one time it had been felt that just as a human agency was responsible for the setting of a mechanical system, so a divine agency was responsible for the setting of a human system: but such a formulation (Max argued) was no longer necessary: humans themselves now had the ability to look down and see what was happening to them on the level of consciousness. This level might be seen as the one on which the requirements of morals and the terrible destructive demands of evolution met; from which the activities of the other levels could be surveyed and perhaps accepted if not controlled. There might always be, that is – for the continuance of life, of evolution – some forms of battle, of self-destruction; what mattered was that these should be contained by a way of looking at them, approaching them, being conscious of them – in a style which was to be learned; which might even result in control.

As a postscript to his papers on cybernetics Max published an article in a small religious magazine (Eleanor joked with him 'You and I are religious not because anyone would recognise us as religious, but because we have recognised all recognitions are of a code'). There were obvious parallels, Max argued, between the idea of cybernetic levels and the efforts that Christians had made in trying to establish their doctrine of the Trinity. At the level of God the Father there was a simple cause-and-effect view of the world – God made his covenants with humans, which was a way of describing something like the mechanical functioning of a thermostat: if humans got too far above themselves then disasters knocked them down; if they got too far below themselves then they were ready to be boosted by the inspiration of a prophet: on this level humans did not have much say in the style of the to-and-fro. At the level of God the Son humans were given information about how to handle such a mechanism: life was indeed a matter of paradoxes – by dying you lived; fulfilment was achieved by sacrifice; you were to love your neighbour as yourself; and so on: but still, in this style humans seemed to experience a somewhat helpless oscillation between ecstasy and despair. But then there was, so it was said at least, the domain of the Holy Spirit, in which humans could be led into responsibility for themselves. This was not so much a level as an ability to move between levels, to see a pattern by means of an inbuilt knowledge of truth – such means, if observed and honoured, allowing ends to look after themselves. But about this style, this spirit, the so-called 'guide into truth', not much more was ever said. And of course this was perhaps necessary, because the point of this activity, this understanding, was that individuals, now being somewhat godlike, might find their own way. But with this spirit humans could keep an eye on (take a walk away from every now and then) the mechanisms that to some extent necessarily ran themselves on the other levels; the nature of the world seeming to be such that this watchfulness, alertness, gave a sense of the miracle of control.

Max ended this article by pointing out the bizarre juxtaposition that the explosion of the first practice Atomic Bomb in which he had been involved had been code-named 'Trinity'; what indeed could be said about this! This had been the beginning of a journey in the dark. But such was the nature of any journey to do with truth, or learning about control.

Max's essay sent Eleanor back to look at the first draft of her work on Judaism of years ago: but whereas news of the suffering of Jews had then discouraged her from publishing it, now news of nationalistic chauvinism had the same effect: she explained to Max 'Of course it is my belief that the true use of power is that seeds of the spirit should be scattered secretly; but then what is the point of saying this?' Max said – 'You mean, if your efforts at control are scattered openly, they fall on stony ground?'

At the end of the 1960s Max and Eleanor were living together again much of the time: Eleanor settled into her psychoanalytic work in London; Max took up a new appointment in Cambridge. Max's mother and father were dead; Max had sold the house with the green lawns and red-brick walls; he bought a cottage on the edge of the estate where he had worked in the early days of the war. Eleanor came here to stay: Max stayed with her when he went to London. They both were now well into middle age: they had been through hard times both together and apart; but still little of this was apparent when they were with their friends. They continued to give to people a sense of involvement and excitement: of life being a successfully going concern. They had each achieved positions of some influence in their professional fields if also a reputation for roguishness – Max still on the borders between physics and biology; Eleanor on the borders between anthropology and psychiatry and with her increasingly thriving analytic practice in London. In this she was noted for the unconventionality of her style: she refused for the most part to use technical jargon; she tried to teach her patients to listen to themselves – to hear, behind whatever screens of language they might use, what might be their fearful or fearsome messages. In their private lives both Eleanor and Max increasingly liked to spend time in the company of people younger than themselves: they each would say that they felt at home in a situation in which there was some transmission of learning. (Eleanor would say 'You like to show off!' Max would say – 'Then aren't I lucky'.) It often seemed, indeed, as if the people around them were their children. Eleanor occasionally regretted that she had not had children herself (she would add 'But the situation would not have been right if I had never been sad about it'). Max occasionally claimed that it had been a conscious and practical decision (then Eleanor would say 'But you can't say things like that!'). What they both did – sometimes together but then again increasingly separately because it seemed that the process worked better that way – was to do what from the beginning of their relationship they had hoped to do, which was to provide settings which they hoped would be nourishing for whatever children, as it were, turned up.

Max had his love affairs: he did not go out of his way to attract girls: he would explain – 'What is love if it is not what turns up out of the dark?' The one time he had gone against this realisation, he used to say, was when he had set out deliberately to get Caroline – and look what had happened then! It had almost killed him. (Eleanor would say 'You set out to attract me!' Max would say 'Ah yes, I sat underneath that tree!') It was when he was quite late into middle age that Max met – quite by chance of course! oh those loops, feedbacks: indeed they can be called 'aesthetic'! – the girl called Lilia.

Max had not seen Lilia's mother since the time nearly thirty years ago when he had been present at the wedding which had taken place in the enormous country house in the wing that was occupied by her grandmother. Max had liked Lilia's father: he was an energetic young arts' student with a passion to make films. When he had joined the army Lilia's mother had gone with him to live near where he trained: then he was sent abroad, and she and the child were on their own. But by this time Max was in America, and so he had not seen Lilia. When he got back from America he learned that there had been a fire in the enormous country house. and it was now a shell: the grandmother had died and none of the family were in the area. Max, of course, retained a romantic vision of Lilia's mother – and indeed of Lilia.

Some thirty years later, then, Max for the first time came across Lilia: they were at some gathering of people protesting about the war in Vietnam. Max had gone to the meeting in the spirit in which he had gone to the anti-nuclear meeting years ago: he himself had ambivalent feelings about the war in Vietnam – he felt that protests should be not so much against this war as against the predilection of humans to make any war – but he had sympathy with the people who were making this particular protest. However, he was also known at this time to be an adviser to the government on scientific matters so it was likely that his presence at the gathering would provoke comment. Max noticed Lilia in the aftermath to the meeting; people were still talking in a crowded room; he thought he might go to her and say – You remind me of someone I used to know a long time ago – and then it would be impossible for him to say any more, the remark having been so commonplace. He was wondering about his ambivalence in such matters when, in a movement of the crowd towards the door, he found himself next to Lilia. He said 'You remind me of someone I used to know a long time ago.' She said 'Everyone says that.' He said 'I know.' She said 'You know my mother?' He said 'Why, who is your mother?' She said 'Everyone always says I remind them of my mother.' Then Max of course felt that he knew who she was, although it was as if he could not know. He said 'I see.' She said 'What do you see?' He thought he might say – I see a broken-backed cottage: something dead coming alive.

Then Lilia said 'What are you doing here? I thought you were supposed to approve of the war in Vietnam.'

He said 'No, I don't approve of it, it's just that if there isn't a war there, there might be a worse one somewhere else. You can try to stop this war, but you can't achieve innocence.'

Lilia said 'God, what a boring attitude!'

Max said 'Yes, it's difficult to talk about it.'

The odd thing about this meeting (this was how Max told the story) was that they each talked as if they knew who the other was – Max as if he knew she was Lilia; Lilia as if the person whom she had recognised as a public figure was the person who her mother had told her had so much influenced her years ago although she had not told her his name – though in fact it was only the next day that they uncovered these parts of their stories. Towards the end of the evening, after they had had dinner together and had talked – perhaps about patterns? about things being apt to return on the curve of the universe? – they had gone back to the small flat where Lilia was staying and she had given Max coffee and had sat straight-backed and smoked a cigarette and backed away as if the smoke were coming after her; and it was then that she had said to him the sentence that had become some sort of talisman for her – 'I must tell you, I never go to bed with people I like.'

And Max had said 'Then that's all right.'

She had said 'Why?'

Max had said 'Because either we like each other or else we will go to bed.'

And she had thought – Oh, if you say that, it can be both?

Max and Lilia set up house together for a time. Lilia's mother and father were away in California – he was working in films; she was doing social work with the homeless. Max and Lilia used to stay in the cottage on the borders of Suffolk and Norfolk: Max would go to and fro between there and Cambridge. Max needed someone once more to adore: Lilia needed someone to learn from. Their affair worked very well for a time, in spite of Max being so much older. But this is the beginning of another story, or set of stories.

Once upon this time there were Max and Lilia; then Lilia's younger brother Bert to whom Eleanor became analyst and mentor; then the girl called Judith who became the lover or beloved of all the male protagonists of these stories; then also Jason, who was or is the correlator of the stories – the writer of this postcript – who loved both Lilia and Judith, who in the end, as it were, is married happily to Lilia. And there is the child who emerges from these stories – as a result of the activities of all the protagonists but in fact, of course, from his mother Lilia. Perhaps too the child is what might come alive in the mind of a watcher or a reader: it is stories, patterns, as Eleanor and Max used to say, that bear the seeds of what is living.

There is also another child, a girl: but this appears at the very end of these stories.

There was always a problem about how to write about all this – liveliness being somewhat secret, being what is experienced on one's own, moving often in the dark between levels. The writer writes: there is that which he writes and that which is what comes alive (or does not) both in his mind and in the mind of a watcher or a reader. Is it you: is it you? It is this that might be like a child. Stories are messages. (Is it not this that Eleanor and Max have been saying?) To exist there has to be a code: messages bring things into existence.

At the beginning it seemed there were seeds; they were like people on a stage; they were in a writer's mind; they were saying 'How do we bring this into existence? – what we would like: in other minds, in the outside world.' The messages, to be effective, would have to be partly in the dark. The questions would be not just what did happen then, not what will happen next, but what is happening now. An actor comes on; he is watched; he watches himself being watched; he watches himself watching. From the recognition of this predicament other questions grow: 'What is acting and what is not?'; 'What is real and what is not?'; 'What is the style that can be seen to be not false but true?' And the answers are not in words: they are (indeed!) what flowers (if any) grow. For creation there will have been some journey through the dark – for an audience, for a reader, for demonstrators in a mind or on a stage: what on earth, after all, is a human being to do? Eleanor and Max and the others wanted to form messages. They might have been linked to archetypes in my mind: but from whatever such seeds, flowers are the flowers that grow.

Lilia split up with Max; Bert was helped to be freed by Eleanor; in time he found what he wanted with Judith; Lilia returned to me, that is, Jason. The stories go to and fro – like a sieve, a riddle. In the end, one might say – There are one or two diamonds!

Eleanor and Max seemed to be our parents or grandparents in

this. But we all felt ourselves to be agents in a strange but indeed not always hostile territory.

I would think – For God's sake, not on our way back to, but for the first time free of, that boring old Garden of Eden!

There was a time when Max, the Professor, was getting old and had become ill; in fact he was supposed to be dying. (I am leapfrogging over the backs of these stories: there may not exactly be an end; but by now there is something living or there is not.) There was this time when Max was supposed to have cancer and to be dying and he was being looked after by his young friend Judith. Judith was also looking after her baby. She was also involved (I think) in writing her part of the story about these years – as indeed all of us had from time to time been trying to do, except perhaps Lilia, but then she was the mother of the child. And we all came to visit Max on his so-called death-bed; on a day that also happened to be his birthday. You imagine the setting (you; or you?): the bedroom of a flat in a Regency building in a town on the south coast of England; the window looking out over a cold grey sea; Max propped up in bed; the new baby in her cot by the window; Judith moving to and fro between death and birth – oh, well, indeed, what is the message! We had come to visit Max; we had also come to see Judith and her baby. First Bert arrived – Bert who might or might not be the father of Judith's baby but what did it matter: what is a father, after all: did not the women in these stories imagine themselves at moments as neo-Virgin Marys? Bert had wanted to marry Judith: he had been quite pleased, probably, when this had not quite occurred; it is easier, after all, for a non-ending to be happy. Bert came into the room and greeted Judith; he stood with Judith by the cot at the window looking down at the baby; oh yes, there are paintings like this. Then Bert went to the bed and stood by Max. He said 'How are you?' Max said 'I'm dying, thank you.' Bert pulled up a chair and sat by Max's bed. Max had closed his eyes. Bert cleared his throat as if he were doing some business on a stage to show that he was trying to get Max's attention. Max smiled. Bert said 'Look here, this cancer you're supposed to have, isn't it true that it occurs when certain cells of the body go into runaway, out of control? I mean, they just multiply and look after themselves without any regard for the body as a whole?' Max said 'Something like that.' Bert said 'And isn't this something you've been going on about all your life – I mean, about the need to stop it?' Max, from behind closed eyes, said 'Yes, that's right.' One could not quite tell, I suppose, whether he was laughing or crying. Bert said 'Well, don't you think, perhaps, that in that case you should stop it?' Max did seem to be trying to deal with some moisture behind his eyes; like someone who might have come across an oasis in a desert. He said 'I've got to die sometime.' Bert said 'But not if you don't want to.' Max said 'I do want to.' The baby, by the window, began to make a slight noise of crying; as if it were a bird very far away. Max said quickly 'And anyway, one has to make room for other people.' Bert said 'Oh but that's up to the other people!' Judith lifted her baby out of the cot and came and sat on the end of the bed: she began to feed the baby from her breast. Max opened his eyes and watched Judith and the baby. Tears appeared on his cheeks like diamonds. He said 'Dear God, what is immortal.'

Shortly after this the other couple who appear in these stories arrived – Lilia and Jason. We came in with our child. The child, a boy, was about eight years old at this time; he had fair hair; he was not dark like his father. He had a face of extraordinary brightness and gravity. He went up and looked at the baby that Judith was holding: this baby was a girl. Lilia and I stood by Max's bed; we were holding hands. Max turned his head to us and said 'You two are together again, are you?' I said 'Have we been away?' Lilia said 'Till life do us part.' Bert said 'We were just talking about how to be immortal.' We, the four of us, stood around Max's bed. It did not seem necessary to talk much. The child turned from watching Judith feed her baby and he came to the head of the bed and looked at Max. His head was at the same height as Max's head, so that he was like a planet spun off from some old sun. He said 'Are you really going to die?' Max said 'I'm trying, but these people won't let me.' The child said 'Why are you trying?' Max said 'I've done everything I want to do: what more can I do?' The skin of Max's face was slightly wrinkled but curiously healthy like that of an apple. The child felt in his pocket. He said 'Have you seen this trick?' Max said 'What trick?' The child said 'It's a trick I do with this medal.' The child took out of his pocket what looked like an old Roman medallion. Max stared at it. He said 'I know that medal.' The child said 'I toss it, and if it comes down tails then you're allowed to die, but if it comes down heads then you're not.' Max closed his eyes. The child tossed the coin in the air, caught it, and turned it over on to the back of his other hand. Then he said to Max 'What do you think it is?' Max said 'Heads.' The child said 'Yes!'

He uncovered the coin and held it out towards Max. Max said 'But you wouldn't let me fix the choice in the first place.' The child said 'It's all the better if you know the trick.' He rocked from side to side with laughter. Bert put out a hand and took the coin from the child: he turned it over. On one side there was the head of a bird carrying what looked like a flower in its beak: on the other there was the image of a snake with its tail in its mouth so that its head, but not its tail, was visible. Bert handed the medallion back to the child: he said 'You're learning.' Lilia had gone to the end of the bed and was making cooing noises at Judith's baby.

I had brought with me a bag that contained a bottle of champagne and some plastic mugs. Judith said 'We've got glasses.' I said 'I suppose I think no one but myself ever has glasses.' Lilia said 'How typical.' We stood round the bed and toasted Max, for his birthday, with champagne. Max held a plastic mug on his chest. He seemed to be having difficulty in opening his eyes. The child had some sips of champagne and was allowed to hold the baby. He took it to the window to show it the sun and the sea.

We were, I suppose, waiting for Eleanor to arrive. The news was that she had been with her horse in the north of England; she had said that she would be with us sometime in the evening. Bert, however, had heard that she had had a fall from her horse. Judith said 'But she's always having falls from her horse.' Bert said 'So, how typical.' We stood around Max's bed: he seemed to like hearing us making these noises around him.

When Eleanor arrived the door swung open and no one came through it for a while: the door was set in a dark alcove: you had to move to see who might be outside. When Eleanor did appear she was on crutches: she seemed to be trying to get herself rearranged: she carried a scarf, a woollen hat, two paper bags: she wore a long multi-coloured cloak which she was draping over her crutches so that they were like wings. When we went to help her there did not seem to be any space in which to do this: she began to laugh; when she came into the room with her bits and pieces it was, yes, as if she were a juggler on a tightrope. She was an old lady with a nut-brown face and dark hair streaked with grey. Before she had appeared it had seemed that it might be Death waiting outside: now, with her cloak like plumage and her movement on crutches that made her seem to float above the ground, it was as if she might be an angel that had won a brief contest with Death in the corridor. By the time she got round the corner of the alcove and thus in sight of Max he had opened his eyes and was watching her. They smiled at one another. There were tears on Max's cheeks: between him and Eleanor there seemed to be bits and pieces of light like a glass screen breaking. It was odd, since we knew each of them so well, how seldom in fact we had seen Eleanor and Max together. He said 'Hullo.' She said 'Hullo.' She moved to the edge of the bed and she put both her crutches in one hand so that she could pivot round to sit on the edge of the bed beside him. Max said 'Why are you on crutches?' Eleanor said 'So I could get up the stairs.' She had managed to lower herself on to the edge of the bed; she now had her back to Max. Jason – or I – offered her a glass of champagne: it seemed that she might produce an extra hand, like one of Shiva's, to take it. Max said 'Then why have I got this cancer?' She said 'Well, why have you?' She seemed to be trying to swing herself round on one hip so that she would be facing Max: this would be a difficult feat; she would have to get half on her back, holding champagne, on her tightrope. Max said 'Perhaps it was so that I could be looked after by Judith.' Eleanor said 'Well, you are being looked after by Judith.' There was a moment when Eleanor was in fact on her back with her arms and legs in the air; she was like some giant baby; then she was over on to her other side, facing Max, her legs coming down over his, her head suddenly a few inches from him. Max kissed her. Eleanor said 'So now, what is it?' Max widened his eyes as if he were about to explode: a sun speeding across a desert. He said 'I can't die!' Eleanor said 'Why not?' Max said 'Because I'm too happy!' Eleanor put an arm round him and held him. They stayed embraced. They were like one of those everlastingly happy couples on an Etruscan tomb. We watched them. The child had come from the window carrying the baby; he seemed to be pointing out to it Max and Eleanor. Max said 'For God's sake, something sometime has to die!' Eleanor said 'I think it is the cancer that is dying.'

The 'Catastrophe Practice' Series of Novels

Humans can learn through catastrophe. Evolution can take a step forwards. We can't change things by efforts of will; what we can do is 'practise' a state of mind that may be able to deal with catastrophe when it comes.

1. *Hopeful Monsters* (U.K. 1990; U.S. 1991): Max and Eleanor are students growing up in the 1920s in Cambridge and Berlin. They have to come to terms with the rise of Communism and Naziism, the crack-up of old ways of thinking in science and philosophy, the self-destructiveness of the Spanish Civil War, the making of the Bomb. What they learn can be passed on, eventually, to the protagonists of the books that follow.

2. *Imago Bird* (U.K. 1980; U.S. 1989): Bert is a student in the 1970s. Through his family he finds himself involved with Establishment politics; through his girlfriend with the revolutionary Trotskyites. He is helped to make his way through this crazy social and political maze by a psychotherapist, Dr Anders—Eleanor from *Hopeful Monsters*.

3. *Serpent* (U.K. 1981; U.S. 1990): Jason is a scriptwriter. He is writing (in the 1970s) a script for a film about the Roman/Jewish war in A.D. 70. He is married to Lilia, Bert's sister, who was previously living with Max. The film people, bored, hatch a plot to break up Lilia and Jason's successful marriage. This is paralleled by the destructiveness/self-destructiveness mocked by Jason in his script. Jason and Lilia have learned to survive—and their child.

4. *Judith* (U.K. 1986; U.S. 1991): Judith is an aspiring young actress in the 1970s. She goes into some sort of crack-up with promiscuity and drugs. She is rescued by Professor Ackerman—Max of *Hopeful Monsters*—who gets her to a healing ashram in India. Later, all the protagonists of these stories come together at an

anti-nuclear demonstration outside an American airbase, where there is an explosion. They have all had a hand in the survival of the child; the child now has a hand in their survival.

5. *Catastrophe Practice* (U.K. 1979; U.S. 1989): This was the first book written of the series—it was the 'seed' of the other books—now it is more clearly seen at the end. (This was the book that earned the 'experimental' tag; the other books are not conventionally experimental.) *Catastrophe Practice* is in the form of four essays, three plays, and a short novel. It was trying to say—what is important about any 'act' is likely to be that which is going on offstage; it is by watching and listening for this that one might be ready for catastrophe—and something new might be born, and survive.

—Nicholas Mosley

DALKEY ARCHIVE PAPERBACKS

PIERRE ALBERT-BIROT, *Grabinoulor.*
YUZ ALESHKOVSKY, *Kangaroo.*
FELIPE ALFAU, *Chromos.*
   Locos.
   Sentimental Songs.
ALAN ANSEN,
   Contact Highs: Selected Poems 1957-1987.
DJUNA BARNES, *Ladies Almanack.*
   Ryder.
JOHN BARTH, *LETTERS.*
   Sabbatical.
AUGUSTO ROA BASTOS, *I the Supreme.*
ANDREI BITOV, *Pushkin House.*
ROGER BOYLAN, *Killoyle.*
CHRISTINE BROOKE-ROSE, *Amalgamemnon.*
GERALD BURNS, *Shorter Poems.*
GABRIELLE BURTON, *Heartbreak Hotel.*
MICHEL BUTOR,
   Portrait of the Artist as a Young Ape.
JULIETA CAMPOS,
   The Fear of Losing Eurydice.
ANNE CARSON, *Eros the Bittersweet.*
LOUIS-FERDINAND CÉLINE, *Castle to Castle.*
   London Bridge.
   North.
   Rigadoon.
HUGO CHARTERIS, *The Tide Is Right.*
JEROME CHARYN, *The Tar Baby.*
MARC CHOLODENKO, *Mordechai Schamz.*
EMILY HOLMES COLEMAN,
   The Shutter of Snow.
ROBERT COOVER, *A Night at the Movies.*
STANLEY CRAWFORD,
   Some Instructions to My Wife.
RENÉ CREVEL, *Putting My Foot in It.*
RALPH CUSACK, *Cadenza.*
SUSAN DAITCH, *Storytown.*
PETER DIMOCK,
   A Short Rhetoric for Leaving the Family.
COLEMAN DOWELL, *Island People.*
   Too Much Flesh and Jabez.
RIKKI DUCORNET, *The Complete Butcher's Tales.*
   The Fountains of Neptune.
   The Jade Cabinet.
   Phosphor in Dreamland.
   The Stain.
WILLIAM EASTLAKE, *Castle Keep.*
   Lyric of the Circle Heart.
STANLEY ELKIN, *Boswell: A Modern Comedy.*
   Criers and Kibitzers, Kibitzers and Criers.
   The Dick Gibson Show.

   The MacGuffin.
ANNIE ERNAUX, *Cleaned Out.*
LAUREN FAIRBANKS, *Muzzle Thyself.*
   Sister Carrie.
LESLIE A. FIEDLER,
   Love and Death in the American Novel.
RONALD FIRBANK, *Complete Short Stories.*
FORD MADOX FORD, *The March of Literature.*
JANICE GALLOWAY, *Foreign Parts.*
   The Trick Is to Keep Breathing.
WILLIAM H. GASS, *The Tunnel.*
   Willie Masters' Lonesome Wife.
ETIENNE GILSON, *The Arts of the Beautiful.*
C. S. GISCOMBE, *Giscome Road.*
   Here.
KAREN ELIZABETH GORDON, *The Red Shoes.*
PATRICK GRAINVILLE, *The Cave of Heaven.*
GEOFFREY GREEN, ET AL, *The Vineland Papers.*
JIŘÍ GRUŠA, *The Questionnaire.*
JOHN HAWKES, *Whistlejacket.*
ALDOUS HUXLEY, *Antic Hay.*
   Point Counter Point.
   Those Barren Leaves.
   Time Must Have a Stop.
GERT JONKE, *Geometric Regional Novel.*
TADEUSZ KONWICKI, *A Minor Apocalypse.*
   The Polish Complex.
ELAINE KRAF, *The Princess of 72nd Street.*
EWA KURYLUK, *Century 21.*
DEBORAH LEVY, *Billy and Girl.*
JOSÉ LEZAMA LIMA, *Paradiso.*
OSMAN LINS, *The Queen of the Prisons of Greece.*
ALF MAC LOCHLAINN,
   The Corpus in the Library.
   Out of Focus.
D. KEITH MANO, *Take Five.*
BEN MARCUS, *The Age of Wire and String.*
WALLACE MARKFIELD, *Teitlebaum's Window.*
DAVID MARKSON, *Collected Poems.*
   Reader's Block.
   Springer's Progress.
   Wittgenstein's Mistress.
CARL R. MARTIN, *Genii Over Salzburg.*
CAROLE MASO, *AVA.*
HARRY MATHEWS, *Cigarettes.*
   The Conversions.
   The Journalist.
   Singular Pleasures.
   The Sinking of the Odradek Stadium.
   Tlooth.
   20 Lines a Day.

Visit our website: www.dalkeyarchive.com

DALKEY ARCHIVE PAPERBACKS

Visit our website: www.dalkeyarchive.com

Dalkey Archive Press

ISU Campus Box 4241, Normal, IL 61790–4241

fax (309) 438–7422